WHITE DAZE

A Rick Attison Novel
By Tammy Coulter

Contents

Dedication

This book is for my late husband, Rob. No matter how much I doubted myself, he never did. He always believed I would be an author and he told me he never cared if I was famous or not. I was to follow my dream and become an author. If I didn't, I'd always wonder. So I did. This was the last book to have his magical touch. From now on, I have to trust myself to get it right. And always remember...teens don't talk like that.

Other Titles by Tammy J. Coulter

Black Knights

Chapter 1

New semester, another chance, Rick Attison thought drowsily as he slapped at his screaming alarm clock. As silence filled his room, Rick flopped over on his back, draped an arm across his forehead and sighed. Staying in bed seemed like a much better idea than getting up and facing another day of accusations and suspicion, especially when he heard his roommate moving around in his room.

"Roommate? Yeah, right, man, just call him a spy and be done with it, idiot," Rick muttered out loud as he continued to laze in bed. He jumped as his alarm shrieked yet again. He sighed as he sat up, rubbed the sleep from his eyes and finally dragged himself out of bed. Rick paused in front of his mirror and stretched. His shoulders protested, popping as the tension from the night eased. As he lowered his arms, Rick continued to stare his reflection, and wondered why it held no answers.

"Morning, Rick. You wanna shower first?" Constable Marshall Andrews asked as he knocked on the open door.

Rick slowly raised his eyes to focus on the man standing in the doorway instead of at his own reflection. Seemingly without breaking eye contact, Rick turned to face someone he had once respected but now had begun to hate. Marshall, at times, seemed to tower over Rick, and yet, in reality, he didn't. It was more for his sheer physical size than anything else that had shackled Marshall to the teen, thanks to Inspector Seamus O'Reilly.

Marshall swallowed nervously as Rick continued to stare silently at the cop. Marshall may have been solidly built, standing at six feet tall, and a trained cop, especially in self-defence, but this teenage boy, at only 5'10" tall, was already as strong as Marshall. With his continued boxing training and working on the horse ranch where he lived with his grandmother, uncle and cousin, 17-year-old Rick was getting stronger every day.

Marshall fidgeted nervously as Rick didn't move or change expression for a moment. The longer Rick stared, the more nervous and fidgety the cop became.

"R...R...Rick?" Marshall stammered, slowly becoming terrified of the teen.

Suddenly, Rick smiled and relaxed, transforming his face. "Chill, Marsh. You first. Gonna work out," Rick said as he grabbed a muscle shirt and threw it on.

Rick turned away from a very relieved Marshall and waited until he heard the shower start up. The teen sighed as he changed his pyjama bottoms for a pair of shorts. Pausing, he looked around his room. "Nice damn jail cell," he muttered sourly and stepped up to the speed bag hanging in one corner of his room.

He took a couple of deep, cleansing breaths, like he'd been taught, closed his eyes and began to punch the bag. *Man, some days I hate my life*, Rick thought. Everything which had happened over the last five months was pure hell. It all revolved around the Black Knights, a group of boys for which, until very recently, Rick was sure he would've died. They had been his family; loyal to each other, fought for each other and had always made sure everyone knew not to mess with any of them. They had meant everything to Rick, at least up until five months ago.

The summer between Grade 10 and 11, though, had been a strange one. Something had changed and Rick suddenly found himself a target of the Knights. He was having to fight his best friends almost daily for just a few hours of freedom to visit his Nana at her ranch, Glencrest, just outside of town or even to spend some time alone. Rick felt as if a noose tightened around his neck each time the Knights pushed him.

More than once that summer, Rick found himself in the emergency room being stitched up, bandaged up, and once, even kept overnight because the leader of the Knights, Johnny "Blade" Chilton had blindsided Rick, knocking him out cold and leaving him with a mild concussion. To this day, Rick had no idea what he had done to anger his leader and it was too late now to try to figure it out.

Later that summer, Rick got to meet a cousin who was less than a year younger than he was and lived only an hour away, but who might as well have lived on the other side of the world. Megan Attison was the only child of Rick's uncle, Ian. A shy, yet extremely strong-willed girl, Megan arrived at Glencrest after the sudden and tragic death of her mother, Ian's wife Diane, from a car accident.

At their very first meeting, Rick recognized something in himself, something he had only felt for one other person in his life, his long-time girlfriend, Jordan O'Reilly. It was an overwhelming desire to wrap Megan in his arms and protect her from the world. Since Rick saw Michael right after thinking Megan needed protection, Rick figured he needed to protect Megan from Michael. He didn't even think of protecting her from the Knights.

In September, back in school, Rick introduced his cousin to his girlfriend, Jordan, and her twin brother, Mickey O'Reilly, as well as the Knights. It turned out to be a busy day for Rick. He and the Knights skipped their morning classes as usual, came back for lunch, got into a fight in the cafeteria and ended up in a week-long detention. All in all, not really how Rick wanted to start his school year, but, hey, *take it like a man,* Blade would say.

All of the Knights received detention, yet Rick knew he was the only one who actually went. His week involved two things: writing an essay about what his life in a gang was doing to his relationship with Jordan, and a continual run of hellish nightmares in which Jordan ended up bloody and beaten. This forced Rick to make a very dangerous decision – it was time to get out of the Knights.

Rick had known from the moment he had slipped on the black leather jacket that symbolized the Knights he was in for life. Blade's number two rule was no one ever left the Black Knights. Number one was no girlfriends. Rick had broken both rules.

Deliberately. Blade seemed to take Rick's decision as a personal insult. However, unlike most other gang leaders who went after the banger who left, Blade didn't come directly after Rick. That's not to say the Knights didn't attack Rick, because they did, but they also attacked Megan and Jordan.

As Rick continued his workout, he realized how many times he had warned everyone there was going to be trouble. He punished himself every day for not having done more to help protect Megan and Jordan. *Was it really my fault they didn't listen?* Rick thought angrily, almost losing the rhythm of his workout.

A not-so-chance encounter with the Knights at a neighbourhood park left Rick with a criminal record, court-ordered counselling sessions with the Youth Justice League and a meeting with the one person who would forever change his life. The League was a counselling program formed by Inspector Seamus O'Reilly – Jordan's dad – and Constable Tony Whitefish, a young Cree cop who had become sick and tired of arresting the same kids over and over without anyone doing a thing to change it.

Rick's first counselling session was brutal. It may have gone better, at least for Rick, if his counsellor hadn't also been his arresting officer, Tony Whitefish. Tony, without Rick's knowledge, had specifically asked to be Rick's counsellor. Rick was sure Tony just didn't realize what he was getting involved in.

The teen smiled as he thought of those first few sessions. *Must've been hell for Fish*, Rick thought, as his workout shifted pace. At least until Tony forced Rick into the boxing club at the youth centre. Rick still remembered the first time he stepped into the gym and Tony's command to the boxing coach to 'make Rick sweat.' By the time Rick had left that day, he was exhausted, yet he felt like had finally come home. Coach had even called him a natural.

Thank God for Coach and his training, Rick thought gratefully. The boxing training had saved his life more than once already when fighting the Knights. Unfortunately, it had also added to his reputation for brutality. After all, why become a boxer if he wasn't going to use that strength for something even more sinister? Right after Rick joined the club, Megan and Jordan were the victims of an insidious and sneaky campaign designed to injure them as much as possible and focus the blame squarely on Rick.

Rick threw a few hard punches at his speed bag as he thought about how close the campaign actually came to working. Every single time Rick turned around, Megan or Jordan was being attacked, physically and mentally, and Rick was always blamed, even if he had someone to vouch for him. It was a campaign in terror, cleverly executed and only Rick seemed to be able to figure out the Knights were behind it.

Actually, Tony knew it too – he just couldn't prove it. Unfortunately, that lack of evidence really hurt Rick just after Thanksgiving. Jordan's father had put his foot down and had forbidden Jordan from speaking or even looking at Rick, something Jordan's brother, Mickey, took very seriously. So seriously, in fact, Jordan ended up sneaking away from Megan and Mickey to spend a few precious minutes with Rick.

She never made it.

Instead, she ended up in a seldom-used classroom, beaten and unconscious. Rick could still see her laying in that crumpled heap, her long red hair fanned out around her pain-ridden face, her hands stretched out towards him as he stood in the door, shocked. It was only a few seconds later Tony, Megan and Mickey came into the room to find Rick standing over Jordan, and Rick realized it looked bad for him.

A week-long incarceration at the local young offenders' centre while Tony struggled to find any evidence left Rick a bitter young man. He knew he hadn't done anything, Tony knew it, and Jordan certainly knew it, but once again, they just couldn't *prove* it. Deep in his heart, Rick believed Seamus knew it too, but that didn't stop the head cop from dropping a bombshell on Rick the day the teen arrived home from the youth centre.

Marshall Andrews was Tony's partner and physically, the only one strong enough to take Rick on when he was in a blind rage, or at least he *had* been the only one strong enough. Now, Rick figured no one on the force would be able to take him without using a Taser or mace or something like that. No matter how Rick tried to look at it, though, Marshall was still there as a watchdog. A jailer. A spy. The constant pressure, both at home and at school, was getting to Rick.

Rick changed the pace of his workout yet again – faster, sharper, more staccato in its rhythm, attempting to forget a day he was certain no one else ever would.

Rick had never understood why, after all of the attacks and everything else which had happened to Megan since Rick left the Knights, his Uncle Ian had allowed Megan to go for a cross-country ski run by herself on Remembrance Day. While alone, Megan had been attacked and left lying in the snow. Ian had blamed himself for her injuries because he hadn't been there to protect her. It had been Rick's bad luck to be found standing over Megan's beaten and unconscious body, and once again, everyone had jumped to the most logical conclusion based on what they saw. Rick was arrested for assault, and it seemed as if Tony and Rick were the only ones who were sure everyone was wrong.

To this day, Rick had no idea how Tony managed to get him through the almost two-month long incarceration at the young offenders' centre, but he was grateful Tony had.

Lord knows I treated him like crap more than once, Rick thought absently as he returned to the beginning of his workout and let the soothing rhythm wash over him once again. He closed his eyes and continued to reflect on the man who had become best friend, surrogate father and big brother, all rolled into one. It was more Tony's inability to find any true evidence against Rick, or anyone else for that matter, which had led to Rick's release this time.

The judge saw Rick as innocent, but Seamus saw it as a case of insufficient evidence. So once again the Inspector dragged poor Marshall out to Glencrest and set him over Rick as a spy, nothing else. It was something Rick only agreed to after forcing Seamus to let Jordan live her life and agreeing to let the couple see each other. *Not like he kept to his part of the bargain, either*, Rick thought ruefully. No matter how much time he got to spend with Jordan, he was beginning to think it wasn't worth all this trouble.

As Rick continued working out, Marshall just stood in the doorway, watching, doing his own thinking. He hated what Seamus was making him do. It made him feel like a dirty cop. He'd even told Tony that after Megan's attack. Marshall firmly believed if he hadn't been at Glencrest, watching Rick, the boy would've never lied to the cop and slipped away, only to be found standing over Megan. Marshall wondered how much longer Rick would be able to last before he did it again.

"Quit staring, Marsh," Rick said suddenly, his hands never slowing. "It's distracting." Rick spoke without any rancour or anger. He had come to accept the watchdog. Kind of.

"Sorry, Rick. Came to get you so you could shower and I got caught up in the rhythm," Marshall said as he sat down on Rick's desk chair.

Rick finished with a flourish and grabbed a towel to wipe away the sweat pouring down his face. "Fish says the same thing. Says it sounds like the drumming when he dances," Rick said as he downed half a bottle of cool water. He could tell from the way Marshall sat something was bothering the cop, but Rick wanted a shower before confronting him.

"I'm off to shower, Marsh. You cooking?" Rick asked as he grabbed his robe.

"Pancakes okay?" Marshall asked as he waited for Rick to leave the room, giving the teen plenty of space, something he had never done before.

Rick nodded absently as he passed the cop and shut the bathroom door softly behind him, when he really wanted to slam it. Hard. He leaned against the door and swallowed back a bitter sob. He realized what was wrong with Marshall. The cop was scared of Rick, of his strength, his power and more importantly, his anger. Rick was so tired of fighting the fear. Somehow, he had to find the strength inside himself to go on, only he wasn't sure if he had it in him anymore.

Rick stood under the pounding, scalding hot water for almost 10 minutes, trying to ease the tension that had knotted up his shoulders, erasing whatever good his workout had done. It didn't do a damn bit of good, just like he knew it wouldn't, so, as the teen was drying off and getting ready for school, he realized he was going to have to confront the source of the tension, no matter how unpleasant it might become.

Rick smiled as he realized even a couple of weeks ago, he wouldn't've been able to do what he was contemplating. He would've exploded, usually at Tony during one of their sessions, and then the cop would talk, seemingly forever, until Rick had calmed down and could deal with whatever was bothering him.

"Thank God for Fish," Rick muttered for about the millionth time since this year had begun as he gathered up his books, shoved them in his backpack, snagged his jacket and strode into the kitchen.

Marshall had already dug into his stack of pancakes, but leaned back to grab a stack for Rick, thrusting the warm plate at him. Rick occupied himself with fixing up the pancakes the way he liked them; all the while, he could feel the tension rising with him in the room.

Lowering his eyes to his breakfast, Rick watched Marshall surreptitiously as he ate. The cop's breakfast was less than half-eaten, and yet he only picked at what remained. His coffee remained untouched and he'd only taken a couple of sips of his orange juice.

"Marsh, what the hell's wrong?" Rick finally snapped, unable to stand it any longer.

"Wha'cha mean, Rick?" Marshall stammered. He had jumped when Rick snapped at him and Rick tried not to yell at the cop as he noticed how Marshall almost cowered in his chair.

"What do I mean?" Rick asked incredulously. "Look at you, man. You sat as far away from me as you could in my room. You gave me more than enough room to pass by you when I left for my shower, like you didn't want me to touch you. You haven't touched your food since I sat down. You're sitting in your chair, cowering like I'm about to pound you flat and you ask me what I mean when I want to know what's wrong? C'mon, man, give me some credit," Rick said with a snort.

Marshall remained silent. He didn't realize he'd been *that* obvious about how he felt. He thought he had hidden his fear, but it was obvious, now, that he hadn't. *How do I tell him?* Marshall wondered as he stared down at his breakfast. *How do I tell him I'm terrified of him without setting him off?*

"Marsh, c'mon, man. Talk to me. Please?" Rick begged.

Marshall hesitated a couple more seconds. "This morning, in your room, the way you were staring at me, I guess it made me bit...nervous, that's all," he finally said softly.

Rick continued to look at Marshall who could see there was some anger, some hatred still left over even after Rick's workout. And that bothered Marshall the most. He had no idea how to handle this kid, not the way Tony could.

Rick sighed. "You want the truth, Marsh? About this morning?" he asked, running a hand through his damp hair, trying to keep the frustration out of his voice.

Marshall nodded, not trusting himself to talk.

"Truth is, man, I'm angry and tired. Angry at Seamus for making my home a jail cell and tired of fighting, not just Johnny, but my family and everyone who's supposed to be my friend. Unfortunately, since you're here, you get it all," Rick said with a shrug.

"What did I do to deserve that?" Marshall demanded hotly, stunned out of his silence.

"Well, nothing, Marsh, but I've noticed how tense I get when I see your shadow or even hear ya move around. I see your face and I get angry. We both know angry guys can get violent," Rick said with another shrug.

Marshall paled as he realized the implications of Rick's comment. "Oh my God! Do you mean you would've..." the cop whispered.

"Yes," Rick said shortly as he began to gather up the remains of breakfast. Martha, Nana's housekeeper, would come down later to tidy up and wash up the dishes, but the food had better be scraped into the garbage or put away in the fridge, or Rick would hear about it later from Nana.

Marshall couldn't move as Rick worked around the stunned cop. He tried not to shake as he finally admitted to himself exactly how terrified he was of Rick. *The boss can fire me if he wants. I don't care*, Marshall decided finally. *This ends. Today.*

Chapter 2

Rick turned back from the sink and laughed at the look on Marshall's face. He grabbed his jacket and book bag as he continued to chuckle. "Marsh, relax, will ya? I don't plan on creaming ya today," Rick said and slapped him on the back, causing Marshall to jump once again.

Leaving Marshall to get his stuff together, Rick grabbed up his boxing gear he had tossed by the door and headed out the door. He threw both bags into the back seat of his Firebird, a gift from Nana on his last birthday, and looked up to see Marshall coming out of the house and a blue and white Chevy short bed pick-up stopped in front of the main house. Mickey O'Reilly climbed out, nodded at Marshall, ignored Rick completely and sauntered up to the main house to get Megan.

Laughing at how absurd Mickey was being, Rick knocked on the passenger window of the truck. Jordan giggled as she opened the door and climbed out into Rick's embrace. They stood that way for a couple of minutes until Rick pulled back to give her a kiss.

"He doesn't change, does he, sweets?" Rick smiled down at his girlfriend.

"Of course not, love," Jordan laughed. "Did you honestly expect him to? My brother, like my father, still doesn't trust you and honestly, he probably never will."

"I know. I guess I was just hoping that today, maybe, just maybe, he'd cut me some slack..." Rick's voice trailed off as he felt an overwhelming feeling of dread come over him. He took a shaky breath and closed his eyes, hoping the feeling would quickly pass.

"Rick? What's wrong?" Jordan asked quietly, as she recognized the signs.

"Megs just came out, didn't she?" Rick asked. Without turning to look, he knew Megan was standing on the porch saying good-bye to Nana and her dad. Rick let the feeling wash over him until he couldn't stand it anymore. Jordan held him quietly while he shook, overwhelmed for the moment.

This feeling was new, one Rick didn't like one damn bit. It was something that had just begun since the turn of the New Year, especially since Rick had left the young offender's centre. The worst part was Rick couldn't explain what was wrong. All he could say, when anyone asked, was someone was coming after Megan and Rick somehow knew he'd be too late to save her.

"Rick? Come on, love. Talk to me," Jordan encouraged as she had been taught by Tony when she asked him what to do the last time this had happened when she was with Rick. The sight of him staring off into space, not focused on anything, talking into a monotone yet with an undertone of fear.

"He's coming, babe. He's coming after Megs and I can't stop him. I'll be too late," Rick said tonelessly. He'd opened his eyes but they were focused on somewhere far away.

"Can you see who it is this time?" Jordan pressed gently, feeling Rick's hand tense in hers at the question.

"I don't know, dammit. I never have," Rick snapped roughly. Jordan just held his hand.

"Come on, boy, move it!" a deep gravelly voice said from behind Rick before Jordan could say anything. A hand landed suddenly on Rick's shoulder, squeezing slightly. Rick had flinched at the sound of the voice, but when the hand landed on his shoulder, he reacted instinctively. He pushed Jordan towards the truck, grabbed the attacker's hand with his left hand and jerked him forward. Then Rick's right fist flashed out and connected solidly with his attacker's jaw. The offender collapsed to the ground.

Rick barely heard Jordan shout, "Rick! No!" as he reacted to the perceived attack. He stood there, shaking, breathing heavy, and trying to focus. He shook his head to clear it and when he finally could see again, Marshall lay in a heap at Rick's feet, blood flowing sluggishly from a split lip and Rick's fist was beginning to bruise slightly.

"Marshall!" Nana cried, as she rushed up to the fallen cop. Marshall struggled to his feet and couldn't help flinching as Rick reached out to steady him.

"Dammit, Marsh, I warned you about this just ten minutes ago! What the hell're ya thinking?" Rick demanded hotly. "I could've really hurt ya and we both know it!"

"I know, Rick. Think about it – this was an attack I deliberately provoked and look what happened. Now how bad would it be after you'd been angry all day and I accidentally startled you? Cop or not, you'd probably kill me and not even realize it until it was way too late. Even worse, what if it was Jordan?" Marshall said his voice muffled as he held a wad of tissue to his mouth.

He pulled it back and looked at a very sober Rick. "O'Reilly can fire me if he wants, but I'm leaving you alone. I'm packing up and heading back to do real police work," Marshall said firmly.

Rick was even more stunned. Seamus hadn't cared what Marshall wanted or not wanted. The inspector had forced the cop away from his partnership with Tony and made Marshall into a spy. After what just happened, Marshall didn't care if he lost his job.

"Marsh, you sure? I mean, really sure? Y'know what Daddy'll say," Jordan pointed out.

"I'm done with all of this, Jordan. It's just too hard on me and my nerves. I live every day wondering, honestly wondering, if Megan's attack was my fault, or if Rick's gonna blindside me one of these days," Marshall said softly. The cop looked at the four teens standing awkwardly in front of him.

"No, Rick, no more," Marshall said firmly. "Like it or not, it's time we started to trust you." Marshall turned towards Rick's house and would've fallen if Rick hadn't caught him.

"Whoa! Gottcha, Marsh. Must've connected harder than I thought. Get the girls to school, Mick. Let Delaney know I might be late and why," Rick said over his shoulder as he helped Marshall back to the house.

Shaking his head, Mickey helped Megan then Jordan into the truck and tossed all three book bags into the back. He angled himself behind the wheel, started the truck and pulled away from Glencrest. As he hit the end of the driveway, he sighed explosively.

"What's the matter, lad?" Megan asked as she settled into her accustomed place with Mickey's arm wrapped around her shoulders.

"Rick. New semester, same old story," Mickey said disgusted. "He still can't control his damn temper."

"That's not it at all, Mickey and you know it! Think about it for a second. How'd you like to have someone come up behind you and scare the crap out of you? How's he supposed to react, for crying out loud? Get real," Jordan snapped. She couldn't believe how stubborn her brother was being.

Mickey was silent for a moment, then chuckled. "I guess — like Rick. You're right, sis. He *would* react that way, wouldn't he? I keep forgetting he's still got the gang mentality at times. But still, you'd think he'd have some kind of control by now," Mickey said with some acidity.

"You know, bro, Marsh's right. We've gotta start trusting Rick sometime. Daddy may not like it, but the courts *have* cleared him. Unless new evidence or crimes come to light, Tony says Rick can't be charged for these crimes again," Jordan pointed out. Sometimes it paid to be a cop's kid — other cops tended to tell you things especially when they concern your boyfriend.

Mickey didn't say anything for a couple of moments as he manoeuvred around a slower car. "Megan, didn't you mention something about Rick asking you if you'd been bugged at school?" Mickey asked absently.

"Yeah, he did. During a ride we took with Marshall just after Rick came home. He started acting...odd, I guess is the best way I can describe it," Megan began hesitantly.

"Sitting still? Staring straight ahead? A blank, distant look on his face?" Jordan asked quickly.

"Yeah, now that you mention it, it was like that. Marshall kept asking him what was wrong, what he saw, and Rick said something about watching a video or something and something about someone coming after her, but he'd be too late. I don't really remember the rest," Megan said with a shrug.

"What're you getting at, sis?" Mickey asked as he slowed at the city limits.

"Remember how Rick got Daddy to leave me alone? To leave us alone?" she asked. Mickey nodded. "Well, we've been talking during lunch and he keeps mentioning a funny 'feeling' he's been having. He can't ever really describe what he's feeling, or sometimes 'seeing', and that's always how his face looks, just kinda blank and distant. All he really knows is this 'feeling' seems to be focused on Megs. He firmly believes the Knights're involved, but he can't say for sure," Jordan explained quickly.

"So what, sis? What's that gotta do with him creaming Marshall? That wasn't really what I was going for anyway," Mickey said as they approached the school.

"Well, I guess what I'm wondering is with Marsh always around, always watching him — what if that's making these feelings of Rick's worse? Making Rick angry? What if it's making everything worse?" Jordan asked logically.

"Well, I guess that's a possibility," Mickey said distractedly, still really wondering where his sister was going with this.

"Besides, we both know Daddy only put the guard on Rick because he doesn't trust him," Jordan said sarcastically.

"Well then, Marsh is right and I'm gonna tell Dad that, too," Mickey said firmly.

You could've heard a pin drop, the silence in the truck was so loud. "Don't tease, lad," Megan whispered.

Mickey didn't lower his voice as he replied. "I'm not, Megan. I'm damn serious. Marshall and Jordan're both right — Dad has to trust the system and leave Rick the hell alone, especially before Rick does something worse than punch Marsh in the mouth," Mickey said firmly. He didn't even have to say who he thought would be hurt, since Jordan already knew.

His sister couldn't've been more stunned if Mickey had hit her. The strain that had been between the twins since Christmas and especially New Year's had been almost too much for Jordan to handle. The twins had barely talked since Rick's arrest after Megan's attack in November and it had forced them apart so much Jordan had been able to sneak away from school with Tony's and Tom's help and ran off to see Rick at the young offender's centre.

In doing so, though, Jordan had deliberately disobeyed her father, something he never tolerated. When Seamus had found out, needless to say, he reacted badly. Jordan absently rubbed a barely faded scar on her right wrist. When Seamus had found out what Jordan had done, he had grabbed that wrist and squeezed so hard, the bracelet Rick had given her for Christmas had cut her wrist deeply.

Seamus had also forced Mickey and Jordan to be 'shackled' together until Rick had, in turn, forced Seamus to leave them alone. At least they were talking to each other again, but now Mickey was no longer protecting Jordan from a faceless shove in the back. It was no longer just Blade and the rest of the Knights. Now Mickey had to protect his baby sister from her own father.

"Speaking of Daddy," Jordan said dryly as they pulled into the parking lot at the school.

"And he looks a little unhappy," Megan added just as dryly as they parked and climbed out of the truck. No one noticed Rick's car pulling in as they walked towards the front doors.

Indeed, Inspector Seamus O'Reilly was a little unhappy. Actually, he was well beyond unhappy, had blown right on past angry and had hit ballistic. He was standing at the front doors talking with the principal, Mr. Delaney, his face as red as his hair. The students flowed around them into the warmth of the school, calling out greetings to each other, seemingly oblivious to the drama unfolding between the Chief of Police and their principal.

"Do not yell at me, Seamus O'Reilly," Delaney said calmly as the trio of friends joined the pair at the front doors.

"Furthermore, you do not dictate policy in this school. The only people I have to answer to are the school board and the superintendent, and right now they happen to agree with me. Rick's marks have improved dramatically and the courts have cleared him of any wrongdoing. Rick has done nothing wrong in my school since his return and I refuse to punish him any further," Delaney continued, his breath steaming in the cold morning air.

Seamus ground his teeth in frustration. "Ye're willin' to risk the lives of me children and the rest of yer students because that boy did nothin' while locked in a room where he could be observed all day long?" Seamus asked. "Of course he did nothin'! How could he?" the cop demanded.

"Alright, Daddy, that's enough! Let him be!" Jordan snapped as she stood in front of her father with her hands on her hips.

"She's right, Dad. Cut the guy some slack for once. Lay off," Mickey agreed.

"Isn't it time you trust the system you swore to uphold?" Rick asked quietly as he arrived.

"Where's Marshall?" Seamus demanded immediately.

"Back at the station, doing the job you actually *pay* him for," Rick explained as he slipped his arm around Jordan's waist, as if daring Seamus to say anything.

"What the hell does he think he's doin'? I never gave him permission to return to duty," Seamus growled.

"Correct me if I'm wrong, Mick, but he said something like "O'Reilly can fire me if he wants. I'm done with this." Right?" Rick looked at the older O'Reilly twin for confirmation.

Mickey nodded. "Like it or not, Dad, we've gotta leave Rick alone," the teen said. Rick could've cheered to hear one of his biggest critics become one of his cheerleaders, if only for a moment.

"And when he starts after the girls again?" Seamus said ominously, glaring at Rick who glared right back.

"*If* that happens, we'll just deal with it then," Delaney said firmly. "Kids, you're gonna be late for Homeroom. Rick, can you please stop by the office before you leave today? Tony asked me for some papers and he said you could bring them after school. Thank you."

Rick nodded and led the way into the school where he had just enough time to kiss Jordan good-bye and hand her over to their good friend and Jordan's escort, Tom Shelley, once a victim himself of the Knights. Tom had formed a group called the Grey Angels shortly after Rick's arrest in November. Their sole purpose was to take Colonial High back from the Knights who were terrorizing the school and the students. By the time Rick came back to school in January, the Angels had been in very real danger of becoming a hard-core gang, just like the Knights, but, somehow, some way, Rick managed to convince Tom of the danger he and the rest of the Angels were in.

"Hey, Champ," Tom said by way of greeting. It was the boxing club and the Angel's way of acknowledging Rick's superior fighting skills and the fact no one had beat the teen in the ring, even though he'd never had a sanctioned fight. Their coach didn't think Rick could handle it quite yet.

"Take care of her, Kid," Rick replied, nodding at Carl, who was Megan's escort.

"Like always. You at the centre today?" Tom asked as the group walked towards their Homerooms.

"Yep. Bad morning. Need to go a couple with Carl here. Later," Rick said as he, Megan and Carl turned towards their Homeroom.

None of them seemed to notice the boy trailing after them. Like Rick, he had blond hair and blue eyes. He was slightly shorter than Rick, and definitely less muscular. He was dressed in a black and silver jacket, with black jeans, white tee and black boots. He had a cold, calculating look in his eyes as he stared at the friends scattering to their classes. Brian "Brain" Townsand wondered, not for the first time, how long this plan of Blade's was really gonna take and if it was really gonna work.

Brain sauntered down the hallways, turning automatically, noticing everything, yet seeing nothing, until he arrived outside Blade's Homeroom. He waited, leaning nonchalantly against the far wall, until the bell rang and the door opened to a crowd of noisy students.

Blade came right over, as if he knew Brain would be waiting. "Yo, man. Whassup?" Blade asked quietly.

"He's back, and in the main population again. Not locked away. When?" Brain asked just as quietly.

Blade thoughtfully paced, planning, trying to figure out the timing for what he planned.

"Blade?" Brain asked again.

"Leave 'im fer now. We'll figure the timin' out tonight. My place. Pass the word." With that, Blade turned and headed to his first class while Brain pulled out his cell phone and sent Crank and Pup, the last two members of the Knights, Blade's message.

As Blade settled into his desk in English and ignored the teacher's hesitant query about why the teen was so late, all the leader of the Knights could think of was how much fun this semester was going to be.

Chapter 3

While the kids settled back into their school routine, Seamus returned to the station a very frustrated cop. In his heart, he knew his kids were right, but it didn't make it any easier for him. His head stubbornly said Rick was to blame, but with no actual evidence, the judge was right – Rick was innocent, and it was time to cut him loose.

If only it was that easy, Seamus thought as he stomped into the station. He saw Marshall at his desk, talking quietly to Tony. Seamus' eyes narrowed as he looked over at his two best cops, regardless of how many years' experience some of the others had.

"Get ready, Marsh. Here he comes," Seamus heard Tony tell his partner as the elder cop strode up to their desks.

"Constable Andrews. Ye mind telling me what ye're doing here instead of at the high school watching over a certain teenager?" Seamus demanded, stopping at Marshall's side and glaring down at the young cop.

"My job, *Inspector*," Marshall said, without looking up, his anger barely held in check and making Seamus' title sound like something he'd like to throw out with the trash.

"Yer job, as I recall it, is whatever I tell ye to do," Seamus replied, trying not to wince at Marshall's tone.

Marshall looked up at Seamus for a few moments, then around at the rest of the police bullpen. Everyone was quiet, waiting to see how this latest drama would play out. Marshall didn't want to air the boss' dirty laundry out for everyone to hear, but he would if he had to. Marshall nodded to Tony and the partners stood.

"Boss, c'mon. Let's take this into your office," Tony suggested quietly. "Don't think you want this coming out in front of the boys."

Seamus nodded and led the way to his office. He paused as Tony and Marshall slipped into the office and looked out at the rest of his officers. When he spoke, it was quiet. "Sorry, boys. Won't happen again." With that, the inspector turned and closed the door behind him.

"What won't happen again, Seamus?" Tony asked as Seamus sat down behind his desk.

"Arguing with anyone in front of the rest of the boys," Seamus said. "I was taught better than that. Now, Marshall, mind telling me why ye're here and not where ye're supposed to be? Especially since I can see that he hit ye. Again," Seamus said, pointed to Marshall's bruised lip.

"Inspector, look. We've all sworn to uphold the law, right? Right?" Marshall asked harshly when Seamus didn't answer right away. Seamus nodded reluctantly. "Well, I'm a cop, and I just couldn't spy on Rick any more. Not and look myself in the mirror in the morning. And it's the first time Rick's ever hit me. Face it, boss, you've made me feel like dirt, making me spy on the kid. This morning, I realized I was probably doing more harm than good. The more I hung around, the tenser and angrier Rick became," Marshall defended himself.

"So?" Seamus replied as he frowned at the partners.

"Would you rather Rick hit me, someone who can take it, when I startled him deliberately, than Jordan when she did it by accident?" Marshall pointed out logically.

"All the more reason fer ye to still be watching over him," Seamus said stubbornly.

"All the more reason for Marsh to back off!" Tony said quickly, defending his partner. *What's it gonna take to convince him?* Tony wondered. *Jor back in the hospital?*

Seamus didn't reply for several moments. "Marshall, was this really yer idea or did the boy put ye up to this?" Seamus finally asked.

"The boy has a name, dammit, Seamus! Would it kill you to use it, even once?" Tony demanded as Marshall gave a wordless growl of protest.

- 21 -

"Well, Marshall? Did he?" Seamus asked again, ignoring Tony's protest.

"No, Inspector, Rick didn't put me up to this. If you really think that, we're done here," Marshall groused and stormed out of Seamus' office, not bothering to hide from everyone else how angry and hurt he really was.

"Nice going, boss," Tony said dryly, as he closed the door behind Marshall and returned to his chair. "Make him feel even worse than he already does."

"Don't tell me how to run me department, Constable," Seamus snapped, stunned at Marshall's sudden, angry departure.

Tony's patience was finally gone. "Alright, then. Fine. Keep on treating one of your best cops like crap, force him to do something he hates. Turn him against everything he believes in and see how much longer he remains a cop! I'm warning you, boss, return him to Glencrest and Nana'll probably file that formal complaint she's been threatening to do since October.

"And when we finally end up having that formal inquiry, and I'm asked why I continued to turn a blind eye to your obvious obstruction of justice, I'm also gonna have tell them about a certain altercation between you and Rick and how a 14-year-old kid managed to get his hands on your service piece!" Tony argued hotly.

Seamus paled as he finally realized what Tony was saying. "You'd be out of a job faster than you could say hello," Tony pointed out, calming down only slightly.

Seamus stewed for a few more minutes, then nodded sharply. "Alright fine, Tony. We'll do it yer way. Fer now. Marshall's back here, with ye," Seamus agreed reluctantly.

Tony flashed Seamus a grateful grin. "You won't regret it, boss," Tony said as he stood.

"I'd better not, Tony. Nothing had better happen to those girls or I'm holding ye personally responsible. Now, get back to work," Seamus ordered. Tony nodded and headed for the door. "Hey, Tony?" Seamus stopped Tony just as quickly as he had dismissed him.

"Yeah, boss?" Tony said, turning back to face Seamus.

"What did Marshall mean? When he said I made him feel like dirt?" Seamus asked quietly. He was kinda dreading the answer, but he knew he had to ask.

Tony didn't hesitate. Seamus needed to hear it, no matter how much it hurt him. "You've made him feel like a dirty cop, boss, as sleazy as the one you know's taking money from Mendez. Did you know he blames *himself* for Rick's arrest after Meg's attack? He figures if he hadn't been forced to stay at Glencrest, Rick wouldn't've left the house and wouldn't've been found standing over his battered cousin," Tony said harshly.

Seamus didn't say anything as Tony poured salt on the open wound. "'Course, who knows what might've happened to Meg if Rick hadn't come along when he did. So I guess you can feel good about forcing Marsh to be a spy." Tony dug the barb in a bit more as he opened the door, leaving Seamus sitting in his office, feeling worse than he'd ever felt before.

The rest of the day, Tony brought Marshall up to speed on the current cases on their desks, including follow-ups on the attacks of both Jordan and Megan, as well as what had been happening while Marshall had been at Glencrest. "That's about it, partner. Good to have you back," Tony said finally, snapping the last folder closed and tossing it over to Marshall.

Marshall finished making his notes and looked over at Jones' empty desk. "Thanks, partner, it's good to be back. Now, where're we on Mendez?" Marshall asked, nodding towards the empty desk. Carlos Mendez was a local bookie, suave, sophisticated and vicious towards anyone who got behind on their payments. It was well known, at least on the street, Rick's dad, Michael, was several hundred thousand dollars in debt to Mendez and yet, strangely enough, Mendez hadn't done anything to Michael, not even threatening his family.

Somehow, Carlos Mendez had managed to buy or threaten his way into the police station and had sunk his hooks deep into one of the cops. No one knew for sure who it was; at least no one would give voice to their suspicions. Tony figured Seamus had a suspect and wondered if it was the same one he and Marshall identified. Neither cop liked the fact one of the longest serving cops, a ten-year veteran named Jones, was selling information to the bookie, but there wasn't anything they could do about it right now.

Tony snorted. "Nowhere, man. Seamus tried to suspend Jonesy after he pushed too hard on something or other, but Jones threatened to go to the union and Seamus backed down. So, for now, we wait until Jones makes a mistake. At least *we* know what he's doing, but let's keep it quiet for now. I'm sure the boss knows, but no one else is saying anything. We need to focus on Rick and the Knights. We still can't pin a single thing on them, y'know," Tony pointed out.

"I know, I know. Well, leave these with me. I'll take a fresh look at them and see if something new jumps out at me. Aren't you due at the centre?" Marshall pointed out, looking at the clock.

"Yep, I'm outta here. Catch you in the morning, man," Tony said, snatching up his coat and heading out the door.

When Tony met up with Rick at the centre, Tony noticed his young friend seemed a bit preoccupied. Tony didn't say a word other than to greet Rick before leading the way to their office. As Tony pulled his gun and extra clips off of his gun belt, locked them away and then pulled out Rick's file, he noticed Rick hadn't sat down. Instead, Rick stood, leaning against the wall, arms folded across his chest, slowly breathing, eyes focused on something only he could see.

"Champ? What's going on?" Tony finally asked, his voice loud in the quite room.

Rick didn't move. "Nothin', Fish," he said, distracted.

Yeah, right, Tony thought, not believe Rick for a moment. "C'mon, son. Don't give me that," Tony said dryly. "Try again."

Rick didn't move. His voice was tense as he spoke in low tones. "I keep thinking back to this morning and what Marsh did. Fish, I'm sure I could've killed him, I know it. If I hadn't pulled him down so I could only hit him once, I hate to think what I could've done to him," he said finally.

"Marsh told me what you said to him. You know he provoked you deliberately, right?" Tony asked as he perched himself, as usual, on the corner of the desk.

Rick nodded. He no longer trusted himself to speak. "He knows he upset you by doing that, but he wanted you to realize he was causing the problem, although he said you knew it. But I don't think that's the real problem, is it?" Tony asked shrewdly.

Rick shook his head and finally flopped into his chair. "I've been waiting all day for Marsh to show up. So where's he hiding?" Rick asked sourly, looking around the room, as if Tony had his partner hiding somewhere in the spartanly furnished room.

Tony smiled. "At the station," Tony explained.

"When's he coming back to the ranch?" Rick demanded.

"He's not. We've convince Seamus, for now, that having Marsh at Glencrest was doing more harm than good. So you're not gonna have him back," Tony said.

"Until O'Reilly decides he can't stand having nobody spying on me," Rick said sourly.

"Now, c'mon, little brother. Let's give him the benefit of the doubt. At least for a little while," Tony laughed.

Rick got up and began to pace restlessly. After the silence stretched on for several minutes, Tony sat forward and asked, "Something happened you wanna talk about?"

"No," Rick replied roughly as he paced.

Inwardly, Tony sighed. They were back to Tony having to fight tooth and nail to get anything more than one-word answers out of Rick. So instead of leaving Rick to pace and stew, Tony thought he'd push, carefully, and see what happened.

"Is that 'No, nothing happened,' or 'No, you don't wanna talk about it'?" Tony asked logically.

Rick turned to face Tony, stared at his friend for a long time, then finally sighed. "Other than beating up Marsh, no, nothing happened," Rick said as he returned to leaning against the wall. "And, y'know what? I think that's what's bugging me, man. They didn't do anything to any of us, all day." Rick was amazed he hadn't realized this before.

"Nothing? To anyone? Nothing?" Tony asked quickly. "That *is* weird," Tony agreed.

"Nope. Nothing. No vandalism. No attacks. No fights. And I have it on good authority they never left school once today," Rick confirmed.

Tony sat, as puzzled as Rick. For the Knights to ignore such a fantastic chance at Rick and the girls didn't make any more sense to the cop than it did to Rick. None at all. *What's going on now?* Tony wondered.

"The only thing that happened all day was Brian followed us to Homeroom this morning. He was close enough to touch any one of us and yet he left us all alone. Fish, any ideas, bro? 'Cause I'm fresh out," Rick said from where he stood.

"Lemme ask you something first, Champ. Did you see Johnny today?" Tony asked instead of replying to Rick's question. Rick nodded and Tony continued. "That funny feeling? The one focused on Meg? Has it gone away?"

"No." Rick shook his head for emphasis. "In fact, today, when I first saw her at the ranch, it slammed into me like a freight train. It gets unbearable when I see Johnny and if I happen to see both of them at once..." Rick's voice dropped to a whisper as he looked past Tony to focus on the far wall. "It's almost overwhelming."

Despite everything Rick had done to warn Megan, he still felt it wasn't gonna be enough. As he stared past his friend, all Rick could see was Megan, bound, beaten, still as if she were dead. Her hands were bound behind her back and it seemed to be pitch-black around her. Rick knew he didn't see the clearing but something much, much worse.

When he finally spoke again, his voice was so low Tony could barely hear him. "He's planning something big, Fish. He's gonna come after her and I won't be able to stop him. I'll be too late to save her."

"Rick, c'mon, son, focus," Tony said, trying to keep the worry out of his own voice.

Rick shook his head slightly and grinned sheepishly at Tony. "Sorry, bro. Sometimes it just comes out of nowhere and hits me. Hard, y'know," he said with a shrug.

"No doubt. This is something totally new for both of us, so it's gonna take some getting used to. Now, anything else going on you wanna talk about today or can I turn you over to Coach? You look like you could use a couple of good rounds against Carl," Tony said, not really expecting an answer.

Rick hesitated, then sat down in his chair right in front of Tony. "Fish, tell me something and I want you to be honest, 'kay?" Rick asked. He lowered his head so Tony couldn't see his face.

Tony frowned. "Rick, I'll always tell you the truth, no matter how painful it is for either of us. You should know that by now. I swore to you months ago I would always trust you and I would never, *ever* lie to you," Tony said quietly, wondering where this was heading.

"Marsh's terrified of me, isn't he?" Rick asked quietly. "That's why he left, isn't it?"

Tony wanted to deny it, but he knew Rick would see right through him. Besides, hadn't he just said he'd never lie to Rick? He took a deep breath and said, "Yes."

Rick raised his head and Tony could see a questioning look in his eyes. There was also a lot of despair, too.

"Are you?" Rick finally had the courage to ask.

Tony smiled. "That's what's been eating at you all day? Whether or not I'm afraid of you?" he asked, relaxing his suddenly tense shoulders. Rick nodded as he waited for Tony to continue.

"I won't lie to you, Rick. When we first started, I was absolutely terrified of your anger. You were so strong and quick, it took all I knew just to keep up with you and stay out of your way. Then once I got you into the boxing club, thinking it would help, it made it worse for a while. The day before your birthday, the situation with Mick's truck? You remember?" Tony asked. He sat down so Rick didn't feel like he was being towered over.

Rick swallowed a couple of times, recalling what he had nearly done that day. "Yeah. Of course I do, man. How could I ever forget the day I could've killed my best friend?" he asked. Tony chuckled.

"That night taught me a couple of things. One – I was really out of shape, and two – I always needed to keep your strength and anger in the back of my mind whenever we talked. If I didn't, there'd always be a good chance you'd do it again," Tony explained.

"But now, right now, are you?" Rick asked again, desperate to hear Tony's answer, which was quick in coming.

"No, little brother, I'm not. I *respect* the power and strength you have, especially when you're angry. I'd be a fool not to, and my mom didn't raise no fool. But I'm not afraid of you or of being in the same room with you when you're angry. Does that help?" Tony asked.

Rick nodded, visibly relieved.

"Don't get me wrong, son. You still have a lot of anger buried in there," Tony said, tapping Rick's chest. "And one wrong move'll cause it to come exploding out."

"Wha'cha getting at, Fish?" Rick asked as he stood up, grabbing his jacket and duffle bag.

"Like you said, Johnny's probably up to something. Even Delaney's noticed a change in the Knights at school. And if they *have* targeted Meg again, when they make their move, I honestly doubt you'll be able to stop yourself from reacting," Tony pointed out. Rick nodded thoughtfully.

"What do *you* think's going on, bro?" Rick said as the two friends left the office and headed to the gym.

Tony shrugged, but didn't say anything as he left Rick with Bob. He watched the club for a while, thinking about Rick's question. The cop sighed as he watched Rick and Carl spar and finally answered Rick, even though he knew Rick couldn't hear him.

"I wish I knew, Champ. I wish I knew."

Chapter 4

That night, while Rick enjoyed a quiet meal with Nana, and Tony brooded over their latest session, the Knights met in the private back room of the pool hall where the manager, Antonio, would guarantee their privacy – for a little while, anyway. Crank and Brain arrived well before Blade and Pup. As they settled into a booth to wait, Crank seemed to be a bit preoccupied.

"Man, what's up, Crank? Yer being a pain in the ass and have been for the last couple weeks," Brain asked quietly. *Like I don't know,* Brain thought as he shrugged out of his jacket. *He's been crabbing about it since I told him Blade's plan.*

"Guess I still don't get this whole thing Blade's lookin' at doin'. I mean, really, whassa point, man?" Crank finally asked.

Brain shrugged and shook his head. "Don't know, man, but I'm not gonna argue with 'im. Not after the last beating he laid on the Slayers. You wanna go a couple with him?" Brain asked dryly.

"Not really," Crank replied quickly. "Especially not after what he wanted ya to do to Moneyman's cuz last year. Hell, he wanted her dead, man, not just roughed up. And now he's got some whacked idea just to get some money? He need it that bad, man?" Crank wondered.

Brain shook his head. "Naw, least not that he's really said to me. He figures if we do this and get away with it, we can move up with Mendez. Blade's gots plans for the Knights, man, big plans. Anyone figures they're gonna challenge 'im better just follow 'im instead," Brain pointed out. The Knights' second in command didn't like the thought of becoming friendlier with Mendez, but what Blade wanted, Blade got.

Crank was going to comment when the door opened, and Blade sauntered in with Pup right behind him. Pup said something in a low tone to Antonio, then followed his cousin over to the booth. A couple of minutes later, Antonio came back in with drinks and snacks. He served everyone then left, closing the door firmly behind him. *What I don't know, I can't tell,* Antonio though as he walked away and back behind the counter. *I don't wanna know what he's planning this time. Last time was bad enough.*

"Boys," Blade said, nodding at Brain and Crank.

"Blade," Brain said while Crank just nodded and made room for his leader. Pup slid in beside Brain and grabbed a handful of nachos for himself.

Brain downed half of his drink and got right down to business. "Okay, Blade, question fer ya. Yer sure ya wanna do this? Really sure, man? I mean, we get caught, we're gonna go away fer a long time, man, even as juvies."

"'Course I'm sure. Why not do it? It's gonna be fun," Blade replied immediately.

Fun? Brain thought as he continued to mull his plan as the others talked, eating and drinking. *He thinks this'll be fun? Doesn't he care if we get caught?* As Brain chewed over his plan, he realized Blade really didn't care if they got caught. He just wanted to prove he could do something like this. The timing, Brain knew, would have to be absolutely perfect. And he had a couple of different plans, depending on Blade. Still, Brain hesitated until Blade forced his hand.

"Okay, boys, Antonio ain't gonna let us have the room all night. Brain, what's yer plan?" Blade asked as he leaned back in the booth.

"That depends on two things, man. One, when do ya wanna grab'er and two, are we doin' a snatch'n'grab or get 'er by creating a diversion?" Brain asked.

"Snatchin 'er while she's with Mickey Mouse ain't gonna work, Blade," Crank said immediately. "We'd need a fifth guy – someone we could trust to keep his mouth shut – to be Moneyman or no one'll even look at 'im. That's figurin' yer gonna blame Moneyman," Crank finished.

"'Course, idiot. Brain, he right?" Blade drawled, as he took another long pull on his drink.

"Yeah. I've thought up a couple of different ways, but the easiest is gonna be getting them to do half the work for us," Brain pointed out.

"Wha'cha mean?" Blade asked. He had pulled out his knife and was playing with it idly.

"If we do this right, we can trick Megs and the others into doing the work for us. We do this right, we have all the fun and Moneyman catches all the blame," Brain said clearly, dropping what he called his "gang-speak", something he only ever did when he needed to clearly state his point, and that was usually only in class. Never with the boys.

"Okay, Brain. What's the plan?" Blade asked again.

"When do you wanna grab 'er?" Brain replied again, trying to keep his patience.

Blade fell silent. When *did* he wanna do this? He'd already talked to Mendez about the whole thing, and the bookie had even given him several ideas about how to do it. Mendez had liked the idea of having some younger members in his organization, guys he could use to get a foot in the door of the high school. He had encouraged Blade to tell him everything, and had agreed if the Knights could pull this off he'd welcome them into his organization gladly.

"Today's what? Beginnin' of February? How's about we snatch 'er 'round middle of next month? That's about six weeks or so, right? That work fer yer plan?" Blade finally said, looking at Brain as he took a pull on a beer.

Brain mulled over his plan and the timeline. That long would mean a few adjustments, but still very doable. *Especially if we delay the start, give Moneyman time to relax, then move slowly until all hell breaks loose,* Brain thought as he finished his drink.

"Think so, Blade. Might mean a few adjustments, but it's good. Okay, so first things first. There's an absolutely no contact rule as of *right now*. We leave *all* of them alone, understand? Got it,

Blade? All of them, no matter how much you wanna go after Moneyman," Brain warned.

"Why?" Crank demanded.

"Because sometimes, Crank, you and Blade don't know your own strength. None of this'll work if Moneyman's in jail, the hospital or locked in Delaney's office! Moneyman needs to be out with everyone else. Otherwise, we might as well stop planning right now," Brain explained angrily.

"Chill, boys. We can leave 'em alone fer now," Blade said with a dismissive wave.

"Okay, here's what we're gonna do. First, we're gonna delay the start of *anything* for a couple of weeks. Let Moneyman relax into school. That's also gonna give me enough time to set up the letters and something with the phones, see if I can get 'em to show Moneyman's number. I also wanna spend some time and get her routine set to I can figure out exactly how we're gonna grab 'er," Brain explained.

"So once you do get going, how long do ya figure?" Blade drawled.

"I figure a couple of weeks to follow her, then ease into the stalking. By the beginning of March or so, I'll go full out, give 'er a couple of days of freedom, then grab her a couple days after that. Around mid-month for sure," Brain outlined his timetable.

Before Blade could say anything, Brain continued, "The best part of the whole plan, though, is what we do once we grab her," he said and continued to detail everything.

By the time Brain was done answering questions, Blade was laughing. "Perfect, man. Best plan ya've ever done fer me!" he chortled.

"You planning on talking to our employer again?" Brain asked as the Knights stood to leave.

"Prob'ly. Why?" Blade asked.

"Need some cash, man. Wanna see a man about a special piece and need something to grease the palm," Brain said as they stepped into the cold night air.

"I'll get it fer ya soon as I can," Blade promised as the four friends went their separate ways.

Chapter 5

For the next two weeks or so, Brain did just what he told Blade he was going to do – study Megan and her routine. School was a piece of cake, since he had most of his classes with her. He watched her every move, dogged her every step and worked on his plans every night. Brain knew he was drawing Rick's attention to him, but he really had no choice.

After school and weekends were harder for Brain until he realized Megan had a routine there, too. Spending time with her horse and long rides, usually by herself, were daily occurrences. Then supper, barn chores, sometimes with Rick helping, sometimes not, studying at her desk near her balcony window, a goodnight call to her boyfriend, getting ready for bed and finally lights out.

Every night, Brain would sit in his room, writing, planning, and figuring out how to fit anything new he had learned that day into the overall plan, his mind going a hundred miles an hour trying to finalize everything. Two weeks after their initial meeting, Blade and Brain planned to meet at Blade's house. Since his mom worked a lot of evening shifts, it was easier to meet there. What the Knights failed to count on was chance.

And Fate.

Rick and Jordan were walking hand-in-hand during a quiet moment at school. Rick had a spare right after lunch this semester and Jordan had ended up getting a free period due to a problem in the Biology lab. They had met up at the library, where Rick was spending his spares, working as hard as he could to maintain his marks.

"Y'know something, Jor?" Rick asked as they wandered the quiet halls. Tom was behind them, guarding and protecting the pair because he wanted to, not because he had to. It was a compromise

Rick had agreed to, albeit very reluctantly. *Anything to keep Jor safe* was Rick's only thought. *Even if I don't like it.*

"I know lots of things, love. Did you have anything specific in mind?" Jordan giggled. Rick found a spot to lean against the wall and pulled Jordan to him. They stood there for a couple of minutes, arms wrapped around each other. Rick looked over Jordan's shoulder as he thought he heard a thump and a soft groan. Tom was nowhere to be seen, but since Rick and Jordan were kind of tucked into a small indent in the wall, Rick really didn't think anything of it. *Oh well*, Rick thought as he turned his attention back to his girlfriend. *Must be my imagination.*

"I'm the luckiest guy alive," Rick said as he looked down at Jordan.

Jordan had buried her head against Rick's chest as she snuggled against him. "How so?" she asked, her voice muffled.

Rick moved her back a bit so he could lift her head up and drown in her deep emerald green eyes. "I've got the prettiest girl in school to love, some really good friends who watch my back, my own pad that doesn't cost me anything and wheels. What more could a 17-year-old guy ask for?" he asked rhetorically.

The sound of a boot scuffing across the floor brought Rick's head snapping up. Grinning in front of them stood three of the four Knights. Tom hung, out cold, between Crank and Brain. Pup was standing just off to one side, chuckling.

"Sorry 'bout yer little pal, Moneyman," Brain drawled as they dumped Tom on the floor, just out of Rick's reach. He nudged the unconscious boy with his toe, but Tom didn't move.

Rick pushed himself easily away from the wall, and slid Jordan into a more protected spot behind him. He schooled his face to show no emotion, even though inside he was babbling to himself trying to figure out how the Knights had snuck up on him. He'd heard nothing! Nothing! He took a couple more steps forward and shifted enough so Jordan would have a clear chance to make a break for it.

"Wha'cha ya want, Brian?" Rick asked. He stood, relaxed, hands hanging loosely by his side, ready for anything. Only Jordan could see how tense Rick really was by the angry set of his shoulders.

"Long time no see, Moneyman. Yer looking good," Brain continued to drawl, sounding more and more like Blade. Brain nudged Tom again and laughed. "Y'know somethin', man? I'd heard this little brat was a pretty good fighter. Looks like he sleeps better than he fights." He grinned at the rest of the Knights who laughed nastily.

Rick looked around the hall quickly. Blade was nowhere to be found and that worried Rick. "Where's Johnny? Thought he'd be here holding your leashes. No? Tells me Johnny has no idea you're here. Not smart, Brian, not at all," Rick said quietly. His guts rolled as he thought of what Blade could be doing while Rick was distracted, but he knew he had to keep his head here, and not worry about what anyone else was dealing with.

Crank growled low in his throat.

"See? Just proves my point, guys," Rick said, shaking his head sadly, with a mocking smirk on his face. "He barks an order and you blindly follow like a pack of dogs," Rick continued to taunt the three Knights.

Jordan couldn't believe what she was hearing her boyfriend say to his ex-friends. The insults were coming fast and furious now. She could see Brain's face getting redder and redder as he struggled to control his temper. "Rick, what ARE you doing?" she finally hissed.

"Trust me, sweets," he hissed back, never taking his eyes off of the Knights. He figured they were almost ready. A couple more insults and then they'd attack, even though Rick was pretty sure they weren't supposed to.

Brain was so angry, he was almost vibrating. "Screw you, Moneyman," he snapped. "Yer too damn chicken to take on all of us. Trust me, boy, we'd clean yer clock just like we did Tomboy here."

"Yeah, Brian, really brave of ya, man. Three-on-one and the one's only half your size, ya idiot," Rick said sarcastically. "How's 'bout going a round with the Champ?" Rick tensed as he saw Brian's eyes narrow.

"Champ? Chump, you mean." With that, Brian threw himself at Rick.

"Jordan! Run!" Rick shouted as he easily dodged Brain's rush.

Jordan didn't hesitate. She fled, her boots ringing sharply on the tile floor. Rick ignored the sight of her fleeing, and just prayed he hadn't sent her straight into Blade's clutches. Brain had circled around behind Rick after his initial rush, leaving Rick to face both Pup and Crank. Ignoring him for now, Rick focused on Pup, since Crank had also backed off.

Pup rushed at Rick, swinging wildly. Rick easily ducked under the kid's flailing arms and swung once. He connected with Pup's jaw, knocking the kid out cold. Rick immediately focused on Crank, since he could still hear Brain moving around behind him. All Rick could think was he was very glad *Blade* wasn't the one behind him, since there'd be a knife in Rick's back had he been back there.

Watch the eyes, Bob's words drifted through Rick's head as he and Crank continued to circle. *The eyes'll tell you.* The merest flicker of Crank's eyes told Rick when to move. As Brain rushed by on Rick's left, Rick landed a solid shot to Brain's left side and ducked to avoid a wild right hand from Crank. With Crank off balance, Rick hit Crank's left side with a short, sharp left followed by a right uppercut to Crank's chin. Crank's eyes rolled back in his head and he fell backward to the floor. Like Pup, Crank didn't move again.

"Yer good, Moneyman," Brain acknowledged grudgingly.

"You here to talk or fight, boy?" Rick grated as he circled, looking for his opening.

Instead of replying, Brain swung. Rick danced easily out of the way. Rick's punch, however, connected solidly to Brain's ribs and Brain grunted with the impact. Before Rick could move out of reach, a lucky punch landed on his right side. Compared to one of Carl's punches, it was a weak one, and Rick easily brushed it off. With a feral grin, Rick saw his opening and struck. As Brain was slumping to his knees, his eyes glazing over, Rick landed one more punch on Brain's cheek, knocking him to the floor, where he lay, not moving.

Rick took a couple of deep breaths to calm his pounding heart, then quickly moved to kneel by Tom, just as Jordan came running back up the hall with Carl and several other Grey Angels. She flung herself at Rick, sobbing in relief.

"Easy, sweets. I'm cool," Rick reassured her, and held her tight.

"Wow! All three! I'm impressed, Champ," Carl said as he looked around.

"C'mon, Tom. Open your eyes, Kid," Rick encouraged his friend. It took a couple more moments before Tom groaned and opened his eyes. Rick breathed a sigh of relief as he knew Tom could've easily been killed.

"Holy crap, Champ, what the hell hit me?" Tom groaned again as his fingers felt a growing bump on his head.

"The Knights, Kid. Y'okay? Can you stand?" Rick asked, holding a hand out. Tom nodded and used Rick's outstretched hand to haul himself to his feet. Surrounded by the Angels, Jordan and Rick headed to the office to report the fight, leaving the Knights in crumpled heaps on the hallway floor.

Later that night, Brain, Crank and Pup had to face Blade after their embarrassing defeat. Crank had never seen Blade so mad in all the years they had known each other. He shouted at the top of his lungs and spittle flew from his mouth. Pup and Crank sat in the two recliners and tried not to be noticed while Blade paced around the living room, ranting and raving.

Brain took the yelling in stride until Blade called them "stupid idiots" for the third time. "Alright, Blade. Enough! We get it, man. We screwed up, alright? Happy now?" Brain snapped.

"No kiddin', Brain," Blade sneered. "Yer tellin' *me* to leave 'em all alone, that *I* couldn't do anythin' to 'em 'cause it'd make 'em all suspicious. I had to leave 'em alone!" Blade snarled as he continued to pace.

"*I* had to, but you guys, no, ya can go ahead and take on Moneyman any damn time y'all want! And he beat ya! *Three* of ya! *Easily!* The least ya could'a done was hit 'im! Once!" Blade shouted.

"It was too good an opportunity to pass up," Brain said weakly. Even to his ears it sounded pathetic.

Blade finally stopped pacing, narrowed his eyes at Brain and snarled, "Next time, try."

Brain didn't flinch as he stared right back. Blade laughed softly as he read the challenge in Brain's eyes. "What, Brain? Yer gonna challenge *me*?" Blade sneered softly.

Brain held his gaze with Blade a couple more seconds and finally dropped his eyes. He knew he wasn't strong enough to take over the Knights and, besides, Blade never followed anyone. He only led. And as Blade's grin widened, Brain felt a noose tighten around his neck. For the first time, Brain kind of understood how Rick must've felt.

"Smart," Blade said, softer than ever.

Brain flung himself onto the couch and reached for the bottle of pop Pup put on the table for him. Silence fell in the living room. Brain knew he had screwed up by attacking Rick, but somehow he'd let emotion overrule common sense. Not that he planned on telling Blade that.

The plan, originally, had been to attack Tom and dump him in front of Rick to prove the Knights could get to him and his friends any time they wanted. And it probably would've worked if Brain hadn't suddenly decided he had to see Rick's reaction. Instead of being patient and following the plan, he rushed at Rick and paid the price.

Blade stared at the rest of the Knights and wondered if they had just blown a chance at the money Michael had promised them. *Screw it*, Blade thought angrily. *We go ahead*.

"Okay, boys. We're moving on. Brain, yer ready?" Blade asked.

"Blade, I'm gonna ask ya this one last time – are ya really sure about this, man? I mean, *really* sure? I start, there's no going back," Brain warned.

"'Course I'm sure," Blade snapped back instantly. "Now, yer ready?"

"Yep. Monday it begins."

Chapter 6

On Monday morning, Megan and her friends met up in the student lounge to catch up on the parts of their weekend they hadn't spent together. As Megan stood by the waterfall with Mickey's arm around her waist, she could feel someone staring at her. Yet when she looked around, the only one she could see was Rick as he walked towards them.

"Hey, Megs, what's up, cuz?" Rick asked as he came up, slipped an arm around Jordan and gave Mickey a nod. Tom and Carl stood just a couple of feet away, as usual, talking quietly and watching the world go by.

"Morning, Rick. Um … did you see anyone watching me, when you came in just now?" Megan asked, still searching past her cousin, puzzled at the feeling.

"When? Just now?" Rick asked, as he, too, turned to look. Megan nodded, still uneasy. "Nope. Why?"

"No reason, really. You know how you can feel someone watching you? Well, I felt that as I was talking to Mickey, but when I looked around, all I could see was you, walking towards me. That's why I asked," Megan explained. Now that Rick had joined them, the feeling had eased. At bit, at least.

"Sorry, cuz. Didn't see a soul," Rick said cheerfully.

"This happen before, lass?" Mickey asked as they all headed to Homeroom.

"Now that you mention it, yeah. The last couple of weeks, especially when I'd go riding," she replied quickly.

Rick laughed. "Blame Uncle Ian, Megs. He'd always sends me or Frank after you, just in case," he explained.

Well, now that's good to know, Brain thought slyly as he followed the group of friends at what he thought was a discrete distance. He filed the tidbit away so he could use it in the next couple of weeks to play with Megan's mind even more.

Rick tensed suddenly, as if feeling Brain's gaze on them. He whipped around so fast Brain had no time to move away. The two just stared at each other for a long time until finally, Brain backed off. "What're you guys up to now, Brian?" Rick said, not realizing he'd spoken loud enough for everyone to hear.

"What's up, Champ?" Tom asked quietly as he motioned for the others to continue on.

"Don't know, Kid. Something feels funny, really funny, y'know? That's the second time in the last couple of weeks I've caught Brian close enough to touch any one of us and both times he's left all of us alone. Now, Megs feels like someone's been watching her," Rick explained as they stood outside Rick's Homeroom.

"Wha'cha thinking?" Tom asked, his arms folded across his chest.

"I think something's beginning and we'd all better be on our guard or things're gonna get real messy, real fast," Rick said sourly as Mrs. Salsbury ushered him into Homeroom.

All day long, Megan kept fighting the urge to turn around to see who was staring at her. Her neck constantly crawled with the sensation, which was making her irritable. It was worse while sitting in class because Megan liked to sit at the front of the room. Therefore, everyone behind her was technically staring at her, so she couldn't very well tell them all to stop.

And walking between classes gave her tormentor ample cover to keep on staring at her. It also made her realize how vulnerable she still felt after her attack. Finally she couldn't take it any longer.

"Carl," she said, exasperated.

"Yeah?"

"I know this sounds kinda weird, but would you please walk right behind me? Maybe that'll help," Megan smiled. Carl nodded once, dropped back a single step and fell into place right behind Megan.

The feeling immediately stopped and Megan sighed. "Now, why didn't I think of that earlier?" she laughed.

With Carl walking behind her, the feeling eased between classes, but it intensified as soon as each class began. And it didn't ease up all week, not even at home. Her Monday ride had just begun when she felt not one, but two sets of eyes, staring at her from somewhere in the woods. It made her skin crawl, but she was determined to continue with her ride. Until she heard the sudden snap of a branch breaking. Suddenly, she found herself racing back to the ranch, unable to control her sudden terror.

Megan thundered back into the yard, just as Rick was swinging up into his horse's saddle. Startled at her sudden appearance, Rick pulled back hard on Cherokee's reins, causing his stallion to rear and paw at the air. "Holy crap, Megs! You scared me," he said roughly as he fought to get Cherokee back under control.

Megan didn't say anything as she sat in Mystique's saddle, sobbing, her face as white as the surrounding snow. Rick jumped down as soon as he saw her face. He knew something had happened to her out on her ride. "Cherokee, stand," the teen commanded, dropping the reins to ground-tether his horse. Crooning softly, Rick grabbed Mystique's reins and then called softly for Frank to come and give him a hand. He didn't want to scare the young mare any more than she already was.

"Joey's got Cherokee, Rick, so give me Mystique. Let's get Miss Megan down from there," Frank said, coming up to the teen and taking Mystique's reins from Rick.

"Megs? C'mon, cuz. Climb down now so Frank can take care of Mystique, sweets" Rick said gently. Megan flung herself into Rick's arms, sobbing hysterically.

"Tack room's warm," Frank offered as he turned the young mare towards the barn.

Rick shook his head. "I'll take her up to Nana. She needs warmth and food," Rick said. He began to head towards the main house, leaving Frank to tend to things back at the barn.

They were about half way to the house when Ian came running towards them. Megan had finally stopped crying hysterically, but soft sobs would still escape occasionally as she clung to her cousin.

"What the hell happened?" Ian demanded, scooping Megan into his arms.

"Don't know," Rick replied shortly as he strode easily beside his uncle. "She came flying into the yard just as I was about to head out after her and she's been crying ever since."

Ian frowned as he stripped Megan's winter coat and boots off and lowered her into a chair in the library. Rick stoked the fire until it was roaring. Megan didn't even notice Ian had tucked a blanket around her legs while Nana brought a tray of hot chocolate.

"How is she? She hurt?" Nana asked Rick as she poured for everyone.

Megan shook her head as she sipped at the mug Nana passed to her and just let the warmth seep through her. "I'm...okay. Now," she finally managed to say.

"What happened, Megs?" Rick and Ian asked together. Rick squatted in front of her, leaving his back to be warmed by the blazing fire. Ian stood beside Megan with his hand on her shoulder.

"I was riding and I could've sworn someone was watching me. At least one person, maybe two," she stammered.

"Like at school?" Rick asked.

"Someone was doing what today where? When?" Ian demanded, his questions tumbling over each other in his haste to get them out.

Megan sighed at Rick's poorly timed comment. It was not how she wanted her dad to find out, but she reluctantly told him what had been happening all day long. "Daddy, it was just like my skin was crawling. And..."

"And what, Megs?" Rick encouraged his cousin.

"I swore I heard the same laughter I did in November. It was deep and slightly hysterical. But very soft," she said. She had lost what little colour she had regained as she recalled the attack, and her hands shook slightly.

"Deep and slightly hysterical," Rick murmured. He left his cousin with her dad and stood by the window.

The library window faced the woods Megan had just bolted from. They were dark now, but not empty. Rick could feel it. He sighed softly. *That laugh could've been Blade*, Rick mused as he continued to stare out the window. *I must've heard it a hundred times, if I heard it once.*

And yet Rick knew he couldn't prove it. Megan wouldn't be able to identify Blade just by his laugh and no judge would be able to do anything. Nothing had happened to her. *Yet*, Rick thought sourly. *Johnny, what the hell're you up to?* Rick wondered once again as he stared into the inky blackness.

"Lad? Rick?" Nana asked, coming up behind her grandson.

Rick didn't move at first. He heard his grandmother calling him from a great distance. It took him a minute to drag his thoughts away from the whole situation with Megan and focus on the here and now.

"Yeah?" he replied finally, turning to face Nana.

"Time for supper, lad," she said and led the way.

After that, Megan refused to go for her rides without someone with her. Usually it was Frank or Ian since Rick was rarely home from the centre until after dark. She never felt like she was being watched again while in the woods, at least as long as someone else was with her, but in the barn when they were gone, the feeling came back. She even began to notice it when she was up in her room studying, alone.

By Friday, Megan was tired of being stared at and not being able to figure out what or who was doing it. Even now, late at night as she was getting ready for bed, she could feel someone watching. Waiting for her to make a mistake.

She was brushing her hair while listening to some music and wandering around her room. Stopping near her balcony doors, she didn't hear them click open.

Megan gasped as she felt the cold air against her legs. She turned around and screamed at the figure in head-to-toe black, standing in the door, the moonlight pouring in behind him.

"Hello, Megs," the figure said in the lazy drawl Megan associated with Rick. "I've been watching you!" He moved to step into her room as he laughed.

After everything else that had happened during the past week, this was too much to take. The room around her faded to black, and Megan fainted.

Chapter 7

When Megan opened her eyes, the first thing she saw was a figure in black. She whimpered and tried to get as far away as she could.

"Whoa, lass, easy," her father's voice came from the farthest part of her room.

Megan blinked several more times and the dark blob melted away to reveal her dimly lit room and her very concerned father standing over her. Near the balcony doors were an equally concerned Seamus O'Reilly and someone who appeared to be dusting for prints.

"Daddy?" Megan whispered. Her father just wrapped her up in a hug.

"Megan, sweetheart, ye okay, me lass?" Seamus turned towards the sound of her voice.

"Someone was on my balcony!" she said, indignant and terrified at the same time.

"Did he hurt ye? Say anything?" Seamus asked as he came over to stand by the bed.

"He said...he said he was watching me," Megan replied shakily. Someone had moved her to her bed and covered her with her comforter. As Ian let go of her, she put her hand on a piece of paper.

"What the hell?" she exclaimed, not seeing the frown her father directed at her for swearing. She tilted the paper to read in the dim light of the lamp on her bedside table. *No, no, no, NO!* her mind babbled as she read. *Not again!* She paled and slumped back against her pillows.

"Megs, what is it?" Rick asked from where he was leaning against the door jamb. His arms were crossed over his chest and he stood like he didn't have a care in the world. He had been downstairs talking to Nana when they had heard Megan scream earlier. It seemed to have taken him forever to get up to her room, and since he was the first to get there, he refused to go further into the room than the door. He'd learned his lesson.

Seamus took the note carefully from Megan, read it once, and then turned to glare at Rick. "If I dinne know ye were with yer Nana at the other end of the house when Megan says the perp was on her balcony, I'd haul yer butt in right now, boy," the inspector growled as he protected the note with a clear plastic sleeve and sealed it.

Rick didn't move or say a word, but his mind was going a hundred miles an hour. It didn't matter what the note said, not to Rick. He was sure it was typed, signed with his stupid gang sign and made the same not-so-vague threats against Megan. *Okay, Johnny, you've made your first move,* Rick thought angrily, *but I'm gonna make the last,* he vowed.

"Inspector?" the crime scene tech called suddenly.

"Yeah, Terry?" Seamus asked, distracted by the note he was still reading.

"Does anyone here wear anything resembling a runner?" he asked as he shone his light around.

"On a farm, especially this farm? Not that I know of. Why?" Seamus asked, puzzled.

"Did anyone move Miss Megan to the bed?" Terry asked instead as he continued to shine his light on the floor, obviously looking at something only he could see.

Seamus looked at Ian and Rick. Both of them shook their heads. "I was at the door first, Inspector, and she was already lying on the bed," Rick said.

Seamus swallowed nervously. He hated to rely on Rick, but he had no choice. "Alright, boy. What did ye see?" the inspector asked reluctantly.

Rick smiled slightly, knowing how much Seamus hated to ask him for anything, but he decided not to rub it in. He closed his eyes for a second to recall the room as he first saw it. He kept them closed as he spoke quietly. "I stopped right here. The room was dark – only the moonlight was coming in. I didn't see anyone in the room but I knew right away she'd already been moved," Rick said softly.

"How?" Seamus asked, curious, despite how he felt about Rick personally.

"Like Jor, Megs brushes her hair out for a long time each night before she braids it for bed. Helps to keep it from tangling. See how her room faces towards my place? I've been on the porch at night sometimes and I've seen her doing it," Rick explained. *Which stops right now before I get blamed for something,* Rick vowed silently.

"So? How do ye know she was moved?" Seamus asked again, impatient now.

"Her hair brush isn't on her vanity," Rick pointed it out as he spoke. "It's on the floor by the window. That tells *me* she was surprised at or near the window. When she fainted, she dropped her hairbrush there. Since we found her, still unconscious, in her bed, not the floor by her hairbrush, she's been moved," Rick said logically. Seamus was silently impressed. He knew seasoned cops who couldn't've seen that much detail, himself included.

Megan's skin crawled at the thought of being touched by whoever had been on her balcony. Rubbing her arms as she sobbed, she threw back her comforter and stumbled to her bathroom to throw up.

"Easy lass, it's okay," Nana said as she handed a cloth to her granddaughter. As she started to wipe at her face, Seamus stopped her.

"I'm sorry, lass, but I can't let ye do that. Not yet. Terry, come here. Be as thorough as ye can, but do it quickly," Seamus said quietly. Megan cringed as the tech combed her hair, checked her arms and did a quick exam of her face. He paused as he was about to search for evidence on her nightgown.

"Boss, I think it'll be easier if I just took Miss Megan's night clothes with me and process them at the lab. I'm making her more than a bit uncomfortable," Terry said, backing away from the grateful girl.

Rick reached around the bedroom door and snagged Megan's terry cloth robe. Without moving into the room any farther than he had to, Rick handed the robe to Nana, then resumed his vigil at the door. He wasn't going to take any chances of being accused of anything. Megan closed the bathroom door behind her to change as Seamus and Ian talked nearby in low tones.

The sound of Aerosmith's "Walk This Way," suddenly filled the room. Rick smiled apologetically as he answered his phone. "Yo," he said quietly.

"Hey, little brother," Tony replied too cheerfully for Rick's peace of mind. Obviously the cop hadn't been told what had just happened.

Rick slipped out the door and walked to the top of the stairs. "Hey, Fish. What's up?" Rick asked as he leaned against the rail.

"Not much, Champ. Just wanna let you know Coach forgot to tell you he'd like to do some extra training this weekend. You up for it?" Tony asked.

Rick hesitated, trying to decide if he should be at the ranch or as far away from Megan as possible. What was the right thing to do? The best thing for Megan? Rick wasn't sure. As he hesitated further, Rick could swear he heard Tony frown.

"Rick, what's wrong? Thought you'd jump at this," Tony asked blandly.

"One condition, bro. Can we talk before I start? Or are you working?" Rick asked. He cringed as he heard Megan start crying again.

"Whenever you need to talk, son, I'm here, but something happen I need to know about *now*?" Tony asked, concerned at what Rick wasn't telling him.

Encouraged, Rick gave Tony a quick rundown of what had happened to Megan, or at least as much as he knew. "O'Reilly didn't show me the note, so I don't know exactly what it said, but given his reaction, I'd say it wasn't good. For better or worse, bro, I'd say whatever Johnny's planning has started. I wish I had more to give you than my gut feeling he's behind this," Rick said sourly.

"Me too, Champ. Did you notice anything else you didn't tell Seamus?" Tony queried his young friend.

"Not that I can think of right now. Sorry, bro, gotta fly. O'Reilly's coming out," Rick said and hung up.

"Fer once, boy, ye did good," Seamus said gruffly. "Oddly enough, she's asking fer ye." Seamus nodded to Ian and Nana as he led the tech out the front door.

"Was that Tony?" Nana asked, indicating the cell phone Rick was tucking away.

"Yeah. Coach wants to do some extra boxing practice tomorrow. Told him I could," Rick said as he began to walk towards his cousin's room.

Rick knocked on the door and eased it open when Megan said so. She was in another nightgown and back in her bed. The last time he'd seen her this pale was in November, just after she came home after her attack. Rick hesitated in the doorway, not wanting to come closer, fearing he'd be blamed for anything and everything.

"Rick, it's okay. C'mere," Megan said, her voice scratchy and raw from crying.

Rick came and sat down on the edge of the bed. He smiled at Megan who finally smiled wanly back. "It's started, hasn't it?" she asked. "Whatever you figured Johnny was gonna do, it's started," Megan said again, choking back a frightened sob.

"I guess so," Rick said sadly. He just wondered how long it was going to be before something happened he'd really get blamed for.

"Megs, what did the letter say?" Rick finally asked. *Not that I really want to know, but I have to,* Rick thought.

"It said he was watching me and he could've gotten to me anytime he wanted. He can't wait to get me alone. I don't matter. Only his pleasure, his fun, matters," Megan said.

Rick stiffened. "It said that? Those exact words? My pleasure, my fun?" Rick demanded with a low growl.

Megan nodded. "I remember hearing that somewhere, y'know," she mused.

"You should. It's Johnny's favourite saying," Rick said harshly. "He only says it at least once a day. Too bad O'Reilly won't believe anything I say about it."

"Johnny was here?" Megan's voice rose an octave.

Rick shook his head immediately. "No, cuz, he wasn't. You'd've been beaten up pretty badly if Johnny was here, no matter what his ultimate plan is. He'd be unable to resist," Rick said, trying to reassure his cousin.

"Rick, I'm scared," Megan finally admitted.

Rick gathered his cousin into his arms, rocking her until she finally fell into an exhausted sleep. He eased her back onto her pillows and pulled the quilt up over her. Climbing to his feet and walking to Megan's patio door, Rick stared into the darkness for the longest time.

Finally he turned to leave. Megan was resting easily as Rick turned out her table lamp. "You're scared, Megs?" Rick whispered. "Then I'm frigging terrified," he said as he closed the door softly behind him.

Chapter 8

Monday came all too soon for Megan and not soon enough for Rick. After Friday night's drama, Megan refused to go anywhere by herself, especially up to her room unless someone checked it out first. It made Megan feel like a wimp, but she was already too scared of the whole situation and she knew it was only going to get worse.

Rick spent as much time as he could at the youth centre on Saturday, taking his frustrations out on Carl and the equipment, the heavy bag more than anything else, not really wanting to hurt his friend and knowing he could. When he wasn't pounding on the equipment, he was with Tony, talking, planning, strategizing, trying to figure out how to avoid ending up in a jail cell this time.

Rick arrived at school before Megan and the twins. He wanted to talk to Delaney before something else happened. For once, luck was on his side.

"Morning, Gloria," Rick greeted the secretary.

"Morning, Rick. His door's open. Go on in," she said with a smile.

"Morning, Rick. What's going on?" Delaney asked as Rick sat down.

It didn't take long for Rick to detail what had happened on Friday. "So, sir, I'm hoping you'll allow me to skip actually going to Homeroom and to just check in with you in the morning. That way, if something happens to Megs in Homeroom or just after it, I can't be blamed," Rick finished. He was a little embarrassed to be asking this, but he couldn't figure out any other way around the only class the cousins had together.

"You think something will," Delaney stated rather than asked.

"It's the only class we have together, so it's really a prime time for them to pull whatever they want. If not then, they'll try before school, between classes, at lunch or after school," Rick said logically.

"There's one way to avoid all of that, y'know," Delaney pointed out with a nod towards the detention room he had in his office. "We can arrange for a tutor for you until this is all worked out."

"Yeah, but I can't hide away forever," Rick said sourly, hurt the principal would even suggest hiding. "We both know they'll just stop whatever they're planning until I'm back in with everyone else and start right where they left off, giving Seamus the excuse he needs to lock me up. No, at least right now, I'm not hiding. I might change my mind later. You never know," Rick said with a shrug.

"Okay, son. Have Gloria send Mrs. Salsbury in and you can hang out in the office until the bell rings for your first class," Delaney agreed.

"I'll come back when the bell rings for Homeroom. Gotta see Jor and explain," Rick promised. He slipped out to the student lounge to tell the others what he was planning to do.

"Dammit, why'd he have to figure that out?" Brain growled. He stomped towards Blade's locker to give his leader the bad news.

"Leave 'er alone this week then," Blade suggested. "It'll make the next couple even better."

The week, at least at school, was so much better for Megan. She still felt like someone was staring at her in class, but she learned to ignore it. At home, though, she always felt like she was being watched. The feeling wasn't there if Rick was at home or when Rick was in the main house with Megan. She took to keeping her drapes drawn over the balcony doors and avoiding her cousin as much as possible. She felt bad about it, but she felt a little safer.

Friday began shiny and new. The sun was just starting to peek over the horizon as Megan showered and got dressed. She was sitting at her vanity when her private line chirped. Glancing at the number, she picked it up with a wry smile.

"Morning, Rick. What's up?" Megan greeted her cousin. Or so she thought.

"Morning, Megs. I'm watching you!" came the singsong voice. "Y'know something, cuz? You look wonderful today. That sweater's just the right colour – blood red. My favourite."

Megan sat at her vanity, frozen with fear. She turned her head ever so slightly towards her balcony doors. She had opened her drapes a bit just a few minutes ago.

"What's the matter, cuz? Cat got your tongue?" her caller taunted.

"What do you want?" Megan asked timidly. She was terrified. In the background, she swore she could hear muffled laughter and whispers.

"I'm not gonna tell you, cuz," the caller drawled lazily. "It's not time yet. So, you just keep on getting ready for school, cuz. I'm enjoying the show."

Megan screamed and threw the phone across the room. She stumbled to her balcony doors and struggled to close the drapes, but they refused to cooperate. She was sobbing loudly and trying to hide at the same time. She was so upset she didn't hear her father come in. She shrieked again when Ian grabbed a hold of her.

"Megan, lass, it's your father," Ian said as he dodged a flying hand.

"Daddy? Oh Daddy!" Megan sobbed, clinging desperately to her dad.

"Sweetheart, what's wrong?" Ian demanded as he held her.

"Phone. Rick. Watching me," Megan continued to sob and began to hiccup as she struggled to calm down.

"What?" Ian demanded, trying to figure out what Megan was talking about.

"Phone call this morning. Rick's number,' Megan continued. She suddenly tore off the red sweater and threw it in the garbage.

"Megan! What're you doing? Your mother gave you that!" Ian said, indignant Megan would throw away a gift from her mother.

"I don't care, Daddy. She'd forgive me! He said...he said it was just the right colour – blood red!" Megan said through another fit of crying.

"Megan? Lass, you ready yet?" Mickey asked, sticking his head into Megan's room. "What's going on?" he demanded as soon as he saw Megan's red eyes. She had pulled another sweater on and tried to braid her hair with shaking hands, but she wasn't doing very well. She stumbled to her boyfriend with a wordless cry and clung to him as desperately as she had clung to her father.

Ian tried to keep an open mind, but when he pulled Megan's phone up from where it fell, he couldn't help but growl when he saw his nephew's number on the call display. "I'll beat him until he can't stand no more," Ian swore out loud.

"Ian, what happened?" Mickey demanded again as he worked to calm Megan down. Ian told Mickey what he knew. Frowning, Mickey pulled his cell phone out of his pocket and called his dad. He listened quietly for a few moments, made his own quiet comments, then hung up the phone. "Dad doesn't want us to do anything different today, Ian. He wants us to leave it for now," Mickey said through gritted teeth.

"Like hell," Ian snapped and stormed out of the room, ignoring Mickey's call to come back.

From where they stood, watching in the woods, Brain and Blade laughed quietly as Ian stormed over to Rick's house and pounded on the door. They couldn't hear what was said but they could see how angry Ian was. Brain swung the binoculars he had taken from his dad back to Megan's window. She still hadn't been able to pull the curtains all the way closed in her hysteria and they could see how upset she still was.

"Man, I don't think that could'a gone any better, Brain," Blade said, his breath steaming in the cool morning air.

"Yep," Brain said, distracted by what he was watching.

"I wonder, then, can we move it up?" Blade asked as they tramped back to Brain's car.

As they sat in the car and warmed up, Brain thought about how he planned to do things. "I don't know, man, depends, I guess," he said.

"On what, man?" Blade demanded.

"On how everyone reacts and if I can get what I need. I gotta see a man about something to help us take her. And I've got to see the doc tomorrow. Hopefully I'll find what I need," Brain explained patiently.

"Why the doc's?" Blade wanted to know as they took off to school.

Brain hesitated, knowing Blade would be angry. "I'm still having trouble breathing from the fight with Moneyman. Ribs still bug the hell outta me when we fight, and we've been fighting a bit more lately than normal, especially with the Slayers," he finally admitted.

Blade just grunted. "Need anythin'?" he asked, choosing to ignore his gang's mistaken attack on Rick.

"Somethin' to grease a palm would be good," Brain said.

"'Kay. You gotta plan fer today?" Blade asked as they approached town.

"Yeah. Got 'er first letter. I'll probably wait until lunch, though. Give 'er time to chill," Brain said with a shrug. He still didn't like the whole damn idea. There was a whole hell of a lot that could go wrong with the entire plan, no matter how good it was.

Blade didn't say anything. "I'm gonna see our employer tonight. I'll see if I can get it then."

The Knights sauntered into school just in time to see and hear another fight between the O'Reilly twins over Rick.

"Same old story, different day," Brain remarked. "Where's Moneyman? Figured he'd be right there with his chick."

Blade looked around the lounge and finally spotted Rick in the shadows. Even from across the room, he could see how hard Rick was working to keep his temper in check. Blade chuckled nastily and nudged Brain, who turned to look.

"Holy Crap! All of this because of one little two-second phone call?! What's gonna happen when we really get going?" Brain spoke softly.

"Can't wait to see, man. Look! He's goin' over! Do it now!" Blade urged.

Looking around to see if anyone was watching, Brain eased around a group of students who managed to block him from being seen by the four friends. He slipped the letter into an open pocket of Megan's backpack before his shield of students began to move again. He stood up, smoothly joined the group walking away and gave Blade a sly grin as they split away and headed to their respective Homerooms, leaving Rick arguing with Megan and Mickey, with Jordan standing firm with her boyfriend.

"For crying out loud, Mick, you just can't resist, can you?" Rick snarled when he finally couldn't put up with the harassment any longer. Mickey had been trying to talk Megan into pressing charges based on a single phone call.

Rick took a couple of deep breaths to calm himself down. He forced himself to look away from Mickey's baleful glare and Megan's red, swollen eyes. As he looked around the rapidly emptying lounge, Rick's gaze locked onto Blade. Rick couldn't quite suppress a gasp as he felt a familiar sensation of impending doom. Unable to tear his gaze away, Rick stood, frozen, frightened of Blade for the first time.

"Champ? Rick, man, what's up?" Tom's voice was low and harsh in Rick's ear.

To his credit, Rick didn't jump out of his skin at his friend's voice. "He's coming. Soon. Too late. Dammit, I'm too late," Rick moaned as if in absolute agony.

For the first time since he had set foot in Megan's room that morning, Mickey actually stopped reacting and listened to Rick. He'd never heard that sound come out of any human throat before. It was the same moan of agony Mickey had heard from his favourite pony when his dad had to put her down after badly breaking her leg. A terror so primitive nothing could match it. And Mickey didn't understand why Rick was that terrified.

"Chill, Champ," Tom said, trying to ease the tension.
"Whatever Johnny's planning, we'll meet head on," the young teen said confidently.

"Carl, get them to Homeroom. Jor, go. Now!" Rick ordered in a low growl, trying to keep himself under control.

Jordan knew that tone, and spun on her heel, totally unfazed. Mickey, however, wasn't going to let that slide, and sent his compassion flying out the window. "You do *not* talk to my sister like that, boy," Mickey snapped.

Jordan quickly spun back to face her brother. "Mick, it's okay. I'm cool. Rick's tense right now and he's just being a bit overprotective. Let's go and leave him alone. Catch ya at lunch, love," Jordan said as if it was the most natural thing in the world.

Once Tom and Rick were alone in the student lounge, Tom turned to Rick with a frown. "What the hell, Champ?" he demanded.

Rick closed his eyes. Blade had left as soon as the twins and Megan had left the lounge with another smirk in Rick's direction. Rick couldn't help feeling sick to his stomach. He stumbled over to a nearby bench and fell heavily onto it. He tried to calm down but all he could see was an extremely still, beaten, and bloody Megan lying in front of him. He actually began to cry softly, begging her forgiveness.

Tom didn't know what to do. He'd never seen his friend like this. Like the Champ was broken. Thinking quickly, Tom pulled out his cell phone and called Tony.

"Whitefish," Tony answered his phone.

"Fish? Tom. Something's wrong with the Champ," Tom said. He glanced up and saw Delaney frowning at them. Tom just shrugged and pointed to Rick.

"What's happened, Kid?" Tony asked. He turned his car around and immediately headed towards the school. If something had happened to make Tom call him, Tony wanted to make sure Rick didn't go head hunting.

Tom quickly outlined the morning. "Rick's sitting in the lounge, crying. He's actually crying, Tony. Johnny's gonna have a field day with this, man," Tom said, concerned.

Tony hung up, flipped on his lights and siren and made it to the school in record time. Between them, Delaney and Tom managed to convince Rick to come to the office, but Tom figured Blade had seen everything anyway. Not that he could do anything about it, Tom realized, but still it was unnerving to think Blade had seen the Champ break down. Tom met Tony at the front door and silently led the cop back to Delaney's office where a still visibly upset Rick sat, his head in his hands, softly whispering, "No. Please, no. Not her."

"Okay, Kid. One more time. What happened?" Tony ordered, ignoring Rick for the moment. Tom once again detailed what had happened. Tony stopped Tom when the teen reached the part about Rick's reaction to seeing Blade.

"Rick actually looked terrified? Of *Johnny*?" Tony asked, incredulous.

"Yeah," Tom said, dejected. *We've finally found someone who can defeat the Champ*, Tom thought, *and all it took was one look.*

Rick finally raised his head and croaked, "Not *of* Johnny, Fish. Of what he's gonna do." Rick drew a shuddering breath, the tears gone for now, but still looked far too upset for Tony's liking. Time was the only thing that would calm Rick down, Tony knew. Nothing else.

"Whatever you do, Delaney, do *not* let him leave this room until at least lunch," Tony ordered the startled principal.

"Why not?" Tom asked, as surprised as his principal.

"If you do, I'll be hauling him in on Murder charges," Tony said seriously. Tom and Delaney looked even more startled as Tony continued. "To you, he's just crying, upset. But I know he's angry underneath that, hurt and frightened and the first time he saw Johnny, that'd be it. Johnny'd be dead, just so Meg'd be safe. Jor, too. Kid, you got someone to stay with him until he calms down?"

Tony looked at Rick who hadn't moved from where he was leaned over, again holding his head in his hands, tears falling silently.

"You're serious, aren't you, Fish?" Tom asked, paling as he thought about what Tony had just said about his friend.

"Deadly," the cop replied, his voice low.

"Well, I guess between me and Carl, we could probably hold him, but I really don't got any *one* Angel who can match him. You know that," Tom said.

With that, Tony left the school, confident Delaney would keep Rick at the office until he truly calmed down. Tom would watch over his friend, keeping the rest of the school safe. Tony was positive he'd heard the last of the situation until it was time for Rick's counselling later that afternoon.

Positive, that is, until a sobbing Megan called him just before lunch. "Whitefish," Tony said when he answered his cell.

"Tony, stop him!" Megan sobbed hysterically.

"Meg, calm down and listen to me for a sec. Okay? Now, tell me what's wrong," Tony ordered softly. He got up from his desk and walked to an empty interrogation room. The last thing Tony wanted was for Seamus to overhear any of this.

"He called me this morning and now I found a note in my backpack from him," she said through her attempts to stop crying.

"What's it say?" Tony asked as he grabbed a pen and paper.

Megan took another shaky breath as she read. "Hey, cuz. Like the call this morning? I sure did. That sweater was perfect. Why'd' ya throw it out? It's so nice. Really too bad. I'll just have to come and get it. Keep it as a little memento. My little prize. Now, gotta question? Want it to all go away? Huh? Sure ya do. Piece a cake, Megs. Just show me some money. Gran's changed the will. Cut my old man out and now he's coming after me. Get Gran to change it back or I'll just have to finish what I started in November. Get me the money, cuz, or else."

Chapter 9

Tony was stunned. *This is about money?* Tony thought, trying to figure out what exactly was going on. *Rick wouldn't need money – he has enough to last him a lifetime.* Tony knew exactly how Nana's will worked and Rick would never have to work a day in his life when he turned 18 unless he absolutely wanted to. Tony was quiet as he thought over the note. Suddenly, it all made sense. Michael was out of money and was still getting further and further into debt with Carlos Mendez, his bookie. Someone had found out about it and was going to use it to intimidate Megan, most likely into pressing charges or something else equally stupid.

Too bad no one else'll see it my way until it's too late, Tony realized as he finished writing down what Megan had told him. *All anyone's gonna see is Rick making another threat against Meg. Just friggin' great.*

Megan couldn't stand Tony's silence. "Tony, is this as bad as I think it is?"

"I admit it's pretty horrible, especially after that call this morning," Tony began. His mind was already turning things over.

"Nana's not gonna change the will. Next year, Rick's gonna get enough money to last him a lifetime," Megan pointed out. "Tony, what am I gonna do?"

"I don't know, sweetheart, but you absolutely must *not* show Mick that letter or tell him about it at all. That boy has a hair trigger temper when it comes to Rick right now, and I'm gonna need some time to figure out what's going on. So I need to you get Mick to bring you to the youth centre after school so I can see the original letter. Can you do that? Tell him his dad wants a formal statement about the phone call and you said you'd give it to me, but swear to me you won't tell Mick about that letter," Tony ordered.

Megan sighed. *Secrets from my boyfriend. The one person I do trust*, Megan thought sourly. *That's just great.* "Alright, Tony, I swear I won't tell Mickey. Yet," Megan said as she hung up.

She took another look at herself in the mirror and sighed. She was an absolute mess. She splashed some cold water on her face, trying to scrub away the tears. She took several minutes to touch up her makeup, then shoved the note, carefully, into her binder, hopefully where Mickey wouldn't see it.

"What's the holdup, Megs?" Jordan asked, sticking her head into the bathroom.

She glanced at Megan's red eyes and, after a quiet word with someone outside, slipped into the room. "Here," she said, reaching for Megan's makeup. "You missed a couple of spots."

"Don't you want to know?" Megan asked curiously as her friend worked quickly.

"Nope. Odds are if you're in here, crying, by yourself, something's happened and you're probably blaming Rick. As usual. So, no, Megs, I don't wanna know," Jordan said firmly as she tossed her friend's makeup back into her bag.

"Oh, okay. At least, I don't have to hide it from you," Megan said as they left the bathroom.

Carl and Tom were nowhere to be found. Instead, Jordan greeted a couple of boys Megan hardly knew, but knew she could trust them. They wore their Grey Angels t-shirts, so obviously Carl and Tom got called away for something else and left these two to watch over the girls. Mickey wasn't far away, chatting with a couple of other friends. Megan forced a smile as she slipped an arm around Mickey's waist.

"You okay, lass? You're looking a little pale," Mickey asked, kissing the top of her head.

"Yep. We're good. Just a touch of indigestion. Should go away once we eat. Tony wants to see me at the centre after school, though. Your dad wants a formal statement about the call this morning and Tony thought I'd be more comfortable doing it at the centre instead of the station. I agreed," Megan explained as they walked to the cafeteria.

Rick, Tom and Carl were waiting for the twins and Megan by the door. Judging by the way the two Angels were standing with Rick, the other three figured something had happened after they had left the lounge this morning. Mickey immediately grabbed Jordan as she went to her boyfriend.

"Champ, don't," Carl said, as Rick tensed over Mickey's action. It was low enough only Tom could hear.

"Let...me...go," Jordan said through clenched teeth.

"Not a chance, sis. Look at him. He'll hurt you," Mickey protested and didn't move his hand.

"And you *honestly* believe keeping me from him's gonna make this any better? Grow a brain, Mick," Jordan said dryly.

Mickey sighed, but let her go. It was getting harder and harder to trust her, especially with Rick's next words. "Keep between me and Megs, Carl. Tom, behind us," Rick ordered as he threw an arm around Jordan's shoulder and walked into the cafeteria. He figured his rolling stomach wouldn't be able to handle a lot of food, so he just grabbed a ready-made sandwich and a bottle of milk. Everyone else loaded up and headed to their regular table.

Rick tuned everyone out as they chatted, trying to keep everything under control. This had been a bad morning. Needing the two best Angels to watch over him instead of guarding Megan and Jordan had just made him madder, instead of calming him down. *Too bad Fish had been right*, Rick thought as he nibbled at his sandwich. *I wouldn't've hesitated to kill Johnny the first chance I got.* It was a sobering thought.

"Speak of the devil," Carl growled as if he had read Rick's mind.

Rick frowned as he watched Blade saunter into the cafeteria as if he owned it. The same feeling of impending doom cascaded over him just as it had this morning, and Rick surged to his feet, fists clenched at his sides. He was determined to stop whatever Blade had planned before it started. Carl and Tom followed suit, but they were only looking at Rick. The Knights continued on past the table with Blade laughing at Rick, who was now being restrained by both Carl and Tom.

Rick didn't struggle against his friends until the Knights were long gone. Then he shrugged their hands off easily. Carl and Tom glanced at each other and nodded, a little afraid of the power their friend had. They both knew if Rick had really wanted to go after Blade, they wouldn't've been able to hold him. Rick turned around and glared at the pair.

"Back off, Kid," Rick snarled and stormed out.

Jordan stood up and followed Rick out, despite Mickey's protests. She just turned and gave him a look he hated – the one that said she was a big girl and to leave her the hell alone. She found her boyfriend sitting on a bench in the lounge, his head once again in his hands. Rick didn't move, even though Jordan was certain he had heard her.

"If I told you to go away 'cause it'd be safer, would you?" Rick asked quietly as Jordan sat down.

"No," she said just as softly.

They sat for a couple of minutes, not talking or touching. Just sitting. Jordan knew he needed her there, but he also needed his space. The silence grew until Jordan couldn't stand it. "Rick? Love, what's wrong? What happened this morning?" she asked, her voice barely above a whisper.

"Tony came to see me today. After you left the lounge," Rick replied, not looking at her.

"So? What's wrong with that?"

"He told Delaney to keep me locked down until lunch. That's why Carl and Tom weren't with you and Megs," Rick murmured.

"Why? What'd I miss?" Jordan wondered. Rick didn't elaborate, just sat silently for a couple of more minutes.

"He was worried I'd kill Johnny if I saw him," Rick finally said. He didn't look at Jordan. He couldn't. *She's finally gonna see me as the monster everyone believes I am*, Rick thought miserably. He forgot how much Jordan believed in him.

"And?" Jordan asked, unconcerned.

"He was right," Rick replied. He waited for the revulsion to hit his girl.

"So? Doesn't matter. Not to me. I know you'd do whatever you had to in order to keep Megs and me safe," Jordan said, shrugging. *Although, I think Daddy'd have a fit if Rick really did kill someone, even to protect me*, Jordan thought with a silent chuckle.

Rick let out a bitter bark of laughter. He turned to face Jordan. He couldn't believe the trust he saw in her eyes. "You really don't care, do you?" he asked, incredulous. "I sit here and tell you I wanna kill another human being and you tell me it doesn't matter? Either you're crazy, I'm crazy or you really do love me," Rick said, shaking his head in wonder.

"If you think it doesn't bother me when you talk like that, you're wrong, but yes, Rick, I really do love you. I understand you're going a little bit nuts trying to keep yourself under control because you're convinced Johnny's gonna do something to Megs.

"But you don't know for sure, Rick. Just like Daddy, you don't have any proof. All you have's this feeling that something's gonna happen. A feeling. And now, all you know is you've already been accused of something you didn't do and you're powerless to stop this," Jordan tried to explain her feelings.

Rick turned to look over his shoulder as he heard someone coming. Tom and Carl led Mickey and Megan into the lounge just as the bell sounded for their afternoon classes. Rick sighed and stood up, pulling Jordan up in front of him so he could wrap his arms around her waist, almost like a shield. It was one united front against another.

Tom hesitated about ten feet away. He was still worried about how Rick was going to react. "Champ? We cool?" he asked warily.

Rick smiled a bit. "Yeah, Kid. We're cool. You're just doing what Tony told you to, right? Nothing personal?"

"Yeah."

An uncomfortable silence fell. It was finally broken by Delaney's booming voice ordering everyone to class. Rick let Jordan go, but didn't head to class. He couldn't. He just couldn't take the chance of running into Blade in class or the hallway. It wouldn't be pretty, Rick knew, for either one of them.

"Rick? Son, you need to get to class," Delaney said quietly, coming up beside Rick who turned to face the principal.

"No," Rick said shortly, trying to keep it under control.

"Just ask, Rick. Don't skip," Delaney sighed. *How's he gonna hang on? He's just so angry all the time,* the principal wondered.

"I...I just need to get outta here. Can I?" Rick asked. Delaney gripped Rick's shoulder gently in understanding and nodded. With a sigh, Rick strode out into the cool February air.

As usual, Rick's departure didn't go unnoticed. Pup slipped away, his shoes silent on the tile floor. He found the other Knights just coming out of the hall that led to their lockers.

He sidled up next to his cousin and spoke quietly. "He's gone."

"Moneyman ran? Yer kidding!" Blade exclaimed, grinning at Crank and Brain.

"Yeah, he's gone, man. Look, Blade, can...can I talk to ya? Just us?" Pup asked, hesitantly, shifting from foot to foot. Brain looked at Crank and raised an eyebrow. They could hear something in Pup's voice. Whatever the kid had just heard had terrified him.

Nodding, Blade moved a short distance away. "Whassup, cuz?" It didn't take a rocket scientist to see something was bothering the smallest member of the Knights.

"Johnny, listen to me. Just listen, 'kay? You gotta stop this plan of yours. It's gonna get someone killed," Pup said in a very low tone, not caring if Blade pounded on him for not using his gang name.

"Where'd ya get that idea from?" Blade asked with a laugh.

"From Moneyman. Wanna know why he wasn't in class this morning?"

Blade shrugged, quizzically staring at Pup.

"Whatever you and Brain did this morning drove 'im so close to losin' it, this cop buddy of his wouldn't let 'im outta Delaney's office until he calmed down. Just overheard Moneyman tell his chick the cop's worried about Moneyman killin' ya," Pup continued. He could see Blade wasn't taking his warning seriously enough.

"What'd Moneyman say?" Blade asked, curiously.

"Said he woulda done it if he'd seen ya today. Don't know about tomorrow. Delaney actually gave 'im the okay to skip, that's how worried they're 'bout 'im blowing," Pup said. His heart fell when he realized he'd just given Blade more ammunition to use against Rick whenever they got him beaten down enough. For the first time, Pup was absolutely disgusted with his cousin. Blade didn't care if someone, even himself, got killed during this. It was always about his fun, his pleasure.

Blade just shrugged. "Let 'im come, Pup. I'm not worried," Blade said as they rejoined Crank and Brain to head to the pool hall. *Just try it, Moneyman*, Blade thought as they climbed into Brain's car. *We'll finally see who's the best.*

It was just around suppertime Blade sauntered into East Side's, looking for Michael. He nodded at Greg, who just glared at the Knight. Blade chuckled as he sat down with Michael at the poorly lit table in the back.

"Michael," Blade drawled as he sipped at the beer Greg grudgingly put down in front of him.

"Blade," Michael replied, looking to see how the teen reacted.

Blade just seethed as he took another swig of his beer. Michael laughed softly as he watched Blade's face. "You know, kid, I must've been really and truly drunk when we first met to not put two and two together."

"What the hell gave me away?" Blade demanded harshly.

"Next time, don't have your mark tell Mendez Johnny Blade's helping. Never saw the man laugh so hard. Told me all about you and the Knights, Blade," Michael said lazily. "'Course, I'd've figured it out eventually. My son did brag quite a bit about you and the rest of his boys." Michael took a couple of bites from the nachos in front of him. Blade just sat, still as a statue.

Michael just chuckled inside as he watched how uncomfortable the teen had become. "So, Blade, does this change anything? You still willing to help me out or are you gonna cut and run?" Michael taunted.

"The Black Knights run from nuthin'," Blade snarled.

Michael laughed. "Good. Now, I wanna remind you of one thing – nothing, absolutely nothing, can be traced back to me. Ever, understand? If anyone figures out that I'm using my son's old gang for this, Mendez might as well kill me right now," Michael explained.

"Just tell Mendez to back off and that I'm takin' care of things. Won't be for a couple more months, but if I was ya, I'd stop betting, man. Ya suck at it," Blade snorted.

"I'll try to remember that. You ready?" Michael sneered and handed a plain white envelope to Blade.

Blade flipped through it, saw what he wanted without even asking and nodded. "We just need a couple more things, but this'll help a lot. Glad to see I didn't need to ask for it," Blade assured Michael as he tucked the money away and stood.

"Call it an incentive. Don't contact me again," Michael said as he waved Blade away.

Blade nodded as he left, throwing money on the bar for Greg. He climbed on his motorcycle and roared over to Brain's, anxious to get the show on the road. He parked in the driveway and walked to the front door. He rapped sharply on it, smiling politely when it was opened by Brain's little sister.

"He's upstairs in his room, Johnny, waiting for you," she said quietly as Blade pulled off his biker boots and left them by the door. He didn't need the distraction of Brain's dad blowing a gasket over any scuffs left by Blade's boots on their precious hardwood floors.

"C'mon up with me, Sarah," Blade said as he threw an arm over her slender shoulders.

Brain's room was right at the top of the stairs. Clenching his teeth, Blade waited politely for Sarah to knock and Brain to open the door. Manners were expected in the Townsand household, by guests especially. Keeping that in mind, and controlling his temper at the farce, Blade turned to Sarah and said, "Thanks, kiddo."

Brain smiled at his sister. "Thanks, sis. Let the folks know Johnny'll be gone before curfew, 'kay?" Brain asked as she closed the door behind her. Brain shifted a bunch of papers off the bed so Blade could crash. Silently, he tossed Blade a can of pop as he returned to his desk to finish some notes.

Blade frowned as he could hear Sarah suddenly sobbing softly in her room next door. He saw Brain stiffen as he heard it, too, and snap the pencil in his hand as he struggled to maintain control in front of his leader. *Bloody chicks're too much of a distraction*, Blade snarled to himself. *Family or not.*

"Sarah still gettin' bugged at school, man?" Blade finally asked when Brain didn't move to continue working on whatever was in front of him. *Better be my plan and nothin' else, not even homework*, Blade fumed.

"Yeah, only now she's not eating or sleeping and Mom's getting worried. Gonna have to go and straighten them out. Again," Brain snarled.

"Focus on our plan, man. Sister or not, Sarah's just another bloody chick," Blade drawled.

"Did you come over for a reason, Blade or just to piss me off by insulting my sister?" Brain growled as he swung around to glare at Blade.

"Michael figured out who I am," Blade finally said, from where he lay on the bed.

"And?" Brain said, anxiously. His plans were already in motion and couldn't be stopped.

"Chill, man. We're good. Yer gonna need this tomorrow," Blade said, tossing Brain an envelope. He'd already taken his share and hidden it.

"Where'd you get this, man?" Brain demanded, paling. It was more money than Brain had ever seen before.

"Michael. Man, you'd think I knocked off a bank the way yer reactin'," Blade laughed. "Enough?"

"More than enough," Brain said, as he relaxed. He really had thought Blade had robbed a couple of stores to get this much.

Blade left about an hour later, after going over everything once more to make sure he had his part down. Brain turned on some music as he threw himself onto his bed. He gasped as fire erupted in his ribs. *Damn you, Moneyman,* he growled silently. Brain shifted around until he was finally comfortable. He lay in bed, thinking. Tomorrow...tomorrow there'd be no going back. Once he walked through that door, Blade couldn't change his mind.

"Damn fool," Brain muttered.

As he finally drifted off to sleep, Brain couldn't help wondering if he was talking about Blade.

Or himself.

Chapter 10

The next morning, Brain sauntered into a downtown shop in Collingwood. It looked like any other shop on the street, but this one was special to Brain. He looked around at the merchandise and thought he spied what he wanted in a locked cabinet. Standing behind the counter was an olive-skinned man, who immediately paled when he saw Brain lean on the cabinet next to him.

Brain just waited patiently as the owner finished with the other customers in the store. He followed the last one to the door, flipped the 'Open' sign to 'Closed,' locked the door and pulled the shades down. Once he was certain no one could see into the store, he turned back to Brain. Even from across the store, Brain could see how nervous he was.

"You promised! You swore to me! Never again, Brian!" he hissed.

"Oh, chill, Elijah. No one knows," Brain said smoothly. It was fun to watch someone quiver and quake when you had power over them. *No wonder Blade loves this*, Brain thought as he watched Elijah fall to pieces.

"I don't care, Brian. I won't do it. Never again," Elijah said, as firmly as his shaking voice could.

"Elijah, Elijah, don't even think about it. I still have the photos and the video. Do *not* make me send them to your wife. Or your lady friend," Brain chided softly.

Elijah paled even more. "No, please. I'll...I'll do whatever you want," Elijah said, defeated. A moment's indiscretion and he was facing this stupid punk's threats of exposure every time he turned around if he didn't do exactly what Brain said.

"Now, I need something special," Brain said, glancing at the guns locked in their glass cases.

Elijah stiffened. "Absolutely not, Brian. I can't do that, no matter how much you threaten me. A knife I can fudge, but not a gun. No way. Forget it," Elijah said. He was much more confident this time.

"Will you please just chill? I don't need an automatic, although it'd probably help," Brain said under his breath.

"Then what *do* you want?" Elijah asked, puzzled.

"That," Brain said, pointing to the gun case. "That one right there. The darts can hold any kind of liquid tranks, right?"

"Yeah, but even that I can't do. You're still not old enough," Elijah said stubbornly.

"Elijah, don't make me call the lady," Brain said softly. Menacingly, he stepped closer and closer to Elijah, manoeuvring the terrified shop owner around until he was pinned against the gun case.

"Brian, I just can't! If the cops found it and traced it back to me, I'd *have* to tell them who I sold it to," Elijah whined. Brain grimaced as the sound grated on his already fraying nerves.

"Fix it up, Elijah. I need it. Now. But this should cover any costs, plus some," Brain said as he pushed the envelope into Elijah's shaking hands. Like Blade, he'd already taken a portion out for himself, and hidden it away.

Two hours later, Brain slipped out of the store and tucked his prize under his seat in the Camaro. He pulled away and grabbed a bite to eat before heading to the clinic. He left his distinctive leather jacket in the car and sauntered in. He didn't have to wait very long once he gave his name to the receptionist. *It's good to go where they know you,* he thought smugly.

"Afternoon, Brian," Dr. Jim Mason said as he came through the door. "What can I do for you?"

Brain couldn't help but grin at the doctor. His deep Texan accent always seemed to precede the doctor by about 10 feet, and he had the ability to make everyone like him. Shifting up onto the table, Brain lifted his shirt to show Dr. Jim the still deep purple bruises on his ribs.

"Well, that's obvious," Jim chuckled.

Still grinning, Brain stripped off his shirt and let Jim's fingers probe gently. "When did this happen?" the doctor asked as he continued his examination. *Better question – how many times did Rick hit you?* he wondered silently, since he knew very well Rick and Brian Townsand were in the same gang – the one Rick was desperate to get out of.

"Couple weeks ago. Ouch!" Brain said and flinched away from the most painful spot.

"Sorry, son. Well, without x-rays I can't say for sure, except for that one spot. That third rib on the left side's definitely broken, but the rest're probably just cracked by now. From the bruises, I can tell you did break a couple of others on each side, but they weren't bad enough to cause you any problems. By now, they've healed to just cracks. Who'd you tangle with?" Jim asked as he taped up Brain's ribs, knowing the teen wouldn't specify.

"An old friend. Owe 'im big now," Brain grimaced as he pulled his shirt on gingerly.

"Well, you need to take it easy for about another week. Quit fighting," Jim cautioned as he made some notes in Brain's file.

"Do what I can, Doc. Oh, hey, can I ask you something?" Brain asked as he stopped with his hand on the doorknob.

"Of course, Brian, that's what I'm here for," Jim said as he looked up.

"Well, it's my sister, y'see. She's being bullied at school and it's getting really bad. She's dropping weight and not sleeping a whole lot. Mom's getting worried and wanted me to ask, as horrible as it sounds, is there something you'd recommend for her? Sarah's 'bout 9," Brain explained. "Something to help her get some sleep at least."

Jim hesitated a moment then led the way to a cabinet full of samples. He pulled out a couple of different pills, looked at them for a bit, put one away and then explained the other one to Brain. "Now, normally, Brian, I wouldn't do this, but I've talked to your mom a couple of times about this, so I've been expecting it. These will help Sarah sleep and one of the best side effects is a slight increase in appetite, especially for someone who's younger. Here you go," Jim said as he handed the sample to Brain.

Brain slipped the samples into his pocket and pointed to a vial of clear liquid that was near to the other sleeping medications. "Would Sarah need something like that if these pills don't work?" he asked innocently.

"Absolutely not," Jim retorted sharply as he locked the cabinet quickly. "That's for use under extremely controlled conditions and only in absolute dire situations. Sarah's nowhere near that bad. Anyone needing that would be in a hospital and under my constant care. That stuff's fast acting and will keep you under for about 12 hours with only a small dose. No, son, trust me. If Sarah ever gets that bad, we'll look at something else."

Absently, Brain thanked the doc as he made some mental notes of the security cameras, cabinet location and the exact name of the drugs they would need. Crank and Pup were supposed to do this part by themselves, but it was going to be too complicated for Pup to handle alone, Brain figured as he drove back to Blade's.

"Yer looking mighty happy, Brain," Blade commented as he let his second-in-command into the house.

"Hullo, Mrs. Chilton," Brain greeted Blade's mom instead of replying as he followed Blade up to his disaster of a room, Pup following closely behind with the pizza and drinks.

"Crank'll be by later," Pup said as he cleared a spot for the food, grabbed some pizza for himself and flopped down on the floor, doing his best to appear invisible.

"Well, Brain? Where're we?" Blade asked as he grabbed a slice.

"Got what we needed from Elijah. Saw the doc, and he was nice enough to show me the tranks I need," Brain said, nodding a silent thanks to Pup for the pop and pizza.

"Can we get at the stuff?" Blade asked.

"Should be able to. Gonna tag along in case Pup's unable to get in and out," Brain said.

"No. Give 'em the info and let 'em do their job. They get caught, it's their own fault. You've gotta be around," Blade said, shaking his head and ignoring the pale face of his young cousin who sat at his feet, already chewing on his second piece of pizza.

Brain just shrugged and turned the conversation to other matters until Crank sauntered in. Brain then walked Crank and Pup through the setup of the clinic and what they were going to be looking for. He explained it a couple of times, just to make sure they understood.

"Wait a couple of days before you hit it, though. Don't want the doc to get suspicious," Brain cautioned, and the four boys headed downstairs to watch a movie.

Monday morning dawned crisp and clear, yet with a hint of an early spring. Having heard nothing else about Megan's phone call or whatever else might have happened on Friday, Rick began his day by doing his workout, completely unaware of how things were at the main house. Unaware, that is, until he heard an angry pounding on his front door.

Grabbing a towel to wipe the sweat from his face, Rick strode to the door, flung it open and saw the purple face of his Uncle Ian. "Morning, Uncle Ian. What's up?" Rick asked politely.

"Don't give me that bull, Richard. You know damn well why I'm here. Again," Ian snarled.

Rick lowered his eyes and counted to twenty. Slowly. "She got another phone call," Rick stated rather than asked. "From here. From me."

"Yes!"

Rick turned quickly and grabbed his cordless. He pressed redial and handed the phone to his uncle. Ian listened, then frowned. "Sorry, Tony. Dialled the wrong number," Ian apologized to the cop.

"Nice try, Ian. Meg's already called me. Now do you believe him?" Tony snapped roughly.

"No. Just because this phone dials your number doesn't mean squat. Richard's smart. He figured out how to do this and not have his number show up. Now, are you gonna arrest him?" Ian demanded.

"No." With that, Tony snapped his cell phone shut.

"Stay the hell away from my daughter," Ian snarled one last time as he threw Rick's phone back at him. Ian stormed out of Rick's house, slamming the door behind him so hard the house shook.

Muttering curses under his breath, Rick jumped as the phone in his hand shrilled. Glancing at the number, he answered with a weary, "Hey, Fish."

"Sorry, little brother. I had just hung up from talking to Meg when you called," Tony apologized.

"How bad?" Rick wanted to know.

"Same as Friday. He's watching her. Watched her all weekend. Reminded her about the letter on Friday. Demanded that Nana change the will..." Tony began.

"Whoa! Hold on! Back up! What letter?" Rick demanded hotly.

"Oh. Sorry, kiddo. You were upset enough on Friday, and I didn't want to upset you even more," Tony said wearily. He was bone tired suddenly.

Rick flopped on his bed and groaned. "First the calls. Now letters. Didn't we go through this in November, man?"

"Don't remind me, little brother. Unfortunately, she's not finding these letters until after Homeroom and since you've basically stopped going, it's gotta be sometime first thing in the morning. See anything on Friday?" Tony asked.

"You mean before my mental breakdown?" Rick asked sourly. Tony laughed as Rick continued. "No, I didn't see anything. I knew the Knights were around, but I didn't see anyone around us. But, honestly Fish, I wasn't really looking. I was too busy trying to keep from bashing Mick's face in," Rick said ruefully.

Tony laughed again. "I remember, son, I remember. You talked a lot about that little altercation in our session."

Rick laughed too. "I know, I remember too. Look, Fish, just so you know, I'm gonna do the best I can to stay away from Megs. I'm not gonna stick my nose out until Mick's picked her up and left. I'm gonna stay away from her at school, even at lunch. I'm not going through this again," Rick vowed as he and Tony hung up.

Brain chuckled as he unhooked his phone from the phone line. "Ahh, technology. Damn, you can find anything on the Internet for the right price," he laughed as he climbed into his car and drove off. And if Moneyman thought avoiding his cousin was going to save her, he was going to find out quickly just how wrong he was.

Chapter 11

Rick was true to his word to Tony. He even waited an extra five minutes after Mickey had pulled out before he left for school. He sighed when he pulled into the lot and realized the only spot left was right beside Mickey's truck. Scowling, Rick pulled the Firebird into the spot and walked into school just as the bell rang for Homeroom.

All day long, Brain was impressed at Rick's determination to stay away from Megan. Even at lunch, Rick and Jordan sat as far away from Megan and Mickey as the table would allow and made sure Megan kept her backpack on the chair beside her.

"Impressive," Crank murmured as he and Brain ate.

"Yeah, but we'll get it done after school," Brain said with a shrug. Then he grinned at Crank. "It's a shame the only spot left is right beside Mickey Mouse, now isn't it?" They both roared with laughter.

By the time Rick arrived at the centre that afternoon, he was positive his plan had worked. That was, until he saw Seamus standing at the front desk, waving another piece of paper at Tony. Livid, Rick turned on his heel and stormed off to the boxing gym, ignoring Tony's call to him to wait.

"Well, c'mon, Tony. Let's go talk to him," Seamus said harshly.

With a grimace, Tony followed his boss to the gym where Rick had already changed, taped up his hands and was pounding on the speed bag in the short time it took for the two cops to arrive. For the first time ever, Seamus actually got to watch Rick and he was impressed. Scared, but impressed. *How'd he learn that much so quickly?* Seamus wondered.

"You sure you wanna talk to him, boss?" Tony asked with a faint smile.

"Um..." Seamus hesitated as he watched Rick's hands fly.

"Gimme a sec, boss," Tony said. He walked to where Bob was talking to Rick and didn't bother to hide his smile at his boss' discomfort.

"Okay, Champ? Understand? Good. Go. 20 minutes," Bob ordered and stood back.

Rick squared his shoulders, nodded once at Tony and began. "New pattern, Bob?" Tony asked quietly as he immediately noticed a change in the rhythm of Rick's swings.

"Yeah. Trying to focus on some different shots. Now, why's O'Reilly here bothering my best boxer?" Bob demanded just as quietly. He frowned as Tony explained.

"How's Rick?" Tony asked, not thinking Rick would be able to hear him over the noise of the bag. He was wrong.

Rick didn't look up as his hands continued their non-stop rhythm. "Pissed, Fish. How'd you expect me to be?" he demanded, loud enough for O'Reilly to hear. "Are my prints even on the damn thing or has O'Reilly just jumped to his usual conclusion?" The pattern never changed, but Rick was swinging harder and faster.

"Uh, Tony, I, uh...I think I'll leave ye to talk to him," Seamus said blandly and strode out. Tony and Bob laughed at how quickly Seamus left.

"Rick, think. At any time today, do you remember being near Meg's bag?" Tony asked.

Rick shook his head. "Not even at lunch. It was on the chair right beside Megs, across the table, with at least three chairs between us. An octopus might've reached it, but not me. Not without actually standing up, and going around the table," Rick replied, hands never slowing.

"Dammit," Tony swore quietly. The only sound for the longest time was Rick's hands connecting quickly and effortlessly. When he suddenly stopped, Tony looked up, startled.

"What?" the cop asked. Rick hesitated and then spoke softly.

"After school, I think. Mick's truck and my car were side by side. Mick just tossed their backpacks into the back of the truck. Not in the jockey box. Meg's was right on top. Can't miss that blue & white bag, man. Nana had them made special for us. The four of us were talking for a couple of minutes beside my car. That was the only time I would've been anywhere near it and we weren't exactly watching them," Rick said slowly.

"That's gotta be when it was slipped into her bag, but damned if I know how I'm gonna get Seamus to see that," Tony fretted.

"Well, I'm not pulling out of school or locking myself in Delaney's office again. Screw that. We're just gonna have to figure out how to stop this," Rick snapped.

"As long as they get a single moment, we don't have a chance to stop them," Tony pointed out dryly.

Rick nodded. "Fish, what're we gonna do?" he asked as he returned to his workout.

"Right now, son, my sole focus is keeping your butt outta jail," Tony retorted. "See you after your workout."

That night, before he was even home, Rick was told under no uncertain terms he was no longer allowed at the main house. "You *will* stay at your house and the hell away from my daughter," Ian snapped and hung up the phone.

"Ian, you're doing it again," Nana chided softly as Ian stomped into the dining room.

"I don't care, Mother. Until Rick stops this, I'm not gonna give him any extra opportunities to get at Megan," Ian said as he sat beside his daughter, giving her a hug.

Megan's eyes were still swollen from crying. She had spotted the letter this afternoon just as the trio climbed into Mickey's truck. She had read it and instantly burst into tears. Mickey hadn't said a word, just driven straight to the station to see his dad. Moments later, Seamus stormed out looking for Rick.

An uneasy silence fell as Megan picked at her dinner, eating a bit here and there. She ignored the conversation between Nana and her dad as she thought about the two phone calls and the letters. They were nastier than the ones in November, and yet the calls would never last as long. The voice was smoother, too, like someone was taking great pleasure in tormenting her. No matter what they said, Megan vowed to be stronger.

"Megan?" Nana said suddenly, startling her granddaughter.

Megan sniffed back another small sob. "Yes, Nana?"

"Sweetheart, I know it's been a rough day, but you need to get working on your homework and unfortunately, your father and I need to go back to Hollyhock's," Nana began.

Megan panicked. "Let me call the O'Reillys. Can you wait until they get here?" Megan begged, desperate to not be alone.

"Of course, lass. We won't leave you alone," Nana soothed.

Mickey arrived less than five minutes after Megan called him, striding confidently into the library where Megan was talking with her father. She smiled gratefully at her boyfriend as he sat down at the table near the window. She frowned as she realized Jordan hadn't come.

"We'll be back in a couple of hours, kids. Mickey, please don't leave until we get back," Ian said as he and Nana left the pair alone.

Megan looked at Mickey expectantly. He sighed. "If she couldn't see Rick, she wasn't coming. Dad said no, so she said no," Mickey said as he opened his textbook. "Rick just means more to her, I guess."

The couple worked happily for the next hour or so, with no interruptions until Megan excused herself to grab a book from her room. Her phone shrilled as soon as she opened the door.

She hesitated and it rang again.

Still she hesitated. The third time, her answering machine picked up.

"Megan!" came the singsong voice. "I know you're there, cuz, so you might as well pick up. No? Oh well. Doesn't matter, cuz. I'll get you to talk to me again soon enough. Want to know how?

"Saw Mickey Mouse arrive and your dad's gone. You're all alone in your room right now and I'm just outside your window.

Wonder who'd get to you first, cuz? Me or Mick." The caller stopped talking.

Megan took a hesitant step towards the door only to freeze when she heard a scraping sound at the balcony doors. Her caller chuckled. "Poor Megs. Don't know whether to run away or stay and fight."

"Why me?" Megan whispered, not even realizing she had spoken out loud.

"So why you, Megs? Simple. I need money and Gran just adores you. One more week, Megs. Gran doesn't change the will, I'll just have to be a bit more...direct, shall we say?"

Megan couldn't stop the scream that clawed its way out of her throat as her caller laughed and hung up. Mickey pounded up the stairs and barrelled into Megan's room just as a black shadow moved across her window. She screamed again as Mickey tore across the room. He struggled to unlock the doors and by the time he managed to get the doors open, Megan's visitor was long gone into the dark night.

"Here, Megan, lass. C'mere," Mickey said, trying to soothe her. He wrapped his arms around his girlfriend and held her as she cried, murmuring soothing comments in her ear.

Megan struggled in Mickey's embrace. "Phone. Message. Tape," she sobbed, shaking.

Mickey pulled out his cell phone. "Dad. Yeah, another one. Phone call again. Don't know, but she said she taped it. Naw, let the machine pick up. Thanks." He snapped the phone shut and continued to hold Megan. He glanced out of the window and frowned as he saw a car pull up in front of Rick's house. *What the hell?* the teen wondered as Megan's sobs began to ease slightly. *Rick wasn't even home?!*

Rick sauntered up to his door just as another vehicle tore into the yard. Puzzled for only a minute, Rick came back and leaned against his car and waited as soon as he recognized Seamus' truck. He had his cell phone out, ready to the make the call he was sure he would need to. He glanced up at Megan's window and grimaced. He could see Mickey holding his cousin. No doubt she'd been crying and Rick wondered what was said this time.

Seamus slammed his truck door and stormed over to Rick. Just as the cop opened his mouth to speak, Rick hit speed dial and handed over his phone. "Just for the record, boss, I'm getting tired of calls you don't believe anyway," Tony snapped when Seamus said hello.

Seamus sighed. "Where's he been?" he asked, resigned.

"With the *entire* boxing club from 3:45 this afternoon when you left the youth centre until he left ten minutes ago. And for once, it's not just me who can vouch for him. We were at The Pizza Place for supper and it had been a celebration until now. Still, I'm sure they'll provide a statement or two. I'm just wondering whether or not to waste my time. You probably wouldn't believe them anyway," Tony finished roughly and hung up.

Seamus slowly snapped Rick's phone closed and handed it back to the teen. "Inspector, I know you don't believe me or Tony, so I'm not even going to bother to say I didn't do whatever it is I'm being accused of. Again," Rick said as he put his phone away, anger clearly evident.

Seamus couldn't move as Rick grabbed his backpack and bag of boxing equipment out of his car and slammed his way into his house. Only a minute later, Seamus could hear a rhythmic thumping coming from somewhere in the house. It took the cop another couple of minutes to begin to walk towards the main house, as he tried to figure out what the hell was going on.

By the time the inspector had made his way to the house, Ian and Nana had made it home. "Seamus, where is she?" Ian demanded hotly.

"Here, Daddy," Megan said, coming out of the door. Her voice was once again hoarse from crying. She handed Seamus her digital answering machine.

"He was on her balcony again, Dad. Where'd he have the car hidden, so he could get back here so quick?" Mickey demanded, as he followed Megan out.

Seamus hesitated a moment, then spoke slowly. "Son, I don't think he did this. At least, not this time."

"What?" came the incredulous cry from both his son and Ian.

"I...um...just got dressed down by Tony. Rick was with him and the entire boxing club at The Pizza Place," Seamus explained quickly.

Nana led everyone back into the house and to the library where they could discuss this further. Everyone settled in chairs around the fire while Nana called Martha to bring tea and hot chocolate. Nana pulled up her own chair, and turned a baleful gaze onto Seamus.

"What, Nana?" he finally said, shifting in his chair uncomfortably.

"Now do you believe him?" she demanded quietly.

"Yes. And no." Seamus replied slowly.

"Seamus!" Nana protested.

"Seriously, Nana. So this time he has a solid alibi, but it's not even a good one. Of course his boxing buddies'll say he was with them all of the time. Even Tony would. He just has too much invested in that boy. Still, I just don't know if I trust anyone to alibi the boy, even one of the best cops I've ever trained and worked with," Seamus said with a shrug, then dug the answering machine out.

"Let's listen to this, shall we?" Seamus said as he plugged it back in.

As the sound of Megan's caller filled the library, Megan whimpered and buried her head into Mickey's shoulder. The tape was mercifully short, shorter than Megan remembered. When it was finished, Seamus unplugged it again and turned to Megan.

"Lass, I know it's hard to go back over this, but, honestly, did ye recognize the voice? Can you honestly say it was...Rick?" Seamus asked, forcing Rick's name out with great difficulty.

Megan sat very still and replayed all of the phone calls in her head, trying very hard to ignore the words and only heard the voice. She was quiet for a long time, but finally she sighed and looked at Seamus.

"No, sir," she said with sudden certainty. "No, I can't."

Chapter 12

It was a long, excruciating week for both Megan and Rick. No matter what Rick did, no matter how hard he worked to stay away from Megan, somehow, someway a nasty letter would find its way into Megan's backpack. She'd usually find it either right before lunch or just after it.

"I don't know what to do any more, Fish," Rick groused as he paced in the office at the youth centre on Friday. He'd already finished his time with Bob and the club, but he didn't feel any better for it.

Tony sighed. He was perched on the corner of the desk, watching Rick very carefully. "Forget about that, little brother. Right now, I'm worried about you." *Keep him calm*, Tony reminded himself. *He looks overwhelmed and I don't need him to blow at me.* "There's something eating at you. Look at yourself. What's going on?" Tony asked quietly.

Rick stopped pacing. He looked down and realized his fists were clenched and he could feel how much he was trembling. He turned and stood, staring, at the wall. It was several long, tense minutes before Tony saw Rick's shoulders relax and his fists unclench a bit. Figuring he was safe, at least for the moment, Tony slipped down from his perch and approached.

"Rick, son, look at me. What's wrong? What aren't you telling me?" Tony asked quietly, resting his hand on Rick's shoulder.

Rick lowered his head for a moment, then turned and faced Tony. The cop could see fear and uncertainty in the teen's eyes. "Fish, I...I...," Rick stammered, his voice catching in his throat.

Patiently, Tony waited. "I'm thinking of leaving, Fish," Rick finally blurted out.

"Where would you go?" Tony asked, not surprised. Hurt that Rick would want to run away, but not really surprised.

"Nana's got a friend down east who runs a boarding house as part of a private school. She thinks Caroline would take me if Nana asked," Rick said, relieved at finally telling Tony what he had planned.

"What about Jor and Meg?" Tony wanted to know. *What about me?* he didn't add, not wanting to be selfish. He'd miss his little brother.

"Fish, if I'm gone, they'll be safe," Rick protested. Tony hesitated, staring at his young friend, arms crossed over his chest, and leaning against the desk. "Won't they?" Rick asked, paling as he figured out what Tony might be thinking.

Tony motioned for Rick to sit down. "Personally, Champ, I don't think so. You still have that feeling, don't you?" Tony asked, then continued after Rick nodded. "So I've gotta ask. Does the feeling get stronger or weaker when you think about taking off?"

Rick sighed and slumped. "Stronger," he finally admitted, defeated.

"So leaving could put them in more danger, right? Besides, don't think your parole officer or the judge would allow you to move that far away," Tony said with a smile.

"Oh, yeah. Right. Sorry. Forgot about them," Rick admitted, a sheepish grin on his face.

"Besides, I'd just have to come with ya, kiddo. I'd miss our daily talks," Tony chuckled, relieved the situation had been diffused. From there, though, the conversation moved to different matters, until Tony decided Rick needed to go back to the boxing ring.

As Tony and Rick continued at the youth centre, they were mercifully unaware of the night's other events. *Night makes great shadows*, Pup thought as he and Crank slipped easily through the darkness to the clinic. They paused by the parking lot and waited until the street was quiet. Pup drew a deep breath and tried to calm his pounding heart.

"Ready, Pup?" Crank whispered. "Know what to do?"

"Yeah," the youngest Knight said with a shaky breath.

"Relax, Pup. Yer gonna be fine, kid. Y'know what yer doin'," Crank said, encouraging his friend.

As Pup eased his way across the parking lot, Crank grabbed his phone and dialled Brain. "He's gone…hell yeah, he's nervous! Remember what his own cousin said 'bout what could happen to 'im if he got caught?" Crank snapped quietly. "Ya'd be friggin' jumpy too, man."

Less than five minutes later, Pup was back, grinning. In his hand, he had the vial and no alarms had gone off. Crank gave him a high-five as they strolled away as if they belonged there. They headed to their favourite place to hang out – the pool hall – where Brain and Blade waited.

It was a quiet weekend for almost all involved. Rick spent most of his weekend either pacing or working out on the speed bag, trying to maintain some kind of control and calm, and failing miserably. Megan spent the weekend with Mickey and Jordan, even spending the night there. Tony and Marshall were asked to investigate an apparent break-in at Dr. Jim's clinic. No leads. And the Knights? They spent the weekend laughing at everyone walking around on eggshells and waiting for another phone call or letter. For them, it was a good weekend.

"Okay, Brain, now what?" Blade asked on the following Monday morning.

"Gonna ramp things up this week. Weather's supposed to break and really warm up. Early spring," Brain said, distracted.

"Fascinatin'," Blade said dryly.

"If we're gonna keep her at yer place, the basement can't be frozen solid, y'idiot," Brain snapped back at Blade's apparent denseness.

Blade just glowered at his second, but said nothing. They were both watching for Megan and Rick to arrive so they could get the party going.

"Dammit," Brain swore softly.

Blade agreed. Megan and the twins had just walked into school, but Rick had, once again, remained outside. Both Knights knew Rick would remain there until the bell rang for Homeroom and then he'd go to the office until the bell rang for the first class, once again wrecking any chance of getting him blamed for the letter Brain had ready.

"Wait, Brain. Look," Blade hissed, nudging his friend. There, in the door, stood an angry Rick. They watched as the teen walked over to the group, and for the first time in a long time, stood right by his cousin. Both Knights could see he wasn't very happy.

Brain eased around and overheard Rick tell the others Delaney was away for the week and his replacement wasn't letting him skip out of Homeroom anymore. Brain smiled and kept on walking. Now, finally, his plan was back on track and he could go ahead like he wanted.

As everyone walked to class, Rick felt more than a little uneasy. He looked around, cautiously, and was horrified to see how close he was to Megan's backpack. *Not good*, he realized and dropped back immediately, leaving both Carl and Tom between him and his cousin. He felt a little better, but not much. He knew exactly where he sat in Homeroom and what was about to happen, no doubt.

Standing in the door, he sighed when he saw the only empty chair was right behind Megan. "Richard, is there a problem?" Mrs. Salsbury asked quietly, puzzled at his sudden appearance.

"Yeah. Delaney's gone this week and his replacement said I had to be in class. Every stinking one of 'em," Rick snarled softly.

The teacher sighed. "Alright, Richard. You're here and I'll mark you as such, and I know you won't sit down. Just...stay put until the bell," she said. It was as if she knew Rick didn't want to be near Megan.

Megan didn't even notice the exchange. She was too busy talking with a couple of other friends about the upcoming prom and what they planned to wear, who was going with whom and other such girl things. Rick frowned as he looked at her book bag, wondering how Brain was getting the letters into it.

When the bell rang, Rick shot out of the classroom, desperate to be as far away from Megan as possible. He was the first one at his morning science class and waited while the teacher opened the door. He couldn't really pay as much attention as he usually did, but since his teacher was showing a movie about…something, it was okay.

Math was one subject to which Rick *had* to pay attention. At least it was engrossing enough he could avoid thinking about Megan. It was also the only class of the day he had with Blade and Crank. As Rick walked in, the two Knights just grinned at their former mate.

Rick sat down after glaring at both of them and counted the minutes until the bell rang for lunch. When it finally did, and Rick stood up, there was Blade waiting, right in front of him.

"Wha'cha want, Johnny?" Rick snapped. He didn't have the patience for this today.

"Like to say yer hide, Moneyman, but not today," Blade smirked as if he knew how much Rick was struggling to stay away from Megan.

In reality, Blade's only purpose in this little confrontation was to give Brain enough time to ensure Megan found the letter. Still, it was fun to play with Rick's mind and make him wonder what Brain and Pup were up to.

"If you're not here to fight, then get the hell outta my way. I'm late," Rick said as he pushed by Blade.

Blade reached out and grabbed at hold of Rick's arm, jerking him back. "Come back here, boy. I'm not finished whi'cha," Blade snapped.

Rick grabbed Blade's thumb and wrist, dug his fingers into the tendons on the underside of his wrist and twisted Blade's thumb backwards. Swearing loudly, Blade dropped Rick's arm and swung at Rick's head. Rick just laughed as he ducked the wild swing and danced away. He continued to laugh as he walked out to meet up with the O'Reillys and Megan in the cafeteria.

Chapter 13

Megan's morning was just as quiet as Rick's, at least at first. She tried not to notice him dropping back away from her, as they walked to Homeroom, desperately trying to avoid being right next to her. She tried to keep an open mind when Rick had stubbornly refused to sit down behind her in Homeroom. It saddened Megan, really, that Rick had to go through all of this and he still couldn't get anyone, including her, to believe him. It just wasn't fair.

As the bell rang for lunch, Megan excused herself, telling Mickey and Jordan to go on ahead, and went to the washroom to freshen her makeup. The note was tucked in the same pocket as her makeup bag, almost like someone knew her routine. She just stared at the plain white envelope, trying to avoid the inevitable nasty letter inside. She actually considered just ripping it up without opening it, but she knew if she did, the next one would be twice as bad.

Her hand was shaking so badly, she almost tore the envelope, trying to open it. She sobbed as she read, fear completely engulfing her once again:

Hey, Megs. Good weekend, huh? Nice. Quiet. No phone calls. No nasty letters. Just two days of relaxing with Mickey Mouse and my Sweet Irish Lady. It musta been really tense, not knowing when the next call would come. Not knowing if ya'd go to bed and if I'd be waiting for ya again.

So what now, ya wonder? Ya ready for what I'm gonna do next, cuz? Maybe I'll just leave ya alone. Go after Mick or Jor, huh? Take them out together? Oh hey, even better – you and Mick. Sorta like Bonnie and Clyde. Wouldn't that be fun?

*Here's the deal, Megs. I'm tired of waiting. I
know Gran hasn't changed the will yet and I'm
getting kinda impatient. And ya really don't want to
see what I'm like when I get pissed, Megs.
November'll be nothing compared to what I'm gonna
do this time.*

*This time, ya won't live long enough to say
good-bye to me, let alone Mickey Mouse, I promise.*

*You're not gonna know where and ya
definitely won't know when. Just keep looking over
yer shoulder, cuz and I'll be there. Waiting. Watching.*

MM

Megan couldn't stop the sobs that burst forth as she finished
reading. This time there was no way to mistake the threats and
Megan knew this time "Rick" meant it. She wouldn't survive.

It took her several minutes before her tears and sobs
stopped. She washed her face with cold water trying to get rid of
her red eyes and redid her makeup. She looked at the letter and
then tucked it away. She'd give it to Tony as soon as she could while
trying to avoid telling Mickey. She left the bathroom, her head held
high and went to the cafeteria, Carl trailing behind her, silent and
steady, wondering what was wrong with her, but knowing it wasn't
his place to ask.

She hesitated a moment when she saw Rick sitting at the
table, but then realized there was more than enough space
between them, and she wouldn't have to look at him if she didn't
want to. And she really didn't want to. She quickly sat, hoping no
one would notice her red eyes or ask her why she'd been so late for
lunch.

She was wrong. Someone noticed.

Rick frowned slightly as he took in Megan's appearance. He
saw the red eyes, the way she quickly avoided his gaze whenever he
looked at her and the way she just picked at her lunch. He also
noticed her book bag on the chair beside her and he could definitely
see the newest letter just peeking out of one pocket. *If she's not*

careful, Mick'll see it, Rick thought. *Then things'll really hit the fan. He won't be able to stop himself.*

Rick couldn't help the soft snarl that escaped. Jordan looked at him, startled. "What'd I do, Rick?" she asked softly. She'd just taken Rick's hand when he'd growled.

"You? Nothing, babe, but Megs has another letter," Rick replied just as softly. "See it?" He pointed casually towards his cousin's bag.

Jordan looked and nodded slightly. "Look how red her eyes are. She's been crying, probably in the bathroom before she came for lunch, 'cause she told Mick and me to go on ahead. She wanted to freshen up as usual," Jordan said, keeping her voice and her eyes down. She didn't want to direct Mickey's attention to his girlfriend.

"And Mick doesn't know or isn't paying attention," Rick noted, glancing at the other boy.

"When do you figure?" Jordan asked.

"After Homeroom, I guess. Only class I have with her," Rick replied, knowing immediately what Jordan meant.

"Now what?" his girlfriend wanted to know as they gathered up their lunch garbage and left for some quiet moments together.

"I wish I knew," Rick said moodily as they sat in the student lounge, with Tom an ever present but discrete shadow a few feet away.

Before returning to class, Megan slipped into the washroom again and pulled out her cell phone.

"Whitefish," Tony's deep, reassuring voice came over the line.

"Tony, Megan," she said hesitantly.

Tony sighed and reached for a pen. "Another one, sweets?" he asked, knowing Megan should already be in class. "Bad?"

"Yeah," Megan sniffled and read the letter to Tony.

Ouch, Tony thought as he listened. *It's getting worse.* "When did you find it?" Tony asked when she finally finished.

"Right before lunch, but Tony, he wouldn't walk anywhere near me in the hallway on the way to Homeroom, and he wasn't anywhere near me in Homeroom, either. He stayed right by the door," Megan said.

"Okay. Well that's a plus for him, at least today. Have you told Mick?" Tony wanted to know.

"No, not yet. I can't handle the instant judgement. I mean, we really can't prove it's Rick, but Mickey doesn't care anyway. Oops, gotta go!" Megan quickly closed her phone as Jordan walked in to check on her.

"Mick's getting worried and wanted me to tell you to hurry up. What'd Tony say?" Jordan asked blandly.

"Who says I was talking to Tony?" Megan protested as she put her phone away.

Jordan put her hands on her hips and glared at her best friend. "Drop the act, Megan Attison," she snapped. "Rick and I both saw the letter poking out of your bag at lunch. We noticed the red eyes, even if my blind brother didn't. And the only person you'd be talking to at this time of day would be Tony, since you'd never worry Nana or your father. Now, what did he say?" Jordan demanded.

Megan was stunned at Jordan's sudden anger. She didn't realize she'd been that obvious. "Nothing. Seriously, Jordan. You came in before we could get into anything," Megan said as the girls left the bathroom. Jordan just snorted, but didn't say anything else as they walked back to Mickey.

"'Bout time. We're gonna be late," Mickey groused as they dashed to Biology.

That night, Tony followed Rick home from the centre to talk to Megan. "Where is it, Meg?" Tony asked as he straddled her desk chair after Martha had shown him to the teen's room.

Wordlessly, Megan handed it over and waited for Tony to finish reading. When he sighed softly, Megan spoke. "Did he deny it?" she asked quietly.

"Yeah, he did. He admitted, however, he saw it sticking out of your bag and he left the cafeteria as soon as he could," Tony said as he slid the letter into an evidence sleeve and sealed it.

"Now what?" Megan demanded. "I'm tired of being a target, Tony! What's it gonna take to get Rick to stop all of this?"

Tony sat up straight. "Easy, girl. There's no evidence Rick's doing this, y'know. His prints don't appear on either the letters or the envelopes and just because his gang sign's on them, that's no proof of guilt," the cop pointed out. Inside he cringed. He didn't know what would happen if Rick found out Megan no longer trusted him. It very well could be the straw which broke Rick, literally.

Megan didn't speak for a couple of minutes. "Maybe. Maybe not, Tony. All I know is every time Rick's in custody, things settle down at school and this crap doesn't happen. Kinda convenient," Megan pointed out.

"Of course it's convenient. Too convenient, if you ask me," Tony replied, crossing his arms over the back of the chair and resting his chin on his hands.

"What do you mean?" Megan asked, puzzled.

"Think about it, Meg. Would you really expect Rick to continue attacking you, physically, or more like verbally, if he's in jail? Considering how closely they're watched at juvy? Honestly, would you?" Tony asked, a small smile on his face.

"Well, of course not," Megan snorted.

"Alright then, let's play pretend for a sec, 'kay? Rick tells Johnny he's leaving the Knights, right? That's fact one. Fact two, we've warned both you and Jor repeatedly that Johnny'd come after you, right? Still with me?" Tony asked.

Megan nodded absently as Tony continued. "Okay, here's the pretend part. Now, if you were really pissed at someone, the easiest thing to do would be to go after that person directly, right? But what if you wanted to really mess with that person's head, screw with him so badly he'd never be trusted again? What would you do?" Tony asked.

"I sure as hell wouldn't attack someone who can't defend herself," Megan snapped, wondering what the hell Tony was getting at.

"That's right, Meg. *You* wouldn't, but *Johnny would* and you're the perfect target, made all the more tempting by the fact you live so close to Rick. Even better, your dad and your boyfriend both automatically blame anything that *does* happen on the one person Johnny wants them to blame – Rick. They're doing half of Johnny's work for him," Tony pointed out.

"Okay, I'll give you that. But what's this got to do with these attacks ending when Rick's in jail?" Megan asked.

"Just this. If Johnny's intent is to blame Rick whenever something happened to you or Jor, that won't work very well if Rick's in jail, now will it?" Tony pointed out logically.

Megan paused before sighing heavily. "No."

"So, of course, the attacks stop until Rick comes back and pick up right where they left off. And everyone makes the only logical connection they can – Rick's back, the attacks now continue and therefore Rick's to blame. Seamus finally gets mad enough to ignore the law and Rick's hauled away. The attacks should stop then, right?" Tony said.

Megan stared, deep in thought.

"It's actually quite brilliant," Tony continued. "And it *will* eventually work unless you can convince yourself, and Mick, Rick's not to blame."

"Tony, when you say it all logical like this, I can see it. Understand it. But…" she hesitated, unable to look Tony in the eye, a faint blush making her cheeks slightly pink.

"But what, Meg?" Tony asked gently.

"But when you get the call or see the letter, read it, and hear all the ugly threats, you react on instinct. You believe what you hear and see. And you just want it to end," she whispered.

Tony had nothing to say to that, so he took his leave and walked slowly down to Rick's house. He knocked absently and walked in without waiting for Rick. The cop found him pacing in the living room, the T.V. on, but the teen wasn't paying any attention to the program.

"Hey, Rick," Tony said, throwing himself into Rick's easy chair. He ran a hand over his face, trying to scrub away the tension his talk with Megan had created. He had no idea how to even begin to talk to his friend.

"Fish? Tony, what the hell's wrong, man? What'd Megs say?" Rick demanded as he sat down on his couch.

Tony hesitated a long time. He didn't want to be the one to tell Rick what his cousin had said, and he couldn't bring himself to say the words. He just sat there, his head in his hands for a very long time.

Rick waited patiently while Tony struggled to speak. When his friend finally looked up at him, Rick could see the compassion, hurt and sadness in Tony's eyes. The silence and tension grew as Rick tried not to get angry at Tony's unspoken words. But Rick knew what Tony couldn't say.

"God, no. Not again." His voice broke as he realized he was all alone.

Again.

Chapter 14

The next morning, Rick struggled from his bed, anxious and exhausted. Tony had left him the previous night to struggle with overwhelming psychological pain. Tony had nothing to say to Rick to ease the betrayal Rick felt; he knew it would take time for these feelings to ease.

As he got ready to face the day, Rick wondered how much more graphic things would have to get before Megan finally broke down and charged him. No matter what Tony said, Rick knew that day was coming and he figured it was coming sooner rather than later.

Rick glanced out the window and saw Mickey hadn't arrived yet. *If I hurry, I can get outta here before Mick shows*, Rick thought and grabbed his bag. He'd just sat down in his car when Mickey pulled in. Rick nodded absently at the twins as he pulled away, avoiding the hurt look in Jordan's eyes.

She pulled out her phone and dialled Rick's cell. "Hey babe, you alone?" Rick asked as he pulled over to talk.

Jordan looked over at her brother, who was listening intently. "No," she replied dryly. She waved Mickey out of the truck. "Okay, I am now."

"Just listen. Don't say anything, just listen," Rick ordered harshly. He quickly outlined what Tony had told him last night about Megan's latest letter and what Megan said she wanted to do. Jordan could've wept at the hurt and defeat she could hear in Rick's voice.

"Why'd you leave so quickly, Rick? I was looking forward to spending a couple of minutes with you," Jordan said quietly. She wasn't ready for the ferocity of Rick's answer.

"'Cause I'm sick and tired of bein' accused of doin' sumthin' I ain't done, dammit!" Rick snapped, slipping into the gang speak he used when he was a Knight.

Jordan gasped as she heard the return of Moneyman. "Rick? Please don't. I'm sorry," she said quickly, her voice quivering.

Rick growled at a sound that just succeeded in angering him even more. "Just drop the scared little girl act, 'kay, Jor? I don't give a damn 'bout a whole helluvalot right now, so just drop it! Trust me, y'don't wanna be 'round me right now, 'cause I'd probably do what everyone's accusin' me of doin' already." Rick snapped his phone closed and sat, shaking with anger and watching the traffic race by him.

Jordan could only stare straight ahead as the dial tone hummed in her ear. She saw Mickey and Megan come out of the door and knew she'd have to act quickly.

"Whitefish," Tony answered his cell when Jordan called.

"Tony, Jordan. Listen, I don't have much time. Moneyman's back," she said and hung up, hoping Tony understood her message.

Tony hung up slowly, Jordan's strange words ringing in his ears. "Moneyman's back? What the hell does she mean?" Tony wondered out loud. He sat in his squad car for a couple of minutes, thinking, turning her words over and over in his mind.

Suddenly, everything made sense, when Tony put it together with what he had told Rick about Megan last night. Tony tore off to the school, praying he wasn't too late to stop Rick from doing something incredibly stupid. Tony pulled up just as Rick was climbing out of his Firebird. Even from this distance, Tony could see the anger, the hatred and the arrogance back in Rick's walk. *Dammit, Jor's right,* Tony thought. *Moneyman's back. Creator help us all.*

Rick jumped back as Tony's car stopped right in front of him, blocking him from entering the school. The window lowered and Tony's voice ordered coldly, "Get in. Now."

Rick didn't hesitate and climbed in; arguing with Tony Whitefish when he spoke in that tone was pointless. Tony peeled away from the school before Rick had even buckled his seat belt.

The teen couldn't believe the anger he could feel radiating from the cop and didn't understand what was wrong. He hadn't seen Tony this mad since the day Rick had almost taken him down after the false accusation of scratching Mickey's truck. Even more disturbing was the phone call Tony made as they pulled away.

"Ma'am, Constable Tony Whitefish. Richard Attison will not be in this morning. I've pulled him out to protect the school. I will let you know if he'll be back this afternoon. Thank you." Tony snapped his phone closed and drove on silently. *Protect the school? What've I done now?* Rick wondered as they drove. He really wasn't at all surprised to find Tony had pulled up in front of the youth centre and they were the only car, aside from the front receptionist, there.

Silently, Tony led Rick to their office. "Sit down, Moneyman," Tony ordered quietly, shocking the hell out of Rick. And for the first time ever, Tony did not remove a single piece of his hardware. The gun and extra clips remained firmly attached to his belt. *What the hell's going on?* Rick wondered as he hesitated at the door.

"I said, sit down, Moneyman," Tony ordered harshly.

Rick hesitated a moment longer before lowering himself into his usual chair. "What'd you just call me, Tony?" Rick said, his voice loud in the sudden silence dominating the office.

"You heard me, Moneyman. Now, I wanna know exactly what you said, and how you said it, when you talked to Jordan this morning," Tony said heatedly. He stood in front of Rick, not Fish, friend, counsellor and big brother, but Constable Tony Whitefish, cop and ready to kick ass and take it to jail.

Rick didn't understand what Tony meant at first. He watched the cop's face get angrier and angrier as he replayed the conversation for him.

"The tone, Moneyman. I want to hear the tone," Tony ordered again.

"What do you want from me, Fish? And quit calling me Moneyman!" Rick retorted hotly.

Tony sighed and hung his head for a second. Obviously whatever Jordan had heard, Rick didn't remember. "Son, Jor called me right after you hung up on her and said 'Moneyman's back.' So obviously she heard you say something in such a way for her to believe Moneyman's come back outta the woodwork and I happen to agree with her. Now, what, _exactly_ did you say to her and how did you say it?!" Tony snapped again, glaring at Rick, trying to make him understand.

Suddenly Rick groaned. "Ah crap, Fish. I must've fallen back into the way I used to talk when I was with the Knights. I probably did it without even thinking about it. I used to do it a lot, remember, when this all started and I got really stressed?" Rick tried to explain and deflect Tony's anger.

It didn't work. "So you thought it was a good idea to threaten her? Brilliant move, Rick. Just be glad she was the only one who heard you say anything," Tony said roughly.

Rick stood up quickly and began to pace. Tony braced himself for the outburst he could see coming and wondered if he'd be able to hold up against the angry teen. "What the hell do you want me to say, Fish? I'm sorry? Fine. I'm sorry. And I really mean it. I never meant to scare Jor and I sure never meant to piss you off. Alright?" Rick said angrily. He knew his hands were clenched and he could see Tony was ready for anything, including another attack. Rick just wasn't sure if he'd be able to hold back if Tony pushed him.

"No, Champ, it's not alright. Do you truly understand what you've said to Jor could be taken as a true threat if anyone, _anyone_, other than Jor heard you say it? Seamus would've had the excuse he needs to lock you up," Tony tried to explain.

Rick stopped pacing and turned to face Tony. "What I said to Jor was stupid and idiotic, but I did _not_ threaten Megs. O'Reilly wouldn't've had a leg to stand on," Rick said quietly.

"No? 'Trust me, right now y'don't wanna be 'round me, 'cause, I'd probably do what everyone's accusin' me of doin' already.' That's just vague enough to be applied to either girl, and Seamus won't wait, not with the letters and the calls Meg's already received. It'd be too much of a risk, one Seamus won't take. Not with the girl Mick loves, and he won't care about breaking Jor's heart if it means keeping Meg safe," Tony said softly.

Rick shook his head, the anger draining out of him a bit. "How could I've been so damn stupid, bro?" he asked, dejected. The teen returned to slump in his chair, his face pale, finally and completely understanding what Tony meant.

Tony sat on his favourite perch on the corner of the desk, shifting his gun unconsciously to be more comfortable. "For once, I think I understand your logic, stupid as it is. Last night, I told you, not in so many words, but told you Meg's basically given up on you. Again. So somehow, you decided you might as well go back to the one group of people who had always believed in you, the Knights, didn't you?" Tony asked.

"Yeah, I guess," Rick said, distracted as he thought about what he had said this morning.

Tony didn't say anything, just sat there, waiting for Rick to realize what he'd just said. It actually took almost five minutes for the words he had spoken to filter down through Rick's distraction and Rick tried desperately to cover up his slip. "No! Wait! I didn't mean that, Tony! I'd never go back to the Knights!" he protested loudly, yet weakly.

"And yet, when you weren't really thinking about it, what was your first reaction to what Meg said? Go back to the Knights, once again, in an attempt to stop all of this, wasn't it?" Tony probed gently.

Rick's face fell. He felt like such an idiot. First the stupid comment, threats really, in gang speak, to Jordan. Now, telling Tony he was more than willing to run blindly back to the Knights. *Have I lost my mind?* Rick thought miserably as he sat still as a statue. *What the hell am I doing?*

Watching Rick struggling, Tony did something he rarely, if ever, did with a counselling assignment, even Rick. He sat down beside his young friend and put a comforting arm around Rick's shoulders and squeezed, trying to provide some sort of comfort to Rick. He sighed as he realized this was something Michael never would have done with his son – comfort him. It made Tony truly understand and appreciate how much he had grown this past year and how far Rick had wormed his way into the cop's somewhat battered heart.

"Son, look, I know you spoke in anger or maybe even fear, and I know you didn't mean a single word of it," Tony said softly as he dropped his arm and Rick turned to face him. "I also know you're doing everything humanly possible to avoid being sucked into whatever it is Johnny may be planning and it's not working."

"No kidding," Rick said dryly.

Tony laughed. "Okay, so we're on the same page on that. Now, we have to figure out how to erase this morning. We both know Jor won't say boo to either her dad or Mick about what you said or did, so we won't have to worry about you getting hauled down to the station, at least not today. I don't want you to stew about this either. It won't do you a damn bit of good, and will do a lot of harm," Tony pointed out. "Even though we'll have another session this afternoon, it'll be too long to wait."

Rick looked at his watch, then back at Tony. "Think Coach's here yet? I could try some boxing," Rick suggested.

"That's only going to help get rid of the physical tension and only for a short while," Tony replied.

"Fish, I can't go back in time and take back what I said, so it's gonna have to do," Rick pointed out dryly as Tony's cell phone rang.

"Hold that thought, son," Tony said as he answered his phone.

"Where the hell *are* you?" Seamus demanded loudly.

Tony winced. "Sorry, boss. Small temporary emergency came up I had to fix."

"Yeah, right. Drive the boy back to school NOW and get your butt back to your real job," Seamus snapped and hung up.

Rick chuckled. "Guess he figured out the emergency," the teen said as he stood.

Tony closed his phone and grinned back at his young friend. "Guess so, little brother. You gonna be okay?" Tony asked as he locked up the office and they nodded to the receptionist on the way out.

"Always was. You've just made me think about a couple of things. But, in case you're worried, I promise to hold it together until this afternoon, Fish, and if I can't, I leave," Rick said with a shrug as he climbed into Tony's car.

Tony didn't say anything as he drove Rick back to school. As he watched Rick saunter into school, his bag thrown casually over his shoulder and nodding greetings to a couple of friends from the club, the cop couldn't help but wonder if Rick really understood how close he was to breaking down and going back to the Knights. If he did, then Tony figured he could help keep Rick under control.

If he didn't, Tony knew things would get real ugly, real quick. *Heaven help this town if Moneyman does come back,* Tony thought as he drove slowly away.

Collingwood won't survive if he does.

Chapter 15

Lunchtime was the first opportunity Jordan had to talk to Rick. She looked at her brother and said, "Can you trust me, *alone*, for a couple of minutes?"

"Depends," Mickey said as they weaved through the other students.

"I just wanna couple of minutes alone with Rick. No one, not even Tom," Jordan said, overriding Tom's protests.

"I guess. As long as you stay at the school, I'm cool," Mickey shrugged as they met up with Rick at the cafeteria doors.

Rick smiled at Jordan, hoping she had forgiven him. "Rick, can we talk? Alone?" Jordan asked, her face absolutely neutral.

His heart sinking rapidly, Rick followed Jordan to the lounge, unconsciously reaching for his knife in its sheath on his hip. If he lost Jordan on top of everything else he'd lost, he figured his knife was sharp enough to end it quickly. He couldn't go on without at least her support. She settled onto a bench, leaving Rick standing by himself, wondering what was going to happen. He knew he had messed up badly this morning – he just wasn't sure how bad. *What'd I do?* Rick wondered as he shifted from foot to foot.

"Rick, we need to talk," Jordan said softly.

"Yeah, I...know," Rick said, just as softly.

"Rick, I need to know..." Jordan began but Rick interrupted her before she could finish.

Rick fell to his knees and took her hand, trying to keep the panic out of his voice. "Jor, I don't know why I said what I did! I'm sorry! I never meant to scare you!" Rick begged.

Jordan smiled her gentle smile. "Hush, love. I know you didn't and I've already forgotten it and forgiven you. What I wanted to know was if you were okay and not angry any more. I don't like being around you when you're that angry and I wanted to know if I should stay away until you've calmed down some more. Are you okay?" she asked again.

"Did you tell Mick?" Rick asked as his heart returned to a normal pace.

"Have you been arrested?" Jordan asked, cocking her head at her boyfriend.

"No," Rick said as he sat beside her.

"Then I obviously didn't tell him. Rick, honestly, what possessed you to leave without talking to me? Mick couldn't believe it when you just blew by us like that," Jordan said.

"I'm sorry sweets, but I'm really getting tired of blamed for all of this and I just couldn't face it anymore," Rick said sourly.

Jordan smiled at her boyfriend again. "Well then, I guess I'll just have to be content with our time here together," she said, leaning her head on his shoulder for a moment. "Can we go eat? I'm starving."

The couple went back to the cafeteria and joined their friends. They had to hurry, but that didn't stop them from chatting. Nor did that stop Rick from noticing Megan's continued silence and how she picked at her lunch again, and that her eyes were red and swollen. *How in the hell's Johnny getting those damn letters in her bag? I wasn't even at school this morning for Homeroom!* Rick wondered as he watched his cousin.

The careful scuff of a well-worn boot on the floor alerted Rick Tony was behind him. Smiling, Rick turned around to greet his friend. His grin faded when he saw, not only Tony and Marshall, but Seamus as well.

"Let's go, boy," Seamus barked. "Ye and I need to have a little, uh … chat."

Rick sat frozen, wondering what was going on. "Fish?" he asked quietly.

"Just a formality, kiddo, relax. Let's go chat, 'kay?" Tony said, trying to keep his tone light, but failing miserably as Rick frowned.

Rick looked around as he suddenly realized the cafeteria had gone stone silent and everyone was staring at him. Taking a deep breath, he grabbed his book bag, stood up, and motioned for Seamus to lead the way. Tony fell in beside him and Marshall brought up the rear. Jordan quickly joined them, motioning for Tony to be quiet. She wasn't about to let her father railroad Rick into anything.

When the whole group finally arrived at the principal's office and the nearby boardroom Tony and Rick had used before, Seamus was forced to take a step back when he saw his daughter standing, defiantly, beside her boyfriend. She just glared at her father, daring him to say a single word.

"Get to class, Jordan," Seamus said, glaring right back at her.

"No," she said shortly.

Seamus' eyes narrowed. "What did ye just say to me, me girl?" he asked quietly. Rick noticed how Seamus' hand twitched, as if he wanted to grab Jordan and how Jordan suddenly paled and put her hands behind her back. *What the hell's that all about?* Rick thought.

"I said no, I'm not going to class. I'm staying right here to make sure you don't accuse Rick of anything, especially without any damn proof," Jordan said, more defiant than before.

Seamus continued to scowl as Jordan put her hand in Rick's and squeezed. Rick turned to Tony with a sour look. "Alright, Fish, what the hell's going on?" he demanded.

"I need to ask you one question before I explain. Did you, at any time today after I brought you back, go and find or talk to Meg?" Tony asked, his voice loud in the quiet room, knowing he wouldn't have to explain anything.

With a snarl, Rick dropped Jordan's hand and stormed to the far end of the room. Seamus started to go after him, but Tony put a hand on his boss' arm to stop him. He could hear Rick muttering and cursing, trying to calm down in order to be able to talk coherently. Even Tony didn't move towards the upset teen, knowing Rick would swing at him if he did.

"Son?" Tony asked from where he stood.

"Not yet," Rick growled without turning around.

Seamus just snorted as he shook off Tony's restraining hand and strode across the room to stand in front of Rick. "Ye don't tell us when we can talk to ye, boy. We tell ye! Now, sit down!" the inspector thundered.

Tony winced. Subtly was never Seamus' strong point. "Um, boss. Trust me, it's definitely safer to wait for Rick to calm down," Tony advised dryly.

"Safer?" Seamus shrugged. "He swings, we taser. End of story."

Rick laughed suddenly, the sound low and sinister. It was one Tony had never heard before, yet one he was sure Moneyman had made more than once. "Ya really think yer fast enough, O'Reilly? Huh? Do ya?" Suddenly, Rick was moving, a blur, so fast Seamus couldn't blink, and then he heard it. The snap of something at the back of his head. Something which sounded horribly like the sound of a gun being cocked.

Seamus froze as he looked at Tony and Marshall at the other end of the room, both pale with shock. Before he could say a word, he felt Rick at his back and thought he felt something digging in. The cop could feel the teen's breath on the back of his neck and Seamus wondered if he would come out of this encounter unscathed or even alive. He slowly reached down and sighed as he realized his gun was still in its holster.

Rick's voice hissed in his ear. "Think again, O'Reilly. I don't do the same thing twice. So, now yer wunderin'. What's he got? Knife? Another piece? Or maybe nuthin'. Maybe he's just gonna rip yer throat out?" Seamus actually shivered at the anger and hatred in Rick's voice.

"Go ahead, boy. I dare ye," Seamus said gruffly, trying to keep his voice from trembling. The one thing he noticed was Jordan didn't seem to be the least bit concerned.

"Rick, no," Tony said softly, unable to move.

"O'Reilly, if you really wanted to know whether or not I wrote or put that letter in Megs' bag, all you had to do was ask me. But no. You had to come into my school at lunch, and, in front of the entire school, basically haul my butt out. You might as well arrest me and lock me up right now, because there ain't a person in this school that's gonna trust me again," Rick snarled and shoved Seamus away. The teen spun away and slammed his fist through the wall without noticing the pain.

Seamus didn't move for a moment then looked at Rick. "Alright, boy. I'll give ye that. I could've done it different, I'll admit. Is that what ye wanted me to say, boy? Huh? I'm just getting tired of getting calls from me boys telling me Megan's got another letter or call," Seamus said, running a frustrated hand through his fiery hair.

Rick turned around, incredulous. Seamus could see the blood dripping from Rick's sliced up knuckles and the cop wondered briefly if Rick had just deliberately broken his hand instead of hurting him. Rick looked down and grimaced. Tony tossed him a towel he found so the teen could wrap his hand and hopefully stop the bleeding.

"*You're* getting tired of all of this? You think this has been a walk in the park for me? You can't <u>prove</u> a damn thing and yet you insist on hunting me. Why?" Rick demanded as he put pressure on his hand. He hissed at the shaft of pain that shot up his arm, and he figured he'd probably cracked a bone or two.

"Right now, boy, I have all the proof I need. The calls all originate from yer phone number and the letters are all signed by ye. I've got the attack in November ye did on Megan, not to mention every other little attack that has happened this year. No judge alive would fail to convict," Seamus said confidently.

"Except for the small fact there's no actual physical evidence, y'know, like fingerprints, DNA, fibres, etc., that can place Rick at any scene. Meg and I cannot say for certain Rick attacked us and she's already told you she can't clearly say it's Rick voice on the phone. All you have, Daddy, is suspicion and innuendo," Jordan stated as she moved without any fear to Rick's side again.

Seamus paused as he watched Jordan carefully peel back the towel and murmur a few questions to Rick. He smiled softly as he replied in a low tone and shook his head. The inspector was almost embarrassed by how open they were in showing their love for each other, even in front of him.

And both kids had a point. There really *was* nothing he could pin on Rick, yet he trusted his instincts, all of which pointed to the boy standing, now hurt, in front of him. And he was hurt because Seamus had pushed him, wanting answers. With a soft snort, Seamus stormed out of the conference room and slammed the door behind him.

Perching on the table to wait Rick out, Tony sighed explosively as the tension eased considerably. "Rick? Son? You okay? I am so sorry about this. I would've warned you if I'd known he was gonna do that," Tony apologized.

With a shrug, Rick said a couple of more quiet words to Jordan and re-wrapped his hand. The cuts were bad, but nothing seemed broken. He could move his hand easier now. He walked over to Tony and stood in front of his friend, doing nothing for the longest time. Tony tensed when he heard the same soft click he knew Seamus had. "Rick?" he asked, trying not to worry.

Rick held out his fist and waited. Tony slowly, hesitantly, nodded. Rick opened his fist, palm up. He smiled and chuckled. In Rick's hand was a key chain with a small charm. It was a charm Tony had seen Rick use many times when trying to train his stallion, Cherokee. Rick closed his fist and squeezed; the charm clicked loudly in the now silent room. Finally, he burst out laughing as Tony sighed, rolled his eyes to the ceiling and shook his head.

Chapter 16

Wednesday, Rick managed to stay completely away from Megan, but it wasn't easy. He showed up at Homeroom just as the bell rang to go to class. He ducked in only long enough for Mrs. Salsbury to see him and nod, then he dashed away. At lunch, he bought a couple of things from the ready-to-eat section, waved to Jordan who was sitting with her brother, then ate out in his cold car, not even bothering to start it, wanting to be miserable. He dashed into his first afternoon class with about a minute to spare.

Rick hoped all of this was worth it. No one bugged him all day about a phone call or a letter, so Rick assumed Megan hadn't received one. By the time the final bell rang, Rick was ready to get as far away from the school as he could, just so he could finally relax. Whistling to himself, he stopped at the edge of the sidewalk when he saw the twins and Megan waiting by his car.

"Rick, could you do me a favour, man? Take Jordan home?" Mickey asked. Rick saw how clenched the other boy's jaw and hands were. It was costing him a lot to ask this but Rick wasn't going to gloat.

"Long as you and your dad know it won't be until after my session with Tony at the centre. Can't be late," Rick warned.

"Yeah, yeah, that's fine. I just wanna spend some time alone with Megan," Mickey explained neutrally. Megan refused to look at anyone, either.

Rick hesitated a moment. *This isn't right*, he realized as he looked at Mickey. Rick narrowed his eyes as he spied the envelope poking out of Mickey's coat pocket and realized Mickey was about to confront Megan. *Jeez, hope she's ready to tell him what's going on*, Rick thought sourly. He also hoped Mickey was ready to deal with what he was about to hear.

"Come on, sweets. Gonna be late," Rick said and opened the door for his girlfriend.

He watched Mickey toss his and Megan's book bags into the jockey box, and then waited until the truck pulled out. He sighed as he pulled out as well.

"What's wrong, Rick?" Jordan asked. "I thought you'd be happy about this. You know, spending time with me without having to beg?"

Rick smiled and squeezed her hand. "'Course I am, Jor. Just...be ready to fight Mick. Again," he said, hesitating slightly.

"He's finally gonna confront Megan," Jordan said with a groan.

"Yep," Rick agreed. "I saw another letter. It was poking out of Mick's pocket, so he's obviously found this one. And we both know what's going to happen then. I get accused without any evidence," Rick said sourly as they pulled into the youth centre.

As Rick and Jordan greeted their friends, Mickey and Megan drove slowly away from the school. Megan didn't even care they didn't head straight home. She sighed happily and settled into Mickey's embrace as close as she could, relaxed as much as she could be for the first time in months.

Megan smiled when Mickey pulled into Inland Park, their favourite place to go for walks when they were in town. There were no other cars in the lot, so they'd probably have the whole park to themselves, something they rarely did. Megan could see the buds on the trees and how the grass was beginning to show some green. Everywhere she looked, life was getting ready to start again.

Silently, Mickey helped his girlfriend down from the truck and locked the door behind her. He slipped his hand into hers and wandered slowly towards an isolated spot near the pond, another of their favourite spots. They settled onto a bench with Mickey's arm across Megan's chest as she stretched out with her head in Mickey's lap. She lay there, enjoying the silence, broken only by an occasional bird chirping in the distance.

Megan sighed as she finally relaxed. It had been such a long week. "This was a good idea, Mickey. Thanks. It's so quiet, so peaceful," Megan said, smiling up at him.

Mickey looked down at her. "So far away from whatever's been bugging you," Mickey replied dryly.

"I don't know what you mean, lad," Megan said, trying hard to keep her voice steady. Her heart pounded so loudly, she swore Mickey could hear it.

"Don't give me that, Megan. Every day this week, right before lunch, you haul your bag into the bathroom and come out about ten minutes later, white as a sheet, with your eyes all red and swollen. You've hardly eaten all week, and you're losing weight. And don't think I haven't noticed how you hardly look at Rick anymore. Now, what's wrong?" Mickey demanded. He wanted to shake her, she was being so stubborn.

"Nothing, lad, really. I'm just not feeling good lately. Must've picked up a bug or something," Megan insisted as she sat up, pulling her legs close to her and wrapping her arms around her knees.

Mickey sighed as he reached into his coat pocket and fingered the letter he had pulled out of her bag. He had spotted it in class and grabbed it before she could realize she had dropped it. Now, he wondered how many of these she had received since that morning when Rick had phoned her at home. Mickey closed his eyes and recalled the letter he had only read once, but would never forget, even as short as it was.

"Hey, cuz. Nice day, isn't it? Last night was sure fun, Megs. At least for me. Did my workout, and all I could see every time I threw a punch was yer face. Every single time. It was so cool!

"Scared probably doesn't even come close to how yer feeling, by now, I'd guess. I'm surprised Mickey Mouse isn't camped at yer house, trying to protect you. Guess that means yer not brave enough to tell him. What about Daddy, Megs? Told him yet?

"I'm getting impatient, Megs. Get the damn will changed, or my next workout *will* be on you instead of my punching bag."

It was signed "MM" and Mickey was sick.

The young Irishman pulled the letter out and held it in front of Megan's wide eyes.

"You dropped this," he said quietly.

Megan could only stare, horrified, at the envelope she hadn't ever wanted her boyfriend to see. She reached out with a trembling hand and took it hesitantly. She turned it over and over, recalling the horrible words hidden inside. She couldn't help the tears that welled up as she thought about the threats and how little she had told her boyfriend, the one person, next to her dad, she was supposed to trust.

"Megan, please. Talk to me. What's going on?" Mickey asked.

Megan sighed. "So much for a nice day," she said sourly. "You really wanna hear this?" Mickey nodded. "Where do you want me to begin?" she wanted to know.

"At the beginning, of course," Mickey replied.

It took Megan a couple of minutes to get going but when she finally began talking, she talked for over an hour. Mickey listened, silently, as she talked. He held onto his temper, barely, as she detailed the calls and the letters. *How in the hell's he getting the letters into her bag if he's not near her in Homeroom and Ian won't let him into the house at all?* he fumed as Megan wound down.

Megan looked at Mickey. She knew he was mad, just by the tightening around his eyes. "And this is exactly why Tony didn't want you to know," Megan accused. "You're upset."

Mickey turned to look at Megan and couldn't stop the snarl curling his lips. "To hell with upset! I'm well passed upset. Why haven't you charged him, dammit?" Mickey demanded.

Megan hesitated a moment then spoke softly. "I wanted to about a week ago, but Tony talked me out of it," she said, unable to look at Mickey.

"Figures. Tony'd do anything to keep the boy outta jail," Mickey said sourly.

Neither spoke for a couple of minutes, each trying to figure out what to do. Megan just stared across the pond and waited. She wanted Mickey a little calmer before they talked again. Suddenly, Mickey sat up, swore loudly and knocked Megan off the bench.

Megan grunted as she hit the ground, hard. "What's wrong, lad?" she demanded once she got to her feet and dusted herself off.

"That bastard's got Jordan!" Mickey said hotly.

Megan grabbed his arm in a surprisingly strong grip. "And they're together at the youth centre," Megan pointed out, trying to calm her boyfriend down again.

"But what about after – when they leave?" Mickey asked, trying to keep the panic out of his voice.

Megan sighed again. She grabbed her cell phone and dialled Tony, who was just finishing up with Rick at the centre.

"Hold that thought, Champ," Tony said as his cell rang. "Whitefish," the cop answered while Rick and Jordan paused by the door.

"Tony, it's Megan. Mickey found one of the letters, and he's really mad. He wants Jordan to wait there for us; can you please ask her?"

Mickey paced nearby as Megan waited for an answer. After a moment, she hung up slowly. "Well?" he demanded.

"Um..." Megan began hesitantly. She took a deep breath and plunged in. "Jordan said no, she wasn't gonna wait for you and she and Rick had plans that didn't involve you, me or your father. Then they left."

"What!? Does Tony know where they're going?" Mickey demanded.

Megan shook her head. "And he told me to tell you if he got a call from either of them, he was gonna charge you. With harassment," Megan said, unable to look at her boyfriend.

Chapter 17

Mickey couldn't've been more stunned if Megan had slapped him. He couldn't believe Tony had threatened to haul *him* to jail if he bothered his sister on her "date." But the more Mickey thought about it, the more he realized his father would never forgive him if he just let his sister go out with Rick and didn't do his best to get the two of them apart.

He turned back to his girlfriend and took a step backwards. Megan was scowling at him, her arms folded across her chest. "No. You're not going after her. I can hear you thinking all the way over here and I know what you're thinking of doing," she said firmly.

Mickey walked over to her and put his hands on her shoulders. "Look, lass. I just can't leave her alone with him. Dad'll kill me. Besides, look at these threats against you. Can you imagine what he's gonna do to my sister?" he demanded quietly.

Megan grabbed Mickey in a tight grip. "Leave her alone! She's old enough to make her own choices, Mickey!" Megan said sharply.

Mickey stubbornly refused to listen. Megan argued with him for a few more minutes then dropped her shoulders in defeat. "Fine, Mickey. You want to go after your sister? Fine, go ahead," she said.

"Good." Mickey turned to go to his truck when he realized Megan hadn't moved.

"Megan, what's wrong? C'mon. Let's go," he said, puzzled.

"You can go after Jordan once you drop me off at Hollyhock's," Megan said as she swept by a confused Mickey.

"Hollyhock's? Why?" he asked as he hurried to catch up with her.

"Because if you're hell bent on going after your sister and getting arrested, you can do it without me!" Megan said angrily. She waited patiently by the truck until Mickey opened her door so she could climb in.

Mickey climbed into the cab of his truck and stared at the empty space beside him. Megan sat, rigidly, on the far side of the truck, almost daring Mickey to say something. They sat that way for a couple more minutes until he finally sighed and drove her to Hollyhock's.

As he drove, Mickey tried to figure out what to do. He knew he should leave Jordan alone, but he just couldn't bring himself to trust his little sister, especially not her judgement, but sitting in that truck and not having Megan beside him was driving him insane. So he did the only thing he could do. He swallowed his pride.

"Alright, lass. You win. I'll...I'll leave Jordan alone. With a maniac, but I'll leave her alone," Mickey said quietly.

Megan sighed as they pulled into Hollyhock's. "Thank you, lad. I know that wasn't easy," she replied.

"You have *no* idea," Mickey said with a short bark of laughter.

"Mickey, I know it looks like Rick's doing this, and who knows? Maybe he is, but no one ever sees him doing anything, so we have to give him the benefit of the doubt," Megan said as she turned to face her boyfriend.

"So you're willing to risk your life just because no one's <u>seen</u> him doing anything?" Mickey asked sarcastically.

"No, now stop that!" Megan snapped back instantly. "I'm just trying to keep an open mind, like Tony asked me to. What if Rick isn't doing this, Mickey? What if someone's trying to frame him?" she asked.

"So what? So what if someone's trying to frame him? What's that gotta do with him hurting you?" Mickey shrugged indifferently.

Megan stiffened, then climbed out of the truck, slamming the door so hard, the whole truck rattled. Mickey was shocked. His girlfriend never got this angry, at least not with him.

Mickey climbed out and reached Megan's bag for her. She jerked it out of his hands and stormed towards Nana's store. Mickey managed to catch up with her at the door. "I'm sorry, lass. Please don't fight with me," he begged. Things were just not going his way today.

"For once, I finally understand why Tony's so...frustrated with all of this," Megan said. "There's always so many accusations and never any proof!"

"Never any proof about what, lass?" Seamus O'Reilly said from just inside the door to Hollyhock's. "Did ye get another letter?" Seamus held out his hand expectantly.

Megan hesitated, then handed him the letter. He read it in silence, then turned to look at Megan. "Are ye wanting to press charges?" he asked quietly as he slipped the latest letter into an evidence sleeve and sealed it.

Megan shook her head slowly. "No, Seamus, I don't want to charge him," she said hesitantly. Mickey fumed, but didn't say anything. He was tired of pushing the issue.

"Alright, Megan. We'll leave it. For now. Mickey, where's yer sister?" Seamus asked. Mickey flushed slightly and told his dad.

"Dang that girl and her stubborn streak. Never mind. Head home, son. Better yet, why don't ye take a ride with Megan, just be home by dark. Okay?" Seamus suggested as he climbed into his car to head back to the station.

Megan spent a very uneasy night once Mickey had gone home. They hadn't gone for a ride, like Seamus had suggested, but they had given Frank a hand grooming some of the horses. Finally, just before darkness fell completely, they saw Rick come home.

"I'd better go, lass, before I beat him to a pulp," Mickey said wryly. He kissed her quickly and climbed into his truck.

Megan stayed out of her room until it was time for bed. She changed quickly, checked her balcony doors to make sure they were locked and the drapes were securely pulled across. Then she turned her phone off so if "he" called, she wouldn't hear the phone ring and her machine would automatically pick it up. Finally, just before midnight, she fell into a troubled sleep.

Thankfully, no phone call disturbed her sleep and morning came all too soon. She went through her normal morning ritual and went down for breakfast. She picked at her toast and muffin, taking a few bites as she thought about how she was growing to hate school.

She sighed as she glanced at her watch and realized Mickey was going to be there soon. That was another thing she didn't want to face anymore – Mickey's constant pressure to give in and charge Rick. Megan just couldn't do it, not yet. Something in her heart kept telling her Rick didn't do anything.

As she finally finished her breakfast, she heard the doorbell ring and Martha greet Mickey. She had just gathered up her book bag and jacket when Mickey came in.

Mickey pulled her into a hesitant hug and whispered, "I'm sorry, lass. Please. Forgive me."

"Me too, lad. Let's go," she said.

They walked out to the truck, hand-in-hand, happy to be together again. As they got nearer to the truck, they both stopped in fear. Jordan's backpack lay on the ground near Rick's car and Jordan was nowhere in sight.

"JORDAN!?" Mickey shouted, his panic rising faster than a surging river after a massive rainfall. He spun around, looking everywhere he could. He was digging frantically for his cell phone when Jordan popped her head out of Rick's front door.

"What?" she yelled back, annoyed.

Angered and more frightened than he ever wanted to be again, Mickey strode over to the door and grabbed her by the upper arms in a painful grip. "Don't you ever do that to me again!" he half-shouted, punctuating each word with a rough shake.

"Stop it, Mick! You're hurting me!" Jordan protested as she struggled in his ever-tightening grasp. Mickey growled and moved as if to pull her close, but continued to shake her instead.

Rick held his temper as long as he could, but the last shake nearly knocked Jordan over. *That's it*, he thought angrily as he threw open the door and charged over to the twins. *How dare he hurt her?* Rick grabbed Mickey's hands from Jordan's arms and shoved the older O'Reilly back away from his sister. Mickey stumbled backwards and almost fell off the porch.

"Don't you ever lay another finger on Jordan," Rick growled as he stood in front of his girlfriend. She was rubbing her arms and muttering under her breath.

Mickey slowly pulled himself up to face Rick. "Move it, boy," he said menacingly.

"Back off, Mick. She's put up with your watchdog act long enough," Rick snapped.

Scowling at the other teen, Mickey reached around Rick and grabbed Jordan's wrist. "Come on. We're late," he said and began to drag Jordan towards the truck.

Jordan jerked her hand from Mickey's grasp and stepped back to Rick's side. She glared at her brother as she snapped, "You can shove that attitude, mister. I'm not going anywhere with you. I'm riding to school with Rick."

Chapter 18

Mickey couldn't speak as he and Megan drove to school. He was shaking, he was so angry at his sister. Megan had dragged Mickey away instead of letting him fight more with Jordan. The silence in the truck was thick enough to cut with a knife and it was hard to stay silent. Megan had debated sitting at the far side of the truck, but figured it would hurt Mickey even more if she did.

Still, she couldn't bring herself to break the silence. Mickey's high-handed treatment of Jordan rankled, but Megan had to admit Jordan brought a lot of this onto herself with her continual desire to flaunt the rules. The road to school never felt as long as it did today.

It was several minutes after Mickey pulled into his usual spot in the parking lot before he could bring himself to say anything. His voice was low and husky, his accent so thick Megan could barely understand him.

"I'm sorry, lass. Don't be mad at me. I just can't stand this constant strain. He's gotta be stopped," Mickey said softly.

"Lad, I know it's gotta be hard, but even if you don't trust Rick, at least try and trust Jordan. She's old enough to make up her own mind," Megan replied. "You've got to stop making accusations without proof and I mean *real* proof."

Scowling again, Mickey climbed out of the truck, then helped Megan. As he grabbed their bags out of the back, Mickey spied another envelope poking out of Megan's backpack. She paled as Mickey pulled it out. They both knew her bag had been zippered closed.

Mickey handed it to her. "Are you sure *you* trust him?" her boyfriend asked quietly.

Her hands were shaking so hard, Megan could barely open the envelope. Mickey clenched his jaw as he watched his girlfriend pale even more. "Lass?" he asked, holding his hand out for the letter.

Megan handed it over and leaned against the truck, trying not to cry. Mickey fumed as he read aloud the very short letter.

"Hey, cuz. Get ready 'cause it's gonna happen any time now. Remember, I'm watching you! ...MM."

"How'd this get into my bag?" she wondered.

"Obviously when we were distracted, looking for Jordan. Dammit, Megan, charge him!" Mickey demanded.

Megan didn't answer as they went their separate ways to Homeroom. Megan kept her bag under her desk between her feet in every class so no one could get near it without her noticing. She just couldn't handle another letter today. On the way to the cafeteria for lunch, Mickey's latest argument with his sister broke through Megan's wandering thoughts.

"When I see that "boyfriend" of yours, sis, he's getting a piece of my mind," Mickey snapped.

"Careful, bro, you don't have that much to spare," Jordan replied sarcastically.

Mickey was so startled by Jordan's comment he stopped in the middle of the hall. Since Megan wasn't paying attention to where she was walking, she ploughed right into the back of her boyfriend. "Ow! Mickey!" she exclaimed, rubbing at her nose. She looked back and forth between the twins and realized she had missed another argument.

"What the hell does that mean, Jordan?" Mickey demanded harshly. He reached out and jerked Jordan to a stop.

"Dammit, Mick, let go! That hurts!" Jordan protested as she tried to pull her arm out of her brother's sudden iron grip.

"Answer me!" Mickey demanded, shaking her once.

Jordan wrenched her arm out of his grasp and stared at him for a minute. When she spoke, her voice was quiet, but there was no mistaking the anger in it. "He did not do anything!"

"Jordan, we found another letter in my bag when we got to school, but I know my bag was zipped up when I put it down by the truck. If Rick didn't put the letter in there this morning, then who did and when?" Megan asked quietly.

Jordan took a step closer to Megan and Mickey. Her voice was barely above a whisper but they heard her anger loud and clear. "I'm gonna say this one last time. Rick...Did...Not...

Do...Anything!" she hissed, emphasizing each word. "From the time you left to get Meg, Mick, until you shouted my name, Rick was *never* out of my sight. Got it, *brother*? I was with him the whole time. So, unless you plan to accuse *your own sister* of stalking your girlfriend, I suggest you never make these baseless accusations in my presence again. Do I make myself perfectly clear, *brother*?"

"Perfectly," Mickey murmured as Jordan turned on her heel and stormed away, with Tom following. Mickey looked at Megan, who could only shrug at Jordan's reaction.

Jordan was still fuming when she found Rick in the cafeteria. Rick smiled as she strode up to him and threw her arms around him. He raised an eyebrow at the ever-present Tom and returned Jordan's hug.

"Mickey," Tom mouthed with a grin.

"Problems, sweets?" Rick asked as they got in line for their lunch.

"My brother," she snarled.

"What'd I do this time?" Rick wondered, although he had a pretty good idea.

Jordan told Rick about the latest note as they sat at a table away from Mickey and Megan but still close enough Mickey wouldn't complain.

"Well, since you and I were together, sounds like I got an alibi he can't argue with, huh?" Rick said with another smile.

Jordan couldn't help but laugh at Rick's attitude. It was infectious. They finished up their lunch and went their separate ways, and by the end of the day, Jordan was almost ready to forgive her brother. Almost, but not quite. She met up with Rick at his car after the last bell and climbed in before Mickey could say anything.

Her brother stood by his truck with his hands clenched tightly, and glaring at Rick, who just glared right back.

"What?" Rick snapped.

"Jordan, get out of that car. We've gotta go," Mickey said, loud enough to be heard through the closed windows.

She shook her head. Mickey flushed, strode over and yanked the door open. "Get out!" he shouted.

Rick was about to come to Jordan's rescue when he noticed the principal coming over. The teen leaned against the car and prepared to watch the show. As he leaned, though, he could feel someone glaring at him and the feeling of unease, which had gone away for a while, was back and very strong. He turned his head slightly and could see both Blade and Brain standing at the front doors.

They were watching the drama unfolding at the car with undisguised glee, as if they *wanted* Mickey to be fighting with Jordan and Rick. They saw Rick looking at them and they began to laugh at him, pointing and talking to each other. *What's going on now?* Rick wondered as he turned away to watch Delaney dress Mickey down.

"Alright, Mickey O'Reilly, I've had enough," Delaney snapped as he stopped by the car. "Leave your sister alone!"

"No. It's my job to protect her!" Mickey replied stubbornly as he tried to pull Jordan from the car.

"Protect her from what? You and your father have to quit doing this. Rick has done nothing wrong! And this constant fighting with your sister's getting on everyone's nerves, mine included, so I can just imagine how your sister feels. Your marks're starting to fall and *all* of *your* teachers're complaining about your inattention in class," Delaney warned.

"So what? I'll gladly fail every class if it means Jordan and Megan're safe from him!" Mickey snarled as he pointed at Rick, who just glared back.

"Lad, we've talked about this – you have to trust her," Megan said from where she stood by the truck.

Jordan closed her door firmly as Rick climbed in. He pulled away carefully and headed to the youth centre. Mickey just stood, fuming, as he watched his sister drive away with someone he couldn't trust, no matter what anyone said to him. Megan waited patiently. She figured Delaney wasn't done with her boyfriend and she was right.

"One last thing, Mr. O'Reilly," Delaney said, drawing Mickey's attention back to him.

"Yes, sir?"

"Leave your sister alone in my school. What you do before you walk in those doors and after you drive off of this lot, I can't control. But once you walk through those doors, you WILL leave her alone. Understood?" the principal said.

"And if I don't?" Mickey asked curiously.

"I will suspend you. Try explaining THAT to your dad," the principal said as he walked away, leaving a pair of stunned teens in his wake.

As Mickey and Megan drove home, Rick and Jordan were pulling into the youth centre. He shut the car off and sat behind the wheel for a couple of minutes. *Something changed today*, he thought as he recalled the looks on Blade's and Brain's faces. *Whatever they've got planned, it's gonna be soon.*

"Rick? What's wrong?" Jordan asked.

Rick smiled at her, trying to dispel his mood. "Nothin', sweets. Just wish your bro would cut me some slack, that's all," he said, climbing out and coming around to her door.

Jordan left Rick at the gym to do his workout with the club while she went to find Tony. As usual, he was working in his office with the door wide open. She could see he was concentrating hard on the paperwork in front of him. She knocked on the door and, when Tony looked up and smiled at her, she slipped into the office, closed the door and sat down. Tony finished up, closed the folder, and came to sit by the young teen.

"So, my sweets, to what do I owe the pleasure of this visit?" Tony asked, smiling.

Jordan hesitated a moment, then spoke in a hushed voice. "I'm worried, Tony," she finally said.

"About what?" Tony asked, now worried himself. Jordan was the one person who hadn't worried about anything in this whole mess.

Jordan told the cop about how Mickey was starting to act and how quickly he was jumping to conclusions. "Today, he grabbed me and shook me when we were at Glencrest." She shrugged out of her jacket and pushed up the sleeve of her shirt.

Tony frowned at the vivid bruise he saw developing there and he was even more annoyed when he saw the matching bruise on the other arm. "Does Rick know?" he asked as he took a couple of pictures.

"Is Mick in the hospital or the morgue?" Jordan replied with a wry grin as she covered herself back up.

Tony laughed. "Okay, point taken. Do you want me to talk to Mick 'bout this? I can actually charge him with assault for this, y'know," Tony pointed out.

"Not without my permission, you can't, and I won't do that," Jordan said quickly. Then she smiled. "But...I wouldn't object to throwing a bit of a scare into him. Maybe then he'd get the point, y'know."

"I'll stop over after Rick drops you off at home, 'kay?" Tony promised.

Jordan nodded. They turned their conversation away from all of the sudden craziness and just talked about school and other mundane things until Rick showed up for his session. Unlike most days when Jordan would wait out near the gym talking with her friends, today Tony asked her to stick around. Biased or not, Tony liked to hear Jordan's views sometimes. She often saw things Rick missed.

"So, Champ, tell me about today," Tony began and then sat back to take notes.

Rick snorted and launched into his day. He talked for about an hour then frowned as he recalled Brain and Blade watching the fight. "I just don't trust them, bro. Whatever they've got planned's gonna happen soon, I just know it. I can feel it, man," Rick said with a growl. *And I'll be too damn late*, Rick knew, trying to keep from panicking.

"Rick, just because they laughed at me fighting with Mick, which I do on almost a daily basis lately, doesn't mean they're gonna do whatever it is you think they've got planned," Jordan pointed out.

Tony nodded, thoughtfully. "I could almost agree with you, Jordan, except for one thing. Meg's this close to pressing charges," Tony said, holding his thumb and forefinger about an inch apart. "One more letter or phone call'll be enough and neither Mick nor Ian'll stand by and not let her press charges then. In fact, they'll probably do it for her."

Jordan sighed. "You're probably right, Tony. Come on, love. You'd better get me home. Daddy's gonna be worried," she said as she glanced at her watch and stood.

Rick nodded. "Later, Fish," the teen said as he opened the door for his girlfriend.

"Later, son. Jor, I'll be over shortly," Tony said as he sat down at his desk.

"He's just coming over to see Daddy, Rick," Jordan said as Rick frowned at her. Not believing her for an instant, Rick held his tongue as he helped her into the car.

When Rick dropped her off at home, Jordan stayed on the porch, watching Rick pull away and Tony pull in only a couple of minutes later. The cop climbed out of his car and grinned at her, Marshall right behind him.

"Ready, kiddo? Remember what to do?" Tony asked as the trio approached the front door.

Jordan nodded as she took a deep breath and opened the front door. "Daddy? I'm home," she called as she hung up her coat and took off her boots.

"Where've ye been, me girl? Ye should've been home a while ago, even if ye did go to the centre with the boy," Seamus said, sticking his head out of the living room and frowning when he saw Tony and Marshall standing in his foyer.

"Sorry, boss, my fault. I saw something at the centre tonight you need to know about, so I kept Jordan a bit longer to discuss it," Tony said, struggling to keep his face neutral.

"Come on in, boys," Seamus said, opening the door wider and motioning for the partners and his daughter to come in. Mickey was lounging in front of the fireplace with one of his favourite books, relaxing before supper.

"Now, Tony, what's this all about?" Seamus said after everyone exchanged greetings.

"A possible assault on Jordan here…" Tony began.

"I'll lock that boy up until he rots!" Seamus interrupted hotly.

"…by your son," Tony finished loudly.

Silence fell. The fire snapped and crackled loudly as Seamus couldn't believe what he had just heard Tony accuse Mickey of. His son was pale, but defiant at Tony's accusation.

"Prove it," was all he said.

Chapter 19

"Prove it," Mickey insisted again, when Tony turned to look at him.

"Why?" Tony replied. Inside, he was chuckling. Mickey had opened the door, just as Tony hoped he would.

"Because ye damn well cannot accuse me son without proof," Seamus pointed out harshly, standing with his hands on his hips and glaring at the partners.

Without missing a beat, Jordan glared at her father and snapped, "Then why do you continue to accuse Rick without any real proof, Daddy?"

Seamus pulled up short. Once again, his daughter surprised him with how much she really understood about what was going on. Frowning, he looked at Tony and Marshall, then motioned sharply for the partners to continue.

"Oh, trust me, boss, I have all the proof I need," Tony said as he turned to Marshall and nodded. His partner pulled out his notebook and began to take notes as Tony looked at Mickey to begin his interrogation.

"Mickey, this morning, at Glencrest, did you or did you not put your hands on your sister, grasp her by her upper arms and shake her – hard – several times?" Tony asked, knowing exactly how Seamus would react to this.

"What?" Seamus exclaimed, turning to his son. This was not what he had expected.

Mickey flushed. "Well, yeah, but she'd scared me, Tony. She disappeared from the truck without telling me," he protested weakly.

Tony looked at Jordan and nodded. She pushed up her sleeves to show the vivid bruises which had already begun to form on her upper arms. "I discovered them at lunch, Mickey, and they hurt!" she said emphatically. Mickey flushed and turned his head away.

Seamus looked at his son. "Mickey, son, while I applaud yer dedication in protecting yer sister, this time, ye've really gone too far. Tony could arrest ye and charge ye with, at the very least, Assault or Battery, depending on how bad the bruises got and there's nothing I could do to stop him. Not legally, anyway," Seamus said solemnly. *What have I turned me son into?* Seamus wondered as Mickey struggled to speak.

"But what about you, Dad? What you did at Christmas? I mean, you actually cut her," Mickey said. His protests seemed weak even to his ears.

Seamus glanced at Tony, who only raised an eyebrow. Here was something the cop didn't know and wasn't sure he wanted to know. "Technically, son, I could've been charged then too. Still could, I guess, but since the only witnesses're me children, it probably wouldn't hold up in court. Besides, I'm gonna assume if Jordan had really wanted to do that, she would've done it a long time ago. However, that's not the issue here, son. What ye did this morning is. Now, who else saw this?" Seamus asked, struggling between being Dad and Inspector O'Reilly.

"Well, Rick and Megan for sure, but I couldn't say if any of the hands saw it. I guess I shouted pretty loud, but I wasn't looking for anyone but Jordan," he finally admitted.

Silence fell once again. Mickey stood in front of the fireplace, his head hung in shame, while everyone else stared at him. *How'd it come to this?* he wondered as he waited for Tony to arrest him. *How's it that I'm the one that's 'bout to go to jail when Rick's threatening Megan? It's not fair!*

Mickey didn't raise his head as he heard Tony approach. "Mick, look at me," Tony ordered quietly.

The teen took a deep breath then raised his eyes. Tony smiled, relieving the tension. "Even if I did arrest you, you know damn well your sister would never actually press charges. But you need to understand something right now, son. This blind anger of yours, especially towards Rick, leads to this kind of behaviour and it's dangerous. I'm only gonna issue you a warning this time, but I need you really listen to me and understand what I'm saying to you. You do anything like this to your sister again, and I'll haul your butt in and give you a taste of what Rick's already gone through this year while you sit in jail for a weekend, even if Jordan doesn't want to press charges. Maybe then you'll give 'im a break. Understand?" Tony threatened.

Mickey mumbled something unintelligible.

"Didn't hear that, son," Seamus said intensely as he stood next to Tony with his arms crossed over his chest. His son really had gone too far over the line.

"I said, yes, sir. I understand," Mickey said in a louder voice, one tinged with anger. He was getting embarrassed and it still wasn't fair.

"Boss? Can I leave this with you now?" Tony asked Seamus. He knew he'd hurt Mickey's pride, but this was a lesson he needed to be taught, sooner rather than later, before he did something stupid, like challenging Rick.

"See ye both in the morning," Seamus said, dismissing the partners with a wave, still looking at his son.

Marshall nodded and waited for his partner at the front door. Tony stopped to have a couple minutes of quiet conversation with Jordan before joining Marshall. They left the O'Reillys and closed the door softly behind them. They exchanged a grin as they walked down the stairs, knowing Seamus probably had something nasty planned for his son as punishment.

"Jordan, I need to have a few private words with yer brother. Why don't ye take yer stuff upstairs, me girl? I'll call ye for supper," Seamus said. He hadn't taken his eyes off of his son, who continued to stand with his head hung low. "Now!" he barked when Jordan didn't move right away. She fled after giving her brother a frightened look. Mickey looked resigned to his fate and gave her a shooing motion, sending her upstairs. *What've I done?* she wondered as she closed the door behind her.

Seamus was angry at his son, but more than that, he was worried. Tony didn't make idle threats to arrest someone. He really would haul Mickey to jail and keep him overnight at least, just to prove a point. Seamus quickly realized he couldn't be angry at his son. After all, he was only trying to protect his sister. Still, Mickey would have to be punished and there really was only one way to do that. It hurt Seamus almost as much as he knew it was going to hurt Mickey.

"Dad? I'm sorry, okay? I didn't mean to hurt her," Mickey finally said when the silence had stretched on for several more minutes.

Seamus sat down. He motioned for Mickey to sit down, too. "Mickey, tell me exactly what happened today. I wanna know if Tony's got a case," Seamus ordered quietly.

Mickey told him everything that had happened, first at Glencrest that morning and then about lunch and finally about Delaney's threat to the teen after school. "I just can't help it, Dad. I'm just trying to protect Jordan like you asked me to. I'm trying to keep her safe," Mickey said, miserable at how things had turned out.

"I understand, son, really I do, but Tony's right. Ye could've been arrested and charged, even if Jordan didn't want to press charges. Really should've been, actually. The bruises're all the physical evidence they'd need, especially if they could actually match them to yer hands. Yer statement and Jordan's could convict ye. Throw in the boy's, which I'm sure would match yer sister's and ye'd have a record," Seamus tried to explain. It didn't seem like his son completely understood what he had done was wrong.

"What're you gonna do?" Mickey asked, knowing his dad was going to punish him somehow anyway.

"The only thing I can do. Sorry, me son, but ye're grounded this weekend. No phone calls as of right now, except to tell yer lass and absolutely no visitors. And no email either," Seamus said over Mickey's groan. "Give me yer phone," Seamus continued. "Ye can use the phone in the hall to call Megan."

"Dad!" Mickey protested loudly. His dad knew Mickey had a date with Megan every Saturday night.

"No buts, son. Think of the alternative. Now, go get yer sister for supper," Seamus ordered.

Mickey left the living room, slowly climbed the stairs and knocked on Jordan's door. "Hey," he said when she opened it.

"Hey yourself. What did Daddy do?" she asked anxiously.

"Grounded me. For the whole weekend. No visitors and the only call I can make is to tell Megan that I'm grounded. After that, no calls or email either. All thanks to you and your boyfriend," Mickey snapped, letting out some of his frustrations at the whole situation.

"Get real, Mickey!" Jordan snapped right back. "Whose hands were the ones that bruised me? Huh? Yours, Mickey O'Reilly, not Rick's."

"Because you scared me! I didn't know where you were! You could've been kidnapped for all I knew!" Mickey shouted.

"Oh, so naturally, you decided to hurt me?" Jordan snapped back sarcastically. She shrugged out of her sweater and showed her brother the darkening bruises. Mickey turned away. He really had hurt his sister.

"Just be glad I didn't tell Rick. You know he'd go to jail again, and gladly, to defend me!" she yelled.

She shoved past Mickey and stormed down to the dining room. She threw herself into her chair and poured herself a glass of water. Her hand shook with her anger, but her father only raised an eyebrow at the small spill. She wiped it up just as Mickey joined them and silently sat down. Seamus didn't say anything to either of his children. He'd heard their argument – after all, it hadn't been their first – and figured it was something they needed to work out on their own.

Dinner was tense. Jordan's bruised arms stared at Mickey, shrieking their accusations at him. Jordan ate slowly, as if to prolong her brother's agony. Annoying as it was, it was a rule in the O'Reilly household that no one left the table until their father determined they'd had enough to eat. Mickey hardly ate at all, since everything sat like a stone in his stomach.

Finally, Mickey couldn't stand it anymore. "Sis? Jordan?" he said tentatively.

"Yes?" she said as she continued to eat, staring at her plate. She wanted him to suffer.

"I'm sorry, 'kay? I really didn't mean to hurt you," Mickey finally managed to get the apology out. Jordan smiled at him, easing the tension.

"Thank you, Mickey. That's all I wanted. Well, that and for both of you to give Rick a break, but hey, I don't expect miracles. Apology accepted." With that, she finished up quickly, got permission to leave the table and then went to her room to do her homework.

After supper, Mickey called Megan and told her about the grounding and why he couldn't take her to their usual movie. She was sympathetic but, to his chagrin, agreed with his dad – it could've been a lot worse. They talked for about half an hour before hanging up to do their homework. Mickey tried to concentrate, but after he had read the same paragraph for the third time, he snapped his book closed with a sigh. He'd take the grilling from his teachers tomorrow.

He climbed into bed and laid in the dark, thinking. He still didn't really understand how he just about ended up in jail and Rick would've still been walking free. Rick's constant harassment with the letters and phone calls were fraying Megan's nerves, and by extension, Mickey's. *What is it gonna take to convince everyone Rick's dangerous?* Mickey wondered as he finally fell asleep.

By the morning, Mickey was sour as an old lemon. He rarely remembered his dreams, but this time, Mickey clearly remembered the one that replayed all night long. He was staring out of the bars of a jail cell while Rick laughed at him. Tony and Marshall were there, too, laughing and pointing at him, making sure the teen was thoroughly humiliated. And now, even though Mickey knew it was only a dream, he was angry.

He showered, dressed and joined his sister for a quick breakfast before heading over to Glencrest. He frowned as Jordan climbed out of the truck and headed over to Rick's so she could go to school with him. *Trust her*, the teen thought firmly as he helped Megan into the truck. *Trust her.*

All morning long, Mickey was distracted, thinking about Tony's visit the night before, the threat to haul Mickey away and the vivid bruises on Jordan's arms. The only reasonable conclusion was that Rick was to blame for all of it, the bruises included. Somehow, he'd found out about them and then turned the cops on Mickey. *Fine*, Mickey thought as he struggled to pay attention in class. *Let's play hardball, if that's what the punk really wants. Then we'll really see who's better.*

Mickey slipped away from Carl and the girls so he could get to the cafeteria to confront Rick. He knew Rick's last class of the morning was closer than theirs so he'd always get there first and secure their table. Sure enough, Rick was waiting by their table, talking with Tom – who had been at the principal's office, leaving another Angel to guard Jordan – and a couple of the other Angels. Before Tom could warn Rick, Mickey came up and shoved Rick hard enough to send the teen stumbling into the table.

"What the hell?" Rick snapped as he recovered. He turned and glared at Mickey.

"I'm sick of ye, boy. Leave Megan and me sister alone," Mickey snarled, his Irish accent as thick as his father's and taking his personal humiliation out on Rick. He knew this was wrong, but he just couldn't stop himself.

"What's it gonna take to convince you I'm not doing anything to Megs?" Rick growled. He backed away from Mickey, knowing the other boy wanted a fight. Rick didn't want to give Mickey this, but something told Rick he wasn't going to have a choice, judging by the angry look on Mickey's face.

Mickey shoved at Rick again, but it had almost no effect. "C'mon, boy. Ye think ye're so damn good, don't ye? All ye're doing is trying to scare Megan. Ye use pen, paper and the phone. For once in yer miserable life, face someone yer own size, and do it face-to-face. Quit hiding!" Mickey yelled and tried to shove Rick again.

Rick took another step back, and took a deep breath. Mickey was pushing all of the right buttons, trying to get Rick to swing first, and if Rick wasn't careful, the Irishman was going to get his wish. "Mick, c'mon, man, stop this! I don't wanna fight you," Rick said, trying to do his best to calm the other teen down. Out of the corner of his eye, he saw Tom and the other Angels form a circle around him and Mickey to keep the other students out of this.

"See? Knew it. Yer too damn chicken to face me, boy. Yer yellow!" Mickey sneered.

With that, Mickey swung at Rick's head. Rick easily ducked the punch, then caught another movement out of the corner of his eye. Tom stood at his friend's back, ready to help if needed. Rick shook his head. There was no way he was going to let anyone else get involved in this and get them suspended. This was his fight.

"No way, Kid. My fight. Alone. Y'hear me? Stand down," Rick warned Tom as he faced Mickey just in time to duck another punch. Before Rick could swing, Mickey caught him with a lucky shot in the ribs. Compared to Carl's shots, it was extremely weak and Rick absorbed it with a nasty grin. He'd hoped this would cause Mickey to back down, but there was no stopping the young Irishman.

Rick returned Mickey's punch with one of his own, being cautious to hold back as much as he could. As it was, it was still enough to drop Mickey to his knees, gasping for breath. Rick backed away, giving Mickey a chance to get to his feet and stop this insanity. *C'mon, man,* Rick thought miserably. *Don't keep coming. Back off before I really hurt you.* He could hear the other students cheering and it made Rick sick. He shook his head as he watched Mickey climb back to his feet and get ready to attack again. That was the last straw.

Fine, Rick thought angrily. *You won't back off? Time to end this. Before I get sick.* Rick circled just out of Mickey's reach, seeking his opening. When he finally saw it, he grinned and struck. His hands flashed so quickly, Mickey had no chance to defend himself. He slumped to the floor, dazed.

Breathing heavily, Rick straightened up, looked around and groaned. Standing in front of him and Mickey, arms folded across his chest, was a very unimpressed Mr. Delaney. He glared at Mickey, but when the principal looked at Rick, the teen could've sworn Delaney winked at him.

"What in the hell's going on here?" Delaney demanded in the now silent cafeteria. "Richard?"

"Hey, I was just defending myself, sir," Rick protested. He pointed down to Mickey. "He started it."

"I really don't care who started it, Richard," Delaney said, waving off Tom's protests as well as Rick's. "You know the rules."

Rick sighed, then grinned. He knew the rules, alright, having violated most of them over the last couple of years. Did Mickey? "Yes, sir. One or three?"

Delaney smiled. "Just the rest of today, Rick. You've worked way too hard to avoid this for so long. Okay?" Rick nodded, grateful he hadn't been truly suspended. Blade would've struck for sure. "See you Monday morning, 'kay?"

The principal looked down at a still-dazed Mickey. "By the way, Mr. O'Reilly, that goes for you as well. You're suspended until Monday morning," Delaney said firmly.

Mickey struggled to his feet, shrugging off Megan's helping hands. "You're suspending me?" he asked, incredulous. *Could things get any worse?* Mickey thought. *Dad's gonna kill me.*

"You're lucky I don't suspend you for a week, Mickey, first offense or not. I warned you yesterday about this. I know for a fact you deliberately provoked this fight and Rick gave you at least two opportunities to stop, but you chose to continue. You've made your choice, Mickey. Now you deal with your father."

With that, Delaney left the cafeteria, trusting the two boys would obey. Rick turned away from the still angry Irishman and wrapped an arm around Jordan. He grabbed his book bag and sighed. He knew he needed to get out of the school before Mickey came after him again. If the other boy did, Rick knew he wouldn't be able to hold back this time.

"Sorry about this, sweets. You watch your back, 'kay? Johnny may try something with both me and Mick gone," Rick said softly, turning to look for the Knights, grateful he didn't see them.

Jordan hugged him again, then turned to smile at Tom, who nodded at Rick. "Don't worry about me, Rick. With Carl and Tom, Meg and I'll be fine. I'm sure we'll have a full Angel escort anywhere we want, won't we, Tom? But what 'bout you?" she asked as they walked out of the cafeteria.

"I'll go and get something to eat, then head to the centre. Take my frustrations out on the bags for a while 'fore the club gets there for practice, just so I don't kill someone, y'know? If you can, meet me there, 'kay?" Rick asked as he took a hold of Jordan's arm to guide her around the bench she was about to walk into.

Jordan couldn't help her sudden cry of pain. Rick had just grabbed one of her bruises and they hurt worse today than yesterday. "Jor, what did I do, baby?" Rick asked, concerned, letting go immediately.

Jordan hesitated, then shrugged off her jacket to show Rick the bruises on her arms and told her boyfriend where and how she'd got them. Rick saw red. "He accuses *me* of hurting you when he's done *this*?!" Rick fumed. He turned to go back into the cafeteria when Jordan grabbed him.

"Rick, no!" Jordan pleaded. "You'll get kicked out for sure. Besides, Tony's already taken care of it." Jordan told him what Tony had done to her brother. Rick roared with laughter. He could just see the look on Mickey's face when Tony came to arrest him.

"Okay, Jor. I'll give Fish this one. I'm sure he scared the bejeezes out of Mick. Later," Rick smiled and kissed her good-bye. He left the school and climbed into his car, sitting there, fuming for a few minutes. Why he hadn't backed away from the fight, Rick didn't know. He fired up the Firebird, cranked the music and tore out of the parking lot.

He grabbed himself a quick lunch before he headed to the centre. But when he pulled up in front, he just sat in his car, thinking, trying to figure out what was going on and what he was going to do about it. In fact, if he were Blade, he'd grab both Megan and Jordan today, before the end of the day, especially with both Rick and Mickey gone. The longer Rick sat and stewed, the angrier he got.

He finally glanced at his watch and realized he'd been in the car for almost two hours. He had another hour before Tony'd be there, so it was probably a good idea for Rick to work off the extra anger.

Rick changed his clothes and strode into the gym. Bob raised an eyebrow. "Aren't you 'bout an hour early?" he asked dryly, glancing at the clock.

Rick chuckled and told his coach what had happened at lunch. "So I'm gonna have a go at the speed bag for a while. As angry as I am right now, the weights might kill me," Rick said with another grin.

Bob nodded. "Okay, Champ. Go back to your first pattern. I wanna leave that new one I showed you the other day for later on. Sound good?"

"Sure thing, Coach." Bob watched Rick close his eyes, take a deep breath and swing into the very familiar routine. Bob continued to watch for several minutes to make sure he wasn't going to have a repeat of the incident just before Thanksgiving.

Rick showed no signs of slowing, but Bob could see no true anger in the swings. Just a strange mixture of relaxation and concentration. Bob was positive Rick was going to be using this time to plan his next move, as he was certain the Knights were doing. The coach left Rick alone while he finished up some paperwork, the rhythmic sounds soothing to his ears.

An hour later, Bob looked up in time to see a very unimpressed Tony walk into the gym. The cop frowned as he watched his young friend. This fight had done nothing to redeem Rick in Seamus' eyes. *How could've he done this? With Mick?* Tony wondered as he continued over to Bob.

"C'mon, Tony, cut 'im some slack, man," Bob said quietly so they didn't disturb Rick's rhythm just yet.

"No way, Coach. How the heck could he lose control like that? And with Mick of all people!?" Tony growled, not trying to keep his voice low.

Rick heard his friend's voice, and the anger in it. He gradually slowed the pace of his workout until he could end with his usual flourish. He stood in front of the bag, covered in sweat, but relaxed and breathing deep and easily. There was no anger, just the most relaxed Tony had ever seen Rick. Outwardly, Tony showed no emotion but the anger Rick had heard. Inside, though, the cop was impressed. *Guess he's learned a few things after all,* the cop thought.

"You know something, Champ? You're a bloody idiot," Tony said harshly, coming over to stand in front of Rick at the speed bag.

"No kidding, Fish," Rick replied dryly.

Tony blinked, his anger draining away at Rick's completely unexpected response. "I...um...," Tony said, unsure of what to say.

Rick laughed. "I should've walked away, bro, and I know it. I was thinking with my fists again, but he really did push a couple of the right buttons today. Was O'Reilly...upset?" Rick asked hesitantly.

Unable to stop himself, Tony burst out laughing. "You could say that. I'm just not sure what he was angrier about – the fact Mickey got in a fight and got suspended, or that Mickey got in a fight and lost. To you," Tony said, as he continued to chuckle.

"Coach, can I take twenty and talk to Fish before I start practice?" Rick asked, turning to Bob.

"Sure thing, Rick, just try not to cool down too much. Sparring with Carl in twenty, since I think you've warmed up enough." Coach turned to the rest of the boxing club, giving directions while Rick and Tony went to talk. They met up with Jordan at the front desk and the two teens followed Tony to his office.

After putting his gun and clips away and locking the drawer, Tony perched on the corner of his desk while Rick and Jordan sat in front of him. "Gotta question for you, champ," Tony began.

"What's wrong, Tony?" Jordan asked.

"Son, honestly, did you feel better, putting Mick on the deck like you did?" Tony asked quietly, ignoring Jordan for the moment.

Rick hesitated then nodded reluctantly. "A little, until it was all over and I could hear all of the students cheering me on. After that, I just felt sick, although I do have to admit I really enjoyed the look on Mick's face when Delaney suspended him. I think he thought he wouldn't get suspended because he was fighting me and O'Reilly's his dad," Rick said with a grin.

"Well, Daddy's not gonna be any happier with him. He's already been grounded this weekend because of the bruises, so, personally, I'm not really all that anxious to hear how much more he'll get," Jordan said dryly. *Seeing as I was the one who got him grounded this weekend,* she thought sourly.

Tony chuckled. "Okay, son. I guess you get it. Now, what did you need to talk about that couldn't wait until session?" the cop asked.

Again, Rick hesitated, then spoke quietly. "I did a lot of thinking going at the bag and I think it'd be a lot safer for both girls and the school if I pulled out," he said slowly. He couldn't help feeling sick to his stomach at the thought of the girls being there without him, but he still believed they'd be safer if he was somewhere else.

"Rick, why?" Jordan protested. She clutched at his hand. She didn't want to be left alone at school. Tom was a fine protector, but she always felt safer when she knew Rick was only a scream away.

"I don't *want* to, but I have to. Honestly, sweets, the longer I stay at the school, the more of a target everyone is, myself included. Whatever Johnny's got planned's gonna end up targeting everyone, I know it. This fight today could even play into his hands," Rick said. He got up and began to stretch. He could feel his muscles tightening with the tension he was feeling and he didn't want Coach mad at him.

"What're you talking about, young man?" Tony demanded. "And hold that stretch properly!"

Rick flushed at Tony's tone, but did as he was told. He knew he had just given Tony something else to worry about, and his friend wasn't really mad at him. He was scared. As the teen straightened up, he said, "Think 'bout it, bro. Mick finally reaches his breaking point after watching his girlfriend slowly being frightened to death. He's powerless to stop the letters because no one knows how the hell they're getting into Megs' book bag. But Mick *thinks* everything points directly at me. So since Megs won't do anything, Mick decides to take matters into his own hands."

Rick fell silent as he did a couple more stretches. Jordan and Tony were mesmerized by his tale. "So Mick comes looking for me. He finds me, pushes all the right buttons so I end up fighting with him. You know how Delaney feels about fighting, so we both end up getting suspended. Now, both Megs and Jor have only the Angels to protect them. Don't get me wrong, Fish, they're good, but they're just not me and Mick. And honestly, if I were Johnny, I would've grabbed both girls, not just Megs. Today, right after school. It would've killed not just Mickey but me as well. You know I would've gone head hunting right then," Rick said as he finished stretching and faced the cop.

Tony paled. "Jor, where's Meg?" he demanded harshly.

"With my brother. He picked her up right after school. He didn't wait for me, since five of the Angels, including Tom and Carl, walked me here. I was totally surrounded," Jordan said, chuckling.

Tony calmed down only slightly. He turned to Rick and said, "Okay, little brother. I guess I understand your logic. It's twisted, but I understand it. I just hope it works. But, *before* you do anything permanent, do me a favour and take the weekend to think about it. Deal?" Tony asked.

Rick nodded. He left Jordan and Tony to do his training. This was no longer just anger management, although that was a big part of it. Rick knew this training was going to save his life one day. This training was going to be the one thing he would do on his own, with no help from anyone, especially not the Knights.

By the time he was done, Jordan was gone. As he sat down with his counsellor for their session, Rick sighed as he finally realized he could've just seen his girlfriend for the last time.

Chapter 20

Rick did as he promised Tony. He really thought long and hard about pulling out of school and whether or not the girls would really be safer without him there. Between brooding about pulling out and a sudden return of the horrible nightmares which had plagued him at the beginning of the summer, Rick wasn't getting much sleep. The nightmares changed nightly and since he was having them two or three times a night, the constant stress didn't help his mood. And they all ended up the same way anyways – Megan beaten, bloody, lying in darkness and Rick could never tell if she was alive or dead.

Rick stayed housebound all weekend long, not even taking time to go for a ride on Cherokee. By lunchtime on Sunday, he had made up his mind and his plans were firmly set in his head. He was going to pull out of school, finish Grade 11 by correspondence, and pray the girls stayed safe.

"Hey, Rick? You here?" Tony and Marshall called from the front door.

"Living room," Rick called back as he searched for a late season hockey game on TV.

He nodded at the partners as they sat down on the couch. Rick didn't look at either of them for quite a long time. He didn't need to. He knew something was up because his friends weren't there as friends – they were there as cops, in full uniforms and both had sombre looks on their faces. Something bad had happened and Rick was about to be blamed. He clenched his teeth as he continued to flip through the channels.

"Um, son," Tony began hesitantly as Rick continued to ignore them.

"No, Fish. Whatever's been said or done to her, no, I didn't do it," Rick said. He continued to watch TV, refusing to look at either Tony or Marshall.

"Rick, Seamus sent us here to...to...," Marshall stammered to a stop. He couldn't say it. He couldn't say they were there to arrest the teen.

Once Rick had found his hockey game, he'd put the remote down and picked up his glass of water. The sudden sound of shattering glass exploded in the room, startling both cops. Tony swore as blood began to drip from Rick's hand.

"Oh hell, Champ, Coach is gonna kill me if you've wrecked your hands!" the cop snapped as he jumped to his feet. He grabbed Rick's unresisting hand and gently pried it open. He sighed as he realized none of the cuts were really that deep. He picked the glass out of the cuts as he continued to talk to Rick, who seemed to be focused on the game, not what his best friend was saying.

"Take it easy, son. You should know by now that, until Seamus has clear, untainted proof you're behind any of this, I won't take you in no matter what Seamus or Ian wants. Supposition *is not* proof," Tony said as he cleaned the cuts and then wrapped Rick's hand carefully.

"All right, what did *I* do this time?" Rick demanded as he jerked his hand away. He began to pace, struggling to regain his composure.

Tony sat back down. "I don't know, little brother. Seamus won't tell us. All I do know is Meg's received either a phone call or a letter or maybe even both this weekend and Ian's had enough. *He's* the one actually pressing charges. Or trying to, at least," Tony explained.

Rick stopped pacing and stared at Tony. "Uncle Ian? Can he even do that?" the teen asked, horrified.

"Well, yes and no. Because the calls're coming into his house, he can, technically, charge you with harassment at the very least, probably trespassing because he's told you not to come into the house, I guess, but that probably wouldn't stick since you live on the same piece of property. *He* can't charge you with stalking or

- 145 -

anything like that since the calls and letters aren't actually directed at him, and so far, Megan continues to refuse to press charges," Marshall spoke up, while Tony cleaned the glass and blood.

"So then why the hell're you here?" Rick demanded hotly.

"More or less to warn you, Rick, I guess. If Seamus or Mick finally convinces Meg to press charges, it won't be us sent to arrest you," Tony pointed out.

"And?" Rick asked dryly, knowing there was more to it.

"And if I get enough warning...I'll try to come up with some kind of plan to get you outta here until we can prove your innocence," Tony said with a shrug, ignoring the protests from both Rick and Marshall.

"Are you nuts, Tony? Seamus'll kill you if he finds out," Marshall shouted.

"Don't care, Marsh, not anymore. I'm not gonna have Rick railroaded into jail because Seamus is too blind to see someone's framing this boy," Tony said, angry he was even being questioned.

"Tony, I did what you asked me to do and I've thought about it all weekend. I'm still gonna pull out. I think it'll be better for everyone. I can go to the centre and work with a tutor or finish school by correspondence during the day, have our sessions right after school and training with the club, then come home after Meg's in bed. That's the best I can do," Rick said.

Tony nodded, still not happy with what his friend was doing. "I guess you're right, Rick, but why does it feel like we're just putting you in another jail?" Tony groused.

"Better a cell at the centre than a real one at your office," Rick retorted with a grin.

With that, the partners left. What Tony didn't tell Rick was he already had a plan for getting Rick out, one he'd hoped he never had to use, and the partners knew exactly why Seamus had sent them to arrest Rick.

Tony grimaced as he recalled the hysterical call Megan had placed to him that morning. The phone beside Tony's bed had been set to 'shrill,' since the cop tended to sleep like the dead when he was totally exhausted. When it shrieked less than three inches from his head, he grabbed it before the first ring had finished. "Whitefish," he said sleepily.

"Tony!" was all Megan had to say. Tony bolted up in bed, completely wide-awake.

"Meg, hon, what is it?" Tony demanded.

"Just listen," she begged and began to read.

"Well, time's almost up, cuz. Since Gran hasn't changed the will, I'm gonna have to be a bit more direct. I'm gonna have to take my anger and disappointment out on ya. I'm gonna squeeze and squeeze. There'll be no escape this time.

"Can't wait. Can ya, Megs? Do ya wanna know when it's gonna happen? Well let's just say, yer not gonna see Easter at school. How's that? Y'all excited now?

"So now ya know. Make sure ya say good-bye to Mickey Mouse today. Ya won't have time later, Megs." Megan's voice had fallen to a whisper.

"It ends with his gang sign."

"Holy crap!" Tony whispered when Megan had finished. *We've got a timeline now,* Tony realized, *but it's a damn short one. This is not good.* Tony knew he didn't want to know the answer to his next question, but it was one he had to ask.

"First, Meg, when did you find this letter? And, second, what do you want to do?" Tony asked, wincing at what he knew Megan was going to say.

Megan hiccupped as she tried to stop sobbing. "This morning in my bag, but it's probably been there since Friday since I didn't do any homework until today. But, Tony, it's not just the letter this time. I just don't trust him. Not anymore," Megan said, finally broken by everything that had happened.

"Take it easy, Meg," Tony said, trying to soothe the young girl. He sat up in bed, shifting around until he was comfortable. "Now, I want you to take a couple of deep breaths, and we'll talk about this some more. But not until you've calmed down, 'kay?"

It took almost five minutes, but Megan managed to stop crying finally. Her voice was raw when she continued. "It's not just the letters or calls anymore, Tony," she reiterated firmly. "It's Rick himself. Tony, he never even blinked when he was suspended. He *always* argues when he gets suspended, even if he doesn't deserve it. Friday? He never even questioned Mr. Delaney. And that fight? He enjoyed it! He was actually grinning at the end. He could've killed Mickey and he grinned like it was nothing!

"I'm sorry, Tony," she continued, trying to control the hysterics once again. "I can't do this anymore. He scares me! His power. God, his strength! No, no more, Tony. Monday, I'm pressing charges," she said firmly.

Tony's heart sunk like a stone. This was the one thing he'd been working so hard to avoid for the whole year and now there was nothing Tony could say or do that was going to change Megan's mind. "Meg, please don't. Why would you wanna do that? Especially now?" Tony asked sadly.

"Because whenever he's gone, this all stops! And nothing you say, Tony, will change my mind this time!" Megan replied sharply.

And she was right. Nothing Tony could say would convince Megan this wasn't going to work. She wouldn't believe him when he said Blade wasn't going to quit this time. Charging Rick would just play into his overall plan. Nothing mattered. Megan was firm. She was pressing charges. The only thing Tony got her to agree to was to wait until Monday to tell Ian or Seamus.

Then, just before lunch, Tony got a call from Seamus saying Ian was pressing harassment and stalking charges against Rick since Megan was refusing to do so. Thanks to some fast and fancy talking, Tony managed to get Seamus to hold off until at least Monday afternoon. That was when Tony got together with Marshall and came up with a plan to get Rick away from Glencrest before he could be arrested. Tony prayed he never had to use it.

Knowing how little time Megan actually had, and therefore Rick, too, was enough to make Tony ill. He hadn't told anyone about the last letter Megan read to him. He had to figure this out on his own, he knew, because he didn't even trust his partner to not tell Seamus, just to keep Megan safe. Unable to control his anger for a change, Tony slammed his hand against the steering wheel in frustration. Marshall raised an eyebrow at Tony's uncharacteristic outburst.

"Something you wanna get off your chest, partner?" was all he asked.

"Ever feel like you're trying to hold sand in a sieve? Time's running out, Marsh, and I can't stop it. I don't know what to do!" Tony's voice was almost as shrill as Megan's had been.

Marshall had no answers for his partner as Tony dropped him off at home. The rest of Sunday was quiet, but Tony couldn't help wondering when the hammer would fall. He knew it was going to be bad when it did, but no one, not even Tony, realized just how bad it would be.

Monday morning, Rick rose and took a very long, hot shower, after a short but intense workout. The more he thought about pulling out of school, the more right it felt. He didn't feel like the girls would be in any *more* danger if he left. He knew Mickey, at least, would be happy with Rick away from school. And he had to trust the Angels would be enough to protect everyone.

Rick dressed slowly for his last day of school. He paused by his dresser and saw Jordan's bracelet from Christmas. He picked it up and ran it through his fingers. He choked up when he realized Jordan probably would never wear it again. *Not as long as Seamus hates my guts*, Rick thought as he put the bracelet back on the dresser.

He sat on his front porch, waiting for the O'Reillys to arrive. It would be the last time Jordan and Rick would be able to ride to school for a long time. Rick sighed. Pulling out might be the right thing for the girls, but it really, really sucked.

He was thinking so hard he didn't hear the truck pull up. It wasn't until he heard the top stair squeak that Rick turned to see Jordan standing there, looking at him. He smiled and rose to take her in his arms.

"You're pulling out," she said as she pulled away.

Rick nodded. "I don't think there's really any other choice, Jor. I'm causing too much stress and there's too much danger. Not just to you and Megs, but to the school, too. It's just better for everyone if I leave," Rick said as they walked to his car.

"Not everyone," Jordan disagreed tartly.

Rick smiled as he helped Jordan into the car. Mickey and Megan were still in the house when Rick pulled away for their last ride to school together, one Rick made as long as he could. They talked as they drove and made what plans they could, not knowing their plans would never come to pass.

It was a long morning for Rick. He took a couple of minutes after each class to talk to his teachers about his decision. All were disappointed it had come to this, but they all understood.

"Perhaps it *will* settle things down," his Science teacher said as they walked towards the office. "I'm sorry to see you leave, though, Richard. You've made some remarkable progress since you left the Knights. You're doing so much better, not just in your marks. Good luck, Richard. I'm positive I'll see you back next year."

With that, the teacher left Rick standing outside the office. He hesitated a minute or two, then visibly steeling himself, he opened the door and stepped in. *I'm doing the right thing,* he promised himself. *They'll be safer.*

"Hello, Richard," the secretary nodded a greeting.

"Hey, Gloria. Delaney in? I need to see him," Rick replied.

"My door's open, son. Come on in," Delaney called.

Rick slipped into the office and sat down. He looked around and realized he'd been in here an awful lot this school year and, oddly enough, he was going to miss it.

Delaney looked up and smiled. "What can I do for you, Rick?"

"I'm out," Rick replied shortly.

"There's got to be another choice, Rick," Delaney protested.

Rick shook his head. "No, sir, there's not. I'm not just putting Megs and Jor at risk anymore. It's the whole school," Rick said. He couldn't help the sudden shiver that went down his spine at his choice of words.

"Really, Richard," Delaney said in disbelief.

"Quit calling me Richard," Rick snapped. Then he frowned. "Look, Delaney, it's like this. You know I think Johnny's got some kinda plan, one that directly involves me and Megs. And until he tires of this game of his, *everyone's* in danger. Johnny'll destroy this school down to the last brick to get what he wants," Rick said roughly.

"Megan," Delaney nodded in agreement.

"Megs. She's his target, I'm sure of it, and he won't care if others get hurt," Rick said.

Delaney rested his arms on his desk and looked at the troubled teen before him. "Well, Rick, I figured this day was coming and I've been prepared for it. Sorry that it has, because you worked so hard to get your grades back up, but not surprised. What's Nana got to say about this?" he asked as he grabbed the paperwork necessary to get Rick set up on correspondence.

"Like you, Nana don't like it, but she agreed with me once I laid out my reasons. I've decided to go to the youth centre every day and do my work from there. That way, I'm far enough away Seamus can't blame a damn thing on me," Rick said as he signed the papers Delaney held out to him. He fell silent as the principal talked quietly to his secretary.

"Gloria'll have everything ready for you in a couple of minutes. I just hope you know what you're doing, son. If this doesn't work, I'm gonna have a bloodbath in my school," Delaney said ominously.

"The Angels'll go after him with all guns blazing, that's for sure. If I see Tom, I'll warn him," Rick agreed as he got his correspondence materials from Gloria.

While Rick walked to his car and threw his stuff in the back seat, Jordan and Mickey waited in the cafeteria for him. That is, Jordan waited, but Mickey and Megan continued an argument they had started in the truck on the way to school. Jordan gritted her teeth against the shrill tone of Megan's voice. Even Tom winced.

"I told you to back off!" Megan shrieked.

"And I told you – I even swore to your dad – I will protect you from that boy," Mickey yelled back, trying to keep from losing it completely.

Rick sauntered into an awkwardly silent cafeteria. He could see Crank and Brain sitting at the Knight's table, talking quietly, but enjoying the show. Rick winced as he realized the feeling of impending doom he'd been experiencing wasn't gone, like he'd hoped. In fact, it was suddenly stronger than ever. *Maybe this isn't such a good idea,* he realized. *Great move, idiot, giving them the opening they needed. Oh well. Too late now.*

"And what a wonderful job you've done, too. First, you can't stop these letters from getting into my backpack, no matter what you do. Then, you try and fight Rick and you fail – miserably, I might add. He knocked you flat with one punch! Some protector *you* are!" she yelled back. Like Jordan and Tom, Rick winced at Megan's shrill tone.

He strode quickly over to the couple, nodded absently at both Jordan and Tom and spoke quietly, trying to calm his cousin down. "Yo, guys, cool it. Everyone, including the Knights, are watching. Take it outside."

Mickey glared and shoved Rick back. "Stay outta this, punk, before I pound you flat," he snarled.

Rick heard Tom snicker. "Yeah, right. Whatever, Mick. Look, if it makes you happy, I'm outta school as of today, so things should settle down. You don't have to worry about me anymore," Rick continued.

"Oh that's just great, Rick. Just bloody great. Now you'll have more of an opportunity to come after me," Megan snapped, glaring at her cousin with her hands on her hips.

Rick paled. His mind couldn't understand, really comprehend, what his cousin was saying. "What're you talking about, Megs?" he stammered. He clutched at the table trying to keep his knees from buckling as the room spun. He couldn't believe what he was hearing.

"You know damn well what I mean! You've threatened me for the last time, Richard! I won't see Easter at school, huh? Well, you won't see the outside of a jail cell for a very long time!" Megan said, brushing hot tears from her eyes.

"You're...you're pressing charges?" Jordan asked, horrified. Rick couldn't speak, he was so stunned at the sudden turn of events. With a sudden shriek, Jordan launched herself at her best friend, hands reaching out to grab a hold of Megan's hair or whatever else Jordan could get a hold of.

"Sis, no!" Mickey said firmly as he grabbed Jordan in a bear hug. Jordan twisted and turned, trying to get away from her brother. As she glanced back at Rick, he was still frozen at Megan's words.

"Meg, you can't do this!!" Jordan demanded loudly as she continued to fight with her brother. She could hear Mickey laughing at Megan's sudden turnaround. Jordan twisted out of Mickey's arms and turned to see his triumphant grin.

"Just watch me, Jordan," Megan insisted. "I'm pressing charges. Today. After school."

"Why?!" Rick finally demanded. "I haven't done anything to you!"

"Because I figured if I didn't say anything, I was protecting Jordan. She's my best friend and I didn't want to hurt her. But I've had a lot of time to think about all of this, and I know it was you who attacked me in November, and you probably attacked Jordan, too. It was *your* jacket I saw that day and *your* laughter I heard. And it's been *your* voice I've heard on every stinking phone call," she said hotly.

Megan continued for several more minutes, but Rick didn't hear a word of it. All he could hear was the realization someone had managed to poison her against him. As he stood facing his cousin, he could see Mickey chuckling uncontrollably.

Rick knew now who had turned Megan against him. The anger he had worked so hard to push down since he first met with Tony came roaring back to the surface. Everything and everyone around him seemed to turn red. *This is all Mick's fault,* he raged. *He's put her up to this!* And the more Rick saw and heard, the angrier he got. Underneath that anger, though, was a feeling of absolute despair. Mickey had done exactly what Seamus had wanted – isolated Rick from everyone he possibly could. The trust Rick was so desperate for was now completely gone.

Suddenly Rick couldn't stand it any more. He lashed out blindly, and when the haze cleared, a stunned Megan was sprawled on the cafeteria floor, a red welt on her cheek. The cafeteria was silent as a tomb as Rick towered over his terrified cousin. His face was a brilliant shade of red and contorted with fury.

"Ya think I've hurt ya, cuz? Really? Guess it wasn't bad enough. Next time I get my hands on ya, I'll finish the job right."

Chapter 21

Rick stormed out of the silent cafeteria, vibrating with anger. By the time he got two steps out of the room, the students were buzzing at what they had just witness. The sudden explosion of anger from Rick had finally convinced everyone *except* the Angels and Jordan. The Angels knew, if Rick had really meant to hurt Megan, she'd've been on her way to the hospital right now with a broken jaw. Jordan trusted her heart despite what her eyes had just seen.

Megan struggled to her feet, waving off Mickey's help, while Jordan just stood apart from everyone, trying not to break down and Carl was a few feet away, talking quietly on his phone. He snapped his phone closed and looked at Tom. Neither one looked really happy.

"Okay, Fish says to keep an eye on her until he can get here, but it probably won't be until after school," Carl said quietly. Tom nodded and issued his orders quietly, praying it was going to be enough. Neither Angel counted on the Knights.

Crank and Brain had watched the whole fight with sadistic glee then slipped out of the cafeteria to find Blade. They couldn't help but grin and high-five each other. Rick had just played right into their hands.

They hurried to the metal shop, catching Pup up on their way through the school. Brain needed to catch Blade before he cut out for the day. Only Blade could give the green light to go ahead and actually take Megan. As they rushed to catch their leader, Brain quickly ran over his plan. He nodded to himself when he realized he had everything ready to go. They could take care of her today. It was time for Rick to pay.

"Yo, Blade. Hold up, man," Crank called as they came around the corner.

"What?" Blade growled. He was tired of the constant delays. He wanted to move and soon, no matter what Brain said.

"Man, have we got news fer ya!" Crank said excitedly.

"What?" Blade snapped again. The other three gang members took a prudent step back. There was no mistaking the tension Blade felt. He had his knife in his hand and was tossing it around. He came awfully close a couple of times to hitting his cousin, but didn't seem to care. Pup moved behind Crank's shoulder, trying to be as quiet as possible about it.

Crank gave Pup a tight smile as he detailed what he and Brain had just witnessed in the cafeteria. The more he talked, the happier Blade seemed to get. The gleam in Blade's eyes, when Crank told him how Rick had threatened Megan, actually scared the normally unflappable teen. Suddenly, Crank wasn't so sure about this plan of Blade's.

"He actually threatened her, Brain?" Blade asked, turning to his second, who immediately confirmed Crank's story.

"It's just too good to pass up, Blade," Brain said enthusiastically.

"Ya got everythin' ready t' go? Can we take 'er today?" Blade demanded roughly.

"It was gonna be this week anyway, so yeah, I'm ready. Just say the word, man, and I'll put it in motion," Brain said confidently.

"Wish I could see Moneyman's face when we do this," Blade sneered. "It'll be the best day of my life."

- - - -

This is the worst day of my life, Megan thought. She was distracted all through Physics. And sore! She couldn't believe how sore she was just from falling onto the floor. Granted, she did fall awkwardly over one of the chairs, but still...

There had been one brief argument with Mickey after Rick had stormed out. Mickey insisted on skipping class and heading straight to his dad to press charges against Rick. But Megan was equally stubborn, insisting it would wait.

"Enough, lad. Stop pushing me. You've already called your dad and he's gonna have everything ready after school. It can wait until then," Megan said with finality.

Grumbling, Mickey backed off and then turned to his sister. "Jor, you okay? You've been awfully quiet since lunch," he said, worried.

"Just...thinking," Jordan replied, distracted. She was still trying to figure out what she'd witnessed. Her head finally agreed with Mickey, but her heart remained stubbornly loyal to her boyfriend.

"What's there to think about? Rick's finally proven to everyone else what Dad and I've known all along – Rick attacked both of you. Now, he's taken off and it's just a matter of time before Dad gets to haul his butt to jail," Mickey shrugged as they all sat down in Physics.

In Computers, their last class of the day, Megan could let her mind wander freely. She was beginning to regret what she had said to her cousin. She still wanted to press charges, but she figured she shouldn't've said anything to Rick. Who knew what he was going to do now? And that scared Megan a fair bit.

The sudden scream of the fire alarm startled everyone. No one moved for a long moment until their teacher starting giving crisp commands. The class quickly gathered up their stuff, closed the windows and left the classroom, the last student out closing the door behind him. As soon as they got into the hallway, though, they began to cough at the heavy smoke. The fire was clearly near their classroom.

In the chaos, Megan and the twins were separated. Carl and Tom were nowhere to be found either, and Megan was suddenly scared. As she got closer to where the smoke seemed to be the thickest, there was a lot of pushing and shoving. There were even fists thrown as the younger students in this end of the school began to really panic. There was nothing the teachers could do or say that would calm everyone down.

Tears streaming down her face and coughing from the smoke she'd inhaled, Megan tried to push through the bodies, but it just wasn't possible. Still coughing, she spied an empty hallway that led to another exit, one no one else seemed to see. *I'm outta here,* Megan thought as she turned down the hall.

She stopped for a moment, coughing and trying to catch her breath. She felt a small jab of pain as she coughed again. She grimaced as she realized falling over the chair had, indeed, injured her. She glanced back over her shoulder and realized the smoke was still pretty thick and the fighting was getting worse. She turned back to the beckoning exit sign and strode forward purposefully.

Halfway down the hall, Megan suddenly became very nervous. Her cowboy boots were loud against the hard floor. She continued cautiously down the hall, only now realizing the fire alarm wasn't shrieking here. She paused again, wondering if she should go back and fight through the smoke instead of continuing down the hall.

Her common sense asserted itself and Megan started forward once more. She had just passed the final classroom in the hall when she heard the softest of clicks and then felt a sharp poke in her neck.

"What the heck?" she exclaimed, startled. As she turned back towards the dark classroom, her knees buckled and she fell heavily to the floor. She struggled to focus as the walls around her began to spin. She finally collapsed onto her side, the blackness forcing her eyes to close. Just before the darkness pulled her down completely, she saw at least four black clad figures enter her waning vision. A distorted voice said, "Don't worry, Megs. Rick'll take care of everything."

Then nothing.

As Megan was being eased into the back seat of Brain's car, Mickey was outside, trying hard not to panic. He couldn't find either girl, and he knew something was wrong. He could feel it with every fibre of his being. He stopped a couple of friends, asking if they had seen either Megan or Jordan. He couldn't help the groan he let out when no one could tell him where his sister or girlfriend was. He'd just pulled out his cell phone to call his dad when he heard his name called. He turned and grunted with the impact of Jordan's body against his.

"Oof, easy, sis," he said as he clung to her. "Have you seen Megan?" he asked as they finally let go of each other.

"She's not with you?" Jordan coughed, trying to clear the smoke from her lungs.

Shaking his head as Jordan coughed again, Mickey called his dad. He could hear the sirens in the distance and figured his dad was on his way, but the teen wanted – no, needed – to hear his dad's gruff voice. It would all be better then. The fire department was already on site, working to extinguish the fire.

"O'Reilly," Seamus barked when he picked up the phone.

"Dad, Mick," Mickey began then paused as Jordan began coughing again.

"Son, thank God! The girls there with ye?" Seamus asked, relieved to hear his son's voice, although he frowned when he heard Jordan coughing in the background.

"Jordan is. She's inhaled some smoke, but I can't find Megan, Dad. She might just be with another class, but I don't think so." Mickey told his dad what had happened at lunch, including Rick's threats, while Jordan was looked at by a paramedic.

"I'm almost there, son. Dinne worry about anything. Grab a couple of those Angel kids and start looking fer her, but don't let yer sister outta yer sight!" With that, Seamus hung up and manoeuvred around slower traffic, his lights flashing and siren blaring.

Still coughing, Jordan pulled the oxygen mask off over the protests of the paramedic. "I've gotta find my friend," she said firmly as she climbed off of the gurney. She motioned to Tom and Carl.

"What's up, Jor?" Tom asked, trying to keep his voice steady. He felt absolutely miserable – he'd just failed both Tony and the Champ. He already knew what Jordan wanted and Megan was nowhere to be found. He'd already looked for her and couldn't find her.

"We can't find Megan. Help us look," Mickey ordered then ran off, Jordan right beside him. Tom and Carl looked at each other as Delaney joined them.

"Do we tell them?" Carl asked hoarsely, as he drank some water to help clear the taste of the smoke from his mouth.

Delaney shook his head. "No, not yet, boys. We'll go through the motions of looking for her until we're absolutely positive she's actually gone. I'm gonna give Tony a call and let him know. Just…go around and double check, just in case we missed her." The principal turned away and began to call Tony.

The two Angels did as their principal ordered and met back up with the twins at their computer class. Seamus had arrived and did *not* look happy. "Are ye sure she's not here? She's just not mixed in with another class?" the inspector said roughly. Marshall stood by, hoping and praying things turned out better than they appeared right now.

Mickey shook his head sadly. "No, I'm so sorry, Dad, but we couldn't find her. Tom? Carl? Any luck?"

Tom winced at the despair in his friend's voice. The Angels shook their heads, unable to say a word. They felt bad enough and didn't need Seamus to tell them how bad they had just screwed up. Marshall looked at Seamus who began to bark orders. "Mr. Delaney, I need a list of all of the kids here today, especially any that've already left for the day. Marshall, have the teachers move the students into the gym, but keep the classes together. It'll make the interviews that much faster and easier. No one's to leave until we talk to them. Once we've got everyone in the gym, come find me," Seamus ordered.

"What about me, boss?" Tony asked, striding up to the group. Marshall left quickly to help the teachers get everyone back into the school. He didn't want to be anywhere near Tony when Seamus gave his next order.

Seamus looked at Tony for a long time. "Yer gonna get back into yer squad car and go back to the station, Tony Whitefish. Yer <u>not</u> gonna be part of this," Seamus said firmly. He tried not to wince at the anguish he saw in his constable's face.

"What? Why not?" Tony demanded, stunned.

"Because we both know Rick's taken Megan and yer way too close to the boy to be objective," Seamus snapped back, trying to contain his anger and fright. He knew the fire could've been a lot worse. No one had been seriously injured and so far, Megan was the only one missing. *Not including Rick*, Seamus thought sourly.

"Do you know that for sure, Seamus? Do you have true, unbiased evidence Rick took his cousin or are you just guessing? Are you even 100% sure she's gone and not lying injured somewhere in the school? Has the fire department completely cleared the school and told you she's not here?" Tony demanded quickly. He couldn't believe Seamus had ordered him away from the investigation. He knew they'd need everyone they could get their hands on to find Megan before Blade harmed her.

"As for me being too close to Rick, okay, boss, I'll give you that. But I honestly think you hate Rick too much to be any more objective than *I* would be, so *you* shouldn't be on the investigation either," Tony continued quietly. The young cop motioned to several Angels to move on as they hesitated near him. He glared at them when they didn't move right away.

"Watch it, Constable. I've fired men for less," Seamus cautioned.

"You think that bothers me any more, Inspector? Rick and Meg mean an awful lot to me and I know Meg means a lot to you, too, just because she's Mick's girl. So why would you send away the *one* person who knows how Rick thinks almost better than he does himself?" Tony pointed out logically.

Seamus shook his head immediately. "I know ye know the boy really well, but I'm not gonna take a chance. Ye head straight back to the station, hear me?" Seamus ordered again.

Tony nodded. Once. Not trusting himself to speak, the cop turned his back on his boss. Seamus grabbed Tony's arm roughly and turned him back to face him. Tony could see how angry and upset Seamus was, but it was no excuse to manhandle him. "I'm serious, Whitefish. Back to the station. Do not call him. Do not warn him. *Do not cross me*," Seamus hissed softly. Tony could hear the desperation in Seamus' voice. The young cop knew his boss was worried, and was only taking it out on Tony because he was there. It didn't make being ordered away any easier.

Tony jerked his arm out of his boss' grip and glared at Seamus. "I'll go, Seamus, but I want it noted it's under protest, understand? And, boss? Do everyone a favour – don't lose focus this time," Tony said over his shoulder as he stormed back to his car.

He sat, fuming, behind the wheel as he watched Seamus give orders to the other officers. A couple of them hesitated and looked back at Tony, wondering what was going on. Another bark from Seamus sent the officers hurrying to their assignments. Seamus turned back to Tony and motioned sharply for the cop to leave.

Tony grimaced and pulled out of the lot, but he had no intention of obeying Seamus. Not until he knew *exactly* what had set Rick off. Tom and Carl only told Tony Rick had blown up at Megan and stormed out of the school, but offered no other details, at least on the phone. Tony pulled around the school and parked by the back end of the gym. He could see the exit doors had been opened to allow fresh air to circulate while the entire student body sat on the floor, waiting to be questioned.

Tony peeked into the gym. He pulled his head back quickly as Seamus strode by, looking for his kids. The Inspector paused near the open door and began to speak.

"Jordan, me girl, ye okay? Mickey said ye inhaled some smoke?" Seamus asked as he squatted by his daughter.

Jordan coughed as she nodded. "I'm okay, Daddy. What about Meg?" she demanded, waving away his concern.

"We're gonna start looking now. We had to wait until the fire marshal said it was clear. Ye just stay here and rest until I come back for ye, okay?" Their dad stood and walked away when they both nodded.

Tony waited patiently while Seamus issued his final orders to the officers who remained in the gym. They started talking to the various classes. The inspector motioned to Marshall who reluctantly followed his boss. As soon as Tony saw the gym door close behind his partner and the three remaining cops turned away to begin their work, he slipped into the gym. He found Tom and Carl first, standing apart from the rest of the Angels.

"Fish, I'm sorry, man. I screwed up," Tom said immediately. Carl nodded sharply. He didn't trust himself to speak. He was so mad at himself for letting Megan disappear Tom had already had to hold him back from hunting down the Knights. The Angels, who had begun to gather around Tony, knew who had done this.

"It's okay, Angels. You did the best you could, under the circumstances. Now, anything else you wanna tell me about lunch?" Tony asked as he glanced around.

Tom and Carl hesitated as another couple of Angels swore softly. Tony's heart sunk. "C'mon, guys, talk to me. What happened? Tom? Carl?" the cop demanded.

Carl motioned sharply to the O'Reillys. "You'd better ask Mick, man. He's the one who pushed the Champ over the edge, laughing at him," Carl said roughly. Tom could only nod as he glared at the twins.

Sighing, Tony eased his way over to Mickey and Jordan. They were huddled together, leaning against the wall. Mickey had his arm wrapped around his sister so she could lean against him. Every now and then, she would cough, long and hard, ending up slumped against him, exhausted.

"You, young lady, need to go to Emergency," Tony said quietly as he stopped in front of them. "You sound like you got a lot of smoke in those lungs, sweets."

"Tony, have you found Megan?" Mickey asked immediately.

Tony shook his head. "Sorry, Mick, but I'm not even allowed on the investigation, thanks to your dad," Tony said bitterly. The twins both winced at the cop's tone.

"Daddy thinks Rick did this and you're too close to Rick to be objective in his eyes. Damn his stubborn Irish pride!" Jordan stated sourly. She coughed again.

Tony sat down in front of the twins, looking more serious than they had ever seen him. "That's right, Jor, and when I asked Carl and Tom what happened today, they wouldn't tell me. They just told me to come and talk to you, Mick. Said you pushed Rick over the edge. Laughed at him. Now what the hell happened at lunch?" Tony demanded harshly.

Mickey hesitated for several moments, then told Tony his tale. Tony winced when Mickey described Megan's reaction at lunch. *Hearing that would've definitely set Rick off,* Tony thought, wanting to shake the Irish teen in front of him.

"How'd Rick take it?" Tony asked blandly.

"Badly, Tony, really badly. He couldn't speak at first, then he kinda stammered and stuttered and finally was able to demand why," Jordan said quickly.

"Hush, Jor. I wanna hear this from Mick," Tony ordered gently.

Mickey flushed at the soft rebuke then said, "She's right, Tony, he took it really badly. As soon as Megan began to talk about pressing charges, he got all pale. Then, the longer she talked, his face got all red, and you could see him start to shake. Tony, it was scary, man," Mickey said as he recalled the scene in the cafeteria.

"Mickey O'Reilly, do not lie to me!" Tony snapped heatedly, running a frustrated hand over his braids. "That alone wouldn't've been enough to set Rick off like this. I've taught him too well to be able to walk away from this type of crap. Something else pushed him over the edge. Now *what the hell happened!?*"

Mickey hesitated again then spoke softly. His voice was so soft Tony almost couldn't hear him. "Yeah, I, um, I laughed at him, Tony. A lot, I guess. I just couldn't help it. I just thought he was getting what he deserved, after all!"

"What the hell're you trying to do to this town, Mick!? Destroy it!?" Tony demanded, disgusted at what had happened. Mickey flushed and stammered a couple of times, trying to defend himself. Tony interrupted harshly. "Never mind. What happened next?"

"He hit Megan, knocking her over a chair. She tripped and fell onto the floor. Then he threatened her!" Mickey said, indignant.

Tony hung his head. *What a nightmare,* the cop thought. "What, *exactly,* did he say, Mick? The words, dammit. I wanna hear the words," Tony said quietly.

Mickey looked at Jordan who sighed. "I don't remember the words exactly, Tony, but it was basically if she thought he'd hurt her before, the next time he got his hands on her, he'd finish the job right," she said sadly. Mickey nodded, feeling vindicated for the first time since Tony had begun to question him.

"He said *what*?!" Tony yelped loud enough for heads to turn, including the other cops. They turned back to their interviews, ignoring what Tony was doing. "And this was *after* you laughed at him, Mick? Great job of screwing everything up, Mickey O'Reilly. Just friggin' great!" Tony couldn't help the scorn and anger that crept into his voice.

Mickey nodded again, miserable over what had happened. He knew he'd screwed up, and badly, judging by how Tony was reacting. He knew Tony was upset with him, but he couldn't help what he'd already done. "Tony, why'd you ask if I was trying to destroy the town? I don't get it," Mickey finally got brave enough to ask.

"Because your little stunt today could be the straw that literally breaks down the barriers Rick and I have struggled so hard to build up between Rick *and* Moneyman. If Rick ever decided to go back to the Knights, and he's threatened it more than once to stop all of this, this town would swim in blood. You'd be the first on his hit list and Rick would not care anymore," Tony said. He had a sour taste in his mouth and he felt like throwing up.

"Tony, you okay? You're looking kinda pale, and that's a pretty good trick for you," Jordan said, leaning forward to touch Tony's hand.

"No, sweets, I'm not okay. I'm sick. Literally sick. How on earth could he've done something so abysmally stupid?" Tony demanded, trying to understand how everything had gone so wrong so quickly.

Mickey was silent for a very long time. When he finally spoke, he was thoughtful. "Tony, I think I finally get what you've been trying to say all along. Y'know, about how much Rick's been beaten down? Well, today finished him completely. He gotta feel like he's got anything left – no family, no friends and, thanks to me and my dad, no trust. He probably even thinks Jordan and Nana don't love him anymore, and I know that's not true, especially Jordan. And it's all my fault, man. All my damn fault," Mickey said, his voice dropping so low Tony struggled to hear him through his own anger.

"Damn right it is," Jordan snapped, slapping her brother on the leg as she broke out coughing again.

"Alright, enough, you two. I've got to figure out how to keep Rick outta jail, so do me a huge favour – don't tell your dad. Please?" Tony begged, climbing to his feet.

"Too late, Tony. I, um, told Dad when I called him about Megan being missing," Mickey said softly, his head in his hands.

"I swear by all I hold dear, you hate Rick more than your dad does, Mick. Anything else you want to throw at me now? Like a knife? 'Cause killing me's probably gonna be a hell of a lot easier than dealing with the mess you've created!" Tony growled. He knew he was being hard on Mickey, but this was *exactly* why he'd been pushing Mickey to go easy on Rick. It was going to be hard, if not impossible, to keep Rick under control even if Tony found him first. The cop knew he had a long road ahead of him. And he wasn't looking forward to it.

"I'm sorry, Tony, alright? Dammit, *I am sorry*! But I can't change what I've already done, so what else do you want from me?" Mickey demanded hoarsely, raising his voice finally.

"I want you to use the brains the Creator gave you and start thinking for once," Tony replied harshly as he stormed out of the gym. He just prayed he got to Rick before the boy did something even more stupid than he had at lunch.

Like return to the Knights.

Chapter 22

As Tony stormed out of the gym and tore off to Glencrest, leaving Mickey and Jordan in the gym, clinging to each other, Seamus, Marshall and Mr. Delaney met up with the fire marshal at the door of Megan's last class.

"Hey, Smoke, wha'cha find?" Seamus asked after shaking the marshal's hand.

Garret "Smoke" Simons looked at the inspector and said, "This could've been absolutely deadly, Seamus, absolutely deadly so just keep that in mind. If the alarm had gone off even five minutes later, no one in this class probably would've come out alive, or at the very least unharmed. It's a pretty bad set up."

"Me daughter was in here and has smoke inhalation, so I can believe that. What else?" Seamus asked. Marshall stood behind his boss, calmly taking notes, trying not to think about what could've been.

"As you've probably guessed by now, it was definitely deliberately set. We found some rags and possible accelerant, but I'm not sure exactly what kind yet. It can take weeks, if not months, to get an analysis from the city lab, depending on how backed up they are. I don't know if we'll be able to get you any evidence you can use, but I'll do my best," Smoke said as he turned back to his job.

"I knew ye will. As always, Smoke. Lemme know when yer report's ready. Thanks." As the fire marshal turned to talk to his people, Seamus looked around and saw the books strewn about, as if dropped in a panic.

Delaney saw what the inspector was looking at and nodded. "Since the fire started there," the principal said, pointing down the hall where Smoke worked with the rest of his team, "there were quite a few kids trying to get out that door down there." The inspector turned to look down where the principal pointed in the opposite direction. "Several told me the smoke was really getting thick and some of the younger students began to panic. Fights broke out, the smoke got thicker, and well, you get the picture."

Seamus nodded absently. "So if Megan came up behind these panicking kids, would she fight her way through?" Seamus asked Marshall, thinking Marshall would know better than he would how the young girl would react in an emergency.

Frowning, Marshall turned around slowly, looking for options. He stopped when he saw the dark hallway with its beckoning EXIT sign at the end. "Not likely, Seamus. After everything that's gone one, I'd say she'd take the path of least resistance in her haste to get back to Mickey or her Angels," Marshall said, indicating the hallway. "Especially if she suddenly felt threatened or alone."

Grabbing their flashlights, Seamus and Marshall slowly began to walk down the hall, looking for evidence. Delaney reached around the corner and flicked the lights on. Muttering an oath under his breath at the sudden light, Marshall paused to let his eyes readjust. He opened the first classroom door and looked around, making sure Megan wasn't hiding or lying injured under any of the desks.

He sighed as he closed the door, shaking his head at Seamus. They moved down the hall, methodically clearing each room. By the time they got down to the last classroom, Seamus and Marshall had come to identical conclusions – Megan had indeed gone missing.

From the far end, Delaney watched the two cops conduct their search. He saw them pause by the last classroom, and, even from the other end of the hall, Delaney heard them both curse. Needing to know, the principal hurried down towards them. After all, he was responsible for the students while they were at the school.

"Two techs, Terry. Double time," Delaney heard Seamus order as he approached.

"What did you find?" Delaney asked as he stopped a safe distance away.

"Megan's book bag for one. We're gonna assume she was taken here," Marshall said as he indicated the books scattered around the floor.

"Looks like a struggle to me," Delaney agreed.

"No, I don't think so. Her book bag looks like it was just dropped and the books scattered by gravity," Seamus disagreed slowly as he slowly turned around in place, looking at the scene in front of him. Something wasn't right.

All three fell silent as Marshall and Seamus continued to look around, trying to figure out what had happened. As Seamus' flashlight passed near the lockers, it caught a flash of silver on black. He paused, stared at it for a moment, then used his flashlight to nudge the cloth open. He wasn't surprised to see "Money" stitched on it.

"Oh, c'mon, man. That's just too bloody obvious," Marshall protested when he saw what Seamus was looking at. "Talk about trying to point us in a specific direction."

"On the other hand, ye do have to admit the boy is our prime suspect, what with the letters and all, even if he's not actually doing anything. Which I don't believe, by the way," Seamus said, slowly, hating to admit Marshall and Tony might actually be right. He stood to one side, thinking.

"C'mon, boss, don't start. Let's not close our minds already. C'mon, Seamus, admit it. This is just too obvious," Marshall said sourly. He prayed Seamus wouldn't jump to conclusions.

Seamus didn't say anything as he watched the crime scene techs begin to process the evidence while Marshall stood in the doorway of the last classroom, careful not to touch anything, but trying to piece together in his head what happened. Neither liked where the evidence was pointing to.

"Seamus, judging by where the books fell, I'd say her attack occurred or started from here," Marshall said, thoughtfully. He squatted down a bit to Megan's height to see things from her point of view. His flashlight caught another flash of silver from just behind the lockers. Wedged into the tight space was a small bag.

"Interesting," Marshall said softly. He waited for a tech to mark the spot and take several pictures of it before carefully wiggling out the black bag with a silver zipper.

"Wha'cha find, Marshall?" Seamus asked, coming over to stand by the cop.

"This was shoved behind the lockers, boss. Check out what's inside," Marshall said as he opened it. Peering inside, there appeared to be several darts and a bottle of clear liquid.

"Well, now we know how. Did ye find a gun of any kind? At least, I assume those things're supposed to be used in a gun," Seamus said uncertainly.

Marshall shrugged and nodded absently. He handed the bag over to the crime scene tech and stood with his hands on his hips. Seamus was right. They were looking for some type of gun – one obviously not here at the scene. "Okay, Seamus, we've got who, where, good estimate of when and how. But why? Honestly, why Megan? Why not Jordan?" the younger cop demanded. "I know he lives on the ranch with Megan, but Jordan's his girl. To me, honestly, she's the better choice to be taken, even with all of the letters and calls to Megan."

"Does Rick really need a reason?" Seamus said sharply, forcing himself to ignore the idea of Jordan being kidnapped.

"Seamus, c'mon, please? Don't lose focus. Not already. We've just begun the investigation," Marshall groaned.

Seamus stopped on the far side of the door and peered closely at the wall. "Well, here's another nail in his coffin, Marshall. Take a look at this," Seamus said and pointed to the wall.

Marshall groaned again as he read the words scrawled in blood-red marker: "Rick'll take good care of her."

There was nothing more damning to Rick than those words. Between the letters, the calls, Rick's attack at lunch, the bandana and now this, Seamus wasn't going to stop until Rick was locked up again and for a very long time. Yet, the longer Seamus stood, looking at those words, the bigger his frown got.

"What's wrong, Seamus?" Marshall finally had to ask.

Seamus sighed and shook his head. "Ye're right, Marshall. This is just *way* too easy. I mean, really? Why not just hit me over the head? Okay Marshall, ye win. We'll do this the right way. I'm gonna stay as open to suggestions as I can, but no real promises. We both know I've got too much baggage when it comes to the boy. Check outside, too. I'm sure they didn't haul her unconscious body back through the smoke and out the front doors. After we're done here, I wanna talk to the boy, because he remains a suspect until he's cleared. Sooner rather than later," Seamus said as he went to talk to the very worried principal. Marshall sighed. *At least he's willing to look at everything before deciding Rick's guilty,* Marshall thought as he worked.

As Marshall continued to search for clues to Megan's disappearance, Tony pulled up in front of Rick's house. The cop looked around and sighed happily as he realized only Rick was at the ranch. Both Nana and Ian were nowhere to be found. *With luck,* Tony thought, *I may just pull this off.* He eased out of his car and slipped into Rick's house. He could hear Rick slamming things around in his room.

"Rick?" Tony called as he walked down the hall. The last thing he wanted to do was startle the Champ. As angry as he figured Rick was, Tony knew he'd wake up next week and Rick'd be long gone.

"Go away, Fish. After I hit the bank and a gas station, I'm outta here," Rick snapped as he threw some more clothes into a duffle bag and zipped it closed.

Tony just leaned against the door as he watched Rick pack away his entire life in two large duffle bags, including all of his boxing gear. It was sad, really, when a person's life could fit into two duffle bags, *no matter how old they are,* Tony thought as he watched his friend.

"So that's it, huh? Just gonna cut and run? Did you even bother to check with your parole officer or do you even care?" Tony asked, blocking the doorway.

"What the hell's my parole officer gotta do with this, Fish? Why would I need a parole officer in jail? Face it, Fish, Johnny's won! Nobody trusts me anymore. All Johnny's gotta do is look at me and I lose it! I can't control my temper. Talking and boxing don't help much anymore, sorry bro, and I'm getting damn tired of being treated like I'm some kinda disease! So hell yeah, Fish, I'm just gonna cut and run. Now move it!" Rick growled.

Tony hesitated, then nodded and moved aside. He waited until Rick was about halfway down the hall before he spoke quietly, "Alright, kiddo. I'll let you go. But what would you like me to tell Megs when we find her? If we find her?"

Rick stumbled, his duffle bags falling loudly to the floor in the sudden silence. He turned around slowly and faced Tony. The cop couldn't believe how white Rick was. The teen slumped against the wall and Tony was afraid Rick was going to pass out. Yet the cop remained standing where he was. Now was not the time to be comforting. Not yet.

"Tony, what do you mean, when you find Megs? She's not at school? Not with Mick?" Rick whispered, horrified at what Tony seemed to be implying.

Tony shook his head slowly. "No, son, she's not. She's gone. Taken during an apparent fire at school during the last period. Although, honestly, I don't know much. I'm not allowed to be part of the investigation, 'cause I'm too damn close to you. So, you still planning on running now?" Tony demanded. He stood with his arms folded across his chest and looked down the hall at the now-frightened teen before him.

He continued before Rick could open his mouth. "And if you really run, you'll only confirm to Seamus you've acted on your stupidity at lunch. By the Creator, Rick! How could you say something so monumentally stupid in front of the school and to Meg? Are you *trying* to get locked up?" Tony demanded hotly.

Rick fell heavily to his knees. His head swam from the enormity of what he had done at lunch. He shook his head, but he couldn't get the sudden image of Megan's lifeless body out of his mind. Everything suddenly made horrible, sick sense.

"What the hell've I done, Fish? God, bro, I'm gonna be too late, too damn late to save her," Rick groaned, lowering his head to his hands and struggling not to cry.

Tony winced at the pain he could hear in Rick's voice. He pushed away from the wall and moved down the hallway to squat in front of the teen. He hesitated, then put a hand on Rick's shoulder in sympathy. He, too, had put everything together, and like Rick, realized the fight had played right into whatever the Knights had planned.

"Look, son, moaning about what's done isn't gonna help us find Meg. We both feel in our guts Johnny and the Knights took her, but can you think of any way to prove it?" Tony asked quietly.

Rick pulled himself to his feet and sighed. "Of course I can't prove it, Tony. If I could've found the proof, I would've given it to you long ago. Face it, bro, Johnny's won," Rick snapped.

Tony rose to his feet as well. "Hey, none of that! He has not won. We will figure this out," Tony snapped back, his own tension and worry now out in the open for Rick to see.

That brought Rick up short. "Sorry, Tony. I forgot about everyone else. Hell, this is gonna kill Nana, and if Uncle Ian didn't hate me before, he sure will now," Rick groused. He stood, shaking and trying to control himself. He knew if he didn't, he'd probably end up hitting Tony by accident. Growling low in his throat, Rick whirled away from his friend and slammed his fist through the wall. Tony winced at the damaged wall, but didn't say anything to Rick. Simply put, Tony felt the same way – he just couldn't vent his anger as easily as Rick.

"I know that didn't help, did it, son?" Tony asked with a wry grin.

Rick shook his head as well as his hand. "No, not really. Now what, Tony? I can't stay here, can I? Seamus'll be after me in no time, won't he?" Rick asked softly.

Tony nodded. "I'm actually surprised no one's been sent out here yet. So now we plan. I've gotta get you outta here before Seamus finds a real reason to arrest you," Tony said and led the way to the kitchen.

Chapter 23

Jordan lay on her side with her head pillowed in Mickey's lap. They were alone and still under guard in the gym, while their dad continued to look for Megan. It had already been a long day and it didn't look like it was going to end any time soon.

She sighed. Mickey looked down at his sister and smiled slightly. "I thought you were asleep, sis. You haven't moved in over an hour,' he said quietly. His one arm was across her ribs, holding her close, while the other held his cell phone waiting for some kind of update, any kind of update.

"No, Mick. I'm too worried to be asleep. Shouldn't've we have heard something by now?" she asked plaintively.

The cop who had remained with the twins looked up. Lieutenant Billy Jones was one of the longest serving cops in Seamus' precinct, who also had a terrible secret. He was fairly certain most of the cops in Collingwood didn't have a clue about his secret, but he was also fairly certain Seamus, Tony and Marshall did. And that terrified him.

He glanced at his phone as he felt it vibrate. He swore silently as he saw who was calling him. "Yeah?" he said quietly, moving away from the twins.

"Status report," came the soft Spanish voice.

"You're clear. For now. Boss is focusing all of us on a kidnapping. And, no, I don't have any more info. I'm not in the loop right now," Jones replied.

"Get in the loop. Or else." With that, Jones' caller hung up.

Or else Carlos Mendez would send some not-so-innocent pictures and video to Seamus, the paper and probably Jones' wife. A bad night at one of the many poker tables in Mendez's casino led to Jones spending the rest of the night in the willing arms of a woman who wasn't his wife. The next morning, Jones was introduced to Carlos Mendez and given a choice – either start providing Mendez with inside information on whatever Mendez wanted, included planned raids on his facilities, or Mendez would send the pictures of Jonesy's indiscretion to his boss and his family, not caring about ruining the reputation of a good cop.

Some choice, Jones thought for the millionth time as he sighed and walked back towards the twins. He attempted to put Mendez out of his mind for now, needing to focus on Megan's kidnapping. Jordan turned her head to look at the approaching cop.

"Shouldn't've we heard *something* by now, Jonesy?" she asked again.

Jones smiled down at Seamus' daughter. "Not necessarily, Jordan. Every step she took after the fire alarm has to be looked at and retraced. But, lemme check with your dad and at least see if I can take you home so you can wait in comfort? How's that?" Jones asked, trying not to wince at the exhausted pair in front of him. He knew it was going to be a long time before this ended.

At Jordan's nod, the cop pulled out his cell and dialled the inspector. "O'Reilly," Seamus barked when he answered.

"Inspector, Jonesy. All of the other students've been sent home. Your kids're the only ones left and they're tired and hungry. Can I take them home?" Jones asked.

Seamus sighed as he looked at his watch. Jones was right – the twins had been there way too long. "Sorry, Jonesy. I've been a bit busy. Tell them I'll be there in about five minutes to talk to them." Seamus snapped his phone closed and looked at Marshall who was just coming back inside.

"Anything?" the inspector asked hopefully. His hopes faded when Marshall just shrugged.

"Nothing concrete. Terry's gonna try and cast the tire tracks, but he said to tell you he's not expecting much. The treads look too shallow. Sorry, boss," Marshall said. He ran a hand over his face trying to scrub away some of his exhaustion.

Seamus looked around and sighed. "Okay. Tell him to do his best. Stay here, Marshall, and finish up. I don't think ye'll find much more, but we'll be very thorough, okay?" Seamus said again as he began to walk away. "Then go get something to eat. I'll meet ye back at the station as soon as I can." *And pray Tony's there too,* the inspector thought as he walked up the hallway.

"Where'll you be, Seamus?" Marshall asked.

"Breaking me kids' hearts," was his gruff answer. Marshall winced at the pain he could suddenly hear in the inspector's voice.

"Good luck, boss," Marshall said softly as Seamus turned the corner and went out of sight. As soon as he was sure his boss was gone, Marshall pulled out his phone to update his partner. Tony didn't need any more surprises.

Seamus paused at the gym doors. Mickey and Jordan had relocated to the stage and sat, waiting as patiently as they could, for their dad. They were talking with Jonesy and looked a little more rested than when he'd first seen them just after he'd arrived at the school. He could also see his daughter was still fighting the smoke she'd inhaled.

"Dad!" Mickey called as he caught sight of Seamus. He jumped down from the stage, then turned to help his sister down. Seamus hurried over when Jordan began coughing again.

"Jordan, are ye sure ye're okay, me girl?" Seamus asked. She nodded as she caught her breath. "Ye need to go to the hospital and get treated," her dad ordered, not believing her for a minute.

"I'll be okay, Daddy, once I've had a good chance to rest," Jordan said with a shaky breath.

Seamus put his arms around his children and held them close for a couple of minutes. He tried to figure out how to tell his kids what he now knew. Nothing came to mind as he held them even closer.

"Daddy! What's wrong?" Jordan said, her voice muffled against her dad's broad chest. She struggled to move from the strangle hold her dad had on her.

"Dad? C'mon. Did you find Megan? Is me lass okay?" Mickey demanded at the same time.

Seamus sighed. "There's no easy way to say this son, so I'm just gonna say it. We've looked everywhere, Mickey and we've found where we think she was attacked, but no. We didn't find Megan. I'm sorry, son, but she's gone," Seamus said. He could see the sudden flash of pain in his son's eyes and inwardly he swore. He couldn't stand the loss of innocence the students of Colonial High had faced this year, *and that included Rick,* Seamus acknowledged privately. *None of these kids should be living like this, scared of what's around the corner.*

Mickey, stood, transfixed, horrified by what his dad told him. "No way, Dad. Ye've gotta go back. Ye've missed her. She's gotta be hiding somewhere. She's not missing, ye hear me, Daidí? She's not missing!" Mickey continued to deny what he heard.

Finally, he fell silent. He couldn't tear his eyes away from the sympathetic gaze of his father. "Dad, please. Please tell me ye're lying? Dad? Please?" he begged.

He couldn't help the sobs and tears that started to fall when his dad slowly shook his head. "I'm sorry, son. I really wish I was," Seamus said softly.

As Jordan held her brother, trying to give him what comfort she could, she couldn't help but wonder how long it would be before her father blamed Rick. "What else did you find, Daddy?" she asked warily as Mickey dried his eyes.

"Before I answer, Jordan, I swear to both of ye that we will find her and figure out who did this, okay?" Seamus promised.

His children nodded, knowing that went without saying and Seamus continued. "The unfortunate part, Jordan, is I do need to find Rick and fast."

"Why must you always blame him, Daddy? I mean, really! Do you at least have something like evidence this time or are you just assuming again?" Jordan snapped, hurt.

Seamus smiled at her fiery spirit, even though he was sick to his stomach. "Right now, me girl, all of the evidence I have points right to the boy. No, Jordan, just listen to me for once!" Seamus snapped suddenly when Jordan opened her mouth to protest. "If ye take the letters and calls at face value and assume they really *are* from the boy, then add in the fight with Mickey and his attack on Megan today at lunch, that *alone* would be enough to bring him in on probable cause. When ye add in what we've found from where we believe Megan was taken, including his bandana again and the writing on the wall, and the fact I'm pretty sure he's not at Glencrest, well, it just all adds up to him being a prime suspect. I have to follow the evidence, me girl, no matter how much it hurts you for me to do that. Understand?"

Jordan swayed in shock as her dad laid out the evidence before her. Mickey grabbed a hold of her to steady her. "What writing, Daddy?" she whispered, not wanting, but needing to hear, what her father had found.

"Someone scrawled on the wall, near where we found her back pack, "Rick'll take good care of her," in what looks like blood red ink," Seamus said quietly.

Jordan, like her brother before her, stood transfixed, trying to come to terms with what her father was telling her. She shook her head in denial. "No, Daddy. No. Not my Rick. He'd never do something like this. Not to me! No!" she cried. She shrugged off Mickey's restraining hands as she stumbled blindly from the gym. She managed to find her way out of the school, and past Mickey's lonely truck.

"Jordan! Wait! Come back here!" Seamus shouted as he watched his daughter run away.

Turning to his son, Seamus said sourly, "Go on, son, go after her. Take her home. I'm gonna head back to the station and try to figure this thing out."

Mickey grabbed their book bags then turned back to his dad. "Be honest, Dad. Did Rick take her?" his son asked.

Part of Seamus wanted to tell his son, yes, he believed Rick had taken his cousin, but the other part wasn't so sure anymore. Like Seamus had pointed out to Marshall when they found the bandana, the way they had been pointed by the evidence was just too obvious. Of course Rick was a suspect, but Seamus was trying to keep an open mind.

"Dad?" Mickey asked again.

"Son, I...I just don't know. Right now, all of the bloody evidence I have is pointing straight at the boy, but I'm not sure I can trust some of it. Not yet. Now, go. Take care of yer sister," Seamus said. He watched his normally proud son shuffle from the gym. His shoulders were slumped in defeat as if he'd already given up hope of ever finding Megan. Seamus thought he'd also heard his son choke back another sob. Silently he swore as he watched his family get torn apart.

"Inspector?" Jones asked. "Inspector, you okay?"

"No, Jonesy, I'm not. I've just destroyed me family. Megan's missing and Jordan's boyfriend's me main suspect. Me kids're angry, hurt and there's nothing I can do right now," Seamus said roughly, fighting back his own sudden tears.

"Now what?" Jonesy wanted to know as the two cops left the gym and headed to their cars.

"Now, we figure this out." With that, Seamus climbed into his car and drove away.

Mickey watched his dad pull away from the school as he sat in his truck, trying to figure out what was going on. When he had arrived and realized Jordan wasn't there, he panicked, thinking someone had grabbed her, too. When his common sense reasserted itself, Mickey was just angry and hurt. *Where the hell did she go?* Mickey wondered as he threw their backpacks into the back of the truck.

And sitting in the cab by himself, Mickey realized how quiet it suddenly was. Megan was gone, he realized as fresh tears gathered. There was no Megan to snuggle with as he drove. No Megan to kiss good-night. No Megan. Period. It was as if she had never existed.

"Dammit," he swore as he realized he'd been crying for almost a half an hour. He needed to find his sister, before someone else did.

Swallowing another sob and wiping away his tears, Mickey pulled out of the lot, trying to figure out where his sister might be. For some reason, he headed to Inland Park, his and Megan's favourite place to walk. He knew Jordan and Rick loved the park, too, since she was the one who had shown it to him. If she was anywhere, he figured it would be there.

Sure enough, as he pulled up and parked, he saw his sister sitting under a tree near the pond. Her head was buried in her arms laid across her knees. Even from the truck, Mickey could see her shoulders shaking, so he knew she was still crying. He forced himself to walk through the park and tried not to think about the times he'd been here with Megan.

He sat by Jordan. She didn't resist as he pulled her close and just let her cry. He figured he'd better take a moment, though, to call his dad to let him know he'd found Jordan so he didn't worry anymore.

"How's she doing?" Seamus asked, concerned.

"She's hysterical, Dad. But that's understandable, I guess, considering what you told us. Any news?" Mickey asked as Jordan continued to sob. *Idiot*, he thought as soon as the words were out of his mouth. *Like there'd be any change in less than an hour.*

"Sorry, son, nothing. How're ye holding up, Mickey? Jordan's not the only one who's gotta be upset by what happened today," Seamus asked as he sat down behind his desk.

Mickey swallowed a sudden sob. It wasn't often he actually heard how much his dad loved him — it wasn't manly, you see, but today, it was right there. "Not great, Dad, to tell ya the truth, but better than Jordan, I guess. At least, I'm not crying right now," Mickey said as he shifted his hold on his sister.

"Alright, son, take care of her. Get her home and call Jim if she won't quit, okay?" Seamus said quietly.

"Sure, sure, Dad. What about you? You gonna be home soon?" Mickey asked as Jordan's sobs finally began to slow.

Seamus snorted. "Not before midnight, I'm figuring. Tony's MIA. Rick, if he's still around, isn't answering his phones, not like I really expected him to. Still, criminals have done dumber things," Seamus said with a nod to one of the boys and the report he laid on the inspector's desk.

Mickey paused. If he knew his dad, he probably hadn't eaten anything since breakfast. "Don't forget to eat, Dad, okay? Please? I'll get Jordan home. You just find Megan," Mickey said as he hung up.

Jordan lay against her brother's shoulder, dry coughs mixed in with the dry sobs. She looked up at Mickey with tears in her eyes. "Anything?" she croaked. Her throat was absolutely raw from the smoke she'd inhaled and all of her crying.

Mickey shook his head. "No, sis. Nothing. Now Tony's MIA. He's probably gone after Rick," Mickey said. He sat up, shifting Jordan to a more comfortable position on his shoulder.

"To bring him in or hide him?" Jordan wondered as she pulled away from her brother.

Mickey climbed to his feet and helped Jordan up. "Knowing Tony, sis, he's burying that boy as deep as he can before Dad finds him," Mickey said as the twins finally headed home.

Oddly enough, though, Mickey wished the cop luck, figuring things were about to get a whole lot worse before Megan was found.

Chapter 24

As Mickey and Jordan headed home for a cold supper, Seamus was at the station, working with the team to process the little evidence they had found. He ordered the team to go over every letter, call and attack Megan had suffered since school started. Now, sitting in his office, listening to the phone ring and go to voice mail – again – Seamus was about ready to snap.

"Dammit, Tony Whitefish, I told ye to come back here and to leave the boy alone! Call me! Now!" Seamus snapped as he left his third voice mail for Tony in under an hour.

Tony only glanced at the cell phone when it rang, knowing who it was and that Seamus was angry. The first two voice mails had made that very plain. He had piled Rick's bags into the trunk of his car while Rick sat at his kitchen table, writing a letter to Nana to explain his disappearance. Now, Tony sat, waiting impatiently for Rick to finish.

Tony glanced nervously at the kitchen clock. "C'mon, son. Hurry up. I've gotta get you outta here before Nana and Ian get home or this ain't gonna work," Tony urged.

Rick nodded as he quickly signed the letter. "Sorry, bro, but I was just making sure it was right. It's done now," the teen said. He placed the letter in the middle of the table, reaching into his pocket and slammed something into the letter, pinning it to the table.

Tony was stunned. He swallowed nervously as he realized the knife quivering in the table could've gone several places other than the table. *Including me*, Tony thought. Rick was glaring at the knife and his hands were clenched into white-knuckled fists.

"Rick? Kiddo, you ok? Time to go, son," Tony said, as he tried to keep his voice from shaking.

Rick continued to stare at the knife in the table for several more moments. Tony had thought, at first, that Rick had used his gang knife, but then realized Rick would keep that for whenever he confronted Blade. And that confrontation was coming soon; Tony could feel it in his bones. No, this was another switchblade Rick must have had lying around.

"That's for Megs, you son of a...," Rick snarled.

"Champ! Time to go. Now!" Tony snapped, interrupting Rick quickly.

Tony took a look around the yard; seeing no one, he motioned to Rick. "Hurry up, Rick. Back seat and squish down low," Tony hissed. Rick softly closed his door then hurried to the back of Tony's car. Jumping in the open door, he laid down as low as he could. Tony threw a blanket on top of the teen in an effort to hide him better. As the cop straightened up, Frank appeared out of nowhere.

"Constable," Frank said dryly. Rick and Tony both froze. *Please, God,* Rick prayed. *Don't let him know or say anything.*

"Frank," Tony acknowledged the lead ranch hand with a nod. Inside, the cop was freaking out, but outside he was cool as a cucumber.

"Seeing as you have Rick hiding in your back seat, I'm gonna assume something's happened and he's about to be blamed. Again," Frank said. He stood, with his arms crossed, in front of the car, blocking their escape.

"And what do you plan to do?" Tony wondered without really acknowledging Frank was right.

Frank didn't hesitate. He turned away and said over his shoulder, "Nothing. Good luck, Rick."

Tony leaned against the car, unable to believe his luck. Shaking, he climbed behind the wheel and pulled out of the driveway. Rick stayed hidden until he felt the car come to a stop. Raising his head carefully, Rick saw Tony had pulled onto a dirt road.

"Fish?" Rick asked quietly. He sat up, shrugging the blanket off.

"That, Rick, is the closest I ever wanna get to being caught doing something like this," Tony whispered. He clenched the wheel and laid his head on his hands. Rick could see his friend shaking. Reaching over the seats, Rick touched Tony's shoulder.

"Tony, you sure 'bout this? Really sure? About hiding me, I mean?" Rick asked.

"You wanna go to jail?" Tony snapped suddenly.

Rick sat back, stunned at the cop's sudden anger. "Um...no, not really, but you look like you're gonna puke and I just thought maybe this wasn't such a good idea. I mean if it's gonna make you act like this, I don't know if it's really worth it," Rick said uneasily.

Tony shook his head immediately. "No, Rick. I'm not gonna be sick. And yes, hiding you's a very good idea," Tony said, raising his head.

"Then what's wrong?" Rick demanded.

"I never even saw Frank until he came up to the car, yet he was apparently watching long enough to realize I was hiding you. And instead of turning both of us in, he just walked away and wished you luck. I'm shocked we're not on our way to jail," Tony explained with a chuckle.

There wasn't much Rick could say to that. He scrunched back down out of sight, pulling the blanket over himself again. Tony pulled away and headed back towards town. Rick could hear Tony talking on his cell and winced as he overheard stuff he was pretty sure he wasn't supposed to.

"Talk to me, Marsh. Wha'cha got? Okay, so we're certain she's gone? Damn. Any evidence? Just the bandana? Nothing else? Marsh, c'mon, don't beat around the bush, man. I'm too exhausted for this crap," Tony said. Rick nodded as he could hear the exhaustion in his friend's voice.

"Damn, that's bad, but not a complete loss. Not until we confirm it's his. The boss? Oh. Well, I'm not gonna be back for another hour or so. I'm heading to the safe house. No, I came up with another idea and it's already in motion. Later." Rick heard Tony sigh and snap his phone closed. *What have I gotten my big brother into?* Rick wondered as Tony continued to drive around.

Rick waited patiently until the car finally stopped. "Okay, son. Coast is clear for now. You can sit up. Just be ready to run if this doesn't work," Tony said quietly.

"Where are we?" Rick asked as he sat up. He looked around but didn't recognize the neighbourhood.

"A safe house," Tony replied tersely. He wasn't really happy about the location, but beggars couldn't be choosers.

"You don't sound so sure," Rick said, leaning forward a bit.

"When I made arrangements for this, I didn't realize where it was located. It's a lot more exposed than I'd like. You're gonna have to keep your head down and the curtains closed, no matter what time of day it is," Tony explained tersely.

"Dammit, a prison cell," Rick groused. He wasn't happy about having to hide but he knew it was necessary.

"Be glad it's not a real jail cell," Tony snapped angrily, disappointed at Rick's reaction.

"Because if you cause me one ounce of trouble, young man, it will be," a new voice drawled.

Rick jumped and turned around to see Dr. Jim standing at the door of the car, a frown on his face. Rick and Tony followed Jim silently into the townhouse. The teen dropped one of his duffle bags down beside the door and looked around at his new home.

It was warm and comfortable, sunlight streaming in the living room window until Jim jerked the drapes closed. The furniture was used, but not worn out or too unbearable. He could see the TV, DVD player and figured there was probably satellite, too. The food was limited when he looked into the fridge and cupboards, but Tony said he'd bring whatever Rick wanted.

They all sat around the kitchen table and Jim was the first to speak. "Look, Tony, I know I agreed to this, but now I'm worried. Do you realize how much I could lose if anyone found out? I'd lose the clinic for sure, and probably my freedom," the doc said. He was really worried, Rick could tell.

"I know, Jim. I don't like putting anyone else at risk, but I have no where else to turn. If I keep him at my place, Seamus'll find him for sure. I need time, Jim, please?" Tony begged.

"Fish, if the doc's gonna get in trouble, take me home, man. Or to the station. I can't get him in trouble like this," Rick protested.

Tony was stunned. For the first time ever, Rick was thinking about someone else instead of just himself or Jordan. Tony was so proud of his friend he could've burst. He smiled at Rick. "Commendable, son, but no, I'm not gonna take you home or to the station. Seamus'll just find you, lock you up and throw away the key, then twist the evidence around to make it fit you. You don't have that kind of time and neither does Meg," Tony insisted.

Rick hesitated a moment then looked at Tony. "Doc's not the only one who could get into trouble, is he, bro?" the teen asked shrewdly.

Tony nodded. "At the very least I could lose my job, Rick. At worst, I can be charged with aiding and abetting a wanted fugitive, obstruction of justice or even accessory after the fact," Tony said. His tone was matter of fact, but he, too, was sick inside from how much trouble he really was in.

Rick's face went white at the thought of what Tony and Jim could both lose. He looked at them and shook his head. "Oh hell no, bro! Absolutely not! No way am I gonna let either of you sacrifice your lives for me. I am *not* worth that!" he said hotly. He stood up and stormed to the door, totally prepared to go and turn himself in.

Tony's quiet voice stopped him before he could get out of the door. "Rick, please. Sit down."

Rick hesitated, his hand on the door knob. "Rick, please?" Jim asked.

Still, Rick hesitated. "I'm so not worth this, Tony. For you or Jim," he insisted again as he returned to his chair.

"We happen to think you are, young man, so trust us when we say we're willing to take a chance," Jim said, refilling Tony's coffee, who nodded his thanks.

"Look, Rick. We both know you've made some mistakes. That fight with Mick last week and today's idiocy with Meg in the cafeteria were due to stress, and only a few would blame you for them. When you do anything, it's by instinct, not by any kind of plan. You wouldn't go to the trouble of writing letters and making phone calls. I've always believed if you attack either Meg or Jor, it would be straight at them – not by hiding in the shadows. I just need time to prove it," Tony said wearily. He could feel how tired he suddenly was. *I've gotta get some sleep,* Tony realized sluggishly. *I make too many mistakes when I'm this wasted.*

Jim was solemn when he turned to face Rick. "Rick, I know what you've been accused of. I've treated you often enough since you joined the Knights, and since you've left, to know how brutal they really are. I've treated both girls and I know for a fact Jordan's voice'll never be the same and Megan still has nightmares from being attacked in November. Her nightmares're so bad she occasionally takes sleeping pills so she can sleep and not dream. I don't even wanna think about what she'll be like when we get her back. And yet, I do not believe for a second you've actually attacked either girl.

"But understand this, young man. You cause any kind of trouble while you're staying in this house and I'll turn you in myself, and damn the consequences," Jim said quietly.

Rick sat up and looked back at the doctor. "Don't worry, Doc. I cause you any trouble, I'll hand you the phone myself.

"My word on that."

Chapter 25

Tony pulled up in front of the station almost an hour later. It seemed like every light in the place was on. The focus would be on Megan's kidnapping, Tony knew, but life as a cop didn't stop for just one crime, no matter how bad it was. There would be other crimes to investigate, and Tony wondered idly whom he'd get as a partner since Seamus had made it very clear Tony wasn't going to be helping out on the most important investigation of Tony's life.

Glancing at the clock, Tony sighed. He'd been on the go since his shift had started that morning at seven after being on shift all weekend. It was now after six, but Tony knew he wasn't going home any time soon. He couldn't even remember the last day he'd had off, and now he needed to account for being MIA for the afternoon. He'd got Rick the groceries he'd wanted as well as some cash from his own bank account, just in case, and then left for the night. Rick was on the couch in front of the TV watching...something.

Tony rubbed the back of his neck. *Man, I am so tired,* he thought. He tried to remember what Rick had been watching and couldn't. The cop couldn't even remember what, if anything, he and Rick had talked about once Jim had left. Tony prayed it hadn't been vital to the case. He sat, staring out of the front window, trying to remember.

With a shake of his head, Tony realized he had no idea how he'd even managed to make it back to the station, and that another half hour had just disappeared while he'd been sitting here. "Crap," he muttered as he climbed out of his car and up the front steps.

Everywhere Tony looked, he could see his fellow cops rushing around in organized chaos, moving evidence, writing reports, booking arrestees, the low hum of voices lulling Tony almost to sleep. He jerked awake at the sound of his name being called above the noise.

"Fish!" Marshall called, weaving his way through the traffic.

Tony just nodded to his partner. Marshall caught him as he stumbled with exhaustion. "Whoa, man. Easy does it. Here, sit down before you fall down. Hank, grab me a cup of coffee. Strong and black. Thanks," Marshall said as he guided Tony over to their desks in the bullpen.

Tony took the coffee a very concerned Hank handed him and drank the bitter brew gratefully. "Bring me another, Hank. Thanks," Tony said.

Marshall waited until the coffee'd been brought and the partners were left alone. Pulling his chair closer, Marshall asked, "Where the hell've you been, man? The boss was pissed when he got back here almost two hours ago and you weren't anywhere to be found and not answering your cell. Now, according to a preliminary call to Glencrest, Rick's gone but his car's still there." Marshall's voice was barely loud enough for Tony to hear.

Tony looked down at his hands. He hated hiding things from his partner, but he had to in this case. Marshall didn't need to be caught up in Tony's crazy plan. "All I'm gonna tell you is he's safe. What you don't know you can't tell. Now, I'd better go and check in," Tony said. He finished the coffee, then hauled his tall frame to its feet, trying to stay awake. He prayed the caffeine would kick in soon.

Before he could take a step, Seamus bellowed Tony's name from his office, as if he knew Tony was back. Squaring his shoulders, Tony walked to the inspector's office, his head held high. The cop had absolutely no regrets about what he'd done. No matter what Seamus did or said, Tony knew he'd bought Rick enough time to prove his innocence or to at least find the clear, unbiased evidence Tony had been seeking to convict him.

Seamus didn't look up or acknowledge Tony as the younger cop closed the door behind him and sat down. The inspector continued to read the report in front of him, adding his own notes occasionally, while Tony was forced to wait him out. Tony could see a diagram of what appeared to be a hallway in the school, but the details were too small for him to read clearly, even if the words weren't swimming in front of him. Seamus continued to read, or so he wanted Tony to believe.

In reality, Seamus was trying very hard not to curse out loud and call Jim to put his best cop in the hospital. Tony looked like death warmed over. His hands were shaking slightly and he constantly rubbed his eyes, as if he was trying to make them focus. His hair had come out in several places from his braids and he was constantly brushing the stray hairs away from his face, distractedly. Seamus knew Tony and Marshall had spent the weekend struggling to keep Megan from pressing charges, even though she really wanted to and the inspector wondered when the last time Tony ate a decent meal or slept properly. *Hell, when's the last time the fool had a real day off?* Seamus wondered.

None of that mattered right now, though. Seamus had to go through the motions of reaming Tony out. Even when he'd ordered the young cop back to the station, Seamus knew in his heart Tony wasn't going to do it. He figured Tony'd hidden the boy away and damned if he knew what to do about it.

Clearing his throat softly so Tony didn't go through the roof when he finally spoke, Seamus tried to keep his voice gruff. "I seem to recall ordering ye back to the station this afternoon, Constable," he said, closing the folder and leaning back in his chair. He ignored how Tony looked, but it was damn hard.

Tony nodded wearily. "Yes, sir. You did," he agreed, brushing his hair back absentmindedly.

"Ye were told not to contact the boy in any way or to warn him," Seamus continued.

"I believe you did say something like that," Tony agreed again.

Seamus sighed. "Dammit, Tony Whitefish, where is he? No one's seen him since lunch today," the inspector said, weary already and the investigation had just started.

"Don't know, boss, and wouldn't tell you if I did," Tony lied easily.

"Tony, I will not put up with a cop who lies or obstructs an investigation, do ye hear me? Now where is he?" Seamus barked, hoping he could trick the answer out of Tony.

Tony just laughed. "Man, is that a joke, Seamus? *You* accusing *me* of obstructing an investigation! You've thrown so many obstacles in our way this year we might never figure out exactly what happened. I can tell you've already decided Rick's to blame, so I'm already gonna question the forensics, no matter who did the collection. And you want me to give him up? Even if I did know, I wouldn't tell you," Tony snapped back. Harsh words, he knew, but true nonetheless.

"Okay, Tony, fair enough. So let me tell ye what we've found." For the next few minutes, Tony listened impassively as Seamus outlined the evidence they found, hiding his uncertainty about all of it. When Seamus finished, Tony said two words.

"All circumstantial."

Seamus grimaced, holding onto his temper. Barely. "What's it gonna take to convince ye the boy's guilty?" he demanded finally.

"Why won't you believe he's being framed?" Tony retorted.

"Give me the evidence," Seamus said.

"Give me a motive," Tony replied softly.

Grateful for the opening Tony'd just given him, Seamus ruffled through the letters he was reviewing. He selected one, pointed to it, and said, "Yer motive's right there, Tony."

Tony laughed as he read what Seamus had pointed to. "Money? You think Rick's done this for money? No way, boss. In one year, when he hits eighteen, Rick gets a large trust fund, no questions asked. Then, whenever Nana passes on, he gets 30% of Nana's fortune. Not to mention, according to Nana, he's Michael's sole heir, because Michael cut Nelson out of his will. That is, if there's anything left when Michael dies," Tony said, dismissing Seamus' idea of a motive easily.

Seamus nodded sharply. "That's what I think, Tony. Michael needs money. The boy's probably doing this to get his dad out of trouble," Seamus said. *Not that I really believe that, but I have to give Tony something*, Seamus thought wryly.

Tony laughed again. "Oh, c'mon, Seamus. You honestly don't believe that, do you? After the way he's been treated by Michael? Rick wouldn't lift a finger to help his dad if he was the last man on earth. He'd gladly see him in whatever hell Mendez wants to put him in. No way, boss. You'll have to do better than that," Tony admonished, wagging a finger at Seamus.

"Ye've hidden him away, Tony, I know ye have, so where is he?" Seamus said wearily.

"Even if I have, I won't turn him over to you, Seamus. Not until we've done a lot more investigation and we've discovered as much evidence as we can. Now, can I go? I'm sure I've got other investigations that need to be done," Tony said, as he stood.

"No, Tony, ye don't. As much as I don't wanna have ye on this investigation because of yer close ties to the boy, I'm thinking maybe ye should be on it. Ye're right about one thing – ye know how the boy thinks almost better than he does and we'll need every advantage we have to figure this out. Marshall, on paper, will remain lead, but ye'll be the one who reports to me. Besides, Marshall's never led a major investigation like this and he's gonna need all the help he can get," Seamus explained.

Tony stopped at the door. "He doesn't wanna tell Nana and Ian, does he?" Tony asked shrewdly.

Seamus shook his head. "Do ye blame him, Tony? He's never had to do any kind of notification before and he doesn't want his first to be someone he knows. I know ye've done some before, and besides, Nana'll take it better from ye than anyone else. I'm gonna assume the boy's not still at home, but bring him in for questioning *only* if he is." Seamus' voice trailed off. Tony could hear Seamus was almost as tired as he was. The coffee wasn't kicking in yet.

"Seamus, how're the twins?" Tony asked quietly.

"Devastated, Tony. How'd ye expect them to be? Mickey's lost the best thing he's ever had and Jordan's...boyfriend's me main suspect," Seamus said sadly.

Tony came back to his boss and put a hand on Seamus' shoulder. "Don't worry, Seamus. We will find her and she'll be okay," Tony said reassuringly and strode from the office.

Seamus said nothing as he watched Tony leave, closing the door softly behind him. Tears suddenly welled up as Seamus looked at the picture on his desk of Megan, Mickey, Jordan and, yes, even Rick. It had been taken at the beginning of the school year, just after Rick had told the Knights to shove off. All four were smiling and they didn't have a care in the world. Seamus was certain none of them knew how screwed up their year was going to be.

"I pray ye're right, Tony. God, I pray that ye're right," Seamus whispered to the empty office.

Tony didn't waste any time after leaving Seamus. He grabbed Marshall and headed out to Glencrest. There was a small disagreement when Marshall, rather firmly, told Tony he was not driving. "I'd like to get home in one piece, Fish. You're exhausted and you're not driving! Now, give me the damn keys," Marshall said firmly, holding his hand out.

Now on their way to Glencrest, the partners talked over the evidence Marshall and the CSIs had found. It was pretty damning, Tony admitted privately, but still circumstantial.

"You know, Ian's gonna be pretty upset we've waited over four hours to tell him Megan's missing," Marshall said as he manoeuvred around a slower vehicle.

"Upset?" Tony replied. "Upset? He's gonna wanna kill us!"

"Yeah, I guess I would, too, if I was in his shoes," Marshall admitted. "So how do we do this?"

"We can say we didn't wanna tell him until we knew for sure. Besides, he can handle it. It's Nana that I'm worried about. I don't know how much more she can handle. She loves Rick and won't stand any more accusations against him," Tony said worried.

"Wonder why they haven't reported anything," Marshall asked as he pulled in.

"Probably figures she's with Mick. Curfew isn't until eleven, even on a school night," Tony said as they approached the front door.

"Constables," Martha greeted the partners. "Mrs. Attison and Mr. Ian're just finishing a late supper. Please, wait in the library while I tell them you're here."

Tony smiled as he flopped into one of the comfy leather chairs by the fireplace. The fire crackled and threw shadows around the stacks, warming the room. "I love this room, Marsh. I always feel at peace here. There's never anything wrong when I'm here, even when the world's coming to an end," Tony said, his voice low.

"Me, too. No matter how bad things are gonna get, Fish, I'll just remember this moment. Before all hell breaks loose," Marshall agreed, staring into the dancing flames.

"Well, that's not exactly a good way to start a conversation, Marshall," Ian chuckled as he and his mother walked in.

Tony surged to his feet. Nana smiled as he gave her a quick hug. "Evening, Nana."

"Tony, Marshall. Nice to see you both. Please, sit down," Nana said as the four sat down around the low table near the bookshelves and away from the heat of the fire.

Nana waited patiently as Martha poured tea for everyone, then retired. "Now, what can I do for my two favourite policemen?" she asked, smiling slightly.

"Have either of you heard from Meg today? Or Rick, for that matter?" Tony asked after a few seconds of awkward silence. No matter that he'd done notifications before, this was Nana, and she'd been hurt enough.

"Megan? Not since she called me this morning and told me she'd finally decided to press charges against her no-good cousin," Ian replied. Nana paled as she put two and two together and came up with nothing good.

"Tony, stop it! What's wrong? Where's Megan? And what's happened to Rick?" she demanded shrilly.

Tony winced. "There's no easy way to say this, Nana, so I'm just gonna come out and say it," Tony said softly as he knelt by her side and took her hand in his. "Meg's missing."

She went as white as a ghost and clenched even harder to Tony's hand. "I'm sorry, Nana," he whispered.

"What happened? What do you know?" Ian demanded hoarsely, trying to understand what Tony had said.

Marshall quickly outlined what evidence they had found. "Unfortunately, right now, all of the evidence we have points right at Rick," he finished with a heavy heart.

"No! Not my lad!" Nana protested, sitting up and showing some of her old spirit.

"C'mon, Mother. Open your eyes for a change. That boy's nothing but trouble. He's greedy, just like Michael. You're the only one too blind to see it," Ian snapped.

"Ian!" Tony protested, climbing to his feet.

"That's enough, both of you. Son, I've told you before blood is blood, and I will support Rick no matter what. And he's <u>nothing</u> like his father, do you hear me? Nothing! You may not see it, but I do. Rick's kind, gentle, loving. And unlike Michael, Rick never asks for anything, even when he needs to! I don't care what the evidence says – Rick didn't do this!" Nana's voice continued to be shrill.

Ian just snorted. "Fine, Mother. Believe what you want. But I'm gonna side with Seamus on this, and I'll bet you're here to arrest the boy," Ian demanded as he looked at Tony.

The cop shook his head quickly. "We haven't got a warrant for his arrest, not yet, anyway. But we do have to bring Rick in. Just for questioning, Nana," Tony reassured her at her cry of protest.

Nana sighed. "You swear you're not gonna arrest him?"

Tony smiled, trying to reassure her again. "I swear on the Creator, Nana. I'm not gonna arrest Rick today," he said.

Nana frowned as she realized what Tony hadn't said – he wasn't making any promises about tomorrow. She remained sitting in the library, silent tears falling on the picture of Rick and Megan she held in her hand.

Ian led the way to Rick's house, walking into the house without knocking, not caring how Rick may react. It didn't take long for everyone to determine Rick was long gone. Everything had been cleared out, including his boxing equipment.

"He's run, just like the coward he is," Ian said, coming back into the kitchen. He was more than a little disgusted with his nephew.

"Look at what I found," Tony said, indicating the letter pinned to the table. "No, don't touch, Ian. It's evidence."

Ian leaned in next to Marshall and read the letter aloud:

"Dear Nana,

"By the time you find this, I swear I'll be long gone. I'm leaving the car 'cause it costs too much to keep it going and I don't know where I'm gonna end up. Sell it or keep it, I don't care anymore.

"I pulled outta school to try and keep them safe, but I don't know if it'll help. I hope so. I'm sorry, Nana, but I can't do this any more. I can't be someone I'm not. I'm not a good kid, no matter what Fish says. So I'm not gonna try anymore.

"Since no one's trying to clear my name, I'm gonna do it myself. Seamus can go to hell for all I care – I didn't do anything to Megs or Jor.

"Sorry, Nana. I know you tried to help, but it just didn't work out. Tell Jor I'm sorry. I'm not good enough for her and now she can find someone who is. Love ya, sweets.

"Fish, if you're reading this, sorry, bro. You tried, but I ain't worth losing a job over. Peace, man. Tell Coach and the club I won't forget them or the lessons I've learned. And tell the Kid to keep the Angels on the right path.

"I probably won't be back, Nana, but I'll write if I can. Love ya!

"Moneyman."

Chapter 26

Hell, that's where I am, Megan thought as she slowly regained consciousness. *Otherwise, I wouldn't hurt so damn much.* As she struggled to open her eyes, she became aware of the dank wetness in the air. Her clothes smelled like smoke, and the stink of sweat seemed to be hanging around. There was also a subtle scent she couldn't quite place, yet she knew it from school. Not one she could associate with Mickey, Rick or Tom, but from school nonetheless.

As Megan lay in the darkness, she could hear the sound of a tap dripping somewhere close by. In the distance, she heard a telephone ringing and ringing. No one seemed inclined to answer it and it finally fell silent. When she shifted, Megan heard the skittering of a mouse and she gave a muffled cry of panic. Megan hated mice and rats.

Now that she was completely awake, Megan could feel how cold she was. It had sunk into her very bones and it made her ache. The pillow beneath her head barely qualified to be called that, it was so thin. The mattress she was on was lumpy and well worn, so much so Megan could feel the steel frame of the cot beneath it. She couldn't help shivering as the cold seeped further into her body.

The shivering was so strong it shook Megan for all she was worth. Now she could feel her legs tied to the bed frame with coarse rope and her arms were wrenched behind her so tight she couldn't feel her fingers. Her shoulder screamed in pain, just like it had that cold winter day and all she could think was she'd gone back in time to November again. That would explain the cold and being tied up.

Panicked, she fought against her restraints as hard as she could, her muffled screams unheard by anyone. Panic couldn't sustain her for long, though and soon she slumped back on the cot, struggling to breathe. She choked on the dirty rag that had been shoved down her throat. As she started to calm down a bit, she could feel blood dripping into her hands from where the ropes had cut into her wrists.

A low chuckle sent Megan scrambling as far back against the wall as she could. Overhead, a dim light was snapped on, causing her to wince. Her eyes now watering, Megan struggled to focus on the four figures standing just outside of the straining light. As one, they stepped into the light and her heart sunk like a stone.

Head-to-toe black and silver and a white t-shirt. The black bandanas tied over their hair. Outfits so familiar to Megan she could've wept. The Black Knights stood in front of her, arrogantly believing they were going to get away with this. So arrogant it took Megan a minute to realize they hadn't bothered to hide who they really were.

And because they didn't hide their faces, Megan realized there was no way she was going to get out of this alive. Tears fell silently as she finally believed Rick. *He really is innocent*, she thought. *Lord, please get me outta this and I swear I'll never not trust Rick again.* The longer Megan looked at the Knights, the more she realized who Brain really was. Brian Townsand sat right behind her in every one of her classes, giving him perfect access to her book bag. And now he stood before her, grinning as she figured out what was going on.

Brain chuckled as he looked at Blade. "Think she's figured it out, man," he drawled. Megan winced as she recognized the voice on the phone. And as she studied Brain, she could see how much he and Rick actually looked alike, and now she understood how it had been so easy to think Rick had hurt her in the woods. *Rick, I am so sorry*, she thought miserably.

"Be nice, Brain," Blade drawled as well. "After all, man, she's a guest. Show 'er the same...hospitality as last time." Megan almost laughed as Blade struggled with the big word.

But when Brain knelt by the bed with his hands reaching out towards Megan's throat, she no longer felt like laughing. She was terrified. Again, she tried to squish herself as far back as she could, but, as she was tied down, it wasn't nearly far enough. Brain grinned as he wrapped his hands around her throat and squeezed.

As first, Megan couldn't do anything but stare at the face of a boy who suddenly wanted her not just frightened but dead. It didn't take long before her vision began to grey out and then she began to struggle, battling for her life. All she could think was it was a good thing she hadn't worn the diamond and emerald necklace Mickey had given her at Christmas, like she normally did. As hard as Brain was squeezing, her throat would've been sliced to ribbons.

Megan continued to struggle as the darkness beckoned again. When her struggles finally ceased and she once again fell unconscious, Brain let go and stood back. Blade just stood there, looking at his captive. Suddenly, he leaned down and grabbed a bucket of water no one had seen before. Before anyone could stop him, Blade tossed the whole bucket of freezing water over Megan to wake her back up. Brain was so stunned, he was speechless. This had *not* been part of their plan.

Megan's eyes snapped open as the shock of the water hit her. It soaked her from head to toe, including the ropes, the mattress and the gag in her mouth. She could feel the water trickle into her mouth and towards the back of her throat. Her eyes widened as she began to choke. She struggled to get the gag out of her mouth, but it wouldn't move.

"You, Megs, are nuthin' more than a pain in my ass, so don't think fer a second I won't take ya out if ya cause any trouble. Understand?" Blade snapped, ignoring the struggling teen.

When Megan didn't answer, Blade backhanded her, hard enough for Megan to see stars. "I said, understand?" Blade snarled.

Megan nodded, terrified.

"Good. 'Cause if ya make any kinda noise that can be heard, I'll make ya wish Brain had finished what he started today. Get it?" Blade hissed.

Megan tried to nod, but could only stare in horror at the Knights. Between the coldness of the room and the freezing water Blade had thrown on her, she was shivering violently. The pain in her ribs from falling over the chair in the cafeteria was now worse. The water that had been a trickle in her mouth suddenly seemed to be a torrent rushing down her throat. With the gag in place, she couldn't cough to clear her lungs and now she couldn't breathe. Once again, the darkness threatened.

The sound of Megan's head hitting the wall as she collapsed made Pup turn to look at her. He was pretty sure Megan wasn't breathing. Paling, he risked Blade's wrath and tugged on his cousin's arm to get his attention.

"What?" Blade glared at his cousin.

"Yo, man. Megs ain't breathing!" Pup hissed, pointing at their captive.

Brain turned away from the argument he and Blade had begun to see Megan flopped over on her side. Her normally tanned face was pasty white and she was most definitely struggling to breathe. He yanked the gag out of her mouth and tipped her head forward, trying desperately to get the water out of her mouth. Nothing.

The teen pulled out his knife and quickly sliced the ropes that held her hands, hoping this would help. Nothing. Just as Brain reached to check for a pulse, Megan's eyes snapped open and she took a gasping, shuddering breath. Brain sighed, relieved. *That was too bloody close*, he thought as Megan began to cough weakly.

"Pup, go and get me a glass of water," Brain ordered. Pup didn't hesitate. He flew up the slippery stairs and was back before Blade could protest.

Pup handed the water to Brain, then shook out a thread-bare blanket and covered Megan with it. "It's not much, man, but it'll help 'er until she dries a bit," the youngest Knight apologized to Brain who only nodded. "The other one's too wet."

"Thanks, kid. Crank, cut 'er one leg loose so she can lay down," Brain ordered. He still didn't like how pale Megan was, but he could feel Blade steaming behind him and knew he'd better not push his luck anymore.

Retying Megan's hands in front so she could at least drink the water, Brain leaned in to talk quietly to the terrified girl. "You promise to keep quiet and I won't put the gag back in, 'kay?" he said quietly.

Megan nodded weakly. Although her throat was killing her, she had to know one thing. "Why, Brian? Why?" she croaked. *Now I know how Jordan felt,* she thought as she finished the stale water and handed the glass back to Brain.

Blade laughed. It was the same slightly hysterical laughter she remembered from the woods and Megan couldn't stop the shivers. "Why, Megs? 'Cause I do what I want. When I want. To who I want. My pleasure. My fun. That's all that's ever mattered. And since Moneyman lives right beside ya, all by hisself, yer the easiest. And now, he's gonna pay and pay big time," Blade continued to laugh.

Megan couldn't believe what she was hearing. "Rick? This is all about Rick?" she croaked incredulously. "And you came after me instead of him? I guess it must be easier to attack someone who can't fight back since I know Rick could wipe the floor with you. He's better than all four of you put together, isn't he, *Blade?*" Megan continued, making Blade's name a curse.

"You're weak compared to him and you know it! That's why he won't fight you. He knows it wouldn't be fair. Tony and Coach taught him to be better than that. You've got the whole school thinking you're some big bad gang banger. You're nothing but a bloody coward!" Megan spat, hatred making her voice stronger than it had been since she woke up.

Suddenly, Blade shoved Brain away from Megan and slammed his hand across her face. Her head bounced off the concrete wall, stunning her again. When her vision cleared, she was horrified to see Blade's fist flying towards her unprotected head. She closed her eyes, praying it ended quickly.

"Don't," she heard Brain say softly to Blade. When she got brave enough to open her eyes, she saw Brain holding Blade's arm as easily as she held a pen. Blade's eyes blazed with anger as he ripped his arm away from Brain.

Blade turned that angry gaze onto Megan. "Next time, *cuz,* there won't be anyone to stop me," he growled and stormed away.

Megan shivered at his threat. "I'm so sorry, Rick," she said again as she began to sob quietly into the pillow, remembering Blade's threat about being heard. Cold, wet and miserable, she struggled to fall asleep. As she did, she prayed she would be found soon. Otherwise, Blade was going to kill her.

"Will you just calm down, Blade?" Brain ordered as Blade paced the living room. Pup and Crank had stayed in the kitchen, talking quietly. There was no way they were going anywhere near Blade when he was this angry. Only Brain or Moneyman could ever handle Blade when he got like this, and it had been more often Moneyman than Brain who did.

"If yer thinkin' I'm gonna let 'er talk t' me like that, yer crazy," Blade growled. Brain winced as Blade's knife suddenly appeared quivering in the wall behind the leader of the Knights. He hadn't even seen Blade pull his steel, let alone turn around and throw it.

Still, Brain got right in Blade's face. He figured he was safer with Blade's steel in the wall, and Brain knew he could take Blade easier if it came down to a fight with their fists. "Look, man," Brain said, speaking slowly and clearly. "You don't control your temper and we get no money, man. Nothing, you hear? You keep this up and someone's gonna call the cops. Cops come down on us, we all go to jail for a very long time! What's gonna happen to your pleasure and your fun when we're in jail? That what you want?" Brain snapped. His voice was low, but easily carried to the Knights in the kitchen.

"No, but I'm not gonna let 'er talk to me like that!" Blade raged again.

"I get it, man, but you've gotta follow the plan. Throwing water on her and freezing her to the bone wasn't in the plan and you'd better hope the temperature doesn't drop again or she's gonna get sick. You gotta keep her fed. Give her water. Let her go to the bathroom and keep her clean. Don't beat her any more, no matter what she says or does," Brain ordered.

Crank blinked as he sat down with another pop for him and Pup. "What the hell, man?" he said softly. Even Pup was surprised at what he'd just heard.

"Did Brain just give Blade an order?" Pup hissed.

Crank nodded slowly as Brain continued his tirade. "Blade, I'm serious, man. If you can't stay away from Megs, she's gonna get sick – or worse. Let Pup take care of her; either that, or we move her somewhere where I can take care of her. We want the money, not a dead body."

Brain turned away, trusting Blade wouldn't put a knife in his back. He motioned for his coat hanging on the chair behind Crank. Soberly, the other Knight handed Brain his coat and nodded, once, acknowledging the beginnings of the power shift in the Knights. Brain sighed as he shrugged into his jacket. They didn't need this right now, but he knew he would challenge Blade for the lead if it meant keeping Megan alive and sticking to this crazy plan of Blade's.

"Blade? You gonna listen and leave 'er alone or do I gotta move her?" Brain asked as he stood by the front door.

Blade cursed as Brain issued his subtle challenge. "Don't worry, Brain. I'll take care of Megs," Blade drawled to his second as he shoved Brain and Crank out of the house and slammed the door behind them.

Brain snarled low in his throat. He looked at Crank and muttered as the pair walked away, "That's what I'm afraid of."

Chapter 27

That was the start of a very long week for everyone. While Brain paced in his room, worrying about leaving Blade alone with Megan and Rick did the first of many long workouts on his speed bag, Marshall and Tony returned to the station – without Rick. Tony was relieved at how relatively easily it had gone at Glencrest, once Ian realized Rick was long gone. Marshall, on the other hand, was silent as a tomb as they pulled up in front of the station.

Tony was part way up the stairs before he realized his partner was still sitting in the car. "Wanna get it off your chest, partner?" Tony asked, climbing back into the car.

Marshall stared at his white-knuckled fists clenched on the steering wheel. He took a deep breath and turned to face Tony. His face was tortured and Tony was surprised to see tears welling in Marshall's eyes. "Hey, man. What the hell?"

"You've always believed Rick's innocent, haven't you?" Marshall said quietly, brushing away the sudden moisture.

"Right at first? No. Not until I talked to him as a counsellor and not as a cop. I learned the hard way, the night he took me down at the centre, Rick has to have *one* person, other than Nana or Jor, believe him or he has absolutely nothing. Without me believing him, he's as cold and unfeeling as Blade is," Tony explained. He wondered where his friend was going with this.

"And after that day?" Marshall asked, curious.

"You've seen him, Marsh. He's way too gentle with Jor to do this. Meg, too, no matter what she believes right now. Yet we both know how strong he is. We've seen him control that stallion of his easily. Frank's told me if anyone but Rick tries to ride Cherokee, the horse goes ballistic, and yet with Rick, he's as gentle as a newborn lamb. It's taken a very long time, some very long nights and horrid sessions to teach Rick about that strength. I can't tell you how proud I am of my little brother," Tony replied.

The partners sat in their car while Tony waited for Marshall to wrestle with what was bothering him. Finally, Tony couldn't take the tension anymore. "C'mon, partner. You've asked me about this for a reason. Talk to me, man. What's eating at you?" Tony demanded.

"Ever since Seamus told me Megan was missing, I've been thinking...I screwed up and badly. I'm pretty sure I could've prevented this," Marshall whispered, choking back a sob.

Tony was stunned. "Marsh, take a breath and calm down. No one could've prevented this," Tony said. He couldn't believe his partner actually blamed himself.

That was until Marshall told him about the phone call he overheard in late January between Rick and Blade. "When Rick told Blade to leave the girls alone, he just laughed. He said he did what he wanted, when he wanted, to who he wanted. And when Rick challenged Blade to come after him, I don't think I'll ever forget his reply," Marshall said hoarsely.

"What did Blade say?" Tony asked. He couldn't help but wish Marshall *had* told him about this earlier, but nothing could be done about it now.

"He said, "Tempting, Moneyman, very tempting. But...no. You're not ready yet. I haven't begun to break you. Trust me, little Moneyman, when I'm through with you, there ain't no one that's gonna trust you ever again. What happened before was just child's play. Practice. If you don't believe anything else, believe this. When I get through with them and you, you'll beg me to end it, just to save them." Then he slammed the phone down, laughing," Marshall said, miserably. Now Tony understood how the cop could blame himself.

Before he could stop himself, though, Tony blurted out, "Why the hell didn't you tell me this before, Marsh?"

Tony instantly regretted his words when Marshall flinched and hung his head. Again, Tony thought he heard his partner muffle a sob. "I've really screwed up, didn't I, Fish? I mean, really screwed up?" he whispered.

"No, Marsh. You didn't screw up, man. It's too late now to worry about what-ifs and might-a-beens. Even knowing what I do about the Knights, I might not've put it all together, so you definitely wouldn't've. Okay? These were just words to you, man. They didn't mean anything," Tony said, trying to reassure his partner.

"What now, Fish? What do I do now?" Marshall asked, as he tried to relax a bit. As long as Tony didn't blame him, Marshall wouldn't blame himself so much either. He still felt like he could've stopped this, but Tony was right. He couldn't worry about it now. *What's done is done,* Marshall thought firmly, getting himself back under control.

Tony climbed out of the car and stood by the door, looking across the top of the car at his partner. "For now, nothing, I guess, other than add it as a report to the file – a remembered conversation overheard before the threats started up again. Seamus wouldn't believe you anyway. Not until we have a viable suspect other than Rick," Tony said with a shrug.

Tony left Marshall working on his report at their desk while he went to check in with Seamus. The inspector waved Tony to a seat as he continued to listen to whomever was on the other end of the phone. "Still? Okay, son, call Jim. That's gotta be stopped before she gets sick. And I need ye both to stay close to home for now. I know, son, but I can't look for Megan while I'm worried about where ye are, 'kay? I don't have anyone to spare to watch over ye. How're ye holding up, son? Sure? Okay. Try and get Jordan to eat something, even if it's just soup. I love ye both. Yes, Mickey, I promise I'll eat. Goodnight son."

Seamus hung up the phone with a small sigh. He turned away from Tony for a moment, trying to compose himself. When the inspector turned back, only the faintest of tightening around his eyes betrayed the stress and strain he was under, both here at the station and at home. Pretending not to notice, Tony sat, waiting, for his boss to speak.

"So? Glencrest. What happened?" Seamus finally asked.

Tony sighed. "Nana was about as hurt as Mick and Jor when I told her Meg was gone and Rick was wanted for questioning," Tony said.

"Understandable, don't ye think?" Seamus replied, his tone dry. "And Ian?"

"Ian led the charge over to Rick's house," Tony said, handing over the now-protected letter to Seamus. He said nothing more while his boss read.

Shaking his head, Seamus looked up to see a totally innocent look on Tony's face. "So he wasn't home, huh?" Seamus asked unnecessarily.

"Sorry, boss, but no, he wasn't. Gotta question for you, boss, off topic. How're the twins holding up?" Tony asked. His genuine concern touched Seamus in a way he didn't imagine would ever happen, especially knowing how he'd treated Tony in the past year.

"Bad, Tony, I won't lie. Jordan won't quit crying. Every time Mickey thinks she's done, she'll see something or hear something and start all over again. I'm hoping Jim can help her," Seamus said. "At least Mickey seems to be strong enough to get through this without falling apart."

"Don't be so sure, boss," Tony disagreed. "Right now, he's doing what comes naturally, what he's done all of his life, really. He's taking care of his sister and making sure she's okay. But, trust me, boss, eventually, he's gonna be by himself and then it's gonna hit him, really hit him. When it does, it's gonna be as bad, or worse, than Jordan," Tony warned.

Seamus nodded thoughtfully. "Ye're probably right, Tony. Thanks. I'll give him some time when I get home tonight, so he can do what he needs to do to get through this. Now, back to the boy, if ye don't mind. This is mighty convenient, if ye ask me," Seamus said, tapping the new letter in front of him.

"About as convenient as the bandana Marshall and you found," Tony replied.

Seamus nodded. "I actually agree with ye fer once, Tony. I've thought about it and thought about it and realized everything in that damn hall was placed just right. The bandana was dropped in just such a way ye couldn't help but catch the silver stitching with a flashlight. The more I've thought about it, the more I realized everything was very well staged to point me in one direction," Seamus explained. He hated to admit he'd been tricked, but he couldn't help it.

Tony rubbed at his face. His eyes blurred again with exhaustion. "Gimme the evidence run down again, boss," Tony said, leaning over as if thinking. Even his voice was shaking now with exhaustion and he clasped his hands together, hoping to hide their tremors.

"There's the letters, if taken at face value; transcriptions of the two calls Megan recorded; his threat against Megan at lunch today; and there's the bandana, the writing on the wall and a black bag stuffed behind the lockers near where she was taken," Seamus said, detailing the evidence, pointing out locations of items on the sketch on his desk and desperately trying to ignore the exhausted cop sitting across from him.

Tony sighed as he listened. "All of it points to Rick when taken at face value," he admitted sourly. "Where's the evidence now?"

"Being logged in the evidence room. Why?" Seamus asked.

"Thought a fresh pair of eyes should take a look at it," Tony said as he stood. He didn't seem to notice how much he was swaying on his feet.

Seamus did and snorted, unable to ignore the evidence in front of him now. "Fresh eyes, Tony? Look at yerself, Constable. Ye can barely stand, let alone keep yer blood-shot eyes open. Ye've been here for what? over 15 hours already and knowing ye, ye have no intention of going home anytime soon. Ye need to re-braid yer hair. Ye haven't slept properly in Lord knows how long. When was the last time ye ate anything other than fast food? Hell, when was the last time ye didn't go racing off to help that boy through some crisis or another?" Seamus demanded harshly.

Tony flushed. He didn't realize it was that bad, but still, he couldn't quit. "It's been a while, Seamus," the cop finally admitted.

"But that doesn't matter. Not right now. I'll be in the evidence room with Marsh."

Tony closed the door to Seamus' office with a sigh, leaning against it for a minute, trying to get some energy to get going. He glanced at his watch and groaned. Seamus was right. He'd already been on duty for over 15 hours today and that was *after* putting two more brutal fifteen-hour shifts over the weekend, some of which had nothing to do with Rick's problem. He hadn't slept Sunday night at all, tossing and turning, fighting nightmares that suddenly decided to disturb his sleep.

And food? Real food, not fast food? What's that? Tony wondered as he went to sit at his desk for a minute. The last real meal he remembered having was one Rick had cooked for him a couple of weeks ago when the cop had dropped over to talk. Otherwise, it had been take out, fast food and microwave dinners. He was running on empty and Tony knew it wasn't going to be long before he ran out of everything.

"What happened?" Marshall asked as Tony collapsed into his chair. He nodded as Tony replayed the conversation with Seamus. And like Seamus, Marshall chose to ignore the exhausted cop in front of him. He had to since Tony wasn't going to quit without being forced to quit. Just like Marshall.

"I wanna take a look at the new evidence you got today. Maybe, even as tired as I am, I'll see something," Tony said as he finally acknowledged his exhaustion and struggled to his feet. He wasn't surprised to see he and Marshall were the only ones left from the day shift, but he still didn't want to show any kind of weakness to the other cops on duty.

In the evidence room, Tony and Marshall looked at all of the evidence collected since the start of the school year. Tony sighed. *Dammit, it really does all point to him,* Tony thought sourly. "Okay, Marsh. Looking at it this way, I understand how Seamus would look at Rick and no one else. I didn't realize how damning it really was," Tony said, motioning to everything laid out in front of them.

"Yeah. But you know what's really bugged *me* about all of this? In every other case we've ever investigated, there's always been something which pointed, at least at first, to another suspect we could look at and possibly eliminate. Not in any of these. It's always been Rick," Marshall groused.

Tony frowned as he looked at the evidence and realized Marshall was right. The tire tracks found behind the school had been too shallow to yield any good casts, but Terry mentioned he thought they looked like the ones on Rick's Firebird as well as about a hundred other cars. The writing that had been photographed wasn't a clear match to Rick, yet it was still similar enough no one could be eliminated right now. The bandana (*how many of these stupid things did he really have?* Tony wondered as he looked at it) had been processed and they were now waiting for the results. Finally, Tony picked up the black bag Seamus had mentioned in passing.

Looking inside, he found the same darts and the vial of clear liquid Marshall had noted on his report. Tony stared at everything for a moment, then turned to his partner. "Marsh, I know these're tranquilizer darts, but did you ever find a gun? I don't see one logged," Tony said, holding up the dart in his gloved hand.

Marshall shook his head. "No, I think they took the gun with them, but left that bag behind. And I personally don't think it was supposed to be forgotten," Marshall said with a slight smile at the kidnapper's forgetfulness. He just hoped it would help them break the case open.

"And where does one get a gun like this?" Tony replied with his own smile. His smile faded, though, when Marshall replied.

"Elijah, and I've already sent someone over to question him. Store's closed up, and all of his records, legal and illegal, are gone. When Hank checked with his wife, she had no idea why he'd left town so suddenly. Oh yeah, and the surveillance tapes're gone, too. She told Hank to check with the mistress Elijah thinks no one knows about, but she has no idea either. And neither one knows where he might've gone. The wife's gonna go through all of the inventory left, turn the guns over to us to destroy and then turn the store into something positive," Marshall said. He could see the flash of disappointment in Tony's eyes.

"So much for that lead," Tony muttered, disgusted. He tossed the dart back into the bag and picked up the vial. He just stared at it for a moment, wondering.

"Wha'cha thinking, Fish?" Marshall asked finally.

"Not sure, Marsh, but could you bring me anything and everything we have on the break-in at Jim's clinic? I wanna check on something," Tony said as he made some notes. He didn't hear Marshall leave as he cleaned up the evidence they looked at, making some additional requests for processing. Then, he resealed the evidence bags the partners had opened up and returned everything to the desk to be put away.

Once back at his own desk, he put a call into Dr. Jim. "Sorry to wake you, Jim," Tony said when the doctor answered.

"No worries, Tony, you didn't. I just got home actually. I was at Seamus' for the twins and then Nana called me out to Glencrest," Jim explained.

"Nana? She was fine when we left her," Tony said, worried.

"Relax, Tony. She's still fine. Worn out, of course, but she knows she's gonna need to be able to function. Her "empire" as she called it isn't gonna quit running just because her grandchildren're gone. Life still goes on so she wanted a couple of light sleeping pills so she can get some decent sleep. I'll keep an eye on her," Jim explained quickly.

"Oh. Thank the Creator. I thought something else had happened and Seamus didn't wanna tell me. And Jor? How're the twins doing?" Tony wanted to know.

"That's a different matter. I don't mind saying I'm worried about them, Jordan especially. I had to have Mickey hold her down so I could sedate her. Otherwise, I was gonna put her in the hospital under strict observation. You can't cry non-stop for over five hours and not pay for it. Mickey even asked for a sleeping pill for himself so he could get some sleep. Those kids're a mess, Tony and there's only so much I can do for them outside of the hospital. I'm afraid Jordan may try to hurt herself, she's that upset," Jim said angrily.

"Damn, Jim, that is bad. I'll try to stop over tomorrow to talk to her. Maybe I can help bring her out of this," Tony offered.

Jim frowned as he realized how much Tony was slurring his words. "Thanks, Tony, I'm sure that'll help. But I gotta ask, you okay? You're slurring your words so much I can barely understand you. Do you need me to stop by your place?" the doc offered.

"Naw, I'm okay, doc, don't worry 'bout me. Anyway, I'd like to stop by the clinic tomorrow. I've got some questions for you and something I need to show you," Tony said, trying to deflect everyone's concern. He rubbed his face again, almost asleep at his desk.

He barely heard Jim's answer to come and see him after lunch at the clinic. He continued to scrub at his face, trying to get his head working and back in the game. He couldn't focus long enough to read anything on his desk. He was concentrating so hard on reading the report in front of him he didn't hear anyone approach his desk.

So when he felt a hand come down on his shoulder, he jumped up and swung. His fist went wild and Tony stumbled. He felt himself falling only to be caught before he hit the floor.

When he could finally focus, Tony looked up into the shocked and concerned faces of his fellow cops.

Chapter 28

"Fish? Tony, c'mon, partner, look at me," Marshall commanded in a low tone. Tony struggled to understand the words and then to make his eyes obey. Blinking furiously, Tony finally managed to convince his body to do what he wanted.

Marshall's concerned face gradually swam into focus. Tony was surprised to find himself sitting on the floor facing his partner and the equally concerned face of the Inspector. "Wha' happen?" he slurred, struggling to pull himself up.

Glancing at each other, Marshall and Seamus hauled Tony to his feet and then sat him back down at his desk. "You passed out at your desk, man, without hanging up your phone," Marshall explained slowly as Tony tried to follow his words. He couldn't believe how bad Tony looked. It was even worse than it had been a few minutes ago.

"I went for that report you wanted, and I was on my way back when Seamus called me into his office. We came back out here to find you out cold on your desk. We shook you for at least a minute and you wouldn't wake up. Then, for some reason, you took a swing at us, but at least you're awake," Marshall explained as he tidied up his partner's desk, locking away his current files.

"Was talkin' t' Jim. Seein' him after lunch tomorrow," Tony said as he tried to stand again. He still didn't realize how much he was slurring his words when he talked, but both Seamus and Marshall did.

"The hell ye are. *You*, Constable, are going home and sleeping until ye get up. Then ye're gonna eat a decent meal and go back to bed and sleep again until ye wake up," Seamus ordered. "Or do I call Jim to knock ye out?" the inspector threatened.

Tony swayed as he shook his head frantically. "No, boss, please. I hate sleeping pills. Always feel worse after." With that, Tony turned to go and stumbled again.

Marshall caught Tony before he fell. "That's it. I'm taking you home, partner. No arguing," Marshall said. Over Tony's shoulder, Marshall looked at Seamus and mouthed, "Call Jim." Seamus nodded soberly. He couldn't believe how bad both Marshall and Tony looked. Motioning to Paul Culligan to follow the partners home, Seamus took his own advice. On his way out to his car, he called Jim and then headed home to be with his children.

Tony woke to the smell of strong coffee and frying bacon. He stretched, taking stock of how he felt and realized he felt a lot better. Not a hundred percent, but then again he wouldn't feel that way until Megan was found and Rick was cleared. As he climbed from his bed and headed to the shower, Tony swore he'd pay a visit to his shaman as soon as this was all over.

Ready to face the day after a very hot shower and scraping away the beard that seemed to show up overnight, Tony joined his partner in the kitchen. He accepted a cup of coffee with a thankful nod and then turned up the news on the TV, just in time to hear the weather for...

"Wednesday? What the hell?" Tony sputtered, spraying coffee all over the counter.

"Really, Fish. You don't like the coffee? Just say so, man. Don't spray it all over the damn place," Marshall admonished lightly as he wiped up the counter and plopped a loaded plate in front of Tony. "Eat," he ordered as he fixed a plate up for himself.

Tony turned an accusatory look on his partner. "Not until you tell me how in the hell I've just lost a day on this investigation," he ordered in a deadly quiet voice.

Marshall took a couple of bites of breakfast before he replied. "Jim knocked you out. Seamus thought it was for the best," Marshall said quietly. "Jim happened to agree and so, by the way, did I."

Tony was furious. "After I said no? After I begged you not to? How the hell could you do this to me?" he demanded hotly.

"Dammit, Tony, we did what we thought was best for you! Otherwise, we both know you would've forced yourself awake to go and see Jim yesterday, probably getting into an accident on your way there, maybe even killing yourself in the process. You are *that* exhausted," Marshall snapped back.

Tony stopped. "I? What?" he asked, puzzled.

"Tony, for your information, Monday you looked like death warmed over. Hell, I've seen corpses who looked more alive than you did and I know you would've just continued to push yourself past your limit. Jim couldn't believe how bad you were. You really don't remember Monday night?" Marshall asked, curious.

Tony took a bite of his now cool breakfast as he tried to recall getting home. He finally shook his head. "I don't remember anything after we left the station," he admitted sheepishly.

Marshall nodded. "Frankly, I'm not surprised. You basically passed out again in the car and then Jim and I had to practically carry you into the house after you tried to climb the front steps and fell flat on your face," Marshall explained as he ate.

Tony continued to eat slowly as he tried to recall what Marshall described. "I remember trying to hit someone...and did I say something about feeling drunk?" Tony asked as a snippet of memory came back.

Marshall laughed. "Yeah, you took a swing at me and Seamus just before you fell on the floor behind your desk, and after we finally got you up to your room, you got a little silly. Jim was checking you over and asked how you felt. You looked at him and said, "Drunk, doc. I'm drunk." Then you...giggled, like a little girl. Jim decided then Seamus was right – you needed to be knocked out, no matter what you wanted. He gave you a shot and waited until you were completely under before he left. You fought it for quite a while, actually," Marshall said. He began to clean up the breakfast while Tony thought about what Marshall had just said.

Despite how hurt he was at what they did, he had to admit he did feel a lot better for having slept for close to thirty hours. He didn't even feel as crappy as he usually did after taking something to sleep and that was saying something about how tired he had really been. What he really felt more than anything was embarrassed at letting his partner see him that bad.

"Alright, Marsh, you're forgiven. The boss, too. I guess you did do the right thing. Did you manage to catch some zz's, man?" Tony asked as he went to refill his coffee.

"Yeah. Stayed awake long enough to make sure you were out for good, then crashed and slept until about one yesterday afternoon. Doc came over to check on you and make sure you stayed asleep and I took one of his sleeping pills about supper time and slept until this morning," Marshall replied, sipping at his coffee and relieved Tony had forgiven him. He hadn't wanted to do what he did, but they hadn't had a choice. Tony was needed way too badly by a lot of people to let him go on like he had been.

Tony leaned against the counter, drinking his coffee. "Did we miss anything?" he asked, figuring Marshall had called Seamus for an update.

"Word's out in the press about Megan's disappearance and Rick's wanted for questioning *only*. The boss thought it was best and Nana agreed. They're trying to put as much pressure on Megan's kidnappers as they dare, whoever they are. The crime lab's working on processing the stuff we found in the hallway. They're also gonna re-process all of the evidence from the other assaults once more, just to make sure we didn't miss anything. One tech's focussing just on the couple of phone calls Megan recorded and we're going over Glencrest with a fine tooth comb, looking for anything that might be there and tied to her kidnapping," Marshall said.

Tony digested the information and sighed. "So right now, we're at a stand still until all the forensics're in, aren't we?" Tony said glumly.

Marshall nodded. "What now, partner?" he asked as he led the way out to the car.

"I'm gonna hold off on talking to Jim until we've looked at everything else. For now, we wait. Wait and pray," Tony sighed.

Waiting had never been one of Rick's strong points and being forced to wait while hiding out wasn't going very well. Remembering his promise to Jim, Rick kept as quiet as he could. He turned the basement into a make-shift boxing gym, trying to keep in shape. Rick was pretty sure he was going to need Moneyman sooner rather than later and Moneyman had better be ready.

When Rick wasn't keeping up his weight training, he was keeping up with his school work. He was optimistic Tony would figure out who had taken Megan and, once they were caught, Rick would be able to go back to school. Again, he figured he'd better keep up as best he could, so he spent as much time on his school work as he could stand. But once supper time hit, so did the worry and the wondering.

He'd hoped Tony would call him and let him know what was going on, but day after day passed and no word. By late Friday morning, Rick couldn't stand it any more. He pulled out his cell and called Tony.

"Gimme a minute and I'll call you right back," Tony said quickly when he answered his phone and heard Rick on the other end.

It was another five long minutes before Rick's phone rang. "Hey, bro," Rick answered.

"Sorry, Rick, but I was still in the station and I didn't want anyone to overhear me, not even Marsh," Tony replied. "What he doesn't know, he can't be forced to tell, after all."

"You cool now, man?" Rick asked, leaning back in the recliner. He flipped on the TV and found some music to listen to.

"Yeah. How're you holding up, son?" Tony asked as he pulled his car out of the parking lot. He heard some stress and strain in just the few words Rick had spoken and was worried about how the teen was actually holding up.

"Okay, I guess, a little stressed, but working on it, doing as much training as I can without hurting myself. I've been hoping you'd call me and tell me what's up, even though I'm pretty sure you're not supposed to," Rick said wryly.

Tony laughed. "True, son, true, but there's been nothing to tell you. Literally nothing. We don't know any more than when this all happened. Look, Jim's on his way over to you and so am I. Can you wait for an update until then?" Tony asked.

Rick snapped his phone closed after agreeing to wait for Tony to arrive. He quickly straightened up the kitchen and threw on a pot of coffee. Something told him his friend was going to need it. Rick had heard something he didn't like in Tony's terse words and he was really worried now.

Tony pulled up behind the house, shutting off his car to think about what he'd learned from Jim that morning about the break-in at the clinic. Most of the information didn't seem to make sense until Tony thought about possibly connecting the break-in to the kidnapping. He hoped, by talking it over with Jim and Rick, things would clear up a little.

The cop looked up when someone tapped lightly at his window. Jim motioned for Tony to follow him inside. At the top of the stairs, Tony remembered the stress he'd heard in Rick's voice. "Better let me go first, Jim. He's likely a bit jumpy," Tony advised.

The cop eased the back door open and slipped into the kitchen. He'd only taken a couple of steps into the room when his feet were abruptly swept out from underneath him and he landed heavily on his stomach. Before Tony could recover, he felt someone land on his back, and press a knife to his throat. Tony froze, but just as suddenly as it appeared, the knife was gone.

"Dammit, Fish, you ever hear of knocking?" Rick said, disgustedly. He extended his hand to help his friend to his feet. He gave Tony a quick man-hug and then pulled away.

"Sorry, son, but considering the house is supposed to be empty and it does belong to Jim, there would be no reason to knock. And I did tell you not ten minutes ago I was coming over?" Tony admonished lightly as Jim followed in slowly, shaking his head.

"Guess I expected you to come in the front door, Fish, not the back," Rick said with a shrug.

"Little tense, Rick? I can help," Jim said as the trio sat in the living room. Tony sipped at his coffee gratefully while Rick and Jim drank pop.

Rick hesitated a moment then got up to pace. When he finally spoke, his voice was a bit rough. "Yeah, doc, tense and worried, but no, I don't want anything. It'll take my edge off just when I need it the most. I'm worried about Nana and Megs. Jor's safe as she can be with Mick and her dad, but Nana's got no one for support since I'm sure Uncle Ian's convinced I've taken his daughter. Worried about Megs, how she's doing and what Johnny's probably done to her. Most of all, though, Doc, I'm pissed Johnny's walking free and I'm in hiding," Rick groused.

Tony stood up in front of Rick. "Hey, son, none of that. You could've let me take you in, but you decided it was better to hide. I need to know, right now, little brother – can you hold it together?" Tony asked.

Rick shook his head immediately. "Not if I stay cooped up much longer, bro. Lemme help," Rick begged.

"How?" Jim asked as Tony sat down, leaving Rick to pace away his nervous energy.

Rick paused. "Good question, Doc. I, uh...I don't know. I guess that would depend on what you know, Fish," Rick said.

"Honestly, not much. I'm waiting on fingerprints to be analyzed, along with some other stuff from the kidnap site. Jim's gonna go over some patient files from before that break-in at his clinic to see if we can find a clue or lead there, based on how we believe Meg was taken. Otherwise, all we have is another one of your bandanas at the scene and a little black bag which contains some small darts and a liquid we believe to be a sedative. Again, thanks to that bag, we're looking at couple of other leads, but so far, nothing's panning out," Tony said, laying out the scanty evidence.

Rick sighed. Tony was right – there really wasn't much to go on. He continued to pace, thinking. "You getting anything from the street, Tony?" he asked as he paced.

"Don't have any trustworthy contacts out there, son. Unless *you* know someone we can tap?" Tony asked, curiously as he watched Rick.

Rick stopped pacing and stood staring at the wall for a second or two. "Maybe," he said slowly. "Lemme go and check it out." He grabbed his jacket on the way to the back door.

Tony was stunned. "Now?"

"Yeah. You and doc stay here and chill. I'll be back in about an hour," the teen said as he strode confidently from the room.

Rick slipped out the back door and down the alley, keeping to the shadows. He took back alleys and seldom used roads until he was at Mahoney's. Remaining back in the shadows, he whistled a specific and seldom used sequence. He smiled tightly as Jimmy split away from the group hanging out in front of the store to join the former Knight around back.

"Moneyman," Jimmy greeted Rick softly, bumping knuckles with Rick.

"What's the word?" Rick asked, trying not to flinch when Jimmy called him by that hated nickname.

"Other than you're hot, Rick? Nuthin'. Blade's hidin' out somewhere. The Slayers're huntin' fer him, too," Jimmy said, dropping Rick's gang name. He knew how much Rick hated it. He leaned against the wall, blocking Rick's view of the street. But Rick didn't mind. It also meant no one could see him from the street either.

"Blade's got my cuz. Keep an ear out for me?" Rick asked, handing Jimmy a twenty.

"With you bein' hot, man, how'm I s'pposed to get a holda ya?" Jimmy asked, pocketing the cash.

"Don't worry about that. I'll find you. Jimmy, I'm trusting you, man, not to turn me in," Rick said pointedly.

Jimmy nodded. "Don't worry, man. You ain't never ratted on me, not even to Blade, so we're cool, Rick," Jimmy said and turned away.

"One more thing, Jimmy. You seen Santana or Ricardo lately? Where're they chillin'?" Rick asked quietly.

Jimmy paused. "Ya goin' ta Slayer turf, Rick? After whatcha did ta Ricardo las' summer?" Jimmy asked, stunned. "After what Blade did ta him while ya watched?" *Are you nuts?* Jimmy wanted to ask, but didn't dare.

"Yeah, I know, I'm nuts," Rick said as if he'd heard the unspoken question, "but I need to put some pressure on the Knights and I'm not exactly in a position to do that. I need some help and they're my best bet," Rick said, trying not to recall those brutal beatings.

"Check down by East Side's," Jimmy said over his shoulder, shaking his head at Rick's audacity.

Rick slipped away before Jimmy had moved more than a couple of feet. Again, he kept to the back alleys until he was by his dad's favourite bar. He looked around the parking lot and sighed in relief. He couldn't see either his dad's car or Blade's bike, so he figured he was still safe for a bit. He slipped into the bar and waved Greg over.

"Moneyman," Greg nodded. He knew he should call the cops, since Rick was wanted, but he wouldn't do that. Unlike the rest of the Knights, Greg liked Rick.

"Sorry 'bout this, Greg, but I need some help, man. Looking for Santana or Ricardo. The Slayers around?" Rick asked. "And please, don't call me Moneyman any more. He's dead and gone. It's Rick, 'kay?"

Nodding, Greg pointed to the backroom and walked away, grateful there was no one in the bar who would turn the kid in. Especially since Greg had one or two things going on in his bar that weren't exactly legal and Rick knew it. Taking a deep breath, Rick headed into the backroom. As soon as he walked in, he could see all of the Slayers hanging around and watching Santana and Miguel playing pool, badly, but better than most. Ricardo was leaning against the wall talking with Julio and Tomas.

It took a few seconds for the Slayers to register they were no longer alone and their visitor was the enemy. "Moneyman," Ricardo growled.

Rick didn't move as the Slayers threw down their pool cues and advanced on him. He could see Ricardo still limped from when Rick had re-broken his knee last summer and the Slayer leader automatically turned his battered shoulder away as well, protecting his vulnerable areas. Rick wasn't going to get the drop on him again.

"Ricardo, peace, man. I'm not here as a Knight," Rick said, holding up his hand.

"So what? Think that means anythin' t' me?" Ricardo said angrily.

Rick shook his head. "Prob'ly not, man. Look, gots a problem and was hopin' ya'd help out," Rick said softly. He prayed talking like a gang banger would help get through to the Slayers. Every word out of his mouth just about made him sick, though.

"*You* want the Slayers to help the *Knights*?" Ricardo said incredulously. Everyone but Rick laughed.

Rick shook his head. "No, Ricardo, not a Knight, but an innocent man. I've been outta the Knights since September, man, but Blade's taken my cuz as payback and everyone's blaming me. Maybe we can help each other out. Heard yer lookin' fer him, too," Rick drawled.

Ricardo paused. "Damn Jimmy and his crew. Boy doesn't know when to keep his damn mouth shut. Leave us," he ordered the rest of the Slayers. He motioned for Rick to follow him over to a booth.

"Now, what's this really all about?" Ricardo asked when they were finally alone, dropping all pretence.

Rick quickly outlined what had been going on for the past year. The Slayer listened without any comment until Rick finally fell silent. The girls were innocent and Blade should've been taking his anger out on Rick, Ricardo knew, but something still bugged him about the whole idea. "Honestly, Moneyman, why the hell should we help you?" Ricardo asked bluntly.

"One word, man. Revenge. Johnny's been bragging all year long about how easily he took you out and he's actually surprised you still lead the Slayers. Help me put him away as payback for those beatings and the lies he's spreading about how weak you are," Rick pointed out. He held his breath while Ricardo thought about it.

Finally, Ricardo nodded. "Deal. Don't know nuthin' yet, man. Come back in a couple of days," he said.

Rick looked around nervously. "Sure thing, but not here, 'kay? My old man comes here too much and it's a favourite place for undercover cops. How 'bout the vacant lot by Theo's instead?"

Rick asked. Ricardo agreed and Rick slipped away from the bar. Just as he entered the shadows on the far side of the lot, he saw his dad pull in. He sighed with relief. *That's cutting it a bit close, man,* Rick realized.

More than an hour had passed before Rick finally returned to the safe house. Tony and Jim hadn't moved from the living room, but the files Jim had brought were spread all over the couch and tables. The pair looked up as Rick slipped back into the house. Tony sighed with relief to see Rick alive and unharmed.

"Thought I'd run off, bro?" Rick asked with a grin as he flopped into the recliner.

Tony laughed. "Honestly? Yeah. Anything?"

"Sorta," Rick replied. "I'll have to go back in a couple of days, but I've got some feelers out. By the way, bro, you ever need info from the street, head to Mahoney's and give a whistle like this," Rick said and demonstrated. Tony practiced a couple of times until he was certain he had it down.

"That'll get you in touch with a kid named Jimmy. He runs a gang called Jimmy's Crew. They're pretty good at hearing things around town. If it's out there, Jimmy'll hear it. Eventually. They also are about as non-violent as you can get. If Jimmy can talk his way outta something, he will," Rick said with a grin.

Tony nodded. "When'll you go back?" the cop wanted to know. He rubbed at his eyes and sighed. Any good that had been done with sleeping over 24 hours at the beginning of the week was long gone. He'd pulled two straight eighteen hour days and had nothing to show for it.

Rick frowned as he read the exhaustion and frustration on Tony's face. Without a word, he went into the kitchen and poured a cup of very strong black coffee for Tony. The cop just about gagged at how strong it was, but he drank it gratefully. He blinked in sudden confusion as Rick pulled the drapes over the blinds, darkening the room almost completely.

"Now, what did you two discover in all of this mess?" Rick asked as he sat back down across from Tony. "And why do you look like hell, bro?"

Tony laughed. *Now who's taking care of who?* he thought as he took another pull at the tar in his mug. "I've had less than twelve hours' sleep in the last two days and we still can't find anything. Not eating right and not sleeping the best, but to me, it's worth it. Meg and you're important to me, kiddo," Tony said lightly.

"Megs is worth your health, Tony, not me. Ever," Rick said firmly, stunning both Jim and Tony into silence.

Jim finally cleared his throat, trying to get back to the task at hand. "Nothing here's jumping out at us," he said, motioning to the files strewn around the room.

"Rick, let's review what you know 'bout all of the Knights, family life and that kinda thing," Tony said, pulling out a notepad and pen. "Maybe that'll trigger something." He took notes as Rick launched into descriptions of the lives of the Knights as best he knew.

"Well, Johnny's mom's hardly ever home. Always working two or three jobs, mostly waitressing, if I remember right. Even so, we rarely, if ever, hung out there. Johnny hates it there. We're always at Eric's place. I could tell you how to get to Eric's from the school, but I don't know his actual address. Johnny's neither. I always rode with Brian. If Johnny's dad's alive, he's never around. Only his mom. I think he mentioned an older brother or two, but no idea where they are, either.

"Eric's Johnny's muscle, but also a total gear head. He'd be working in a garage somewhere already if his parents weren't so set on him finishing high school, which ain't gonna happen," Rick continued with a snort.

"How'd he and Johnny hook up into the Knights?" Tony asked, scribbling as quickly as he could to keep with Rick. Rick immediately slowed down since he didn't want Tony to miss anything.

"Junior high, I think. Johnny hasn't always been as beefy as he is now and Eric's always been big like that. They've been friends since they were kids and always hung out together. In junior high, Johnny kept getting bullied and beat up. Eric finally had enough of watching his friend get the crap kicked out of him, so one day, Eric did the kicking. Think that was the start of the Knights right there. Don't you dare insult Johnny when Eric's around. Not if you want to live," Rick said. Something told Tony Rick had done that once and almost didn't live to regret it.

Tony nodded and motioned for Rick to continue as his pen flew across the page. "Mark and Brian? What 'bout them?" Tony asked.

"Well, Mark's only been around the gang for a couple of years. Came to live with Johnny when his parents died in a house fire, but don't ask me exactly when that was. I think Mark's mom was Johnny's mom's sister, so Mark and Johnny're cousins. He's always been the eyes and ears of the gang and Johnny used him constantly as a spy, even on us," Rick said thoughtfully.

He continued before Tony could say anything. "I guess Mark's more like an annoying little brother than a real banger. He's too young yet. Now, Brian's a bit different. He comes from a good family. They're not as rich as Nana or even my dad, but they're not exactly middle-class either. Definitely not poor, like Johnny and Mark. His leather coat's custom made, like mine, but he buys most of his stuff off the rack at like Walmart or places like that, whereas I go to the higher end stores. You get what you pay for man, and my stuff's outlasted his by a long shot.

"He's got a little sister, Sarah and he's damn protective of her. She's kinda shy and quiet. Brian always talked about how much she got bullied at school, too and how many times he's had to go and take the bullies down at least once a month. I also know he's got two older brothers, one or both in jail and both had been in gangs before being arrested. They started the Hit Squad, and one became leader a couple of years later when the other was arrested on drug charges and attempted murder, I think. Both have actually been caught dealing, so a gang life's kinda what Brian grew up watching," Rick explained.

Interesting, Tony thought as he wrote. "What pulled all three of them into gangs?" Tony wondered.

"Nothing pulled them into the life. Their dad pushed them there. They needed the safety and protection," Rick said sourly.

"Mr. Townsand's a really strict guy, whether you're his kid or not. Almost abusive. I've seen bruises on Brian that had nothing to do with any rumble and Brian knows how to defend himself."

Jim looked up, interested. "Think he takes the abuse for his sister?" he asked.

Rick nodded. "I know he does, Doc. Sarah's small, even for her age and fragile, really fragile. I've only met her once, but I know if her dad ever hit her, no matter how gently he thought he was doing it, he'd break something for sure, maybe even kill her. So I don't think there's any physical abuse with Sarah, but there could be other kinds," Rick explained.

The teen fell silent for a moment, thinking hard. "Tell you something, though, bro. The more I think about this, the more I've realized this whole plan's pure Brian. Johnny's not this smart or disciplined. The fire and sedatives? Way too subtle for Johnny to think up, but Brian would. Hell, he probably even cased the clinic as the easiest place to get what he needed for those damn tranks, instead of trying the hospital," Rick said. His comment was idly thrown out, surprising both of the older men.

Suddenly, Jim began digging frantically. Files went flying everywhere as he looked for the one he needed. He finally found it and then looked at Rick. "You said the last name was Townsand?" the doctor demanded.

"Yeah, why?" Rick asked, puzzled. Tony looked at the doctor, interested.

"Something caught my attention when you talked about Sarah and the bullying. Then I remembered Brian had actually come to see me a week or so before the break-in," Jim said excitedly.

"So?" Tony said.

"Well, after I treated his bruised and broken ribs, we talked about his sister, Sarah. Ah, here it is," Jim exclaimed as he opened up a second file.

"What, Jim?" Tony said, impatient now. He leaned over to read what Jim was looking at.

Jim pointed out something in the file. "Her mom had asked me several times about sedatives because Sarah's having trouble in school and not eating or sleeping. What I really remember about the whole conversation was when I gave Brian the samples to take home, he asked me about that vial specifically – and it was the only one stolen from the clinic," Jim said triumphantly.

"Bingo!" Tony said as Jim handed him the first viable suspect other than Rick.

Chapter 29

Rick couldn't check back with Jimmy and the Slayers until Monday morning. Jimmy hadn't heard anything but he promised to keep trying, and asked Rick to come back again that afternoon. When Rick sauntered onto the vacant lot where he'd agreed to meet the Slayers, he saw they weren't alone. Ricardo was face to face with the leader of the Hit Squad, the gang formed by Brain's brothers. The rest of the Hit Squad was chatting quietly behind their leader, while the Slayers shuffled their feet nervously.

Swallowing his sudden fear, Rick walked boldly up to Ricardo and said, "Hey, man. Whassup?"

Ricardo looked at Rick, then back to the other gang leader. "Don't think you ever took on Devon and the Hit Squad, did ya, Moneyman?" Ricardo asked, making the introductions.

Rick shook his head. "If the Knights did, I wasn't around. Nice to meet you, Devon," Rick said, holding his hand out and praying he didn't get killed.

Devon didn't move, and as Rick waited, he heard the tell-tale sounds of someone approaching from behind and to his left. He knew it was a member of the Hit Squad, since all of the Slayers were in front of him.

Rick sighed and moved so quickly no one had a chance to react. He spun away as he was rushed from behind, then spun again to get Devon in a headlock. He was a couple of inches taller than Devon, so he had the upper hand. His knife was suddenly in his hand at Devon's throat and he had the leader of the Hit Squad pulled tight against him. This was what had always made Moneyman so dangerous – he was the quickest of anyone the other gangs knew.

Rick glared at the Hit Squad who were trying to circle him. "Call 'em off, Dev, or they're gonna be lookin' fer a new leader,"

Rick hissed in Devon's ear. To emphasize his point, Rick pushed the knife a little deeper into his captive's throat, drawing a bit of blood.

Devon grimaced and managed to gasp out, "Back off, boys. Now!" Only once Rick could see all of the Slayers and Hit Squad did he let Devon go with a hard shove.

Rick cleaned his steel and slid it into its sheath on his hip. He glared at Ricardo, whose shoulders had suddenly slumped. Ricardo'd just broken a cardinal rule in the gangs – don't double cross someone you've agreed to help. "I trusted ya, man, and this is how ya repay me? I'm risking my life here, trying to help ya put away the one Knight who hates yer guts, and ya try to get me gutted by someone I gots no beef with? I'm outta here, man," Rick snarled, disgusted at what the Slayer had tried to do.

"Moneyman, wait," Devon said as Rick started to storm away.

He stepped back, startled, as Rick turned around and snarled, "Stop calling me that! My name's Rick. Moneyman's gone! You hear me?"

"Jeez, man, chill out, will ya? I'm trying to apologize," Devon said, holding his hands up.

Rick turned away again, trying to regain his hard-fought control. He took a couple of deep breaths, then a couple of more. It took a lot longer than he wanted, but he was finally able to face the other gangs completely in control of himself.

"Accepted, Dev. Now, Ricardo, what's up with all of this? You and the Hit Squad working together's gonna cause the cops a lot of worry," Rick pointed out as he looked around at the gangs.

"We're gonna work together and put some pressure on Blade. We'll flush 'im out fer ya," Ricardo promised. Both gangs nodded, enthusiastic about taking on the Knights.

Rick shrugged, trying to keep his fear from showing. He wasn't sure this was actually a good idea, but he decided to run with it. "Do what you can, all of you, but don't drown this town in blood," he warned as he left. "If ya do, Moneyman'll come back and visit y'all."

As Rick wandered slowly back to his hideout, Tony was just pulling into the station after sleeping in for the first time in ages. Seamus just raised an eyebrow when Tony sat down at his desk to get organized for the day. Tony and Marshall had been in all weekend, looking at the evidence and talking to potential witnesses. On the other hand, the inspector hadn't been seen all weekend, choosing to stay at home with his children instead of working. He trusted his team.

"Thanks for coming in, Tony," Seamus said dryly as the partners sat down in his office.

Tony smiled. "Sorry boss. What a time to forget to set my alarm, huh?" he said as he pulled his notes, trying to keep a straight face. Marshall and Seamus just grinned at him.

"What do ye have?" Seamus asked, pointing to the file.

Tony outlined quickly what he and Jim had figured out on Friday. "Marsh and I dug a bit deeper into Brian's background and there's some potential there as a viable suspect," Tony finished.

Seamus hesitated for a long time. Finally, he sighed. "Another suspect, huh? Someone other than the boy? Great. How good do ye really think this Townsand kid is fer this?" Seamus asked quietly.

Tony looked at the inspector. "Right now, it's too hard to say, but it's another lead to look at, boss. If nothing else, Nana can't accuse you of focussing only on Rick when we can prove we've looked at someone else. We can't eliminate anyone just yet, right?" Tony said.

Seamus nodded. "Alright. Run with it, boys. Tony, I need ye to do something for me first," Seamus said, hesitating on the request.

Tony looked at the inspector quizzically. "Whatever you need, boss, you know that," Tony assured Seamus.

Tony was more than a little surprised when Seamus whispered, "Help me kids."

Marshall didn't need to be told Tony wanted to talk to the boss alone. "I'll be at my desk if you need me, Fish," Marshall said as he left, closing the door softly behind him.

"Boss, what's going on?" Tony asked when they were alone.

"The kids're broken, Tony. I don't know any other way to describe it, but broken. I don't know how to help them. I tried to talk to Jordan all weekend but all she does is scream at me this is all me fault, she hates me and she'll never forgive me. When she wasn't blastin' me with accusations, she was cryin' and lockin' herself in her room. She won't talk to me or her brother," Seamus said. He was more than a little worried about his kids, but his daughter especially. Mickey seemed to be handling things far better than Jordan was.

Tony winced. He didn't realize it was that bad at Seamus' house. "What about Mick?" Tony asked.

Seamus looked even worse than before. "It's bad, Tony, just like ye thought it would be. He doesn't say or do anythin'. If he's not tryin' to calm his sister down, he's just sittin' in the livin' room on the window seat, starin' out of the window, holdin' a little teddy bear Megan gave him. There's no tears, no sound, nothin'. He's got every right to be yellin' at me too, but he won't say anythin'. He just sits there. They won't eat. They won't drink and I'm pretty sure they haven't slept since last week when Jim was there. He's about ready to put them both in the hospital under psych care. I don't know what to do," Seamus said again. It was as close to a plea for help Seamus was ever likely to get and Tony knew it.

"It's actually worse than I thought, Seamus. Much worse than I thought. Lemme and Marsh talk to them before you have Jim do anything, though. I've got an idea that just might work. Let us know if anything new comes in from forensics." With that, Tony grabbed his partner and headed out to Seamus'.

"Thank God, you're here," Seamus' cook and housekeeper said as she opened the door.

"Where are they, Cook?" Tony asked as he entered.

"Miss Jordan's room," Cook said and stood aside.

A bleary-eyed Mickey cracked open the door at Tony's soft knock. Both cops had to swallow hard to avoid gagging at the smell wafting from the room. It was the smell of sweat, tears and unwashed body odour and Tony couldn't figure out if it was coming from Mickey, Jordan or both. Tony shook his head. It was definitely worse than he'd imagined.

"Tony," Mick said wearily. The young Irishman leaned against the door frame, looking about as alive as Tony had when he collapsed at his desk.

The gentle approach won't work, Tony decided, quickly discarding his original plan. *I need to shock them both awake.* Tony brushed past Mickey, strode across the room, yanked the curtains open and threw open the window. Mickey winced in the sudden light while Jordan cried out weakly. She lay on her bed, sheets and blankets scattered about. There was a strong odour coming from her, like she hadn't showered in days.

Tony stood over her, hands on his hips. "Up, Jordan. Now!" he barked.

Marshall cringed. "Uh, Fish, a little tact, don't you think?" he asked, falling into Tony's new plan as if they'd rehearsed it when Tony knew Marshall was just as shocked at the twins' appearance.

"Tact, Marsh? Think the Knights're gonna be tactful when they brag all over school about how they broke the inspector's kids?" Tony asked, not caring if he hurt them more. Right now, he needed to get them both up.

The dry hiccups and sobs ceased immediately as if a tap had been shut off. Jordan raised her head from the pillow and she glared at Tony. "What did ye say?" she hissed, her Irish accent suddenly thick. Mickey stiffened in anger before coming over to wrap his arms around his sister.

Tony glared right back at the teens. "You've missed an entire week of school because you've been at home, bawling your eyes out. You look like hell and a sewer smells better than this room does right now, not to mention how bad *you* stink. Blade and the Knights've broken you, kiddo and you don't seem to care one damn bit," Tony said with a shrug.

"Never," the twins snapped together. Jordan struggled to get up and out of bed, her face flushed with anger.

Tony smiled and helped Mickey to steady his sister. "Welcome back, Jor. Mick, son, let me go draw your sister a bath, then you go and shower. Marsh, have Cook heat up some soup and make some strong sweet tea. We'll talk afterwards," Tony directed.

After helping Jordan get to the bathroom and assuring himself she could take care of the rest, Tony cleaned up her room, stripping the bedding and leaving it piled in the corner for the moment. Cook came up a couple of minutes later and collected it to be washed, quickly making up the bed with fresh sheets and blankets. She also found a change of clothes for Jordan. When Jordan finally emerged, clean for the first time in days, Tony had to help her down the stairs to keep the teen's legs from collapsing.

Marshall and Mickey were already waiting in the den, Mickey sipping gratefully at a large cup of tea. Jordan settled in her own chair with her own mug of tea and a bowl of Cook's fabulous homemade soup. Everyone remained quiet while she ate.

Only once she was finished and had sat back, did anyone speak. "Feeling better, sweets?" Tony asked.

She smiled. "Yeah. Thanks, Tony. I needed that. Guess I forgot about being an Irish cop's kid. We're proud and stubborn. Normally too stubborn to give up. Time to go back and face the school and the Knights head on," she said softly.

Before he could reply, Tony felt his phone vibrate. "Gotta take this. Sorry," he said as he looked at the number.

"Hey, kiddo, what's up?" Tony asked softly as he stood on the O'Reilly's front porch.

"Just wanted to warn ya the Slayers and Hit Squad've teamed up. Working together to flush out Johnny. This could get bloody," Rick said tersely.

"Damn. How'd you hear this?" Tony asked, making a mental note to let the right people know.

Rick quickly outlined what had happened that morning and how close he'd come to crossing the line. "I'm gonna slip out to see Jimmy again later today, but if the Slayers can't find Johnny, Jimmy ain't gotta hope in hell," Rick said sourly.

"Don't turn any potential lead away, kiddo. Give the kid some more time," Tony cautioned.

"Fish, how's Jor? Do you know anything new? How's Nana?" Rick's questions tumbled out.

"Fine. No. Don't know," Tony answered with a smile. He turned his head as he heard someone coming to the door. "Look, son. You just continue doing what you're doing and I'll catch up with you tomorrow after school. We're gonna follow that other lead we talked about. Stay safe, 'kay?" Tony said as he hung up.

Marshall joined Tony on the porch a few minutes later. "Everything okay?" his partner asked.

"Yep. Just another source checking in," Tony said, looking back into the O'Reilly house.

Marshall knew instantly who Tony was talking about. "And is your "source" doing okay?" Marshall smiled as the pair climbed into their car. "I told the twins we'd see them tomorrow at school. Seamus called me to tell us that's where he wanted us tomorrow. Follow-up, he said."

"Yeah, my source is okay. Stressed, but okay. He's looking at putting some added heat on the ones we really suspect," Tony said as they headed back to the station. Marshall nodded his approval and talk turned to other things.

Tony's source was sitting at the kitchen table working on schoolwork while he waited to go and check in with Jimmy again. Rick sighed as he struggled a bit with some of his studies, especially when he tried to do it by himself. He wished he could talk to his teachers when he hit a wall like this, but that would defeat the purpose of being in hiding, he knew. Bending over his books, he forced himself to concentrate.

It was late afternoon when Rick closed his books with a sigh of relief, cleaned up and headed back out to Mahoney's again. He stuck to the back alleys until he got to the convenience store. Jimmy was waiting at the back of the store, nervous and jittery.

"Jimmy, what's up?" Rick asked, suddenly as nervous and jittery as his contact.

Jimmy pulled Rick away from the shop and back down the alley to a spot where they couldn't be seen unless the cops actually turned and looked down it. "First, there's some Angels in the store.

Figured ya didn't want them t' see ya. Second, cops're talking t' my crew out front," Jimmy hissed.

Rick tucked himself further into the shadows. He knew he could trust Jimmy, but the rest of his crew or Mahoney weren't so lucky. "Thanks for the heads up and watchin' my back. Anything else?" Rick asked, handing over some more cash Tony had given him for Jimmy's information.

Jimmy shook his head, hesitating to pocket money for nothing. He looked more than a little upset at his lack of progress. It wasn't normally this difficult. "Sorry, man. Nothin'. It's like the Knights've dropped off the face of the earth. No one's heard from them since your cuz vanished. Last couple days no one's seen Blade or Brain at school, either. Just Crank and Pup," Jimmy said sourly.

Rick hesitated then asked, "Have you heard anything from Mendez's crew? The younger ones?"

Jimmy nodded. "Yeah, and nothin' good. Mendez's given the Knights the green light to come on board, but no one's talkin' bout what or how, y'know?" Jimmy said.

Rick's heart sank. This really wasn't good news. Megan's kidnapping could be nothing more than Johnny's way of getting into Mendez's organization. "Great. Just friggin' great. Megs is caught between the Knights and Mendez," Rick groused.

He started to walk away. Jimmy stopped him and said, "Moneyman, you wanna save yer cuz? Only one way, man. You gotta go back to the Knights."

Chapter 30

Tony and Marshall arrived at the high school just after Mickey and Jordan had been escorted to Homeroom. Waiting for them in the student lounge were the principal and Tom, who were in the middle of a heated discussion that easily carried to the front door.

"...and I've had enough of the Angels head-hunting, Tom. You've begun to be a problem. I allowed the Angels to start, but I *will* shut you down if I have to. Understand?" Delaney snapped.

"But...but...but...," Tom stammered, stunned.

"Whoa, hold up, guys. What's going on?" Tony demanded as the partners approached.

Seeing Tony, Tom lowered his head as his principal continued to berate him. Tony listened impassively while Delaney explained what the Angels had been up to since Megan's disappearance. When Delaney finished, Tony sighed and shook his head.

"Lemme deal with this, please," he requested.

"Gladly. He stopped listening to me a long time ago, and his real leader's nowhere to be found," the principal said as he left.

Tony turned to Tom. "Tom, why're you and the Angels pulling this crap, now of all times?" Tony demanded.

"I promised the Champ I'd keep 'em both safe, Fish. Me, not the Angels. Me. I've screwed up and now I gotta make it right," Tom defended himself.

"Really? By getting arrested for assault?" Marshall asked dryly.

Tom flushed, unable to answer.

"Kid, we need you here with Jor, keeping her safe, just in case," Tony said quietly.

Tom winced. "Do you blame me and Carl, too, Fish?" he asked after a few seconds of awkward silence, hanging his head and shuffling his feet.

"Tom, look at me," Tony ordered. Tom finally raised his head to look at the cop. Tony reached out and grasped Tom's shoulder, trying to convey his feelings to the teen. "I don't blame anyone here for this, Tom. Not any of the Angels, or the students. And certainly not Rick, if that's what you're thinking. The only ones I blame're the ones who actually took Meg and who are blaming Rick. Understand? But you have to trust me that I'll figure this out, okay?" Tony asked.

Tom nodded, but when he spoke again, his voice was filled with hatred. "Don't take too long, Fish. I don't know how long I can hold the Angels, or myself, back," Tom growled.

Tony winced. "Well, I'm not making any promises as to how long this'll take, Kid, but I promise this. If the Angels don't back away from the Knights and their friends, I will haul every one of your sorry butts in. Now, take us to the twins' first class," Tony said firmly.

Standing in the back of the classroom, with his gun and shield clearly visible, Tony tried to figure out where the connection to Megan was. How did someone who wasn't even in the class get these letters into someone else's backpack without help? As Tony prowled, he noticed a blond boy with a shaggy haircut, *just like Rick's,* Tony thought, who was sitting behind the empty desk that had been pointed out earlier as Megan's. Could this be the link Tony had been looking for?

"Mr. Townsand, answer, please," the teacher asked.

Bingo, Tony thought excitedly as the blond boy drawled, "I'm missin' a step, sir. I got three different answers last night."

Tony watched Brain for the rest of the period. Sure enough, Tony could see how easily it would be for Brain to slip a nasty letter into Megan's bag. He was certain Brain didn't write the letters here, but you never knew. Tony followed the teen to the next class and smiled slightly as Brain sat down – right behind Megan's empty desk.

"Meet me in the cafeteria at lunch," Tony said softly as Marshall joined his partner at the back of the class. "I've gotta talk to Delaney first."

As Tony sat down in Delaney's office, the principal asked, "Tony, did you straighten Tom out?"

Tony nodded and smiled. "He's a little...uh, obsessed, shall we say, over a promise he made to Rick, but he's good for now. Keep an eye on him, though and lemme know if he gets out of line again," the cop said. "I'll haul him in if he does. Give him a taste of what Rick's gone through," Tony chuckled.

"Deal. Now, what can I help you with today? I didn't figure you'd be on bodyguard duty," Delaney said.

"I need some information on another angle we're looking at. What can you tell me about Brian Townsand?" Tony asked.

Delaney was surprised. "What could I possibly tell you about Brian that Rick hasn't? He's a Knight, obviously, although you ask him and he'll deny it quickly enough. It's like he's almost ashamed of admitting it. He's from a good family and an extremely smart kid. If I'm not mistaken, he's probably got most, if not all, of his classes with Megan," Delaney explained.

"Yeah, Rick's told me all of that, but what about his family? Rick didn't know much," Tony said, lying slightly as he continued making notes.

"Rick probably doesn't know this, but I've seen bruises on Brian he won't explain. I'm pretty sure they're from his dad, though. He told me that much one day when I pushed him, but he won't let me report him. Tony, really, what's this all about?" Delaney asked.

"I'm not sure, but I think Brian's my link to the whole thing," Tony mused. "I need a place to do some follow-up questions with him. Do I have your permission to do this? While he's here, you're technically his guardian."

"If you're thinking of calling his parents, his mom will be the one to talk to. His dad won't give us permission, no matter what we say," Delaney said, picking up his phone and calling Brain's mother, who he knew would be home. After receiving her permission to talk to her son about the situation, he got up and left Tony sitting in the vice-principal's office while he went to get Brain from the cafeteria. He could see the twins surrounded by the Angels and Marshall, so he didn't worry about them. The principal watched as Tom and Carl broke up a small disagreement between Blade, Crank and two of the smaller Angels. And when Brain joined the group, trying to add more muscle to the Knights' side, Delaney hurried over.

"Tom, take your Angels back to your table. The rest of you, where do you think you're going?" he asked as the Knights began to move away.

Blade turned around with a soft snarl. He needed to get away from the school before he exploded. Brain had been hounding him all morning about Megan and how she was doing. Was Blade feeding her? Treating her right? *Gah, my second's getting yeller,* Blade thought.

"Wha'cha want, Delaney?" Blade snapped sourly.

"Watch your mouth, Johnny. I've had just about enough. Where's Mark? I haven't seen him in a couple of days," Delaney asked.

"Home. Sick," Blade snapped again. He thought of his cousin at home, taking care of Megan. Blade hadn't listed to Brain. He just couldn't stay away from Megan, and this morning she'd goaded him again and he beat her nearly senseless before Pup managed, somehow, to drag him away.

"Right, Johnny. Either he's here tomorrow or I want a note from Dr. Jim saying he's sick. Understand? Brian, my office. Now," Delaney ordered.

Brain glanced at his leader, shrugged and followed Delaney to the office. The teen paused by the door and grimaced when he saw Blade grin viciously and saunter out of the cafeteria. Brain was almost positive Blade was heading back home. *I just hope she survives this,* Brain worried as he continued to the office. *Hell, I hope we all do. Blade's outta control.*

Still, Brain was confident nothing would be able to be traced back to the Knights or their employer. So he was more than a little surprised to be led into the vice-principal's office where Tony sat, waiting patiently.

"What's going on?" Brain demanded, seeing his parents weren't there and the principal had sat down just outside the partially closed door.

"Brian Townsand? I'm Constable Tony Whitefish," Tony introduced himself as Brain sat down cautiously. "I'm sure you've seen me around the school with the O'Reilly twins and Rick Attison."

Brain was worried now. He was sitting across from the one person, after Megan, he feared would figure out what had happened. On the desk were a couple of cans of pop, one already opened and in front of the cop. Brain didn't even blink as he grabbed the other can, cracked it open and downed about half of it, silently studying Tony. Outwardly he appeared calm, but inside he was panicking. *What the hell does he think he knows?* Brain wondered.

Tony sipped at his drink while he made a couple of notes about Brain's initial reaction to seeing a cop waiting for him. As Brain lifted his hand to drink, Tony could see the very slight tremor in the teen's hand. Tony simply sat, waiting and watching. Brain began to shift uneasily in his chair. The longer Tony watched, the more nervous Brain became. *Good*, Tony thought before speaking again.

"Brian?" Tony said, his voice loud in the quiet room.

"Yeah, man, I knows ya," Brain finally acknowledged.

"Alright, then. I'm here to do some follow-up interviews on Megan Attison's disappearance. I know you're a friend of Rick's, but how well do you know Megan and the O'Reilly twins?" Tony asked, taking out a note pad and pen.

"Known the twins since about Grade 2," Brain said laconically. He grabbed his pop again and leaned back in his chair.

"And Megan?" Tony asked.

"Only met Megs this year. Gots mosta my classes with 'er except in last block. Gotta spare and usually cut out early," Brain said. "So?"

Tony made a couple of notes, then looked up. "Gotta different question for you, on an unrelated matter. Did you, by chance, stop by the Attison Memorial Clinic about a month and a half or so ago to talk to Dr. Jim about some mild sleeping pills for your sister, Sarah?" Tony asked, keeping his tone relaxed.

"Yeah, and again, I'll ask. So what? Didn't have anythin' to do with Megs' kidnappin', man. Way yer talkin', yer thinkin' I shot 'er full of drugs or somethin'," Brain drawled, not realizing the mistake he'd just made.

Tony did. He made a couple of more notes, then looked up. "Can I ask you one more question that doesn't really relate?" Tony asked. He continued when Brain shrugged, unconcerned. "Are you a Black Knight or do you have a death wish?"

Brain laughed suddenly. "Don't know what ya mean, man. Ain't a Knight," Brain denied easily, as Delaney said he would.

"Really?" Tony said, acting surprised. "You're wearing a black and silver hand-made leather jacket similar to one I've seen on Rick and I know he's a Knight. Or was, anyway," Tony amended quickly. "Now, how about Rick? How well do you know him?" Tony continued before Brain said anything.

The teen dropped his empty pop can into the garbage can and sneered, "Moneyman? Known him 'bout four years, I guess, really good in the last couple, though. Decent man in a fight."

"Have you seen or heard from him since Megan went missing?" Tony asked.

"Look, man, everyone here knows how close y'all're. If ya don't know what hole Moneyman's dropped down with his cuz, ain't no one around here gonna," Brain laughed again and stood up. "By the way, cop, don't think yer supposed to question a minor without permission," Brain drawled as he put his hand on the doorknob.

"Relax, Brian. I have your mom's permission," Tony replied, keeping his eyes on his notepad. "Besides, you're not under arrest or anything. These're just follow-up questions we're doing with a lot of Rick's friends and classmates, so you won't be the only one. However, since the vice-principal's not here today, Mr. Delaney needed to be available if needed, so he's been sitting right outside that door. Trust me, he's heard every word of this," Tony said.

Brain didn't say anything as he left the office and saw Delaney was indeed just outside the door. Tony waited until Delaney joined him in the office before he used a handkerchief to grab the empty can from the garbage. He hoped he'd finally caught the break he needed.

"Anything?" Delaney asked as Tony sealed the can in an evidence bag.

"Not really. All I managed to get was some minor confirmations, but he didn't admit to anything. I'm really not any further ahead, but life goes on." With that, Tony caught up with Marshall and the twins just after the start of Physics. Tony smiled slightly when Brain stared at him. *Now, he's really nervous,* Tony thought. *Good. Maybe he'll make a mistake.*

Brain was distracted all through Physics, especially with the cops patrolling the back of the room. He was more than a little rattled by the interview, considering he knew he was the only Knight the cop questioned, at least today. So now Brain worried about what he'd screwed up. *What do the cops think they have? And why ask about the visit to the clinic? What did I miss?* Brain thought. These and other questions continued to race around in his mind and left him distracted and annoyed.

The teen bolted from the room as soon as the bell rang, heading for the metal lab and his locker. He was so distracted he nearly missed the note taped to the front of his locker. It wasn't until after he'd thrown his books into the locker and slammed it closed that the fluttering paper caught his eye. It had one word on it – *Blade's.*

Fuming, Brain stormed to his car and drove to Blade's house. *Fool musta left at lunch,* Brain thought, furious at how Blade was acting. *Probably knew I wouldn't get there until after school. Damn him!* Brain drove as quickly as he dared, praying he wasn't too late.

Crank looked more worried than Brain had ever seen him when he let Brain into the house. "Where the hell is he?" Brain snarled.

A muffled cry from the basement told Brain what he needed to know before Crank even opened his mouth. He spun on his heels and rushed down the slippery stairs just in time to hear a loud smack and Blade's maniacal laugh. As Brain rounded the corner to where they were holding Megan, Brain was stunned to see Pup cowering on the floor, holding a bleeding arm and Megan's face bruised and swelling.

Blade had his steel out and seemed to relish threatening Megan with it. Fortunately, he put the knife away before he struck Megan again. Brain winced as her head rebounded off the wall – again – and she tried to cry out. The gag had been shoved back into her mouth, her arms were wrenched behind her and she couldn't seem to catch her breath.

"Dammit, Blade! Stop it!" Brain ordered harshly, stepping between Megan and his leader. He motioned Crank over to check on Pup. Blade just glared at his second.

"Crank?" Brain asked, not taking his eyes off Blade.

"He...he sliced me, man!" Pup stammered, trying to be brave and not cry, but his arm hurt and he'd never been attacked by Blade like this before.

"He'll be okay, Brain. It looks worse than it is, but it'll be damn painful for a while," Crank said as he looked at the cut on Pup's arm.

Brain took a deep breath, struggling to control his temper. "What the hell're ya doing, Blade? Slicing yer own cuz? Beating on Megs? What's next? Slicing her?" Brain demanded hotly.

"Too late," Pup grunted from where Crank was working on the cut.

"Blade, I swear, if you can't control yourself and your temper, I'm gonna move her some place you can't get to," Brain threatened. *Like the damn hospital and screw the consequences,* Brain thought, seething.

"Ya finally gonna challenge me fer the Knights, Brain?" Blade growled quietly.

"Ya gonna grow up and start listening to me? Yer the one who got us into this, but I am the only one who's gonna get us through it," Brain said through gritted teeth. "But only if you start doing what you are told!" Brain finished slowly, emphasizing each word so Blade understood.

Brain turned to Megan and swore viciously. He saw the blood dripping from several shallow cuts on her arms. One eye was swollen shut and beginning to turn a brilliant shade of purple. He yanked the gag out of her mouth and Megan gasped out her thanks.

"Pup, did you bother to give 'er anything to eat or drink since this morning?" Brain snapped as he heard Megan's stomach rumble.

"How'd you think I got sliced and this black eye?" Pup demanded. "He came home and found me trying to get her to drink some soup."

Blade snorted at the whining tone of Pup's voice. "So I didn't let poor Megs eat. Boo hoo," he said sarcastically.

Brain didn't say anything for several seconds as he tried to control his anger. "Pup, go and make some more soup and grab a bottle of water for her. I put some in the fridge when I came the other day. Crank, give her a hand to the bathroom, man, so she can clean up a bit," he finally ordered. He stood between Megan and Blade while Crank untied the ropes and carried Megan up to the bathroom. Neither Brain nor Crank could believe how weak Megan had become in only a few days.

Once they were alone, Brain turned to Blade with a vicious snarl. "Dammit, Blade. I can't trust you with her for a second, can I? How much did you cut her?" Brain demanded, pointing to the cot under the dim light. It was covered in blood.

Chapter 31

"Answer me!" Brain demanded when Blade just shrugged.

"I don't answer to nobody, Brain, especially you," Blade snapped back.

Crank brought Megan back before Brain could reply. Barely keeping a hold of his temper, Brain quickly stripped the cot and flipped the mattress. He knew he'd have to remake the cot with the bloody sheets, but he could at least let Megan lie on the cleaner portion. Crank laid her down as gently as he could and retied her hands, in front once again, and then one leg to the frame.

Megan sipped gratefully at the soup and water Pup handed her. She studied their faces and realized Blade was losing control of himself and his gang. Too bad she couldn't let anyone know about it. *It probably wouldn't do Tony any good anyway*, she realized as she finished the soup.

"Thank you," she whispered as Brain took the cup and handed it back to Pup.

"Sorry 'bout this, Megs," Brain said, indicating the cuts and bruises. "This wasn't supposed to happen."

"Oh really?" Megan replied sarcastically. The food and water had energized her. "You actually believed Johnny and you were gonna kidnap me, and Johnny was just gonna play nice and by the rules?"

Brain flushed. "Yeah, I guess I did," he admitted.

"I may be a bit naïve, but I'm not stupid, Brian. I've heard how Johnny treated Rick when he was a Knight, and that was supposedly someone he actually liked! Hell, I treated some of Rick's wounds. I knew Johnny'd do something to hurt me, just because he hates me almost as much as he hates Rick," Megan said.

Before Brain could stop him, Blade backhanded Megan again, reopening her split lip. "Ya got that right," Blade laughed.

"Will you stop hitting her, dammit?" Brain demanded, shoving Blade out of the alcove and towards the stairs.

Crank and Pup followed more quietly. Pup looked back at Megan as she coughed long and hard. *She's getting sick down here,* he thought as he shut off the overhead light and went upstairs just in time to hear Brain and Blade going at it again. He handed Crank a can of pop, threw himself into a kitchen chair and waited.

"I'm friggin' serious, Blade. If I can't trust you to take care of her properly, I'm gonna move 'er. Tonight if I have to," Brain snapped.

"I am takin' care of 'er," Blade snapped back.

"Yeah, and ya keep takin' care of her this way, and we're gonna need some place to dump a body, and I don't think Mendez'll do that for us," Brain yelled.

Blade just snorted.

"And quit beatin' on her, or treatin' yer own cuz as a place to bury yer steel. Keep her fed. Give her some water. Let her use the bathroom. You've already blown the plan the hell out of the water. Don't screw with it any more," Brain said harshly.

"Ya done, *"Dad"*?" Blade asked sarcastically.

"Ya gonna listen?" Brain shot back.

"We'll see," Blade said noncommittally. Brain seethed again, but decided not to press the issue. For now, at least.

Brain waited almost an hour before being brave enough to ask, "Did the cops talk to any of you?"

All three Knights shook their heads. Brain cursed softly. "Damn. What the hell do they know?" Brain wondered.

"Screwed up somewhere, did ya, Brain?" Blade smirked.

Brain refused to take the bait. "Since yer so cozy with Mendez, tap his source and find out," Brain said instead. "Now, ya finish the letter like ya were supposed to?"

Blade tossed over an envelope. "There's room at the bottom if ya wanna have Megs add a message," Blade said as Brain read.

Nodding, Brain stood up. "That's the first good idea you've had since we started this mess," Brain said and grabbed a pen. "Come on," he urged, nodding his head toward the basement door.

Blade roughly shook Megan awake. She whimpered as pain shot through her arms and shoulders. Mercilessly, Blade grabbed her arms and hauled her to a sitting position, causing her to cry out even more in pain, which led to a sudden spasm of coughing. When she was done, Brain was horrified to see bloody foam around her mouth. What was even worse was how little Blade seemed to care.

Blade untied Megan's hands and shoved a pen into one. "Read this and add sumthin' so's they know it's from ya," he said harshly.

Megan nodded and began to read. Suddenly her head was jerked back. She cried out again as Blade's fist closed in her hair, knotting hair around his hand. "Don't get cute, Megs. And don't try to warn 'em or nuthin'," he growled and shoved her away, not caring about the hair he had just ripped from her head.

Megan whimpered with the new pain while she read the letter. She sat, thinking about what to write to convince everyone the note was actually from her, and Rick wasn't responsible for this, all without making the Knights suspicious. Suddenly, she knew what would work. With shaking hands, she wrote two messages — one for her father and one for Mickey. Then she signed it, managing to slip the other, more secret message into her signature. She just prayed no one, especially Blade, would see it until Tony did. He'd get it.

Brain quickly took the letter before Blade could. That didn't stop the leader of the Knights, though. "Okay, Megs, now something to really prove it's from ya," he snapped harshly as he glared at her.

Megan hesitated, thinking of what she'd be willing to part with, then pulled a delicate diamond ring off. "Take this," she whispered. "Daddy had it made for my last birthday." She handed it over.

Blade caught her hand as something else flashed and caught his eye. "And this one?" he sneered as he pulled off the slender, plain gold band.

"No, Johnny! Please!" Megan begged, holding her hand out for the ring.

"Now, I know it's important," Blade laughed viciously. He grabbed her hair again, wrenching her head back even more painfully than before. "Why?" he demanded, shaking her head.

Megan pulled weakly at his hand as she sobbed. "It's from Mickey," she finally managed to gasp out. She sobbed even harder when Blade laughed evilly and slipped it onto a thick gold necklace around his neck.

"Well, it's mine now," he said softly as he re-tied her ropes so tightly they cut into her already battered hands.

Back upstairs, Brain turned to Pup and said, "Delaney wants ya at school tomorrow, so I'll stay here with Megs."

"And just how're ya gonna explain that to my old lady, Brain?" Blade said sarcastically.

"Um…," Brain hesitated.

"That's what I thought. Pup can go so Delaney quits freakin'. I'll stay here and deliver the note tomorrow," Blade said.

Again Brain hesitated, then shook his head. "No way, Blade. I'm not leaving ya alone with her again. Crank, can ya stay here for a couple of days? Keep an eye on things? Blade, ya can still deliver the letter tomorrow, but sometime after lunch," Brain directed as he stood up.

That was the last straw for Blade. With a shout, the leader of the Knights surged to his feet and flew at Brain. The two traded punches for several minutes until Brain got in a lucky shot that dropped Blade. He laid there, stunned, while Brain towered over him, breathing hard.

"I told ya before, Blade, I will take over the Knights to keep Megs alive and to make sure ya follow the plan. Now, are ya gonna listen and get with the plan?" Brain asked, shaking with anger.

Blade could only glare. Crank and Pup glanced at each other, then made their choice. It only took a couple of steps, but suddenly they were backing Brain, who just sighed. This was not what he really wanted, but Blade was the one really forcing the damn issue.

"Looks like it's three-to-one, man. Now will ya listen?" Brain said quietly.

Blade could only nod. While he might be able to take Brain one-on-one, he wasn't going to be stupid enough to take on all three of the Knights. "Fer now, Brain," he said, climbing slowly to his feet. "But this ain't over, man. No one challenges me. Ever," he snarled.

Brain nodded as he took off, trusting Crank would let him know if Blade continued to screw around with their investment. Brain was concentrating so hard on trying to keep his temper he almost didn't see the gang of boys surrounding his car.

"Brian," one of them said softly.

"Dev, what the hell're ya doing in town? When did ya get back? The folks know yer here?" Brain asked, startled.

"I've been back long enough to take the Hit Squad back and no, the folks don't know. I'd rather be back in jail or dead than go back, Brian and ya know why. Keep it quiet...little brother," Dev said very quietly. No one needed to know about their relationship.

Brain nodded. "What's up?" he asked, leaning against his car after turning his alarm off.

"Word's out, kid. Yer wanted for taking something that didn't belong to ya, and there're some people who might be offerin' a reward," Dev drawled, raising his voice so his crew could hear. He stood in front of Brain with a scowl on his face and his arms folded across his chest. To his crew, Dev looked for all the world like he was scolding a younger brother. *If only they knew,* Dev thought sourly as he continued to glare at Brain.

"So what?" Brain shrugged, unconcerned. He knew there was no reward being offered publicly, but who knew what might be out there privately. Rick's grandmother was loaded, after all.

"There's lots of people interested in finding what ya've got squirreled away, Brain," Dev continued, switching to calling Brain by his gang name, instead of his given one.

"Who's lookin' and why're ya warnin' me?" Brain asked, curious, despite the shiver that went down his back.

"Cops. The Slayers. Jimmy's crew. Us. And…Moneyman, of course," Dev replied. "As for why I'm warnin' ya, well, we'll just say courtesy, man. I don't want ya caught in the cross fire. We've known each other too long. See, I *will* find where yer hidin' her and I'll let the one person who's got the most to lose know where y'are. Then, while Moneyman's beatin' the crap outta ya, the Slayers and the Hit Squad'll take care of the rest of the Knights. I guarantee ya once Ricardo and me finish with Blade, he ain't coming outta this alive. Dammit, boy, ya never, ever touch a chick!" Dev hissed, getting right in Brain's face.

Brain shoved Dev. "Back off, Dev. Ya can't take me anymore!" Brain snarled. He was suddenly jerked back from Dev and held in an iron grip, while Dev took a couple of swings at him, being careful to narrowly miss. Brain struggled against his restrainers, but wasn't able to shift them one little bit.

Dev laughed as Brain struggled, and got in one good shot, just to prove his point. Brain grunted as Dev's shot slammed into his ribs. "I can take ya any time I want, boy. Now ya give Blade a message fer me. You tell 'im if either the Slayers or the Hit Squad find him and the chick before the cops do, we won't play nice. 'Specially if she's hurt. And that's a promise."

With a sharp jerk of Dev's head, the rest of the Hit Squad disappeared, leaving Brain lying sprawled on the hood of his car, gasping for breath. It was several minutes before the teen could stumble into his car. He sat there, shaking, for what seemed like forever.

First, to see his older brother out of jail, cleaned up and in charge of the Hit Squad was enough of a shock, especially when it was evident he'd been back in town for some time and hadn't let the family know. But to have that same brother threaten to beat him up for taking Megan was something else.

It made Brain realize, and not for the first time, this idea of Blade's was absolutely wrong and if he didn't do something quick to make things right, someone was going to end up dead and he didn't want it to be him.

Chapter 32

Brain didn't sleep much that night. He had too much on his mind and no one to talk it over with. Things had begun to spiral rapidly out of control and he had no idea what he was going to do to fix them. No matter what, though, he figured it'd better be him instead of Crank staying with Blade after Dev's warning.

Not that it mattered to Blade. "Don't care, man. I've kicked both of their butts before and I'll do it again. Now, I'm outta here. I'll deliver the letter after lunch. There's some cold pizza in the fridge. Stay in my room in case my old lady comes home. Later."

Blade climbed aboard his bike and roared away. He cruised around Collingwood, watching, waiting, plotting. He saw the Slayers and the Hit Squad looking for him and he laughed as he easily avoided them. He screamed out towards Glencrest, loving the freedom the bike gave him. He parked far enough away no one would see him and walked back to the mailbox. His timing, for a change, was perfect. The mail truck was just pulling away as he approached.

He chuckled as he slipped the envelope into the box. Blade made sure his envelope was mixed in with the rest. He didn't want them to find it too soon. Laughing, he sauntered back to his bike and roared back to town to wait.

When Nana received the mail later that day, she was in her office, arguing with Ian. He, like Tony, hadn't slept much since Megan had disappeared, but unlike Tony, Ian firmly believed Rick was to blame. And he never hesitated to let anyone and everyone know.

"Ian, please. Will you *please* quit pacing? You're driving me batty," Nana said exasperated as she sorted the mail.

"Sorry, Mother, but I can't sit still. I'm too worried," Ian replied as he paced.

"What's it gonna take to get you to sleep?" Nana demanded crossly as Ian continued to storm around the room.

"My daughter home, safe, and your grandson in jail for as long as possible," Ian snapped.

Nana sat up in her chair, her eyes snapping with renewed anger. "Ian Attison, do *not* start with me. Until there's clear and unbiased evidence linking Rick to this, you will *not* jump to the same conclusions as Seamus, especially not in my presence! Understand?" Nana said hotly.

"Dammit, Mother. How can you still be brainwashed by that boy? After everything he's done, you still support him? How?" Ian shouted in frustration.

"Do not raise your voice to me, son and you know exactly why I still believe in Rick. He's blood, family and unlike your brother, whom I *know* for a fact is up to no good, Rick has never done anything wrong but join that bloody gang!" Nana retorted hotly.

Ian fell silent as Nana returned to sorting the mail. Megan's would be added to the pile already on her vanity in her room. Wordlessly, Nana gave Ian his mail and then returned to her own. Bills were put off to the side to be looked at in the morning. Her personal letters she opened one by one, making quick notes about which ones to answer by phone or mail and which ones to ignore.

The final envelope puzzled her. There was no return address and it had "Gran" on the front. She hesitated before she opened it and pulled out the letter inside. Something fell out and rolled over to Ian, who had finally stopped his pacing, over by the fireplace. He bent over and picked up the ring, stifling a sob when he realized what it was.

"Mother, look," he said hoarsely.

Nana's hand shook as she opened the letter and she saw the hairs that had been included. "Dammit," she swore as she reached for the phone.

"Mother, what's wrong?" Ian demanded, recovering his voice somewhat. Whatever was in that envelope had bothered his mother a great deal and Ian wanted to know what it was.

She shook her head. "No, son. Not until Tony gets here. Now, put...that on the envelope," she said quietly, motioning to the ring in his hand.

Ian returned to pacing, wondering what was going on. He was almost ready to grab the note from his mother when Martha showed Tony and Marshall into the room. *Finally,* Ian thought angrily. He couldn't understand why they had taken so long to get to the ranch.

"Where is it, Nana?" Tony asked immediately.

"Here, Tony. I've handled it as little as possible, but there's hair in there, Tony," she said softly. Swearing to himself, Ian no longer had to wonder what was in the envelope. He knew it was ransom demands for his daughter.

Tony snapped on some gloves and approached the desk. He carefully gathered up the strands of hair and slipped them into an evidence envelope and sealed it. He picked up the ring, turning it in his hand a couple of times and asked, "What's this?"

"A ring I gave Megan on her last birthday. Custom made from one of her mother's old diamond rings. She never takes it off," Ian said quietly.

"I'm sorry, Ian, but we'll have to take it and check for any evidence that might be on it," Marshall said gently as Tony dropped the ring into another bag and sealed it. Ian could only nod and wonder if he'd ever see it back on his daughter's hand again.

Then Tony picked up the letter and read it. Ian could see the anger that suddenly appeared on the cop's face and he couldn't take it any more. "Will someone please tell me what the hell's going on?" he demanded, wanting confirmation he was right.

Tony slowly began to read. "Gran, in case ya haven't figured it out, I've got Megs. Don't worry, Gran. I'll take good care of her. Ya want 'er back, Gran, gimme what I want, what I asked Megs for. Money. That's it, folks, show me some money and I swear I'll just fade away.

"Nothing personal, Gran, but what I want's a drop in the bucket compared to what ya have. Six mill, Gran. Surely my cuz is worth six mill. You gimme that, in small unmarked, untraceable bills and ya get Megs back in one piece.

"That's it, Gran. Don't bother to call the cops, since I'll know as soon as you do. I'll call in a couple of weeks to set up the delivery. Don't screw up, Gran. Otherwise, I'm gonna finish what I started in November.

"Think about it, Gran. Just think about it."

Taking a deep breath as he paused, then Tony continued softly. "'Tis Christmas morning, Daddy and all through the house, not a creature is stirring, including your little mouse, but I'm okay. Jordan, Mickey, my best friends in all the world. Jordan, you were right. About everything. Mickey, my dearest love, I have the proof you wanted and the proof we need. I love you, never doubt that. So promise me – no more accusations without proof, okay? And I have the proof." It was signed "Megan."

The room fell silent as Tony slid the letter and envelope into evidence sleeves and sealed them. Nana sat at her desk, pale, with tears running down her cheeks. Ian stewed by the fireplace, glaring at a photo of Rick sitting on the mantle. The cops both noticed a faint tightening around Ian's eyes, just before he reached up to seize the picture.

Marshall caught Ian's hand before he could damage it and took the photo away. "*You* may not like him, Ian, but dammit, respect the woman who does," he said firmly, putting the photo back on the mantle.

"Damn that boy! Lemme at 'im," Ian snarled.

"Enough, Ian," Tony snapped, trying to calm him down. "I need you to focus on this letter. Does that last paragraph make any sense to you?" Tony asked, taking out his notepad and pen, trying to do his job.

Ian took a couple of deep breaths. His voice was still angry when he spoke, but he was mostly calm. "The first part, at least, does, and it proves to me Megan actually wrote that part. It's a variation of something Megan and I say to each other every

Christmas morning. We use it to wake each other up. Her mother came up with it when we lived in Scotland. Only Megan, Mother and I know it," he said with a sudden catch in his voice.

"So it's a message telling you this really is from her and she's okay?" Tony confirmed.

"Yeah, I guess so, Tony. As for the rest, I've no idea, but since it's addressed to the twins, they might," Ian said with a shrug.

Tony dialled Mickey and, when the teen came on the phone, said, "Mick, I need you to listen to this." Tony read the last paragraph quickly.

"Hey, Jordan? Pick up your extension, will ya?" Mickey called. There was a couple of quick clicks, then Mickey said, "Tony, can you read it again?"

Tony read it again. "Does it mean anything to either of you?" the cop asked, puzzled.

"I'm guessing she's changed her mind and now knows I've been right about Rick all along. That's what I get, anyway," Jordan said thoughtfully.

"Mick? Anything?" Tony asked again.

Mickey didn't say anything for a minute. "That part about proof, can you read it one more time?" he asked quietly.

Patiently, Tony read it a third time and this time Mickey sighed. "Yeah, I know what she means. The day before Rick and I fought at school, I took Megan to Inland Park and basically forced her to tell me about the letters and the calls. As usual, I jumped to the normal conclusions. I called you, Tony, and Jordan told me to take a leap because she was going on a date with Rick. Before I left Megan at Hollyhocks, she said one more thing," Mickey explained.

"What? What did she say, Mickey?" Tony wanted to know.

"She told me she finally understood why you were so frustrated with this whole mess because there were always so many accusations against Rick but never any real proof. She swore she'd make no more accusations without proof," Mickey said.

"Hmm. Okay, thanks, kids," Tony said.

"Tony, wait! Is that a ransom note? From Rick?" Mickey demanded before Tony could hang up.

"Mick, you know I can't tell you anything like that, but it is a note and there is a message from Megan's kidnappers," Tony admitted reluctantly.

"A note from Rick," Mick reiterated.

"Mick, no more accusations without proof, please," Tony said as he looked more closely at Megan's signature. Something caught his eye, but he wasn't sure what it was, exactly. "Y'know, Mick. I'm not so sure this is from Rick, but I need to look at it more closely. Later." With that, Tony hung up.

"I'll contact the bank in the morning and arrange for the money," Nana said before Tony could say another word.

"Nana, there's no guarantee, even if you pay, we'll get Meg back. I need you to think about that and be prepared," Tony admonished.

"Tony, why don't you think Rick wrote the note? Or at least the one who's been posing as Rick?" Marshall asked as the partners left Glencrest. "Or am I missing something?"

Tony pointed at the letter. "The one who has her definitely wrote it, but it wasn't Rick. I'm almost positive of that. Look really closely at her signature. See those xx's? She never has those in there. Do you see what they're almost covering?" Tony asked as they drove back to the station.

"Is that...Rick's gang sign?" Marshall asked as he squinted at the paper.

"I'm pretty sure it is, but we need to examine it a bit further to confirm," Tony said, trying to keep the excitement out of his voice.

At the station, Tony and Marshall caught up with Terry at the evidence lock-up. "Hey, Terry. Got something I need you to look at right away," Tony said and handed the tech the sealed letter.

"Wha'cha need, Fish?" Terry asked. Tony pointed out the marks he wanted examined. Terry nodded. "Give me about ten or so to blow that up and see what I can find."

Tony and Marshall waited ten long minutes until Terry came back with the letter and an enlarged copy of the mysterious marks.

He smiled as he handed them over to the cops. "That help you boys?" the tech asked.

"Hard to say. How's the other stuff coming?" Tony asked. He couldn't help but grin at his partner. Hell yes it would help, IF Seamus would actually listen to them.

"Should have the fingerprint analysis finished later this afternoon," Terry promised, as he headed back to the lab.

The partners headed back to the bullpen and dropped their coats over their chairs. Grabbing some information out of locked drawers, they headed back to Seamus' office to update the inspector. Tony tried not to notice Jonesy casually snooping at what they had.

Shaking his head, Tony sat beside Marshall and closed the door. "Hey, boss."

"Problems?" Seamus asked, nodding towards the bullpen.

"Jonesy's been snooping, trying to worm into the investigation, that's all," Tony shrugged. It wasn't something they weren't used to, after all.

Seamus frowned. "Okay. I'll have a chat with him and tell him to keep his mind and his eyes on his own cases. Now, the ransom note?" Seamus asked, holding out his hand.

Tony handed it over and waited while Seamus read it. "We've confirmed with Ian and the twins the last part's truly from Meg, but I'm confident Rick doesn't have her," Tony said.

Seamus grunted as he finished. "Why not?" he asked, tossing the letter onto his desk.

"Other than personal belief, you mean?" Tony grinned as Seamus chuckled. He leaned over and pointed to the spot in Megan's signature which had caught his eye. "Take a good look at those marks, boss. What do you see?" Tony asked.

Seamus squinted, then pulled out an old-fashioned magnifying glass to examine the spot further. "Looks like xx's, like something's been crossed out," he finally said.

"Now look at that same spot magnified," Tony insisted, handing over the blow-up Terry had done for them. Seamus studied the paper in front of him for several moments, then frowned. He could see what Tony was pointing out, but the possibilities were not ones Seamus wanted to look at.

"What do you see, Seamus?" Tony pressed.

"Ye know what I see," Seamus grumbled.

"Say it, boss," Tony insisted. He wanted Seamus to admit what he saw.

"The boy's gang sign's been crossed out," Seamus finally admitted. "That's what makes ye believe the boy didn't write this and he doesn't have Megan?"

Ignoring Seamus' sarcastic tone, Tony pressed on. "Look, boss," he said, pleading his case. "Here's the last letter Megan got before she was taken. Note the signature at the bottom?"

"Yeah, it's his gang sign," Seamus said insistently.

"And what *don't* you see on the ransom note?" Marshall asked.

Seamus looked again, then sighed. "Megan's the only one who's signed this letter. But that doesn't mean the boy doesn't have her," Seamus said stubbornly.

Tony shook his head. "Seamus O'Reilly, you really are a stubborn Irish fool, aren't you?" Tony said. His words were serious, but his tone was light.

Seamus looked at Tony with a small smile. "Aye, stubborn, Tony, but realistic as well. Hear me out, Constable," Seamus said firmly, holding up his hand to stop Tony's protests. "Ye have *nothing* which actually proves the boy doesn't have her other than a couple of crossed out letters in Megan's signature and gut instinct. Right?" Seamus asked.

Tony groaned as he realized Seamus had just turned Tony's own arguments against him. "Okay, boss. I get ya. If you've gotta prove Rick did all of this and he took her, then fair's fair. I've gotta prove Rick didn't. Deal," Tony said sourly.

Marshall and Seamus laughed at his sour tone. "Boys, I trust ye believe this signature is important, so I'm gonna agree – it's important. Let's try to solve this and quick," Seamus said and dismissed the partners.

Marshall took the letter and enlargement back to evidence to be properly processed along with the ring and hair also collected. He nodded at Terry who handed over a folder. "What's this?" Marshall asked, puzzled.

"The fingerprint analysis Fish needed done on the vial and pop can," Terry explained, trying to hold back a grin, but unable to.

Marshall opened the folder and read the details. He grinned back at the tech. "Yes. Thank you. There really is a God!" When he went back to their desks, though, Tony wasn't around.

"He got a call and took off," Jones said.

"He say where?" Marshall asked, putting the new evidence in a drawer and locking it up.

"Nope. Said to have you call him on his cell if you needed him," Jones said and turned back to his desk.

Nodding, Marshall went to tell Seamus about the latest evidence. Jones waited until the squad room was quiet before he eased over to Marshall's desk. He slipped something into the lock, and the drawer popped open easily. The cop rifled through the evidence, making notes as he went.

Jones eased the last report out and read quickly. He knew Mendez wasn't going to be happy since the cop knew Mendez wanted the Knights to be his way into the high school. Whatever the Knights had done was rapidly falling apart. Jones knew he had to report this to Mendez so he could do damage control before things really got bad.

Jones closed and locked the drawer, making sure to leave no evidence of his snooping. He stood up, turned around and swore loudly.

Marshall glared at the other cop. "Looking for something, Jonesy?" the cop asked dryly. "Let's go and have a chat with the boss, shall we?"

Jonesy's heart sunk as Marshall hauled him over to face a very unimpressed Seamus O'Reilly. That he could handle. After all, he'd been doing it for months.

Mendez, on the other hand, was going to crucify him.

Chapter 33

Totally unaware of the drama unfolding at the station, Tony stopped and grabbed some pizza to share with Rick. When the cop pulled up behind the townhouse, Tony could see a light peeking through the upstairs window and he could hear the faint thumping of Rick going hard at the bag.

Tony sighed as he slipped into the house and put the pizza on the counter; hesitating, he headed upstairs. The rhythm he heard was angry, frustrated and worried, leaving him to wonder what the teen had learned from the street over the week.

Tony leaned against the door frame and waited. Rick's eyes, as usual, were closed and sweat poured from his face. Tony nodded as he watched the teen swing. When he pushed away from the door, he made sure he made enough noise so Rick knew he wasn't alone.

"Hey, Fish," Rick said as he wound down.

"Hey, son. You okay? The rhythm sounded a bit off," Tony observed as he straddled Rick's desk chair.

Rick downed a bottle of water before replying. "Trying to figure some things out," he said finally.

"Is that why you called? Need to run something by me?" Tony asked.

Rick nodded. "Lemme grab a shower first. I've been at the bag for a couple of hours, and my weight room downstairs for an hour before that," Rick said.

"I'll wait in the living room. I brought some pizza, so you'd better hurry." Tony left the teen to clean up. He grabbed the pizza and some drinks and stretched out on the couch. He turned on the TV to catch up on the news while he waited for Rick.

It wasn't long before Rick joined Tony in the living room. He mumbled 'thanks' through a slice of pizza and threw himself into the recliner. Tony waited while Rick sat quietly, thinking. *Wait for him to start talking*, Tony warned himself, *no matter how hard it is to wait.*

It was another hour before Rick sighed and looked at Tony. The cop had his head back and seemed to be napping or, at the very least, relaxing. Rick cleared his throat and chuckled when Tony bolted upright.

"Nice nap, bro. Feel better?" Rick asked, getting some more drinks from the fridge.

"How long was I out?" Tony asked, chagrined at having fallen asleep.

"'Bout an hour. Don't worry, man. I used the time to figger out what I wanna do," Rick said as he returned to his chair.

"Okay, Rick. What's going on?" Tony asked.

"Talked to Jimmy on Monday and he told me he's hearing from Mendez's younger members Johnny's got the go ahead to come on board. This could actually be more than trying to get me locked up for life. Megs could be the Knights' initiation into a larger gang," Rick warned.

Tony gave a low whistle. "Not what the boss is gonna wanna hear. Damn. What else?" Tony asked, making some notes so he didn't forget anything.

"When I talked to Jimmy, he had a couple of warnings for me to pass on. While Ricardo and the Slayers wanna find the Knights 'cause of the rumbles and beatings, Devon from the Hit Squad has a personal vendetta against the Knights, but no one'll tell Jimmy what it is. Said it's safer if no one knows. That's one," Rick said, then hesitated.

"And two?" Tony asked.

"That's what I've been strugglin' with and wanna talk about," Rick said roughly.

Tony sat up straighter. He'd heard something in Rick's voice he didn't like. "Put Moneyman back in the cell and slam that door shut. Now, Rick," Tony warned.

Rick got up and began to pace. "Dammit, Fish, don't you think I've tried, but I can't think of nothin' else! I don't even wanna *think* of Moneyman, but there ain't n'other way to get 'er back," Rick snapped.

"I don't care, you are <u>not</u> going back to the Knights," Tony growled, getting in Rick's face.

"As if yer gonna stop me," Rick laughed nastily. The longer he talked, the more he sounded like Moneyman and madder Tony got.

"I did *not* just spend the last eight months fighting like hell to keep you out of that damn gang to watch you throw it all away at the first chance Johnny gives you to go back. Forget that, boy. You're under arrest!" Tony snapped. He spun Rick around and snapped the cuffs on Rick before the stunned teen could move.

"What the hell?" Rick said hotly as he struggled against the cuffs. "Tony, get these damn things off of me!"

"No. Not until you change your mind. And I promise I'll haul your ass to jail to keep you safe," Tony replied just as hotly.

Rick backed away from Tony and took several deep breaths. If he didn't calm down quickly, he was going to do something even more rash than what he was thinking of. "I've had a lot of time to think about all of this, Fish. You haul me to jail, and Johnny'll kill Megs because he won't be able to blame me for kidnapping her. Besides, killing Megs is just gonna prove to Mendez Johnny can handle himself. That's exactly what Johnny wants," Rick said quietly.

Tony tried to calm himself down. "And you honestly believe Moneyman's the only way to save her? From all of this?" Tony asked, incredulous.

Rick nodded. "Tony, please? Uncuff me and I'll try to explain my idea," Rick begged.

Swearing softly in Cree, Tony sighed and pulled off the cuffs. "Sorry, Champ. It's just you startled the crap out of me and I guess I overreacted," Tony apologized.

Rick nodded. He rubbed his wrists as he sat down across from his friend. "Look, bro, I know it's a drastic idea, but I don't think we have a choice. Not anymore. Unless you've actually found

Megs and aren't telling me? 'Cause, to be honest, I don't wanna go back if I don't have to," Rick said.

Tony shook his head sadly. "No, Rick. We're no closer to finding her than when she was taken. We've chased down lead after lead, and all we have is a *very* tenuous link between Brian and Jim's clinic. Otherwise, everything we have points in one direction only," Tony replied, looking at Rick with a small grimace.

"Me," Rick nodded.

"You," Tony agreed. "And you honestly *want* me to let you just crawl right back down into that sewer without a fight? Not bloody likely. Seamus finds you in the Knights, no matter the outcome and you can kiss your freedom good-bye," Tony said firmly.

"I know, Fish, but the only way we're gonna find Megs is to have someone on the inside," Rick insisted.

"No, Rick. It's just too dangerous," Tony protested weakly.

"Any more dangerous than fighting Seamus and Uncle Ian? Or avoiding fights in juvy? What about hiding out here, waiting for the cops to bust in and arrest me?" Rick demanded.

"Yes, Rick, more dangerous than all of that. Combined. Trust me on this, Rick, you're just not strong enough," Tony said seriously.

Rick scoffed. "I can take the Knights easily," he laughed. "I'm way stronger than them."

"Not that kind of strength, Rick, because we both know yes, you can take the Knights on physically. No, I'm talking about the strength to pull yourself back out again. There's no way you'll be able to walk up to Johnny, demand back in, live the life while you get Meg free, if Johnny really has her, then get out. The pull's too strong. Trust me on this, son," Tony tried to explain.

Rick looked at Tony, his face twisted and tortured with pain. "But it would help, right?" he asked. He tried to hide his fear, because the plan scared Rick more than he cared to admit, but Tony heard the fear immediately.

"Of course it would help, son, but just listen to yourself! I can hear the fear in your voice, and you damn well know Johnny will. You'd need to bury that fear so deep Johnny doesn't hear it and kill you! You'll lose everything," Tony protested.

That was the final straw for Rick. "Me! Me! Me! That's all you care about, Tony Whitefish! Megs means nothing to you! What good's having *anything* if we lose Megs to Johnny, or worse, Mendez? How could I look Nana or Jor in the face if we lose her? God, if Uncle Ian and Mick hate me now, can you imagine what they'd say to me if I just laid down without a fight? I'm not that scared, Tony. I won't give her up without trying!" Rick shouted.

Tony was stunned, then hurt at the accusations spewing from Rick. "Rick, calm down a minute, huh? You *are* my main concern, but Meg means a hell of a lot to me, as a friend and not just because she's your cousin and important to you. Okay?" Tony said gently.

Rick could only nod as Tony continued. "And I know you won't lie down and not fight for her. But you need to think of one very important thing," Tony said soberly. He hesitated for a minute trying to figure out how to say this to Rick.

"What're you gonna do once you get back to the Knights, once you get Meg free, and Johnny won't let you go again?" Tony asked quietly.

Rick turned a hate-filled and angry gaze towards Tony. "Kill him," was the snarled reply.

Chapter 34

Nothing Tony could say would change Rick's mind. Rick's patience was nearly gone when Tony reluctantly agreed to help, even though the thought of Rick going back to the Knights made both of them sick to their stomachs.

"Look, Fish, I know this ain't a great idea," Rick said as they sat in the living room, planning. "But unless you've got another idea that'll give you the info you need, it's the only one that's got a chance of working. No matter what Jimmy's hearing on the street, Johnny ain't gonna let a stranger in right now. Too much of a chance the guy'll go straight to the cops once he found out about Megs."

"You really think Johnny'll take you back?" Tony asked.

Rick shrugged. "Hard to say, man. I mean, it's what he's been after since September, so he's either gonna take me back or...," Rick's voice trailed off.

"Or what?" Tony prompted, already knowing what Rick would say.

"Or he'll probably kill me. Either way, my choice, bro. But I'm scared," Rick finally admitted.

"You're only *scared?* Then I'm bloody *terrified*," Tony squeaked, his voice breaking on the last word.

Rick burst out laughing, finally breaking the tension. He couldn't help it. No matter how serious this was, hearing Tony's voice squeak was a riot. "Sorry, bro, but your voice," he sputtered.

Tony grinned, then sobered. "How do you wanna do this? Do you need anything?" Tony asked, trying to ignore how his stomach was sinking.

"My jacket and bandana. I've got the rest here. I went shopping yesterday," Rick said quietly. "Actually, Jimmy did, but, hey, you know what I mean."

"Full gear?" Tony whispered, horrified. *By the Creator, I've lost him as soon as he puts that damn jacket on*, Tony agonized. *Rick'll never survive.*

Rick nodded. "Don't got much choice, man. I show up in anything less than full gear and Johnny'll know I'm not serious," Rick explained.

"But full gear, Rick? Honestly?" Tony continued to protest.

"Yeah, I know. Kinda makes me sick, too, but without the gear, we're just five boys hanging out and chillin', y'know?" Rick said.

"Okay, I'll get your jacket and a bandana, but I've gotta do it carefully. Tampering with evidence'll really get me fired, understand, son? This is extremely dangerous for me," Tony warned, hoping that would make Rick change his mind. *Should've known that wouldn't work*, Tony thought, when Rick just shrugged.

"But you'll do it?" Rick pleaded, suddenly worried Tony wasn't going to help.

"I'll do it on two conditions. One's negotiable. One's not. First, do you think you could wear a wire or something?" Tony asked as he stood and stretched.

"No way. Johnny catches me wired and you'll never find all the pieces," Rick vetoed immediately. "Mine, not the wire."

Tony nodded. "Thought so, but wanted to ask anyway. Now, I don't want an argument on this. Gimme until Monday to see if we can get somewhere without you going back. Gimme at least that much time, Rick," Tony begged.

"No prob, bro. It'll take me a while to get everything else set up. I'll head to Eric's place late Monday afternoon. Can you get me his actual address? I kinda know how to get there from the school, but I don't wanna take a chance of being seen," Rick explained with a faint flush.

When Tony left, Rick wandered back up to the spare room where most of his gear was already laid out. His cell phone chirped as he stood there, hating what he was going to do, but knowing he didn't have much choice. Jimmy was right. This was the only way to get Megan back. He reached for his phone and answered the call.

"Yeah?" he said quietly.

"Word's out. Moneyman's back," Jimmy said and quickly hung up, leaving Rick to wonder how Jimmy got his cell number.

Now Rick knew this crazy idea of his stood a chance of working. Once he got his jacket and suited up, he'd make sure both the Slayers and the Hit Squad saw Moneyman and knew what was happening. They'd have his back, just for the chance to get back at Blade and the Knights.

Rick dropped his phone on the bed and returned to his makeshift gym. All he could do for now was wait for Tony to come through with his gear. Until then, he'd work out and rest.

Tony didn't sleep a whole lot that night. He woke, grumpier than he'd been in a long time, and headed into the station, expecting nothing but more frustration from a lack of progress.

"Morning, Fish," several cops called out as Tony entered the bullpen.

"Morning," Tony replied, doing his best to keep the frustration out of his voice.

He got to his desk and noticed immediately the locks had been changed. "What'd I miss?" he asked as Marshall handed him the new keys.

Marshall lowered his voice and said, "Caught Jonesy with his hand in my desk, including a report you have to see. Seamus suspended him for his next three shifts. He'll be back on Tuesday."

"Ouch. Harsh. Wait. What report?" Tony asked. He read over the analysis twice to make sure he understood it right. Then he looked up to see Marshall grinning at him. "This for real?" Tony demanded.

"Yep. The risk you took was worth it, partner. The fingerprint on the vial is the same as the on pop can. They match. We've also matched these two fingerprints to a certain suspect from a previous arrest," Marshall replied, unable to resist high-fiving his partner.

"He can't ignore that, now can he?" Tony asked rhetorically. He knew Seamus could ignore any evidence he wanted to, but he really hoped Seamus would listen to reason. "The boss in yet?"

"Not yet. He's running late this morning. Why?" Marshall asked.

Tony locked the report up, by habit, and leaned on his desk, thinking. "Let's go for a walk," Tony suggested, snatching up his jacket and heading outside. Puzzled, Marshall followed his partner across the street to the park and sat down at one of the picnic tables.

"Marsh, you know what I've done, and why, right?" Tony began after brooding for several long minutes.

"You mean with your young friend who's our boss' number one suspect? Yeah, of course," Marshall said with an unconcerned shrug.

"Well, as much damage as I've already done to my career, I'm about to add Evidence Tampering to Obstruction of Justice, Aiding and Abetting a Wanted Fugitive, and only the Creator knows what else Seamus'll throw at me when he finds out about this, "Tony said sourly.

"Um, Fish, don't get me wrong, you're a good friend and a hell of a partner, but I really like my job and I don't want to lose it," Marshall said mildly.

Tony laughed. "Don't worry, I've got your back. The only one who'll lose his job'll be me," Tony assured his partner.

"So why the secret meeting, man?" Marshall asked.

"Because I'm gonna need some help to pull this off, that's why. I need Rick's leather jacket and one of the bandanas," Tony said. He quickly outlined Rick's plan to his partner, who responded with several moments of stunned silence. Finally, Marshall seemed to regain consciousness. "Holy crap!" he blurted out. "Does he realize how dangerous this is?"

Tony nodded. "Trust me, Marsh, I spent entirely too many hours yesterday trying to talk him out of this and I got nowhere. It's either this, with my help, or he's gonna go back without my help. Either way, he's going back," Tony said. He was still sick to his stomach at the thought of Rick back with the Knights.

"I wanna get the stuff to him today so he has time to finalize everything, then I wanna find and arrest another suspect before Monday. Otherwise, he's going back," Tony said again.

Marshall paused, thinking long and hard. "Okay, here's what we're gonna do. You're gonna take that report to Seamus and get him to see the light. While you're doing that, I'll go and get what you need from the evidence lock up. Tell Rick not to screw this up, Fish, since my name's gonna be on that sign-out sheet. I don't want this coming back to bite me in the ass, y'know?" Marshall said.

Tony nodded and the partners went their separate ways. He could hear Seamus talking on the phone as the young cop approached his desk. Grabbing the report he needed, Tony knocked on Seamus' door.

"Thanks, Lance. I've got nothing new to report, but Tony's just come in, so that might change. I'll call ye later." Seamus hung up and looked at the cop now sitting in front of him.

"Ye cut out a bit early yesterday, Tony. What's up?" Seamus asked, leaning back in his chair.

"Sorry, boss, but I was working a confidential informant, and he doesn't like me to bring company, y'know?" Tony lied smoothly.

"Anything good?" the inspector wanted to know.

Tony shrugged. "Nothing yet, but I did hear we may have a bit of a gang war starting because of Meg's disappearance. Apparently the Slayers and the Hit Squad've joined forces and are head-hunting. They're gunning and gunning hard for the Knights, but if things don't change soon, they may start going after each other," Tony warned.

Seamus grunted and made a couple of notes. "I'll pass it on. Anything else?" he asked.

"Marshall's still trying to find Elijah, but so far, nothing new on that front. He's gotta couple of rookies doing background checks and more interviews. Who knows? We may find him yet," Tony said and then handed Seamus the report he was holding.

"What's this?" Seamus asked as he began to read.

"Fingerprint analysis you'll find interesting," Tony said. Seamus grunted and continued to read. When he finished, he sighed and put the report on his desk.

"Okay, now why're ye still looking at this Townsand kid?" Seamus wanted to know. "By the way, yer conversation with him at school was just this side of legal, Constable. His dad lodged a complaint, but Lance Blackstone smoothed it over. Just watch it next time. 'kay? Now, again, what've ye got on the Townsand kid?" Seamus asked, knowing Tony would take the warning as it was meant. Be careful and watch his back.

"Noted, boss. As for what we have, mainly circumstantial, but so's the *real* evidence against Rick. When I talked to Brian at school, he confirmed he'd been at the clinic and talked to Jim about sleeping pills for his sister. Jim remembered Brian also asked specifically about that stolen vial of sedatives. Brian actually laughed at me and said the way I was talking, I thought he'd shot Meg full of drugs, something we've never released to the public.

"Second, when I asked him about knowing Meg, he called her Megs, just like Rick does, and admitted to having most of his classes with her. When I followed him to Physics, he sat behind Meg's desk, just like he did in the other classes I observed. He's in the perfect position to slip the letters into her back pack," Tony continued.

Seamus nodded thoughtfully. "Okay, Tony, so far ye have some compelling non-evidence. Convince me Townsand's really worth pursuing," Seamus ordered. He was actually impressed Tony had managed to get what he had, but the inspector needed more.

Tony continued. "When we talked, I asked Brian how well he knew Rick and he said he's known Moneyman for 'bout four years and if I didn't know where Moneyman and his cuz were, no one would," Tony said.

"So? Mickey's called the boy Moneyman plenty of times," Seamus pointed out dryly.

"True, but as an insult, boss. Brian did it automatically as a sign of respect. Gang members're drilled from the moment they join that only the gang names're to be used, nothing else. Even though

Rick's been out of the Knights since September, Brian couldn't call him anything but Moneyman. He also referred to Meg as cuz. Only someone who was around Rick all of the time would call her that since both "Megs" and "cuz" were the only way Meg was referred to by Rick. Something the gang would've known," Tony explained.

"That doesn't eliminate the boy, y'know, Tony. He could've been with Townsand when he wrote the letters and made the calls, and yes, I've also seen how much he looks like the boy. Still not good enough," Seamus said, dismissing Tony's evidence, yet wanting to hear more. Tony never pursued a false lead. Ever.

"Well, then this has to be good enough, boss. I gave Brian a can of pop to drink. I made sure there wasn't a drop of condensation on it and it had been wiped completely clean of all prints. He left it in the garbage can, plain sight, so I grabbed it. Analysis of the print on the can and on the vial're the same. We searched arrest records and found out Brian has one, so we compared the can and vial to his fingerprint card. They were a match," Tony said firmly.

"And since the vial of sedatives was the only thing stolen from Dr. Jim's clinic, and was found, along with what appear to be tranquilizer darts for a small hand gun in that black bag, at the spot we believe Meg was taken, I'm fairly confident Brian Townsand, at the very least, handled the vial in order to fill the tranquilizer darts used to shoot Megan Attison," Tony concluded.

"And ye think that's enough to call Lance and get an arrest warrant?" Seamus asked.

"Call him and find out," Tony replied. He already knew the answer, since Marshall had run it by the lead prosecutor before Tony came to the inspector, but only Seamus could actually request this warrant.

Seamus dialled Lance, leaving the phone on speaker. When Lance answered, Seamus quickly outlined the evidence Tony had against Brain. "What we wanna know, Lance, is there enough here to get an arrest warrant and search warrants for his locker, car and house?" Seamus asked, praying the prosecutor said no. He was disappointed when Lance said yes.

"I believe so, Inspector, so I'll issue the warrants. Tony, stop by in about an hour. They should be ready by then. Good work, both of you," Lance said and hung up.

"Ye've got yer warrants, Tony. Don't make me regret this," Seamus warned.

"Boss, have you checked in at Glencrest? I've been so busy I haven't had a chance. How's Nana and Ian?" Tony asked as he stood.

"They've got the money ready to go at a moment's notice. Ian's called every day demanding to know why we haven't found Megan or the boy. Nana's a lot more polite. She just wants to know how things're going. Either way, they're not doing the best," Seamus said.

Tony sighed. "So many lives changed because of all of this," he said quietly.

Seamus froze at Tony's words. *How true they are, even for Rick,* Seamus realized. "Tony?" Seamus said, stopping Tony with his hand on the doorknob.

"Yeah, boss?" Tony replied, turning back to see an ashamed look on Seamus' face.

"I've been wrong about...Rick, haven't I?" Seamus began, hesitating on Rick's name.

"Well, I can only speak to this school year, Seamus, but yeah, you've been wrong about him. I won't say anything about before I met him, so you'll have to make your own judgement about that," Tony replied honestly.

"Do ye think, if Rick's found innocent in all this, I'll ever be able to make it up to him? Do ye think he'll ever forgive me?" Seamus wondered.

Tony shrugged. "Don't know, Seamus. It'll be up to Rick if he'll ever be able to forgive you, boss, but a good way to start would be to back off and let Jor and him have their relationship. If it survives this mess, I'm gonna say they'll be together for life. And get Mick to back off and accept his sister's Rick's girl," Tony suggested.

Seamus didn't say anything as Tony left the office and returned to his desk. He looked for his partner but Marshall wasn't around. Frowning, Tony sat down, then noticed a folded note taped to his phone. He opened it, read it, put it in his pocket and stood up.

"Hank, tell the boss I'm off to the prosecutor's," Tony said.

"New lead?" Hank asked hopefully. Like the rest of the team, Hank was frustrated by the lack of progress.

"New suspect," Tony replied as the team gave a ragged and tired cheer. He quickly strode out to his car to find Marshall waiting for him with the jacket and bandana.

"Thanks, partner. We've got an hour before Lance'll have the warrants ready. We're going after Townsand," Tony said firmly.

Chapter 35

Tony dropped Marshall off at the prosecutor's office, telling him only he'd be back as soon as he could. Tony drove quickly over to the safe house to deliver the rest of Rick's gang gear, trying hard not to think of his friend back as a Knight.

"Hey, Rick, just letting you know I'm coming in," Tony said when he called Rick a couple of minutes later.

"Basement," was Rick's short reply.

In the basement, Tony found Rick working out, trying to be as ready for what he was planning to do as he could be in such a short time. "Hey, son," Tony said.

"Did you bring them?" Rick asked as he towelled off.

"Before I give these to you, I'm gonna ask you one last time and don't snap at me, 'kay?" Tony asked. Rick nodded. "Are you really sure you wanna do this?"

"Wanna, bro? No, I don't wanna do this, but I need to. We're not gettin' any closer to findin' Megs, and we're both pretty sure Johnny has her. The deal between the Slayers and the Hit Squad's comin' apart, and it won't be long 'fore they ferget 'bout Johnny and go at each other. I've gotta stop this before someone gets killed," Rick said firmly, slipping in and out of the gang speak.

Resigned, Tony nodded and handed over the jacket and bandana. Rick looked at them, sighed and headed upstairs. Tony waited, pacing, in the living room while Rick showered and changed. Twenty minutes later, Tony felt a subtle change in the room, one of arrogance and cockiness. He turned around to see Rick in full Knights' gear once again, leaning against the door jamb, his arms folded across his chest and a sneer on his face. He looked as if he didn't have a care in the world. Yet Tony knew Rick well enough by now to know the teen was extremely uncomfortable with being back in the gear and Rick's next words confirmed it.

"Dammit, Tony, I really hate this crap," Rick said softly.

"Rick, you gonna be able to pull this off? 'Cause if not, I'm not leaving you here in this gear, brooding, just so you can go and get yourself killed, hear me?" Tony said sharply.

"Don't worry, bro. By the time I go back on Monday, Moneyman'll be ready. I just never thought I'd put this stuff on again once you made me throw it out. It's gonna take a while to get used to it again," Rick explained as he sat down.

Tony handed him a piece of paper. "That's Eric's address. I've managed to connect Brian to this and I'm gonna try to arrest him today. I'm hoping he'll give me the information we need so you don't have to do this. Promise me you'll wait until Monday?" Tony begged again.

Rick nodded. "Don't worry, Fish, I'm not in *that* much of a rush to go back. I'll wait, but I won't sit around here and brood. You have my word on that. Moneyman's gonna be seen around town, so try not to send the rest of your team on wild goose chases, 'kay? They'll only get in my way," Rick said with a cocky smile. Moneyman was back.

"Be careful, little brother, please. And if I don't hear from you within two days of you going back, I'm gonna hit Johnny's place with all guns blazing, understand? I won't lose you and Meg," Tony said roughly as he left. Rick was stunned to see Tony basically bolt from the house.

The cop returned to the prosecutor's office to meet up with Marshall and Lance. Marshall had the warrants in hand and was reviewing the evidence they had when Tony was shown in.

"Sorry, Lance. I was meeting with another informant. We good to go?" Tony asked.

Lance nodded. "Good luck, Constables," was all he said as the partners left.

"How do you wanna do this?" Marshall asked as they climbed back into their car.

Tony glanced at his watch. "Call Delaney and see if we can get him at school," Tony suggested.

"Sorry, Marshall," Delaney said when he answered his phone. "None of the Knights're here today."

"Crap. Okay, thanks, sir. We'll try somewhere else," Marshall said and snapped his phone closed.

"Lemme guess. He's not there?" Tony said sourly. *Can anything else go wrong right now?* Tony wondered. He needed to find Brain, arrest him and find Megan before Monday or Rick was going to commit suicide.

"None of them are. So now what?" Marshall asked.

"Try his house, I guess," Tony said frustrated at the delay.

The constables found no one home at Brain's, and they had the same result at Crank's and at Blade's; that is, no one answered their knocks. None of the parents or family could tell them where any of the teens were when the partners went back later that day.

It was the same for the next four days. The Knights had not been at school, either, and by Sunday night, Tony was very frustrated and worried. Being unable to find the Knights when there were constant reports of Moneyman running loose around town didn't help matters either. Tony marvelled at how good Rick was at causing everyone to think about Moneyman and wonder what the teen was up to.

"You know, kiddo, you're very good at this," Tony congratulated Rick as they had supper together. Tony worried this was going to be the last meal they'd share for a while. Something told him this plan of Rick's was going to seriously backfire in the kid's face.

But he never let on. He could tell Rick was nervous enough with what he was doing. "What's the word?" the teen asked as he leaned back.

"Let's see. You've been seen at East Side's – no, Mahoney's – no, the vacant lot – no, the pool hall – no, Theo's. Oh, wait – here's my favourite. You sauntered back into the high school and went back to class as if nothing had happened," Tony laughed.

Rick laughed, too. "I've been nowhere near the school, bro. I'm not nuts," he protested lightly.

"Oh, I know, son, but it's incredible how many places you've been seen. If that wasn't bad enough, I've also heard Moneyman's recruiting his own gang, or gone back to the Knights, or taken over either the Knights, the Hit Squad, or the Slayers. Maybe none of it. All of them or any combination of the three," Tony said, all laughter suddenly gone from his tone.

Rick frowned. "Didn't know that. Damn, I'll have to get to Ricardo and Dev quick to let them know that ain't the case or they'll come after me," Rick said, worried.

Tony began to clean up, falling silent as he thought about Rick having to face three gangs, all possibly wanting him dead. He'd actually thought he'd masked his worry about what Rick was going to do tomorrow. He thought wrong.

"Tony, what's wrong, bro? You went silent on me," Rick said quietly.

Tony sighed. "I'm just worried, kiddo. You've got potentially three very deadly gangs after you and you're still willing to walk into the lion's den. You're gonna end up dead!" Tony shouted, finally giving into the stress and worry he'd been holding back all week.

"And that's *my* choice, Fish. Not yours, or Nana's or anyone else's," Rick said quietly. He knew Tony never shouted at him unless the cop was truly upset or worried. Tony's obvious lack of sleep and proper food wasn't helping either.

"Oh, so this is your choice, and that's just supposed to make me feel all better, huh, Rick?" Tony replied scathingly.

Rick seethed at Tony's tone. "Look, man. I've done what you asked. I gave you the extra time to find Megs and you haven't. Now, it's time for me to do what I wanted to do," Rick snapped back, knowing he was holding onto his anger tenuously.

He continued before Tony could say anything. "You've told me from day one to trust you, Tony, right? *Right?*" Rick demanded when Tony continued to be quiet. Tony nodded, reluctantly. "I've told you things Nana doesn't even know about my dad and what he's done to me. It's been damn hard, but I've learned to trust you.

Now, it's your turn. *You* have to trust *me*. I know it doesn't look like it, but I know what I'm doing.

"Yes, it's dangerous. I know could get hurt or killed, and I could end up sucked back into the Knights and yes, I could end up losing what I've got back this year. Trust me, I am *terrified* I won't pull this off. But I can't go into this if I'm worried about anything other than being Moneyman. And that includes worrying about you, Tony. Now, do you trust me or not?" Rick asked directly.

Tony stood at the kitchen counter, his hands on the counter top. Rick could see his friend's shoulders shaking, as if Tony was crying. Rick couldn't stand it any longer. He went over to the cop and put his hand on Tony's shoulder, forcing him around to face the teen. Sure enough, there were tears on Tony's face. Rick sighed.

"Tony, do you trust me?" Rick asked quietly.

Tony wiped the water from his face and locked down his emotions. Rick was right. He couldn't do this if he had to worry about anything but being Moneyman. "You, son, I trust. It's the rest of these wild cards I don't," Tony said roughly.

Rick didn't know what to say. He continued to hesitate and then pulled something from his pocket. "Fish, I need you to hold onto these for me. If something does...happen to me and I don't make it through this, give 'em back to Jor for me, please? Tell her I love her and I'm sorry, 'kay?" Rick asked.

Tony looked at the bracelet and guardian angel he held and nodded. He knew what Rick wasn't saying. "Remember, if I don't hear from you by Thursday, I'm coming after you," Tony said as he left.

Rick wandered through the house, cleaning everything up. He made sure there was nothing left in the fridge that could spoil. He did another workout before crashing for the night, vowing to clean the basement after doing a final workout in the morning. He fell asleep, promising himself he could do this and Megan was worth dying for.

By just after lunch, Rick was pacing like a caged tiger. He decided he'd better leave and do one final check in with Jimmy before heading to the lot to cool things down with the other gangs.

He left a thank you letter for Jim on the table, along with his school books, closed up the house and then sauntered down to Mahoney's.

"Moneyman," Jimmy nodded as he and Rick met in the back alley. He seemed unsurprised to see Rick in his full gear.

"Back in school? Really, Jimmy? Who'd believe that?" Rick laughed.

"Sorry, man. Got kinda carried away. When?" he asked as he nodded at the gear.

"Today. Anythin'?" Rick asked.

"Nuthin', man. None of 'em have been at school in days, but they're not at home either," Jimmy replied sourly. He'd never failed to find out information before, and he was frustrated.

Rick swore. "Doesn't matter, I guess. I'm outta here. Take care, Jimmy. You've been a big help. Peace." Rick pushed away from the fence and strode away.

It didn't take long to get to the lot where the leaders of the Slayers and Hit Squad waited for Rick. "Ricardo. Dev," Rick greeted them both.

"Ya trying to get killed, Moneyman? Trying to take us over? Think ya can actually take us both?" Dev snarled, getting right in Rick's face.

"No. No. Yes. Now, ya done with the drama?" Rick asked sarcastically. "I don't wanna lead the Knights, man, so what the hell makes either one of ya think I'd wanna challenge ya? I want out of the Life, not back in," Rick snapped.

"For someone who wants out, yer looking an awful lot like yer heading back to the Knights," Ricardo pointed out, nodding toward Rick's outfit.

"Unless ya been able to track Johnny down and know where Megs is, I ain't gotta choice, man. The cops know squat and she's running outta time. I gots no choice!" Rick repeated.

Dev shook his head immediately. "Sorry, man. Nothin'. No one knows who's got 'er or where. Or if they do, they ain't talkin'. Blade's got everyone in this damn town that scared of him," Dev said sourly. He was more than a little angry at his little brother. No matter how hard Dev tried, Brain had been too sneaky to lead him to where Megan was.

"Then I'm outta here. Thanks for trying to help. And hey, don't go back after each other once the Knights're gone, 'kay? If ya wanna keep the gangs, fine, but no more fighting. Split the town in half and stick to yer own sides. This town can't handle any more blood," Rick pleaded, leaving the two rival gang leaders to settle their differences. The Knights were still fair game, though, *if* they could find them.

Rick wandered around until dusk and then headed over to Crank's. He stood, hidden in the shadows, watching, waiting. He grinned when he saw Crank's family walk out and throw several suitcases into the trunk of the family car and then climb in. Crank's dad came out, walking towards the car while Crank remained on the porch.

"I'm serious, Eric. No parties. No booze. Nothing. You can work on the bike for Johnny and I've left the keys for the Rabbit on the key chain, but none of them're allowed over. Understand?" Crank's dad asked.

"Yeah, Dad, I got it. Just like every other time you've mentioned it," Crank said, bored with the constant reminder – no one over when he was home alone.

The loaded car pulled away and Crank slammed back into the house. Rick waited another ten minutes before he walked up to the front door and knocked. Rick could hear Crank muttering as he came to the door.

Chapter 36

As the door swung open, Rick swallowed a laugh at the look on Crank's face.

"What the hell're ya doin' here, Moneyman?" Crank blurted out.

It was better than Rick thought. Crank was totally unprepared to see him again, especially in full gear. He smiled lazily.

"Sorry to drop in on ya, man, but I heard Blade was lookin' fer me. Figured you'd be the easiest to find, Crank," Rick said. He tried not to wince when he used the gang names, but a sudden flash of Megan lying motionless in the darkness reminded Rick of why he was doing this. *For Megs,* he swore silently while Crank continued to stare at him.

Rick looked around and said, "Look, Crank, I'm wanted, man. Do we have t' stand out here and talk? I mean, if I wanna have the cops come and pick me up, I'da gone home."

Crank hesitated then opened the door enough to allow Rick to slip in. Rick followed the flustered teen up to his room. While Crank paced, getting more and more nervous, Rick lounged on his bed, watching, more relaxed than he'd been in a long time. Inside, the teen was roaring with laughter at Crank's reaction. Outwardly, he was calm as only Moneyman could be. Moneyman was known to have ice water in his veins. *Time to throw another monkey wrench into their plans*, Rick thought gleefully.

"Crank, where's Blade chillin'?" Rick asked casually.

Crank didn't answer as he paced. Here, in his room, was the one person who was supposed to take the blame for all of this. He was supposed to be on the run or hiding away with his cousin, not sitting here with him. *What the hell am I supposed to do now?* Crank panicked.

"Crank?" Rick asked again.

"Yeah, man?' Crank replied, still pacing.

"Where's the rest of the Knights, man? Where's Blade?" Rick asked. *Where Megs is what I really want to know,* he thought.

Crank finally stopped and looked at Rick. "Why're ya here, man? Wha'cha want?" he asked quietly, trying to keep the panic out of his voice.

"I want back in," Rick said clearly, stunning Crank.

"Ya what?" he blurted.

"Word's out, man. Blade and the Knights're into sumthin', and I wanna slice, man. Ain't got nuthin' since my old man took off and my uncle kicked me off the farm," Rick drawled.

"Right, man. What makes ya think we wants ya back?" Crank said shortly, calming slightly. *He don't know nuthin',* Crank thought, relieved.

Rick gave a short bark of laughter, startling Crank. "C'mon, man. Blade's been after me to come back fer months now, and yer askin' why I want back in? Knight fer life, remember?" Rick drawled again. This wasn't going quite the way he'd planned, but he wasn't worried. Yet.

Crank resumed pacing. He was muttering under his breath as he walked as if trying to convince himself of something. Finally, he stopped and glanced at Rick. "Stay here. I gotta check in with Blade," he growled.

Crank thundered downstairs and dialled Blade's number frantically. He returned to pacing as he waited for Blade to answer. "C'mon, Blade, dammit, pick up. Leave Megs alone and pick up, man," he muttered loud enough to be heard outside the kitchen where he paced.

Rick froze on the stairs. Crank had been making so much noise he hadn't heard Rick following him down. Now, Rick had just heard Crank admit Blade had Megan. *Thank God,* Rick said to himself. *We were right. Now, just gotta get the info to Tony.*

"Blade? We gots a damn huge prob, man," Crank blurted out, panic rising again.

"Chill, Crank. What's the prob?" Blade drawled lazily, not expecting the next words out of Crank's mouth.

"Moneyman's here. Right now! At my house!" Crank hissed.

"What? When?" Blade snapped.

"Moneyman showed up here about ten minutes ago. He's in full gear and wants back in. Says he heard on the street we're into sumthin' good and he wants a slice, man. What the hell am I supposed to do, man?" Crank almost shouted.

Rick grinned wildly. He'd made the right choice for certain. Crank would've been the only one who'd panic this badly. It was easy to listen when someone was talking at the top of their lungs. He quickly turned his attention back to the babbling Crank.

"What the hell am I supposed to do?" Crank demanded again.

"First, calm down," Brain snapped. He'd grabbed the phone away from Blade when he actually heard Crank shouting.

"Brain, what am I gonna do? This plan of yers ain't gonna work if Moneyman's back in," Crank said anxiously.

"Calm down, dammit, and lemme think for a second!" Brain snapped again. "Now, can he crash there until tomorrow?"

"Yeah. Family's gone to the city for a couple of days," Crank said.

"Good. I know Delaney wants us all at school tomorrow, especially Pup, so I've gotta chance leavin' Blade here with her. Don't let Moneyman outta your sight and keep low. Bring him over after school and I'll have a plan to deal with him by then," Brain ordered. He rubbed his forehead and wondered how much more screwed up this plan could get.

"No problem, Brain. I can skip another day. But really man, ya trust Blade with Megs?" Crank asked, calming down. It was easy when Brain was controlling things.

"Trust him? Oh hell no, but I'll lay down the law again," Brain said sourly.

"Tell 'im I'm backin' ya, Brain. Firmly backin' ya this time. Blade ain't very stable right now. He's gonna kill Megs if he ain't careful," Crank said.

Rick had heard enough. He slipped back upstairs to digest what he'd heard. Too bad it was all hearsay and Tony couldn't use it. Yet. Until Rick actually saw Megan at Blade's, he had nothing to go on but Crank's words. Still, it gave the teen hope he was right.

When Crank returned to his room, Rick looked like he'd never moved. Tossing Rick a cold pop, Crank said, "Blade wants to talk to ya, but can't get free until after school tomorrow. Ya cool with that? Ya can crash here tonight, since the family's away for a couple of days. Spare room's free."

Rick stood up and drained his pop. "Thanks, man. I know this could bring the cops down on ya, but I really appreciate it. I'll catch up with ya in a couple hours. Need to grab a nap. Been on the run for too long and haven't been able to sleep properly," Rick said and followed Crank down the hallway.

In the spare room Crank showed him to, Rick laughed quietly. No wonder people thought he'd taken over the Knights so easily. Blade hadn't even whimpered when Brain took over. *Sounds like their plan, whatever it is, is going south in a hurry,* Rick thought gleefully. He just wished he could call Tony and let him know what he'd overheard, but he knew Crank would be keeping a very close watch on him. He'd have to plan his check-in carefully.

To say Tony was frustrated with not being able to arrest Brain before Rick had to go back to the Knights was a mild understatement. Tuesday morning, Tony arrived at the station, ready to tear the town apart to find Brain before Lance decided they really didn't have enough to go after the teen. The cop sat down at his desk, and reviewed every piece of evidence they had collected so far, looking for anything that would lead him to Megan.

"Delaney just called. Brian's in school today, but not Johnny," Marshall said just before lunch.

"Let's go," Tony said immediately.

The partners rolled up to the school and met the principal at the front door. "Officers. Any news?" he asked, hopefully.

Tony shook his head. "Nothing new. Is he still here?" he wanted to know.

"In the cafeteria having lunch. Shall we go ruin his appetite?" Delaney asked as he led the way. Tony didn't even care if the other Knights were there to see this, since the cop was certain Blade would hear about it no matter what.

"He's right there," Delaney said, pointing to the far side of the cafeteria. Tony nodded and moved quickly as it looked like Brain was getting ready to leave.

"Brian Townsand?" Marshall asked as the partners approached the table.

"Yeah?" Brain sneered at the cops. He was stunned when Tony spun him around and slapped on the cuffs.

"Brian Townsand, you're under arrest for Break and Enter, Theft, Assault, Assault with a Deadly Weapon, Stalking, Harassment and Kidnapping," Tony said loud enough to carry to all corners of the cafeteria.

The cafeteria was silent for only a moment before the Angels started cheering and cat-calling insults as Tony led the Knight away. As they walked, Tony read Brain his rights and Marshall paused by the twins' table for a quick word. "We haven't found her yet, Mick, but we're closer. Give us some more time. No, Jor, we don't know where Rick is either. Again, give us time. Okay? Gotta go." Marshall left the twins grinning with relief.

"Do you understand your rights, Brian?" Tony asked as Marshall rejoined the group outside the school.

"Yeah," he said sourly.

"Mr. Delaney, do me a favour, please. Contact his parents to let them know what's happened. They can see Brian at the station," Tony said. He knew exactly what Brain's dad would do if he received that phone call.

"Don't bother, Delaney. Don't care if they're there or not," Brain snapped as Marshall led the teen to their car. Brian slumped in the back seat, trying to figure out where things had gone wrong. He kept coming back to that interview he'd done the week before with Tony. He couldn't think of anything he'd said or did that should've tipped these two cops onto him, yet he couldn't help thinking he'd screwed up the interview.

The principal watched Tony pull away with Brain in the back seat before heading back into the school. Despite Brain's reaction, Delaney would still have to call his parents and let them know their son had been arrested. Everything had gone so smoothly that most of the kids were still at lunch. Delaney was picking up some discarded paper in the lounge when he saw a small shadow moving quickly towards the front door.

"Going somewhere...Mark?" Delaney asked dryly.

Pup jumped and swore. "Watch your language, Mark. Now, where're you going?" Delaney asked again.

"Nowhere," Pup snarled and turned back to the cafeteria. He hoped he could slip away when the bell rang for class.

No such luck. Delaney showed up just as the bell rang and escorted Pup to his class. The principal told Pup's teacher to make sure the teen stayed in class until the bell rang and then escort him to his next class. Pup seethed at Delaney's smirk. *Screw this*, Pup thought angrily. *I'm a Knight. I'm outta here at the bell.*

When the bell finally rang, Pup strode from the room, ignoring the teacher's call to wait. *To hell with Delaney*, Pup thought as he left the school. *I'm a Knight and I don't ask permission.* As soon as he was out of the school, Pup began running. Blade needed to know about Brain and now.

When he got home, though, he hesitated. He really didn't want to be the one to push his cousin over the edge, but Blade had to know. Brain and Crank were worried Blade was seriously unbalanced right now and the one who would pay would be Megan. Still, if Pup didn't tell Blade, someone else would.

"Blade? Yo, man, ya home?" Pup called.

There was dead silence to his call. "Blade?" he called up the stairs, hoping his cousin was in his room. Nothing. Pup sighed. He knew exactly where Blade was then, in the basement beating on Megan, again or still, take your pick. Cringing, the youngest Knight opened the basement door and cringed as he heard Megan sobbing, Blade laughing and the sound of skin hitting skin.

"Blade, man, ya down here?" Pup called as he hurried carefully down the stairs.

"What the hell're ya doin' home?" Blade snarled as Pup rounded the corner and froze.

Megan was sobbing quietly as Blade towered over her. Pup could see her shoulder muscles straining, her arms were tied back so tight. She was shivering and it looked like Blade had thrown more water on her, soaking her and her bed once again. Pup didn't even try to count the fresh bruises on her face and arm, and were those fresh cuts?

"Dammit, Blade, ya gots to quit slicin' 'er up, man. She can't take much more! Yer killin' 'er," Pup said, angry at what he saw.

"Screw that. What're ya doin' home?" Blade demanded once again.

Pup hesitated a long time while Blade just glared at his cousin. "Brain's been arrested, man!" Pup finally blurted.

"He's been what?" Blade hissed. He turned to glare at Megan. Her heart sunk like a stone when she saw how Blade looked at her. She was as good as dead.

"Arrested, man, by Moneyman's cop buddy. He came in at lunch, slapped the cuffs on Brain and charged 'im with Assault and Kidnapping and a bunch other crap. Blade, they gotta know, man. They gotta," Pup babbled.

Blade shoved Pup into the wall, hard enough to stun the younger teen. "Shut up, Pup," Blade snarled and turned to Megan. "How'd you get a message to them?" Blade roared and began to pummel Megan unmercifully.

With her arms tied behind her, Megan had no way of defending herself. She cried out weakly as Blade's fists struck again and again. Shaking his head to clear it, Pup struggled to pull the much larger Blade away.

"Johnny? Son, you home yet?" a voice called from upstairs.

"What the hell's she doin' home already? Dammit. Pup, get up there and keep 'er busy," Blade snarled, running a hand through his hair. Everything was going to hell.

Blade turned back to Megan, who was huddling against the wall, more terrified now than she'd ever been. "I don't know how the hell this got so screwed up, but I'm warnin' ya now, Megs. Not a peep. If I gots to come back down here, yer gonna wish ya were dead," Blade snarled softly. He threw the still damp blankets back over her, snapped the light off and stormed back upstairs, yelling at someone as soon as he slammed the basement door closed.

Megan couldn't pull the blankets any closer as she began to shiver uncontrollably in the cold and damp basement. From the moment she'd woken up in this hell hole, she'd never been warm. She was so hungry and thirsty she'd welcomed the water Blade had thrown on her. At least she got something to drink. She couldn't remember how long it had been since she'd eaten that bowl of soup Brain had given her and she was so dehydrated she had no more tears left to cry.

Even worse, she was getting very sick. Whatever injury she'd got when Rick knocked her over that chair in the cafeteria had been made worse by the constant beatings, and now she was coughing up blood. And as much as Blade had injured her, Megan figured she wasn't going to make it out alive, especially with no one around to control him. *Tony, for once, your timing really sucks*, Megan thought as she finally managed to get her shivering under control so she could sleep a bit.

"You know, Johnny, today of all days, I could really use some help around here," Blade's mom complained as she cleaned up the kitchen. "I work hard enough at my jobs cleaning up after my customers. I don't need to come home for the few minutes I have between jobs and clean up here, too," she continued.

"Back off, Ma, or else," Blade snarled. His mother backed away a couple of steps, terror in her eyes.

"Relax, Aunt Marian. I've got this," Pup said quickly. *I'll do anything you want to get you the hell outta here before your son blows,* Pup thought angrily.

Marian sighed. "Fine. Thank you, Mark. Johnny, I've ordered a couple of extra large pizzas for you and your friends, as I'm sure they'll show up eventually. The pizzas'll be here in a couple of hours and they're paid for. Do me a favour, though. Clean up after yourselves and keep the noise down to a dull roar. Mrs. Lazowski's been complaining again and I don't need another call at work," Marian said as she pulled on her coat.

Blade didn't say anything as his mom left and Pup continued to clean up the kitchen and living room. The young teen was never so grateful to see food arrive, since it gave Blade something to do instead of pace and toss his steel around. Pup was never sure if he was going to end up with it in his back, cousin or not.

The two were about half way through the first pizza when Crank walked in with Rick in tow. Blade nodded at Crank, now his number two guy, and glared at Rick, who'd sauntered into the house as if he owned the place.

Looking at Blade, Rick could see he hadn't changed at all since September, except the rage in Blade's eyes made him appear thinner and meaner. Blade returned the gaze, seeing how strong, physically and more importantly, mentally Rick had become in his months away from the Knights. Blade swore silently, knowing Rick could take them all down without breaking a sweat.

"Moneyman," Blade finally acknowledged.

"Blade," Rick nodded back.

"What the hell'm I gonna do with ya?" Blade drawled as he continued to eat.

"I want back in, man. Yer inta sumthin' good and I wanna piece of the action," Rick said lazily, trying to match Blade's indifference.

Blade didn't say anything. He just continued to eat, letting the silence grow. Rick found himself shifting from foot to foot, feeling like he'd been hauled into Delaney's office again. *Screw this,* Rick snarled to himself. *I'm sitting.*

He threw himself into the chair across from Blade, who ignored the pizza in front of him now. Pup stood behind his cousin, nervous as all hell. He kept glancing towards a door on the far wall. Rick figured, based on its location, it led to a basement and, seeing how jumpy Pup was, something was down there no one was supposed to know about. *One'll get you ten it's Megs,* Rick thought gleefully. *Mark's about as subtle as a brick in the face.*

Rick leaned back in his chair, trying not to stare at Blade, but knew he couldn't turn away from him either. As Blade finally leaned forward to pick up his pizza, Rick caught a flash of gold around Blade's neck. A gold ring hung on a gold chain. Rick knew it was Megan's since Blade didn't have a girlfriend. He could see the little diamond shapes cut into the slender band Mickey had given his girl on New Year's Eve.

Rick felt like jumping to his feet and crowing at the top of his lungs. Megan was definitely here. *I'll get you out, Megs*, Rick vowed silently. *I swear it.*

Blade was seething inside while maintaining an outward façade of calm. *Brain's been arrested. Moneyman wants back in. My own boys're turning against me. What the hell else can go wrong?* Blade fumed. He needed some time to figure out what to do, but with Rick sitting there staring at him, daring him to say or do something, Blade knew he was out of time. *Ferget it, I ain't losing my money. Moneyman's gotta go*, Blade decided and made a quick motion with his head.

"What the hell?" Rick jumped as Crank's arm snaked around his throat and began to cut off his air.

Chapter 37

Well, hopefully I won't die right away, Rick thought as he struggled to breathe. Crank's arm tightened even more, cutting Rick's air off completely. The room began to spin as Rick fought to remain conscious, batting and tugging at Crank's arm.

"Somehow, Moneyman, I just don't believe ya. Ya figured it out. Y'know what's going on. I know y'know," Blade snarled as he stood over Rick and Crank.

"What the hell're ya talking about, man?" Rick managed to croak out as he continued to tug weakly at the arm around his neck.

"Ya, right, Moneyman, yer were warned. Ya'll beg me to end it." Blade's voice faded out completely as the world went grey before Rick finally blacked out.

"What now, Blade?" Crank asked as he held his arm in place.

"Pup! In the basement, near Megs, there's more rope. Move!" Blade snapped. Pup thundered down the stairs and skittered around the corner to grab the rope.

Megan struggled to open her eyes at the sudden noise. "Mark?" she whispered. Great shuddering coughs racked her body until she was gasping for air. "Mark, please? Water?" she begged. Her voice rasped and she began coughing again. When she finally stopped, red-flecked foam and spittle lay on the bloody pillow.

"I can't, Megs, Blade's got..." the young boy hesitated, shrugged and fled, leaving Megan alone in the dark once again.

Upstairs, Pup threw the rope at his cousin. Blade swiftly cut several lengths, lashed Rick securely to the chair and told Crank to release Rick. Rick began to cough weakly as he slowly regained consciousness.

Rick growled when his head finally cleared. *No kidding I'll beg,* he snarled to himself as he struggled against the ropes, even though he knew Blade would've tied them too tightly for Rick to break loose. *You're too damn chicken to let me defend myself.* And Rick knew why, too. Blade was scared, even three on one, Rick would take them all again.

"Y'know, Johnny, it's too bad y'all're so scared of me," Rick taunted. Blade's first punch landed on Rick's jaw, hard enough to stun him momentarily. He shook his head to clear the cobwebs and kept the jabs coming. If he was going to die, he'd land a few shots of his own. Verbally, at least.

"Yep, sure is a shame. I'd've loved to find out which of us really was stronger," Rick said with a sardonic grin, since he knew which one of them would win. He grunted as Blade landed a hard blow to his ribs. He could actually feel the bone crack and breathing suddenly became very painful.

"Me. Yer too yeller," Blade grated as another blow landed on Rick's ribs.

"Don't think so, Johnny. See, it takes more guts to walk away than to fight," Rick gasped as more fire erupted in his chest. "Fish taught me that."

Rick continued to taunt Blade as more blows fell. "Tell me, Johnny. Did Megs fight? I'll bet you were too chicken to face her head on, weren't you, Johnny?" Rick chuckled weakly at the image.

"Keep laughin', Moneyman. I like to see a man die laughin'. It's gonna be a pleasure to break ya," Blade gloated as he swung again.

"If it gets you to leave Megs alone, then it's worth it," Rick said shortly as another blow fell on his jaw. *Now I know how Tom felt*, Rick thought, dazed. His ears were ringing and he could barely focus.

"Only if she's lucky, Moneyman. Yer just guessin' she's still alive," Blade said harshly as he grabbed Rick's hair and yanked his head up. One eye was already swollen shut and Rick struggled to focus the other one on his former friend.

"I know she is. Ya haven't bragged 'bout finishin' her off. Ya'd never be able to keep *that* quiet. Ya'd want me to hear about it. Word on the street sez yer hidin', man. Scared of someone?

Mendez, maybe? Yer boss not too happy ya branched out on yer own?" Rick hissed as Blade struck again and again. Rick never even noticed how his speech slipped from normal to gang speak and back again.

"Don't worry 'bout Mendez, Moneyman. He's cool with this. I'll get paid, he'll get paid and I get rid of ya," Blade laughed and struck again. Blow after blow fell on Rick's ribs and head, but Blade paced himself. He wanted this to last a good, long, painful time.

He laughed again as Rick's head lolled against his chest, blood dripping from a couple of cuts on his face. Every gasp the teen made was like pouring liquid fire on his battered lungs. He had had enough broken and cracked ribs over the last few months to know Blade had broken at least a couple and cracked most of the rest. God, he hurt and he knew it had only begun.

"Yer turn, Pup," Blade said lazily as he stood back and enjoyed the show.

Rick's head was jerked up again and into his vision swam a swaggering Pup, who stood looking at Rick for a moment, before he began his share of the beating. Rick struggled to remain conscious as Pup rained short, sharp blow after blow down on his head and face. He could feel his skin tearing and dazedly remembered the youngest Knight usually wore a large signet ring. Rick had no idea how long Blade let his cousin pummel him. He was sure it was only a few minutes, but it felt like hours. He moaned softly as Pup slowly stepped back and Blade once again stood in front of the battered teen.

"Had enough yet, Moneyman?" Blade taunted Rick as he circled behind the chair. Rick cringed. He braced for the killing blow, but Blade only jerked Rick back against the chair and tightened the ropes, not even caring the ropes had started to cut into Rick's wrists, dripping more blood on the floor.

Rick groaned again as his wrists and shoulders screamed in pain. Blade moved around to face Rick and, with another bark of laughter, slammed his boot into Rick's shin. A second blow fell as Rick cried out weakly. His leg had to be cracked, Rick was positive. Blade was wearing his biker boots, after all.

Through his one swollen eye and the haze of pain, Rick heard, more than saw, the approach of the final Knight. Rick could hear Crank circle around and stop right behind him. *What next?* Rick wondered in a daze.

"My turn, Moneyman," Crank said softly and threw his first punch. The blow landed, not on his ribs like Rick was expecting, but on his bound arms. Rick howled in pain as he felt the bones bend, but not break. Yet.

Downstairs, Megan stiffened. "My God, Johnny, what're you doing?" Megan whispered as she shivered and tried to wrap herself tighter in the thin, worn blanket, but with her hands tied behind her back, it was almost impossible. Before she could even begin to think about what was going on upstairs, the shivers grew more violent, and she began to cough. Before she was done, there was more blood on the pillow and she had slumped down, unconscious once again.

Rick screamed weakly as Crank's next blow fell again on his arms. This time, Rick did feel the bones break. He couldn't think because of the excruciating pain in his right wrist, but that was nothing compared to the pain which came from the multitude of blows Crank rained onto Rick's right shoulder. Under the strain, the bone broke, forcing from Rick a guttural howl of pain.

Blade sauntered back over to Rick, who hung by the bloody ropes, and nudged Rick's broken shoulder. The battered teen had no strength left to cry out, but he managed a soft groan. "Sorry, Megs," he whispered so low Blade didn't hear him. "I tried, cuz. I really tried."

"Gonna beg, Moneyman?" Blade asked softly as Crank moved away, a sick look on his face as he saw what they had done to Rick.

Rick somehow found the strength to raise his head and forced his eyes to focus on Blade. His heart sunk like a stone when he saw the flash of steel. Still, despite the fear he felt, Rick remained defiant. His voice was weak but steady when he finally spoke.

"No, Johnny. I won't beg. Megs'll never forgive me if I give up. She hasn't," Rick whispered defiantly.

"Yer still so sure she's alive?" Blade said as he toyed with his knife.

"Yes," was all that Rick managed. He knew Megan was in the basement.

"Well, Moneyman, I gotta tell ya sumthin', man. She ain't fightin' nearly as hard as she did in the woods," Blade laughed. "Gonna beg?" the leader of Knights demanded again.

Rick remained defiant, even in the face of certain death. "Never."

Rick cried out weakly as Blade plunged his knife deeply into Rick's left shoulder, all the way to the hilt. With a savage jerk, Blade yanked the bloody blade out and held it before Rick's swimming eyes.

"While yer dyin', Moneyman, think 'bout where this'll end up next," Blade hissed and plunged the knife in again.

Too weak to protest anymore, Rick could only stare numbly at his former leader as Blade stabbed him over and over. A vicious backhand sent Rick plunging into darkness again, dragging his chair over onto the floor, where the other two Knights joined in on the beating again. Blade egged Crank and Pup on, encouraging them to land blow after blow.

Finally, Crank pulled back, disgusted. "Enough, Blade. God, enough already. He can't die here, man," Crank said harshly. He was panting and he was drenched in sweat. The beating was vicious and made Crank almost sick to his stomach.

"C'mon, man, think, dammit. Yer old lady could come home any time. Neighbours could've heard him and called the cops. He's gotta go, unless you plan on holdin' him downstairs with Megs," Crank continued as Pup went to get some towels and a mop.

"He ain't coming to any time soon, Blade," Pup said as he came back. *If ever*, the young boy thought grimly. It was one of the worst beatings Pup had ever seen and been part of. On the one hand, he was sickened by what he had done, but loyalty to his cousin wouldn't let him say anything to Blade. With a shrug, he tossed Crank an old blanket to wrap Rick in.

"Dump him and make sure he's not found," Blade ordered and went to clean up.

"Cut the ropes, Pup," Crank grunted as he manhandled the blanket near Rick. The unconscious teen groaned as the two gang members rolled their former mate onto the blanket.

"Gimme the ropes and those towels, too," Crank ordered before he wrapped Rick up tight. He struggled to lift Rick's dead weight onto his shoulder. *Man, he's heavy,* Crank thought as he shoved Rick into his back seat.

Driving quickly, but carefully, Crank sped out of town. He had briefly thought about dumping the body at Hollyhock's, but realized it was too busy. He'd be seen for sure. He could hear Rick groaning in the back seat and drove faster. He didn't want to be caught with the body.

"Don't ya dare die on me yet, Moneyman," Crank muttered angrily as he turned down the road to Glencrest. He pulled off onto a small access road and stopped. A quick glance showed no one was coming.

"Out ya go, Moneyman," Crank said as he pulled Rick out and dumped him unceremoniously onto the side of the road, mostly in the ditch. He was out of the way, and probably wouldn't be found until someone came out here to check the fence. By then, Crank figured it would be way too late.

"Sorry, Moneyman, but ya shouldn't'a left," Crank said philosophically as he climbed back into his car. He gunned the motor and sprayed rocks everywhere.

Rick groaned as the rocks pelted him awake, stinging his cuts. His foggy brain realized he had been dumped somewhere. Where, was anyone's guess, but he knew he had to get out to a road. Megan's life depended on him being found, alive, and sooner, rather than later. Inch by agonizing inch, Rick dragged his battered and broken body up the side of the ditch. Several times, he slid back down a small distance, but he gritted his teeth and continued to pull himself up, tears streaming down his face, mixing with the blood still flowing sluggishly.

Finally, after hours of climbing, or was it only minutes? Rick's fingers encountered no more grass, only rocks. "I'm coming, Megs," he whispered, his throat raw from screaming. "Hold on." Through his battered eyes, he recognized where he was – a short access road that led to one of Nana's pastures, and fortunately for Rick, one checked frequently. It was only ten feet to the main road, but to Rick, it might as well have been five miles.

"Gotta move," Rick whispered as he pulled himself along. "Gotta save Megs." It was a mantra which kept Rick moving. He had to be found. He had to save Megan. Then he could rest.

It was almost dark by the time Rick had managed to pull himself to the road. He could go no further and collapsed – once more unconscious and bleeding heavily. Luck was finally with Rick, though. Someone came down the gravel road, their vehicle's headlights glinted off the metal on Rick's jacket.

With a muttered oath, Ian swerved to avoid the lump in the middle of the road. He almost skidded into the ditch to avoid it. "What the hell is this?" he muttered as he climbed out of the SUV, grabbing a flashlight as he went.

He gagged as he got closer. The smell of blood was overpowering and the flies had already started to arrive. He shone the flashlight over the area and realized he was looking at a body. He hesitated for only a moment, but finally turned the body over and stared in horror at the barely recognizable face of his nephew.

Chapter 38

It was very tempting to just get back into his vehicle and drive away. Rick wasn't his problem – Megan was. He could just hear his mother, though, never letting Ian forget how he left his nephew to die. With a sigh, he gathered Rick up and dumped him on an old horse blanket and then gathered the bloody blanket, towels and ropes Rick had crawled out of into a spare garbage bag. All the while, Rick didn't move or make a sound.

"Dammit, boy, don't you dare die on Megan," Ian growled as he slammed the door and ran to the driver's side. Jumping behind the wheel, he tore off towards Collingwood, dialling Tony, ignoring the honking horns and flashing lights of oncoming traffic.

"Whitefish," Tony said, distracted by a report he was reading.

"Tony? Ian. Meet me at the hospital," Ian said tersely as he continued to dodge traffic.

"What's wrong?" Tony snapped. "Nana?"

"No, Rick. Found him dumped on the road to Glencrest. I don't think he's gonna make it," Ian said as he negotiated a corner.

"On our way," Tony said and slammed down the phone.

"Seamus! Marsh!" Tony shouted as he grabbed his coat. Marshall stuck his head out of the conference room just before Seamus flung open his office door, demanding to know what the hell was going on. Tony waved for them to follow him quickly. The three ran to the car while Tony filled them in on Ian's call, even as he was dialling the hospital to let Jim know.

They screamed over to the hospital and were waiting at the emergency doors when Ian screeched to a halt. Jim yanked open the back door even before Ian had stopped. "My God," the doctor whispered as he stared at the battered teen. Tony nudged Marshall who immediately began snapping photos, trying to document the horror they saw before them.

"Move!" Jim snapped at the cops as the trauma team swarmed over Rick. The three cops moved away to let the doctors do their jobs, too stunned to say or do anything.

"Jim?" Tony finally asked, layering several questions in the doctor's name.

"If I can, I will," Jim said. What he couldn't say was he wasn't sure if Rick was even alive.

Silently, Tony grabbed the evidence out of Ian's truck and moved it over to his car while Seamus called for a couple of techs to come and process the mess and to have a couple of others go out to the access road where Ian had found Rick.

"Damn, Tony, he's bad," Seamus murmured as he stared at the door Rick had just been rushed through. Off to one side, Ian called Nana, telling her what he had found and urging her to come to the hospital.

"Should I call Jordan?" Seamus wondered as they went in.

Tony hesitated a long time. "Hold off, boss. Do you really want her to see him like this?" the young cop said as he left the room, a glimmer of an idea forming.

He found Jim arguing with another doctor outside the trauma room. "Don't argue with me, dammit! Get the bleeding under control, Jason. The bones can wait! Save his damned life first!" Jim snapped. "Interns," he muttered as he turned to Tony, handing him a bag filled with Rick's clothes, knowing the cops would need to process them.

"How bad, Jim?" Tony asked, dreading the answer.

"Bad, Tony, as bad as I used to see in Texas. I won't lie. He's lost almost all of his blood and somehow he's still alive. Broken wrist, broken shoulder. Several deep stab wounds. I think every rib's either broken or cracked. Looks like his one shin's cracked as well. I can't count the number of blows he took and I've no idea what kind of internal injuries he has, and that's just based on the first glance. I don't even have time to do X-rays or scans. Not if I wanna save his life," Jim sighed. The cop was stunned. He couldn't speak for several long moments as Jim's words began to sink in.

"How's he still alive?" Tony wondered softly, holding himself up against the door jamb.

"Sheer bloody determination. And I do mean bloody. There must be some reason he's still alive. Maybe he has someone to live for," Jim shrugged and turned to go back into the operating room.

"Jim, wait. I've got an idea that might keep him safe. His life won't be worth spit if the Knights find out he's survived and we both know that," Tony said, hesitating. Jim turned back, his face flushed with anger, as he figured out immediately what Tony was asking him to do.

"You asking me to let him die? You want me to walk into that operating room and tell them to quit trying to save his life? Are you crazy?" Jim asked, incredulous. "I thought you gave a damn about that boy!"

"I do, Jim, you know I do! No, Doc, all I'm asking you to do is *tell* everyone he's gone," Tony said softly. His idea was insane, but it was the only way he could think of to save Rick's life.

"My God! Now, you want me to walk into that room and tell a woman I admire more than my own mother her favourite grandson, a boy she's never given up on, has died when, in reality, he's still alive? You want me to lie? To Nana? *You* want *me* to lie to *Nana*? Do you have any idea what that'll do to her?" Jim demanded hotly. For once, Tony's logic baffled Jim.

"Yes I do, and no, Doc, I wasn't thinking about lying to Nana. She'd figure it out too quickly. You know I can't lie to her. No one can. No, I'm thinking of how the hell I'd tell Jor and the Angels. They're the ones I'm really worried about," Tony said, as he leaned even more heavily against the wall.

"Do you really think this is necessary?" Jim asked quietly after looking long and hard at Tony. The cop was rubbing at his face and exhaustion clearly ruled his body. "Dammit, Tony Whitefish, not again! When was the last time you slept? I mean really slept and I don't mean when I knocked you out?" Jim asked suddenly, grabbing the cop's arm. He could feel Tony trembling as he struggled to remain standing.

Tony waved away the question and shifted the conversation back to where it belonged. "Don't worry about me, I'm good, Doc. Focus on Rick, 'kay? I mean, look at him, Jim. You know as well as I do who did this to him. The Knights were scared enough to do *that* to him on the slimmest idea he *might* know something, I'm sure of it. Imagine what'll happen if they find out he's alive and possibly talking. Blade'll get in somehow and slice the Champ's throat. Come to think of it, I'm surprised he didn't," Tony said, pushing himself up. He couldn't show any weakness, not now or Jim would knock him out.

"He didn't have to. He expected the stab wounds to do that for him," Jim said and fell silent as he thought about Tony's request. "You realize this goes against everything I stand for? Everything I swore to uphold? But you'll tell Nana? Promise?" Jim insisted roughly.

Tony sighed in relief. "Thanks, Jim. I know it's hard, but it's gonna work out. I promise – Nana, Seamus, Marshall, you and me'll know. Ian'll know only if Nana says so. Should we keep him here?" Tony asked, looking around.

Jim shook his head immediately. "I want him somewhere I can control access to him, until he's stable. I can't even control everyone who comes into ICU. My house across the street, the safe house he just left, will probably be best. You, me and Marsh. That's it. Nana can't know. Send Ian home and take the others up to the VIP lounge by ICU. Ian doesn't need to know," Jim said decisively and strode back to the operating room. "Oh, and Tony," he said, sticking his head back out the door.

"Yeah, Doc?" Tony replied, turning back.

"Tell Jordan face to face. Don't you dare let her read about it in the paper or hear this from a stranger," the doctor said as the door closed behind him.

"Sorry, Doc," Tony muttered as he headed back to the waiting room. "That won't work. She'll see right though me if I tell her face to face." He dumped the bag of bloody clothes off with the techs who had arrived to process Ian's truck and went to find the others.

He stood at the door and watched as Ian consoled Nana, and Marshall and Seamus talked quietly. What Tony was thinking of doing to this family, to his friends, was horrible, but if it kept Rick alive long enough to find Megan, then it was worth every bit of pain he was about to cause. *At least, I hope it is*, Tony thought wearily as he entered the room.

"Did ye talk to Jim?" Seamus asked quietly as Tony came up to him and Marshall.

Tony nodded. "Ian, why don't you head home in case the kidnappers call? We'll take care of your mother," Tony said quietly as he crossed the room.

"Mother?" Ian asked. He didn't want to leave, but someone had to be home for Megan.

"Go, lad. I'll be okay," Nana said with a sad smile.

Ian nodded and left quietly. Tony looked around and said, "Jim said Rick's pretty bad and he doesn't know how long he'll be. He suggested we wait in the VIP lounge by the ICU."

"This way, lads," Nana said and led the way briskly to the third floor. The lounge was very plush and had its own kitchenette, fully stocked, and a washroom, complete with shower. Tony looked at the couches and realized they could be pulled out into beds. It was also only a few feet away from the ICU and Jim's office. Nana put a DO NOT DISTURB and OCCUPIED signs on the door and finally turned to face Tony.

"How bad is bad, Tony?" she demanded as soon as the door closed.

"Nana, do you really wanna know?" Tony asked. At her curt nod, Tony rattled off the injuries Jim had told him about. "He didn't have time to go into any more details. Not if he wanted to save Rick," Tony finished.

Nana sank into a chair, her face going white at Tony's words. Tony sat beside her and took hold of her hands. They were icy cold. "Come on, Nana, easy. Jim doesn't need another patient right now," Tony said, trying to soothe her, but knowing that was impossible.

A couple of minutes later, some colour had returned to Nana's face and she was not shaking quite as badly. Tony smiled at her. "Better? Good. I've gotta question for you, boss. How long do you think it'll be before the Knights find out about Rick? Being alive, I mean?" Tony asked, looking at his partner and boss.

"Doubt it'll be long, especially the way we all tore out of the station," Marshall said thoughtfully. "Why?"

"I've got a crazy idea, one that *may* keep both Rick and Meg alive," Tony began hesitantly and then stopped. He really didn't know how to ask Nana to do what he wanted.

"Tony Whitefish, you know I hate it when people beat around the bush. What do you wanna do?" she demanded.

"Nana, how would you feel if we told everyone Rick had died?" Tony finally asked when the silence had stretched on for several minutes.

"Tony, you just said he's alive! Now you're saying he's dead? Which is it?" Nana snapped, colour again fading from her face.

"Alive, Nana, but just barely," a new voice entered the conversation. Jim accepted a cup of coffee from Seamus as he sat down across from Nana. He was tired and still in his blood covered surgical scrubs. No one spoke for a long time.

"He's alive, Nana. Just keep that in mind for the next few minutes. How he's alive, I have no idea, but he's alive. I've got the bleeding stopped for now, especially from the stab wound in the left shoulder. We found a punctured spleen, lacerated liver, and a collapsed lung. All are being taken care of. I have a brilliant intern working on setting his badly broken right shoulder and wrist, but until he's stronger, we won't do the fine work," Jim said tiredly.

"If he's alive, why do you want me to lie and say he's dead?" Nana asked Tony, puzzled.

"I'm scared, Nana, plain and simple. As bad as he is right now, the real danger'll come when the gang finds out Rick's alive. When, not if, Nana. Right now, until we have evidence to the contrary, we have to assume the Knights did this. They're the only ones who hate him that much. Seamus and I're pretty sure the gang has Meg, but again, we don't have any evidence to say they do or that they don't. We don't know if Rick knows anything, but the Knights can't take that chance. If they find out Rick's alive, Blade'll come and finish that boy off," Tony explained, turning to face Seamus.

"Ye really think this'll help?" Seamus asked, doubt colouring his voice. Tony nodded as he continued to outline his basic plan.

"Especially if we have an article in the paper about it, announce it at school, maybe a full funeral..." Tony's voice trailed off at the shock on everyone's faces.

"Bury my boy?" Nana said, aghast.

"Look at it this way, Nana – we'll bury Moneyman. This'll allow us to get rid of the gang member for good. Rick'll be free," Tony said quickly as he took the older lady's hand in his.

"Jordan's gonna freak," Seamus said suddenly.

Tony nodded. "Not to mention the Angels, but it can't be helped, Seamus. *Their* reactions have to be the most natural or this won't work," Tony apologized to his boss. Seamus hesitated then nodded. He didn't like it, but he was beginning to understand Tony's logic. Even if it meant hurting his kids.

"Nana, you alone can know the truth, but not where we've got him. Because I'm not keeping him here, I can tell you that, but that's it. What you don't know, you can't tell," Jim said. He stretched and stood. "I've gotta get back to the operating room to make sure that you don't need to plan this for real." He came over and gave Nana a hug.

"Take care of him, Jim," Nana begged. The doctor nodded and left the room.

"Now, Tony, how do you wanna do this?" Nana asked, turning back to the young cop, once again all business. She knew Tony wouldn't ask her to do this if he really didn't think it would do Rick any good.

"Carefully, Nana. Very carefully," Tony said and laid out his plan, hoping, praying his partner and his boss would come up with something, anything, else.

"You realize any one of these bloody ideas could go horribly wrong and blow up in our faces," Marshall pointed out roughly an hour later as they scribbled down the details of Rick's obituary.

"I know, Marsh, but unless you wanna spend 24-7 at his bedside and not in the field looking for Meg, we've got no choice. You don't like this? Fine. Gimme a better idea, partner. This might be the *only* thing that'll keep him, and Meg, alive!" Tony said roughly. He rubbed at his eyes, wishing he could just collapse for about a week, but knowing if he did, he'd lose both teens.

Jim stuck his head in the door again. "He's settled in the ICU for now, Nana, if you wanna see him, before I move him again," the doctor said, clearly exhausted.

Jim led the way to the lone occupant of the ICU. Nana gasped as she stared at her grandson. "That's Rick?" she asked, in disbelief, pointing at the bed.

Jim didn't answer. He couldn't. Rick lay, pale, on the stark hospital bed. His head had been shaved to deal with all of the lacerations in and around his face and his breathing was aided by a respirator, its hissing loud in the silence of the room. A heart monitor beeped rhythmically, a sound Nana found a bit reassuring, although not much. Rick's face was so swollen the only way Tony was sure the body in the bed really was Rick was by Jim's word.

"Nana, honestly, can you do this? Can you tell everyone who loves him he's gone and cry for him at a fake funeral?" Jim asked quietly, not liking Tony's plan at all, especially now he'd been fully briefed.

"Easily. It won't be my grandson who I bury. It'll be that horrid gang member. Now, please, all of you leave me alone. I need some time with him," she said as she sat down beside her grandson and held his hand, trying very hard not to cry.

As they left, Seamus couldn't help beginning to be a little worried about Tony's plan. "Tony, are ye sure about this?" the inspector asked for the hundredth time.

"Hell no, boss, but I can't think of anything else that's going to keep him alive. Can you? And don't forget about Meg. The Knights find out Rick's alive, do you honestly think they'll leave her alive? Do you really?" Tony snapped harshly, glaring at his boss and running an agitated hand over his head. He was bone tired of protecting Rick and fighting for him, but someone had to.

Seamus had no answer for Tony. He just stood at the door of the hospital as Tony and Marshall walked to their car. "Easy, Fish, don't jump all over the boss. I don't like the plan either, but I happen to agree with you. This is the only way to keep the kids alive. But this is gonna to be hardest on you," Marshall tried to soothe his partner as they drove away. Tony didn't answer as he dropped Marshall off at the station and then headed home. He had a very hard death notice to write before he tried to crash for the night.

The next morning an exhausted Tony met Seamus and Marshall at the school office after dropping the notice and article off at the paper, just in time to make the day's edition. The other two cops had already talked to the principal and arranged for the student assembly to be called, without telling him any more than they had an update on the search for Megan. Seamus nodded a greeting to Tony as he continued to talk to Delaney, ignoring the dark circles under Tony's eyes and the exhausted way the young cop stood. *If he doesn't get some sleep soon, I'm gonna have to call Jim again*, Seamus thought as he responded to a question from the principal.

"Talked to Nana last night," Tony said quietly as he and his partner headed towards the gym. The sea of students swirled around them, a few calling out greetings to the two popular cops, but most of them just leaving the partners alone as if they knew something was up.

"She set a date?" Marshall asked as he steadied a kid who had been bumped into his path. He kept trying to ignore how his partner looked, but, like Seamus, was becoming very concerned. An exhausted cop was a dead cop.

"Saturday. Three very long days from now." Tony looked around and spied Tom, Carl and the O'Reilly twins. "This is gonna kill 'em," Tony said softly, motioning to the four friends. Marshall nodded. *Not to mention what it's doing to me*, Tony thought miserably as he entered the gym and joined Delaney on the stage. *Will she ever forgive me? Will any of them?*

"Okay, settle down, people. Take your seats, please. Hurry up, now!" Delaney called over the microphone to the last few stragglers. Tony watched as the last three remaining Knights stood alone at the back of the gym. *Good,* he thought as he nodded to his partner. *They'll hear it right from me.* Marshall eased himself towards them.

"Okay, kids. Sorry for the interruption but we have a special guest today. Constable Whitefish is here to bring us up to date on the Megan Attison kidnapping. Constable," Mr. Delaney said and handed Tony the mike.

Tony sighed as he looked out over the crowd. Seamus was standing with his kids, his arm around Jordan's shoulder and waiting for the harsh words Tony was about to utter. Tony took a deep breath and began to speak. "Morning. Normally we don't do this, but because of how popular Megan Attison is, we wanted to let everyone know the search for her is continuing and we continue to explore several leads. However, Richard Attison, one of our original suspects, has now been eliminated. In the course of our investigation, we found Rick, late last night, dumped on a gravel road leading to Glencrest. He'd been badly beaten and stabbed several times. Despite the valiant effort of Dr. Jim Mason and the trauma team at the hospital, I'm personally sorry to announce Rick succumbed to his injuries and passed away last night."

Chapter 39

Heads turned as a horrified scream sliced through the stunned silence. Seamus struggled to hold Jordan, who screamed "NO!" over and over. Her reaction was worse than Tony had imagined. He watched as several Angels joined Seamus to help keep Jordan on her feet. Mickey just stood beside his family, his face a blank mask.

Tony wanted to tell her the truth, but as he watched the rest of the students, especially the Knights, he knew he was right. The Knights were all laughing and high-fiving each other, while some of the other students didn't seem too torn up at Rick's death, either. It took a lot for Tony and Marshall to let the Knights just boldly walk out of the gym. *This will work out,* Tony swore to himself. *It has to.*

"Understandably, Rick's family's asked for privacy right now, to deal with both Meg's disappearance and now Rick's death. For those of you who wish to attend, the funeral will be on Saturday. There'll be a private church ceremony, which some of his friends'll be asked to attend, followed by an open graveside ceremony, starting at 2:00 pm at the Attison Cemetery," Tony continued over the sobs and the angry muttering he began to hear from the students. The cop was pleasantly surprised to see there were many more students upset at Rick's loss than were happy about it. The school had come a long way, thanks to the Angels.

"His friends, especially the Grey Angels, can rest easy as this now, of course, removes Rick Attison from our list of suspects in Megan's kidnapping and we are actively investigating Rick's death as a homicide. I promise you, his attackers *will* be found," Tony finished ominously. He handed the microphone back to the principal. It was several long minutes before a stunned Mr. Delaney could speak.

"This is a deep shock for those who counted Richard as a friend," the principal finally said in a shaking voice. He took a deep breath before continuing. "For those of you who didn't, and we all know who you are, please have some sympathy for those who did. I won't tolerate any laughing or snide comments, especially to the O'Reillys. Leave 'em to make their peace with their loss. Understood? Good. Dismissed."

"Tony?" Mr. Delaney said, catching the young cop's arm, as the teachers began easing the stunned students out.

"Yes, sir?" Tony turned back.

"Is he really gone? How? Why?" The principal didn't bother to wipe the tears running down his face.

"I'm afraid so, sir. You really don't wanna know how. Hell, I saw him and I don't wanna think about how. It was bad, really bad. As for why, well, we're assuming he got too close to Meg's kidnappers, and paid the ultimate price for it. Somehow, that boy hid himself away and was doing his own investigating, I think. I just wish he'd told me what he knew. Now, it's too late," Tony said quietly. He looked out over the gym towards Jordan sobbing and struggling in her father's embrace. "Sir, if you'll excuse me. I need to be with them."

To get to the O'Reilly's, though, Tony had to pass Tom and some of the Grey Angels, most of whom were also in the boxing club. He stopped as soon as he heard the anger in their voices. "Fish might not know who killed the Champ, but we do, don't we, boys? Today, after class, we finish this. Eye for an eye," Carl said roughly, brushing away angry tears. The others nodded grimly.

"A wise man once said, 'When you embark on a path of revenge, first dig two graves,'" Tony interrupted gently. He had to end this before it got started or he'd be standing in a lot of blood.

"You telling us to just let this slide, man? You know who did this, Fish, don't tell us you don't, man. Dammit, he was one of us," Tom said hotly, tears pouring down his face. The others murmured agreement.

"Listen to me, all of you. Yes, we have a pretty good idea who did this, but *we have no proof!* And if you go after them, you'll end up in jail instead of them. Or worse. Dammit, Angels, I have to bury one boy already because of this mess. Don't make me bury any more," Tony said, his voice breaking, unable to hold back any longer.

He hung his head and finally let his own grief out. His shoulders shook and he fell heavily to his knees as great wrenching sobs were torn from him. Despite what he knew, he still felt he had failed both Rick and his friends. Rick was lying near death, Megan was still missing and the Knights had walked out, scot free. It wasn't fair!

As he cried, Tony felt the arms of several of the students wrap around him, offering their support, their murmured comments falling between his sobs. Several long minutes later, Tony drew a shuddering breath and raised his weary head. Around him, supporting *him* for a change, were Tom, Carl, Mickey, Jordan and to his surprise, Seamus.

"Feel better?" Seamus asked, offering a hand. Tony shook his head as he hauled his tall frame up.

"Hell no, boss. You know what he looked like last night. I couldn't cry last night, it wasn't real," Tony said as he dried his eyes. He looked at Jordan, and held open his arms. "Now, for some reason, it is and it just hit me. I'm sorry, sweets. They tried," Tony continued as he held the young teen. He gently wiped away the tears that still ran down her cheeks.

"Did you get to say good-bye to him at least?" she asked softly.

"No time, Jor. They rushed him straight into the operating room. They just couldn't replace the blood fast enough. Damn, I'm sorry, sweetheart. You didn't need to hear that," Tony said quickly, seeing how her face fell.

"C'mon, kids, time to go — off to class with ye now. Mickey, Jordan, wait a moment," Seamus said, shooing the others off. Tom hesitated until Tony gave him a small shove.

"Me son'll keep her safe enough fer right now, Tom, and we'll make sure she gets to class safely. Both of 'em," Seamus amended with a sad smile as the Angels reluctantly left.

"Dad, you really don't think Rick took Megan?" Mickey demanded as he gathered Jordan's book bag up. Jordan snorted. *Still the stubborn Irish fool,* she thought as she snatched her bag from him.

"Mickey, Jordan, I need to show ye something and ye won't like it," Seamus replied instead and pulled out a couple of photos. He handed them to his children. Jordan gasped and turned away, burying her face in Tony's shoulder. Mickey could only stare at the battered face. *That's Rick?* he thought, shocked, as he stared at the photos for a moment longer.

"That was taken shortly after he arrived at the hospital, son. Ye tell me, Mickey. Ye *really* think Rick took Megan? No, son. I can't. Not any more. Based on this beating, we think he found Megan, but died before he could tell us anything. Now we have to do it on our own," Seamus said as he took the photos back.

"She's still missing, then. Dammit, Dad, how much longer do we have to wait?" Mickey demanded harshly, turning away, his own fresh tears falling. Seamus grabbed his son roughly by the shoulders, turned him back to face him and stared at him, trying to make him understand.

"As long as it takes, son, but I promise ye, we will find her and ye'll have her back. Alright? Now go to class. And take care of yer sister. I'll see ye both at home later tonight. Oh, and Nana's asked for some space. We'll go over on Friday, not before," Seamus said and let his son go after a hard hug. He watched his children walk away, hoping this pain was worth it.

"That was hard, boss," Tony said finally as they joined Marshall outside.

"Just remember, this was yer idea. I don't like hurting her," Seamus growled.

"You think I do?" Tony snapped back. Seamus flushed in shame.

"No, of course not. Sorry, Tony. Now what?" Seamus wanted to know.

"You saw their reactions?" Tony asked as he opened his car door.

"We have, as of yet, to put the rest of them anywhere near her kidnap site or at Rick's beating," Seamus said as Tony and Marshall sat down. "All we have is Townsand."

Tony sighed. "Look, Seamus, I just wanna go and veg for the rest of the day. She's lasted this long – she'll hold on until tomorrow," Tony said as he rubbed his neck. It was stiff and sore and he was just exhausted. *At least I hope she'll hold on,* Tony thought as he continued to rub his neck.

"I'll have the techs process what was found with Rick and go over everything we have so far. We'll be ready fer Monday. Ye two need a break. Go home. Rest. Come back on Monday. This weekend's gonna be hard enough on ye," Seamus ordered and went to his car.

Stunned, Tony just sat in his car as he watched his boss pull away. "Did he just give us the next four days off?" Tony asked his equally stunned partner.

Marshall managed a dry chuckle. "Yep. I, for one, will enjoy it. You?"

Tony shrugged and Marshall just snorted with derision. They both knew Tony would spend his time working from home, instead of resting, trying everything he could to solve this case sooner rather than later and not caring if he collapsed again. "I'll be at Jim's for some of today. Then, when I get home, I'm gonna call my shaman, something I should've done a long time ago. I'm not the only one who could use a healing," Tony said as he guided the car back to the station.

He quickly cleared his desk and left some instructions for the crime scene techs regarding the evidence. "The Inspector, Marsh or myself're the only ones who see the results. No one else, no matter how much they beg or try to pull rank on you, understand? If you need me before Monday, I'll be on my cell. Clear?" Tony said.

The head tech hesitated, then nodded. "Is there a problem? With Jonesy?" he wanted to know.

Tony shook his head. "Nope. The boss just wants very limited exposure right now," he said on his way out.

Tony waited until after lunch before going to the townhouse across from the hospital. He sighed as he stared at the mainly darkened house, remembering all the planning and time he and Rick spent hunting for Megan before Rick had ended up a broken, bloody mess. *Where did it go so damned wrong? When?* Tony wondered as he climbed up the front stairs. Jim himself let the cop in before he could ring the doorbell.

"How's he doing, Doc?" Tony asked immediately.

"He's a bit stronger, Tony, and the bleeding's under better control, but I don't think it's quite stopped internally. His vitals keep fluctuating wildly. We're gonna operate again tomorrow to finish setting his broken bones, make sure we didn't miss anything and get the bleeding stopped finally," Jim said as they sat in the kitchen.

"I had to come and see him, Jim," Tony said slowly.

Jim looked at the young cop's face. "Was it bad?" Jim asked, kindly.

"Horrible, doc. It was the hardest lie I've ever told, and I've told a few. I had to stop the Angels from going head-hunting. I've never seen them so mad. Even Jor took it better than Tom and Carl," Tony said as silence fell.

"Tony, go and see him," Jim said after a couple of uneasy moments, motioning Tony towards the living room. "We've sterilized it to death, but I still need you to mask and gown up. The smallest infection'll kill him just as sure as the knife would right now," the doctor said and helped Tony to get dressed.

The respirator hissed rhythmically and Tony could see Rick's chest rise and lower in time. The beating looked even worse now that the bruising had started. He noticed the room was warmer than the rest of the house, thanks to a portable heater, so the sheets could be lowered away from the raw stab wounds.

Tony froze at the sight of Rick just lying there. It just wasn't the boy he knew. Where was his little brother? Where was the Champ? He had to force himself to walk over to the bed. He sat down next to his friend and gently took Rick's left hand in his. For the longest time he couldn't say a word. All he could do was stare at every wound, memorizing them. As he sat there, he vowed, by all he held dear, Blade would pay for each and every one.

"Well, little brother, we knew this could happen, didn't we? God, Rick, how'd you make it this far? What did you see that pissed Johnny off so damn much?" Tony asked, not expecting an answer.

He took a deep breath before continuing. "I'm sorry, son. I don't know what else to say, but I'm sorry. I promise you – I'll find Meg. You won't go through this for nothing. I swear it," Tony said as fresh tears began to fall. He lowered his head and just cried, his sobs echoing in the silent room.

Jim stood outside the door and watched Tony fall apart. *He's worn out again,* Jim thought. *How much longer's he gonna last before Seamus calls me again? He's been going too hard for too long.* It didn't take Tony long to stop crying and, oddly enough, he felt a bit better. As he dried his eyes, he felt his cell phone vibrate and reached to answer it.

"Answer it out here, Tony," Jim said, startling the cop.

"Answer for me, will ya', doc? I wanna say good-bye first," Tony said and tossed the phone over.

As Jim walked back to the kitchen, Tony turned back to Rick. He reached down and carefully squeezed the boy's left hand again. "You hold on, little brother. You hear me? You need to get better. Jor needs you. So does Meg and I won't let you die, either. You hear me, boy? So you hang on, understand?" Tony whispered and squeezed Rick's hand. Was it his imagination or did Rick squeeze back?

He quickly stripped off his gown and mask and joined Jim in the kitchen. "Yes, Nana, he's doing better. A little stronger, but still unconscious. No, ma'am, you may not. The bruising's started so he looks ten times worse than last night and you don't need to see that. Hang on, here he is," Jim finished and passed over the phone.

"Hey, Nana, how're you?" Tony asked as he sat down at the kitchen table, nodding his thanks as Jim set a cup of strong coffee in front of him.

"Better than you, I hear. Seamus called and said this morning was bad," Nana said sympathetically.

"It was the hardest thing I've ever had to do, Nana. After her initial reaction, Jor seemed okay with it. It was the Angels who were the most upset. They wanted to go head-hunting," Tony said dryly, after taking a couple of sips of the coffee. He winced at how strong it was.

"I take it you managed to stop them," Nana said, horrified.

"All it took was asking them not to make me bury two boys. One was bad enough. How're things going for Saturday?" he asked hesitantly as he continued to sip at his coffee.

"Okay, I guess. I've figured out how to do this. Rick was so badly injured I've decided to have him cremated," Nana choked a bit on the words. "I've told the pastor at the church what's happening, after swearing him to silence, and he's agreed to help out by not filing the actual funeral documents with the government. Rick won't legally be dead. It'll just be a farewell ceremony, not a funeral."

"Good idea, Nana," Tony approved.

"I'm gonna need your help for the honorary pallbearers, though. I just don't know…," her voice trailed off.

"Tom, Carl, Marsh, me and Coach Bob. You could ask Frank or Mick for the last one. Personally, I'd go for Frank before Mick, but that's up to you," Tony advised. Jim tapped the cop on the shoulder and motioned to himself. "Actually, Nana, Jim said he'd be the sixth. I'd still ask Frank and Mick, though," Tony said.

"Thanks, Tony. I'll give everyone a call tonight and ask them. But that's actually not why I called. I got home today and there was a message on my machine. Listen," Nana said and snapped on the answering machine, holding the phone close.

"Well, thanks to the cops and the newspaper, I know Moneyman's dead. Good. One more outta the game. I also know he didn't talk or the cops woulda been all over me. Ya want Megs back? In one piece? Bring the six million in a plain black briefcase Saturday night to the Pitts. Be there by midnight.

"But I don't trust any of ya. I don't want anyone but yer son, Michael, to bring me my money. No wires. No cops. Just Michael. Ya don't do this – Megs dies." The message ended and Nana snapped off the machine.

Tony's mind worked furiously. *Why this way? Why Michael?* he wondered.

"Tony?" Nana asked, interrupting the cop's thoughts.

"Nana, I need that tape. Can you get it to me? Or should I stop by?" Tony asked.

"Stop by, lad. I'll give you the tape and a good meal. I have to ask, though. Does any of this strike you as odd?" Nana asked.

"Every word on that tape's odd," Tony snorted. "The biggest question is why Michael? How's he connected with this mess all of a sudden?"

"Mendez, maybe?" Nana suggested.

"Anything's possible, Nana," Tony sighed. "Listen, I'll be over there shortly. Don't let Ian get a hold of that tape. He'll go crazy if he hears it," Tony said and hung up.

"What's up, Tony?" Jim asked as he poured the cop another cup of coffee.

"Ransom demands for Meg. They said they saw it in the paper," Tony said.

Jim nodded and handed Tony the paper. There, on the front page, was the story of the "murder" of Rick. Tony could only stare. Despite having written the article and the death notice, it was still hard to read about it. It was hard to imagine the battered face shown in the paper was really Rick's.

"Tony, go see Nana, then go home. You've worn yourself out taking care of that boy in there. You need to take care of yourself. I'd give you some sleeping pills if I thought you'd take the damn things," Jim said dryly. Tony shook his head. He had taken sleeping pills before, and he hated how they made him feel out of it for more than just overnight.

"Thanks, Jim, but no thanks. I'm gone," Tony said as he left.

"Hmph. Stubborn fool," Jim said as the door closed. The doctor sighed and went to check on his patient, trying to figure out what he was going to do with a very stubborn cop who was fading faster than the boy lying in the hospital bed.

Chapter 40

As Tony tried to figure out why Michael was suddenly involved in all of this, Blade was on his way to speak to that very same person. The Knight was very proud of how things had progressed since Brain had been arrested. He was getting his money and Moneyman was gone. All in all, life was good.

As he sauntered into East Side's he could see Michael sitting at his favourite table, nursing a drink. He watched Greg, the bartender, go over with a plate and an "I'm so sorry," look on his face. Blade just sat back and enjoyed. From the look on Michael's face, he hadn't seen a paper or heard a news report. Blade chuckled as Michael raised his voice.

"What the hell do you mean, Rick's dead?!" he demanded loudly.

"Last night, man. I thought...I thought you knew. Everyone else in town does," Greg stammered.

"I've been outta town for the last week. The last thing I'd heard about my son was Megan had disappeared and he was the prime suspect, but he'd vanished as well. Dead?" Michael asked again, stunned. Greg nodded and dropped the newspaper on the table beside Michael's supper.

"I'm sorry," he said again as he walked away, leaving Michael to grab the paper and devour the story instead of his supper.

Michael could only stare in shock at the picture of his son. He really didn't care for the boy, but he didn't want him dead, either. *Christ, he took a hell of beating,* Michael thought as he slugged back his drink and waived for another. He wondered who had done this and why his mother hadn't bothered to call.

"'Lo, Michael," Blade said quietly, dropping into a chair on the other side of Michael's table.

"What the hell've you done, boy?" Michael snapped, realizing now who hated his son enough to beat him this bad.

"He'd tracked me down, and I took care of the problem," Blade said with a shrug, not really caring what Michael thought.

"You took care of the "problem?" Rick wasn't a "problem" until you made him one," Michael snapped loudly as he poked Blade roughly in the chest.

Blade glared and batted Michael's hand away. "Like ya care, and lower yer damn voice."

"I may not've given a damn about the boy, but I sure as hell didn't want him dead. I don't ever recall asking you to "take care of him"," Michael said hotly.

"Worried this'll be traced to ya?"

"Damn straight."

"Don't worry. After Saturday, yer'll have yer money. Yer gonna pay me and my boys and Mendez, and then I suggest ya take a vacation. A very long vacation," Blade said quietly.

"If nothing can be traced to me, why should I leave?" Michael pointed out logically.

"'Cause no matter what happens, yer always gonna be a suspect, even if there's nuthin' to tie it to ya. Once word hits the streets Mendez's been paid, in full, and right after Megs has been paid for, yer life won't be worth spit. Take my advice – sell yer house and business and disappear Saturday night."

"How're you gonna get the money out of wherever?" Michael asked as he quickly made plans. He noticed Blade never said anything about returning Megan at all, let alone alive, and Michael was suddenly worried Blade meant to finish her off. That also told him Blade wasn't joking about getting out of town quickly and quietly. *No one's gonna miss me,* Michael decided.

"Simple. Yer not gonna take it in."

"I thought I made it very clear I wasn't to be involved."

"Yeah, but this way, ya get yer money, less my share, and I don't have to track ya down to give ya yer split."

"You had no intention of giving me my money, did you, Johnny?" Michael asked wryly as he downed another rye and finally dug into his rapidly cooling supper.

"Not really," Blade admitted. "But, then I figured if I didn't, you'd rat me out just to save yer hide from Mendez."

"So, just how does this plan of yours work?" Michael asked. As Blade outlined his latest idea, Michael just nodded. It'd be easy. He'd be gone by early Sunday morning.

"This is the last time we talk, Michael. Don't double cross me," Blade threatened as he stood.

"After what you did to my son?" Michael pointed out dryly as his phone rang.

Blade just walked away. Despite his cocky attitude, he was worried. The cops said Rick hadn't talked, but Mendez's boy on Tony's team couldn't be positive. He was suddenly out of the loop. He didn't even know what evidence had been recovered.

She's gotta be moved, Blade decided suddenly as he arrived back at his house. He entered the kitchen Crank and Pup were scrubbing down once more.

"Aunt Marian called and said not to wait up," Pup said as he dumped his pail of water down the sink. "She's going out after work."

"She say anythin'?" Blade asked as he sat down.

"She saw the paper this morning and asked if he's one of our friends. I couldn't lie. I told her yes," Pup said, distracted as he wrung out the mop.

"What now, Blade?" Crank asked, leaning against the counter.

"We're gettin' our money on Saturday, but I'm worried. What'd Moneyman say 'fore he croaked? No one knows nuthin', not even Mendez. Dammit, why ain't Brain here when I need him?" Blade snarled suddenly and slammed his fist down on the table.

"'Cause someone, somewhere, got sloppy. We'll just have to make do," Pup reasoned.

"Why're ya worried, man? The cops said he bit it 'fore he could say a word," Crank pointed out as he got a drink.

"So they say, Crank, so they say, but no one's seen the body since Moneyman arrived at the hospital," Blade said. "Mendez couldn't find out anything from his snitch neither."

"Makes sense, man. His obit says he's been cremated. Won't be a body for anyone to see. So wha'cha wanna do?" Crank asked again.

"Move 'er," Blade said shortly. Crank coughed as his swallow of pop went down wrong.

"Where, man? Brain's in jail and I don't have a basement," Crank said after getting his coughing under control. His mouth was suddenly dry as he realized what Blade wanted to do.

"No, but ya still have that room over the garage," Blade said slyly, looking at Crank.

"Yeah, and I live in it most days. My folks'll wonder when I move back into the house," Crank pointed out as calmly as he could. Meanwhile, his brain was screaming this was a very bad idea.

"Since Pup and I'll be staying with ya for a few days and that room ain't big enough fer one person, let alone three, they won't even blink. I'll tell 'em the house's bein' painted and my old lady won't let us stay here. Poor Pup's lungs, y'know. We'll hafta wait 'til they go ta work in the mornin', though. I don't want 'em ta see Megs," Blade said sharply.

"Move her now, then, if ya have ta. Mom's at Bingo and Dad's out fer the week," Crank said. Inside he was cringing. This was a very bad idea. His parents would freak when they found out, and Crank just knew they'd find out somehow.

Besides, after what he had seen earlier in the day, he didn't think Megan was strong enough to be moved. She was so sick and the whole plan Brain had come up with was going south in a hurry. Blade was right – where the hell was Brain when they needed him?

Earlier that afternoon, Pup had gone down to the basement to check on Megan, something they could only do when Blade wasn't in the house, and had flown back up the stairs, panicking and white. "She ain't breathing, Crank," the young boy had cried.

Shaking his head and thinking Pup was overreacting, Crank followed Pup back downstairs and could only stare in shock at

Megan. She was white and indeed it looked like she had stopped breathing. He could see the blood on the pillow and the thin blanket thrown over her didn't do much to cut the damp cold of the basement. Not very big to begin with, Megan was now rail thin. *What the hell happened to her in less than a month?* he wondered as he stared at Megan.

Suddenly, she gasped and started to cough. She shook and thrashed as she struggled to breathe. Helping her to sit up seemed to ease some of the spasms, and knowing Blade hadn't fed her in who knew how long, Crank sent Pup to make some soup. Megan was so weak she could hardly hold her head up to get even that little bit of food in her.

What the hell was he going to do? He didn't want Megan at his house. There'd be no way to keep his parents out of the garage and they'd hear Megan coughing for sure, because the walls weren't that thick. He didn't want to go against his best friend, but knowing Blade wanted to move her, Crank had a serious dilemma.

Snapping out of his thoughts, Crank turned to Blade. "I'm not sure about this, man. Have ya looked at her lately? She's dying," Crank said hesitantly. "I don't think she'd survive."

"No way," Blade scoffed.

"We checked on her this afternoon while ya were gone, and I'd swear she'd stopped breathin' fer a few minutes. There's blood on her pillow, a lotta blood. Blade, she ain't good, man," Pup said earnestly.

Blade sat there for a couple more minutes, trying to digest what the other two were telling him. He spied the article in the paper about Rick and wondered what the one for Megan would say.

"Well, if she's dyin', we could always just finish 'er off," Blade said nonchalantly. Crank and Pup looked at him like he had grown another head.

"Get real, Blade. All I'm saying's I don't think we can move her. She's too sick," Crank said angrily.

"Sucks to be ya, don't it, Crank? Get some more blankets while Pup packs our gear," Blade ordered. Crank hesitated for a long moment, and stared at Blade, who shouted "MOVE!" Crank shrugged and did as he had been ordered.

Once everything was loaded, Blade led the way back down to where he held Megan. *Crap, they're right – she don't look good,* Blade realized. Then he thought about his money and knew he was going to do whatever he needed to. He wanted his money too badly to lose it now just because one little girl was sick. Besides, he never said he was going to give Megan back – alive or dead.

Megan was slumped over awkwardly on her left side and her breath rattled in her chest, but she was awake. She tried to focus but her vision was so blurry all she could determine was someone was there. She gave a small cry as Blade snapped the overhead light on.

"Well, well, well, Megs. Looks like yer not feeling too good. Little sick? Huh? Answer me," Blade snapped harshly and smacked Megan across the back of her head.

She couldn't control a cry of surprise and a cough at the attack. Megan sobbed weakly at the sudden pain. "Water, please, Johnny," she croaked. She licked her cracked lips and tried again to focus.

"Don't think so, Megs, and since yer so sick, maybe I should just finish ya off. Y'know, like I did Moneyman," Blade said idly and slid his knife out of its sheath.

"Rick? What do you mean?" she whispered, paling even more. *What's going on now? What's happened to Rick?* she wondered.

Blade pulled out the paper and flipped it open to the obituary, struggling to read the words clearly. "It is with extreme sadness we announce the sudden passing of our beloved grandson and nephew, Richard Donald Attison, at the tender age of 17. His passing leaves a large hole in our family. He was predeceased by his grandfather and aunt and leaves behind to mourn his passing his Nana, father Michael, mother Kara, brother Nelson, uncle Ian, cousin Megan, and many friends, too many to list individually.

"A private funeral service will be held for family and select friends at Sacred Heart Church on Saturday at 1:00 p.m. An open graveside service will be held at 2:00 p.m. at the Attison Family Cemetery. In lieu of flowers, donations may be made to the Moneyman Foundation Scholarship, a program for graduating students of the youth centre's boxing club so they may continue their training and education."

"No accusations without proof." Blade finished reading and snapped the paper closed while Megan sobbed quietly. Now, she knew who had been upstairs the other day and what her cousin had gone through, just to find her.

Blade laughed at Megan. "Aw, poor Moneyman, huh, Megs? So wha'cha think, boys? Should we give 'em two to bury?" Blade asked and suddenly plunged his knife deep into Megan's left shoulder. He had moved so quickly no one had a chance to react. Megan just stared up at him in shock, too shocked to even whimper.

"Christ, Blade, what the hell're ya doing?" Crank yelled and jerked the knife out. He grabbed the blanket up and pressed it against the rapidly bleeding wound.

"Leave it," Blade said indifferently, as he cleaned his steel.

"Like hell! Ya want her dead before we get two feet out the door?" Crank snapped back.

"It don't matter. Look," and Blade shoved Crank away to stab Megan several more times, though not as deep as the first one.

"What did I ever do to you, Johnny?" Megan whispered as she slipped into unconsciousness. Crank jumped to his feet and threw Blade against the wall, hoping beyond hope Megan wasn't already dead.

"Pup, water, bandages, towels. Move!" Crank snapped.

"Just get the bleeding stopped. We've gotta get moving," Blade said as Pup dashed upstairs.

"What the hell do ya think I'm tryin' ta do, ya bloody idiot? Ya killed 'er," Crank said furiously as he tried to staunch the bleeding.

"So what?" Blade was nonchalant. Crank struggled to control his temper. *Do not hit him,* Crank told himself over and over again. *You'll end up just like Moneyman.*

"We was to give her back after we got our money," Crank reminded Blade as he pressed on the bleeding shoulder.

"Yeah, right, Crank. Now, who's bein' the idiot? Think about it, man. She's seen us. She knows who went after her and Jor, and she knows damn well it wasn't Moneyman. How long do ya think we'll enjoy our money if she goes home alive?" Blade pointed out dryly.

"What about Brain? How're we gonna get him out? Mendez?" Crank asked as Pup skittered to a stop and thrust the first aid kit at Crank, who bent to his work.

"Tough. He's been arrested. Nothing we can do now. Finished?" Blade demanded, brushing aside Crank's concern.

"Gimme a couple of minutes. These're damn deep." Glaring at Blade, Crank returned to his work, for once thanking his dad for making him take an advanced first aid course. He quickly bandaged the shallower cuts, but the one in the shoulder refused to stop bleeding. Eventually, he managed to get the bleeding to slow by actually sticking a couple of face cloths over it and taping them down tight. He just hoped it would hold.

He reached back and grabbed Blade's steel to slice the ropes holding Megan, not liking how she just fell over. Silently he handed the knife back and gathered Megan up in the warmer blankets. He still couldn't believe how much weight the young girl had lost in the last month.

"I'm gonna tell ya this once, Johnny, ya lay off, y'hear? No more slicing. I didn't agree to this so ya could kill two people. I just wanted some easy money and to have a little fun with Moneyman," Crank said over his shoulder.

"Johnny? What the hell?" Blade snarled. *When did I lose it?* he wondered.

Crank shook his head. *Of all things for him to worry about, it's his friggin' name,* Crank thought. "Forget it, Blade. Just lay off, alright? I won't rat ya out, but ya can't kill her," the teen said hotly and carried Megan upstairs.

"Leave it," Blade ordered shortly as Pup moved to clean up the basement. As his cousin nodded and moved past him, Blade grabbed him.

"Ya still loyal, Mark?" he hissed.

"Yers fer life, Blade," Pup assured him and sauntered up the stairs, trying not to show Blade how scared he really was.

Crank had Megan settled in the back seat when the other two Knights came out the door. "Pup, in the back with her. Blade, up front," Crank ordered as he opened the driver's door.

"Yer giving orders now, Crank?" Blade said softly as he slammed Crank backwards into the car.

"If it protects my investment, damn straight. So either get in, sit down and shut up, or stay here and explain that basement to yer old lady," Crank growled, not the least bit scared of Blade at that moment.

With an answering growl, Blade shoved Crank again and stormed around the car. He slammed the door and just sat there, steaming. He didn't say another word as Crank navigated the traffic and pulled up in front of the garage.

He climbed out of the car while Pup helped Crank get Megan through the messy garage and up a set of narrow stairs. "Open the blinds for a second, would ya, Pup?" Crank ordered as he laid Megan on the bed. She whimpered and turned her head away from the sudden light.

"She's bad, ain't she, Crank?" Pup asked as he tucked the blankets around Megan. The young girl was shivering despite the layers of blankets and the warmth of the room.

"Yeah she is, Pup. I don't think she's gonna live. It's gonna be bad enough ta go down for one murder, let alone two. Damn him anyway. I've never seen him this obsessed. He's got no intention of givin' 'er back — alive or dead," Crank said sourly as he moistened a cloth and pressed it to Megan's lips. Even as unconscious as she seemed, she drank greedily. Crank remoistened the cloth and just left it lying on her lips so she could drink whenever she needed to.

"Let's go. He's gonna be in a state by now. Someone's gonna have to stay here, other than Blade, that is, to take care of 'er, no matter how much Delaney wants us in school," Crank said. Pup just nodded. He paused with his hand on the door and looked back at the motionless body on the bed. *What the he'll've ya done, Johnny?* Pup wondered as he slowly closed the door and joined Crank and Blade in the house.

Their leader was waiting in the living room. He was steaming mad at Crank's highhanded tactics, but he now knew what he was up against. He had forgotten how stubborn Crank could be when he wanted something, and it seemed like Crank wanted the money.

Not Blade. He wanted the money, but he also wanted Moneyman out of the way. Couldn't have one without the other, Blade knew. *Think about the money,* he thought as he cracked a beer and settled down to watch T.V. *It's all about the money.*

Chapter 41

Despite being given four days off, Tony couldn't rest. Something told him if he waited until Monday, it would be too late for Megan, so he decided to check out an untapped source – the street kids Rick had talked about many times during their sessions.

He pulled up in front of Mahoney's convenience store and stared at the group of kids in front. *I hope I know what I'm doing,* he thought sourly as he climbed out of the car. He whistled the specific sequence Rick had taught him, and watched as one tall, lanky boy pulled himself away from his friends.

"You Jimmy?" Tony asked as the boy got closer.

"Depends on who's asking – the cop or Moneyman's friend?" Jimmy replied, as if he knew exactly who Tony was. But then Tony had counted on that.

"Both," Tony replied shortly. Jimmy nodded and looked back at the rest of the boys outside the store. No one seemed concerned, so he turned back to the cop.

"Word's out he's gone. That true?" Jimmy asked as he leaned against the car and took a drag on his bottle of pop. Tony nodded as he leaned against the car, too.

"Yeah, dammit. I need some help and he suggested I talk to you if I ever needed help. Any word on Blade? The Knights?" Tony asked and slipped the kid $40. Jimmy didn't say anything for a few minutes as he weighed what he knew and what he had figured the cop already knew.

"Not much and all bad. Word is Brain had something on Elijah and that's why he's split. Somethin' 'bout a married chick and some video. They say Brain made 'im give 'em somethin' ta help take the girl," Jimmy said as he pocketed the money.

- 329 -

"So far, not really news. We figured that part out when Elijah did his vanishing act," Tony said wryly. "What else?" *C'mon, kid, give me something to work with*, Tony begged silently.

"Parta this is 'bout Mendez. Wants the Knights ta be his, I guess," Jimmy continued with a shrug.

"Okay, that's new, but it doesn't help me find Meg," Tony pointed out, making a note to check up on Mendez's organization again.

"Can't help you there, cop. Yet. Ain't nobody seen or heard nuthin' from Blade since Moneyman kicked off. Tell ya this much, man. Blade better get his mind back on the Knights or this is town's gonna be a mess. Slayers want revenge fer whut the Knights dun ta Ricardo las' summer, and the Hit Squad're just pissed – but they ain't talkin'," Jimmy said, turning to leave.

Tony shook his head. Not what the cop needed to hear, not right now. Seamus was going to freak if the gangs went at it. "Hey, Jimmy?" Tony called. The teen turned back and stopped. "What would it take for you to call me if you find out where Blade's holed up?" Tony asked, handing the kid a card.

Jimmy cocked his head to the side, considering Tony's offer. "You ain't got enough, cop. Not if I wanna live. You want Blade? Really want him? Talk ta that idiot you got on ice," Jimmy said and walked back to his friends, pocketing Tony's card with a wink.

Smart kid, Tony thought as he drove home. There, he put a quick call into the crime lab to check on the progress of the evidence, specifically the tape from Nana's.

"Sorry, Tony, but I can't isolate anything of interest. I just don't have the right equipment. We *could* send it to the lab in the city, but I've heard you're looking at a three-month wait, *minimum*, no matter how critical the case and I don't think we can wait that long," the tech said with a sigh. *Now what?* Tony thought several times over the next couple of days before Rick's "funeral".

Saturday, Tony woke to the smell of strong coffee and frying bacon. He could hear some soft chanting in the kitchen and he smiled. *Everything's gonna be okay now,* he knew. Pulling on his jeans, he went to talk to his visitor.

"Runningbear, how'd you get in?" Tony grinned at his shaman and poured himself a coffee. Just seeing his shaman made Tony feel up to facing the crappy day this was going to be.

Runningbear snorted good-naturedly as he continued to make breakfast. "Don't gimme a key if you don't want me walking in when you invite me, Whitefish," the elder native said with an answering grin as he buttered some toast.

"I know, shaman, I know," Tony laughed uneasily as he sat down and took the plate Runningbear handed to him. It was loaded with bacon, eggs, and toast. They ate in friendly silence, Tony already beginning to relax.

"I talked to your doctor friend," Runningbear said suddenly, making Tony jump. The shaman noted the reaction and just nodded to himself.

"And? Will he allow it?" Tony asked as he calmed his pounding heart.

"With a couple of changes that aren't important, yes, but not until Monday," the shaman replied. "But if you don't mind me saying, my son, you look like hell. You should've called me sooner. Why didn't you come home?" the shaman asked pointedly.

Tony turned away from the piercing gaze of his shaman and sighed. He had wondered how long it was going to be before Runningbear brought this up and had hoped it would be longer than this. "No time, shaman. I've been trying to find one who's lost and protect another before he goes to the Creator. The rest of my kids're just as worn out as I am and I couldn't just leave them to indulge myself," Tony replied quietly, but defensively.

"Healing yourself so you can help others is *not* being self-indulgent, Small Fry," Runningbear said softly, calling Tony by his childhood nickname.

Tony smiled. "Would you object to healing a couple more?" he asked as he cleaned up, trying hard not to think about what Runningbear was saying.

"One or three, the ceremony's the same," Runningbear said with a shrug. He knew he had to leave Tony alone, for now. The seeds had been planted and it would only take some careful watering to make them grow. The shaman stood up and brushed the crumbs off of his hands. "I'll be outside preparing."

By the time the church service was done, Tony was ready for the day to be over and it had really only just begun. His nerves were shot and the stress was overwhelming. He didn't remember anything from the church other than holding Jordan while she cried, so Seamus could give what comfort he could to his son, who finally seemed to understand how important Rick had become to all of them. Nana wasn't much better, leaning on Ian's strength. No one held Tony up, and all Tony really wanted to do was forget.

At the graveside ceremony, Tony was pleasantly shocked at the number of people who had gathered. Rick had come to mean something to a lot more people than even Tony had realized. The Angels were there in force, of course, all wearing black armbands with both "Moneyman & Rick" stitched on them. They were still so angry, Tony could tell and the young cop just didn't know how to help them anymore.

Nana stepped up and placed the urn with Rick's "ashes" in it in the hole with a small sigh. "Goodbye, lad," was all that she said, tears streaming down her face. She returned to Ian's embrace, trying to find some comfort.

One by one his friends and family stood up to the grave and said their goodbyes. Some said a few quiet words. Some could say nothing, including Marshall and Seamus. Each of the Angels, some openly weeping, others stoic, placed their armbands on and around the headstone. But it was Jordan and Mickey who brought everyone to tears.

Jordan knelt by the headstone with a small box in her hand. In it, Tony knew, was the guardian angel she had given Rick at Christmas. Tony, as promised, had given it back to her when Rick had "died." She opened the box, took out the necklace and hung it over the urn. "Good-bye, love. Here's an angel to guard you in death, as you guarded me in life. I'll miss you, and I promise not to forget you, but somehow, I'll find the strength to go on without you. There'll never be any more accusations without proof," she said through the sobs. A general murmur of agreement went through the crowd.

As she stood up, Mickey joined her, wrapping an arm around her shoulders. "I'm sorry, Rick. For everything. I know it's too late to say it to your face, but I really am sorry. Please, forgive me," the young man said, a few tears falling down his cheeks. Soon, Tony knew, he'd be able to say that in person. *Once Meg's safe*, Tony vowed.

Tony, by his own request, was the last to speak. As he stepped up to say his good-byes, a sudden cry shattered the grave silence. Startled, Tony looked up to see Black Eagle circle lower and lower, finally landing on Rick's tombstone. He cocked his head this way and that, almost as if he wondered what was going on, then gave a soft, sad cry, one that tore at Tony's heart.

Oblivious to everyone watching, Tony reached up and scratched the eagle's head. "I know, old boy, I know how much it hurts. But we tried, didn't we? No one can say we didn't. So it's okay, isn't it? We can let him go, huh?" Tony asked. The bald eagle chirped in agreement and dropped a feather into Tony's hand.

"Good-bye, little brother. Swift flight to the Creator," Tony said brokenly as he laid the feather in the grave beside the urn and stepped back. With another cry, Black Eagle launched himself away. With that, everyone began to move towards their cars to head back to Glencrest for refreshments and to remember Rick.

"Tony?" Nana said, touching his shoulder.

He turned away from watching the eagle disappear and smiled sadly. "Go home and rest, lad. It's been a long enough day," Nana said, giving him a hug.

"You really don't mind me cutting out?" Tony asked. Nana shook her head. "Thanks, Nana. My shaman's here and he's gonna do a Healing Ceremony on me," Tony continued as he escorted Nana to the waiting limo where Ian stood. He didn't have to say what Nana already knew – he needed this badly.

"Not at all, lad, not at all. You shoo and take some time for yourself," she said as she climbed in. Tony closed the door and then looked around quickly for the twins.

"Jor! Mick! Hold up a sec, will ya?" Tony called, sprinting over to them as they were getting ready to climb into their limo.

"Hey, Tony, that was just beautiful," Jordan said sadly, wiping away another tear.

"You too, sweets, but someone forgot to tell Black Eagle he wasn't invited," Tony said lightly. He was pleased when they all laughed. "Listen, how would you two like to come to my place instead of Nana's? I have something there that might help you both," Tony said.

"Daddy?" Jordan was clearly torn.

"Listen, ye two, ye've had enough of everyone saying, "I'm sorry." I know what Tony's got going on at his house and I think you'll like it. Go, we'll talk later. I'll be interested to know how things turn out," Seamus said with a smile and sent them on their way.

"Tony, is that...smoke coming from your house?" Jordan asked ten minutes later as they pulled up in front of Tony's two-storey house.

"Hope not, sweets. Unless Runningbear forgot to unplug the coffee pot this morning," Tony laughed as he got out of the car.

"Runningbear? Who's that?" Jordan asked nervously.

"My shaman, sweets. He's come to help me out and I thought he could help you two as well," Tony said. He led the way around back where Mickey and Jordan saw the smoke was actually drifting gently away from a full-size teepee.

Jordan hesitated as Tony opened the flap of the teepee and motioned the twins inside. Strangers, especially adults, had always bothered her a little bit and she never really knew why. She wasn't sure about any of this.

A disembodied voice came from inside. "Healing takes many forms, little one. Will you not take the opportunity to lay down some of your heartache?"

"It's only a Healing Ceremony, Jor, a chance to dump your problems on the Spirits who, thankfully, have much larger shoulders than we do," Tony encouraged. "Trust me, Jor. Like always. I won't ever hurt you."

Visibly steeling herself, Jordan ducked her head, stepped into the dim light of the teepee, and gasped. All around were masks, dream catchers, drums and weavings. Everywhere she looked, Jordan saw Tony's heritage, mostly made by his own hands. A part of his past they knew nothing about.

"Wow!" was all Mickey managed as he, too, paused to look around. The artwork was incredible. He reached up to run a finger along one of the dream catchers and studied the detail in the weaving.

"Amazing, isn't it? He's very talented." Runningbear stepped out of the shadows and faced Tony and the twins. He was older than Tony, of course, his brown face starting to wrinkle. His midnight black hair was untouched by any grey and pulled into two braids, hanging down his back. He was shorter and more slender than Tony, but then he didn't need Tony's bulk to do his job. He wore buckskin breeches but no shirt. When he shook his head, Jordan could hear small bells jingling. None of that mattered when his eyes caught and held her attention. They were dark, foreboding and piercing – endless pools she could easily drown in.

Until he smiled, that is; then his eyes gleamed. He nodded to Tony who reached up behind Mickey to grab a drum. "Thank you, Whitefish. You were right to bring them. They need me, too. Come, everyone. Let's begin."

The shaman led the way to the fire dancing in the middle of the teepee. The little bit of smoke the fire made drifted up through the opening at the top. He settled Jordan and Mickey across from each other on hand-woven rugs, with Tony across from where Runningbear would stand. "Comfortable?" he asked all three as he took his spot.

At their murmured assents, he stood and softly began to chant. At the end, he threw some herbs into the fire. There was more smoke, not unpleasant, but unexpected nonetheless and Jordan sneezed several times.

Runningbear chuckled. "Sorry, my daughter. An unfortunate side effect if you aren't used to the herbs. Now, children, breathe deep. That's it. Deep and slow. Relax and focus on the flames. See how they dance. How they flicker. Breathe deep." The shaman continued for several moments, his voice low and soothing.

He watched as all three settled more comfortably on their rugs. Tony was the easiest of all to settle. After all, he'd done this many times before. Runningbear was more worried about the twins. He had no idea how the native herbs would affect them. Some white men handled them just fine – others, not so well.

He moved to check on them. Jordan was clearly relaxed, focused on the fire, her breathing deep and easy. Mickey, on the other hand, was fighting.

"Why do you fight, my son? The herbs're to help you relax, nothing more," Runningbear asked as he squatted beside the young man.

"I'm scared," Mickey finally admitted in a low voice. "Tony's told me about the vision quests he's been on and I just don't know about this."

"Relax, son," Runningbear said again. "This is a Healing Ceremony, not a quest. You may see things in the flames or you may not. Either way, don't worry. That's not the purpose for today."

"Trust me, Mick, just breathe deep and relax," Tony said in a slightly dazed voice. The shaman moved back to his spot and began to drum softly.

Tony continued, his voice almost slurred. "When he begins, you won't understand the words. They're Cree, but it doesn't matter. Just listen to the rhythm of the drum and the words. Make your heartbeat match, if you can. As he drums, he's asking the Spirits to come help us," Tony said.

"How, Tony?" Jordan asked, in just as dreamy a voice as Tony.

"Imagine your cares and heartaches're like the smoke, sweets. Just let them drift away." Tony's voice faded as he fell silent.

Runningbear began to strike the drum harder and spoke as he settled into the rhythm he needed. "I don't care if you're black, white, or red. Everyone hurts and everyone needs to heal. I've found over the years, for most, the traditional form works best, but for Whitefish, for some reason it never has. This is a special ceremony I created for him alone several years ago, and I think it's gonna do wonders for both of you.

"Like I said before, as you look in the flames, you may see things. You may not. It doesn't matter. Listen to the drumming with your heart as well as your ears," Runningbear said as he increased the volume of the drumming and began to chant again.

For the longest time, Jordan sat with her eyes closed, listening to the rhythm and did as the shaman suggested. She just wished her cares away, although she couldn't help but think about Rick. Her chest tightened, but she was so tired of crying. Sighing, she finally opened her eyes and, there, in the flames, she saw Rick.

He was wearing the last thing she remembered, from the day Megan disappeared. The dark blue, button-front shirt was opened at the neck and she could see the Guardian Angel necklace gleaming at this throat. His face shone and there were no scars marring his handsome appearance. He smiled at her and Jordan could swear he was trying to tell her something.

"Oh Rick, I miss you so much," she said softly and couldn't stop the tears this time. Over her sobs, she could hear a hiss as Runningbear threw something into the fire.

The pressure in her chest was easing as were her tears and she suddenly felt at peace. "Feel better, little one?" Runningbear asked as he stood beside her. Something in his voice compelled Jordan to look at him.

As she raised her head, Jordan could see Mickey, laying on his side, breathing deeply. Out of the corner of her eye, she could see Tony swaying in time to music only he could hear, his lips moving in a silent chant and his gaze fixed firmly on the flickering flames. She pulled her gaze back to Mickey, yet didn't feel concerned as she finally looked into those dark pools of Runningbear's eyes.

"Rest easy, Jordan. Your brother only sleeps, healing body and spirit as he does, and Whitefish seems to be questing, seeking *his* answers in the Spirit World, as I figured he would. You, on the other hand, need some special healing. Your heart's so weary and your spirit's almost broken. You have faced more than your brother," the shaman said, stating it as a fact, rather than asking.

"I'm lonely, Runningbear. I miss him so much," Jordan said softly.

Runningbear didn't move for a couple of minutes, trying to decide the best course of healing for her. *Smudging'll help*, he decided and lit some herbs in a bowl in front of him. Softly he began to chant again and gathered the smoke in his hands to spread it over her.

It was several long minutes before he set the bowl aside and looked at the young girl in front of him. *She's nearly ready*, he decided. Her eyes were almost closed and she swayed gently to the beat of the chant he had just finished. When Runningbear finally spoke, it was softly. "You should miss him, my daughter. He was your soul mate. The other half of your spirit. It was why you were always ready to fight for him. You'll see him soon, I promise. Now, you need to heal. Sleep, little one." With that, Runningbear reached over and touched her forehead. With a gentle push and a sigh from Jordan, she collapsed into a deep sleep.

Nice to know those herbs still work, the shaman thought as he threw some light blankets over the twins against the cool night air. *Rest is all they really need to heal.* He then turned to Tony. *Unlike this stubborn fool who waited way too long.*

Tony continued to chant soundlessly and sway in time to the silent drums heard only in his head. He stared into the fire and Runningbear could see the sheen of sweat on Tony's forehead and the tears running down his face. Whatever the young native saw or sought was clearly upsetting him. It was time to end this.

"Look at me, Whitefish," the shaman ordered quietly, touching Tony on the shoulder.

Tony couldn't pull his gaze from the fire. "Yes, Runningbear?" he breathed.

"Do you see the past, present or future?" the shaman asked as he resumed drumming softly. There was obviously something Tony needed to talk about before the shaman could finish healing his young friend. After all, that was what he was here for.

"All three. I see him as I did the first time, dressed in black and silver, tall, arrogant, defiant. And asking for help, even though he didn't really know that's what he wanted," Tony began quietly.

"The past, then," Runningbear said, unconcerned, changing the rhythm.

Tony nodded as he continued. "It changes. He's in his blue jeans and a cowboy shirt, dressed the way he was when Meg disappeared, but it shifts, quickly. Now, he's just lying at my feet, battered. Broken. Dead," Tony said, tears flowing freely. *I'm sorry, little brother* was all that ran through Tony's head as he stared at the flames.

"The present, then. But Whitefish, you know he's not dead. He lives," Runningbear pointed out. "What of the future, my son?"

"He's standing there, reaching towards me, trying to tell me something. I can't hear him, but he continues to try. The only thing he doesn't do is accuse me. He's smiling. Happy. At peace. Unlike me," Tony finished, hanging his head in shame.

"Look at me, Whitefish," Runningbear commanded again. Slowly, Tony lifted his head to face his mentor. The drums continued softly, in a pattern Tony didn't recognize and Runningbear swayed in time. There was something so compelling about the movements Tony couldn't help but follow.

"You asked me to come and heal you. Are you healing, my son?" Runningbear asked, knowing the answer.

"No, shaman. There's no time. I just can't. It hurts too much," Tony breathed again, his eyes never moving from Runningbear's. *What's happening to me? This isn't right. I know this isn't right,* he wondered wildly as he continued to listen to the drums. He couldn't move. He couldn't think. All he could do was stare into Runningbear's endless black eyes and follow the shaman's swaying movements.

"Who heals the healer, my son? They're counting on you," Runningbear said softly. He dropped to his knees suddenly and reached for the smouldering bowl beside them. He knew Tony needed to heal, but, thanks to a lengthy talk with both Jim and

Seamus, Runningbear also knew Tony needed sleep more than anything else.

Tony didn't blink as the shaman moved. He sighed as Runningbear began to smudge him, the smoke and words cascading over him. The white sage assailed his senses as he continued to sway to the drums in his head.

Suddenly, Tony felt something snap inside and realized what hurt the most. "I failed, Runningbear! I failed!" Tony cried suddenly.

"How so, Whitefish?" Runningbear asked calmly, continuing to smudge the cop.

"I failed to keep him safe. Now he's almost dead and I can't help him anymore. She's lost and I can't find her. They're all hurting so bad and I can't help them. I've nothing left to give," Tony said, his voice breaking yet again, tears falling unchecked down his cheeks.

"Why didn't you ask for help?" the shaman asked calmly. "I would've come." The shaman put the smudging bowl aside and picked up the drum again.

"There was no time, Runningbear. I couldn't take the time. I had to find her or they'd both be lost. I couldn't and now I've failed," Tony whispered as he stared at Runningbear and began to move in time to the drumming again.

"You haven't failed, Whitefish. You took a scared, wild young man, befriended him and tamed him. You taught him how to think of others and how to love. You've become brother, father, friend and teacher to him," Runningbear said. He tossed another handful of herbs into the fire. Tony inhaled deeply and relaxed even more, once again recognizing the ceremony.

"But you've given too much of yourself. You have nothing left. You forgot to take time for yourself. You forgot to heal. You need to heal, Whitefish," Runningbear chided softly as he ceased drumming and laid the drum aside. *Ask me, Tony,* the shaman urged silently. *Unlike them, I can't help you unless you ask. That was the way you always wanted this.*

Tony hesitated for a long time. He knew Runningbear's ceremony would be finished while he slept, but it meant giving up his hard-earned control. Tony continued to sway and hesitate.

Finally, unable to bear it any longer, he looked at his shaman. "Help me, Runningbear," Tony begged. Swiftly the shaman reached across to touch Tony's forehead, but Tony stopped him.

"Will you be here later?" Tony asked, sounding like a scared little boy, instead of the confident cop.

"Of course, Whitefish, as always. Now sleep, my son. Sleep and let me heal you." With that, Tony let the shaman go. He watched as Runningbear gently touched his forehead and with a sigh, Tony let himself fall into darkness.

Chapter 42

Tony slowly climbed out of the deepest and most relaxing sleep he'd ever had to an insistent tugging on his hair. He reached up and felt feathers. He chuckled and batted playfully at the bird's beak.

"Enough, Black Eagle, leave me alone. I'm awake," Tony said with another laugh and sat up. He took stock of how he felt and knew Runningbear's ceremony had worked. How long it would last was anyone's guess, but it had worked for now. Standing and stretching, Tony swiftly tidied up the few things that had been left out and went to find the others.

Jordan and Mickey were sitting at the dining room table talking quietly with Marshall. "Afternoon, Sleeping Beauty," Marshall greeted his partner with a grin.

Tony stopped short. "Afternoon? Sunday afternoon?" he asked, horrified.

"You needed to heal, Whitefish. That's what you asked me to come here and do," Runningbear said as he came in from the kitchen. He handed Tony a cup of coffee.

"Dammit, Runningbear, you knew I needed to be at the Pitts last night. I needed to be there," Tony repeated heatedly.

"Do not snap at me, Tony Whitefish. I did what you asked for. You needed to heal more than you needed to go on another useless search," Runningbear snapped back.

Tony was stunned. His shaman never lost his temper, no matter how hard he was pushed. Tony knew then how much the triple ceremony had taken out of his shaman.

"Fish, relax. You weren't needed. It was more important you got some damn rest. You tend to push yourself until you collapse," Marshall said dryly.

Tony sighed. They were right. "Sorry, Runningbear. You too, Marsh. I *did* need this more," Tony apologized.

"Enough, my son. I understand," Runningbear said, dismissing the apology with a wave. He settled down with his coffee.

"Jor, Mick. How do you feel?" Tony asked as he dug into the food Runningbear had put in front of him.

Jordan smiled the first real smile Tony had seen on her face in a long time. "Rested. At peace," she said, fingering a necklace Tony hadn't seen before, but figured Runningbear had given her. It looked like a Dreamcatcher done in her favourite colours. He did recognize the style and whispered a soft prayer of thanks to his mother.

Mickey nodded. "Me too. Thanks, Tony. So what do we do now?"

"We continue to look for Meg and who attacked Rick. You two go on with your lives as best as you can and if you ever wanna do this again, just let me know. I'll call in the cavalry," Tony said with a smile and a nod towards Runningbear, who also smiled at the twins.

"There's a cop outside to take you two home," Marshall said and shooed the twins away.

"What happened?" Tony demanded as soon as they were alone.

"I'll tell you on one condition – you don't lose your temper. Agreed?" Marshall asked. At Tony's reluctant nod, Marshall continued. "Just before midnight last night, Michael walked into The Pitts, with the money in a briefcase. Ten minutes later, he left the briefcase and walked out. We didn't take our eyes off that case, and by two, I figured something was wrong. So we opened the case, and it was empty," Marshall said, disgusted.

"And Michael?" Tony wanted to know.

"You won't believe me," Marshall said with a shake of his head.

"Try me," Tony said dryly. "Nothing 'bout this mess surprises me anymore."

- 343 -

"He was gone this morning when we went to talk to him. He's sold his house, sold his business to a junior partner, paid Mendez off, deposited the money from the house and business into Rick's account and dropped off the face of the earth," Marshall said as he sat back.

Tony blinked in astonishment. "Okay. That surprised me," he laughed.

"Like Mickey said, *now* what do we do? The only real evidence we have's against Brian Townsand and we're no closer to finding Megan than we were yesterday," Marshall said soberly.

"Right now, we do nothing. I want Runningbear to see Rick first. We need him to tell us what he knows, if he can. We need to finish processing all of the evidence and see where it might lead us. We also have to push Townsand. We need him to crack and soon. Meg ain't gonna last long now that they have their money," Tony said.

"Do you plan on telling Seamus about hiding Rick now?" Marshall asked as he sipped another coffee.

"Think I should?" Tony asked, a little worried.

"Well, Seamus doesn't blame Rick anymore, so now's probably the best time to tell him. Before it comes out at trial," Marshall pointed out.

"Whitefish, you have to remember to spread the weight around. That's why you're so run down," Runningbear jumped in suddenly.

Tony sighed. Runningbear and Marshall were right. Seamus needed to know. He reached for the phone and dialled Seamus. His boss answered on the second ring. "O'Reilly," he answered, distracted by the traffic.

"Seamus, it's Tony."

"Tony, how're ye feeling? Yer shaman help?" Seamus asked as he manoeuvred around a slower moving car.

"Better, boss. Centred. Definitely more rested and at peace," Tony said softly. "I need to talk. Where're you?"

"Heading to Glencrest. Nana wanted to do some brainstorming now that the funeral is out of the way. Wha'cha need?" Seamus asked as he negotiated the corner.

"Marsh and I'll meet you at Glencrest," Tony replied instead.

Seamus pulled up in front of Nana's house before saying anything else. "Tony Whitefish, do not take that tone with me. Now, what's wrong?" he asked bluntly.

Tony hesitated. "Something that needs to be discussed face to face, boss," Tony said finally.

Seamus snorted. "Okay, then. Suit yerself. See ye shortly."

Tony hung up and looked at his partner. "Gimme half an hour to clean up and we'll go see the boss," Tony said as he stood.

He stood under the pounding water for more than ten minutes, letting the water wash away the rest of his worries and cares. Thanks to Runningbear, Tony felt better and more focused than the young cop had been since before his first session with Rick, but he knew it wouldn't last. Marshall was right – he pushed himself until he collapsed. It wasn't the first time and probably wouldn't be the last.

He jumped out, dried off and dressed in comfortable jeans and a t-shirt. He grabbed his jacket, gun and badge on his way downstairs. Marshall chuckled at the transformation in his partner. Gone was the worry and exhaustion. Before him stood the old confident Tony Whitefish. Too bad everyone knew it wasn't going to last.

"Ready, Fish?" Marshall asked, brushing that worry away. He'd cross that bridge when he came to it, because he knew he'll be right there with his best friend.

"More than ever. Don't wait up, Runningbear," Tony replied on his way out.

The partners drove to Glencrest, chatting about anything but the case. That would come soon enough. For now, they focused on everything else. They pulled up in front of Rick's house and saw Nana and Seamus walking towards them.

"Afternoon, Seamus, Nana," Tony greeted them.

"Afternoon, lad. You look better," Nana said as they climbed the stairs and opened the door to Rick's house.

"We thought it'd be better to talk in here. Ian can't overhear us then," Seamus explained at Tony's questioning look. "It's all clear."

"Now, what was so all-fired important that ye had to track me down?" the inspector continued as they settled in the living room.

Tony continued to hesitate. He knew how much trouble he would be in when he told his tale. At least he was proud of what he did. "Lemme ask you a question first, Seamus. Do you believe Rick did any of this? The letters? The calls? The attacks? The kidnapping? Any of it?" Tony finally asked. He stood with his back to the room and stared out the window.

Seamus sighed as he shook his head. "Like I told me son, I can't. Not anymore. I know he hid himself away after Megan disappeared and he had to have help to do it, but no. I don't believe he had anything to do with this. He's too badly beaten to have done this. He found out something and it cost him," the elder cop said without any hesitation.

"Tony, what is it?" Nana asked when she noticed Tony hesitating.

"You're right, Seamus. Rick did have help hiding from you. Me. I helped him," Tony said as he finally turned to face his boss.

Seamus shot to his feet, his face mottled in anger. "Ye what?! I told ye not to cross me, boy!" he thundered.

"Dammit, Seamus! I did it to save Meg! At least hear me out before you call the damn firing squad!" Tony shouted back. Without any hesitation, Tony plunged into his story. He detailed everything from hiding Rick away at Jim's to how he had subtly manipulated the investigation away from Rick and towards another suspect.

"Did ye plant that vial so I'd look another direction?" Seamus demanded.

"Get real, Seamus. I told you once before I wouldn't create evidence to help you convict Rick. So how the hell can you think I'd

- 346 -

create evidence to acquit him? That's not me and I thought that wasn't you, either," Tony snapped back and continued his story.

For more than an hour, Tony talked and through it all, Seamus just stood in front of his best constable with his arms folded and a scowl on his face. Once Tony fell silent, Seamus hung his head and sighed mightily.

"Damn, Tony. Do ye know much trouble ye could be in if this ever got out? If Regimental found out?" Seamus finally demanded, his anger long gone.

"At best, I'd only lose my job. At worst, I'd be arrested and charged, probably with obstruction and aiding and abetting. If it helps solve this mess, then it'd be worth it. So yes, boss, I've thought about it," Tony said.

"Yet you still went ahead and did it. Why, Tony?" Nana asked in the silence.

"I did it for Rick. I've always believed him. You know that, Nana," Tony said firmly.

Seamus couldn't speak for the longest time. What Tony had done violated almost every rule in the book and yet, Seamus was slowly beginning to understand why. Still, he had to ask. "Why did ye wait so long to tell me?"

"Because until I had evidence, good, hard evidence pointing to someone else, you couldn't be trusted to do a proper investigation. You'd've focused on Rick and stopped. Now we have another strong suspect sitting on ice. Now, it's safe to tell you," Tony replied hotly.

Seamus could only nod. "Ye're right, Tony," Seamus said, shocking both of his cops. "I probably would've just focused solely on the boy and got Megan killed. Now, with what we have against Townsand, even I have to admit the boy's been framed," Seamus said roughly. Tony wanted to cheer, but he knew how much that cost his boss to admit.

"The boy has a name, boss. It's Rick," Marshall pointed out quietly. Seamus just chuckled.

"Look, Seamus, what's done's done. I can't change it, but we can move on. Now, Nana, have you heard from Michael or the kidnappers?" Tony asked, taking control of the investigation once again as he finally sat down in Rick's favourite chair.

"No. Should I have?" Nana asked, puzzled.

"Well, yes," Tony replied, just as puzzled.

"We've paid the ransom, and by now, they should've called with instructions for the exchange," Seamus explained. His heart sunk as he realized what this meant. Megan wasn't going to be returned.

Nana sighed. "Nothing. I should've known it was too easy. Damn," she said, softly yet with venom, and resigned to the fact that Megan was still missing. "But why would Michael have called? He's been kicked out of the family," she pointed out.

"I know I saw him at the funeral, and I know he took the money for the payoff, but yeah, boys, why would he phone?" Seamus asked, as puzzled and angry as Nana.

"Sorry, boss, but we didn't wanna tell you last night. The money's gone, right from under our noses. I'm pretty sure Michael never even took it in," Marshall explained and tossed a photo in front of Nana.

"What's that?" she asked, even more puzzled.

"The case you gave Michael the money in," the cop replied, now as puzzled as Nana.

"No, it's not. Mine was plain black with gold latches. Not silver. And no initials. That's the case I gave Michael years ago when he opened his brokerage," Nana said. Her heart was sinking rapidly. Somehow, some way, her son was involved in this.

"What else happened?" Seamus asked, beginning to figure out where this conversation was heading.

"Michael's gone. The house has been sold and the money put into Rick's bank account. The office sold to one of his partners, and closed until the transfer can be completed, with instructions to put the money in Rick's account. And…." Marshall hesitated.

"And?" Seamus growled, liking less and less where Marshall was heading.

"Word is Mendez has been paid. In full. When we went to talk to Michael, he was gone and no one knows where. Nana?" Marshall asked. Nana was frozen, but only for a moment.

She reached for her cell. "Gerry? Megan Attison. Thank you. Really? That's great. It'll really help out those boys. Listen, I need you to do me a favour regarding Michael. Freeze it. All of it. You heard me. All of Michael's accounts, credit cards, assets. All of it. I should still have power of attorney, and even if I don't, with Rick's gone and Nelson out of the country, I'm still his mother. Thank you." She snapped the phone closed and looked at the three men.

"Now, once the money in his hand's gone, he'll have nothing," she said ruthlessly. "And the way he gambles, it won't take long. Then he'll be forced to get a job and you can find him and haul his sorry carcass back to face me," she snapped.

"Remind me never to make you mad," Tony said, stunned at her swift response.

"My son's dead to me. Dead and gone. He obviously set this up," Nana said, jumping to conclusions.

"That's possible, Nana, but we have no proof. For now, let's focus on Megan and Rick," Seamus said. Tony hid a smile. Rick's name had just come out of Seamus' mouth and he didn't even think about it.

"Do you have any idea where he might've gone?" Marshall asked again.

"Michael? No, but if it was me, I'd get out of the country," Nana said with finality, dismissing Michael once and for all.

"Now what, Seamus? It's your call," Tony said, deferring to his boss and not even caring they were discussing an open case in front of a civilian. Nana knew things around Collingwood and often had good suggestions on how to do things.

"Until Rick comes to and can tell us what he knows, we're at a bit of a standstill. Marshall, any word on Elijah?" Seamus asked.

"No. No one knows where he is. There's been nothing on the street, either. No one bragging about taking him out. Sorry, boss, but I think we've seen the last of him," Marshall declared.

"Chicken," Tony snorted. Seamus just nodded.

"Tony, tell the doc to move Rick back to the hospital. Marshall, I want ye in that room with him. I'll send a rookie to guard the door. I think we fooled the kidnappers with Rick's funeral, but let's not take any chances. I want him protected, but he needs to be where the doc can take care of him properly," Seamus said.

"Done. I'll take Kelsey," Marshall said, naming a young cop who had just graduated from the Academy.

"Good choice. Tony, get to the station and press Townsand. I want him singing as soon as possible. Now that they have their money, there's no reason to keep her alive," Seamus continued as Tony nodded. He thought he knew how to break the kid.

"What about Ian and myself?" Nana asked as they stood to leave.

"Pray, Nana. Pray we find her soon," Seamus said ominously.

Chapter 43

Tony took Runningbear to see Rick Monday morning, before heading to work. The shaman and Tony had talked long into the night, as Tony wanted to catch up on with family and friends who still lived on the reserve. Thanks to Runningbear's stories, Tony's sleep was easy and dreamless.

"Morning, Kelsey," Tony greeted the young cop outside Rick's hospital room.

"Morning, sir. Who's with you, sir?" Kelsey asked, blocking the door. The rookie took his job very seriously.

"My shaman, Runningbear," Tony explained without a smile. "Jim's expecting him."

The young cop checked a clipboard at his side and then nodded. He opened the door and waved the pair inside. Marshall looked up from his book and smiled.

"How's he doing?" Tony asked quietly.

"Better, Fish. Doc says the bones're all set now and the bleeding's finally under control," Marshall said, nodding a greeting to Runningbear.

"You said he was bad, Whitefish, but I didn't expect this," Runningbear said, shocked.

"Can you really help?" Tony asked his shaman.

"I won't know until I try. But you have things to do, Whitefish. I don't need you here," the shaman said, dismissing Tony as he began setting up.

"Fish, what's he doing?" Marshall asked as he watched.

"A Healing Ceremony, Marsh. It's not the traditional Cree ceremony you've seen before on the reserve. It's created just for me, so enjoy," Tony said as he left.

He met Jim in the hall. "Tony, your shaman's here?" Jim asked.

Faintly the sound of drumming came from inside the room. "Yeah. No, Jim, don't," Tony said, catching the doctor's arm as Jim moved to enter the room. "You'll distract Runningbear now that he's started. A ceremony like this can be very hard to regain the rhythm of if it's interrupted."

"How long will he be?" Jim wanted to know.

"As long as it takes, Doc. Mine probably lasted a couple of hours before I finally collapsed," Tony shrugged and left before Jim could ask any more questions.

Once back at the station, Tony met up with the crime scene technicians to go over the evidence in the whole case. Photos of each piece were spread out on the table in the interrogation room. Tony arranged things to his satisfaction, then called to have Brain brought up.

The normally impeccably-dressed Brain was rumpled; he needed a shave almost as much as he needed a shower. The teen stumbled and almost fell into his chair. Tony chuckled and Brain growled in response. The teen hadn't slept well or much since being arrested.

Reminds me of Rick after his first night in jail, and this kid's been here more than a week, Tony thought, as he waved his thanks to the two cops who had brought Brain. Tony pulled out a tape recorder and snapped it on.

"Morning, Brian. Or would you prefer Brain?" Tony asked politely.

"Whatever," Brain said as he slouched. *Man, I'm beat. Gotta be careful,* he thought as he rubbed his face. Tony took note of the movement, but said nothing.

"Brian, I wanna be clear before we move on. I know you've waived your rights but you can have a lawyer or a parent present during questioning. Are you sure that you don't want one? I mean, really sure?" Tony said mildly, not wanting this interrogation to be thrown out at the trials. There was no way Tony was going to be accused of denying the Black Knight his rights.

"Nope. Don't wanna call my folks. My old man'll save ya a helluva lotta trouble. He'll kill me just fer gettin' arrested. And since I ain't talkin', I don't need a lawyer," Brain said sharply.

"Just remember you can stop this at anytime, then. Now, I just have a few questions for you," Tony said, his tone still mild.

"Told ya I ain't talkin'. I know what ya want. Ya want me to rat my boys out an' say they took Megs," Brain snapped back. "Tough, cop. Ain't happenin'. Everyone knows Moneyman did it." Tony didn't respond. He simply verified Brain's name, known aliases, date of birth and address. Then, he paused, waiting several long minutes until Brain was fidgeting in his chair, before he finally began the interrogation.

"Brian, where were you on the Friday two weeks after Thanksgiving when Jordan O'Reilly was attacked at Colonial High?" Tony asked.

"Chillin' with my crew," Brain said with a shrug.

"I didn't ask you what you were doing, Brian. I asked you where you were," Tony snorted impatiently.

"No where near where the chick was hit. We were at the pool hall all afternoon," Brain lied smoothly. "Just like almost every afternoon."

"Fair enough," Tony said as he made a couple of notes. He waited a few more minutes before continuing.

"How about Remembrance Day? The first time Megan Attison was attacked near Glencrest Ranch? Where were you that day?" Tony asked. He looked at Brain and noticed a faint sheen of sweat on the kid's face.

"Dad's ex-army. He dragged me to the cenotaph," Brain drawled. He stretched his legs out in front of him then stretched the rest of his body as best he could in the uncomfortable chair.

"Anyone verify that? Other than family, that is," Tony asked, making more notes. *Break, damn you, break*, Tony thought angrily. *They don't have time for these games.*

"Lotsa old guys, but I don't know any names," Brain shrugged. *So far, so good,* he thought as he rubbed his face again.

"When'd the program end?" Tony pounced quickly. Having been there himself, Tony knew exactly when it ended.

"About 3," Brain said. Tony made some quick calculations. The cenotaph was in the cemetery by the edge of town, but on the opposite side from Glencrest. Since Tony knew the service had ended around 11:30 and the luncheon had ended at 3 p.m., he also knew would leave plenty of time for Brain to get across town and get to Glencrest in time to attack Megan, since she was attacked at around 4 p.m., just as dusk was beginning to fall. Only Brain would know for sure. Tony knew he needed to keep pushing and digging.

"Plenty of time to get to Glencrest and attack Megan," Tony pointed out.

"Cop, yer crazy. Everyone knows Moneyman whacked both girls. Ya can't pin nuthin' on me or my boys," Brain said with a short bark of laughter.

Tony shook his head, amazed at Brain's stubbornness. He tried a different tactic. "Y'know, for someone who claims he's not a Black Knight, you sure do act like one. I mean, look at you. You're wearing the gear. I know one kid who was damn near killed just for wearing a coat that *slightly* resembled the one you're wearing.

"You call Rick Moneyman and only another gang member does that on a regular basis. Everyone else uses it as a sign of fear and respect. I've seen you hanging with Blade and Crank and I know for a fact the three of you beat Rick up at least once, since I caught you doing it. Now, do you *still* wanna deny you're part of the gang?" Tony asked dryly.

"Fine. Ya want me t' admit it? Yes, I'm a Knight an' damn proud of it. Ya happy?" Brain said aggressively.

"Just wanted to set the record straight," Tony said with a grin. "Tell me, Brain, why won't Blade let Rick go?" Tony asked, switching to Brain's street name. "Why does he want the kid back so bloody badly? What is it about Rick Attison Blade just can't bear to be without?" He was really interested in the Black Knight's response.

"No one ever leaves, man. Once yer in, yer a Knight fer life," Brain said, sitting up proudly. "Moneyman knew that when he

- 354 -

joined. Blade made it very clear. Moneyman jus' needs to be shown the errors of his ways," Brain said with a shrug as he sat back.

Hardly believing the opening just handed to him, Tony pulled a few photos out of a file and laid them in front of Brain. "I wanna know something, Brain. Is this how Blade shows someone the 'error' of their ways?" Tony asked quietly. "Look at them!" he ordered sharply when Brain didn't move.

Without moving, Brain just glanced at the pictures and shrugged. "They're of some punk. So what, man?" he drawled, wondering where the cop was going with all of this.

"Take a good look at them," Tony ordered again.

With a growl, Brain sat up and looked at the photos. Tony watched the teen pale, then flush in anger. *What the hell've ya done, Blade?* Brain babbled to himself. *Ya ruined everything!*

"That's what was left of Rick *after* someone got through with him. The only person I know of who hates him that much is Blade." Pausing, Tony lowered his voice. "He didn't make it," Tony growled, finally venting some of the anger he felt towards the Knights.

"What the hell do you mean, he didn't make it?" Brain said hoarsely, dropping all pretence of being a gang member.

"Just what I said. He died on the table. I buried that boy on Saturday. Now, that same day, we paid the ransom for Megan and we haven't got her back. You see my problem, boy? I wanna know where the hell Megan is!" Tony yelled, jumping to his feet and slamming his hands on the table.

Brain just sat there, stunned at what he saw and heard. Rick was dead, Blade had been paid off, Megan hadn't been returned and Brain was left holding the bag. Tony tossed several more photos on the table and pointed to them, one after another. "This is the writing on the wall near where Megan was taken. Recognize it? You should. It's yours, confirmed by your English teacher, Mr. Robson," Tony said quietly, back in control of himself and the situation.

"This vial was stolen from the family clinic a couple of days after you saw Dr. Jim and talked to him about sedatives for your little sister. He's confirmed you asked about this specific vial. This is the print we pulled off of it," Tony said, pointing to a third photo.

"Can't prove it's mine," Brain said quickly.

"Actually, I can. Remember this pop can? I had wiped it clean before we talked that day at the school. These're my prints. This is yours," Tony said as he continued to point to photos.

"Based on this alone, I have a search warrant for your house. Guess your parents're about to find out you've been arrested and charged," Tony continued.

"Charged? With...with what?" Brain stammered, his poise rapidly disappearing.

"Assault and Battery, Assault and Battery with a deadly weapon, Break and Enter, Possession of Stolen Property, Possession of a Firearm Underage, Possession of an Illegal Firearm, Uttering Threats, Kidnapping, Harassment, Stalking, Destruction of Private Property for the fire at the school and Conspiracy to commit the above crimes. I'm pretty sure if I try hard enough I can also include Destruction of Private Property for the neighbourhood park Rick was accused of wrecking. And even though I know you were in my jail when Rick was attacked, I'm very tempted to see if I could pin a Murder charge on you. Now, where is Megan Attison?" Tony snarled, resisting the urge to grab the arrogant punk in front of him.

"Y'ain't gettin' 'nother word outta me," Brain said, suddenly stubborn.

They sat there for several minutes while Tony tried to figure out what was going on in Brain's frightened mind. "What do you get outta this gang?" Tony asked finally.

"Something ya'd never understand, cop," Brain said shortly.

"Try me," Tony advised.

"Loyalty. Friendship. Respect," Brain said softly, his eyes focused on the wall. He couldn't bring himself to rat his boys out.

"Loyalty? Brian, look around. Do you see anyone else in this room, another Knight? If they're so damn loyal, why're they letting you take the fall for this?" Tony said, pouncing on that first word.

Brain sat there, struggling to understand what had gone so horribly wrong. How could Blade have killed Moneyman? Why hadn't he given Megan back? That was the plan, even though she had seen them. *What had gone so wrong?* Brain wondered again.

"Brian?" Tony said quietly.

"Forget it! I'm not sayin' 'nother word," Brain said and slumped back in his chair.

Tony sighed, staring at the stubborn kid. As he gathered up the pictures and turned to leave, he paused. Looking over his shoulder, he thought for a moment and then spoke softly.

"Brian?"

"What?" the Knight snarled.

"Just keep this in mind as you sit in that jail cell alone. If Megan dies, you could've saved her. Think on it," Tony said as he left the room.

"Take him back to his cell, then make sure he gets a lawyer," Tony said as he passed the two cops at the door. They nodded, grabbed Brain, and locked the door behind them.

Tony sat at his desk and just stared into space. He had failed Megan yet again. He was no closer to finding her than he was before talking to Brain. *Now what?* Tony wondered. He was running out of ideas.

"Hey, Fish?" Jones interrupted Tony's musing.

Tony snapped the file closed before Jones could see anything. "Yeah?"

"Boss wants to see you," Jones said, as he tried to look at what Tony knew.

"Thanks," Tony replied shortly. He gathered up all of the evidence and took it to Seamus' office. He ignored the frustrated look on the other cop's face.

"Yeah, boss?" Tony said as he sat down across from his boss, but left the door open.

"Jones see anything?" Seamus wanted to know immediately as Tony handed over the evidence folder.

"Don't think so, but you never know. Before you ask, Townsand didn't say a thing we didn't already know," Tony said, disgusted.

"Campbell? Get in here!" Seamus barked into the intercom.

"Yes, Inspector?" Tony didn't recognize the cop who stuck his head in the door.

Seamus handed the other cop a folded piece of paper. "Take Benson and Spicoli over to Brian Townsand's house and execute this warrant. Don't forget the crime scene techs," Seamus called as the cop left the office.

"Close the door, Tony," Seamus said quietly.

Tony shut the door and sat back down. He couldn't help the sudden dead feeling in the pit of his stomach.

"What's happened, Seamus?" Tony asked. *Please let him be okay*, Tony prayed.

"Jim called. While ye were talking to Townsand," Seamus began.

"Boss, please. Is Rick okay?" Tony begged.

"He opened his eyes and started breathing on his own," Seamus grinned suddenly.

"He's okay!" Tony said, giddy with relief.

"No, Tony, we both know he's not okay and he won't be. Not fer a long time, but he's awake. Do you wanna go see him?" Seamus asked kindly.

"Hell yes!" Tony said, wiping the tears from his eyes.

"Tony, when can we tell Jordan?" Seamus asked. He was glad Rick was awake, but he really wanted to give Jordan some good news for a change.

"Not yet. I'm sorry, boss, but until we have Meg back, she can't know," Tony said as the inspector's face fell.

"Make it soon, Tony. Make it soon," Seamus said as they got to their feet. He locked the info away in his safe, just in case.

"Jones, Tony and I need to go out. We're on our cells," Seamus said as they walked by the cop's desk.

Jones nodded. He waited until Seamus and Tony walked out before picking up the phone and dialling a number.

"Yeah, it's me. They've just left. No, they still won't tell me anything, but I don't think the kid's really dead. O'Reilly got a call from the hospital and said something about it was good he was awake. Okay, man, I'll try, but you'd better warn them," he said and hung up.

Seamus sighed a couple of minutes later and hung up. "He made the call. Dammit, I really wanted to be wrong about him," he said sadly.

"Problem is, boss, we've nothing on him," Tony said with a shrug. "All he's really done's call Mendez and warned him we've left. He's done nothing wrong," Tony pointed out.

"I'll put him on the night desk after this is all done. That'll keep him out of trouble," Seamus growled.

Tony didn't want to think about Jones being Mendez's mole. He was one of the longest serving cops on the force, and had been Tony's first partner until Marshall and he had meshed so well together. Now Tony wondered what had made the cop turn on everything the badge stood for.

The two cops pulled up to the hospital and parked beside Nana's truck. She had just arrived with Ian, looking happier than she had been in a while. She hugged Tony and whispered, "I can't believe he's awake."

"Come on, Nana. Let's go see him," Tony grinned back.

Once they got up to ICU, though, they had to wait while Jim ran some more tests on Rick. Impatient, Tony paced in the V.I.P. lounge, anxious to see his young friend. Seamus let him pace for a couple of more minutes, then finally had enough of hearing Tony's car keys jingle with every step he took.

"Tony Whitefish, will ye *please* sit down?" Seamus snapped good-naturedly.

"Sorry, boss," Tony said sheepishly and sat down. He couldn't keep his fingers still, though, as they began to tap Runningbear's drumming rhythm on the arm of the couch. He just didn't want to wait any longer.

Fortunately, they only had to wait a few more minutes. Jim came in with Runningbear who looked tired, but content. Tony jumped up and got his shaman a cup of coffee.

"Thanks, Whitefish," he said as he sipped.

"How is he?" Nana asked Jim.

"Better, Nana. He's still really weak, but he's awake and asked for you right away, Tony," the doctor said.

"Whoa! Hold on here! What do you mean he's awake? Who's awake?" Ian demanded roughly as everyone started towards the door.

Turning back to face Megan's dad, Tony hesitated for a long moment. "Rick," he said finally.

"Like hell! I helped my mother bury him two days ago, Tony," Ian snapped.

"I'm sorry, lad. It was necessary to save Rick's life. We wanted – no, needed – to keep him safe until he woke up and could tell us what he knew," Nana apologized.

"It was almost as necessary as Tony hiding him away after Megan disappeared," Seamus said distractedly. Tony groaned at his boss' careless remark.

Ian was stunned. *Tony had done what?* He couldn't believe what he had just heard. The very idea Tony had hidden away the prime suspect in his daughter's kidnapping instead of looking for her was enough to make Ian see red. What was worse was Seamus seemed to be okay with it.

"I don't believe this!" Ian snapped in the awkward silence.

"What's the matter, son?" Nana asked, puzzled.

"Rick, Rick, Rick. This is all about Rick. All he's done since Megan and I arrived at Glencrest is cause trouble. Now your own man has admitted to hiding him away instead of looking for my daughter! Everyone remember her?" Ian continued harshly, not caring about the hurt look on Tony's face. "Young thing. Spitting image of my mother. Been missing for over a month now? Oh wait! Lemme guess. Tony's had her hidden away, just so the rest of us could be worried sick. Tell me something, Tony? Did you enjoy Mother's money?" he demanded sarcastically.

"Ian," Nana protested, shocked at her son's accusations.

Seamus stood up and towered over Ian, despite being almost equal in height. "Don't ye *ever* accuse me men of not doing their job! I may have screwed up in the past when it came to Rick, but Tony and Marshall've always been focused on finding Megan. I swore to ye I'd find yer daughter, Ian and I meant it. She means as much to me as she does to you. She loves me son and that makes her precious to me. Me boys have worked double and triple shifts, to the point where Tony's collapsed more than once at his desk from sheer exhaustion. Think about the lie he's had to tell to me daughter and to Rick's friends? How hard do ye think that was for him? Screw ye, Ian, I won't let ye get away with this," Seamus said angrily.

"Ian, I know you hate me right now, and you've got the right, but I want you to understand something. I did what I did in the hopes of finding your daughter. We just couldn't do that if Rick was sitting in jail," Tony said softly.

"Why not?" Ian asked belligerently.

"Because I wouldn't've let them and ye know it. Rick would've been me sole focus and I would've twisted the evidence to fit him," Seamus said softly, finally admitting what he had done, much to everyone's relief.

"Believe it or not, Ian, we're pretty sure who has Meg. It's the same guy who beat the crap out of Rick. Trust me, he wouldn't be this bad off if he didn't know something," Tony said.

"Problem is we just don't have the evidence to bring him in and we don't know where Megan is. Please, just let us do our job and trust us," Seamus said and motioned for the others to follow.

"Hold on, folks," Jim said, holding up his hands and standing in front of the door.

"What now, Jim?" Nana asked, impatient to see her grandson again.

"Lemme make something very clear right now. That boy's extremely weak. One wrong move could undo all the healing that's been done up to now. If he talks, fine, but *do not* push him. I will *not* hesitate to order everyone out to save that boy's life. Do I make myself clear?" the doctor demanded, his hands on his hips, glaring at Tony and Seamus.

"Perfectly," Tony said as everyone murmured their agreement as well.

Nodding, Jim led the way to Rick's room, where Tony let Nana have some time with her grandson as he stood with Runningbear at the door.

"He's strong, Whitefish. He'll survive," the shaman said softly, putting a shaking hand on Tony's shoulder.

"At what cost, though, Runningbear?" Tony asked quietly.

"Doesn't matter, my son. Just remember this – you're no good to him if you collapse. Now I need to rest. It was a very long healing." With that, the shaman left.

As Tony stared out the door, he heard his name whispered in a sudden silence. "Fish?"

Tony turned towards the bed to see Rick straining to reach him. Swiftly, Tony moved to the bed to push Rick back. "Hey, little brother, none of that. Rest," Tony said, easing Rick back onto the pillows.

Rick collapsed back against the pillows, whiter than Tony ever remembered seeing anyone, including corpses. The cop sat beside his friend, his hands resting on the bed next to Rick while Marshall and Seamus stood at the end. Nana was on the other side, across from Tony and Ian stood on the other side of the room, still fuming.

"How do you feel, lad?" Nana asked.

"Like crap," Rick whispered. "Find Megs?"

"Not yet. We don't know where she is," Tony replied. "We've been waiting for you."

"Rick, Jim doesn't want us to ask, but I have to. What happened?" Seamus asked roughly from the shadows.

"O'Reilly?" Rick asked, trying to see Jordan's dad through his badly swollen eyes.

"Yes. Do ye want me to leave?" the cop asked hesitantly as he stepped forward. He hoped Rick wouldn't mind him being there, but Seamus would understand if the teen asked him to leave.

Rick shook his head once, then winced with the pain. "Need to hear. Promise one thing?" he whispered.

"What, Rick?" Seamus asked, grateful.

"Don't be mad at Tony. Did this for me," Rick pleaded. He reached toward Tony's hand and held it tight.

"Rest easy, boy. Tony's not in trouble," Seamus said gruffly.

"Am I?" Rick asked wearily. He sighed and rested for a few minutes before beginning to tell his story in broken sentences.

"First week, hardest. No news. No leads. Started sneaking out, second week," Rick said in a raspy voice.

"Why?" Seamus wondered, amazed at Rick's boldness. "Ye could've been seen."

Rick snorted, then coughed for several moments. When he was done, he lay back, exhausted. "Not likely. Where went, cops don't follow, even with reason. Sought Slayers. Hit Squad. Pressure on Johnny. Worry him," Rick continued, struggling to speak clearly.

Tony squeezed the hand he held. "Rest for a bit, Rick. Take your time. We'll wait," Tony urged. He could see little flecks of blood at the corner of Rick's mouth he wiped away with a soft tissue.

"No! I'll be too late!" Rick whispered, panicked.

"What good will you do her, lad, if Jim sedates you?" Nana asked, trying to keep the fear out of her voice.

"Please, just rest," Tony begged, struggling not to cry. It was several long minutes later before Rick could continue and then his voice was so quiet it could barely be heard over the sound of the monitors.

"Street talk no good. No one seen Johnny. Knew had to get back in. Only way. Argued with Fish. Didn't want me to," Rick said. His eyes never left Tony's, as if he was using Tony as a focus for his tale.

"Why not?" Ian demanded harshly. "It would've helped find my daughter!"

"Because Rick and I knew this could very well happen. Dammit, Ian, that funeral on Saturday could've been real. You know how bad he was. Hell, you brought him in!" Tony snapped back. Ian didn't say anything. He just stood on the far side of the room, scowling.

"Funeral?" Rick whispered, tugging at Tony's hand to get his attention.

"We told everyone you'd died, Rick. I couldn't take a chance," Tony replied.

"Jor!" Rick cried suddenly as Tony's words sunk in. He struggled to sit up.

It was Seamus who calmed Rick for once. "Hush, boy, take it easy. Yeah, she thinks ye're gone, but think for a moment. Who'd've needed to react the most naturally for this to be believed?" he asked as Tony pushed Rick back down gently.

"Jor," Rick replied, brokenheartedly.

"Trust me, boy, that lie hurt me and Tony more than ye think. I hate lying to me kids," Seamus said sourly.

"Can you go on, Rick?" Nana asked, concerned. Her grandson was too pale and weak for her liking, yet she knew he had more to say.

"Yeah. Told Tony. Need gear. Got jacket and bandana from station. Went looking for Johnny weekend. Found Eric on Monday. Panicked," Rick gasped. Seamus just glared at Tony who shrugged.

"Easy, Rick. Who panicked? You or Eric?" Marshall asked, quietly writing.

"Eric. Called Johnny. Went to Johnny's house Tuesday. Asked to come back. Johnny wearing Megs' ring from Mick. Johnny didn't believe me. Said I knew. I said no. Still didn't believe me. Had Eric choke me. Came to tied up," Rick gasped, his sentences coming rapidly.

"Rick," Jim warned as he looked at the monitors by Rick's head. They weren't painting a very good picture.

"No! Save Megs! Gotta save her!" Rick said, desperately. He couldn't understand why they weren't taking him seriously.

"Guys? Can I have a few minutes? Please?" Tony asked, looking around the room.

When they were alone, Tony turned to Rick and said, "Look, little brother. I know you have lots to tell us, but it's not gonna do Meg any good if Jim knocks you out or you pass out from the pain," he scolded softly.

"Megs important," Rick insisted stubbornly.

"Hey, son, guess what? So're you. Especially to me. Now listen to me for a moment. I want you to rest. Just lay there quietly. Don't speak. Don't think. Just rest. Deep breaths. That's it.

Remember how I taught you to calm yourself down? Breathe as deep as you can, son," Tony urged softly.

Rick sank back into his bed, but couldn't help begging, "Don't leave."

"I'll be right here, little brother," Tony promised, taking a hold of Rick's hand again.

Rick rested for more than an hour before he felt strong enough to continue his tale. Tony let everyone back into the room where they all settled back into their spots.

"Ready, Champ?" Marshall asked, pen poised above his notebook.

"What happened when ye found yerself tied to that chair?" Seamus asked. He forced himself to ignore how battered Rick looked, how pale he was and how he was struggling to speak. He tried to see him only as a witness, not a victim, but it was so damn hard. *No one should have to go through this,* the Inspector thought angrily, *let alone a kid. Even one I hated.*

"Beating. Johnny first. Then Mark. Was wearing ring. Slashed face. Then Johnny again. Broke leg?" Rick looked at Jim.

"Hairline fracture. Won't slow you down too much. Left shin," the doctor said confidently.

"Eric next. Stood behind me. Broke arm and shoulder. Felt them go. Hurts," Rick whimpered. He hated feeling weak, even when he had a good reason.

Jim quickly administered some painkillers through Rick's I.V. The lines of pain eased almost immediately and Rick seemed to perk up. But he still rested another ten long minutes before deciding to go on.

Tony noticed Rick visibly steeled himself before continuing and wondered what was so horrible he almost couldn't continue. "Johnny again. Could hardly see. Shoved knife in face. Said Megs not fighting like in woods. St-st-st-st...," Rick's voice faltered. No matter how hard he tried, he just couldn't say the word.

"Johnny stabbed you," Tony finished for him, realizing what Rick couldn't say.

Rick nodded gratefully. "Held knife in face again. Said think where knife end up next. Hit me. Don't remember anything else. Enough?" Rick asked, clearly exhausted. He couldn't stop the tears that fell down his face and Nana gathered her grandson into her arms. He had no energy left to sob, but just let the tears flow freely. He hurt so much and they were no closer to finding Megan.

"Rick, is there anything else ye *need* to tell us right now?" Seamus asked quietly, emphasizing the word *need*.

"No," the exhausted teen whispered as Nana finally let him go.

"We'll leave ye to rest then," the elder cop said and led Ian and Nana from the room. Marshall sat down in his chair at the foot of the bed, and finished up his notes.

"Marsh? Can I take your notes?" Tony asked quietly.

"Sure, Fish. I've filled in some words so they make more sense," Marshall said, handing over the notebook.

"Thanks, partner. Give me a few minutes alone with him, okay?" Tony asked. "I'll call you in a minute, doc. I'm gonna convince him to take some sedatives," he said in a low voice. Jim nodded, relieved.

Tony stood there, looking at the broken body in the bed. Rick's breathing was shallow and laboured. Tony shook his head. *How's Rick gonna get through this?* he wondered.

"I know you're there, Fish," Rick croaked without opening his eyes.

"Can't fool you, can I, little brother?" Tony said as he came and sat by the bed.

"Did I screw up, Fish?" Rick asked quietly, opening his feverish eyes to focus once again on Tony, who sighed.

"I don't know, Rick. I just don't know. It'll depend on what Seamus wants to do. Don't worry, Rick. We'll find her and she'll be okay," Tony said with forced confidence. *Please let her be okay,* Tony prayed. *It'll kill Rick if she isn't.*

"Sorry, Tony. Should've listened," Rick said with a sigh. "I was too late to save her," he said, even more quietly.

"Rick, you need to rest. Doing this took way too much out of you. Let Jim give you something to help you sleep. Please?" Tony begged, ignoring Rick's last comment.

Rick sighed. "Okay. Tired. Sore," he whispered finally, closing his eyes.

Tony went to the door and looked out. "Jim? He's agreed," the cop said.

The two went back to the teen, who continued to labour to breathe. "It'll take a couple minutes to kick in," Jim said softly to Tony as he injected Rick's i.v. again.

"Son? Jim's given you something to help you sleep," Tony said quietly. He wasn't sure Rick had even heard him.

Rick's eyes fluttered open. Tony could already see the dazed look in them from the drugs. "Bro? If I die, tell Megs I'm sorry. Sorry I was too late. But I tried. I really tried." With another painful sigh, Rick gave into the sedative and fell into a deep sleep.

Tony thought his heart would break at those soft words. He walked out with his head lowered and tears in his eyes. He blindly entered the V.I.P. lounge and stood off alone for a long time before anyone even noticed he was there. Marshall nudged his boss who looked over at a very worried young cop.

"Tony, what's wrong?" Seamus said, keeping his voice low and coming over to put his hand on Tony's shoulder.

"I couldn't stop him, boss. I tried to talk him out of this and he was adamant he do this. Now look at him," Tony said miserably.

"This is *not* yer fault, Tony! If there's one thing I've learned about Rick Attison, it's once he makes up his mind about something, he goes after it whole-heartedly. Look at how focused he's always been on me Jordan," Seamus said with a smile.

"But look at him!" Tony repeated stubbornly, motioning back towards the room where Rick rested.

"He just needs time to heal, Whitefish," Runningbear said confidently.

Tony took a couple of more minutes then squared his shoulders. "Boss, do we have enough to go after Johnny for the attack on Rick?" Tony asked.

- 367 -

"We'll need to review the evidence, some of which may now be compromised," Seamus said reprovingly.

"I'm not sorry I took them, Seamus. You know as well as I do there was nothing on them before. Now, we might have some trace," Tony said, defending his actions.

"Whatever. I'll talk to Lance and the judge tonight and see if I can get a warrant based on Rick's statement alone," Seamus said.

"Meet you at the station tomorrow, then, boss?" Marshall said, as he headed back to his vigil, but Seamus stopped him.

"Yeah, and ye too, Marshall. I need me best boys on this. Kelsey's enough protection, I think," Seamus said as he left.

"Take care of my boy, Jim," Nana said as she left, taking Ian with her.

Tony was the last to leave the hospital. He sat by Rick's bedside for the longest time, just looking at his friend. Someone who had taught him as much as he had taught Rick. Now, as Tony watched Rick fight to breathe, to survive, he made a vow.

"I swear to you, little brother, I will find her. I won't be too late."

Chapter 44

Tony arrived at the station the next morning awake, alert and ready for just about anything. He had slept fitfully at first, but finally fell into a deep, dreamless sleep around midnight. He called out greetings to several officers before settling at his desk to answer his growing pile of messages and memos.

The first one he called proved to be the most interesting. "Jimmy's the name. Selling info's my game," the kid answered the phone.

"Whitefish here. You called?" Tony said, leaning back.

"Yeah. Blade showed his face at the pool hall las' night. He's recruitin'. Says he's inta a good thing," Jimmy drawled.

"He hook you?" Tony wanted to know.

"Naw. Not my kinda thing. Not inta violence and hatred like he is, man. Sez he's on Mendez's payroll now and that ain't me. Don't like how Mendez works the kids, y'know. And sez he has inside info," Jimmy said wisely, knowing he didn't have to say inside *where*.

"Gimme something to work with – names, boy," Tony growled good naturedly. Out of the corner of his eye, he could see Jones listening hard.

"Blade wouldn't say, 'xactly, but he said his recent investment's protected. I know it ain't much, but I'll keep workin' it," Jimmy said defensively, wanting to impress Tony.

Tony sighed. "Just be careful, kid. I'll see you tonight at Mahoney's. I'd rather have no info than dead info, y'know?" Tony sighed again as he hung up the phone. *Great, now Johnny's getting info from here*, Tony thought angrily. *Mendez's really expanding his borders.*

"Fish? I gotta bone to pick with you. And the boss," Jones said hotly as he stood by Tony's desk.

"What's up, Jonesy?" Tony replied, distracted as he sorted the rest of his messages. He threw several in the garbage and stacked the rest. Same went for the memos.

"Why've I been shut out suddenly?" the older cop demanded. "I'm senior investigator. I should be leading the Attison kidnapping, not you and certainly not Andrews."

"Talk to the Inspector, not me, Jonesy. He's the one who decided who was in charge and he's the one who put the limit on who knows what," Tony said with a shrug. "Oh, and don't go listening at any doors, either. O'Reilly really hates that."

With that parting shot, Tony sauntered over to the conference room where the rest of his team had assembled. The young cop stopped abruptly at the sight of all the food on the table.

"Grab a plate, Tony," Seamus said from the other side of the pile. Tony didn't have to be told twice.

"Okay, boys, here's where things stand. Talked to the prosecutor in light of some new evidence and he gave me a warrant for Chilton's place. Campbell, I need ye to finish at Townsand's today. Have you found anything?" Seamus asked as he and Tony sat down to eat.

"Some letters and stuff. His clothes're kinda probative, but so far, nothing really firm. Sorry, sir," the rookie apologized. Seamus just waved the apology away.

"How'd his parents take it?" Tony asked, curiously, as he dug into the first real breakfast he'd had since Runningbear had left.

"I'm quoting, "That jackass is no son of mine. Look as long as you want." End quote. We've been given a green light to come back again today. And tomorrow if we really need it," Campbell said with a grin. The rest of the cops just laughed.

"The rest of us, boss?" a veteran cop named Hank asked.

"We're hitting Chilton's place right after breakfast," Seamus said with his mouth half full. The rest of the team gave a ragged cheer and dug into their food.

Tony leaned in. "Jones stopped me and asked me why," he said softly.

"Wha'cha say?" Seamus sighed.

"That he'd have to ask you. Boss, we're not gonna be able to stop him from calling," Tony pointed out.

"He probably already has," Seamus said sourly.

"You have to decide sometime, boss, or we'll never get Mendez. Either bring him back in, or fire him," Tony advised. "Morning, Marsh," he greeted his partner in a slightly louder voice as Marshall sat down after dumping his empty plate.

"Morning, Seamus, Fish. Talked to Kelsey this morning. He's awake again. Says he's a bit stronger. What's the plan?" Marshall asked Seamus.

"Everyone done? Good. Let's go. Quickly," Seamus said, standing.

He led the team from the room. They dispersed quickly but instead of following right away, Seamus stomped over to Jones' desk. "Ye gotta problem with how I run me department, Jones, transfer. I decide who's in an investigation. Not Carlos Mendez. And ye can tell him I said that," Seamus said as he walked away from the startled cop.

It didn't take long to get to Blade's house. It was in a nondescript part of town, plain and beginning to look as rundown as it felt. It was easy to see why Blade was in the gang. He had nothing at home, Tony knew, no father and a mom who worked all the time. Unlike Rick, who only *thought* the gang was his family, for Blade, the Knights *were* his family.

"Ready, Tony?" Seamus asked as they walked up to the door and rang the bell.

"Let's just hope we find her, boss. If they've hurt her…," Tony said ominously.

When Blade's mother opened the door, she sighed. *Either cops, or Welfare*, she thought immediately, resigned as she wondered what was going on now. "Yes?" she said a bit timidly.

"Do ye have a son named Johnny, Mrs. Chilton?" Seamus asked gruffly.

Marian sighed again. Cops, then. Welfare never cared about her son, just her nephew. "Yes," she replied. She hated to admit Blade was her son.

"Ma'am, may we come in? We need to talk and I'd really rather not do it on the steps," Tony said before Seamus could continue his barrage.

"As much as I'd like to say yes, I'm sorry, officer. No. We'll talk right here," she said, easing the door closed somewhat.

"This is a search warrant for this house and property, ma'am," Seamus said, not bothering to keep his voice down so the neighbours on their front porches could hear him. He handed her a sealed, folded piece of paper. "Do ye still wanna talk on the front porch in front of yer neighbours?" he asked pointedly, lowering his voice slightly. Flushing, she looked around and shook her head. She may have had a crappy life, but it didn't need to be aired for the whole neighbourhood to hear.

"Come in, then," she said, reconciled to whatever was about to happen. As Tony and Seamus entered the kitchen, they immediately noticed a really strong smell of bleach. *Someone tried to clean up, at least once*, Tony thought, gleefully. *Something* did *happen here.* Through the open kitchen window, they could hear Marshall direct the officers outside.

"We're good to go outside, Inspector," he said, striding confidently into the room a couple of minutes later.

"Officers, please sit and tell me what the hell my son's done this time," Blade's mother said sourly as she sat down and motioned for the rest to join her around the kitchen table.

"Marsh, wait! Don't touch that chair!" one of the CSIs snapped suddenly. Startled, Marshall stumbled away from the chair, trying not to fall down.

"Gotcha, partner," Tony laughed as he grabbed Marshall.

"What is it, Terry?" Seamus demanded quickly.

"Looks like blood, sir," Terry said as he pulled out his kit.

"Blood? What're you talking about? What's going on here?" Marian demanded, looking from one cop to another.

"Ma'am, when was the last time you saw your son?" Tony asked as he and Marshall finally sat down, after Terry cleared the rest of the chairs.

"Last week sometime. Tuesday, I think," she replied softly, after thinking for a couple of minutes. She really didn't like the dead feeling in her stomach. Something was seriously wrong.

"Ma'am," Tony began but Marian quickly interrupted with "It's Marian, please."

"Marian, have you ever heard of the Black Knights?" Tony continuted.

"Yes. My 'son' leads them," she replied with a dry emphasis on 'son.'

"How about Megan Attison? Or Rick Attison?" Tony questioned.

"Only what's been in the papers and on T.V. in the news. She's missing, if I remember correctly and he's dead. Poor family," Marian said sadly.

"The reason we're here's we believe the Knights, and that includes your son, took Megan and killed her cousin, here in this house. We desperately need to search the house, Marian, please. Even though we have a warrant and could force you, I'd like it to be with your cooperation. Do we have your permission to search?" Tony asked. She nodded quickly, raising her hand to her mouth in shock.

While Seamus stayed to talk with Marian, the CSIs, Tony and Marshall headed upstairs. They made a quick search of Marian's room, not really thinking there'd be anything in there. As expected, they found nothing. There didn't seem to be anything in the bathroom, either, but Tony had a tech process everything for blood, just in case.

"Hey, Fish, you've gotta see this," one of the techs called from down the hall.

"Coming," Tony replied, distracted.

"He sure idolized his cousin, didn't he?" the tech said, standing outside Pup's room.

Tony could only shake his head in amazement. Idolize was too mild of a word to describe what they saw. Pup's room was a shrine to his older cousin. Blade's picture was everywhere, along with weights and books on gangs. Tony saw the inevitable gang wear and then spied a large ring on the night stand.

"Take that ring, man. Rick's face was pretty torn up. That could've done it," Tony pointed out.

"Hey, Fish? What about the weights?" Marshall asked, hefting one up, testing the weight of it.

"Swab them, I guess, but I think there would've been a lot more damage if Rick had been hit with them, especially if Eric or Johnny had used them, don't you? No, Mark's the smallest. He's probably just trying to bulk up," Tony pointed out logically. Marshall nodded, but still handed them over to the techs to be processed and eliminated.

There wasn't much else in Pup's room, but they took their time processing the scene, just in case. Over an hour later, Tony finally called a halt.

"We still have the rest of the house, boys and we're running out of time. Do you think there's anything else in here?" Tony asked Terry, who shook his head.

"Probably not, Fish. We'll move on," Terry replied, looking around. He'd come up to grab another tech to work on the kitchen, while he remained with the main group. "We can always come back if needed."

"Johnny's room, then," Tony said and led the way down the short hall. He hesitated and then pushed the door open.

"Jackpot!"

"Bingo, Fish!"

"Dibs on the closet!"

"Got the desk!"

"Holy crap!" Marshall said over the excited babble of the techs.

Tony couldn't move. Everywhere they looked, they saw how much Blade hated Rick, especially two pictures on the wall opposite the door, both riddled with knife marks.

Megan's face was still relatively easy to discern, but Rick's was almost completely gone. It wasn't just stab marks, either. There was a multitude of slashes and gouges, some very deep. The only thing not destroyed were Rick's eyes, staring out into the room, defiant as always.

With Tony frozen in the doorway, the techs had to shove past him to process the room. Tony didn't even hear their excited chatter, as he stared at the photos, or what was left of them. He slowly walked across the room and stood in front of them.

"Tony?" Terry called.

"Damn, Marsh. He was playing. Practicing. We may already be too late," Tony whispered, horrified at what he was looking at. He reached up and gently touched Megan's picture. He couldn't bring himself to touch Rick's.

"Tony?" Terry called again, this time more urgently.

"What?" Marshall replied, knowing Tony was too upset to talk.

Terry came over, carefully holding a piece of paper by the corner. "Doesn't matter how late we are, Fish. We've got him," the tech said, grinning, holding it up for the partners to read. Marshall read it, then read it again.

"He couldn't be that stupid!?" he exclaimed.

"Yes, he is," Terry grinned and slid the paper into a clear evidence sleeve and sealed it.

Tony finally snapped out of his stupor. "What did you find?" he asked harshly.

"Just a draft of the ransom note," Marshall said. Tony just shook his head in stunned amazement.

"How about copies of a couple of the letters sent to Megan?" another tech called.

"I've got at least one of Rick's bandanas," someone else added excitedly.

"Holy crap. Sorry, Fish, but...um... I've got some bloody clothes in the hamper. Really bloody clothes," a third chimed in hesitantly, holding up the shirt he had found. Silence fell as everyone looked to Tony.

"Wow," someone whispered, as they looked at the young cop.

Tony's face was flushed, his jaw had tightened and he'd clenched his fists so hard the knuckles were white. Marshall couldn't believe the change in his partner, but what scared him the most was the look in Tony's eyes. Black and cold, they looked like someone was going to pay for this. Marshall shivered. Somehow he needed to reach Tony before he destroyed the room in his anger.

"Fish, you need to calm down," he said. His voice was loud in the suddenly silent room.

Tony turned slowly. "What the hell did you just say?" he growled low in his throat. Marshall shivered again at the anger he heard, but stood his ground.

"Look, Tony Whitefish, don't you dare take that tone with me! I'm just as angry as you, but destroying evidence because you're pissed ain't gonna help her," Marshall snapped back.

"Marsh," Tony warned and began to turn away. His partner grabbed him roughly before he could move more than a couple of feet and shoved him towards the door.

"Think about it, Fish. We've panicked them enough that they didn't clean up after themselves. We have enough *in this room alone* right now to put him away for a long time. Don't lose it now," Marshall said as he roughly steered Tony out of the room.

"Let go of me!" Tony groused as he struggled in Marshall's iron grip. Marshall slammed the door behind them and continued to shove Tony down the hall. They finally ended up in Marian's bedroom. Tony jerked his arm out of Marshall's grip and stalked over to the far wall, turning his back to his partner.

"C'mon, man, you know I didn't wanna do that, especially in front of the rest of the team," Marshall said quietly, praying he hadn't just wrecked their friendship, let alone their partnership. Marshall could see how hard Tony was taking what he had seen in that room. Not that Marshall was handling it any better, but at least he wasn't about to hit someone.

"Leave me the hell alone," Tony grated, his voice throbbing with hatred and what Marshall thought were unshed tears. Tony was taking this *way* too personally.

"Like hell, *partner*," Marshall said roughly. He stormed over, grabbed Tony by the shoulder and spun him around, not caring what Tony did to him. He knew he had to keep Tony from doing anything stupid.

"Stop reacting and start thinking, Tony Whitefish! If you blow and contaminate the evidence, *Johnny walks*! Worse, Rick, your little brother, that kid you care so damn much about, will've gone through that beating for nothing!" Marshall said quietly, but intensely, finally getting through to Tony.

Tony stared into his partner's eyes. Sighing, he sat down on the bed for several minutes, trying to get himself under some kind of control.

"Sorry, partner. But to see that room, those pictures..." Tony's voice trailed off. The thought they could already be too late to save Megan was almost too much for Tony. In the silence of Marian's bedroom, away from all of the hustle in the rest of the house, the partners tried to collect their thoughts and tighten their resolve.

"Better, Fish?" Marshall asked finally.

"No, but I'll get over it," Tony said, his calm voice belying the anger he tried to bury.

"Tony, look, whether we find Megan okay or not, we can bury Johnny with that evidence," Marshall said. "Remember what Runningbear said? You're no good to them if you've collapsed? Well, the same goes if you're in jail. You're no good to anyone, especially me," Marshall pointed out. "And, dammit all to hell, man, I need your help or this ain't never gonna get solved."

"Marsh, I know you did what you thought was right just now, but don't ever do it again," Tony said roughly as he stood up.

"Only if I have to," Marshall muttered as the two walked out.

They passed Blade's room and Tony stuck his head in. "Sorry, boys. Bag and tag everything. Be thorough," he ordered, ignoring the looks directed at him.

Downstairs, Seamus was still questioning Marian. "So he's been gone about five years, then?" Seamus asked as Tony and Marshall came in.

"Yes. Y'know, that's about when Johnny began to get into real trouble," she replied thoughtfully.

"Boss, we got 'im," Marshall said, interrupting.

"What did ye find?" Seamus asked as he looked up at his cops.

"Copies of the ransom note, letters sent to Meg. There's some bloody clothes up there, too," Tony said roughly. His eyes wandered around the room, searching for anything that could help them.

As he looked around, Marshall leaned over and spoke quietly in Seamus' ear. Seamus just frowned. "I'll talk to him. Later," the inspector promised in a low tone so Tony didn't hear.

"Marian, where does that door lead?" Tony snapped suddenly, pointing to the closed door near the back entrance.

Marian cringed. She could hear how angry the cop was. Whatever they had found upstairs must've been really bad. "The...the basement," she stammered when Tony turned to her. "Johnny never let me go down there. Too dangerous, he'd say," she explained softly.

Tony looked at Marshall and nodded. "Send Terry down, Seamus. I'm sure we'll need him," Tony said as they approached the door.

"There should be a light switch about half way down," Marian offered.

"Thank you, ma'am," Marshall replied, gratefully.

With his flashlight in his hand, Tony inched his way down the creaky stairs, searching for the light switch. He hit it about half way down, just as promised, and snapped it on. Light weakly flooded the whole basement and Tony realized he'd still need his flashlight if he was going to see anything. As Tony got to the bottom, he slipped slightly on the damp bottom step.

"Careful, Fish," Marshall cautioned as Tony caught himself.

Tony snorted as he moved into the room. He shivered in the cold air. The dampness seemed to soak into his bones. He could taste the mud and wondered if there was a problem with the foundation. Everywhere he shone his flashlight, Tony could see the dampness on the walls.

"She'd've frozen down here, man, no matter how warm it was outside," his partner said as he moved around to the left side of the room.

"Can you taste the mud?" Tony called.

"Yeah. See the wires? Exposed bulbs? This place is a fire hazard and should be condemned, man. Damn, this sucks, Fish. His mom? She works three jobs and still can't make ends meet. If Megan was here and this place burned down, we'd never've found anything," Marshall said, noting the slippery spot at the bottom of the stairs as he joined his partner.

"Anything?" Tony asked. He had regained some of his natural calm, but he was still very angry. He just wasn't sure if he was angrier at Marshall for what he had done upstairs or at himself for losing control.

"Nothing. Literally nothing. No furniture, no garbage. Nothing. I don't think she's here, partner," Marshall said as he shone his flashlight around.

"Let's try behind the stairs here," Tony said as he led the way around into the shadows. His flashlight caught a light switch, and Tony snapped the dim bulb on.

"Oh God, no!" Marshall swore loudly.

"Get Terry. Move!" Tony snapped. Marshall didn't argue. He raced back up the damp stairs, shouting for Terry.

Tony stared at the army cot with its thin mattress. There were a couple of very thin pillows and Tony saw red at the blood flecks on one of them.

"Lemme in, Tony," Terry said from behind. Tony moved quietly aside.

"Blood, Terry?" Marshall asked.

The tech tested it quickly. "Positive. And human," he said as he studied the results.

"Take your time. By the way, I think there's some rope under the bed. Bag everything you can. Can we take the bed without contaminating it further?" Tony asked.

"I'll figure out a way, Tony. Trust me. No matter what happens to Miss Megan, I'll get you the evidence to put these slimy bastards away," Terry vowed. Tony couldn't believe the anger he heard in the tech's voice. It matched his own.

"She's important to a lot of people. She just has that ability to make everyone like her," Marshall said thoughtfully as they walked away. Tony needed a couple more minutes before he could face his boss and the mother of the boy who had kidnapped Megan.

"Fish? C'mon, partner. Let's go bring the boss up to date," Marshall said, slapping his friend on the back.

"Well, boys, what did ye find?" Seamus asked as they came back upstairs.

"An awful lot, and yet not very much," Tony admitted reluctantly.

"There's a little nook under the stairs that's probably where Megan was held. There's an army cot with a thin mattress and pillows. Maybe a blanket. It's cold and damp and a hell of a fire trap down there. If she was held there for the last month or more, she's gonna be pretty bad, boss," Marshall said, then hesitated.

"What aren't ye telling me, boys?" Seamus asked shrewdly.

"There's blood on the pillows, Seamus," Tony said after an awkward silence.

"A lot of blood," Terry said, coming upstairs. His arms were full of evidence bags and Tony jumped to help him before he dropped something.

"Thanks," was all he said. "Gimme a second and then I'll explain." He gave some instructions to his team in a quiet voice, then turned back to the partners as others went downstairs to continue to collect evidence.

"I pulled out the bed to get at the evidence you saw, Fish, and I saw a darkish stain on the underside of the mattress. I flipped it over and found a large blood stain," Terry explained quietly, stunning everyone in the room.

Marian gasped. Her horrified look matched how the three cops felt. "Problem is right now I can't tell you who that blood belongs to or how old it is. I do know this – there's not enough there to indicate someone died there, but someone was definitely either beaten or stabbed there," Terry finished, then hesitated before continuing quietly. "Possibly multiple times."

"Marian, I'm sorry, but we're gonna be here fer several more hours. Is there someone ye can stay with for a while?" Seamus asked.

"Yes, my best friend. But can I ask *you* a question?" Marian asked before she stood.

"If I can answer it without compromising the investigations, I will," Seamus promised.

"When was that boy, Rick, found?" she asked quietly.

Now that's a strange question, Seamus thought before replying. "Early evening, last Tuesday. Why?" he asked.

"Do you have a photo of him? The paper only showed his battered face for some reason," Marian said. Wordlessly, Tony handed her a school picture of Rick he kept in his wallet.

"That's what I thought. If this happened on Tuesday, I may have seen some of it. In fact, I'm sure of it. See, Tuesday's my long day. I literally worked from 5 a.m. until 3 a.m. Wednesday morning. I'd already worked two jobs and had come home to change for the third. I must've come home early," Marian said quietly.

"What makes you say that?" Tony asked as Marshall took more notes.

"Mark came dashing up from the basement, trying to push me out the door and Johnny was nowhere to be found, as usual. Suddenly there he was, right behind me. He was so angry, I remember," Marian said.

"Are ye scared of yer son?" Seamus asked, noticing Marian shivered whenever she mentioned her son.

"Who isn't? Anyway, I remember thinking something was wrong, because Mark kept rushing me out the door. That's probably why I forgot my money pouch and had to come back. I wish to God I hadn't," she said fervently.

- 381 -

"Why?" Tony asked, dreading the answer.

"I arrived at the door and heard an argument through the window. Shouting, then a loud smack. I stood up on a wooden box I keep near the back door and looked in the kitchen window and saw Johnny hitting your boy. I stood there, shocked, as Mark walked up and just pummelled him, all the while Johnny was egging him on, encouraging him to keep going. The other boy just stood there and didn't say a word or try to stop Johnny. I could see the blood everywhere on my floor. Then the other one, not Mark or Johnny, broke his arms. As I stood there, I watched my own flesh and blood stab your boy. I stood there and watched him die. I fled. I was late for work and lost my job. I was so upset, I never called the police about this. I'm sorry," she sobbed.

Tony sighed. Here was a woman so scared of her son she wasn't aware she had been living over a young girl for the last month. One who was probably sick, beaten, and maybe dead. Blade truly ruled his gang and his home.

Seamus motioned to Hank. "Marian, this officer'll escort ye to yer room. Ye can pack a bag, but I need ye to come to the station and make a formal statement about what ye saw that night. Don't be surprised if ye get asked the same questions more than once. We don't wanna miss anything," Seamus said. Marian stood up and went to follow Hank to her room.

"Marian, one last question. Do you have any idea where your son might be?" Marshall asked as he put his notebook away.

"Sorry, officer, but no. Johnny never talked about where he went or who he was with. I honestly don't recall ever seeing your boy here any other time, but that doesn't mean anything." With that, she left the room.

"Whitefish, outside, now!" Seamus barked suddenly.

"Thanks a lot, partner," Tony said sourly, knowing he was about to get the chewing out of his career. Marshall just shrugged. He had done this for Tony's own good.

"What the hell do ye think ye're doing in that house?" Seamus asked harshly as they stood by the squad cars.

"Look, Seamus, you didn't see Johnny's room. There were two photos – one of Meg and one of Rick. Both were riddled with holes. Rick's was the worst. His face was sliced to ribbons, except for his eyes. Johnny hates him with more than a small passion. He's obsessed. So I got a little hot under the collar. I don't see what the problem is," Tony said with a shrug, unprepared for Seamus' reaction. Seamus pushed Tony up against his car and got right in his face.

"The *problem*, Constable, is ye're the lead investigator on an investigation ye should *never* have been involved in, let alone leading it. In that, Jones is right. Ye can*not* give into emotion. If anything, ye've gotta be the most unemotional cop ye've ever been, or the evidence could be tossed at trial. Ye have a personal interest in keeping Rick out of jail, so I don't want anyone to accuse ye of creating evidence, especially evidence to clear him, understand? Ye need to be focused and calm, not ready to rip yer partner's heart out and feed it to him while it's still beating, and especially not in front of the rest of the team!" Seamus said hotly, trying to keep his voice down while maintaining his intensity.

Tony hung his head while Seamus scolded him. Seamus stood in front of his two best cops and sighed, all of his anger suddenly gone. "Look at me, Tony," he ordered softly. Tony slowly raised his eyes to meet the compassionate gaze of his boss. Seamus gripped Tony's shoulders in understanding.

"I know now how much Rick means to ye. I saw it, God, was it only yesterday? when we were talking to him and he just continued to fade. You looked like Mickey the day Megan was taken – heartbroken. That boy means the world to ye because ye've been able to get to know him. When ye see him hurt, ye hurt. When ye see him attacked, ye feel attacked, but ye have to remember one thing, Tony," Seamus said intently.

"What's that, boss?" Tony said quietly.

"Jones may not be the only one and I don't wanna hand Mendez any more ammunition or someone that bugger thinks he can turn," Seamus pointed out. He let Tony go and watched as the younger cop struggled with the events of the day.

"Any sign of weakness plays to him, Fish," Marshall agreed. Tony leaned against his car and didn't say anything. He couldn't. They were both right.

Terry came out a couple minutes later. "Better, Fish?" he asked. Tony nodded.

"Look, Tony. I was thinking. Word on the street's Blade's holed up somewhere, but no one knows where. His mother doesn't know. His rivals sure as hell don't know," Terry said as he put some evidence on Tony's car.

"Wha'cha getting at, Terry?" Tony asked, puzzled. He wondered where Terry was getting his information, but it could be from anywhere. Terry was a Collingwood original.

"You have someone who knows. Make 'im talk," Terry said with a shrug. "There's enough in that box alone to scare the crap out of any kid, hard core "gangster" or not." He nodded and went back inside to continue processing the house.

"He's right, Tony," Seamus said. Tony squared his shoulders and nodded.

"Let's go, Marsh. I've gotta promise to keep," Tony said as Marshall placed the evidence in the trunk, then climbed in.

"Promise? What promise?" Seamus asked, curious.

Tony stopped and looked at his boss. "I promised I wouldn't be too late." With that, Tony pulled away, his car's tires squealing.

Chapter 45

Tony was quiet on the way back to the station. The tongue lashing Seamus had just delivered rankled, but deep down, Tony knew his boss was right. He had to be above reproach, and since they didn't know if Mendez had his hooks in someone else, Tony couldn't afford to give him any ammunition.

"What was that promise?" Marshall asked quietly. He had already sat down in the car when Tony had replied to Seamus.

"Remember how Rick kept saying he'd be too late to save her? Right from the very beginning of this year?" Tony asked. Marshall nodded as Tony continued. "Last night, just before I left, he asked – no, begged me – to tell Meg he was sorry that he was too late. I promised him *I* wouldn't be," Tony shrugged. He kept the rest of Rick's words to himself. Marshall didn't need to know Rick figured he was going to die before they found Megan.

Marshall fell silent as they pulled into the parking lot. They both watched silently as a black limo pulled away. *Wonder if Jones has any skin left?* Tony thought as they parked the car.

"Mendez actually had the nerve to come and do his own chewing out? Man, that's ballsy. Fish, when're we going after him?" Marshall asked as he grabbed the evidence box.

"One disaster at a time, partner, one disaster at a time. Don't worry, though. Since we've now confirmed how he's getting his info, it's gonna be a lot easier to control the leaks," Tony said, wishing it was that easy.

They marched into the interrogation room, where they pulled out what Terry had given them. They carefully arranged the evidence on the bulletin board so Brain would see everything in bright, vivid, damning colour. Then, to complete the image, Tony sat down, resting his feet up on the table and looking for all the world like he had no cares, no worries and certainly not a missing teen on his mind.

Once again, Brain was led into the room. He had showered and shaved and his nicely tailored gang clothes had been replaced by a set of bright orange jailhouse coveralls. Marshall removed the cuffs and motioned to a chair. Brain flopped down without a sound, only glancing at the bulletin board before staring at the far wall.

"Hello again, Brian," Tony said from where he sat, determined that today, Brain wasn't leaving without giving Blade up. "Once again, I must ask. Do you want a parent or lawyer present while we talk?"

"Y'ain't gettin' 'nother word outta me, cop, so shove yer parents and yer lawyer" Brain sneered. Tony noticed the teen looked everywhere but at the bulletin board. The cop just smiled grimly.

"That's okay, Brian. Just wanted to make sure nothing had changes. See, I wanna show you a few things we found today," Tony said as he pointed to the display. Brain refused to look anywhere but at his feet. "That's not very nice, Brian; Marsh, I think our young friend here doesn't appreciate all of our hard work," Tony said sadly.

Marshall grabbed Brain's chair and dragged him over to sit in front of the board. "Don't know about you, boy, but I'd look at this wall. See, my partner's ready to rip something, or someone, apart, and I'm just angry enough myself I'd turn a blind eye to whatever the hell he has planned," Marshall said harshly in Brain's ear, noting how Brain stiffened at the threat.

He pointed to the sliced photo of Rick. "I had to drag him from the room when he saw that. And that was *mild* compared to his reaction when we found the basement," Marshall went on.

Brain looked at the damning evidence in front of him. He had told Blade to burn the letters, but his "friend" just never listened. Still, he remained stubbornly silent.

"Brian, y'know where we found this stuff. We have the letters, the rest of Rick's bandanas. I even have the bloody clothes Johnny was wearing when he killed Rick. You wanna know what else we found, Brian? We found the room and the cot where we believe Meg was held for the last month," Tony said idly. He acted like he was bored and was talking about the weather for all the emotion in his voice.

He sat up suddenly, his boots thudding loudly on the floor in the strained silence of the room. It was so sudden Brain jumped. "Y'know what else I found in that room, you little punk?" he growled as he got right in Brain's face.

"What?" the Knight growled back.

"Blood. Lots and lots of blood. If it matches Rick or Meg, you're going down for two counts of Murder 1. *Alone. Do not* expect your gang to come running. They're actively recruiting to replace you and Rick. You still wanna be a clam?" Tony asked harshly.

Constable Campbell stuck his head in the door. "Sorry to interrupt, sir, but the Inspector thought you might wanna see this. We found it at your prisoner's house," the young cop said as he handed Tony a spiral notebook.

Unable to stop himself, Brain groaned. He had thought he'd hidden the notebook very well, but he'd forgotten how determined these cops could be. What they'd find in there would be enough to sink him, and the Knights.

Tony quickly thumbed through the book. "Take him back to his cell, Marsh. We have everything we need right here," Tony said with a satisfied grin.

Without a word, Marshall hauled Brain up, spun him around and slapped the cuffs back on. Brain was too stunned to move. For a brief moment, he thought about keeping silent. Then common sense reasserted itself.

"Screw this!" Brain snapped as he wrenched his arm out of Marshall's grasp. He stumbled back to the table and glared at Tony.

"No way, cop. There's no way in hell I'm taking the fall for this alone. It wasn't my idea to begin with. You want Blade?" Brain snarled. *Loyalty be damned*, he thought angrily.

"I want Meg. Alive. Then I want Johnny," Tony said quietly. *I want his head on a platter*, Tony growled to himself.

Brain hesitated for a long moment. Despite what had happened, he wanted to remain loyal to the gang and the only brother he felt he'd ever had, Dev not included. Yet now it looked like Blade was willing to let his Second take the fall. Alone. Blade had to know Brain was in jail, and yet had never called or contacted him to find out if he had talked. Besides, now the money would only have to be split three ways, instead of four.

"You talking or am I walking?" Tony asked quietly.

"Well obviously, Megs wasn't at Blade's or we wouldn't be talking," Brain began hesitantly.

"Obviously," Tony replied dryly, knowing what it was costing Brain to rat out the gang.

"Dammit, we already know she's not at Johnny's place, and she's not at yours! Where would they take her?" Marshall shouted. He tried not to scream at how long this was taking. It was so frustrating to watch people circle around and try to protect Blade and the Knights.

"Megs'll be the same place Blade is. Since they're not at my place, and they're not at Blade's, they gotta be at Crank's," Brain said logically.

"Again, obvious. Million-dollar question, Brian. Where does Crank live?" Tony asked. They already had Crank's address, but they had to get it from Brain in order to make it stick.

"No way, man. I won't do that. Check out Crank's real name – Eric Jones. Once you show up there you can say you got his address from Delaney or something. Just not me," Brain growled.

"You afraid of Johnny?" Tony said as the three left the room. *It's not much, but it might be enough,* Tony thought.

"Man, get real. 'Course I am. You'd have to be crazy – or Moneyman – to not be scared of Blade. By the way, right hip, near the back pocket," Brain said as a parting shot.

"Right hip, near the back pocket?" Tony repeated, puzzled, as he reached for his back pocket. There was nothing wrong there.

"Boss wants to see you," Jones said sourly. The cop was packing up his desk and had a scowl on his face.

"What happened, Jonesy?" Tony asked as they paused by his desk.

"Suspended until further notice. Had it out with O'Reilly and the bastard suspended me. Said I needed to get my priorities, and my bosses, straight," Jones said as he slammed the final drawer shut.

"Oh," was all Tony could say. Marshall shrugged and led his partner to Seamus' office.

"You've taken a hell of a chance, Seamus," Marshall said as the two junior cops sat down.

"Had no choice. He openly challenged me authority, right out there in the bullpen, telling me I had no right to shut him out of the investigation since he was my senior investigator, not either one of ye. So I suspended him indefinitely. We'll look into this more once we've put the Black Knights away. Townsand give ye anything?" Seamus asked, turning the conversation back to the matter at hand.

"Not much, but he finally broke down enough to say we should look at Eric's house. It's the only place Johnny has left to go, I guess, unless Mendez decides to get involved and hide him away," Marshall said.

"Why the hell didn't we send a team to Eric's house?" Tony groused. He ran an agitated hand over his hair. "We've had at least two teams at Brian's and we've been all over Johnny's house. How the hell did we forget Eric?"

"Fish, c'mon, man, we're exhausted. We've been pushing ourselves until we can't go anymore, then pushed on some more. Look at yourself, man. You've collapsed at least twice at your desk, from sheer exhaustion, before the funeral and at least once since. I know Runningbear came to help you, but any rest you might've got on Saturday's long gone and you're not sleeping properly again. I know you're not eating properly, since all I've seen you put away is fast food, and junk at that. You haven't spent any time with Sheona or your family for that matter and you have enough stored anger right now to rival Rick at his worst. We've just stopped thinking clearly," Marshall said with a rough sigh.

Tony leaned over and put his head in his hands. There was no denying he was still so damn tired, and he couldn't deny how angry he was, either. But, to him at least, that was no excuse for not thinking. If Megan died, he'd never forgive himself.

Marshall looked at Seamus as Tony sat as still as a statue. The inspector didn't say anything, but promised himself he'd give these two a long, paid vacation after all of this was over. But until then, his boys would push themselves, as he would. *That's what makes them such good cops,* Seamus knew.

As he let Tony rest for a few more minutes, Seamus put a quiet call into the prosecutor. "Lance? Seamus. Yes and no. He said to look at the last gang member's house. Eric Jones. Yeah, got it here. Minor stuff. Couple arrests, but no convictions. Warnings. Looks like they tried community service, but no good. He never completed it and it was never enforced. Search and arrest, please. For all three, since I'm pretty sure they're there together. That long? Okay. See ye then." Seamus hung up the phone and looked at Tony. The young cop still hadn't raised his head and Seamus was beginning to worry.

"Quit staring, boss. I can't think," Tony said with a low chuckle.

"Ye've half an hour. Blackstone can't get here before then. But I've some good news," Seamus said with a grin.

Tony stood and stretched. He felt his back pop and some of his strain was gone. "You found Elijah?" he said, sitting back down.

"We'll never find him, Tony, y'know that. No, even better. Rick's awake again," Seamus replied. "Stubborn cuss, ain't he?"

"How is he?" both cops demanded at once.

"Better. Still terribly weak, but better. Jim said he'll get stronger with the blood loss completely replaced. They had to do more surgery on both of his shoulders. The broken one hadn't set properly and the one stabbed had the beginnings of an infection in it," Seamus continued.

"But he'll make it?" Tony asked intently.

"Yes, Tony, he'll make it," Seamus reassured his young friend.

The next half an hour was the longest in Tony's life. He paced back and forth near his desk, his boots echoing on the tile floor. Marshall wanted to make him sit down, but figured the pacing was better. It was helping to burn some of the energy clearly evident in his partner.

"How're we doing this, Fish?" Hank asked as the team approached while Seamus talked to Lance Blackstone.

Tony stopped pacing and faced them. "I've got the front with Marshall and the inspector. Hank, you take the rest of the team in through the back. We go in with guns drawn, of course, but *do not fire* unless you are attacked first. Consider all three to be armed and extremely dangerous, and watch for civilians," Tony said, firmly. Hank just nodded.

"Here's the warrants, boys. Remember – we need these suspects alive. Megan's life depends on it," Seamus said as he came up behind Tony.

The teams pulled up and parked near Crank's house. Seamus decided to approach on foot without lights and sirens, so they didn't flee. Tony led the way to the front door slowly to give Hank and his team more time to get set up. He quietly tried the front door. Amazingly, it was unlocked.

He keyed his mike and spoke quietly. "Hank?"

"In position," was the reply.

"Front's open," Tony said quietly.

After a moment, Hank came back. "Back, too."

"Watch for innocents. The family may be home," Seamus said, then looked to Tony. It was his investigation and they would go on his mark. "Ready?" Tony nodded, took a deep breath and gave the most important order of this whole investigation, perhaps his career.

"Move in!" Tony snapped and flung the front door open.

"POLICE! DON'T MOVE!" Marshall and several other cops shouted.

There, in the front room, were three very stunned Black Knights. They were sitting around, drinking, smoking, and having a good time. In fact, right in front of them, were three piles of money.

Blade was frozen for only a second. Then he exploded out of his chair and reached for something behind him. Suddenly, Brain's comment made sense. Blade was going for his knife.

"Hank! Right hip pocket!" Tony yelled at the cop coming in the back door.

Blade froze as Hank pressed the steely cold barrel of his automatic to the back of Blade's head and cocked the gun. "Gimme a reason, punk. Now, move your hand, *slowly,*" the cop growled. Blade removed his hand from his knife and stood, fuming, as Hank pulled out the knife, gave it to a CSI and snapped the cuffs on.

Tony winced as Hank jerked Blade over to the kitchen and threw him into a chair. From the anger on most of the cops' faces, Tony realized his team members, especially those who had kids, had taken this case to heart. It seemed the team was determined to find Megan before what happened to Rick happened to her.

However reassuring that was, Tony couldn't allow his team to hurt anyone. Police brutality never portrayed well, no matter the reasons. Marshall and Campbell brought Crank and Pup into the room and pushed them roughly into chairs.

"Easy, fellas. Don't bruise them," Tony said calmly. He swung a chair around backwards and sat down facing the trio. He crossed his arms, leaned on the back of the chair and grinned at them.

"Fell apart on you, didn't it, Johnny?" the young cop said quietly.

"Blade," Blade snapped back. He fidgeted under Tony's baleful gaze.

Tony just sat there and stared at the leader of the Knights. Here was the one person responsible for a year of hell, not just for Rick and the girls, but for the whole town.

"Marsh, take Eric and Mark outta here. I wanna talk to Johnny. Alone," Tony said quietly. Marshall motioned to a couple of cops, who hauled the other two up and out, but there was no way Marshall was leaving his partner alone with Blade. Seamus motioned the rest of the team out to search for Megan.

As soon as they were alone, Seamus stalked over to Blade and yanked a chain off from around the teen's neck. Hanging there in the loop was a slender gold ring.

"Seamus!" Tony warned, but didn't move to interfere with his boss. He knew what that ring was and why it was so important to Seamus.

"I'll have yer badge, cop!" Blade growled.

"I'll gladly give it up just to have this off yer slimy neck," Seamus growled back.

"Seamus," Tony warned again, as if he was the Inspector and Seamus the Constable.

"Don't worry, cop. I know what he wants t' know. Ya really wanna know?" Blade chuckled nastily. Tony could tell he was enjoying every minute of this.

"Me son gave Megan this ring and I wanna know where she is!" Seamus yelled.

"Wouldn't ya love to know? Tell ya this, though cop, she didn't fight me fer very long. She definitely prefers local boys to the imports, that's fer sure," Blade smirked, leaving the adults to fill in the blanks.

Snarling, Tony launched himself at Blade, who just laughed as Marshall grabbed his partner and struggled to hold him back. Seamus left the room, but they could all hear his bellow of rage and the sound of shattering glass. Their reactions just made Blade laugh louder.

"Campbell? Get in here now!" Marshall shouted. The rookie rushed in, saw Marshall struggling to hold Tony and wisely dragged Blade from the room, the teen's laughter ghosting back to them.

Tony wasn't even aware Blade had left. All he could see was that arrogant smirk as Blade bragged, and all he wanted to do was grab that knife that they both knew had been used to stab Rick and plunge it into Blade as many times as he had stabbed Rick all year long.

Holy crap, he's strong, Marshall thought as Tony thrashed back and forth, struggling to break free. "Enough, Fish!" Marshall yelled in Tony's ear. It was loud enough to make Tony wince.

It was also enough to bring Tony to his senses and make him realize he could've just seriously screwed the whole case. He was still shaking with anger as Marshall shoved him into a chair. It took Tony a good ten minutes to calm down and focus on the room again. He finally looked up at his partner who was holding a towel full of ice against a bleeding nose.

"Sorry, partner," Tony said wearily. "Now I know how one of Rick's rages feel."

"Now I know how hard it was for you to hold him," Marshall said, his voice partially muffled by the towel. Tony just chuckled as he went over to his partner.

He peeled the towel away carefully and took a long look at Marshall's nose. "Just bleeding, my friend. Not broken. Still, sorry 'bout that, man. I owe you a beer. Now, let's go find her," Tony said, determined not to leave the house without Megan.

"How can you be so sure she's alive?" Seamus asked as Marshall washed his face in the sink, after clearing it with Terry.

"He's all bluff, Seamus, y'know that. He's too chicken to kill in cold blood," Tony said confidently.

"I don't know about that, Fish. I mean, look what he did to Rick," Marshall shook his head.

"Oh, sure, Marsh, I'll grant you, in the heat of the moment, seeing Rick saunter back in like he owned the joint, hell yeah, Johnny could kill. But standing face to face with someone, no way, boss, he just doesn't have it in him," Tony continued. "Now. Let's find our girl."

More than two hours later, they had torn Crank's house apart, looking in every nook, cranny and closet. They were standing in the driveway, feeling frustrated, when Crank's parents showed up, demanding to know what was going on.

"Tony, you ever get the feeling we're missing something?" Marshall said, as they stood waiting for Seamus to finish talking to Crank's family.

"You mean other than Meg?" Tony replied sarcastically.

"Yeah, other than Megan, wise ass," Marshall asked, smacking Tony lightly on the back of the head and grinning at him, despite how serious the whole situation was. "What're we missing? Where haven't we looked?"

"Have you looked in Eric's room in the garage? He normally lives in that damn room, but hasn't for the last week or so," Crank's father explained, just as Campbell came out of the garage, shouting for Tony.

"We found a locked door in the back of the garage, sir. We jimmied it open. There's a staircase leading up to another door," the rookie said excitedly.

She was there, Tony could feel it. "Seamus, get the ambulance ready, just in case," Tony said as he entered the garage. Seamus reached for his radio, trying not to get his hopes up, yet believing with all of his heart Megan really was in that room.

Campbell led the way through the various piles of clutter to where Hank stood at the bottom of the stairs. With a nod, Tony drew his weapon.

"Why're we being so cautious? We have all the Knights in custody," Marshall said quietly as he followed his partner up.

"Johnny's been actively recruiting, Marsh. He may have someone we don't know about up here," Tony replied as they reached the top.

"Ready?" Marshall whispered.

"Go," Tony ordered and slowly eased the door open.

They both gagged at the stench that rolled over them. Thick in the air was the coppery smell of blood, both fresh and old. Just as overwhelming was the stale smell of urine and fear.

"God, Tony, what the hell?" Marshall gagged. Tony could only shake his head as he snapped on the light. Looking around, he forced himself to take short, shallow breaths.

It was a small room, one the light bulb hardly lit. Tony could see there were a couple of lamps next to the bed, which dominated the space. Tony couldn't see a toilet, which could account for part of the stench, he supposed.

They moved cautiously, shining their flashlights around the room. *She's here*, Tony kept saying to himself. *She has to be.*

As he shone his light around, it glinted off of something on the bed. A weak sob caught his attention. He had thought the lump in the bed was just more blankets, but when he pulled them back, he could only stare at Megan's battered body.

Chapter 46

Megan tried to turn away from the light that shone into her barely opened eyes, but she just didn't have the strength to move anymore. Her shoulder had continued to bleed sluggishly, she couldn't catch her breath, and she hadn't eaten since the Knights had moved her ages ago.

"Megan?" Marshall whispered, horrified at what he saw.

Tony didn't hesitate. He scooped Megan up in his arms and rushed to the door. "Hold on, sweets. Marsh, get down there! Get the ambulance!" Tony snapped.

"Damn, Tony, leave her. You'll hurt her more. Wait for the medics," Marshall said even as he automatically moved to obey.

"No time! The gurney won't make it up the stairs. It's too narrow!" Tony yelled. "Hold on, Meg," he begged as he manoeuvred down the stairs.

Megan struggled weakly, her breath rattling in her chest. She didn't want to believe her eyes or her ears. In her mind, Blade was moving her again and she just had to get away.

"Meg, stop struggling, honey. I'll drop you," Tony said in her ear. "Trust me, sweets, it's Tony."

She finally managed to open her eyes enough to focus on the haggard looking face of Tony Whitefish. She really was safe. "Tony," was all she managed to croak before collapsing in his arms, unconscious.

Waiting at the door were the paramedics. They grabbed Megan from Tony's arms and placed her on the gurney. They didn't hesitate, working to stabilize her as the ambulance screamed away. Tony just stood there, in the door, his shoulder covered in blood. "Thank the Creator, I found her in time," Tony whispered, bowing his head.

"Terry, get a team up there and process that room. Hank, escort the Jones' to the station and take their statements. Adam, ye, Campbell and Marcus take those three gang members, in separate cars, get them booked and get them lawyers. Make sure ye keep 'em apart," Seamus barked. The Knights just stared at the ambulance as it tore off down the road. Blade glowered at the cops, his easy money gone, just like that and wondered where the hell it had all gone wrong.

"Where will you be, Inspector?" Hank asked, as he began to guide the Jones' to his car.

"On me cell, with Tony and Marshall. At the hospital," he replied tersely.

Tony quickly stripped off his bloody shirt, and handed it off to Terry. He grabbed a clean tee out of a duffle bag in the trunk of his car and threw it on, then climbed in beside Seamus while Marshall followed in the partners' car.

Seamus handed Tony his cell. "I've already called Nana. She and Ian'll meet us at the hospital. Keep trying me son. I got no answer," the inspector said shortly.

Tony pressed redial and listened as the phone rang and rang. He was just about to hang up and try again when Mickey finally picked up.

"Hey Dad," Mickey said, distractedly. "Jor, *come on*. Hurry up!" he called away from the earpiece.

"Mick, it's Tony. Listen, I need you to meet me at the hospital," the cop said, holding on as Seamus rounded a corner on two wheels.

"Tony? What's wrong? Where's Dad?" Mickey demanded quickly.

"He's fine, Mick, trust me. No, son, we...we found Meg," Tony said quietly.

There was stunned silence on the other end of the phone. "Mick?" Tony asked, wondering if the teen had collapsed in shock.

"Mick? Bro, what's wrong?" Tony heard Jordan ask.

"Megan," Mickey whispered, stunned.

"Hello? Tony? Daddy? What's this about Megs?" Jordan asked as she snatched the phone away from her stunned brother.

"It's Tony, sweets. We found Meg. She's bad, but alive when I found her. I need you two to get to the hospital," Tony said and snapped the phone shut.

Mickey sat in his truck, too stunned to move, tears streaming down his face. *They've found me lass*, he thought in wonder. *She's alive and they've found her.* Jordan just held onto him while he cried.

"Bro, c'mon, let me drive this once. You can't. Not safely," Jordan said and held her hand out for the keys. Mickey shuffled over into the passenger seat while Jordan climbed behind the wheel. She eased her way out into traffic, a little slower than Mickey liked, but nonetheless sped to the hospital.

"You're to go to the V.I.P. lounge, kids," the emergency room nurse said after the twins identified themselves. "Your friend'll be brought up shortly. Down the hall to the elevators. Take the one on the left. On the key pad, enter the code 0522. The elevator'll take you to the restricted floor."

The twins rushed to the elevator. They had to enter the code twice because their fingers were shaking. The elevator rose agonizingly slowly to the top floor. As the doors opened, they saw Tony and their dad standing with Nana and Ian.

"She's in surgery and we're just gonna have to wait," Marshall was saying, trying to reassure a very upset Ian.

"Dad?" Mickey said, touching his dad's shoulder.

"Kids," Seamus said, as he gathered them into a hug. This part of the nightmare, at least, was over.

"How's Megan?" Mickey finally asked.

Seamus sighed. *How much to tell them?* he wondered. "Look, son, let's go sit down," he replied finally, pulling Mickey along despite his protests.

After they had settled in the lounge, Seamus turned to his kids. "Mickey, I won't lie to ye. She's bad, really bad. Jim popped up as they were prepping her for surgery and said she's very ill. Dangerously so. She's been starved, probably since she was taken.

- 399 -

Definitely been beaten and more than once and extremely dehydrated. He wasn't sure, but he thinks she's been strangled at least once. And she's been stabbed," Seamus said quietly.

Mickey sat there, even more stunned than he had been in the truck. He could feel Jordan's arms wrap around him as he began to sob again. *How could she survive all that?* he wondered as he cried. He wasn't sure what he was crying more for – how bad Megan had been hurt or that she had been found alive at all.

Tony leaned over to his boss. "I'll take Jordan to see him and you stay with your son," Tony said in a low voice. Seamus just nodded, relieved the lie was about to end.

"Jor? Can we talk outside for a minute?" Tony said as he touched Jordan's shoulder to get her attention. "Please?" he insisted when she hesitated.

Puzzled, Jordan left her brother with her dad and followed Tony out. He nodded to Kelsey and asked the rookie to give them some privacy. Tony stood in front of the shuttered window. He could just see Rick lying there in that bed and knew Jordan was going to be mad as hell at him. He closed the blinds completely so she didn't see Rick before Tony wanted her to.

"Jor, if you had Rick here, right now, what would you say to him?" Tony asked without turning around.

Jordan wondered at the odd question. She stood beside her friend and looked at their reflections in the window. "I know he always wanted me to forgive him for being a Knight. I couldn't ever convince him I didn't blame him or hate him for it. I loved him as he was. I forgave him for that a long time ago. As long as he was himself when we were together, I could live with what he did as a Knight," she replied quietly, wondering what had brought this on.

"What else?" Tony wanted to know.

"That I love him. I miss him, Tony, but oh, how I still love him. Even knowing he's gone, I can always feel him close to me. Like he's watching over me," Jordan said, her voice breaking slightly.

Tony turned to face her. He was about to do the hardest thing he had ever done and he just hoped she would forgive him.

"Jor, I've something to tell you, something you'll probably hate me for, but I want you to promise me you'll listen to everything I have to say before you judge me," Tony said quietly.

"Of course I will, Tony, don't be silly. But you're making it sound like it's the end of the world," Jordan said with a slight smile.

"It just might be. Jor, you can hate me all you want, but I've gotta tell you I've lied to you and hurt you more than you can ever know," Tony said, hanging his head in shame.

"Tony, what're you talking about? What lie?" Jordan asked, exasperated.

With a sigh, Tony opened the blinds and let the teen look into the room. It took Jordan's eyes a few moments to adjust to the near-darkness of the room, but when she finally was able to see into the room, she gasped as she realized who was in the bed.

"Rick!" she cried, shocked. "Tony, how could you?" she demanded immediately. She turned to him and glared with so much hatred Tony took a defensive step backward.

"You promised to listen, Jor," Tony protested weakly.

"That was before you showed me this! How could you lie to me like that, knowing what he means to me?" she replied heatedly. *How could you?* she cried to herself, hating Tony.

"And it was the hardest thing I've ever had to do! Those tears in the gym that day? Those weren't just for Rick. They were for you and what I was putting you and the rest of his friends through. Dammit, Jor, it hurt like hell to stand on that stage, lie to you and watch the rest of the Knights walk out scot free, knowing what Rick had gone through. He's my friend and so are you. It hurts like hell now," Tony said roughly and turned back to the window. He didn't want her to see the fresh tears gathering in his eyes.

Jordan couldn't say a word as she stood with Tony at the window and looked at Rick. Tony knew Rick's eyes were closed and his breathing wasn't as laboured as it was the last time Tony was there. He wasn't out of the woods yet, but he was better.

"Understand this, Jordan, before ye judge Tony and me so harshly," Seamus said, coming up behind his daughter. He continued before Jordan could say anything. "Rick really could've died. As it is, he still could. He's extremely weak and the slightest overexertion could undo all the healing he's already done. Trust me, he looks a 100 times better than the last time I saw him and that was just two days ago. We did what we did to save his life and Megan's. We needed to give him enough time so he could recover enough to talk. *We did it to save Megan.* She would've died very quickly, I think, if the Knights thought Rick had lived long enough to talk."

"Daddy, that still doesn't forgive you for this. Either of you. I stood by his grave and said good-bye. Now...," she said, brushing away hot, angry tears, unable to continue and not knowing what she would say if she could continue.

"I know, honey, but we did it for Rick and Megan," Seamus said again as he stood with his arm wrapped around her shoulders, looking into the room. "We only found her by sheer dumb luck. Rick's statement alone helped us get the warrant we needed for the place where he was attacked, but it was Tony and Marshall who put it all together. Don't hate him, sweetheart, either of us. We did it because we just couldn't take the chance Rick might be finished off before he could tell us anything. Ye know how much I hate lying to you both," Seamus said.

"If you knew, why didn't you tell me before you came to the school? I could've faked the tears," she said indignantly.

"Maybe, me girl but that's not the way we needed ye to react. We needed everyone to respond naturally, especially ye and the Angels. We needed to see who might've helped the Knights. Thankfully, we should have enough evidence to pin all of this on those four," Seamus explained patiently.

"Can I see him? Please, Daddy? Please, Tony?" she begged. Seamus looked at Tony with a raised eyebrow.

Tony looked at her, relieved she seemed to have forgiven them. "I'm not sure, Jor. Lemme check on him and see how he's doing. I don't wanna startle him," the cop said as he eased open the door.

He stood in the dimly lit room and let his eyes adjust. Jim had taken to keeping the room as dark as possible to ease the constant pain Rick complained about in his head. Walking softly, Tony sat down in the chair on the left side of Rick's bed and gently touched Rick's shoulder. Rick jerked awake, panicked until he realized who was beside him.

"Hey, Fish," Rick croaked. He reached for Tony as if to prove to himself he really had his friend next to him, that it wasn't a dream.

"Don't strain, Rick. I'm right by your left hand," Tony said quietly and grasped the hand Rick was holding out towards him. Rick quickly closed his eyes again and sighed. He was still safe.

"How do you feel?" Tony asked after a few minutes.

"Lousy, but better. Head hurts the most, at least today. Megs?" Rick asked, struggling to open his eyes.

"She's in surgery right now, but Rick, I found her in time," Tony told him softly.

"Surgery? Hurt? Bad?" Rick demanded. He struggled to sit up, but fell back into the pillows with a soft groan.

"Young man, you do that again, and I'm taking back your surprise," Tony said angrily and a bit frightened. He couldn't believe how quickly Rick went from almost healthy looking to pasty white. Rick laid back, his breathing laboured and shallow. Only once the teen got some colour back in his face and Tony thought he could handle the shock of seeing Jordan, did Tony stand up to go get her.

He opened the door and stuck his head out. Jordan was pale. "You saw that I take it? Now you understand what your dad meant. Stay as close as you can so he doesn't strain. Don't get him worked up or Jim'll knock him out," Tony warned softly as they entered the room.

Jordan saw Rick had closed his eyes again. She could hardly bear to look at him. The rugged good looks she had fallen in love with would be forever marred by the scars that ran down his left cheek.

Rick just lay there, hardly daring to breathe. He could smell Jordan's perfume but he was so scared he was dreaming he didn't want to open his eyes. After several long, painful moments, he couldn't stand it anymore. He opened his eyes and for the first time in over a month, beheld his girlfriend.

"Jor," he whispered raising his hand slightly.

"Rick," she replied just as softly.

"Sit here, Jor. He can hold your hand, but don't talk unless he wants to. Just...be together. He still tires easily, so don't be surprised if he falls asleep on you, 'kay?" With that, Tony left the two alone, choosing to stand outside and watch them through the window. Jordan had moved her chair so close Rick could easily cradle her cheek in his hand.

"Thank ye, Tony," Seamus said quietly. "Don't worry, me friend. She'll forgive ye in time. Mickey? C'mere, son," he ordered quietly.

Reluctantly, Mickey stood at the window. He saw the love of his sister's life and the bane of his. Yet, as he watched them, like his dad, he had to admit Rick didn't do anything to his sister and his girl. *I've been such a fool,* he thought sadly.

"Hard, isn't it, son?" Seamus asked dryly, seeing the struggle on his son's face.

"How do you forgive someone you've hated for so long?" the teen asked, bitter.

"Start by saying I'm sorry and then taking it one day at a time, Mick," Tony said kindly. "Less than a week ago, you said sorry at his grave. What's stopping you now?"

"Stubborn Irish pride, I guess," Mickey said with a sad smile.

Anything else he was going to say was interrupted by the sound of the elevator's bell. Jim preceded Megan's gurney off of the elevator and directed the nurses to settle her in the room next to Rick's. The doctor looked tired, but satisfied.

"Let's talk, shall we?" he said and led the way back into the lounge.

"Jim! How is she?" Ian demanded at once.

"Actually, Ian, she's a lot better than I thought when she first came in. The dehydration'll be the easiest to fix. We'll just continue to give her fluids until she's re-hydrated. Most of the cuts were shallow, although there were at least three that needed surgery.

She and Rick'll have matching scars. Her shoulders've been stretched and strained again. There's a couple of broken ribs, lots of bruising and stuff like that," Jim explained.

"Will she make it?" Nana asked, in the silence that fell.

"She should, Nana. She also has a bad chest cold, probably pneumonia. That's gonna slow her down the most," Jim continued.

"She'll make it. That's all that matters," Mickey said firmly. "Can I see her?"

"She's still unconscious and I don't know how long until she wakes," Jim cautioned.

"I'll be there when she does," Mickey vowed.

"Nice try, son, but school comes first," Seamus said with a small grin. Mickey grimaced but nodded reluctantly.

"Slip in and say hello, lad, then join us in Rick's room," Nana said with a smile.

Mickey didn't need to be told twice. He slipped into Megan's room and stood by her side. She was breathing on her own, but he could hear how it rattled in her chest. She was pale and thin. He bent over and gave her a quick kiss. It was killing him to see her like this.

"Rest easy, lass, and get better soon. I need you," Mickey whispered. He turned away and joined the rest of his family in Rick's room.

"She's resting, but she looks terrible," Mickey said as he stood beside his dad. He looked down at Rick and winced at the beating the other boy had taken. As the awkward silence lengthened, Mickey remembered Tony's words. He took a deep breath and spoke before he lost his courage.

"Rick, look, man, it won't be easy, but I'm sorry. I...I...I was wrong," Mickey finally said.

"That was hard, huh?" Rick whispered. Mickey nodded and Rick could see he was getting upset at Rick's short words.

"As hard as saying I'm sorry, Mick," Rick continued hoarsely. He struggled to make a complete sentence. "I'm sorry I wasn't fast enough to save her." Rick couldn't help the small sob that escaped. *This is all my fault*, he thought miserably.

"Rick," Jim warned, looking at the monitors again. "Easy or everyone's gone."

"Sorry, Doc. Can't help it," Rick said, trying to calm down. "Fish, safe now?"

"You're safe from the Knights, Champ. They've all been arrested," Tony began hesitantly.

"Fish, I'm too damn tired for this. What's wrong?" Rick snapped, showing a little bit of his former self.

"There's always the Slayers and the Hit Squad. They've broken up their coalition, so they could come after you, especially Ricardo. What about any of Johnny's other friends, the ones not in the gang, but always there for him in a fight? Mendez might be tied to all of this, or none of it. And no one knows where the hell your dad's taken off to, so we don't know what role he might've played," Tony said and instantly regretted his words as Rick flushed in anger.

"What's that about Dad?" Rick demanded angrily. *If Dad had any part of this, I'll kill him, I swear to God*, Rick vowed to himself.

"All you need to know, lad, is Michael's sold the house and the business, given you the money, and left town," Nana said firmly.

"Nana's right, boy. Don't worry about anything, except getting better," Seamus said. He turned to the other adults and said, "C'mon folks. Let's give the kids some time."

When the three teens were alone, Rick and Mickey just looked at each other. The young Irishman knew he would have to make the first move. Rick had always forgiven Mickey, no matter what, never the other way around. And to know Rick had willingly taken such a brutal beating for someone who believed she hated him was truly amazing.

"What is it, Mick?" Rick finally asked quietly.

Mickey sat down beside his sister. "You really love Jordan, don't you?" Mickey asked.

"Yeah," Rick replied. He was getting tired, but didn't want the twins to leave. He was lonely for some company, other than Tony.

"Would you do anything for her?" Mickey asked, almost too casually.

"I'd die for her," Rick replied fervently. *What else do I have to do to prove myself to you, dammit?* Rick thought angrily. *Actually die?*

"Mickey Liam O'Reilly, where're you going with this?" Jordan demanded. "'Cause if you're thinking of asking Rick to stay away from me, I won't do it."

Mickey shook his head. "No, sis. I'm just wondering if he'd be willing to give me time and a chance, like we promised him we would do and if he'd do it for you," Mickey said, hanging his head in shame.

Rick took as deep a breath as his battered ribs would let him. Mickey was asking for a lot of trust, something Rick wasn't sure he had right now, especially for the one boy who had almost single-handedly turned his cousin against him. Then he looked at Jordan and saw the sadness in her eyes, almost as if she could hear his anguished thoughts.

"Mick, if you're asking for time to learn to trust me, you have it," Rick said quietly, easily forgiving his girlfriend's brother. "Just promise me one thing?"

"What, Rick?" Mickey asked, grateful Rick hadn't refused outright.

"No more accusations without proof," Rick said as he held out his hand.

Without hesitation, Mickey took the peace offering. "No more accusations without proof," the teen agreed, gently shaking Rick's hand.

Chapter 47

Tony turned away from the window with a smile. He hadn't wanted to leave the three alone, but knew it was important for them to start their own healing process. He met up with his boss and his partner in the lounge, thinking about the huge step Mickey and Rick had just taken.

"Those three're gonna be okay," Tony said with a grin at his partner.

"Of course they are. Now what, Seamus?" Marshall asked, grinning back.

"I'm gonna ask Blackstone to question those three we just arrested. Sorry, Tony, but ye'd end up killing Chilton if ye were in a room alone with him or any of the others and I'm not sure I can trust anyone else on the team, either, including meself. This was just too hard on everyone," Seamus said with a snort. "Marshall, I want you in Megan's room until she wakes up," he continued.

"Not a problem, boss," Marshall agreed and went to arrange for a second bed in the room.

"What about you, boss?" Tony asked. Seamus didn't even have to tell him he was to remain with Rick. Someone needed to keep the teen under control when the dam finally broke. Tony just hoped he was up to it.

"I'm gonna take me children, hold them for a long time, then take them out to dinner. I've gotta lot to make up for," Seamus said quietly.

"Start with this," Tony said, handing over a jeweller's box. In it was a slender gold bracelet and, with a cringe, Seamus recognized it as the I.D. bracelet that had just about driven his daughter away. Tony was right – it was a good place to start.

The two cops returned to Rick's room where the three teens were talking quietly. That is, Mickey and Jordan were talking while Rick listened, his breathing still rattling in his chest.

"How're ye feeling, Rick?" Seamus asked as they interrupted.

Rick tensed. He wasn't sure how long this new Seamus would last but, like Mickey, he knew he had to forgive in order to move on.

"Better, sir. Tired, but better," Rick said warily. Seamus just smiled at the hesitant response.

"Like me, it's gonna take a while, Dad," Mickey said wisely. The two adults just laughed at his tone.

"Jordan, Mickey, time to go. Rick needs to rest and I'd like to take ye both out for dinner. We've a lot to talk about. Especially this, Jordan," Seamus said and handed her the box.

She opened it up and gasped. "My bracelet!" she cried, holding her wrist out for Mickey to clasp it on.

"O'Reilly, where did you get that?" Rick demanded hotly.

"Easy, Rick. I had it, remember? You'd left it with me when you went back to the Knights," Tony said with a smile. Rick looked at Seamus with a bit of distrust, but subsided.

"Take care, boy, and we'll see ye after school tomorrow," Seamus said as he led his kids out.

"School? Aw, dammit, Fish, what am I gonna do about school?" Rick asked quietly. He shifted on the bed trying to get more comfortable.

Tony raised the bed until Rick sighed. "We'll worry about that later," the cop said as he settled into a chair next to the bed.

Rick almost sobbed when he saw Tony pull out a notepad and a pen. "You're not serious?" the teen asked, incredulous. *Not now, not yet,* Rick cried inside, trying not to let the panic show.

"Well, yes and no. These're Marsh's notes from a couple of days ago when you first came to. You were trying to get so much out we've missed a few details, I'm sure. Over the next little while, we'll be going over these notes, detail by agonizing detail," Tony said, as he flipped open the notebook, unaware of the pain he was causing Rick just by having it there.

"I can't, Fish, I just can't. The nightmares! It's too soon," Rick said brokenly, giving into his terror and wondering why the hell Tony was trying to hurt him like this.

"Relax, little brother. I didn't mean tonight. *I* still need to go over them to find out what I need to ask. But, Rick, I gotta know – is it just the fear or is there something else?" the cop wondered, putting the notebook away.

"There's fear," Rick agreed immediately. He hesitated then continued. "And anger. Lots of anger. Anger over the constant accusations, every damn last one of them false. Anger at Johnny and the others for doing this. Anger at Mick for turning Megs against me. Anger at my dad and my mom. Anger at O'Reilly for always picking on me. You know, he could've prevented all of this," Rick said bitterly. He laid back, what energy the anger had given him gone, but still fuming at what had happened to him.

Tony sat quietly. He knew Rick wasn't done. Sure enough, a few minutes later, Rick took a deep breath, and continued quietly. "Most of all, I'm mad at myself. I keep asking myself what I could've done differently. I wanna know what went wrong," Rick sighed. The conversation was taking too much out of him. He wasn't ready for this yet.

Before Tony could say anything, a nurse opened the door and brought a cot into the room. Without a word, she set it up and quickly made it. Before she left, though, she checked on Rick.

"Any pain, Rick?" she asked softly as she checked Rick's vitals, made a couple of changes on the monitors and notes on his chart.

"Hey, Mabel. Not as much. Sitting up helps. I'll ring," Rick replied, keeping his sentences short to conserve energy.

The nurse left them alone and Tony picked up their conversation. "Rick, you did the best you could with the cards you were dealt. Who knows how long it would have taken us to find Meg if you hadn't tried to go back?" Tony said as he settled onto the cot.

"Fish?" Rick said tentatively.

"Yeah, son?" Tony said, his eyes already closed and his breathing steady.

"Will you be here all night?" Rick couldn't help the waver in his voice.

"All night, little brother, all night. Just keep calling me until I wake up," Tony replied sleepily and drifted off, laying quietly in the darkness, waiting.

Rick laid in his bed, listening to the steady breathing of the only father figure he had now, and wondered if he could do what Tony asked of him without going crazy. He tired so easily because he couldn't sleep very long. Sleep was hard when you had nightmares of blood and pain every time you dared to close your eyes.

And the anger he had felt was just waiting for the smallest of cracks to appear before boiling to the surface, and since Rick knew it was going to be months before he'd be allowed to box again, he had no way to get rid of that anger. Talking rarely helped any more. And he wondered if he could hold on that long.

"You wanna talk, little brother?" Tony asked quietly.

Rick squeaked in surprise. "I thought you were asleep, Fish," Rick gasped, trying to calm his pounding heart.

"I would be, but I can hear you thinking all the way over here. Figured you wanted to talk. Was I wrong? Do you want to brood by yourself?" Tony asked.

"I'm scared, Tony," Rick finally admitted after the silence stretched on for several minutes.

"Of what?" Tony asked. He remained lying on the cot with his arms folded behind his head. *Let him talk it out at his own pace,* he warned himself.

"Of the fear and the anger. It's gonna be months before Doc'll let me box and I know I won't be able to hold on that long," Rick admitted, proud of being able to get the whole sentence out without have to stop to take a breath.

"That's why I'm here, little brother. You need to talk? I'm ready to listen. No matter what time of day," Tony said patiently.

"Talk, Fish? What if all I wanna do's whine and try to make you feel sorry for me?" Rick asked, curious.

"I *do* feel sorry for you, Rick. The last two weeks, coming on top of the rest of this year, have been pure hell for you. You've been beaten to a pulp and you damn near died on me more than once, to tell you the truth. You're sore and in a heck of a lot more pain than you let on 'cause you don't wanna appear weak to anyone, including the nurses," Tony said with a snort. "Maybe especially to no one here in the hospital 'cause you're not sure if it's gonna get back to Johnny and if he'll use it against you. You're also waiting for everything to go back to the way it was before."

"Wha'cha mean?" Rick asked, even more curious than before.

"Mick and Seamus. You can't believe how nice they're being and you're waiting for the axe to fall. Again. I can hear it in your voice when you talk to them, especially Seamus," Tony explained. "Even if they don't."

"Wha'cha expect, bro? Been fighting the bastard for too long. Hard to believe he's giving up without a fight," Rick protested weakly.

Tony was quiet for a long time. "I think if you hadn't been so badly beaten or if we had found Meg with you in the gang, it might be a different story. But when he saw you lying in the back of Ian's truck, Seamus realized you wouldn't be that bad if you hadn't found something," Tony said. He sat up and swung his legs over the side of his cot. He knew Rick needed to talk. About what would be up to the teen.

"Fish, need to know. Be honest. How's Megs?" Rick asked finally. He was tiring quickly, but he needed to know.

"You'll have matching scars in your left shoulders," Tony said promptly, knowing he couldn't hide anything from Rick any longer. "They've starved her and she's really dehydrated. Some broken or cracked ribs, I think Doc said. She's probably gotta bad case of pneumonia. Cuts and bruises for the most part, but honestly, Rick, it's not as bad as it could have been," Tony pointed out.

"Bad enough!" Rick snapped heatedly.

Tony came over and looked down at his friend. "Rick, c'mon, man, quit beating around the bush. What's eating you? It's not school. It's not Seamus or Mick. It's not even worry about Meg. What's wrong?" Tony demanded softly.

"I don't know!" Rick cried in frustration.

Tony sat down and looked at Rick. His face was flushed and Tony could see how frustrated the teen was at not being able to articulate his feelings for once. "Relax, son. You're getting yourself worked up and Jim ain't gonna let me stay if you do. So, try this. I want you just to focus on a point on the wall. Take a deep breath and relax. When you're calm, what's wrong'll just come out," Tony soothed.

Rick did as Tony asked and it didn't take him long to calm down. He then made the mistake of closing his eyes. Tony chuckled softly as Rick's breathing deepened and he settled himself more comfortably in his hospital bed. The cop inched his way slowly back to his cot, making sure to not wake Rick. As he lay there, Tony realized his own mind was going a mile a minute and he couldn't sleep either. Taking his advice, he focused and relaxed, finally settling down to sleep once again.

It took him a few minutes the next morning to figure out where he was, especially when he heard Nana and Ian talking to Jim. Tony rubbed the last of the sleep from his eyes and sat up.

"Jim, did you give him a sedative last night? I've never seen him sleep so deeply, even before any of this had happened. He just doesn't sleep like this," Nana said, panic tingeing her voice slightly.

"Of course not, Nana. I never came back in here. He's just sleeping for the first time since the attack," Jim said, trying to soothe the distraught woman.

"Morning, folks. What's up?" Tony said as he stood up and stretched.

"Rick won't wake up," Nana said quickly.

Rick just lay there in his bed, breathing easily for the first time in a week. He had more colour in his face and Tony could see there was a lot fewer pain lines visible. He smiled slightly as he could see Rick wasn't really asleep any more. *What an actor*, Tony thought as he approached the bed. *Can't he hear how upset his Nana is? I should box his ears!*

"Wow! I guess it really worked," Tony said, playing along with Rick.

"What worked?" all three adults demanded.

"Rick's having a hard time dealing with all of this, including the pain. He's scared, scarred and angry. Yet, he couldn't tell me what was wrong last night when we tried to talk. All I did was ask him to do a meditation technique Runningbear taught me and, instead of calming down so he could talk, he fell asleep," Tony smiled, looking down at his friend.

Rick couldn't stand the worried look on Nana's face any more and he opened his eyes. "Hey, Fish, what's up?" he asked his friend.

"How do you feel?" Tony asked.

"Better. I think...I can talk now, a little anyway. Nana, you okay?" Rick asked, noticing the relief in his grandmother's eyes.

"Sorry, lad, but when I came in, I couldn't wake you. I thought you had relapsed or something," Nana explained with a sheepish smile.

"Naw. I was just resting. I've been awake for a while. I just didn't wanna open my eyes. Sorry, Nana," Rick smiled. She gave him a look that spoke volumes about what she wanted to do to her trick-playing grandson after breakfast.

"I'm gonna grab Marsh and get some breakfast. I'll be back later to talk, Champ." Tony gave Rick a small salute and went next door, leaving Rick with his uncle and his grandmother.

He eased the door open and saw his partner sitting next to a still-unconscious Megan. "Morning, partner. You move at all from that chair?" Tony asked quietly.

Marshall grinned. "Morning, Fish and yes, I slept quite nicely on that lovely cot, right over there. Hungry?" Marshall replied, putting his book down. Tony nodded as he looked down at Megan.

"Get better quick, sweets," Tony whispered, squeezing her hand gently.

The two cops grabbed breakfast in the cafeteria and sat outside in the warm spring morning. They chatted about unimportant things while they ate, relaxing before they had to worry about the two teens upstairs again. Only once they were done eating did their attention turn back to the investigation.

"Rick talk last night?" Marshall asked as he nursed another cup of coffee.

"He tried to, but he fell asleep," Tony chuckled and told his friend about the conversation with Rick the night before.

Marshall roared with laughter. "All you wanted to do was relax him?" Marshall asked, once he caught his breath.

"Yep. Instead he slept through the night without any pain meds. Did him a lot of good, too. He looks way better this morning, at least once he actually opened his eyes and quit scaring Nana. Meg wake up?" Tony asked as he took another drink of his coffee. Some days the cop felt like he lived on the stuff.

"Never even moved, but Jim's not too concerned. At least, not yet. He figures once she's more hydrated, she'll come to," Marshall explained with a shrug. As long as the doc wasn't concerned, he wouldn't be either.

As Marshall continued to sip his coffee, Tony checked in with the station. "Morning, boss," he greeted Seamus when the inspector answered.

"Morning. How're they?" Seamus asked, leaning back in his chair.

"Meg's still unconscious. Rick had a good night's sleep and we're gonna talk some today. What's happening there?" Tony asked.

"They've all lawyered up. They didn't say much 'fore their lawyer showed up and told them to shut up, either," Seamus snorted. Seamus had no intention of telling his cops who had come in to represent the Knights. He figured the trial was going to be soon enough for them to learn about the heavyweight who had just waded into the fray.

"Great, just friggin' great. How long do we have?" Tony asked with a sigh. Marshall just raised an eyebrow at Tony's words.

"Relax, Tony. Blackstone isn't rushing anything. Rick's still gotta fill in some blanks and Megan has to tell her story before anything else happens," Seamus pointed out.

"Okay, boss. We'll take care of things here. Later," Tony said and hung up.

"Now what?" Marshall asked as the partners went back up to the rooms.

"The Knights all lawyered up, but the prosecutor isn't rushing anything. Yet. I get to torture my friend in there and you get to get comfortable with a good book until she wakes up," Tony said with a chuckle as he left Marshall at the door to Megan's room.

He found Rick alone in his room, his eyes closed. "Y'know, Fish, that relaxing thing you did last night really works," the teen said softly as he opened his eyes.

"You even sound better. No more broken sentences," Tony replied happily as he settled into his chair and pulled out his notebook. He took a quick glance at his notes and then focused on Rick. This was not going to be easy, on either of them.

"Now, you managed to get most of your story out when you first came to, but we still have some major holes to fill in over the next few days. I know it's gonna take a lot out of you, so we're gonna start slow. We're gonna focus on one thing or day at a time, and you tell me when you need to stop, 'kay? Today, I want you to start with what happened when you started slipping out of Jim's," Tony said and pulled out his pen.

Rick sat up slightly and nodded. "Okay, Fish. Wha'cha wanna know?" he said confidently.

They talked for the next couple of hours until Rick's pain got the better of him and he finally had to quit. He even let the day nurse give him a small amount of pain killers just so he could sleep. He knew it was the only way he was going to heal quick enough to get out of the hospital. While he knew in his head he was safe here, he still didn't *feel* safe. He figured he'd only feel safe when he was back at his house. Tony just waited until the teen was truly and deeply asleep before he left to go and talk things over with Marshall.

They spent the respite in Megan's room, playing cards and chatting. The partners just enjoyed the lack of real stress for the first time in several months while waiting for the O'Reillys to show up after school.

That was the routine for the next few days. Tony would spend the mornings talking with Rick until the teen couldn't handle any more. While Rick rested, Tony would sit and talk things over with Marshall in Megan's room until lunch. The afternoons were devoted to working with Rick on his schoolwork until Jordan and Mickey would show up. After supper, Nana and Ian would visit before everyone settled down for the night.

Each day, Rick was a bit stronger and able to talk a little bit longer. But he still couldn't talk about Blade actually stabbing him. It was like he had a mental block. And the anger continued to build.

"Look, Rick, eventually you're gonna have to talk about this," Tony said, exasperated, when Rick danced around the attack once again. It was the only thing left he had to detail and Tony was honestly getting tired of the variety of tactics Rick used to avoid it.

Rick's jaw clenched and his left hand curled into as tight of a fist as he could make. His eyes flashed and Tony knew if Rick hadn't still been attached to the i.v., he would've swung at the cop. Tony also knew he was making Rick mad, but he couldn't help it. They had to deal with this now, not at the trial.

"Look at you, kiddo, you're shaking, you're so angry. Talk to me," Tony encouraged.

"I can't, dammit, Fish. I just can't," Rick snarled back. It wasn't the first time Tony had pushed Rick to talk about it and Rick knew it wouldn't be the last.

Tony had had enough. He surged to his feet and snapped his notebook closed. "Fine then," the frustrated cop snapped back, his own anger coming through loud and clear to the startled teen. "Sit here and wallow in self-pity, for all I care. Forget about the fact your cousin's still unconscious and this is all gonna come out at the trials, one way or another. If you won't deal with it now, then screw it. I'm done here!" Tony threw down his notebook and stormed out of the room, slamming Rick's door so hard the glass next to it rattled.

Rick was stunned. In all the long, brutal sessions he had had with the cop, Tony had never stormed out, no matter what Rick had said or done. The cop's patience was legendary. But what Tony asked him to do was just too hard. With a growl, Rick drew several deep breaths and fell into a troubled sleep.

Tony, meanwhile, stood outside Rick's room, shaking with his own pent-up anger. Marshall stuck his head out of Megan's room. "Fish? What the hell's going on?" he demanded quietly. "I could hear you yelling in here."

"Rick," Tony growled, motioning to the closed door.

Marshall shut Megan's door and dragged Tony into the V.I.P. lounge. "He still won't talk about the actual attack?" Marshall asked shrewdly.

Tony paced for several minutes before replying. "He'll talk about everything except Johnny stabbing him. He's told me about everything right up to when Johnny actually plunges the knife into his shoulder. He just stops and, no matter what I say or what I do, I can't get him past that point," Tony said heatedly.

"What does Rick say when you push him?" Marshall asked, leaning back in his armchair with his leg draped over the side.

"All he says is 'I can't. It's too soon.' God, all he does is whine! I swear, all I wanna do is smack him!" Tony grated and stopped, horrified at what he had just said.

"Whoa, Fish, take it easy, partner!" Marshall said, sitting up quickly.

Tony threw himself into a chair across from his stunned partner. He rubbed his face and sighed. "Listen to me, Marsh. I'm no better than his old man. But, hell, he's made me so frustrated and mad at him right now that...that..."

"Tony, look at it from his point of view for a minute," Marshall interrupted. "He's finally had to face a hard truth – Johnny was willing to kill him, something we've both warned him about and he just never believed. He's scared and scarred. Who wouldn't be?" Marshall pointed out calmly.

"What's your point, Marsh?" Tony asked curiously.

"Well, maybe this little blow up of yours was just what Rick needed to push him past that block. He's never had you get this mad and walk out on him. Everyone knows how patient you are with that kid, no matter what he says or does. Now he knows you can actually be pushed too far," Marshall said logically.

"You think I should just leave it?" Tony asked.

"For now. Make 'im come to you," Marshall advised.

Marshall left Tony sitting in the lounge, brooding, as he stood outside Rick's room, staring at the teen sleeping. Rick was tossing and turning, as if caught in a terrible nightmare. The longer Marshall watched, the worse Rick's tossing was. The teen even made a couple of attempts to pull out his i.v.

"Tony, quick. I think Rick's in trouble," Marshall snapped as he stuck his head in the lounge. Tony wasn't sure what to expect when he opened Rick's door, but it wasn't the sight of Rick tearing at his i.v., trying to escape.

"Marsh, grab his arm. Hold him! Rick! Rick! Wake up!" Tony yelled loudly in Rick's ear as they struggled to hold him down.

It took several more moments to get Rick to wake up and when he finally did, his wide eyes were filled with panic and fear. Tony just held onto him while he sobbed.

"I'm sorry, man. I'm sorry," Rick sobbed over and over, clinging to Tony's arm.

"Let 'im go, Marsh. I'll deal with this," Tony said as Rick continued to cry and apologize.

"Call if you need me," Marshall said as he left, confident Tony had things in hand.

"C'mon, son. Talk to me," Tony urged as Rick collapsed back into the bed. This time Rick didn't hesitate, the words just tumbled out.

"I'm sitting in the chair, tied up. He's pulled the ropes tighter. My arm's broken. Shoulder's gone, too. I can hardly see, 'cause my eyes're swollen shut and I can feel the blood just pouring down my face," Rick said between sobs. Tony wrote it all down, wanting to get it all, hesitating to interrupt, but he had to ask.

"Who, Rick? Who's pulled on the ropes?" Tony asked quietly.

"Johnny. It was Johnny," Rick said roughly. He tried to stop the sobs that racked him, hurting his ribs more and more.

"What happened next?" Tony asked softly. *Don't stop now, son, you'll never go back to it if you do*, Tony encouraged silently.

"Johnny's in front of me, standing there. I hear him pull his knife, 'cause I can't see squat. He's toying with it. He's taunting me, but I just can't remember what he's saying. I won't beg, though. I know that's what he wants. I won't give up. I don't know what I said, but he's so mad he stabs my left shoulder. I can feel him push the hilt in, it was so deep.

"It hurts so much I can hardly think, but somehow I stay awake. Johnny just laughs as he holds the knife in front of me," Rick continued quietly. He finally got his crying under control, but he hurt so much from the sobs it didn't matter. He took a couple of breaths before going on.

"Do remember this – as Johnny holds the knife in front of me, he says, "While you're dying, Moneyman, think 'bout where this'll end up next." Then he stabs me again and again. I don't remember anything else until I'm in that ditch, clawing my way up that bank and crawling out to the road. I vaguely remember Uncle Ian saying to hold on. Fish, I don't think I'll ever be able to look at Megs again without hearing those words, knowing now what he did to her," Rick finished as his voice trailed off.

Tony didn't say anything as he finished his notes up. It was worse than Tony had ever imagined and now he understood why Rick hadn't wanted to go back to it. Yet, he also knew he would have to cover this several more times with Rick, because they were going to need to know exactly what Blade had said, but for now, Tony could let Rick rest. He'd done enough.

"Good job, Rick, seriously. I know how hard that was," Tony said quietly. He put his notebook down and sat on the edge of Rick's bed. He ran his hands quickly over Rick's i.v. to ensure it hadn't been dislodged. He was surprised Rick's medical team hadn't come in.

"Fish, you still mad at me?" Rick asked tentatively.

Tony shook his head and smiled down at his friend. "Don't think I ever really was, son. More like frustrated. You just wouldn't listen. It was like our first few sessions. You kept fighting me and it made me mad. Then again, I'm so damn tired from this whole year that anything would have set me off eventually. I'm sorry I stormed out," Tony apologized.

"It wasn't enough, though, was it, Fish?" Rick asked shrewdly.

Tony shook his head sadly. "No, but no more today. You made a major breakthrough and it's been painfully hard. You told me what happened and we needed that. Later, we'll focus on what Johnny said," Tony said as he stood up.

"I'll try," Rick promised softly.

"Now, how about a couple of hands of poker?" Tony asked, as he pulled up his chair, the bedside table and the deck of cards. As he dealt the hand, only part of his mind was on the game. The rest of it was working hard, desperate to drive from his mind the images Rick's tale had created before he had to go to sleep that night.

Tony didn't think they ever would.

Chapter 48

By Monday afternoon, Jim decided Rick was strong enough to have the i.v. removed and start on a liquid diet. Rick just grimaced when they brought his first real food in two weeks – chicken broth, apple juice, milk and green Jell-O. *Why couldn't it at least've been tomato soup? That I like,* Rick thought miserably as he took his first slurp.

"It could be worse," Tony laughed, watching the expression on Rick's face as he ate.

"How?" Rick asked sourly. Nothing had any flavour.

"It could be bread and water," Tony said, laughing at the disgusted look Rick threw at him.

"I think what I hate the most is how weak I still am," Rick said. His hand shook and his soup was cold by the time he finished, but he absolutely refused to be spoon fed. He wasn't a baby. He lay back, heartily sick of tiring easily. He rubbed at his chin, feeling the week's worth of stubble on it. Thinking back to the sponge bath the nurse had given him that morning, Rick realized he still didn't feel clean.

"Hey, Fish?" Rick asked, hesitantly.

"Yeah, little brother?" Tony replied, coming out of the bathroom.

"Could you help me get rid of this beard?" the teen asked, embarrassed he had to have someone else do this for him.

Tony didn't even notice the faint flush on Rick's cheek. He knew how much a young man prided himself on doing things, like shaving, for himself. "Sure. Just gimme a couple of minutes," he agreed and ducked back into the bathroom to grab what he needed.

Rick felt human for the first time in a long time when Jordan came in for her daily visit. Mickey checked in with Tony and chatted quickly with Rick for a moment or two before he went next door to sit with Megan. He found Nana, Ian and Seamus talking with Marshall and Jim.

"Look Nana, I know it's been more than a couple of days, and I know you're worried, but it really is okay. She's sick and she's gonna need time to heal. I'll start worrying when she's been unconscious for two or three weeks. Please, trust me, 'kay?" Jim asked with a small smile.

"I just want her to wake up," Ian muttered.

Leaving the adults to talk in the corner, Mickey leaned over and kissed Megan gently. "Hey, lass. I'm here," he said softly, just as he had every day since she had been found.

To his shock, Megan's eyes fluttered open and she smiled wanly, "Hello, lad. Missed you," she replied just as softly.

She might as well have shouted, everyone in the room was so silent. Just as quickly as everyone fell silent, they were all clamouring around Megan's bed. The cacophony of voices made Megan wince and cry out in pain.

"Stop! Enough! Please!" Mickey said loudly over the adults. "You're hurting her!"

"Lass, thank God. We've been so worried. How do you feel?" Ian asked as everyone settled down. No one noticed Marshall slip out of the room.

"Terrible, Daddy," she whispered. She began to cough weakly and struggled to breathe. Pressing a button on the bed's rail, Jim raised the head of the bed until the coughing eased.

"Megan, I know this is the last thing ye wanna do, me girl, but I have to ask. Can ye tell us anything about what happened? I don't want the whole story, because me son's gonna kill me fer asking this, but whatever ye can tell me right now's gonna help," Seamus asked quietly as his son glared at him.

"If nothing else, I have to say this. Rick's innocent. He didn't do anything, except push me that one time in the cafeteria when I blamed him for all of it. This is all my fault, Seamus," she said quietly, but with certainty.

"We'll argue that point later, missy," Seamus said with a small chuckle. Then he became serious again. "Do ye know who choked ye, Megan?" he probed.

"Brian Townsand, Seamus. I have classes with him, Daddy. He even admitted he attacked Jordan. I'm scared," Megan said with a small sob. Mickey just held her, giving her strength when she had none of her own.

"I've one more question and then I'll let ye rest, lass. I can get the rest later," Seamus promised.

Megan nodded and waited.

"Do ye know who stabbed ye?" the inspector asked quietly.

Megan shuddered. "Trust me – I'll never forget," she said dryly as she closed her eyes. She could still see the obscene joy on Blade's face as he plunged the knife into her shoulder. "It was Johnny. It was right after he told me Rick was dead. He was so happy about that, Seamus. He gloated about it. He asked the others if they should give Nana two to bury on Saturday. Nana, is he really gone?" Megan sobbed.

Ian gathered his daughter away from Mickey and just rocked her like the little girl he remembered until her tears eased. As much as he still didn't like his nephew, it was clear Megan no longer had any questions about Rick. "Megan, lass, I've some good news," Ian began.

"What, Daddy?" she whispered, her throat raw from the tears.

"I'm alive, barely at times, cuz, but getting better," Rick's voice drifted in from the door. Tony pushed his young friend into the room and over to Megan's bed. If it was possible, she paled even more when she saw how badly injured he was. This *is better?* she thought, shocked. *What did he look like before?*

"Rick," she said, reaching for him. He grasped her right hand in his left and held on as tightly as he could, frowning at how weak he really was.

"Hey, Megs. We're gonna be okay," Rick said softly.

"He told me you were dead. What? How? Why?" she stammered, almost unwilling to believe her eyes.

- 424 -

"Why's the easiest – to save you. We thought Johnny'd be less likely to hurt you if he thought I'd died. I'm sorry it didn't work," Rick said as he touched her left shoulder. Fresh tears rolled down their faces as they realized what the other had gone through.

Nana motioned to the adults. "Let's give them some time alone," Nana said quietly.

Ian touched Rick on the shoulder. "Go easy on her, please, kay?" he said gruffly. It took a lot of trust, no matter what had happened, to leave Rick alone with his daughter.

"No more than 10 minutes, tops, Uncle Ian," Rick promised. "Hey, Fish?"

Tony turned as Ian slipped past him out the door. "What's up, Rick?"

"I saw Megs' ring around Johnny's neck. Did anyone get it back?" he asked.

Seamus pulled the ring out of his pocket and gave it to his son. "I forgot I had this. I personally pulled it off of the punk's neck," he said with a smile. No one even questioned why it wasn't in evidence.

Mickey slipped the ring back onto Megan's left hand, but with all the weight she had lost, it was loose. Megan didn't care as she smiled down at it. It was one thing she had never thought to see again. That and her cousin alive.

Rick sat in his wheelchair for a long time before he spoke and when he did, his voice was thick. "Look, Megs, I'm not gonna lie to you. Johnny beat me bad 'cause he *thought* I knew what he was doing. Just 'bout killed me, but every cut, every bruise, every broken bone's been worth it," Rick said roughly.

"Why?" Megan asked. It was like they were the only two in the room.

"'Cause I managed to tell 'em enough so they could find you. I couldn't lose you, especially 'cause Johnny wouldn't take no for an answer," Rick said. He took a shaky breath before he continued in a low voice.

"All I could think about, cuz, every day I was waiting for you to be found, was I hurt you the last time I saw you. I'm sorry," Rick apologized.

"And my last words to you and Mickey were angry accusations. I'm sorry too, Rick," Megan said softly.

"Look, none of us behaved very well," Jordan said firmly, making the two teens jump. "But we have to move on." She took Megan's hand and then Mickey's. Her brother reached across the bed to grasp Rick's left hand, while Rick somehow managed to lift his broken right arm to clutch Megan's.

"No more accusations without proof. Right, Rick?" Megan said softly.

"Right!" the other three teens agreed.

Rick sat back. He was tired, but something was bothering him. "Megs, I gotta know," he began hesitantly.

"You wanna know when I realized it wasn't you?" Megan interrupted gently. Rick nodded. "Oddly enough – right at the very beginning. They all stood together, but you weren't there, ever. They were so proud of what they were doing. They just laughed when I asked them why. They just kept saying that it was because they could. They didn't even bother to hide their faces or disguise their voices," Megan said. Suddenly, she began to cough again, great tearing coughs that, once she was done, left her gasping for breath.

"We'll leave you to rest," Rick said gently.

Megan shook her head in a panic. "No! Don't go!" she rasped. She grabbed at Rick's hand and held on, afraid to let go. "Please don't leave me alone! They left me alone for so long, I thought they had abandoned me," she cried.

After a few moments, she continued. "You wanna know when, Rick? It was when Brian attacked me. It was just like you said, Jordan. He reached down, placed his hands gently around my throat and squeezed, harder and harder. I remember tugging at his hands, trying to get them off.

"I must've passed out, because I remember being shocked awake after getting water thrown on me. They just laughed and I

- 426 -

recognized the same crazed laughter I heard in the woods. They never let me dry off and I got so cold. When I fell asleep that night, I dreamt about the attack in the woods," she continued quietly.

"I remember, vaguely, seeing you running into the clearing, Rick. You fought for me then. You nearly died for me now. And it's all because of me," Megan finished with a sigh. Her eyes fluttered closed as she rested.

"No, not 'cause of you, Megs. Never 'cause of you. What happened to me's 'cause of the choices I made," Rick said quietly. Megan never moved, and Rick wasn't sure if she heard him. He let her hand go and motioned to Jordan. "I'm exhausted, sweets. Take me back to my room?" he asked, suddenly weary of it all and knowing it wasn't going to end any time soon.

She nodded and pulled Rick back towards the door. Mickey didn't move from where he had settled with Megan against his shoulder. "I'll stay with her for now," the young Irishman said softly. "She won't be alone."

Before Rick and Jordan could make it to the door, Tony entered. He thought he had opened the door quietly enough not to startle Megan, but her eyes flew open with a strangled gasp.

"Easy, lass. It's only Tony," Mickey said as he tightened his grip on her.

"Sorry, Megan, but I wanted to talk to all of you together, without interfering parents," the cop said quietly as he closed the door behind him.

He took a deep breath as he stood beside Megan's bed. "How's everyone feeling?" Tony asked, trying to delay the inevitable. Rick narrowed his eyes. He knew the cop had bad news.

"Tired, but fine," Megan said softly.

Rick wasn't so polite. "Quit stalling, Fish. You've gotta problem. Spill it. We're both too tired for this crap," Rick snapped, anger making him strong again.

Tony winced. Rick had regained some of his old fire, that was for certain. "I've just talked to Lance Blackstone, the head prosecutor. He wanted to know when you came to, Megan. He said to tell you he's glad you're awake and he knows it's gonna be a few days before you're probably gonna feel up to it, but strong or weak, by June 1, he wants both of your stories, the complete stories, and directly from your mouths," Tony said finally.

Rick sighed. He knew what that meant. More brutal sessions, trying to recall every word, every action, every little detail from everything over the past few months. And from the look on Tony's face, he wasn't looking forward to this, either.

"And so it begins," Rick said softly and pulled Jordan close.

Chapter 49

The next couple of weeks dragged on for Rick and Megan. They continued to heal, physically, but Rick wondered if he'd ever even *begin* to heal mentally. Tony spent hours with Rick, talking, analyzing, reviewing, remembering. Every session brought fresh memories and new details. And new nightmares and fresh anger sat there, simmering, right below the surface, waiting for the crack Tony knew would come one day and sooner rather than later.

Megan was also healing, physically at least. She commented one day to Marshall she was healing faster than Rick, but the cop pointed out she did have fewer broken bones than her battered cousin. Nights were the worst for her. She would often be awakened by the sounds of Rick's sobs or angry words from the next room, if her own nightmares didn't wake her first.

It took Megan a few days to start talking about her kidnapping, but once she did, she couldn't stop. Marshall just listened patiently and made sure they explored every little detail. He wanted to have her complete statement before she left the hospital so she could start her own healing. It made him feel like he was finally doing something productive in the investigation instead of just sitting around taking notes. He finally felt like he belonged here.

"Well, Champ, you and Meg get out tomorrow," Tony said late in May as he sat by the window in the sunshine.

Rick just grunted as he continued some physio for his leg. He finished up, then did a slow stretch, being careful not to overextend his stabbed shoulder. He felt his back crack and he sighed. It always felt better when it did that.

"Lie down," Tony ordered good-naturedly as he saw Rick rubbing at his shoulder. The cop grabbed some muscle cream as

Rick eased off his shirt and stretched out on his bed. The teen gasped as Tony spread the ointment on his shoulder and gently massaged it in, exactly as the massage therapist had shown him.

"Did Jor tell you what Delaney did last week?" Rick asked, as Tony massaged his back.

"Nope," Tony replied, distracted as he worked on a particularly tight set of muscles. Rick grunted as Tony pressed a little harder, then sighed as the muscles finally relaxed.

"I guess O'Reilly gave Delaney permission to tell the school what happened," Rick said, his voice muffled by the pillow. He continued as Tony's strong hands eased the still tense muscles in his back. "This is what Jordan told me happened:

"Alright everyone, settle down please. C'mon kids, hurry up. I don't wanna keep you too long," Delaney ordered as the stragglers coming in were directed to the vacant seats by the teachers.

When everyone had settled down finally, Delaney stepped up to the microphone again and cleared his throat. "Alright, kids. I've called you here to provide another update on the Megan Attison case," he began, then paused as he looked at the Grey Angels surrounding Jordan and Mickey. *This is gonna kill them,* Delaney thought. He was still hurt by Tony's explanation, but he finally understood why Tony had done what he'd done. The teacher in Delaney didn't like lying to his kids. The pragmatic man understood why he'd had to.

"Okay, first thing's first. Megan has been found. Alive," Delaney said. He had to wait until the loud cheering subsided before he could continue.

"She's alive, but under guard in the hospital. She's been badly injured. Because this is an ongoing criminal investigation, I'm not allowed to say what those injuries are, even if I knew them. Also, she's not allowed visitors at the hospital as she wants to concentrate on getting better. Once she's home, she'll allow visitors. I've also been informed there was sufficient evidence to arrest those who appear to be responsible. Again, I cannot and will not answer any questions about Megan's condition or the arrests of those responsible," Delaney said and again had to wait for the cheering and cat-calling to subside.

"Yes, everyone, I will confirm The Black Knights, with the sole exception of Rick Attison, have been arrested as the responsible parties. That is *all* the information I have been provided with. We will just have to wait until the police release more information and that may not be until the trial or trials. Understood? Now, I have one more announcement to make and this was just as much of a shock to me as it will be to you.

"I will preface my statement to you with this. Every now and then, decisions are made that hurt people in the short term, but have been done for the greater good. No one faces challenges like this more often than the police. This case posed some unique challenges and forced the Collingwood police department to make a hard choice," Delaney explained, then fell silent as he struggled to figure out how to say what he had to.

Jordan quickly made her way up to the stage when she heard how much the principal was struggling. Holding out her hand, Delaney gratefully handed her the mike. If anyone could explain this, it was going to be a cop's kid, and he knew Jordan would handle it with grace and elegance.

"This is not an easy thing to discuss. Everyone here knows who my boyfriend is. I mean, was, and you all remember how devastated I was when Tony stood up here and said Rick was gone. I've buried that man. However, I have now learned Tony stood here, in this very spot, and told a heart-breaking and difficult lie. So they could do everything they could to find Megan alive, Tony told us Rick had died," Jordan said, her voice trembling only a little.

As she was about to continue, Tom's angry voice ripped over the muttering students. "Are you saying the Champ's alive, Jordan?" he snarled.

Jordan looked at the Grey Angels and saw their anger. Hell, if she really admitted to herself, she was still angry at Tony, but she understood why he'd done it. Now, she just had to convince the Angels Tony had done the right thing. If she didn't, there would be a lot of Angels going hunting for Tony's head.

"Yes, Tom, that's exactly what I'm saying and before you all blow at Tony, lemme tell you a couple of things. First, Tony's just as broken over lying to Rick's family and friends as we are at him lying to us. Remember I thought I lost the love of my life and Tony lost his little brother and a good friend. That lie hurt him a lot and those tears he shed weren't faked. Second, Tony said they did what they did to protect Megan. The Black Knights have been arrested for Megan's kidnapping, that's true. But since they didn't have Megan when Rick was found, the police decided it was safer for Megan to say Rick was dead so whoever beat Rick up wouldn't come back to finish him off."

Jordan paused as she looked at the Angels again. "Tom, when I found out Rick was alive, Doc Jim took me aside and explained all of the injuries so I didn't hurt Rick more by accident. When Tony stood up here and said Rick had died, he didn't know Rick had actually died – twice – on the table that first day as they struggled to get him stable enough just to live. He sort of died once more while they were waiting for him to wake up. So, honestly, Tony didn't lie to us. He just didn't know the whole truth," Jordan said and handed the mike back to the principal so he could dismiss the students back to their classes.

Delaney watched Jordan convince the Angels not to go after Tony. He wasn't sure what the young teen said to the others, but soon they were all hugging each other and heading on to their classes.

"I guess Delaney and Jordan explained what happened and why you did what you did. Most understood, but the Angels, especially Tom and Carl, were really pissed. Jor managed to get them to deal," Rick said finally as Tony finished the massage and cleaned up.

"How?" Tony asked as he flopped back down into his chair.

Rick pushed himself up carefully and sat on the edge of his bed. He was still uncomfortable talking about the Angels. Somehow, he had been put in charge of the Angels, if you could call it that. Tom was his second-in-command, according to Jordan. "She told them Moneyman was gone for good, and I was coming back. I guess

Tom figures I'm leading the Angels. I don't want that, Fish. I'm no leader, especially not a gang," Rick said harshly.

Tony sighed. He, too, had heard the story straight from Tom and wasn't too happy with the Angels either. "I hate to break this to you, Rick, but to them, you are. You're probably the only one, next to Tom, who'll be able to keep that group from *becoming* a true gang. You won't let 'em because you hate the life, especially now, and Tom's been scared away from it. Just talk to Tom and tell 'im that you'll be there for him to lean on, but you don't wanna take over. He'll understand," Tony said philosophically.

"Fish, did you know I sorta died three times in those first couple of days?" Rick asked quietly.

Tony shook his head. "Not until you said it right now. And I've very glad I didn't. I wouldn't've made it through everything if I had known," Tony replied honestly.

Marshall knocked on the door before coming in. "Hey, guys. The boss just called. Seems there's a transfer hearing next Monday. They wanna transfer Brian and Johnny to adult court," the cop said as he sat down. Before anyone could move, another knock sounded on the door and Megan and the twins came in.

Jordan gasped when she saw Rick sitting there without his shirt on. For the first time, she saw all of the wounds Rick had sustained over the year. Most of the scars were just white lines, but the most recent were still a vivid red, and only partially healed. He jumped down and walked over to her.

"It's okay, sweets. I really am healing," he said as he gathered his girlfriend to him. "It looks worse than it really is, I promise."

"God, Rick, I've seen fewer injuries on some accident victims," Mickey said. Rick tensed as Mickey slowly walked around him, then stopped right behind him. His arms tightened around Jordan so much, she couldn't breathe. Rick's own breath quickened as fight was beginning to overwhelm flight.

"Mick, for the love of the Creator, if you value your life and your sister's, move! Now!" Tony barked. Puzzled, but knowing that tone, Mickey moved to the side.

"Rick, c'mon, let Jordan go. Please? He's not behind you any more," Megan said quietly before Tony could utter a word.

It took several more tense moments before Rick could convince himself it was okay to let Jordan go and when he finally did, she took a couple of steps back from him into the safety of Marshall's arms. Rick could see the fear in her eyes and knew she was scared of him for the first time. *Damn you, Mick,* Rick growled to himself as he tried to figure out how he could reassure his girlfriend.

"Rick, c'mere," Tony said quietly. The cop glared at Mickey as Rick slowly walked back to stand near Tony's cot. He faced away from everyone in the room and stared out the window, while Tony stood back-to-back with him. He could feel himself shaking, with anger or fear, he didn't know.

"Mickey Liam O'Reilly, how stupid could you be?" Tony asked hotly. "You know what he's been through! How the hell could you calmly walk around and stop right behind him?! Do you have some kinda death wish?"

Mickey lowered his head at Tony's barrage. "So I forgot, Tony. Sue me," he finally snapped back.

"Look at your sister, dammit! Look at how scared she is," Tony continued loudly.

"I said I was sorry! What more do you want?" Mickey shouted, his face flushed with both anger and embarrassment.

"Mick, you have any idea what I could've done to you?" Rick asked quietly, not turning back to face the angry teen.

"Yes," Mickey replied shortly.

"Good. Remember that the next time you get the dumb idea to walk behind me. 'Cause, just for the record, next time, promise or not, I will flatten you," Rick warned. The silence stretched on for several minutes as Rick thought back to that night with Crank behind him, and the blows that fell on his arms. He absent-mindedly rubbed his broken shoulder and arm and wondered if he'd ever really be free of the Knights.

"Rick, you still wanna come down for supper?" Megan asked tentatively, a little worried Rick might blow.

Rick took as deep a breath as he could with his sore ribs. He smiled over his shoulder at his cousin and nodded. "Sure. You guys head on down and I'll follow as soon as I'm dressed. 'Kay?" he said and smiled again when she nodded. Rick couldn't help but grimace at how quickly Megan fled from the room, the twins right behind her.

Everyone left but Tony. Rick sighed explosively as soon as the door closed behind Marshall. "Fish, that was close," he said grimly, turning to face the cop.

"Way too close, Rick. You okay?" Tony asked, grasping Rick's shoulder carefully.

"Honestly? No. I could've killed Jor. I couldn't let her go, man, no matter how hard I tried, I just couldn't let her go. Fish, I've gotta figure out a way to get rid of the tension, before I explode. Talking just isn't doing enough right now," Rick said as he manoeuvred a t-shirt on.

"Think Jim would okay some running as part of your physio?" Tony asked on the way down in the elevator. "It'll bring back your endurance, if nothing else."

Determined to put the whole episode behind him, Rick said "I'll ask him in the morning," as they sat down in the cafeteria.

The next morning, the first Monday in June, Jim arrived early to do a final examination on both teens. As Rick sat on his bed and Jim explored all his wounds, Nana packed up her grandson's clothes.

"Glad to be going home, Rick?" Jim asked as he probed Rick's ribs.

"Ow! Careful, Doc. Yeah, it's good to be getting out," Rick replied, flinching away from the last tender spot. Jim nodded at his reaction.

"Sorry about that, Rick. That's the last rib to heal, but, considering it was actually broken in three spots, it's not doing too bad. The rest've healed. The shin's good. The wrist's in the cast another month or 6 weeks. The stab wound's healed, but there's no strength in that shoulder. Your broken shoulder's gonna take a lot longer, I'm afraid," Jim said as he wrote down his observations in the file.

- 435 -

"Doc, will I ever be able to box again?" Rick asked worried as he got dressed.

"If you rehab those shoulders properly, yes. Tony's arranged for a physiotherapist to work with you at the youth centre, I believe. Stretches and strength exercises'll be the best for now. Maybe in July, we can look at adding some *light* work on the speed bag for the left shoulder," Jim continued, stressing light. He knew how important boxing was to Rick and he knew the teen wanted to get back into the ring sooner rather than later.

"Jim, what about running?" Tony asked, finally sticking his nose into the conversation.

"Actually that's a good idea, Tony. You can start with walking over to Jordan's farm and work your endurance up from there, Rick. When you think you can handle it, try riding, too, but maybe not on Cherokee for the first few. Easy trips around the farm for the most part, okay? I'll see you at the end of June at the clinic for a follow-up," Jim finished and snapped Rick's file closed.

Rick pulled on one of his long sleeved cowboy shirts and slowly did up the snaps before putting his left arm back into the sling. He came over to the man who had saved his life, literally. "Doc, in case I haven't said it before – thanks. For helping me out and for saving my life. I don't know if I can ever repay you," Rick said quietly. Smiling, Jim carefully gripped Rick's outstretched hand.

"Just go and live a long, healthy and happy life with Jordan by your side and that'll be thanks enough," Jim said and left the teen to finish packing.

Rick went into the bathroom and sighed. He lathered his face, picked up his razor and tried to shave. His arm shook and he cursed. Loudly.

"Language, my lad," Nana cautioned with a laugh as she continued to pack.

"Gimme that!" Tony laughed as he looked into the bathroom and took in Rick's struggles with a glance.

He sat Rick down and shaved his face with long, slow strokes. Nana just smiled as she watched the two. Tony had indeed become Rick's father and older brother. *My boy's growing up*, Nana

- 436 -

thought as she closed the suitcase she was working on. *Too bad Michael didn't want him.*

"I meant to ask you, Fish. Where'd you learn to do this?" Rick asked as he rinsed his face. He stared at the scars running down his left cheek. It was the only visible scar Rick saw every day and it would always bring back memories.

"I had to do it for my father and grandfather. They both were alcoholics and neither was steady enough to shave properly. Someone had to do it so I learned. Life on my reserve, I'm afraid," Tony said with a shrug.

Megan stuck her head in the door. "You ready yet, Rick?" she demanded, impatient to be gone from the hospital.

Rick laughed. "I'm ready, cuz. School first?" he asked, wincing as he picked up his knapsack. There was no way for him to carry it on either shoulder, but it was too heavy to leave dangling. Tony wordlessly showed him the wheels and the handle he could use to pull it along behind him. Rick grimaced. *Great – a sissy backpack,* Rick thought, disgusted while Tony struggled to keep from grinning. *What next? Training wheels on my horse?*

"Mickey said to meet them in the cafeteria since he figured it'd be lunch by the time we got to school," Megan said as she discovered her knapsack did the same thing, making the embarrassment easier for Rick to handle.

"Along with Jor and her Guardian Angels," Rick smiled. He turned to Nana who had finally finished packing away all of the cards and gifts which had flooded in once the students had known Rick and Megan were safe.

"Nana, you sure you don't need a hand?" Rick asked as he paused at the door.

"Go, you two. We've got things handled here," Nana assured her grandson.

"See you at the centre after school. You know where to find me," Tony called as the door closed behind the two teens.

They stood outside in the bright sunshine, enjoying their first real taste of freedom. Rick breathed as deeply as his still-tender ribs would let him. Jim was right – the physical injuries would heal in time. Rick just wished the emotional scars would heal, too. He wondered if the nightmares would ever go away.

Megan turned as she heard Rick mutter under his breath. She shivered at the unfocused look in his eyes and noticed his jaw was clenched. It brought back all the horrid memories of the weeks leading up to the kidnapping. His warnings. His vague feelings. Megan began to shake as she tried not to run back into the hospital looking for Tony and panicking.

"Rick? Rick, don't do this to me. Please. I'm not ready. I don't wanna be alone," Megan begged, trying to keep the panic out of her voice.

Rick remained frozen. Taking a deep breath, Megan, very cautiously, touched his arm. "Rick, do you see something?" she finally asked, locking her fear away for the moment. Right now, she needed to focus on her cousin and help him through this. Then, she could fall apart.

"That damn, bloody knife. I can still feel it plunging in, over and over," Rick growled.

"What else?" Megan pressed gently.

Rick suddenly sighed and shook his head. "Nothing, but I'm scared. For you and Jor," he admitted. Forcing himself to look at his cousin, he shoved the ugly memories away.

"But not for yourself," Megan said, her voice low and even.

"No, never for me. I made my choices a long time ago, Megs, good or bad. But you and Jor never asked for any of this," Rick said as he took another deep breath and looked down at Megan's scared eyes. *Gotta remember not to do this to her,* Rick thought as he pulled his cousin into a one-arm hug. *She's less ready to deal with this than I am.*

Megan wanted to continue to talk, but sensed Rick wasn't in the mood. Instead, she led him over to his newly painted Firebird. Rick stared, slack jawed, as Megan handed him his keys.

He walked all around his car. Gone was the black and silver paint job. It had been replaced with ice blue and white, Glencrest's colours. On the hood was the most incredible picture of a thundering stallion in full gallop. It took Rick a second to realize it was his stallion, Cherokee. It was a magnificent gift from his Nana and it made it a lot easier for both Rick and Megan.

Rick grinned as he opened Megan's door. As she went to sit, Rick put his hand on her arm. She looked up at him, puzzled. "Megs? You sure about this? I mean, really sure? Tony could drive you, after all," he said hesitantly.

"I don't want Tony to drive me, Rick," Megan replied confidently.

"Do you trust me?" Rick finally asked the question he'd been dying to since he'd first seen his cousin in the hospital.

Megan didn't hesitate. "Absolutely." With that, she sat down and Rick closed the door.

The drive to school was mercifully short. The tension in the car was almost unbearable. Rick's fingers were tapping and his legs twitched at every stop. He wasn't sure he could just walk into school like everything was normal and pretend this year hadn't happened.

"Rick, are *you* okay?" Megan finally asked.

"Just nervous, I guess. Nothing's ever gonna be the same," Rick said quietly as he pulled into the school parking lot.

He parked the car next to Mickey's truck, climbed out, got both of their book bags out of the trunk and stood, staring at the doors of Colonial High. *So much has happened here*, Megan thought as she stood beside her cousin. *How our lives've changed.*

"You sure you wanna do this, Megs? We could always wait until next week," Rick said quietly, noticing Megan was in less of a hurry than he was to go through those doors.

"Would waiting make it any easier, Rick?" Megan asked logically.

"No, probably not. Shall we?" Rick said. Megan, nodded, visibly steeled herself and walked to the front doors, with Rick beside, but slightly behind her. As soon as she opened the doors, the deafening silence assailed Megan's ears. Even at lunch, when most of the students were in the cafeteria, there was always a student or two in the atrium, and someone on the p.a. system, making announcements.

Today, though, the only noise was the sound of the water trickling into the pond. The silence made Megan nervous. It reminded her of the dark hallway where Blade had grabbed her. Frozen just inside the door, she couldn't help the tiny sob that slipped out.

Rick immediately wrapped her in a hug. "Easy, Megs. It's okay. I've got you. He's not gonna get you. I swear I won't ever let anything happen to you again," Rick soothed her and held his cousin while she cried. Inside, he was fuming. *Where the hell is everyone?*

Chapter 50

The silence in the rest of the school became obvious when the teens walked into the cafeteria. The entire student body screamed "Welcome Back!" as they walked through the doors.

Mickey and Jordan were the first to greet them. Megan was shaking and trying to calm her pounding heart. "Sorry, lass," Mickey said as he chuckled at her. "We couldn't resist."

"Next time, try. You beast," she said, slapping his arm lightly.

"Rick? Love, you okay?" Jordan asked, frowning. Rick had pulled her to him and she could feel him trembling.

"Hell no, babe. It's taking all of my self-control not to run, screaming, outta here. You scared the crap outta me," he replied harshly, his face flushed with shame.

Standing behind Jordan, as ever, was Tom. When he finally got his shakes under control, Rick raised his head to see his friend grinning at him. Rick still couldn't believe this strong, confident teen was the shy, slender kid nearly killed by the Black Knights less than a year ago and he had helped them do it.

"Champ, good to have you back. Again," Tom said, as his eyes quickly roamed the cafeteria. He motioned to a couple of Angels standing near by to go and break up a shoving match, but Rick no longer worried about the Kid. Tom had learned his lesson. The gang life was not for him, or the Angels.

Rick finally let go of Jordan and gripped Tom's arm. "Kid, I won't lead," Rick said quietly, trying to get that through to him. "I can't lead a gang, man, not after this."

"Tell the Angels that, man. They want you at the top as a constant reminder. It's not my call, Champ, and I'm not gonna fight them. Or you. I'll run them if you want, but they want you to lead," Tom replied just as quietly. Rick nodded, accepting the inevitable. He understood he would indeed end up leading the Angels. *Whether I want to or not,* he thought wryly.

"I ever thank you for looking after my girl?" Rick asked as he pulled out a chair for Jordan, who'd already picked up a tray for Rick.

Tom did the same for his girlfriend before turning back to Rick. "No, but no worries. Just put 'im away for good and that'll be thanks enough for all of us," Tom said as he sat down.

But Rick just couldn't relax as he sat with the others. He could constantly feel someone coming up behind him, but whenever he looked, there was never anyone there. Finally, his nerves couldn't take it any more. He reached over and tapped Tom on the shoulder.

"Hey, Kid," Rick said softly with a jerk of his head. With a knowing smile, Tom nodded, stood up and just directed the traffic around the table. Rick finally settled down to eat. The same couldn't be said for Megan. Mickey could never react fast enough to keep friends from coming up behind Megan. It wasn't long before she was a nervous, sobbing wreck, with her head buried into Mickey's shoulder. The look of anguish in his sweet cousin's eyes just about broke Rick's heart.

Without thinking twice, Rick made his first decision as the leader of the Grey Angels. "Carl," he ordered, pointing to Megan.

"Done, Champ," Carl said and jumped up. Tom just smiled at Rick's natural response and said nothing. Rick could say he wouldn't lead, but Tom knew the truth and was perfectly happy with it. The Angels were Rick's, the way they should've been from the start. Carl stood behind Megan and, like Tom, just kept the traffic moving smoothly past their table so everyone could eat in peace.

As they were eating, Tom's girlfriend kept looking over at Rick, as if trying to decide if she wanted to ask him a question or not. "Tom says you're a Knight," she finally said shyly during a lull in their conversations.

"Yvonne was the first person the Angels ever helped. I told you about it at Christmas," Jordan explained as Rick looked over at his girlfriend for an explanation.

Tom turned back to the group. "First, she was grateful. Then friendly. Now, we're in love," the young man grinned, as he squeezed her shoulder.

"Well, are you?" Yvonne demanded again. Rick could tell she was more than a little worried to be sitting so close to him.

"I *was* a Knight, Yvonne. I left the gang more than six months ago and I've never looked back. That's why I look the way that I do, 'cause of them. Even when I was a Knight, though, I *never* hit a girl and I *never* laid a hand on anyone smaller than me. Ask Tom. He'll tell you. Don't worry about me, sweets. You're the Kid's girl. I'll protect you, not hurt you," Rick swore to her. She sighed, relieved, and turned the conversation to more mundane matters, never mentioning the Knights to Rick again.

"You cool for a couple of minutes, Champ?" Tom asked suddenly. "Gotta situation to take care of." Rick looked up, saw the scuffle going on and nodded. The rest of the teens just sat and talked, catching up on the news of the school and Rick relaxed for the first time all day.

"Megan. Rick. Good to have you both back. Could you please come and see me after lunch?" Mr. Delaney asked. Startled, Rick jumped up, putting a couple of feet between him and the principal. *Where the hell did he come from?* Rick wondered in a panic. He could feel Tom right behind him and felt a little safer, although he was still embarrassed at his reaction. *Why didn't I hear him? It's not that noisy in here.*

"Yes, sir," Megan replied for both of them, all the while staring at her cousin and wondering if he was about to bolt.

"Rick, it's okay. He's been there for a while," Jordan reassured her boyfriend as Rick slowly sat back down and held his trembling hand in hers.

"Why didn't I hear him? I should've heard him," Rick protested weakly as he struggled to calm his pounding heart.

"It means you're finally able to relax, at least with us. You're not always on your guard," Mickey pointed out.

Rick didn't agree with Mickey, but he didn't argue. By the end of the lunch hour, he had relaxed again, but then Tom was there, guarding his back. Carl escorted the twins to their class, while Megan and Rick went to visit the principal. Tom, without being asked or saying a word, was right there behind them.

"Y'know, Kid, you don't have to do this anymore," Rick said with a chuckle.

"Champ, you're not getting rid of me. Johnny still has lots of friends, any one of which would love to take on Moneyman. Until you have both arms *and* your strength back, you have a permanent shadow. Me," Tom said firmly. Rick just smiled. Yep, the Kid would be just fine.

Delaney couldn't help but smile too, as Tom went to settle into a chair. "Get to class, Tom, until the end of the period. I'll make sure they wait for you," the principal promised. Tom nodded at Rick, threw him a jaunty salute and left.

"What was that about, Rick?" Delaney asked as he led the way to his office.

Rick sat slowly in his chair with a sigh. Damn, he was already tired and the afternoon had just started. "According to Tom, I'm the leader of the Angels. Something I really don't need," Rick said sourly. He looked around at the too-familiar office and sighed again. "I never thought I'd be back in this school again, never mind sit in this chair," he said softly as he tried to settle his broken arm more comfortably.

"You *have* sat in it an awful lot this year, son," Delaney agreed with a smile. The smile faded as Delaney looked across at Rick. "Honestly, Rick, how're you doing?" he asked.

"Physically? Most of the cuts and broken bones've healed. The ribs're still a little tender in a couple of places. My right wrist and shoulder're slowly healing, but they were badly broken. My left shoulder has a deep stab wound, like Megs, that's taking a while to heal," Rick said clinically. He found talking as if the beating had happened to someone else kept some of the nightmares away, but not all of them.

"And psychologically?" Mr. Delaney wanted to know. He was worried about the teen. After everything else Rick had been through this year, this was not going to help him get better or deal with the gang.

Rick shrugged. "What can I say, sir? I'm told the nightmares should ease in time. But seriously, I doubt they'll ever go away. I'm jumpier than I've been in a long time and I constantly have to fight the Fight or Flight response. At lunch, I always felt someone behind me, yet you came up without me hearing a thing. As bad as Johnny wants to get rid of me, that's not good. It puts everyone in danger, not just me," Rick said bluntly.

"While I admit I was surprised to get that close to you without you turning to face me, I must also admit it's nice to see you relax in a crowd. Honestly, though, I don't think you have to worry about anyone coming up behind you. Those instincts'll come back quick enough, and with the Angels behind you, you'll be safe until they do. Whether you wanna lead them or not, they're now your Angels," Mr. Delaney said firmly. And gratefully, if the truth be told. There was no one better able to lead that group than Rick. "Besides, I missed seeing you in that chair," the principal finished with a straight face.

"Yeah, right," Rick laughed, relaxing again.

"Sir, you didn't call us in here to talk about Rick and his chair, did you?" Megan interrupted politely, wondering what was going on.

"You're right, Megan, I didn't. I need to talk to both of you about your schoolwork. Now, Rick, Tony gave me the work you did while in the hospital. You've managed to keep up fairly close to your classmates. At most, you're only about two weeks behind. And your marks've actually improved a great deal since the beginning of the semester. Megan, unfortunately, you're about two months behind," Mr. Delaney said apologetically.

"Now, granted, we all know it's not your fault, Megan," Delaney said quickly, noticing how the young teen's face fell with

- 445 -

the news. "I'm more than willing to advance both of you based on your marks before all of this started. Unfortunately, the school board's not so willing. Especially you, Rick. They wanna hold you back and make you repeat as much as possible, because of the Knights. What a load of bull," the principal snorted.

Delaney sighed and went on. "The school board also wants to keep both of you out of school until they meet again to decide what to do. But *that* meeting won't be until the end of the month – and school'll be over. I think we need to make a decision before then, don't you?" Delaney asked with a smile.

"And?" Rick drawled, slumping down in his chair as much as he could comfortably.

"Richard, stop that! You sound like Johnny!" the principal snapped automatically.

"Realistically, sir, what can I do about it? If they wanna fail me, what can I do?" Rick said philosophically. He shifted again, trying to ease the pain in his arms.

"Well, I've talked to your teachers and, for the next couple of weeks, as long as you make an effort to catch up, they're willing to evaluate you based on what they have. I think if you also agree to summer school, the board might be willing to see reason," Mr. Delaney advised.

"If not, I'm sure Nana'll make them see reason," Megan said with a small grin.

"What about Megs, though? I mean, she's more than two months behind. She's not gonna be able to make that up," Rick pointed out.

"Again, let's see how the next two weeks go, okay, kids? Now Megan, I'm gonna give you an option. You may drop Computers, if you wish, without failing. In fact, your teacher's already said you'd get an A. Even the school board agrees. I don't want you to have to go near that hall if you don't wanna," Mr. Delaney said gently.

Rick watched his cousin. He could see how she struggled and wondered how it would feel to walk past the spot where someone had come up behind you, knocked you out and hid you away for over a month, beating and tormenting you. His nightmares were nothing compared to facing that.

"Megs?" Rick asked as the bell rang.

"C'mon, Rick. I've Computers and you've History, if I remember correctly," she said, quickly making her choice.

Outside, Carl and Tom waited. Rick frowned. "Who's got Jor?" Rick demanded harshly.

"Relax, Champ. I got our number three, well, I guess number four, guy, David, with her. She told, okay, *ordered* me to come and get you," Tom said, holding up his hands in surrender.

Rick hesitated, then nodded. "Megs, I'll see you after class," he said as he and Tom walked away. Mrs. Salsbury was waiting for them at the door, smiling as she saw Rick.

"Welcome back, Richard. Now, I've moved your desk off to the side here. Constable Whitefish came and talked to me last week and said you wouldn't want anyone behind you right now, and I don't wanna just dump you in the back of the class, either," she said, still smiling.

Rick nodded gratefully and sat down. He was so damned tired and he still had a long day ahead of him. "Jesse, you're up," Tom ordered as he left. A tall, lanky teen got up and stood next to Rick with his arms crossed over his chest. His Grey Angel tee fit snugly and there was a subtle power about him. Rick breathed a bit easier. Tom was definitely looking out for him.

"Just lemme get the rest of the class going and then we'll talk," Mrs. Salsbury said as she moved to the front of the room. The rest of the class ignored him like he'd never been gone.

"Jesse, do me a favour?" Rick said quietly.

"Lemme guess, Champ? Quit towering?" Jesse replied with a chuckle.

"And close the door, please," Rick said. With a nod, Jesse closed the door, grabbed a chair and sat down. The two chatted until Mrs. Salsbury came over to review what Rick had done since he had been gone.

"Well, Richard, I have to say I'm impressed. You've managed to keep up quite well. Here's the last five assignments you missed.

- 447 -

See how many you can get done by the end of the semester. And I'm exempting you from the final, like most of your other teachers will, I'm sure. If they don't, you just let me know. I'll talk some sense into them. You've got enough on your plate right now," she said emphatically. Rick smiled at how indignant Mrs. Salsbury was.

"Thanks, ma'am. I'll do my best," Rick said and settled down to work. Fortunately, Jesse was willing to give him a hand, even while doing on his own work. At the bell, Rick waited until the classroom had emptied before he and Jesse left. They met up with Tom halfway to their lockers and the three boys just laughed and talked, like the past several months had never happened. It felt so good to be acting like a normal teen-age boy, not someone to be feared.

Jordan was waiting at Rick's locker with her new Angel, David. Without meaning to, Rick immediately sized him up, looking for obvious weaknesses. Finding none, he nodded his approval to Tom and introduced himself to the Angel. His girl would indeed be okay.

"18-34-7," Jordan whispered when Rick hesitated in front of his locker, unable to remember his combination. Rick smiled gratefully, spun the combo and pulled open his locker. He stood there, amazed. All of the gang marks he remembered being there were gone. He wondered who had done that. *Must've been Jor,* Rick thought as he grabbed his jacket. *I so don't deserve someone like her.*

After throwing what he wouldn't need for the night into his locker and slamming the door shut again, he slipped his arm carefully around Jordan's waist and walked to his car, with Jordan carrying his bookbag for him. Tom and Yvonne were right beside them and David and Jesse weren't far behind. Rick felt comfortable for the first time in months.

Jordan gasped when she saw the repainted car. "Rick, that's magnificent!" she said, admiring the new paint job.

"Nana did it for me. I love it!" Rick grinned. He turned to Mickey and Megan. "I'm heading to the centre, Mick. You okay to take Megs home?" he asked.

"You bet. Take care of my sister and we'll see you later," Mickey said as he helped Megan into the truck.

"Wow! He didn't even argue," Rick said, amazed. He waited until Mickey pulled away before settling Jordan into the passenger seat. As he stood up to go around to the driver's side, he tensed. He could feel someone staring at him, but when he looked around, he didn't see anyone. *I'm just imagining things,* Rick thought suddenly, with a shake of his head. *Johnny's gone for good. So're the others.*

"You okay, love?" Jordan asked as Rick sat down, wondering why he'd paused after shutting her door.

"Yep," Rick replied. He didn't want to frighten her, but he was worried. He pushed the new...watcher out of his mind and enjoyed the drive to the centre while Jordan chattered about this and that and Rick made distracted answers.

Tony met them at the front doors and led them to his office. Rick wanted to visit the boxing club right away, and maybe arrange with Bob to help out a bit, but Tony obviously had other ideas. Tony closed the door behind the trio, then moved to lock up his gear as normal.

Rick groaned when he saw Tony's notebook sitting on his desk. "Crap, Fish. Not now. Not after today," Rick groused. He ran an agitated hand through his hair and flopped into his chair with a vivid curse.

"Actually, no, little brother. All I want today is for you to look over what we've already covered and tell me where the obvious holes are so we can start talking about them tomorrow. We need to fill in a lot of details, but I want *you* to determine how we go about this. And how fast," Tony said, surprised at Rick's sudden and violent reaction.

"Tony, why're you pushing him?" Jordan asked as she sat beside her boyfriend. She tried to grab Rick's hand and hold on, but he jerked his hand out of her grasp with a grunt. She knew she had to leave him alone.

"Believe me, sweets, I know what this does to him and I wouldn't do this if I had any other choice. I've been putting him through hell for the last couple of weeks in the hospital, and I know how it's gonna end. I mean, look at him. I haven't asked him a single question and he's already pissed. At me," Tony said, pointing to Rick's bouncing legs and clenched fists.

"Look, son, all I want you to do is read over what we have, that's it. Let's just start with the day you went back. Read over that. If something jumps out at you, great. Tell me about it. If not, think about it when you go home. We'll try again tomorrow," Tony said again as he handed Rick the very thick notebook.

With a sigh, Rick took the book and read over everything he had already told Tony about the night he nearly died. Several times, he swallowed hard, trying to keep the contents of his stomach where they were supposed to be. The more he read, the more he realized there was only one thing that really jumped out at him.

"Fish, did I ever tell you what Johnny actually said that day?" Rick asked as he finished flipping through the notes and tossing the notebook back down on the desk with another sigh.

Tony shook his head. "You've never been able to get back to that part," Tony replied. "I don't think you completely broke down the wall so much as cracked it open a bit. I think you're still blocking the actual words out."

Rick surged to his feet to pace for a couple of minutes, as if composing himself for what he needed to do, then returned to his chair. He closed his eyes and, quickly, returned to that horrible night. He by-passed everything else until he was once again at the point right before Blade stabbed him. Suddenly, he cried out, making Jordan jump and Rick acted as if he felt his right shoulder break again. His wrist was already gone, he knew. His ribs were burning and his leg was killing him. Who knew that such a small crack could hurt so damn much?

Tony reached out and very carefully touched Rick's shoulder, trying not to disturb what Rick was reliving. "Rick, son, talk to me. Do you remember something?" he asked quietly.

"I'm tied to the chair, bleeding badly. I can't see. I can't breathe. All I can feel is pain. My wrist and shoulder're gone. I can't even lift my head; it hurts so damn much. Johnny's in front of me, holding his steel, toying with it. I can see the light flashing off of it," Rick said, his voice thick and ragged, his eyes still closed.

"Rick, we know what he did. I need you to focus past the pain and hear what he said," Tony encouraged quietly. "Understand?" Rick nodded wearily.

As Rick sat there, trying to hear the words he was desperate to forget, Jordan sat beside him, wanting to reach out and hold him, but Tony's warning glance kept her in her chair. What she saw, though, was truly frightening. Rick twitched and shifted as if he was trying to avoid the blows she couldn't see.

"Tony, what's going on? It's like he's reliving every blow he took," Jordan said quietly as Rick gave a particularly violent wrench and slumped in his chair as if tied to it. She was truly frightened at what she was seeing.

"In a very real sense, he is, Jor. It seems to be the only way he can remember anything now. He's already buried it so deep inside it takes more and more to recall it. Now hush, sweets," Tony said, intensely watching his young charge.

Rick hadn't heard a word of their exchange. He raised his head, holding it as if he could barely lift it. His voice was so quiet Tony could barely hear him. "As he stands in front of me, Johnny's playing with his steel. I know I'm as good as dead. He asks me if I'm ready to beg yet. I tell him, "No, 'cause Megs would never forgive me for giving up. She hasn't." Johnny asks if I'm so sure she's alive. I tell him yes, 'cause he hasn't bragged about it," Rick said hoarsely.

"What else, little brother?" Tony pressed, knowing this would be the only time Rick would ever talk about this part of the attack, and he'd have to get it all now or never.

"Right before he stabs me, Johnny said Megs wasn't fighting nearly as hard as she did in the woods. Then he drives that blade in as far as he can. God, it hurts, I can hardly breathe. He holds it up in front of my face. I can barely focus, but I can see my blood dripping from it. As he holds it there, he says to me "While you're dyin', Moneyman, think 'bout where this'll end up next," and then he stabs me again and again and again. I'm dying and I can't stop him."

- 451 -

Rick began to sob, his head hanging while great wrenching sobs tore at him.

Jordan couldn't stand it any more. She knelt in front of Rick, wrapped her arms around him and just held on. Rick grabbed onto her like a drowning man grabbing for a life preserver. He tried to stop the memories, but everything just overwhelmed him. Tony's soothing voice came to him, but from a very great distance.

"Rick, son, c'mon, just let it go. Let go of those memories. He's not gonna hurt you any more, I promise," Tony said calmly. He continued until Rick's sobs eased.

As Rick dried his eyes and raised his head, he saw Tony move behind him, yet he didn't panic, which, considering what he'd just relived, was a major miracle. He felt Tony gently begin to massage the tense muscles in his shoulders and neck, and Rick lowered his head again. It took several minutes before Rick felt the knots finally ease and he sighed gratefully.

"Better, little brother?" Tony asked as he continued to massage Rick's neck.

"Yes. And no. God, Fish, I can't do this any more. I'm gonna have to do this for the trial and I just can't stand talking about this again," Rick said raggedly, trying desperately to catch his breath.

Tony didn't say anything for a long time while he continued to massage the tense muscles he found in Rick's shoulders. Then he came up with an idea that might save Rick somewhat, his sanity at least. "How about this, Rick? Keep a journal. Write down anything that comes to mind, day or night. Keep one for the trials and a separate one for the nightmares. You wanna talk about them in session, fine. Otherwise, we'll just talk about whatever you want. But you're right. I can't do this to you anymore, either. It's killing me, little brother," Tony said quietly as he came around to sit on the corner of his desk. He was just as drained as Rick was.

No one said anything for a time. Tony worried about Rick's intense reaction to just *thinking* about what had happened. *What's it gonna be like when he has to talk about this in front of the Knights?* Tony wondered as he rubbed his own face, exhausted. *How much more can one kid take? Hell, how much more can I take?*

Rick stood up and pulled Jordan up from the floor. "We done, Fish? I'm beat," Rick said. Tony could see him shaking from the exhaustion and stress.

"Here, yes. Bob and the boxing club wanna see you and we're gonna begin your physio today. C'mon, Champ," Tony said, throwing Rick's very thick file into a drawer and locking it tight.

As Rick walked through the doors into the training area, he felt like he was truly home. The sounds of the gloves thumping into the bags and bodies was welcomed indeed. He could see Tom going hard at one of the speed bags while Carl was in the ring, and calling out instructions was....

"Fish, that Derrick?" Rick asked incredulously, pointing to the tall man standing next to the ring.

"Sure is. He couldn't handle juvy anymore. Said it wasn't the same without you and the boxing training there. He tried to talk them into getting a boxing program started, but they fought him. Said it wouldn't do the kids any good. That you were the exception. So he left and joined up here. He's the only one getting paid to do this. Bob doesn't. And Derrick's finally where he can do some good. He loves it and it's doing guys like Carl a world of good to learn a different style than Coach's," Tony said with a grin.

The object of their discussion was Derrick Tomonavich, one of the many guards Rick had encountered while staying at the young offender's centre over Christmas. He was a large man, easily challenging Tony's 6'5" height and was much more muscular. But Rick knew Tony was stronger. It had been Derrick who had helped Rick through some of the toughest training Coach Bob had ever thrown at him and, in doing so, also earned the hardest thing for Rick to give — his trust.

Rick hurried over to the ring, arriving just as Carl finished up his training. "Hey, Champ. Welcome back!" Carl said as if he hadn't seen Rick a couple of hours earlier.

Derrick turned around and grinned at Rick, the grin fading as he saw the damage. "Wow, Rick. I never realized," Derrick said, appalled.

"It's okay, Derrick. I'm getting better," Rick reassured the former guard.

"You coming back soon, Champ? No one wants to spar with me," Carl said mournfully. Instead of the best young boxer in the club, next to Rick, that is, Carl sounded like a little boy who had lost his favourite toy.

Rick laughed. "Lemme get the cast off first and do some physio, Carl. Probably mid-August at the earliest," Rick promised, laughing again as Carl's face fell.

Bob came over to the ring. "Carl, heavy bag. Derrick, you have Tom and Danny. Danny's new, so go easy. Champ, good to see you. Come with me," the boxing coach ordered, just like Rick had never left.

He led Rick over to the speed bags where another man stood talking to Tony. Rick hesitated when he saw the stranger. Bob stopped when he realized Rick was no longer walking with him. *Here we go*, Bob thought grimly. Knowing what Rick had been through all year, Bob had figured this wasn't going to be easy for the kid.

"Rick?" Bob asked quietly as he came back to the teen.

"Who's that, Coach?" Rick asked just as quietly. Why the sight of a stranger would suddenly bother him so much, Rick didn't know, but he just knew he wasn't comfortable.

"A physiotherapist who specializes in physio for boxers. Didn't Tony tell you about him?" Bob asked, puzzled.

"No. He only mentioned I'd be getting some physio. He didn't mention any strangers," Rick said quietly.

Jordan came up beside Rick. "C'mon, love. We'll face him together," she said as she took his hand. It was as if she knew exactly what was wrong and figured she'd help fix it.

Rick was nervous, Tony could tell, but like Rick, he wasn't sure why the sight of a stranger would bother the teen. He hadn't been attacked by a stranger, after all. *It must be the fact it's someone new he has to trust*, Tony realized quickly.

"Aaron, this is Rick Attison. Rick, Aaron Deerling," Tony made the introductions while keeping himself right next to Rick. He didn't

- 454 -

want Rick to panic and swing, and judging by how much Rick was shaking, swinging would be likely. Damaged shoulders or not.

"Nice to meet you, Rick," Aaron said. He shook Rick's outstretched left hand.

"You, too," Rick replied warily.

"Did I do something wrong?" Aaron asked Tony, hearing Rick's hesitation.

"No, Aaron, it's me. I'm a little nervous around strangers lately," Rick explained, trying to swallow his fear.

"Rick's a former gang member, so trust's hard for him to give. Strangers in general tend to make him nervous. He's also recovering from a brutal beating," Tony explained and quickly outlined Rick's injuries.

Aaron looked at the hand he had just shaken and nodded. He had figured out who Rick really was once Tony said gang member and beating. It had been in all the papers, after all, including the "funeral." "Okay, Rick, here we go. I want you to squeeze my hand as hard as you can. Left first," the physiotherapist said. Rick grabbed the proffered hand like he was going to shake it and squeezed.

"Good. Very good, in fact," Aaron said with approval. Rick snorted. "It's probably weaker than *you* remember, but good nonetheless, considering what's happened to you," he said. "Now, how about the right?"

Aaron carefully went through a whole range of tests with Rick, seeing his strengths and weaknesses. "Okay, just about done. I need to do one more test," Aaron said and moved around behind Rick. Rick immediately stiffened and moved away.

"Aaron, stop! Do not move!" Tony's voice cracked like a whip. "Rick, listen to me. I'm gonna be right behind you. It's gonna be okay," Tony said as he and Aaron walked behind the tense teen. "Don't touch him without telling him exactly what you're gonna do, or you'll be peeling yourself off the floor, broken wrist or not," Rick heard Tony say to Aaron in a low voice.

"Rick, I'm going to reach up and grasp your left shoulder and then lift your arm, okay? Here we go," Aaron said after a moment's hesitation.

It took all of Rick's self-control to stand there and let someone grab him from behind. Jordan stood next to her normally strong boyfriend and watched him become a quivering mass. Suddenly, she understood a bit what Rick had gone through.

"Rick, look at me. Focus on me, not on what's going on behind you," she said, moving quickly to stand right in front of him.

Rick stared at Jordan gratefully while Aaron probed, gently at first, his left then his right shoulder. It was only a couple of minutes, but to Rick it was forever. His breathing became more rapid and he began to shift from foot-to-foot. He couldn't stand it any longer.

"Tony," Jordan warned as Rick's eyes dilated and he began to breathe even faster.

"Aaron, move! Now!" Tony said, dragging the startled physiotherapist away.

Not a moment too soon. Rick fled back to Tony's office, ignoring the startled looks on his friends' faces as he ran from the gym. He slammed the door behind him, and stood there, his heart pounding, his breathing even more ragged than it had been in the gym. He couldn't believe what had just happened. He had fled like a wimp. He had been broken, just like Blade had promised.

"Damn you, Johnny," Rick muttered quietly but with venom.

He forced himself away from the door and sat in Tony's chair. He stared at the desk, not really seeing anything until he calmed down enough to make himself raise his head. There, in the doorway, stood a very concerned Tony. Once again, Rick hadn't heard a thing. *What the hell's wrong with me?* Rick wondered in a panic. He'd never had this many people sneak up on him before, and it was scaring the crap out of him.

"You cool, little brother?" Tony asked. He moved from the door, not wanting to make Rick feel any more trapped than Tony guessed he already did.

"No. Fish, what's wrong with me?" Rick asked, ashamed.

Tony closed the door and sat down; silence dominated the small office. "Fight or flight, Rick. It's bred into all of us and when faced with a choice, we choose the one best suited to the situation," Tony said finally.

"I've never run from anything in my life like I just did," Rick protested weakly. "Not even Johnny."

"So the question becomes why? Why did you run?" Tony asked logically.

"Straight up, Fish? I was scared. All I knew was Johnny was behind me. Every touch was the knife or a punch. I was scared," Rick repeated softly.

Tony sighed. This was going to be a lot harder than he thought. "You knew I was behind you, Champ. Not Johnny, and I'd never do anything to hurt you," Tony pointed out. Rick jumped to his feet immediately, shaking his head in denial.

"No! No way, Fish, I wouldn't've run from you. It was Johnny! I know it. I could...I could feel it! He was standing there, waiting. I wanted to beg him to stop, but I just couldn't do it! Megs would've hated me for giving up. But it hurt so much! I just wanted him to stop! Please make it stop! I'll come back, Johnny, please just make it stop!" Rick begged, dropping suddenly to his knees.

Tony heard the crack as Rick's forehead hit the desk and he shot around to the other side. "Christ, Rick!" Tony said, holding a handkerchief to Rick's bleeding head. He wrapped his arms around Rick and just held onto his "little brother" until Rick collapsed from exhaustion, the panic draining him completely.

And when Rick finally began to talk, his voice hoarse and hard to hear, Tony learned about the nightmares that came, day and night, in vivid, damning, horrid detail.

Chapter 51

As Rick struggled at the youth centre, Megan and Mickey enjoyed their first full afternoon together outside of the hospital. They spent most of their time walking, hand in hand, through their favourite park, remembering the better times, until Megan grew too tired to continue. As they walked back to the truck, Megan told Mickey about the discussion with Mr. Delaney about her schoolwork.

"I guess Rick's only about two weeks behind," Megan said sadly. She was worried. She'd always been an honour student. Now, she was probably going to fail most of her classes.

"How's that possible?" Mickey asked, puzzled.

"As I understand it, Tony had him doing correspondence work while he was in hiding and then he's been working at the hospital about two weeks longer than I have. I wasn't that lucky," Megan said sadly.

"No worries, lass. I'll help you," Mickey promised as they climbed back into the truck. Megan snuggled right next to her boyfriend, feeling safe as soon as his arm settled carefully around her shoulder.

"I missed this," she said happily.

Mickey kissed the top of her head. "Me, too, Megan. Me, too," Mickey replied as he drove to Glencrest.

As they pulled up to the house, Mickey frowned. "Wonder what Dad's doing here?" he said as he parked.

"You can ask him yourself, lad. He's on the porch with Nana, Daddy and...a stranger," Megan said hesitantly. Like Rick, she was suddenly leery of anyone she didn't know.

"Stay here for a sec, Megan. I'll find out who he is and what's going on. Lock the door behind me," Mickey said, jumping out of the truck. Megan watched nervously as Mickey's dad introduced his son to the fourth person on the porch. Mickey frowned, argued for a couple of minutes, then shrugged and walked back to his truck.

"What's wrong, Mickey?" Megan asked as she rolled down her window.

"The other guy's Assistant Chief Prosecutor Charles Adams, and he's here to ask you some questions," Mickey said sourly. *I don't get why Dad said this couldn't wait*, Mickey fumed as Megan paled.

"Already? I haven't even been home yet!" Megan protested weakly.

"I know, lass, but he says it can't wait. It has to be done today," Mickey said sadly and opened the door to help her down from the truck.

Megan came up to the porch and stopped at the bottom of the stairs. "Daddy, Nana. What's going on?" she asked quietly, struggling to hide how upset she was at this invasion. All she had wanted to do when she got home this first day was to sit on the porch with her family and soak in the sun. An officious young man pushed past everyone on the porch to get right in Megan's face.

"Miss Attison? I'm Charles Adams. I'm with the Prosecutor's office," Charles said, coming down the stairs to shake her hand. He paused, confused, as Mickey stepped in front of Megan and glared at him.

"Sir, is this really necessary? I've spent so many hours going over everything with Constable Andrews while I was in the hospital I can almost recite my entire testimony in my sleep," Megan began quietly as she unashamedly hid behind Mickey.

"Yes, yes, I know you have, but I wanna hear everything from you, not read a piece of paper," Charles interrupted impatiently, dismissing her statement with a wave of his hand.

"Young man, curb your attitude!" Nana snapped. "Or I'll tell Lance to replace you with someone with some compassion."

"I'm sorry, Mrs. Attison, but we really don't have time to be gentle. The transfer hearing *is* on Monday and I need to go over your granddaughter's story while it's still fresh in her mind," Charles said firmly, trying to figure out what was going so wrong.

"Mr. Adams, trust me, there's no way I'm ever gonna forget what happened to me," Megan said dryly. "No one will."

"Look, I think we've managed to get off on the wrong foot here. Could we just sit down and talk? Please?" Charles asked, motioning to the porch.

Megan hesitated, then climbed the stairs to sit beside Mickey in the swing while the adults sat in the patio chairs. *Some homecoming*, Megan thought acidly. *I don't even get to set foot in my own house before Johnny traps me again.*

"I'm gonna be blunt, Mr. Adams," Megan began once they were all settled and Martha had served them drinks.

"Knowing your family, Miss Megan, I don't expect anything less," Charles smiled as he pulled out paper and pen.

"I don't like this. Not one damn bit. I was just released from the hospital this morning. I've spent a rather rough afternoon in school, trying not to jump out of my skin when well- meaning friends came up behind me. I'm about two months behind in my schoolwork and I have the school board threatening to hold me back from advancing in my classes because of something I didn't do. Now I don't even get to come home before you jump all over me about a situation I've gone into full detail with a man I know and definitely trust far more than you, Mr. Adams," Megan said harshly as she sipped at her iced tea, trying very hard not to show how much she was shaking.

Mickey, however, knew exactly how bad she was shaking and how much she was hurting. His arm was around her shoulders and he could feel it. "Dad, why're you doing this to her? Why today?" Mickey protested, glaring at the Assistant Prosecutor.

"Son, I don't like doing this any more than ye like me doing it. But Lance wants Megan's statement," Seamus explained patiently.

"And they have it! Megan's given it to Marshall. At the hospital," Ian pointed out. He was just as angry as Mickey.

"I'm sorry, folks, but I don't understand. Why's everyone so upset?" Charles asked, puzzled. "All I want is to hear her story straight from her mouth, instead of reading a piece of paper. What's so wrong with that?"

Megan pulled away from Mickey. She sat up, the sudden anger she felt giving her the strength she needed. "What do you wanna hear, Mr. Adams? Do you wanna hear how the Knights grabbed me from the school, a place where I was supposed to be safe? Do you wanna hear how they used stolen drugs to knock me out? Do you wanna know how they beat me, starved me, strangled me, tried to drown me more than once?" Megan snapped harshly.

"Easy, Megan," Mickey soothed, trying to gather her back into his arms. She shoved him away angrily.

"No, Mickey. He wants to hear it. Well, Mr. Adams? How about how I could hear them trying to kill my cousin? How they gloated when they read me his obituary?" Megan continued hotly, trying not to give into the tears that threatened to fall.

She undid her blouse, pushed it open and pulled off the bandage to expose the still slightly raw stab wound that had started to bleed a tiny bit. Charles turned his head away from the sight. "Would you like to know how Johnny laughed as he asked Eric if they should give Nana two grandkids to bury right before he plunged his knife all the way to the hilt into my shoulder? In exactly the same spot as Rick's stab wound? Don't turn away, Mr. Adams. You wanted to know, now look at it!

"Would you like to know how I'm such a nervous wreck my own boyfriend, not to mention my father, doesn't know if he should hold me or just leave me be? Or how, just sitting here talking to you's making it all come back in horrible, vivid, damning colour and all I wanna do is this?" Megan bolted into the house and up to her room. They could hear her sobbing as she fled, slamming the door behind her.

"Mickey, son, go to her. Make sure she's okay and stay with her until she's calmed down," Seamus said.

Mickey closed the door behind him a great deal more gently than Megan did. Seamus sighed explosively. "Ye've just ruined yer chances with that girl," the inspector said harshly.

"Wow! I never guessed. This is the first case of its kind I've ever worked," Charles said. *And probably my last,* he realized as Nana glared at him.

"Mr. Adams, I want you off my property and off this case. I don't ever want you near either of my grandchildren or my family ever again," Nana said firmly.

Charles nodded. He wasn't surprised by her reaction. How he had blown everything so badly was beyond him. He handed Nana a binder filled with paper. "We've marked the passages Lance wanted more detail on. Honestly, I'm really very sorry for any trouble I've caused," he said. As he stood, Nana's cell began to ring shrilly.

"Leave it. We'll do our best," Ian said sharply as his mother answered her phone. The young lawyer left, talking on his own cell phone.

"Oh Tony, is he okay?" Nana asked as Charles drove away. She listened for a couple of minutes, then said, "Bring him home, lad. We'll figure something out." She snapped the phone closed and sighed. *What an afternoon,* Nana thought as she stared out at the ranch.

"Mother? What's wrong?" Ian asked, pouring more iced tea for everyone.

"That was Tony. Rick had some kind of panic attack while at the centre. Tony was getting some physio for him when he bolted," Nana said as she sipped her drink.

"Like Megan just did?" Seamus said shrewdly.

"Do you blame them? Either of them?" Ian asked harshly. "Dammit, Seamus, I can't get her to talk to me, so I can only imagine what she's actually going through. And Rick? He's probably three times as bad as my lass. That idiot lawyer didn't help matters any. To get what Lance needs, you're gonna have to bring in Marshall, I'm figuring."

Seamus nodded. "Probably, and no, Ian, I don't blame either one of them. This isn't gonna be easy for anyone to get through, let alone those two kids. No matter how much I may have, well, hated Rick, I would never wish this on anyone. A couple of days ago, Tony let me read just a couple of Rick's memories...," Seamus' voice trailed off, as he stared off into space.

"Bad?" Nana asked shrewdly.

"Nana, y'know I grew up in Belfast in Northern Ireland and I've seen some pretty bad things. This was ten times worse. It gave *me* nightmares, and Tony said it was one of Rick's *milder* memories. What're the ones Rick won't or can't talk about really like? The ones that've probably woken him up in the middle of the night, leaving him drenched in sweat and screaming in terror? No, I'm not surprised he's having panic attacks. Megan, either. They've both been through a hell no adult should go through, let alone a child," Seamus said and firmly turned the discussion to more mundane farm matters. Tomorrow was going to be soon enough to deal with this again.

The three adults were still on the porch when Rick arrived home. Nana wasn't surprised to see Jordan driving her grandson's car and Tony pulling up behind them. She walked over to the house to open the front door while Ian went in to see if he could finally get his daughter to talk to him and Seamus remained on the porch, trying to relax.

"Rick, we're home, love," Jordan said as she shook him awake.

Rick groaned. He undid his seat belt, opened his door and fell onto the ground. God, he was so tired. He felt strong hands lift him up and he struggled, weakly.

"Easy, little brother. It's Fish. I've got you," Tony whispered in his ear. Rick leaned on his friend as they slowly walked up to his house, his legs shaking so badly he was surprised he could walk at all. Jordan followed silently along, carrying Rick's book bag, worried.

"Here, Tony, bring him in here," Nana said as she opened the front door and led the way into the living room. Tony eased Rick down on the couch, leaving the teen lying there, unmoving, and as pale as he'd been in the hospital.

"Rick? Lad?" Nana asked, touching her grandson's shoulder, not liking his pale face and sluggish response.

"Hey, Nana," Rick replied quietly. He had thrown his left arm over his eyes against the bright light of the afternoon sun streaming in the window.

"Are you hungry, lad?" Nana asked gently as Tony lowered the blinds and Rick lowered his arm. He grimaced at how much it throbbed just from a few moments raised over his head.

Rick nodded carefully, trying to keep the room from spinning any more than it already was. "I'll make you some soup and a couple of sandwiches. How's that?" Nana asked. Rick just nodded again. He could hear everyone moving around, yet oddly enough, he didn't feel panicked now, just totally exhausted.

"Jordan, ye here?" Seamus called loudly from the front door. Rick winced again.

"In here, Daddy, and quiet, please," she called back as quietly as she could while she bathed Rick's face with a cool cloth.

"Christ, Tony, he looks like ye've put him through the wringer. Again," Rick heard Seamus mutter. *Matches how I feel, O'Reilly,* Rick thought sourly as Jordan continued to mop his brow.

"The worst part, boss, is I get to do this to him again and again, over and over. All I'm doing's causing him more nightmares. I gotta figure out a way to help him get through this when I'm not here, 'cause they don't always come when I'm around to help him. He's gotta learn how to deal with them. Alone. Dammit, when's it gonna end?" Tony said angrily. The cop whirled and slammed his fist into the door, denting it, finally giving into the pent-up anger he had held in all year long.

Seamus just shook his head. He had no answer for his young cop or the teens who looked to him for those same answers. He sighed. "Feel better, Tony? Didn't think so. Just make sure ye fix that door, 'kay? As for when this is all gonna end, well, I guess it'll end when the trials're over. Though, I honestly doubt he's ever gonna be totally free of the Knights and, well, ye'll just have to deal with it," Seamus said. Tony just grunted as he rubbed his sore hand.

Rick sat up slowly. The room swam and he gritted his teeth until the nausea passed. He hardly remembered the last couple of hours. He'd talked, he knew, because his throat was dry and scratchy, but he couldn't remember a single word of what he had said. He hoped like hell Tony knew or he was going to spend the night thinking and worrying.

"Here, Rick. Try and eat," Nana said, putting a tray on the living room table.

"Thanks, Nana," Rick managed to reply. His favourite, cream of tomato soup and grilled cheese sandwiches, sat in front of him. *Could it get any better?* Rick smiled as he slowly ate.

"Jordan, honey, time to go home. Ye've school in the morning," Seamus said quietly a few minutes later. Rick nodded for her to go as she hesitated. "I'll go and get yer brother. Tony, ye gonna be here for a while?" Tony nodded as he watched Jordan give Rick a hug and kiss before following her father out of the house.

"Tony, if you're gonna be here, I'm gonna check on Megan," Nana said from the doorway.

"Megs? What's wrong with Megs?" Rick demanded quickly, surging to his feet, swaying and would've fallen if Tony hadn't caught him.

"Easy, son. Sit back down," Tony said, easing Rick back down to the couch.

"Yes, Rick, take it easy. She's okay. It's just she was blind-sided by the prosecution. They sent someone over to take her "statement" today when she got home. It blew up in his face when Megan bolted," Nana explained sourly. Rick growled. *How the hell could they do that to her?* he wondered angrily.

"I'll call Marsh to come and see her after school at the centre tomorrow or here if she's more comfortable with that. Go on, Nana. I'll take care of Rick," Tony said, closing the door behind her.

He watched Rick slowly eat his soup and sandwiches. The cop was glad to see some colour back in the teen's face, but he was still too pale for Tony's peace of mind. Rick leaned back once he had finished and closed his eyes. He heard Tony clean up supper and wondered what his friend would want to talk about.

"Rough day, huh, little brother?" Tony finally said, after sitting in the recliner and watching Rick for several minutes.

"Hell, yes. Fish, what went wrong?" Rick had to ask. He hadn't moved or opened his eyes. For the first time all day, he was relaxed and comfortable.

"Honestly, Rick, I'm not really sure. The only thing I can think of is you were completely overwhelmed today. You've just got outta the hospital and you insisted on going right back to school, instead of easing back into it or finishing the year by correspondence. I heard you didn't have an easy day today, either. Delaney called me to warn me," Tony said when Rick looked at him. Rick chuckled as he leaned back and closed his eyes once again.

"Then, like an idiot, I pushed you for more info, knowing you'd had a crappy day. Last, I decided to bring in a stranger who I didn't explain anything to and who scared the crap out of you by being behind you," Tony said thoughtfully. "Although why a stranger would bother you, I'm not sure and we'll just have to learn to work with it."

"And I overreacted?" Rick asked, finally sitting up and opening his eyes. The room still spun, but it was definitely less.

"I wouldn't call it overreacting, necessarily, although that'll do for lack of anything better. You're still trying to recover physically, never mind mentally and emotionally. We haven't talked at all about how you're feeling – I'm struggling to just get you to tell me what happened, never mind how you're dealing, or more likely, not dealing, with it. Today, it just all came out," Tony said.

"Do you think it'll get better as I go?" Rick asked. He rubbed at his neck.

"C'mon, Rick. I think a massage'll do you wonders," Tony said instead and led the way to Rick's bedroom. Rick stripped off his shirt and laid down on his bed. As Tony began to massage Rick's tense muscles, he continued the interrupted conversation.

"I don't think things'll get any better until you get the Knights outta your system and that includes trying to deal with the memories. That's why I suggested the journal. You've gotta get it out," Tony said as he worked on Rick's shoulders. Silence fell while Rick just let his mind wander.

"Fish, what did I talk about this afternoon?" Rick finally asked.

"What do you remember?" was Tony's prompt reply.

"We talked about what Johnny said when he stabbed me," Rick recalled after a couple of minutes. "Jor was there and I know I scared the crap outta her. I told you I couldn't do this anymore and you suggested the journal. I think."

"Good. That's right. What next?" Tony asked, encouraged.

"We were in the gym. I was talking to Carl and Derrick and then Coach asked me to come and meet the physiotherapist, Aaron, wasn't it? He made me do some tests," Rick continued sleepily. He was starting to drift off.

"Then what?" Tony asked, as he wiped his hands on a towel. He sat on the floor by the bed where Rick could look right at him without straining.

"All I really remember he's suddenly behind me, and that's when I panicked. I wasn't in the gym any more, I was at Johnny's. I could feel someone behind me, and I couldn't figure out if it was Johnny or Eric. All I knew was I was gonna die," Rick said quietly. It was the first time Rick had admitted he really could've died that night.

"Do you remember what happened in the office?" Tony asked.

Rick nodded as he touched the lump on his forehead. "Kinda. I remember freaking out and saying it wasn't you, it was Johnny and then begging him to make it stop, 'cause it hurt so much. I remember falling to the floor, but after I hit my head, I only remember you and I talked. I don't know what I said," Rick replied honestly.

"Let's just say, kiddo, I'm gonna have a few nightmares of my own. I don't know how you deal with it, honestly," Tony said ruefully.

As Rick lay there, fighting sleep, he suddenly remembered some of what he talked about. It was all about the day at Johnny's, but it was more about what he felt, since he couldn't see a lot of things through his swollen eyes. How he could feel the beating and the stabbing. He knew he had been graphic in the details and he could see how his friend, no, his brother, would have nightmares. *Lord knows I have enough*, Rick thought.

"Rick, son. Look at me. I don't think either one of us thought this would be easy," Tony said quietly as he stared at the teen.

"Nothing worth doing ever is. Didn't you say that to me a long time ago?" Rick replied quietly as he sat up. The tension was gone for now and Rick felt so much better. He always did after one of Tony's massages.

Tony laughed. Trust Rick to remember that one sentence from a lifetime ago. "Yes, I did, little brother. Right at the very beginning, right after you'd left and we had a session at the school. Johnny had broken into your house and grabbed your jacket and bandanna, and they forced you to put it back on. You were late for our session and I tore a strip off of you. Remember that session? It was a doozy, wasn't it? Well, do you think you can sleep now?" Tony asked as he climbed to his feet.

Rick looked at the clock. It was barely six. He shook his head. "Eventually, bro, but it's way too early. I go to sleep now and I'll be awake, nightmares or not, around three and I need my beauty sleep. Did Aaron give you those exercises? Cool. Let's do that and then, how about a couple of hands of poker? I think you're still up on me, aren't you?"

Chapter 52

It did get better over the week. It wasn't always easy to stand there and just let Aaron manipulate his arm while standing behind Rick, but with Jordan's help, he managed. Rick had also taken Tony's suggestion to heart and began to write it all down. It wasn't just the things he remembered about trying to go back to the gang. Every little detail about the whole school year he remembered got written down, too.

Memories, details, and feelings spilled out at the oddest times, so Rick got used to carrying a small notebook in his back pocket so he could jot things down. Every day, he and Tony would go over anything new and expand his statement. Every night, the nightmares ruled his sleep. But, just as with the details for his statement, Rick would write down every detail of the nightmares. Both men hoped, by writing them down, the nightmares would eventually go away.

Megan was encouraged to do the same, but she didn't let anyone go over a word until Tony told her he wanted to see her on Friday at the centre.

"Come on in, Megs," Rick said as he led the way into Tony's office.

Megan looked around and smiled at Tony. "So this is where you and Rick've lived this year," she said as she sat down.

"Mick, Jor. I'll bring them to the gym in about an hour," Tony said as he closed the door on the twins waiting in the hallway.

"Yeah, Meg, Rick and I've spent many hours in here," Tony agreed as he sat down on his favourite corner of his desk. He grinned down at the two teens. Rick just smiled back.

"What's up, Fish? Why're we here?" Rick asked as he adjusted his sling.

"Rick, you and I need to review your statement one last time before I send it over to Lance, although I think we've got it licked," Tony stated as he handed Rick his statement. "Meg, you've been going over your statements from the hospital, right?" Tony asked while Rick continued reading, seemingly ignoring the other two in the room.

Megan nodded hesitantly and handed over the binder left at her house earlier. "I tried talking to Marshall, I really did, and I'm sorry it didn't work. It just got too hard to say out loud any more, no matter what we tried. Then Rick told me how you suggested writing down anything he remembered whenever he remembered it. I finally started doing the same. I put them in the binder where they belonged, I think. I hope they help," the young teen said as Tony began to flip through the binder.

He was quiet for several minutes as he read through everything. Then he smiled. "Great job, Meg. You've filled in the holes nicely and Lance'll be pleased. Do you feel better?" Tony asked, putting the binder down on the desk.

"It helped Daddy and Mickey a lot more than it did me," Megan said with a smile. "They were able to finally see why certain things bothered me and why I couldn't always explain what was wrong or why I felt a certain way."

"Did it help *you*?" Tony pressed again.

"Yeah, I guess it did, at least for a little while, anyway. I haven't had a nightmare in a couple of days. Some bad dreams, but not a true nightmare," Megan said finally.

"Fish, do you know what's gonna happen on Monday?" Rick asked as he put down his statement abruptly. He stood up and began to stretch, trying to work out some kinks.

"Hold those stretches properly, Champ," Tony ordered as Rick shorted one stretch. Rick flushed at the gentle rebuke and redid the stretch properly as Tony watched.

"Much better, son. Now as for Monday afternoon, you get to sit on the stand and face the Knights," Tony said dryly. *And probably have a day from hell*, the cop didn't add as Rick flinched at the thought.

"What exactly *is* a transfer hearing, Tony?" Megan asked curiously.

"In a nutshell, it's a hearing to have a young offender moved to adult court. This is only done in rare cases where the crimes're particularly violent, like this one. The prosecution wants to both Johnny and Brian transferred," Tony explained.

"Tony, I've heard the most a young offender can get is 3 years. Is that true?" Megan asked tentatively.

"Unfortunately, yes, at least for the most part. Sometimes, if the crime is particularly bad or the prosecution makes a good case, they can get about 5, but the time never fits the crime, I'm sorry to say. They can get sometimes get adult sentences, if the judge agrees, even if they're found guilty as a young offender. Repeat offenders can be the worst. It doesn't seem to matter what they did – they don't get any more time. Programs like this one're a great alternative for those who can be reformed before they get dragged too far into the system," Tony said with a smile at Rick.

"What're the odds, Fish?" Rick asked, smiling back as he continued to stretch.

"There shouldn't be a problem with Johnny, based on your testimony alone. But Brian may be a problem. It's all gonna come down to what evidence Lance presents and how the judge sees that evidence and your testimonies, I'm afraid," the cop said. He glanced at the clock and then stood up.

"Now, little brother, you have physio with Aaron and I need to go over a few more things with Meg to finalize her statement. You okay with yours?" Tony asked.

Rick thought about the statement he had just finished reading and nodded. "I think so. I haven't thought of anything new in a couple of days," Rick said as he opened the door.

He left Tony and Megan talking and wandered to the gym. He stood just inside the doors and watched the club doing their training. He ached to get back to boxing, but for now, it was strength training, stretches and mobility. *Soon,* he promised himself as he wandered over to the only treadmill in the gym to spend some time walking away from his troubles while waiting for Aaron to show up.

Megan and Tony arrived in the gym just as Rick was finishing up his physio. The cop was happy to see Rick wasn't freaking out having Aaron working on his shoulders from behind, but the tension was still there.

"Aaron, enough, man. You're killing me," Rick finally said, pulling his shoulder out of the physiotherapist's grasp.

"That's cool, Rick. If you can work it to the point of discomfort, like I did today, it's gonna improve," Aaron said, coming around to face Rick, making sure to keep a running dialogue up the entire time.

"Now, how's the strength coming? Squeeze," the physiotherapist said, holding out his hands. Rick grasped at his hands, squeezed and even pulled back a bit while Aaron resisted.

"Good! Keep it up and we should be able to get you back to some light boxing workouts in about three weeks or so," Aaron said as he left.

Rick let out a whoop of joy. Tony just laughed. "Good is right, Champ. You're doing a lot better than I thought you'd be," Tony said. "Sore?" he asked as he noticed Rick rubbing at his shoulder.

"Yeah, he's pushing me a bit," Rick admitted finally.

"You're done here, Champ. Why don't you take this beautiful lady and head home? You've earned a weekend free from me. Call if you need me, but otherwise, talk to you Monday at the courthouse," Tony said with a grin.

"Your chariot awaits, my lady," Rick said extravagantly as he held out his hand to Jordan.

"See you at home, bro," she called to Mickey as she and Rick left. The couple walked slowly to the car, stopping and chatting with friends along the way, enjoying each other's company, knowing it was going to come to an end soon.

The ride home was far too short for Rick. He had fought so long and hard to win her back and he didn't like to leave her. Seamus would still scowl at them a bit but at least he never interfered. Seamus was slowly learning to tolerate Rick and Jordan being together.

All too soon, they pulled up in front of Jordan's house. Rick walked her to the front door, and pulled her in for a slow, lingering kiss. They jerked apart as the front door opened.

"You've been invited to Miss Megan's for supper, Miss Jordan," Cook said and closed the door, totally ignoring Rick.

"Why couldn't've they said something at the centre?" Jordan asked, exasperated.

Rick just grinned. "C'mon, sweets, who cares? We get to spend more time together. How's about we slip away later?" he said with a sideways glance.

Jordan blushed at his subtle suggestion. She settled back into the car and they shot over to Glencrest, parking in front of Rick's house.

"Dammit, now what?" Rick growled low in his throat. Jordan silently agreed. Standing on the porch was a very familiar figure and Rick was less than impressed to see him there.

"Marshall Andrews, I do *not* need a body guard," Rick snapped as he tossed his knapsack in the front door.

Marshall just chuckled. "Relax, Rick. I'm not here as a spy. I haven't seen you or talked to you all week and I was wondering how you were doing," Marshall said as he leaned against the rail. "I thought we were friends."

"You really aren't here to be my body guard? O'Reilly didn't send you?" Rick asked suspiciously. He stood by the rail and looked at Marshall out of the corner of his eye.

Marshall shook his head. "Honestly, Rick, I'm not. Nana invited Fish and me over for a celebratory dinner. Didn't she tell you?" Marshall asked.

Rick shook his head. "Oh well, guess she had too much on her mind. Besides, you're kinda important to me, kid. I can't imagine why," Marshall grinned.

"Fish tell you about this week?" Rick asked. Jordan snuggled up beside Rick, his arm around her waist.

"He mentioned a panic attack and some physio, but no great detail. What happened?" Marshall asked. Rick stared out at the ranch while he told Marshall about his week. It felt weird to confide in someone other than Tony, and yet oddly right. After all, he and Marshall had been through a lot together in the last few months.

"Y'know, Rick, you could've called. I would've come over to talk, play poker or just be here in case you needed something," Marshall pointed out. He knew why Rick hadn't — it meant he was still too weak to take care of things himself and Rick was tired of admitting that.

Rick didn't say anything as he turned to watch another lone figure walk towards them. Jordan felt Rick sigh and wondered why the appearance of his lawyer would bother him.

"Afternoon, Counsellor," Marshall said dryly.

"Owen," Rick greeted the lawyer sourly.

"Afternoon, folks. Rick, I'm not here to hound you, so gimme a break. I've read your statement and I'm impressed," Owen said with a smile.

"Any chance it could just be read in court and I could avoid testifying?" Rick asked hopefully. His face fell when Owen shook his head sadly.

"Sorry, Rick, but the defendants have the right to face you in court in person," Owen apologized. "But that's not why I'm here."

"What's up now?" Rick asked, resigned.

"I found out late this afternoon you've been summoned in front of your favourite judge Monday morning at nine," Owen said, handing Rick a copy of the summons.

"Did he say why?" Marshall demanded. *Why indeed?* Rick wondered as he read.

"No. All it mentions is it has to do with all the charges against Rick," Owen said as the four walked up to the main house. Owen kept his thoughts to himself. He was pretty sure Monday would bring some closure for Rick, but he didn't want to get the kid's hopes up. After all, Lance could change his mind in a heartbeat.

"I guess we'll find out Monday," Rick said as they entered the library.

"Promise me you won't brood all weekend. You need to be calm on Monday. Both in the morning and in the afternoon," Owen reminded his young client. Rick nodded as he moved to sit in a chair on the far side of the room.

Tony was standing near Rick's chair and had watched as Rick settled into it, taking his drink from Jordan. He was pale and shaking. *He's tired*, Tony thought as he sipped at his drink absently. *He's pushing himself too hard.*

Nana waited until everyone had got something to drink before she rapped on the mantle to get everyone's attention. "A toast," she began. "First to family and friends. Thank you for being with us through all of this."

She looked at Megan and Rick. "To my grandchildren. Megan, you never gave up, no matter how bad it was. Yes, I know you were pushed into some things you really didn't want to do, but it all worked out in the end. Rick, my lad, for all the hell you've faced this year, I'm just glad you survived," she said, with a slight catch in her voice.

"That makes two of us, Nana," Rick said dryly.

Everyone laughed as Nana continued. "To Jordan and Mickey. For both of you to have enough patience to help Rick and Megan get through this. I know trust is gonna take a while, but please, try.

"Finally, Tony and Marshall. Thank you. For your determination in trying to solve the attacks and everything. Marshall, for your patience with Seamus' antics, thank you. Tony, thank you for believing in my boy. Without you..." Nana couldn't continue.

Tony looked down at Rick as everyone raised their glasses to Nana's toast. The young teen was embarrassed by his grandmother's comments and trying not to show it. "Well, Rick, how're you doing? Truly?" Tony asked as the conversations swirled around them.

"Honestly, Fish, I'm tired. It's been a long week," Rick began hesitantly. He stiffened slightly. He could sense someone coming up behind him. Delaney had been right. The reflexes he had learned in the gang were coming back and quickly.

Before he could so much as move a toe, Jordan said softly," Easy, Rick, it's only me. I had no choice."

Rick relaxed as his girlfriend sat on the arm of his chair. He looked up at Tony. "Fish, have I thanked you?" he asked quietly.

Tony smiled. "No thanks needed, little brother. I'm just glad you're around to harass," Tony said, marvelling at the change in Rick. Even as little as 6 months ago, Rick wouldn't have said thank you to anyone, even Tony. *I can't believe how much he's changed in such a short time*, Tony thought, impressed.

"It's not enough," Rick insisted.

"You wanna thank me? Really thank me?" Tony asked. Rick nodded. "Talk about the life," Tony said, much to Rick's surprise.

"Fish, you already know about that," Rick snorted.

"Not to me – to other kids. At the centre, the school. Hell, even juvy," Tony explained.

Rick was stunned at Tony's request. He had never thought about doing anything like that and he wasn't sure he could do what Tony wanted. His friend wanted him to remember something Rick just wanted to forget.

He remained quiet and thoughtful throughout supper, wondering what he would say to anyone about the life. Not even an argument between Tony and Marshall about who was the best boxer, after Rick that is, could distract the teen. As supper ended, and everyone else headed out to the back porch, Rick looked sideways at Jordan.

"Shall we?" he murmured, motioning to the door.

She nodded and the two eased out of the dining room and walked down to the barn. The horses whickered at them as they leaned against the rail, giving scratches and pets to those who wanted them. Content to just be together, Jordan didn't say anything for the longest time.

Finally, she couldn't stand the silence any longer. "You're awfully quiet, love. Is something wrong?" she asked as she snuggled under the arm Rick settled around her shoulders.

"Am I?" Rick replied, distracted as he scratched his stallion's neck.

"You hardly said two words during supper. In fact, you've hardly said anything since Tony asked you to talk about the life," Jordan continued hesitantly.

Rick sighed. "It was a bit of a shock, I'll admit. Look, Jor, I know I promised you some quiet time together tonight, but I'm beat. Can I take a rain check?" he asked.

"Of course, Rick. You can call me later," she said, unconcerned.

Rick felt like a world-class heel as they returned to sit on Rick's front porch. He could tell Jordan was a little disappointed in the way he was acting, but he was just too distracted by what Tony wanted him to do to do anything with his girlfriend. He sat on the porch long after Jordan left, thinking, wondering if he could really do what Tony wanted. Could he really face the nightmares that would come every time he drew himself back into the hell that was the Black Knights?

When he finally dragged himself to bed, he was no closer to a decision than he had been when he first sat in the swing with Jordan.

Chapter 53

Remembering his promise to Owen, Rick spent a quiet weekend, mostly by himself, trying not to worry about Monday morning. He wondered around the farm, helping Frank and the other farm hands when he could, but mainly he just sat and thought about everything that had happened over the last few months. He even managed to drag his sore, battered body up on his stallion, Cherokee, for a couple of short rides.

He had just come back from one such ride with one of the farm hands late Sunday afternoon to find Megan waiting for him on the porch. She was as pale as the white shirt she was wearing and he could tell she'd been crying.

"Hey, cuz, what's wrong?" Rick asked as he sat down beside her.

"Lance Blackstone came over again today," was all she had time to say before she burst into tears. Rick held onto her as she cried.

"Megs, you've gotta get past this," he said soothingly over her sobs.

"I know, Rick, but, no matter what I've told Tony, I still have nightmares and they come back any time I think about this, especially when I see that scar. I've started showering in the dark so I don't have to look at it," she said brokenly. Taking a shaky breath, she brushed away the tears and looked up at him. "How do you do it?" she wondered, awed at the strength Rick constantly showed. He was a rock and never seemed bothered by anything.

Rick hesitated for a moment then stood up. "C'mon. I'll show you," he said finally, and led the way to his bedroom. There, he picked up a very thick notebook. Again, he hesitated before handing it over to his cousin.

"Don't get me wrong, cuz, I don't think the nightmares'll ever stop for me, no matter what anyone says. But they're all in there. Every stinking, horrible, mind-blowing one," Rick said quietly. As she flipped through the book, Megan was shocked at how graphic some of the dreams were. *How does he remain sane with these images in his head?* she wondered.

"Rick, Tony know about these?" Megan asked as she closed the book and handed it back to her cousin. She watched as he put it down with another notebook, but didn't want to ask what was in that one. She was too afraid of the answer.

"Nope. These're for my eyes only. They're the only way I can get back to sleep at night. If I don't write them down, they come back. Twice as bad," Rick said as he rubbed his aching shoulder.

Spying his muscle cream, Megan motioned to her cousin to sit in front of her. "Lemme help, Rick," she offered.

Rick didn't hesitate. He stripped off his shirt and sat down. Megan smoothed the cream into his muscular shoulders, carefully massaging until he sighed in relief. He found it odd Tony and Megan could do this and he would never panic, but even if it was Jordan behind him, someone he knew for a fact would never hurt him, having someone behind him still sent him over the edge.

"Better?" Megan asked finally, drying her hands on the towel Rick handed her.

"Yeah. You?" Rick said as he stood up. He didn't put his shirt back on and Megan stared at all of the scars on his body. Most of the new wounds had healed, but it still bothered her to look at them. The only wound with any stitches in was the stab wound in his left shoulder. The casts on his right arm had come off early, but his arm remained in a sling as a reminder to not overuse it.

"No, but I'll be okay. Tonight, at least. See you in the morning?" she said, somehow sensing Rick didn't want to come up for supper. Rick nodded as he walked his cousin to the door and watched her walk back up to the main house. He sat on his porch for a while, thinking, before deciding to call up to Nana and beg off from supper. He really didn't feel like he'd be any kind of company, let alone good.

"No problem, lad. Martha'll run down a plate for you, if you want," Nana said.

"Thanks, Nana. Sorry about the short notice," Rick apologized again.

"It's okay, Rick, really. Megan said you didn't look good. Tired, she thought. You're not worried about tomorrow, are you?" Nana asked shrewdly.

"Yeah, a bit," Rick admitted after a short silence.

"Don't be. No matter what happens, we'll get through it as a family. You're not gonna be alone. Martha'll be down shortly. Good night, lad and see you in the morning," Nana said.

"See ya, Nana," Rick replied and hung up. After a great meal, he sat in his recliner and re-read the nightmares he had shown Megan. He had lied a bit to Megan – Tony knew about some of these nightmares, just not the ones that woke him time and time again, getting worse and worse over time. The only good thing was each nightmare brought out fresh details about the attacks. Once Rick calmed down enough to write everything down, that is.

He tossed the notebook on the table and flipped on the TV. He fell asleep shortly after he turned it on and plunged headlong into the nightmares again. This time, though, was one of the worst he'd ever had. Standing there in front of him, each holding their own knife, was Jordan, Megan, Tony and Marshall while the Knights stood behind them, egging Rick's "friends" on. No matter what Rick did, he couldn't wake from the horror of the knives being driven in repeatedly. It was the pure joy on Jordan's face as she stabbed Rick one last time that finally drove Rick to wake up, screaming and crying. For a good five minutes, he couldn't do anything but see that look in his girlfriend's face while he begged for his life.

Sobbing, he grabbed the notebook and pen and wrote it all down. Every painful, horrible detail was written down as he shook with emotion. It was a long time before he could convince himself to go back to sleep. A very long time.

When his alarm went off, he was exhausted and grouchy. He stood in the shower and let the hot water pummel his tense shoulders. He reviewed everything he could remember from the nightmare while he slowly got dressed and tried to figure out why he would dream something so horrible.

"I need to talk to Fish," he muttered out loud as he shaved carefully. He finished quickly and snatched up the phone in his room, dialling Tony's number without really thinking about it.

"Whitefish," Tony answered sleepily. He groaned softly as he realized it was way past time to get up, and he really didn't want to move. He was warm and comfortable.

"Fish? It's Rick," Rick began hesitantly.

Tony was instantly awake. "What's wrong, son?" he demanded, sitting up quickly. Just the tone of Rick's voice made Tony worry.

"Can I meet you a bit early? I need...I need to talk to you. Face to face," Rick said, still hesitant to tell his friend what was wrong.

"Rick, what's wrong? I can hear it in your voice," Tony asked again.

Rick looked at his clock. "Can we meet in an hour at the courthouse?" he asked instead. "That'll be about 8:30, if that's okay."

Tony knew he wasn't going to get anything else out of Rick. He was just going to have to be patient. "All right, little brother. I'll meet you in the park across from the courthouse at 8:30," Tony promised.

"Thanks, Fish," Rick said and hung up slowly. He knew he had worried his friend, but he just couldn't talk about the dream without seeing Tony's face. He made himself some breakfast and ate slowly. As he ate, he re-read the dream and added a detail here and there. Breakfast sat heavily in his stomach as he gathered up his stuff to head into town. Alone, but not for long.

Tony was at a picnic table, waiting for Rick. "Morning," he greeted him.

Rick handed Tony a steaming cup of coffee and a muffin. "Sorry to drag you out early, bro, but I had to show you something," the teen said as he sat down with his own coffee.

"What happened last night?" Tony asked as he sipped his coffee.

"Nightmare you need to read," was Rick's short reply as he handed over his notebook. "The one you want's the very last one," he continued as Tony flipped through the pages. With a sip of his coffee and a bit of his muffin, Tony settled down at the table to read, not realizing how bad things were about to get.

Rick stared off into space, slowly drinking his coffee and nibbling on the muffin he'd bought for himself as Tony read. "No way! Oh, hell no!" Tony snapped suddenly.

"Got to the part about you, huh?" Rick asked, not looking at the cop.

"Why would you...?" Tony couldn't go on he was so hurt.

"Keep reading, Fish. It gets worse," Rick said dryly. He still didn't look at his friend until he heard the thud of the book on the table. Only then did he look up into the pale, horrified face of his friend. Tony just sat there, reeling in shock at what he had just finished reading.

"You okay, Fish?" Rick asked, knowing the answer.

"Hell no!" Tony repeated harshly. "How could you possible think this?" Tony finally managed to ask, after several failed attempts to make his voice work at all, let alone properly.

Rick shook his head. "I've no idea, man," he said. "I never once thought of this, even with all the crap I've put ya'll through, and yet, last night, that's what I dreamt," Rick said, tapping the notebook with his finger.

Tony read over the details again, trying not to be sick. The mere idea Rick thought Tony capable of stabbing him was hard to take. As he read, though, Tony focused on a couple of details which made the whole thing make sense. Sick sense, but sense nonetheless.

"Rick, question. Do you remember what name we called you?" Tony asked, putting the book down and taking a drink of his coffee to steady his nerves.

Rick thought for a moment and then said, "No one ever called me Rick, if that's what you mean," he replied slowly.

"That's exactly what I mean. Look at this. You've described yourself wearing your gang stuff. Every piece of it, kiddo. So this is how I see it – we attacked Moneyman, not Rick. If we'd attacked Rick, you'd be wearing anything but the gang wear," Tony said finally.

"Why would I dream that now? Why today?" Rick demanded. *Tony's nuts*, the teen thought, shaking his head.

"You're about to face them for the first time since that night. I wouldn't be at all surprised if you're a bit stressed. Remember the funeral?" Tony asked suddenly.

"Yeah. So?" Rick said, puzzled.

"What did I tell you about it?" Tony asked.

"You told me you buried Moneyman, not me," Rick said slowly. Suddenly he realized what Tony was saying. "And for some reason, last night, I dreamt you killed Moneyman, so 'Rick' could face them today?" Rick asked incredulously. "Tony Whitefish, that's the most ridiculous thing I've ever heard!"

"Gotta better idea?" Tony pointed out, popping another piece of muffin into his mouth and washing it down with a gulp of coffee.

"No, but it's still ridiculous," Rick snorted as he stood up and stretched.

Tony looked at his watch, polished off the rest of his coffee and muffin and stood up as well. "C'mon, Champ. Time to see the judge," he said as he threw out their garbage.

The two friends walked over to the courthouse, continuing to talk quietly. "Do you want this back?" Tony asked, holding out the notebook.

Rick shook his head. "You keep it, Fish. I'll start another tonight," he replied and nodded a greeting to everyone who stood outside the courtroom. Tony winced at the implications of Rick's off the cuff remark.

"Morning, folks," Owen said, walking up to the group. "Rick, they've called us," the young lawyer said and led the way in. Once again, Rick sat at the defendant's table. This time, though, he had no idea what was going on or why he was there.

"Good morning, Rick. Everyone ready? Good. Mr. Blackstone, you mind telling us why we're here?" Rick's favourite judge said, banging his gavel as he sat down.

Lance Blackstone stood, adjusted his tie and cleared his throat, nervously. "Your Honour, as you know, the defendant, Richard "Rick" Attison has been accused of several heinous crimes over the past 10 months, including Assault, Uttering Threats and Destruction of Private Property," the prosecutor began hesitantly. This was not going to look good for his office but he had no choice. Rick had been wrongly accused and his record needed to be cleared.

"Having presided over the trials in the cases, I am well aware of the crimes of the accused. Your point, please?" the judge encouraged, trying to keep the sarcasm out of his voice.

"Through some very determined and gritty detective work by Constables Whitefish and Andrews, it has come to our attention Rick has apparently been framed for these crimes," Blackstone said neutrally. *That's the understatement of the year,* the judge thought, trying not to laugh out loud.

"Evidence, Mr. Blackstone, evidence," the judge encouraged again.

"Your Honour, in executing a search warrant at one Brian Townsand's house in the course of the investigation into Megan Attison's kidnapping, we found this spiral notebook. In it, I'm sure you'll agree, is a very clever campaign designed to frame Rick," Blackstone said as he handed the notebook to the judge.

The judge flipped through the notebook for several minutes, making notes as he went along. Finally, he looked up and looked right at Seamus. "Inspector, perhaps you would like to explain to this court, and the Attison family, why it has taken more than *five* months for this particular evidence to come to light?" he demanded as he brandished the notebook.

Seamus hesitated and the judge continued. "I recall ordering you and your men to reinvestigate all the crimes Rick was accused of, after I had cleared him of the original assault of his cousin in January due to a horrendous lack of evidence. We all knew something was up then. I wonder if the family would like to place the blame for what has happened to their two teenagers squarely on your shoulders, Inspector. If it was me, I would, but then, my personal opinion doesn't matter. Why don't you *try* to explain yourself?" the judge snapped harshly.

Seamus looked at Rick for a long time, then back at the judge. "I *have* no explanation, yer honour, at least nothing ye'd accept. All I can say's I was obsessed with keeping Rick away from me daughter. So obsessed, in fact, I technically obstructed justice in an attempt to put and keep him in jail, and honestly, probably more than once," Seamus finally admitted. *You did what?* Blackstone thought, horrified, whipping around to glare at Seamus. Even the judge looked less than impressed.

"Please tell me you didn't create evidence," the judge said, holding his head in his hands.

"No, yer honour. I managed to avoid that. I just tried to twist evidence so it pointed to Rick and ignored it if it proved he was innocent," Seamus rumbled, his face flushed with shame.

"And may have seriously compromised my cases against the Knights! For crying out loud, Seamus O'Reilly, do you have any idea what the hell you've done?" Blackstone demanded.

"Mr. Blackstone, please. One person yelling at him at a time, if you don't mind. Now, Mr. O'Reilly, what in the hell led you to do this?" the judge asked harshly. Everyone in the courtroom winced as the judge dropped Seamus' title.

Rick stood quickly, wincing as he jostled his shoulders. "Actually, your honour, to be perfectly honest about it, I did," he said quietly, taking pity on Seamus.

"You did, Rick? How?" the judge wanted to know, shocked Rick would actually defend Seamus and take any blame for what had happened.

"Well, it started the day before I got sucked into the Knights," Rick explained and proceeded to tell the story of the fight between Seamus and himself, with one small deletion. He figured Seamus didn't really want the part about his gun coming out.

When he finished, silence fell in the courtroom. Seamus stood between the defendant's and prosecutor's tables with his head hung low. He knew what he had done was wrong, but he couldn't change it now. He just hoped the judge would understand he did what he did out of love for his daughter, not out of any real desire to obstruct justice.

"O'Reilly, I ought to throw you in jail, y'know that?" the judge said, disgusted. "You realize you stand a hell of a good chance of losing your job because of this?" he demanded after letting the silence drag on for several minutes.

"Yes, yer honour, I do," Seamus replied without raising his head. He deserved whatever he got and he knew it.

"You've done just about everything wrong you possible could in the last ten months. I'm placing the blame for what's happened to Rick and Megan squarely on your shoulders. The Knights may've been the ones who actually attacked them, although that has yet to be proven in a court of law, but why this happened is entirely your fault! My God, do you realize what you've done, to them, their friends, this community, *your own children*?" the judge snapped, pointing at Rick, Megan and the twins.

"Yes, yer honour, I'm...beginning to," Seamus said quietly.

"Personally, if it was my family and my choice, I'd slap a lawsuit on you so fast, it'd make your head spin. However, knowing the Attison family as I've come to, I'm pretty sure you'll be spared that embarrassment. Pity. Unfortunately, there's no way I can avoid reporting this gross dereliction of duty to Regimental Headquarters. You'll probably face an inquiry. There'll be an official reprimand in your service record by the end of today. I also suggest you take a leave of absence and decide if you can honestly continue to lead this detachment in an unbiased and fair manner," the judge continued in a scathing tone. Seamus flinched at the barely contained anger he could hear. The judge took a deep breath before continuing.

"And there's one other probability you're gonna have to face. There's no way to keep this out of the press. Especially once the trials start. You're gonna have to work extremely hard to regain the trust of this town, if you ever can. You've made your bed, now lie in it, Mr. O'Reilly," the judge snapped, making Seamus feel like he'd already been fired. *I made me choice,* Seamus thought sadly. *I did this fer Jordan, and now I'm gonna pay fer it.*

Rick was stunned. Seamus had just paid a huge price for what he had done, and with a sinking heart, Rick realized Tony could be forced to pay the same price when his role in the whole mess came out. Rick watched as Seamus turned to leave. He knew he had to say something, and quick, or Seamus would forever be blaming himself for a situation not entirely his fault.

"Inspector?" the teen said in the suddenly silent courtroom.

"What, boy?" Seamus replied, sourly.

"I forgive you," Rick said softly, knowing, somehow, this was the right thing to say to the cop.

"What? How? After everything I did to ye?" the inspector asked, surprised. *How can he?* the inspector wondered.

"Easy, sir. Jor. Just...think about it," Rick said, and turned back to face the judge. Seamus continued walking to the courtroom door, still surrounded by the loud silence, when his daughter called out to him to stop.

"Daddy, I understand why you did it," she continued quietly.

"Dad, we both do, and we'll stand by you. No matter what," Mickey said just as soft. Megan nodded her agreement as she gripped Mickey's hand with hers.

"Thank ye, kids. All of ye." With that Seamus left and never looked back, but he left holding his head high.

"I'm assuming you want this book back for the trials, Mr. Blackstone?" the judge asked the prosecutor.

"Yes, sir. We don't need it this afternoon, but we'll definitely need it for the trial of Brian Townsand," Lance said unsteadily. He was as stunned by Seamus' confession as he was by the harshness of the judge's reaction.

"Very well. Rick, please stand," the judge ordered. Rick stood slowly. He was already tired and the day wasn't even close to being over.

"Well, son, we've been through a lot this year, haven't we?" the judge said. He acted as if he and Rick were the only two in the courtroom.

"Yes, sir. I just wish it was all over," Rick replied honestly.

"Soon enough, son, soon enough. Now, what with the inspector's confession and what's in this notebook, there's more than enough evidence to completely clear your name. I hereby order your record completely cleared of all charges. The record is expunged. You, Rick, are free and clear. Do you have anything to say?" the judge asked. He finally smiled as the courtroom filled with cheers.

"Just thank you, sir. Without you, I don't think I'd ever would've been able to make it through this year," Rick said as the shouting died down.

"Do you plan to continue with the counselling?" the judge asked, curiously.

"Yes, sir. It's the best thing that's ever happened to me, to be honest. Tony's been a huge help, especially since the attack. I can't box, so the anger remains," Rick said as he hefted his arm carefully.

"You still have anger issues?" the judge asked, a frown creasing his forehead. He had assumed after all of the sessions Rick would've had some control over that.

"He probably always will, thanks to how his dad raised him, more so than the gang life," Tony spoke up quickly.

"Well, I'm sure the story'll be very interesting to hear. We need to get outta here, though. So, young man, since there's nothing further, I have just one last thing to say to you," the judge said, still smiling.

"Yes sir?" Rick asked, hesitantly.

"Get the hell outta my courtroom! I don't ever want to see you in here again." The gavel banged down and Rick was free.

Chapter 54

They found Seamus sitting on a bench outside the courtroom. Rick could see Jordan's dad had been crying. It had cost him a lot to admit what he had done and now he faced a pretty bleak future. One Rick wasn't even sure he deserved. Seamus had done what he did because he loved his daughter. Rick could understand that.

"Seamus?" Nana asked.

"Hello, Nana, kids," Seamus replied, drying the remaining tears on his face. He saw Rick and grimaced.

"Hard to admit you screwed up, isn't it?" Rick said quietly.

"Don't start, boy!" Seamus snapped back quickly.

"O'Reilly, I meant what I said in there. I forgive you. No matter what anyone says about you, I never thought you were a bad cop. Just a little too focused on one person, but not a bad cop. If I'm asked, I don't even want them to demote or fire you," Rick said roughly.

"Why not, lad? He does deserve it after all," Nana said pointedly while Seamus winced at her candour.

"Because he did what he thought was right, and he did it because he loves Jor. Who could fault him for that?" Rick said, pulling his girl close and smiling at her. With that, Rick dismissed the role Seamus played in the last year from his mind.

"Owen, you joining us for lunch?" Nana asked as the group walked towards the cafeteria.

"No, Nana, but thank you. I'll just have to grab a quick bite or two in between work. I've got some paperwork to finish with Lance in order to get Rick's record completely cleared and then I need to prep for this afternoon's session. You do realize you'll be questioned? By both sides?" Owen asked Rick suddenly.

- 489 -

"Yeah. And I really wish I could just forget everything, especially that day," Rick replied, his voice already shaky.

"The rest of you better go on. Rick needs to talk," Tony intervened quickly before Rick broke down and led the teen back across to the park where they had met earlier. They sat on a bench where they could stare back at the courthouse and the police station. *Man, I really hate this place*, Rick thought sourly.

Tony sat beside his friend and waited, patiently, for a few minutes before speaking. "Talk to me, little brother. What's eating you?" Tony finally asked.

Rick didn't respond right away. "Is there any way to get outta testifying, at least today?" Rick asked, staring straight ahead.

"Sorry, son. Not really. Even though it's only a transfer hearing, they still have a right to face you and your testimony in open court. They have the right to question you. Trust me, they don't wanna be tried in adult court. I've seen the list of charges Lance's throwing at 'em, and conviction on any *one* of them in adult court could result in a life sentence with little or no chance of parole," Tony explain.

"What about *my* rights, dammit? The right to live my life without fear? The right to not have nightmares anymore?" Rick demanded, turning to face Tony.

Tony just laughed. "Sorry, kiddo, but that's not considered a right in the courts," Tony said, still chuckling. Rick smiled wanly as he struggled to figure out why he was so tense.

"C'mon, son. Talk to me. What's wrong?" Tony pressed. Still Rick sat, motionless, staring across the road. Finally, he began to talk, quietly.

"I hate this, Fish. I'm gonna have to go into that courtroom and face them. Their lawyers're gonna try and twist everything I say and make it look like I had something to with all of this, and I hate it," Rick said again.

"A possibility," Tony said, calmly. He leaned back and waited. There was still more to this, he could feel it.

"And once we're done here today, I get to do it all over again at the trials, no matter how many there are. Now you want me to talk to the kids at the centre and juvy about this," Rick continued, trying to control the shaking which had begun again.

"Again, all possible," Tony said patiently, ignoring the tremors. He had learned to have infinite patience when dealing with Rick. While time was limited, they had all the time Rick needed. Tony would make sure of that, even if it meant being late to this afternoon's trial.

"I really have to testify?" Rick asked again, trying to keep from bolting suddenly.

"Sorry, little brother, but yes. Think about it, though. You know Johnny's gonna fight the hardest and that means you *have* to tell your story. Rick, remember this – *you could've been killed*! By Johnny!" Tony emphasized.

"That doesn't make it any easier to face them," Rick pointed out. He couldn't control his legs any longer and finally just let them bounce.

"Rick, c'mon, kiddo, what's really wrong? I know you, son. There's something eating at you. What is it?" Tony asked again, still ignoring Rick's bouncing legs.

Rick sat, staring across the street. He wasn't sure what his problem was. He was just as nervous, tense and jumpy as he remembered being at his first sessions with Tony. He figured if someone came up behind him right now, he'd swing first, then run as fast as he could.

He sighed. *That was it*, he realized suddenly. He just wanted to run and hide. Not talk to anyone about anything any more. He didn't even want to talk to Tony, his best friend, any more. *Some tough gang banger I turned out to be*, Rick thought miserably.

"Rick, talk to me," Tony encouraged quietly.

"Honestly, Fish? I'm scared. I'm so damn tense right now if someone came up behind me and even whispered "boo," I'd probably swing first and ask questions later. Much later. Like, whenever I stopped running," Rick said finally. "If I ever stopped, that is."

Tony just waited. He figured there was more and he was right. "Most of all, I'd just like to hide forever in my house. Not talk

- 491 -

about this stuff any more. Not leave for any reason. I'm sorry, Tony, but I can't deal with this. Not any more. I'm just not strong enough. There's too much pain, physical and emotional. Johnny's won. I'm so broken I don't recognize myself any more. He broke me just like he promised. I just wouldn't admit it," Rick said softly, staring down at his hands, unable to look at his friend.

Tony snorted, startling Rick. "Broken? You? Not the Champ. Not my little brother. C'mon, Rick, think about it and stop reacting for a moment. You're nervous and jumpy because you're still expecting the Knights to come after you. You know they probably will, but it won't be them. It'll be their friends, the ones you won't see coming. Hell, you still expect Seamus to take Jor away again and Mick to act like a first class idiot," Tony said with a soft chuckle.

Rick couldn't say anything as Tony continued. "Rick, *think*, don't react, for a minute. Just follow me for a minute. You've handled a brutal situation much better than most *grown* men would've. I know I wouldn't've handled it half as well as you have. Plus, you took a hell of a beating and you're still trying to recover physically, never mind mentally. I'm honestly surprised you haven't ended up in the local loony bin with some of the nightmares you've told me about, and I know you haven't told me all of them. I'm sure I'm not gonna like reading that book you gave me this morning. Trust me, kiddo, you're not broken. Just...bent a little," Tony said with a small grin.

Rick finally looked up at his friend. "How can you say that? Look at me, Fish," Rick said, pointed at his bouncing legs with shaking hands.

Tony dismissed that with a wave. "That's because you're worried about this afternoon, that's all. Besides, if you'd really been broken, little brother, you never would've been able to stand up and tell the story of your fight with Seamus in court. The only ones who knew about that fight was you, me and the boss. Having someone else tell it was a lot easier on Seamus than trying to tell it himself, and don't think I didn't notice you never mentioned the gun," Tony pointed out dryly.

"You've finally broken free of Johnny's and the Knight's influence, but it's taken this beating to do it. You've only been bent a bit," Tony said again. "Know how I know?"

"How?" Rick asked curiously.

"Because you've enough guts to admit it's possible to be broken. It's those who can't admit they've been changed by something like this that'd be broken, at least to me. You've struggled to overcome some huge obstacles and, for the most part, you've succeeded. I'm proud of you, little brother. Very proud of you. In the short time we've known each other, you've gone from a bullying rich kid who sauntered into my office at the youth centre in September. You're someone who knows his strengths and weaknesses, his limitations. You've learned, the hard way I might add, others matter and you know walking away from a fight takes more strength and courage than actually fighting." Tony paused for a couple of minutes, trying to figure out how to get through to Rick.

"Rick, remember this – I believe you. I believe *in* you. I trust you. Besides, what kind of friends would we be if we truly let you be broken?" Tony finished with a smile.

Rick whirled as he heard the snap of a twig behind him. He crouched in front of the bench, his heart pounding. There, grinning like a trio of Cheshire cats, stood Marshall, Carl and Tom. Rick breathed a little easier, and tried to calm his pounding heart.

"What're you doing here?" he demanded to Tom and Carl.

"I may have to testify today, Blackstone said," Tom said as they came around to stand in front of Rick and Tony.

"And you?" Rick drawled to Carl. He knew something was up.

"Moral support, Champ. Marsh figured you'd be having a pretty rough time," Carl explained with a shrug.

"Rick, you've got four people right here who think you're doing pretty good," Marshall pointed out.

"That which doesn't break you makes you stronger," Tony quoted. "Trust us. You're gonna be just fine."

Rick smiled. "Bend but don't break, huh, Fish?" he said with a sly grin.

- 493 -

"Absolutely, little brother," Tony agreed. Rick sat and thought about what everyone had said and realized he wasn't the only one who had been changed by everything that had happened. Then he frowned. Something just didn't add up.

"Wait a minute. After all the trouble I caused, y'all still consider me a friend?" Rick asked incredulously. "Are y'all nuts?"

"*You* didn't cause any of this, Rick," Marshall snapped. "All *you* did was try to get away from a gang hell bent on getting you in as much trouble as they possibly could."

"You took the situation and ran with it as best you could, Champ. Sure, you made mistakes this year. Who hasn't? But, hopefully, we've all learned from them. C'mon, kiddo. Time to gather your courage and get back in that courtroom. Time to put them away. For good," Tony said firmly as he stood beside his partner. He knew he could encourage Rick all he wanted, but the ultimate decision about getting back in the game was going to be the teen's.

Rick remained on the bench. He thought about the two cops in front of him. One forced to become Rick's jailer and one forced to hide the teen away just to save his life. Yet they considered him a friend.

Carl watched him take down a cop in blind anger, yet accepted him into the boxing club. Tom had nearly been killed by the Knights as Rick had stood by and watched, and yet had come back strong enough to be Rick's friend. And protector.

These four hadn't given up on him and the more Rick thought about it, the more he realized he'd be damned if he gave up on himself. Not now. He was better than that.

Rick finally stood up. He squared his shoulders as he looked at the courthouse he hated. Yes, he knew he was still nervous and jumpy. He probably always would be, thanks to Blade and the Knights. But, as long as he remembered he wasn't alone, he'd be okay.

"Let's go. I'm not letting him win. Never again," Rick said as he led the way to the cafeteria where they joined Nana, Seamus and the rest of their friends for lunch.

"Better, love?" Jordan asked as Rick slid in beside her with his tray.

"Yes and no," Rick said with a shrug. Jordan just squeezed his leg, somehow understanding his need for silence.

Rick finished his lunch quickly and left the others in the cafeteria. He needed some more time alone to compose himself. This afternoon was going to be painfully hard and he knew it.

He sat on the same bench Seamus had and stared at the courtroom door. All too soon, he was going to have to walk through it and face Them.

For good or bad, what happened in there was going to depend solely on him keeping his temper. He just prayed he would be strong enough. He thought about the glee on Blade's face when he was driving the knife into Rick's shoulder and the way he just pounded on Rick that night. It seemed like a lifetime ago. And if he failed today, Blade would walk away with only a slap on the wrist.

"No way, Johnny. You're not winning. Not this time," Rick vowed softly as he waited for the rest of his family to show up. *Over my dead body,* Rick swore as he stared at the courtroom doors.

Over my dead body.

Chapter 55

Rick was still on the bench when his family and friends showed up half an hour later. He had leaned his head back and close his eyes, as relaxed as he could be under the circumstances.

Tony stopped in front of him, reaching out to gently touch his shoulder. Rick chuckled low in his throat. "Don't bother, Fish. I heard ya," the teen said, sitting up and opening his eyes. Tony smiled down at him, and hoped his young friend could keep that calm composure for the rest of the day.

"Megan? Rick? Ready?" Owen asked.

"Ready as we'll ever be, I guess," Megan replied. Rick nodded as he heaved himself up. They followed Owen into the courtroom and sat down with their lawyer in the first row right behind the prosecutor. Their family and friends settled around them.

"Worried, Rick?" Megan asked. She didn't miss his bouncing legs and clenched jaw.

"Yeah. You?" he asked, reaching out to hold her hand. She squeezed it gently.

"Scared to death, to be perfectly honest. But determined, too," she replied.

At precisely 1:30 p.m., the door next to the judge's chambers opened and Blade and Brain were led into the courtroom, followed by a single lawyer. He was dressed in a dark pinstriped suit with a pristine white shirt and sedately coloured tie. He had piercing gray-green eyes that focused immediately on Rick and Megan. His thin mouth stretched into a sly smile.

"Oh crap. Not good. This is not good at all," Owen said quietly, glancing at Tony.

"What's wrong?" Tony demanded quickly.

"That's Julien Tarbot, a high powered attorney from the city. Brian's parents're obviously paying for the best for their boy. He only takes the cases he thinks he can win. He's absolutely vicious on cross and has been known to deliberately provoke witnesses. This is *not* good, Tony. He's not gonna be able to stand up to Tarbot," Owen said again quietly, looking at Rick, who puzzled at the sudden whispered conference between Tony and the two lawyers. *What the hell's going on?* Rick wondered as the trio kept glancing at him.

"What do you wanna do, Owen? He's your client," Blackstone asked quietly, making some notes quickly. While Lance had known about Tarbot, seeing him there with the two Knights just made it way too real. He didn't know what he was going to do. "Not put him on the stand? I can do it if you really want, but..."

"What *can* we do, Lance? Without Rick's testimony, Chilton, especially, ain't going anywhere but juvy, which will mean three years max and these kids'll have to hire bodyguards for the rest of their lives. And that's *if* he's convicted. Just be prepared to do a lot of objecting, 'cause if you don't, I will," Owen warned. Lance nodded.

Throughout the whispered conference, Blade stood in front of the defendant's table, grinning at Megan and Rick. Megan had buried her head against her cousin's shoulder as soon as the Knights had walked into the courtroom, and shook with silent sobs, unable to look at them, while Blade stood there, laughing, mocking her fear. Carl and Mickey surged to their feet and had to be held back by Tom and Seamus, anger contorting all of their faces.

"Sit down! All of you!" the judge snapped as he came into the room. With a growl, Carl and Mickey threw themselves back into their chairs and Tarbot led his clients to their table.

"Easy, Megs. Don't let 'im see you're scared. Face him. C'mon, cuz. Face him down," Rick encouraged, all the while wanting to wipe the arrogant smile off of Blade's face with a right hook he couldn't deliver.

"Ladies and gentlemen, are we ready? Good. Court is now in session. The Right Honourable Judge Rory Neils presiding," the court clerk intoned.

Finally knowing what his favourite judge's name was, Rick watched as he slowly sat behind his bench and looked around the room. "It must be my lucky day," he said dryly. "First I get to dismiss charges against one member of the Black Knights. Excuse me, Rick, former member," the judge corrected himself quickly as Rick grinned up at him.

"Now, this afternoon, I seem to be here to preside over a hearing for two more. Mr. Blackstone, you've petitioned the court to transfer these two defendants to adult court. Perhaps you could start off by explaining what the charges are," Neils asked formally.

Lance Blackstone stood. His light tenor filled the courtroom as he read the charges. "Brian Townsand and Johnny Chilton, also known as Brain and Blade respectively, members of the Black Knights Gang, are both charged as follows: Destruction of Private Property, Assault, Assault & Battery, Harassment, Stalking, Vandalism, Uttering Threats, Kidnapping, Conspiracy to Commit Assault and Conspiracy to Commit Kidnapping. Separately, Mr. Townsand's also charged with Break & Enter, Theft, Possession of Stolen Goods and Possession of an Illegal Firearm," Mr. Blackstone said.

"All of that for one defendant? You've apparently been busy," Neils said, making his notes while looking at Brain. "Any further charges for Mr. Chilton?"

"Yes, your honour. We're also charging him with Unlawful Confinement, Extortion, Assault with a Deadly Weapon and five counts of Attempted Murder, specifically, Megan Attison twice, once in November and once this past May, Jordan O'Reilly, Tom Shelley and of course, Richard Attison," Blackstone said. The judge just stared at the defendants.

"They're both what? 16? 17? These're some very serious charges, Mr. Blackstone and I can see why you're petitioning the court for the transfer. However, I need more than just a list of the charges to warrant the move," Neils pointed out.

"To answer that, your honour, we'd like to call a couple of witnesses. Their full testimony won't be necessary until trial, so I'm gonna just focus on the events surrounding the kidnapping of Miss

Attison," Blackstone advised. "We believe this'll be sufficient for the court to make the right decision."

"Very well. Call your first witness," Neils ordered, as he finished making note of all the charges.

"Miss Megan Attison," Lance said and motioned to the young teen.

Megan caught her breath. She stood up and immediately stumbled. Blade and Brain snickered, making Megan flush with shame. "I got you, cuz," Rick said as he steadied her. He escorted her to the stand and whispered, "C'mon, Megs. You can do this," as she settled into the witness stand.

Rick walked slowly back to his seat, glaring at the two boys he would've gladly laid down his life for at one time. He paused in front of the table, struggling with the almost overwhelming desire to leap over the table and throttle the pair. The two Knights just glared right back.

Tony's voice was loud in the sudden tense silence of the courtroom. "Rick? C'mon, son. Just walk away and let the court do its job," Tony advised.

"Gladly, Fish. I wouldn't wanna soil my hands on their stinking carcasses," Rick snarled. He sauntered back to his chair and sat where Megan had a clear view of him.

"Too close, Fish. We wouldn't've been able to stop him," Marshall murmured. Tony just nodded as Blackstone got his case underway.

"Okay, Megan? Now, although I wanna focus on the kidnapping and captivity, I would, however, like you to give a brief synopsis of the school year. What's it been like?" Lance began as he stood in front of her.

"Hell," Megan said shortly and launched into a review of all the letters and calls she'd received over the school year.

"Your honour, I have here transcripts of several phone calls and letters Megan received over the year. Again, I don't think they all need to be read into evidence, but I would like to read the last one," Lance said, handing over the stack of papers.

"Proceed, Mr. Blackstone," Neils replied distractedly as he read. Megan tried not to cry as the last threatening letter was read into evidence.

Rick paled as he heard the words for the first time. *No wonder she wanted to press charges*, he thought. Tony sighed as he knew the question Lance had to ask, but, man, he hated to hear it.

"Megan, do you remember this letter?" the prosecutor asked.

"Yes sir," she replied softly, unable to look at Rick.

"Do you remember what happened next?" Lance asked. He didn't want to ask about it either, but if he didn't, then Tarbot would, and it wouldn't be politely either.

"After I found it, my boyfriend, Mickey O'Reilly, confronted me. By the time we finished arguing, I'd decided Rick was after me again and I needed to press charges. To this day, I don't know if I did it because I really thought Rick was responsible, or because Mickey wanted me to.

"At lunch, I confronted Rick and told him I was tired of the harassment and I was pressing charges after school," Megan said, her voice hardly louder than a whisper and she couldn't look at Rick.

"What happened?" Blackstone asked gently. It was hard to do, but he had to.

"Rick slapped me, knocking me down. It was his words, though, that got everyone's attention. He said...he said...." Megan couldn't go on. She finally broke down, the tension of the last few weeks coming out and she sobbed, holding her head in her hands.

Unfortunately, those words were forever burned into Rick's memory and he spoke them quietly. "I said, "Ya think I hurt you, cuz? Really? Guess it wasn't bad enough. Next time I get my hands on ya, I'll finish the job right." Then I stormed out," he said. *I was such an idiot*, he thought sadly, knowing he was truly to blame for what had happened to his cousin. If he hadn't said those stupid words, this might never have happened. *Maybe it wouldn't've happened*, he thought wryly, knowing Blade would still have gone after Megan some other time.

"Thank you, Rick," Blackstone said. He turned back to Megan who was trying to get herself back under some kind of control.

"Megan, need a minute?" Lance asked softly as he handed her a tissue to dry her eyes.

She shook her head and continued softly. "After Rick stormed out, Mickey wanted to take me to see his dad right away, but I said it could wait. I wish to God I had listened," Megan said with a sigh.

"What happened?" Lance presses, anxious to get this over with. Megan looked like she was on the verge of passing out, she was so pale.

"During my last class, Computers, the fire alarm blared and we were told to leave, to follow the standard fire alarm drill procedures. I got separated from the O'Reillys and my Angel guardians and then found the main entrance blocked by smoke and panicked students. I decided to go down a dark hallway and out another exit," Megan explained.

"Did you ever make it out that door?" the prosecutor asked.

Megan shook her head emphatically. "No, sir. I was almost there when I felt a sharp sting in the back of my neck. I remember getting very sleepy and then nothing until I came to, tied up in a damp basement with four of the Black Knights staring at me," Megan said. "Those two included," she added pointing to Blade and Brain.

"Let the record show the witness had identified the defendants, Johnny Chilton and Brian Townsand," Neils intoned and motioned for Lance to continue.

Blackstone led Megan through a very thorough description of her month-long captivity. Megan managed to stay calm until he asked how she had received her stab wound. Instead of naming Blade, his name came out as a strangled scream and she couldn't continue for almost ten minutes.

Once she had composed herself, Blackstone thanked her and sat down. Julien Tarbot made a few notes and then stood.

Before he could draw a single breath, Neils gave him a stern warning. "Your reputation proceeds you, Mr. Tarbot. Let me make this perfectly clear right now. No badgering. No verbal insults. And don't push my buttons. Do you understand? Cross that boundary even once and you'll be replaced, no matter who's paying the bills. And be advised, although it's not normal procedure, I *will* accept objections from Owen St. James as he is her lawyer. Do I make myself clear, Counsellor?" the judge warned.

"Crystal, your honour," Tarbot replied sourly, and stepped to the podium.

"Miss. Attison, I wanna go back to something you said earlier. You said Rick was after you again. Again? Are you saying this wasn't the first letter you'd received from your cousin?" he asked.

Megan sighed. She knew this was going to come out, but she didn't have to like it. "No sir, it wasn't," Megan replied but didn't elaborate.

"Well, then, let's go back to that first letter. Do you think you can remember that far back?" Tarbot asked sarcastically.

"Objection!" Owen snapped before Blackstone could even draw a breath.

Neils looked at Tarbot. "This is your only second chance, Mr. Tarbot, and only because I know you need to defend your clients. Behave!" the judge threatened.

"Sorry, your honour," Tarbot said, not sorry at all. He turned back to Megan. "Miss. Attison, please think back to that first letter. Was there anything in it that would point to someone other than my clients?" the lawyer demanded.

Megan narrowed his eyes. She knew what the lawyer was after, but she'd be damned if she was going to make it easy for him. She'd show him who was smarter. "All of the letters referred to me as "cuz," but anyone, including your clients, would've heard him call me at school at one time or another. He never calls me Megan. It's usually Megs or cuz. As those two well know," she said, pointing again at the defendants.

"Anything else?" Tarbot asked. This was not going the way the lawyer had planned, Rick could tell. Maybe, just maybe, they would win this round.

"The letters were always typed, as I recall, never hand-written. See, Rick has a very unique way of writing I've never seen anyone else use, especially a teen-age boy and by typing them, there was no way I'd be able to tell who actually wrote them. They were also always signed, in black, with a pair of stylized M's – Rick's gang sign. Again, something your clients would know very well. However, the few notes I remember getting from Rick in school *before* all of this started, the signature was usually in blue – Glencrest ice blue to be specific, from the special pens and ink Nana had made up for the two of us a long time ago, something your clients wouldn't've known," Megan said confidently.

"What's changed your mind? Why don't you blame your cousin now?" Tarbot asked.

"Two things, really. After the new semester started, I received a phone call which showed up on my call display as Rick's home number. Since my room overlooks his house, I could clearly see he wasn't home from counselling, since he always parks in front of it. And when I confronted him, he promised he'd stay well away from me, which he did, but it didn't help," Megan said sadly.

"And the second thing?" the lawyer asked, not at all happy with the way the questioning had turned around.

"When I came to the first time, tied up in that damp basement, the only face I *never* saw was Rick's. The other four were there, but never Rick. It took me a couple of minutes that first day to realize I knew Brian Townsand. He had every class with me. He actually sat behind me with perfect access to my knapsack," Megan said, then paused to moisten her dry throat.

"I also realized how much he and Rick looked alike, at least at first glance. They're both blonde, with blue eyes and about the same height. When you've been choked almost unconscious or beaten to within an inch of your life and you hear someone encourage "Rick" to keep going, your oxygen-starved brain makes the only conclusion it can. It's only after you come to and really think about it, do you begin to wonder," Megan said softly, finally looking at her cousin.

Rick smiled encouragingly at her. "Doing good, cuz," he mouthed. She smiled at him and took a couple of more sips of water while Tarbot formed his next set of questions.

"Now, during your alleged kidnapping, was there anything either of my clients did to make your stay more comfortable?" Tarbot asked.

Megan stiffened at the implied insult. "It wasn't alleged, sir. Your clients really did this to me," she snapped as she showed her healing shoulder. Tarbot wouldn't look at it.

"Don't turn away from it, Mr. Tarbot, dammit! This is what Johnny did to me after starving me, denying me water and beating me. The only time that *ever* changed was if Brian was around. And even then, Brian had to fight Johnny to let him do anything. But that only lasted until he was arrested. After that, no one could control Johnny. No one. I was scared of him then. I still am," Megan finished.

Julien Tarbot smiled. "Nothing further, your honour," he said quickly, acting as if he had scored a major point.

As Mickey helped Megan back to her seat, the tension in the courtroom increased tenfold as Lance Blackstone turned to the gallery and said softly, "Richard Attison."

Chapter 56

Rick couldn't move. He was frozen to his chair. The moment he'd been dreading for weeks was finally here and he couldn't do it. He couldn't get up and face them. He shook his head frantically as Lance motioned again for the teen to take the stand. Megan leaned over and gave him a reassuring smile.

"C'mon, Rick. You can do this. Face him, just like I did. Don't let him win," Megan encouraged, but Rick just couldn't make his legs move, no matter how hard he tried.

Suddenly, Blade's mocking laughter filled the room. It seemed like no one else heard his muttered comments, but Rick, and Rick heard them loud and clear. "Told ya I'd break 'im, Brain. He's yeller," Blade said to his second as he continued to laugh.

Anger surged through Rick. *Like hell, you bastard*, Rick thought hotly. He surged to his feet and sauntered up to the stand like he didn't have a care in the world. He would face them both down. No way was Blade going to win.

"Rick, I won't lie to you. This is gonna hard for you, brutal even, but without your testimony, I can't prove these two should be tried as adults. Can you hold on long enough to tell me what I need to hear?" Blackstone asked.

"Honestly? I doubt it, Mr. Blackstone. It's been a year from hell and all I wanna do is forget it," Rick said shortly. *But no one will let me*, he didn't have to add.

"Rick, to make it somewhat easier, let's just focus on that month Megan was missing. Start with the fight in the cafeteria and stop, well, you know where I want you to stop," Lance said with a small apologetic shrug.

Yeah, Rick thought roughly, *I know exactly where to stop. The ditch on the side of the road, bleeding and dying.* Rick took a deep breath and began to talk. For more than an hour, he described hiding out at Jim's townhouse and sneaking out to help search for Megan. How frustrating it was to find nothing. The long arguments with Tony about going back to the gang. Through it all, Lance didn't interrupt once. He didn't need to.

Rick paused for a long time before he began to describe that horrible day he tried to go back to the Knights. He spoke with clinical detachment as if he was describing something happening to someone else.

He described the beating, blow by excruciatingly painful blow, all the while refusing to look at the defendant's table. He knew Blade was reliving it all and relishing Rick's discomfort way too much.

"After Johnny stabbed me the first time, I don't really remember anything else until I felt rocks spraying my face as I was lying in the ditch. I remember thinking I had to be found. I had to save Megs. Inch by inch, I remember dragging my butt up that ditch, and down the road. After that, nothing until I heard some strange drumming at the hospital," Rick finished. He ran an agitated hand through his hair. He was shaking so hard he thought he'd vibrate the stand apart, and he knew he couldn't take much more.

"You okay, Rick? Do you need a break?" Neils asked, concerned at what he saw.

"Won't help, Judge. I'll just stew. Let's finish this before I do blow," Rick said shortly. Tony winced at the brutal acknowledgement by Rick. *At last, he finally knows the signs*, Tony thought sadly.

"Mr. Blackstone, anything further?" Neils asked.

"No, your honour. I've...tortured him enough," the prosecutor said and sat down.

Neils nodded and motioned to the defendant's table. With an oily smile, Tarbot stood and adjusted his tie. He buttoned his jacket and slowly walked to the podium. He read over his notes for several minutes until Rick began to fidget nervously.

"Mr. Tarbot, do not try my patience. It's been a long enough day for this witness for various reasons, none of which you need to know about. Now, either ask him a question, or let him stand down," Neils snapped.

Owen looked at Tony. Both were worried. Neils was right. It had already been a long day for Rick and now the defence was doing their best to get to Rick. Unfortunately, they knew it was working all too well.

"Rick," Tarbot began, only to have Rick interrupt him harshly.

"Do not call me Rick. Only my friends can," Rick snarled, biting off each work. Tony was surprised, considering how much he knew Rick hated his real name.

"My apologies, Richard. Now, why did you join the Knights? Did Johnny hold a gun to your head?" Tarbot asked innocently.

Rick almost laughed at that. No, Blade hadn't held a gun to his head, but Rick had held one to Seamus'. "No, sir. I joined willingly. For the longest time, I thought the Knights had replaced my dad. He hasn't really been in my life since I was six, even though I lived with him," Rick said shortly.

"Why did you leave then? I mean, if they meant so much to you, why would you wanna leave?" Tarbot asked curiously.

Rick wasn't sure what this had to do with the transfer request, but he answered the question anyway. "Believe it or not, in a way, they drove me out. I was starting to have nightmares about the gang life. I didn't like what I was becoming. I was a machine, just reacting to what Johnny wanted. I no longer thought for myself. Johnny had a noose around my neck and just kept pulling it tighter and tighter," Rick explained dryly.

Before Tarbot could ask another question, Rick continued. "For example, the first day of school? Johnny started a fight in the cafeteria just because I was sitting with my girl instead of the Knights. It sickened me. There was no reason for it. Thanks to Delaney's detention that week, I came to realize I wanted out. I just wasn't like them. Jor meant more to me than they did. More than beating up the smaller kids and destroying property," Rick said.

"Anything else?" Tarbot asked.

"Yeah, Tarbot, there was something else. Something your clients won't ever understand. Someone took a chance on me. After getting caught in the playground in my neighbourhood the Knights had destroyed, Judge Neils here took a chance. He ordered me into counselling, but more importantly, he actually ordered me out of the gang. Thanks to counselling with Constable Whitefish, I've been able to break free of the gang. It wasn't easy, but I did it," Rick said proudly.

"Okay, Richard. Now back to the alleged assault, the one you say Johnny did. You broke that court order you just talked about, didn't you? Why?" Tarbot asked innocently.

Rick didn't hesitate. "To save Megs," Rick said. He frowned suddenly as he realized what Tarbot had said. *Alleged assault?* Rick thought incredulously. "Don't let him fool you, Tarbot. Johnny did this. Don't let his lies fool you," Rick said sharply. Tony winced at the anger he could hear.

"Keep an eye on him, Owen. It's starting to get bad," Tony whispered. Owen nodded.

"To save Megan," Tarbot said thoughtfully. He paused for a couple of minutes to mull that over. "You say that as if you knew Johnny had her. If he actually took her, that is. So, if he had her, how could you have known that, unless you had helped to kidnap her?" Tarbot pointed out logically.

Rick laughed. "You obviously don't know your client every well, Tarbot. Johnny's been after Megs from day one. I saw it in the way he looked at her when I first introduced them. She was just...a toy to be played with. She's everything Johnny hates. Pretty, confident, but more importantly she's smart and rich. Everything Johnny isn't.

"Besides, when Fish told me how she'd been taken, I realized Johnny'd taken her to get back at me. Even if there wasn't any immediate evidence, we both knew who wanted to take her and they figured out a way. But I can guarantee you this – he didn't plan it. No way in hell's this his plan. Check the notebook they found at Brian's place. It'll all be in there. It's Johnny's idea and Brian's plan. The notes. The harassment. The assaults. All pure Brian. That's the reason we call him Brain," Rick said evenly. It was the first time Rick or anyone else had openly implicated Brain in the whole affair.

Tarbot continued to hammer at Rick, but Rick never wavered from his story, no matter how hard he was pushed. Tony could see the questions were starting to get to Rick, though. His left hand, clearly visible in the sling on the side of the witness box, was clenching and unclenching. His upper body was jiggling so his legs were bouncing uncontrollably and Rick's jaw was clenched. It wasn't going to be much longer before he lost control, Tony just knew.

"Owen, you've gotta stop this. He's beyond upset," Tony hissed. Owen agreed, but he never got a chance.

"Richard, isn't it true you've attacked a cop at least twice and have never been charged? How about that assault on your uncle after you'd been arrested for attacking your cousin back in November? Not to mention the attack in school of three boys, including my client, Brian Townsand? Why've you never been charged with any of these assaults?" Tarbot demanded, suddenly switching his line of questioning.

Before Rick could respond to the verbal onslaught, Tarbot hit him with *the question*. "C'mon, Richard, admit it. Isn't it true the real reason you joined the Knights is because your dad blames you for your mother leaving?"

Rick paled, then flushed in anger. Before he realized what he was doing, he shot from the witness stand and rushed at Tarbot. Stunned at Rick's sudden movement, Tony and Marshall hesitated almost a moment too long then launched themselves over the railing. They caught Rick before he could lay a hand on the lawyer, who stood at the podium, apparently shocked, but Marshall could see the glint of success in Tarbot's eyes. *He got what he wanted alright*, Marshall realized. *Dammit!*

"Rick, NO!" Tony shouted as he wrapped his arms around the angry teen who was fighting with all of his limited strength. Both Owen and Lance were shouting objections while Blade and Brain roared with laughter. Even Tarbot couldn't keep the grin off of his face.

"Holy crap! Injured my ass, Fish. I can't hold him. He's too damn strong!" Marshall growled as his grip slipped when Rick gave a particularly violent wrench.

"Rick, stop fighting me, dammit! You're ripping your stitches! Rick, listen to me!" Tony yelled in Rick's ear. It didn't do a bit of good. If anything, Rick struggled harder.

Jordan couldn't watch anymore. Hardly aware of the sudden silence as she stood, Jordan walked slowly towards Tony. She could see Rick battling to get past his friend. She could also see the anger in her boyfriend's eyes and she could see how hurt he was by Tarbot's questions.

She stopped before the trio and spoke softly. "Rick, enough. Please. You're hurting yourself," she said. Sitting in the gallery, Nana did a double take. Jordan had sounded so much like Rick's mom at that moment, Nana had thought Kara was there.

Rick stiffened like he'd been shot, then dropped to his knees so fast Tony and Marshall had no chance to catch him. He landed heavily and his sobs filled the courtroom as Jordan gathered him to her. Tony watched them for a second to make sure Rick wasn't going to start bleeding then looked at Marshall who nodded in silent agreement. The cops, still breathing heavily and trying to catch their breath, turned to face the defendants, who couldn't stop grinning. Both cops stood there with their arms folded across their chests, as if daring the Knights to try something else.

Tarbot straightened his tie and looked at the judge. "Well, you honour, I think this little demonstration just proves Richard's more than capable of attacking his cousin. I hereby request the motion to transfer my clients be denied. Also, I request all charges against my clients be dropped. After all, they didn't try to attack me, now did they?" Tarbot smirked. Tony clenched his fists, trying very hard not to wipe the smirk off the lawyer's face. *Arrogant bastard!* Tony wanted to yell.

"Your clients have, thankfully, been arrested and charged based on evidence, not emotion, Mr. Tarbot," Blackstone snapped. He still couldn't believe the anger he had just seen explode from

Rick and he now understood what Tony was always so worried about.

"Mr. Tarbot, as much as I dislike violence in my courtroom and knowing I would've had to charge Rick (and don't think I don't know how much you would've loved that!) you're just very lucky these officers were here to keep him back. Even one-handed, I'm sure he would've put you down," Neils snapped. "Despite my earlier warnings, you deliberately provoked him, knowing he'd react this way. And I happen to agree with some of Mr. Blackstone's and Mr. St. James's objections. Rick's parents have *nothing* to do with this case and I'm dismissing those suggestions from my considerations. Now, do you plan on calling any witnesses or are we done here?" The anger in the judge's voice was unmistakable.

"No, your honour, we're done," Tarbot said smoothly. After all, he had achieved what he wanted. Or so he believed.

"Constable Whitefish?" Neils asked, indicating Rick. Jordan continued to cradle her boyfriend as he sobbed like his heart had broken. The only other sound was the Knights continued laughter.

Tony had to take a couple of deep breaths before answering. "Unlike me, your honour, he's in no danger of attacking anyone. At least right now. However, it's gonna take me a long time, a very long time, to get through to him, if I can," Tony said harshly. He took a couple of more deep breaths and stood facing the Knights with his arms folded over his chest. There was no mistaking his message to them. Stay away from Rick. Neils nodded and made a few notes before looking at the defendant's table.

"Wipe those grins off your faces, boys. This is serious business. Now, the defendants will stand," Neils said shortly. The two stood.

"Based on the evidence *presented*, both today and in the application, I've determined the application for Brian Townsand's denied. No matter how serious the charges are, you didn't present enough *evidence* to warrant the transfer, Mr. Blackstone. I only ever heard one mention of Townsand's involvement all day and you did not present the one thing you had that might've worked, so drop it," Neils said over the prosecutor's protests as he wondered why the prosecution never bothered to present the notebook the judge knew they had. It would've been more than enough to warrant the transfer, but since they didn't present it, he couldn't consider it. Lance subsided with a final word of protest. Brain just grinned and nudge Blade who grinned back. Blade's grin faded quickly, though, with the judge's next words.

"Mr. Chilton, on the other hand, will be transferred. There's enough evidence just in Rick's testimony alone, to warrant this, Mr. Tarbot, so I advise you to drop the objections as well. That application's hereby approved. The three juveniles'll be tried together, at the victims' request, Mr. Tarbot. They don't want to tell their stories four times, and I happen to agree with them. Based on what I've heard today, I'm sure it's gonna be hard enough telling it twice as it is. Trial date's three weeks from today, pending confirmation of the presiding judge's schedule. And I can guarantee it won't be me, Mr. Tarbot, so don't worry," Neils said before Tarbot could say a word and as he made some more notes. Silence fell, punctured by Rick's continued soft sobs. Brain shrugged and sat down.

Judge Neils turned to Blade and flipped a couple of other pages and made a note. "Mr. Chilton, your trial'll start approximately six weeks from today, again pending confirmation of the presiding judge in adult court. I suggest you use this time to plan a proper defence, one that's a bit more constructive than trying to provoke that young man over there into more violent outbursts. Trust me, young man, your trial judge'll know exactly what transpired here today.

"Now, Bailiff, get them the hell outta my courtroom!" Neils snapped, banging down his gavel sharply.

Blade and Brain were hauled up by two burly bailiffs, and cuffs snapped on. As they were led away, Blade hesitated for a moment by Rick. Neils snapped, "Don't even think about it, Chilton! Move it!"

Blade just laughed down at a still sobbing Rick. "What a wimp! I warned ya, Moneyman. Told ya you'd beg to end this,"

Blade said softly enough only Tony heard him. The cop just glared at the Knight as Blade continued to laugh while he sauntered out.

"Rick? Son, c'mon, it's Fish, man. Hey, Rick, c'mon, look at me," Tony said quietly as he squatted beside the sobbing teen.

"I'm sorry. I'm so sorry," Rick sobbed over and over as he rocked in Jordan's arms. "Mom, I'm so sorry. I didn't mean it. Please come back." Tony just shook his head and sighed.

"Tony, what happened? I've never seen him react like that," Nana said from the gallery.

Tony sighed again as he stood with his hands on his hips. "He would've been just fine if Tarbot hadn't mentioned his mom. That'll get him every time and no mater how many times I've told him, he still blames himself for her leaving. Michael really did a job on this kid," Tony said. Nana just shook her head, disgusted at Michael all over again.

"Will you be able to get him calmed down?" Marshall asked as the judge came over to check on things.

"Eventually, but it's gonna take a while – a very long time. Uninterrupted time. Look, Judge, I know it's a lot to ask, but can I have this room locked down until I can calm him down? I don't wanna take a chance he'll go berserk on me and possibly break away," Tony explained with everyone looking at him, shocked.

"Is that a real danger?" Neils asked, surprised. When Tony nodded, the judge nodded. "Okay, not a problem, Constable. Fortunately, it's not booked for the rest of the day and I'll make sure everyone knows what's going on in here. You're gonna have a major problem if he does this at the trials, you know?" Neils said philosophically as he left the courtroom.

"No kidding, Judge," Tony said dryly to the judge's retreating back.

"Tony, how'd he find out about all the fights?' Seamus wanted to know as he joined them. "Only ye, me, Ian and Nana knew about them," O'Reilly pointed out, deliberately ignoring Rick. He figured the kid had had enough of people staring at him all day.

"Probably Mendez, through his snitch, and I'm pretty sure Johnny told Tarbot about Rick's mom. I don't think he hid anything from the Knights. Clear everyone out, Marsh. I need to work him through this," Tony said with another sigh. *Again*, the cop thought sourly. *When's he gonna learn?*

Marshall herded everyone towards the door, despite protests from Nana and the Angels. Everyone, except Jordan, that is. Rick clung to his girlfriend like seaweed clung to a rock. "Just leave her, Marsh," Tony said when it became evident Rick wasn't about to let go. "She'll help."

Tony waited until the door closed softly behind his partner before he locked it and approached Jordan and Rick. The cop slid his tall frame down the front of the judge's bench and just waited. This was going to take a long time, the cop knew. Jordan continued to rock her boyfriend as he sobbed.

"Tony, he won't stop. I don't think he can," Jordan said over Rick's sobs.

Tony nodded. "I know, sweets, and normally it's not this bad. It's just been way too much for him today. He had a hell of a nightmare and, no, you don't wanna know the details. Hell, I didn't wanna know the details after I read them, but there's no way I'll ever forget them. Then, after this morning, I had to talk him through some other issues. Now this. Somehow, I've gotta convince him he's not to blame," Tony explained. "That he's never to blame."

Not knowing what to say, Jordan just held Rick as he slowly began to calm down. Ten long minutes later, Rick drew a shuddering breath and sat up. He was tired and shaking, not to mention extremely dry. Once again, he remembered very little of the past few minutes. He smiled at his girl as he knew she was the one who'd managed to help him this time.

"Thanks, babe. You okay?" he asked softly as he scrubbed at his face. He was almost asleep he was so tired.

"I'm fine, Rick, but how about you?" Jordan asked.

Rick nodded absently as he looked at Tony. The cop didn't say anything for a while as he tried to figure out how to get through to Rick he couldn't do this any more. "You just about blew it, Champ, y'know that? It's a good thing your favourite judge was presiding today. He understands. The next judge might not," Tony finally said from where he sat.

"Fish, you know what happens when someone mentions Mom," Rick protested weakly. He groaned as he shifted his bandaged shoulder. While he didn't like the constant reminders, he knew Tony was right – he couldn't react, not at the trials, but dammit, it was so hard.

"Here, let me look," Tony said, moving to peer under the bandage at the stitches.

"Just swollen," Tony said with a small grin.

The three just sat there for a couple more minutes as Rick tried to get back under control. "Rick, this cannot happen at trial. Either of them," Tony finally said.

"I get that, Fish," Rick snapped harshly. "Trust me – I get that."

"Well then, we'll just have to change your reaction to this then. I'm sorry, little brother, but if you thought our sessions were brutal before, they'll be a walk in the park compared to what I'm gonna do to you," Tony threatened. Inwardly, the cop grimaced. He hated beating on Rick – it took a lot out of both of them, but this time, it was absolutely necessary.

It took Rick a couple of minutes to understand what Tony was talking about, and when he did, Rick wanted to cry again. He knew what Tony was going to do – deliberately provoke him until he broke. And it wouldn't be just once. It would be over and over and over again. Deliberately. Cruelly. Rick wanted to crawl into a hole and hide.

"How long?" the teen whispered, horrified at the prospect. He'd pushed himself away from Jordan and stood, facing the judge's bench, his back to them. Still, Tony winced as he heard the terror in Rick's voice.

"Three weeks," Tony said with finality.

Chapter 57

Tony was true to his word. Every day, Rick went to school, struggled through his classes and then dragged his battered body to physio at the centre. Only once he was physically exhausted, would Rick sit in Tony's office while Owen fired question after question at him, twisting the teen's words around to try and trap Rick in a lie, just like Tarbot would be doing. Owen would wait until the very last minute when Rick was so angry he was ready to explode at his lawyer before asking *the question*. After that, it was up to Tony to get Rick calmed back down so they could analyze what had happened. Every day it took longer and longer to calm Rick down, and left them both so exhausted they could barely move to make it home.

By the end of the second week, Rick was physically and emotionally exhausted. He stared at the ominously closed door, knowing it would soon open to reveal Owen, Tony and the next punishing session. The longer the teen stood and stared at the door, the more he wanted to run away, but he couldn't make his feet move. *I can't take much more,* Rick realized.

The door opened. "Come in, Rick," Tony said quietly.

Rick hesitated for a long moment, followed his best friend into the office, and then sat down heavily in his chair as Tony closed the door with a soft click. The cop settled on his favourite corner of the desk, silent for a very long time.

"I've put a stop to Owen's sessions, Rick. You've been through enough. You deserve to have some peace," Tony finally said. His voice was quiet, but tense.

"Fish, you sure? I mean, look how quickly I blew yesterday," Rick protested weakly. Not that he really minded, but still, Rick knew how important these sessions with Owen were. Without them, he wasn't going to last very long at the trials.

Tony just snorted. "C'mon, Rick, think about it. We've been beating on you since the transfer hearing and, hell, *I* couldn't take it any more, so I'm pretty sure you're not handling it very well. Sometimes, well, sometimes, kiddo, these sessions're harder on me than you, trying to deflect your anger, while trying to teach you how to handle this yourself," Tony said as he rubbed at his face. His shoulders were slumped and he felt defeated. Once again, he felt like he had let his little brother down.

Rick looked at the cop and shook his head in disgust. "You're not sleeping again, are you, Fish? When was the last time you ate a decent meal, one that didn't come from a fast food joint? Dammit, Tony Whitefish, I need you," Rick snapped harshly, angry and hurt his big brother was doing this to himself and over something that wasn't important.

Tony flushed. "I...I...I'm sorry, little brother," was all that the cop could manage in a barely audible voice. He hung his head in shame. Rick didn't say anything for a long time, stunned at how hard Tony was taking what Rick had said.

Finally, the teen stood up and fished out his cell phone. "Hey, Nana. Okay, I guess. Listen, can I bring a friend over for a ride and supper? No, Tony. Thanks. Love ya. See you soon." With that, Rick snapped his phone closed and looked at Tony. He weighed his words carefully before he spoke.

"Look, Fish, I'm not gonna promise I won't blow in the courtroom. I think we both know I probably will, and we both know it's gonna be bad, but you're right, we need a break. Both of us. Would you be upset, if we stopped counselling for a while, just stopped?" Rick asked tentatively. Tony was a little surprised at the request, but nodded. Rick continued after stretching carefully.

"More than that, though, Fish, *you* need a good meal, a decent night's sleep and some good company. Not necessarily in that order. C'mon, man. I need some fresh air and I'm sure Frank can find you a nice ride," Rick said, grinning suddenly at Tony.

Tony laughed as he jumped to his feet. "Great idea, son. I'll meet you at the farm," Tony said, feeling better already.

Rick left Tony tidying up the office and climbed into his car. He dialled another number after a moment's hesitation and spoke quietly for a few moments. He sighed as he watched a very tired Tony shuffle out of the youth centre and climb in his car. Only when he was certain the cop was coming to Glencrest did Rick ease out of the parking lot and race home.

He pulled into the drive about five minutes before Tony and smiled when he saw Cherokee, Mystique and a young gelding named Rockin' Robin saddled and waiting in front of his house. He changed into his cowboy boots and grabbed a jean jacket. Megan was already on her horse, waiting patiently when Tony pulled up.

Rick swung up into Cherokee's saddle and grinned at his cousin. It felt so good to be back in the saddle, *in more ways than one*, he thought. "Hurry up, Fish," he called as Tony switched his runners for cowboy boots.

The three friends rode out into the woods, unconsciously following the same route Megan had that fateful day in November. They rode quietly and emerged in the same clearing not far from where she had been attacked. She looked around as they climbed down and sighed.

"What's up, Megs?" Rick asked over his shoulder as he loosely tethered Cherokee.

"I was attacked just over there," Megan pointed towards the far side of the clearing. "Just inside the woods. I'd skied through the woods on the edge of the clearing instead of crossing it," she said softly, remembering.

Tony sat down on a fallen log and looked at the two teens who had gone through so much in such a short time. He still wondered how they were going to get through the upcoming trials without going bonkers. Rick especially. The short ride had done the cop some good, but he would kill for a good night's sleep, too.

"Okay, Fish, now what in the hell's going on? Why're you dragging yourself around again?" Rick demanded harshly as he settled on the ground next to his friend. Megan winced at Rick's blunt question.

"Life goes on, Rick, you know that. Marsh and I've been working with the prosecutor on the case, and going over our testimony to make sure we haven't forgotten anything. There's all of the evidence to go over and figure out what needs to be presented in the trials and which trials, and what we might not need at all. There's other cases to work on – life as a cop doesn't stop just because one case is solved. Like both of you, kiddo, I'm just plain worn out," Tony said, so exhausted all of a sudden, he was surprised he was still sitting on the log. He'd actually thought he'd fallen off for a moment. He held his head in his hands, his eyes closed against the bright sunshine.

"Is there a problem, Tony?" Megan asked, worried.

Tony hesitated for a minute then spoke quietly. "No, not really, Meg, at least not with the kidnapping or the two attempted murder charges. We've more than enough evidence for those. No, it's the other parts of the case – the assaults against you and Jordan and the threats only you heard, Meg. We'll be hard pressed to get convictions on those. Even the ones on Tom will be hard to prove. Everything we have forensically points to Rick, not the other Knights. That notebook of Brian's might not be enough," Tony said without raising his head.

Rick, seemingly unconcerned, sat on the soft moss under a large tree, drinking in the glorious early summer day. The birds were chirping back and forth, and there was just enough of a soft breeze to keep the early summer bugs away. He was content to sit in the sun, but his mind was going a mile a minute. *There has to be a way,* he thought, *to get Fish what he needs.* He sat as still as he could and just let his mind sort through the problem.

"Mark!" he said suddenly, sitting up abruptly and startling the horses. He settled them just as quickly with a wordless croon.

"What?" Megan and Tony chimed together.

"Mark may be the key, Fish. Think about it for a sec. I've told you I've always wondered what he got from the gang. I mean, he's always adored Johnny and Johnny used it every chance he could,

- 519 -

but otherwise, what does he *really* get from being a Knight? Nothing, man, nothing. Mark was Johnny's snitch, plain and simple," Rick said. "And he's really only been in the gang for just over a year, since coming to Colonial."

"So?" Tony asked, puzzled, wondering where Rick was going with this.

"So, he hasn't had enough time to really become immersed in the gang. Honestly, Fish, he's more like a hanger-on than a full member. He never became fully involved until he could be with Johnny all day, every day at school. It was like me – one day he was just hanging around, the next he's a Knight," Rick explained patiently. He couldn't understand why Tony couldn't see what he was talking about.

"Where're you going with this, Rick?" Tony finally asked.

"Turn 'im. Every now and then I thought I saw he didn't like what Johnny did. Turn 'im," Rick urged.

"Turn him,' Tony mused, sitting up. *Turn another Knight? The one closest to Blade?* Tony thought.

"Why? What do you think he can tell us, Rick?" Megan asked curiously. She was trying to follow her cousin's logic on this, but for once, she couldn't.

"He's Johnny's shadow, always there, just outta sight. He lives for the brotherhood of the gang – the "spirit" if you will. The idea you always had someone to watch over you. It's the one thing I loved about the gang – it really was a family, no matter what you say, Tony. But, like me, Mark never liked the unnecessary brutality. He was more like me since he never laid a hand on the little guy. He was always in the background, watching, listening, no matter what was going on. Johnny was so used to him being around he probably never watched what he said. Mark'll know everything," Rick said dryly. *And then some, no doubt,* he didn't add.

"What're you saying, Rick? You wanna offer a deal to someone who did this to you?" Megan asked, stunned, as she motioned at Rick's face, his scar bright white.

"Meg, do you *ever* remember Mark hitting you?" Tony interrupted before the cousins could begin arguing. Megan thought for several moments, then shook her head.

Rick didn't say anything as he shifted to sit on the log beside his cousin and when he did, his voice was quiet. "Trust me, I know what he did, cuz, but ask yourself this. Did he do it because he *wanted* to or because Johnny *expected* him to? Did he do it because he didn't wanna disappoint the cousin he adores or because he's a brutal thug? Tony, of all the Knights, Mark's gonna be the easiest to turn. He's still young enough he can have a shot at a normal life. The others never will," Rick said emphatically.

Tony fell silent, thinking about what Rick was asking him to do – offer a deal to someone who had helped almost kill the teen. He continued to think as the trio finally rode back to the farm. As they rode up, Tony snorted at a very familiar figure standing on Rick's porch with his arms crossed, not looking impressed.

"Snitch," he snarled good-naturedly at Rick as he swung down from Robin and handed the reins over to Frank.

"Payback," was Rick's grinning reply as he handed the reins over to one of the grooms.

Seamus took one look at Tony and sighed, whatever anger he may have had disappearing as he stood there. He shook his head and frowned at his best cop. "This is gettin' outta hand, Tony Whitefish. Ye're as bad as when Megan first disappeared. If not worse. So if ye're not gonna take care of yeself, I will, dammit. As of right now, ye're on paid leave, Tony, until further notice. Don't argue with me, Constable, I am dead serious. If ye set foot in the station before Jim clears ye, ye'll be on unpaid leave. Permanently," Seamus said gruffly. He turned to a shadow on the porch.

"Same goes fer ye, Marshall. Ye both see Jim. Tomorrow. 9 a.m. Don't be late," the inspector said as a parting shot and drove away.

Tony was stunned. *Paid leave until medically cleared?* he wondered as Seamus drove away. *Am I really that bad? Are we?* Silently, Rick led the partners into the house while Megan left to clean herself up, telling them she'd see them at supper.

Rick jumped into the shower and emerged, dripping but relaxed, twenty minutes later. He could hear Tony and Marshall talking quietly in the living room.

"Bathroom's free if you wanna shower, Fish," Rick called from his room. The teen pulled on clean jeans and eased a shirt over his healing shoulders. His hands twitched immediately as he glanced at his speed bag gathering dust in the corner. The desire to do a workout was almost overwhelming.

Soon, he promised himself as he did a slow motion run-through of his workout and felt both shoulders protest almost immediately. With a sigh, he finished dressing. *Damn you, Johnny,* he thought as he stood, staring at the speed bag for a long time. He could hear Tony changing in the spare room and then the muffled conversation between the partners picked up where they had left off. Rick slipped silently up to the kitchen door to listen.

"She didn't?" Marshall exclaimed in delight as Rick approached the kitchen.

Settling down in his chair with a chuckle, Tony lifted his drink in a toast to his girlfriend and nodded. "She most certainly did. Switched the sweet grass I had ready and put in Runningbear's mix. I lit them in the tepee intending to meditate for a couple of hours and instead woke up late the next afternoon," Tony laughed. The shower and ride had done him some good, but he wasn't 100% and the cop knew it.

"And yet, here you are, exhausted and worn out," Rick pointed out from the door, causing both cops to jump in surprise.

He sat down across from Tony after grabbing a drink from the fridge. "Why'd you rat me out, son? I'd've found a way to survive," Tony pointed out after a couple of minutes.

"By collapsing like you did after Megs disappeared? Marsh told me all about that, so you can yell at him if you want later. Fish, I told you before – I need you, whole and healthy. I can't make it through the trials alone. *I will need your help!*" Rick said hotly, trying to make Tony understand.

"But paid leave? Paid medical leave? *Stress leave?* Makes me seem like a wimp, Rick. I've worked with major injuries before and he's never given me any kind of leave. Hell, he's never even suggested it. Word gets out that I'm on stress leave and I'll be laughed off the force," Tony protested weakly. He was embarrassed to admit he could use the time off, though. He just didn't like how he was given it.

"Doesn't matter, Fish, not to me. I need your help, so you need to take the time. Now, you tell Marsh about our idea?" Rick asked, certain his point had been made. *Back to the business at hand*, he thought as he took a swig of his drink.

"Yeah, he did. Rick, you sure? Really sure? I mean, look at your face, man. Look at what he helped do to you! And you wanna offer Mark a deal!?" Marshall was incredulous at the mere suggestion.

"I know what Mark did to me, Marsh, every stinking, painful blow. Trust me – I am never gonna forget. This scar's the one visible reminder I face every day," Rick said sourly, pointing to the scar on his cheek.

"And yet you still wanna offer him a deal?" Marshall said, amazed at Rick's willingness to forgive. Rick nodded.

"The final choice is still Blackstone's, though," Tony pointed out as he gathered up the empty cans and tossed them in the recycle bin Rick kept by his door.

"And we won't see him until Monday morning, so this discussion's over," Marshall agreed and changed the subject.

Supper at Nana's was filled with laughter and lots of talk about everything and anything but the trials. Those would come soon enough, everyone knew, so there was no need to remind the two teens about what they would've been through. Once back at Rick's house, Tony and Rick sat on the front porch, Rick watching the light fade while Tony just relaxed, truly relaxed, for the first time since Rick's beating.

"Hey, Fish?" Rick asked finally as the last of the light faded, not wanting to disturb Tony, but the teen needed to talk.

"Yeah?" Tony had leaned back and had closed his eyes. There was less tension in his face but what remained was quite visible. Problem was, Rick knew most of the tension was because of him and he felt like crap for causing it.

"I'm not gonna make it," Rick said quietly after a couple of minutes.

"What?!" Tony's eyes flew up and he sat up.

"Through the trials, I mean," Rick said quickly, easing Tony's fears. "I'm not gonna be able to control myself at the trial. I just know it. Especially if, no, when Tarbot mentions Mom," Rick continued sadly.

Tony sighed. "Look, kiddo, how many times do I have to tell you this – *you're not responsible for what happened between your parents!*" Tony said, exasperated at the one thing guaranteed to derail Rick at trial.

"I don't know, Fish, maybe if I knew she was okay or where she was, maybe I'd be able to accept it. I just don't know," Rick said sourly.

Tony didn't say anything for the longest time. He already knew Kara Attison was okay and where she was. He had made a point of finding her when Rick first came to his sessions at the centre and had contacted her when Rick was in the hospital, just in case he hadn't made it. Tony had found her, but Rick didn't know it and that was the way it was going to stay for a while longer.

"If I *could* find her, what would you say?" Tony asked finally. Rick didn't look at Tony while he thought about what Tony had asked.

"I guess, why? That's all I really wanna know. Why she left and why she never came back or called. I could even handle her being dead, I suppose, but either way, as long as I knew," Rick replied slowly.

Tony stood up and stretched. "I won't promise anything, Rick. Finding someone who doesn't want to be found isn't easy," Tony said, wincing at the small lie, but the cop knew Rick wasn't ready to deal with his mother suddenly reappearing in his life. Not yet.

Rick sighed as the pair finally went into the house. "That still isn't gonna help me get through the trials," Rick pointed out as he flopped on his bed with a groan.

"Wanna massage, Rick?" Tony offered. Rick nodded quickly, stripped off his shirt and laid back down.

"The shoulders look like they've healed pretty good. Still sore?" Tony asked as he gently rubbed the lotion into the teen's back and shoulders.

"Yeah, but they're getting better. I tried a verrrrrrrry slow version of my speed bag today, just a single run through of the motions. Not a good idea. They hurt, but we had just come back from riding and I was still tense from school and physio," Rick murmured sleepily. Silence fell as Tony continued to soothe Rick's tense muscles.

Ten minutes later, Rick had settled into a deep sleep. Tony smiled as he covered the boy and left the room. He settled into the spare bed for the first night of dreamless sleep in a very long time.

Chapter 58

A week later, Rick woke well before his alarm and lay in bed, drinking in the warmth of the early morning, thinking about everything and nothing at all. School dominated his mind at the moment since the year had ended on a mixed note.

Both Rick and Megan had worked hard over the remainder of the school year, somehow managing to finish most of their assignments, and their final marks – Rick's especially – weren't bad. All of their teachers had exempted them from their final exams and had taken their marks solely on what they had accomplished. By agreeing to tutors and some super fast and fancy talking by both Nana and Mr. Delaney, the school board had agreed, albeit a bit reluctantly in Rick's case, to pass the two into Grade 12 in the fall. It was one less stress for Rick, since Jordan had agreed to tutor him. It made sense – both she and Mickey were on the honour roll.

And while everyone else in their class was worried about finals, prom night and summer vacation, Rick and Megan worried about the upcoming trials. *Trials that start today*, Rick reminded himself as his alarm jangled to life. Rick groaned as he crawled out of bed. He stood in the bathroom after his shower and stared at the scars criss-crossing his torso and face.

Time might heal the physical wounds, but it can't make the memories fade any faster, Rick thought as he ran a finger over the last set of stitches in his left shoulder. Jim had removed the first set a couple of weeks earlier, but the wound had refused to heal, so he'd put more in.

He returned to his room and laid his new suit out on the bed. He dressed slowly, trying to put off the inevitable confrontation at the courtroom with the Knights. His phone rang as he struggled with his tie.

"What's the hold up, Rick? Martha's holding breakfast, and I'm starved!" Megan said cheerfully, far more cheerful than Rick felt.

"Morning, cuz. Sorry. I'll be there in a couple," Rick said, glared at the tie, and threw it down in disgust.

"Not me," Rick muttered and left his shirt open at the neck. He grabbed his jacket, threw on his cowboy boots and snagged his sling almost as an afterthought and sauntered up to the main house to join Nana, Ian and Megan at the dining room table.

"Morning, lad. How're you?" Nana asked as Rick filled his plate.

Rick shrugged. "Okay, I guess, Nana," he said distractedly and dug into his breakfast as he continued to think about the upcoming days and weeks.

Ian frowned at Rick's attitude, but Nana just waved it away. It was going to be a long enough day without Ian starting on her grandson, she knew. They finished in silence and left Martha to clean up.

"Rick, honestly. You okay?" Megan asked quietly. She stood next to her cousin's car, close enough to make her feel safe, yet far enough away to keep Rick comfortable.

"Rick?" she asked again, this time reaching out to touch his shoulder gently.

Rick shook his head. He'd been staring off into space, just trying to prepare for the day. "Sorry, Megs. Just...thinking. Yeah, I'm okay, or at least I'm as good as I can be, considering," Rick said with a smile.

"Considering the hell we're about to enter," Megan said dryly. She walked around to the passenger side of the car and got in.

Rick climbed in beside her and started into town. The O'Reilly twins were going to meet them at the courthouse, rather than Rick and Mickey picking up their girls separately. Hopefully there'd be a little time for everyone to spend a few minutes together before going into the courtroom. No such luck. Just as Rick and Megan arrived in front of the courtroom with Rick still settling his arm in his sling, Owen pulled his client into a quiet alcove to talk.

"Rick, you're already worried and tense. I can tell," Owen said immediately. "Can you hold it together today? Blackstone won't call you for a while, probably not until close to the end of his case."

Rick shrugged. "I'm okay, I guess, Owen, but I haven't seen any of the Knights yet, so who knows? I can't promise anything. Do I really have to be in court until I'm called?" Rick asked plaintively.

"Normally, most witnesses aren't, but we can't spare anyone to keep you occupied and not worrying about the trial while you're out here," Owen said as he straightened Rick's collar and settled the sling underneath it properly.

"Thanks, Owen. So I take it you don't want me outta the courtroom," Rick said.

"No. Although it's not normal procedure, I want you to hear all of the testimony to make sure nothing's missed. It's gonna be brutal," Owen warned as they walked back to the rest of the group. Rick gave a short bark of laughter.

"More brutal than fending off lies all year long? More brutal than taking on my best friend at least twice, and winning? More brutal than fighting for my life?" Rick asked sarcastically.

Owen chuckled. "Okay, point made, Rick. But I guarantee you the sessions we had at the centre'll be a walk in the park compared to what Tarbot's gonna do to you," Owen warned again.

Rick looked at the courtroom door and sighed. He couldn't wait for this to all be over. He wanted his life back, as crappy as it could be at times. He followed Owen into the packed courtroom and sat in the front row right behind the prosecutor.

Rick nodded greetings to the Angels, including Tom, Carl and the rest of the boxing club. Tony and Marshall sat on either side of Rick, and somehow, Rick just knew it wasn't just for moral support. Megan sat on the other side of Tony between the cop and Owen, but the twins were nowhere to be found.

A sudden whisper of movement behind Rick caused him to tense for a brief moment until he caught a whiff a very familiar perfume. Relaxing, he smiled, reached over his shoulder and grabbed Jordan's hand. Now he could face anything the Knights threw at him.

"Hey, love," she said as she leaned over and kissed his cheek.

"Morning, sweets," Rick managed to reply before a door on the far side of the courtroom opened and the Knights were led in. The tension in the courtroom increased measurably and, hearing muttering from the Angels behind him, Rick tossed a warning glance their way. They subsided, knowing Rick, and the presiding judge, wouldn't tolerate any disruptions in the trial.

Brain and Crank were followed by a frowning Julien Tarbot, but Pup was followed by his public defender. As he waited for the others to settle at the defendants' table, Pup caught Rick's eye and nodded. Once.

"He still with us?" Mickey asked quietly, leaning on Rick's left shoulder, sending sharp pains down Rick's arm.

"Hey, Mick, watch the shoulder, man," Rick snapped roughly.

Mickey jerked back, cursing. "Crap, sorry, Rick!" the young Irishman said as Rick pulled away with a muttered curse.

Tony eased open Rick's shirt and pressed a handkerchief to the now-oozing wound. He pulled it away, a little bloody, but nodded. "It's okay, Mick, just pulled the stitches a bit. Still, be careful, 'kay, buddy?" Tony reassured Megan's boyfriend who nodded.

"Yeah. He's still with us," Rick said softly as Tony fixed his shirt and jacket and Rick settled his sling again. Oddly enough, it hadn't taken as much as Rick thought it would to convince Mark to turn, either.

The Monday after Rick ratted on Tony to Seamus, Rick, the partners, Megan and the O'Reilly twins met up with Lance Blackstone and the inspector at the station. Seamus relented this once to let Tony and Marshall back into the station to clean up a few things on their desks before Jim had cleared them to return to work. There, in a conference room, Tony and Rick outlined their plan to turn Mark.

"You're sure about this, Rick? Really sure? You really want me to cut a deal with the one who did this to you?' Blackstone asked as he tossed the picture of Rick's bloody and slashed face down on the table. He, like Marshall, was amazed at Rick's ability to forgive.

"Will everyone *please* quit asking me that? I know what the hell Mark did, Lance," Rick pointed out as he refused to look at the picture on the table. "I see it every damn day."

"Yet ye still wanna offer him a deal," Seamus said thoughtfully. Rick nodded sharply. They all discussed the plan for almost an hour before Seamus finally called a halt. Lance looked less than pleased to be offering a Knight a deal, especially the one Rick was encouraging him to make, but, all in all, it really was a fair one, based on what they knew Mark had done.

"It's a risk, Fish. We could end up getting this kid killed," Marshall warned as he stood.

"This whole damn business has been a risk, Marsh! But without someone to back Rick up, Tarbot's gonna cream him on cross. He might anyway. Mark's our best chance to get convictions on the other two!" Tony snapped back, running a hand over his hair and brushing back a couple of strands which had escaped from his braids.

Rick put a hand on Tony's shoulder. The teen could feel the cop shaking, with exhaustion or anger, he couldn't quite tell. "C'mon, Fish, chill. You too, Marsh. Arguing gets us nowhere. I know what I'm doing and what I'm asking, so stop questioning me. Inspector, would you bring Mark up, please? Let's get this over with," Rick said, never letting go of Tony.

Seamus left, taking Lance, Megan and the twins out with him. When the door closed behind them, Rick turned to the partners and said evenly, "No more fighting, you two. If we don't present a united front on this, it'll fall apart." Both cops managed to look sheepish at the gentle rebuke from the teen.

"Sorry, Rick. We're just tired, that's all," Marshall said lamely. He looked as exhausted as Tony, and Rick was concerned about both of them.

"Jim's put us both on a month's leave, to be extended if he deems it necessary, and he wanted to give me some sleeping pills, but I turned him down," Tony said as he stretched. What no one knew was Runningbear had moved in with Tony without being asked and the shaman was determined to help Tony find his balance again.

Marshall didn't have time to answer as Pup and a lawyer were led into the room. Rick sighed as he saw the lawyer wasn't Tarbot. He didn't know what he would've done if it had been, because he was pretty sure Tarbot wouldn't've gone for any kind of deal, especially one guaranteed to put Brain and Crank away for a long time. Tony and Marshall excused themselves to wait outside while Rick tried, on his own, to convince another Knight to turn.

"Wha'cha want, Moneyman?" Pup said sourly. *Like I don't know*, the youngest Knight thought angrily.

Rick motioned to a chair across from him. "Sit down, Mark. I wanna talk to you," Rick said quietly, ignoring his gang name.

Pup slid warily into the offered chair while his lawyer looked around. "Where's Blackstone? Does he know about this? And the cops? Why aren't they here?" the lawyer demanded quickly.

"You know the constables're just outside since you just saw them leave, but I wanna talk to Mark without the cops hovering, and yes, Mr. Blackstone's okay with this," Rick explained, doing his best to calm the lawyer.

"Wha'cha want, Moneyman?" Pup demanded again. He slouched in his chair, trying to show how tough he was, how much like Blade.

"My name's Rick, Mark. The punk you knew as Moneyman's dead and buried. You were there when Johnny killed him. It was the day he tried to kill Tom in September. I'm here to make you an offer – a chance, really – and it's an offer I don't think you can refuse. It's a chance to get free of the Knights like I did," Rick explained patiently.

Pup shook his head emphatically. "Who says I wanna be like ya, Moneyman? Yer not strong like Blade. Yer yeller. Yer weak," Pup snorted, deliberately sounding like Blade. *I will be loyal*, Pup thought proudly. *I'll remain loyal to my boys. Not like Moneyman, the chicken.* The young teen wasn't counting on Rick's next move.

"How the hell does this make Johnny "stronger"?" Rick demanded quickly, throwing down the pictures of Rick and Megan's battered bodies. "Look at 'em, Mark. How does this make you stronger?" Rick snapped, indicating the livid scar on his cheek. "How does being a bully and terrifying a school and a community make you stronger? How does almost killing two people, deliberately, make you stronger? Did you *really* enjoy doing this to me, Mark? Huh? Look at those pictures, damn you!" Rick shouted, pushing more photos across the table.

Slowly, Pup reached out and touched one of the photos. He couldn't take his eyes off of it and Rick swore he'd heard a soft sniffle come from the younger boy. The picture showed Megan's left shoulder and the raw, bleeding stab wound. Pup could also see there was a lot of pain on her face, even though Megan was unconscious. He grew pensive as his eyes roamed over the pictures and the more he looked at the pictures, the more the façade of Pup, the youngest Black Knight, fell away. *Why'd ya do this, Blade?* he wondered silently. *Ya ruined everything.*

"He was...playing," Mark whispered as he traced the wound on Megan's shoulder.

"Before he says another word, I wanna deal," the lawyer said quickly.

Lance Blackstone came in immediately and handed the lawyer a piece of paper. "Hello, Josh. Good to see you again. Glad to see this kid's got someone who'll give a damn about him at trial. Here's the offer. Six months for the assault on Rick and Megan's original assault in November, two for aiding in Megan's kidnapping, two for aiding in Jordan's assault, two for conspiracy in all charges and two years probation. If he stays out of trouble until he's 18, I'll order the records sealed. Time to be served consecutively, but we're willing to look at parole after six months time served, providing Mark behaves in juvy. All goes well, six months total behind bars. If not, it'll only be a year," Blackstone offered. He looked at Mark and his lawyer trying to decide what to do.

Mark hesitated. "He'll come after me, y'know," Mark pointed out.

Rick just chuckled as he came around the table and sat beside Mark. "'Course he will, Mark, but look at me. Johnny's been after me since September. He's beaten me more times than I can count and that was while I was still in the gang. It's been ten times worse since I left. He tried to kill me. Hell, you were there, so you know what he did. How much he enjoyed it. You just learn to live looking over your shoulder," Rick said nonchalantly.

"Live in fear? Of Blade, Crank and Brain for the rest of my life?" Mark protested weakly.

Rick shrugged, then nodded. "Fear? I guess, but not necessarily, just...cautious. Look, Mark, I'm not gonna lie to you. You've got every right to be scared of them. Look at what they've done to me, but I haven't given up. If anything, the instincts, at least before the beating, were honed to a fine point and they're coming back to me quickly. They'll never leave. And it'll be like that for you, too," Rick said with a shrug. "The life of a former gang member is a dangerous one."

"Yet yer still asking me to turn. Where's the loyalty to the boys?" Mark protested hotly, glaring at Rick.

"Loyalty? What loyalty? The Knights have no loyalty to anyone, man, not even themselves. Johnny was willing to let Brian hang for this, alone I might add. Johnny's only loyal to himself. He doesn't care about the rest of you. He's angry and resentful of anyone who's able to make something of themselves, and that includes me. Mark, c'mon, man. Take this deal. Otherwise, you're facing hard time," Rick encouraged.

"The offer's good for another ten minutes," Blackstone said as he walked out the door.

Megan walked in and sat down next to Rick. Mark didn't say a word. He continued to stare at the pictures, but remained stubbornly silent. "Mark, look at me, please, "Megan said quietly.

The young Knight raised his tormented eyes to look at her. "Take this deal, Mark, please. As much as you might adore your cousin, you're just not like him. You always held back when Johnny would "play" with me, I believe you called it. I remember the day you told Johnny about Brian's arrest. Do you remember that beating? God, I do. It was brutal. He was so mad at you. I kinda remember you had a very disgusted look on your face while Johnny beat me.

"I can vaguely remember how horrified you were when Johnny gave me these," Megan finished quietly as she pulled open her blouse and revealed the still red looking wounds. Mark stared at the worst one for a long time. Then he motioned silently to Rick, who immediately opened his shirt to show the matching stab wound on his left shoulder. He looked back at Megan and finally down at all of the pictures arrayed on the table in front of him.

Mark nodded sharply. "You gotta deal, Rick. I still think ya got wha'cha deserved, man, but that didn't need to happen," Mark said, roughly, pointing to Megan's shoulder.

Rick sighed. Thank God, it had worked. They had convinced the kid to turn on his own cousin and the gang. Then Rick grinned at Mark. "Mark, did you have to wear that bloody ring?" Rick asked dryly as Tony, Marshall and Lance walked back in. Mark just snickered.

"Wait a minute. We may've agreed to this deal, Lance, but I want one more thing. Mark doesn't serve his sentence with the other two. His life won't be worth spit once they find out," Josh Grimes, Mark's lawyer, said quickly.

"No worries, Josh. Mark's in protective custody as of right now. He'll serve his sentence here while the others're sent away. As far away as I can," Lance assured them both.

"Done," Mark and his lawyer agreed immediately and settled down to tell Mark's tale.

Mark talked for hours and even Rick had been surprised at what the youngest member had known. Blade often forgot Mark was in the room and didn't really watch what he said in front of the boy. Mark knew everything.

And then some.

Now, sitting in the gallery, Rick knew Mark's testimony would break the Knights. First, though, they had to get Rick through his testimony. He still wasn't sure he'd get through the trial without blowing or breaking down, but at least he had someone to back up his story. Someone no one would be able to refute.

"All rise. Collingwood Youth Court is now in session. The Right Honourable Judge Dmitri Prokovic presiding," the court clerk intoned.

Rising awkwardly to his feet, Rick watched as a stocky, dark haired, swarthy man entered the court and climbed behind the bench. His dark eyes quickly scanned the room and settled briefly on Rick. The teen groaned softly as he recognized the look he was getting. It was almost as if Judge Neils had warned the new judge about Rick. After a couple of tense moments, the judge nodded ever so slightly.

"Be seated everyone. Thank you. Let's get going, shall we? Opening statements please," the judge said, nodding to his bailiffs and the court reporter. "Mr. Blackstone? You first, please."

"Thank you, your honour," Blackstone said. He stood, straightened his suit jacket and made his opening statement. He spoke with elegance and in a calm voice for twenty minutes. The judge didn't say anything as he motioned to the defence table.

The two defence lawyers conferred quickly and then Julien Tarbot stood. He, too, spoke calmly and elegantly, but spoke for only fifteen minutes, then sat, smiling as if being shorter was a victory for the defence. Mark leaned back to look at Rick and smiled slightly, shaking his head at the antics of the other lawyer.

"Very well, gentlemen. Thank you for being so brief. Now a few ground rules before we truly begin. Mr. Tarbot, you're representing two of the three defendants, correct?" the judge asked as he reviewed his notes.

"Yes, your honour. Mr. Mark Chilton has declined my services and has chosen to be represented by Public Defender Josh Grimes. We were advised of this only this morning," Tarbot said, without standing.

"Really? I was informed a week ago. Well, no matter. However, the reputations of several witnesses and yourself have preceded you. No yelling at any witnesses in my court, Mr. Tarbot, nor will I accept any badgering. I know who the witnesses are, so keep a lid on the theatrics as well. Especially on cross, Mr. Tarbot. You know exactly which witness I am talking about, so don't even go there. This is the only warning you get, gentlemen and it applies to both sides. Does everyone understand?" Prokovic warned, glaring at the two tables full of lawyers. Everyone nodded.

"Richard Attison?" the judge called, suddenly.

Rick stood slowly. "Yes, your honour?" he said, his mouth suddenly dry. He didn't think this judge would be as forgiving as Neils. Rick was startled when Prokovic's voice mellowed while talking to him. *He might not be as forgiving as Neils, but he understands,* Rick realized as the judge talked.

"Hello, son. Judge Neils gave me some background on you, young man. I hope you'll forgive me, but I've also taken the liberty of talking with both your counsellor and your lawyer. I'll do my best to keep things under control, and I expect you to do your best to do the same. When you testify, if it gets too bad and you need a break, don't wait, 'kay? Tell me right away and you'll get the time you need to get back under control, I promise. I do *not* want a repeat performance of the transfer hearing, agreed?" Prokovic said. He smiled a bit to take the bite out of his words. He had spent a good couple of hours with Neils and afterwards realized this was one trial he was not looking forward to.

"Yes, sir," Rick said, swallowing quickly. "I'll do my best, sir, but, honestly? I can't make any promises. It usually just happens so quickly." Rick sat down, heavily. Tony just smiled his encouragement.

"That's all I can ask for, son, for you to try. Now, Mr. Blackstone, call your first witness. Let's get this trial underway," the judge said, satisfied that his ground rules would be followed.

"Of course, your honour. The prosecution calls Richard Attison," Lance Blackstone said without turning around.

Chapter 59

Rick sat, frozen. He wasn't scheduled to testify until the very end of the trial, right before Mark. Owen had promised to prep him, based on what they had learned during Tarbot's cross of everyone else. He swore he'd heard wrong. Lance wasn't really calling him to testify, was he? Not yet?

"Lance, what the hell're you doing? He's not ready for this," Owen hissed in the sudden silence, glancing at a white-faced Rick. The courtroom was so silent Owen's hiss was clearly audible to everyone. And Rick was so pale Owen expected him to pass out at any moment, if he didn't get the shakes first.

"I agree, your honour. This witness wasn't scheduled until the end and I'm not prepared for him to testify today," Tarbot protested. He was annoyed, Rick could tell. *Come to think of it, so am I*, Rick said to himself as he struggled to his feet.

"Your honour, you've been briefed on this witness, so you know his history. We all do. Would you rather have him sit and stew while we go over the other testimony, especially the cross by the defence? Would you like to see him in restraints or sedated by the time he's done, if he even makes it that far? Given your ground rules, your honour, I realized I needed to change the order of my witnesses just to save us all some grief. I don't wanna ban him from the courtroom because there's no one to be spared to keep him under control while we're in here," Blackstone pointed out.

"Objection overruled, Mr. Tarbot. I happen to agree with the prosecution. Richard, witness stand, if you please," Prokovic said and watched impassively as the teen stumbled blindly to the stand.

Rick took a deep breath as he swore to tell the truth and sat down. As soon as he did, there was no way to stop the shaking from starting. Tony could see the telltale signs already. "Oh by the

Creator! Great friggin' job, Lance, you've already set him off. Look at him," Tony snapped in a low voice. Owen was glaring at the prosecutor and Marshall looked ready to murder Lance. Seamus wasn't happy with this sudden move and Nana was ready to spit nails.

Blackstone looked at Rick, who was now visibly shaking, then motioned sharply to Tony. "Help him, Tony. Dammit all to hell, how could I've screwed this up already?" Blackstone muttered to himself.

"Rick, look at me, son," Tony said quickly as he walked towards his young friend. The judge looked at the witness stand and sighed. *Already?* he thought sourly. *Neils was right. This is gonna be a* very *long trial.*

After a couple of shaky starts, Rick raised his eyes and Tony could see how panicked the teen really was. "Fish, I'm not ready for this! I can't do this! Not yet! I…I…I…," Rick stammered. He couldn't stop shaking and he was afraid he'd burst into tears at any moment, which he knew Blade would love to see. Moneyman completely broken. Tony grabbed a chair and sat in front of the witness stand where Rick was able to look right at him and more importantly, not past him.

"Rick, trust me, okay? I know you weren't expecting this, but we'll get through this together, alright? C'mon, little brother, look here – right at me. That's it. There's only you, me and Lance here right now. 'Kay? Focus on me. There's no one behind us or around us, understand? No one. Now, deep breath and focus. Right here, son, look at me," Tony said softly, catching and holding Rick's eyes.

Rick took several deep breaths, keeping his eyes glued to Tony's, forcing down the panic threatening to overwhelm him. It took more than a couple of minutes before he could raise his head and nod at Lance, totally ignoring everyone in the courtroom, determined to hold it together as long as possible. The prosecutor began by having Rick talk about gang life as background on the brutality of the Knights.

Rick described in detail how the Knights had attacked Tom outside the library, blow by devastating blow. "Stuff like that? Made me sick, sometimes physically. But I just couldn't walk away from the power of being a Knight, y'know? It was a drug, a craving. The sight of a sea of students parting, trying not to look at you because they know you'll flatten them if they do. Man, what a great high," Rick said. His voice was mostly a flat tone, but in describing the high, everyone could hear how much he had loved that.

"What changed your mind?" Blackstone asked curiously. He stood right behind Tony, so Rick didn't have to look around and risk seeing the Knights. Lance had already heard them snickering a couple of times.

"Two things, I guess. First was that attack on Tom. I refused to lay a hand on the kid 'cause he didn't deserve that. In fact, later I stood up to Johnny and got the crap beat out of me. Slice to the ribs that required stitches and a couple of cracked ribs. The first of many, I might add. I just couldn't justify it, y'know? The kid was new to school and no one told him not to wear our colours," Rick said bitterly. It had been more than a year since that first beating, and it still made Rick sick to think about what had almost happened.

"Your colours? What do you mean?" Blackstone asked.

"Tom made the mistake of coming to school in a black and silver jacket, white tee and black jeans. Those're Knights colours, man. It's all we ever wore, no matter how hot or cold the day. God, the beating was brutal. Mark, Eric and I were on watch, keeping everyone, teachers included, at bay. With only two punches, Johnny and Brian just about killed the Kid," Rick said harshly. He finally looked into the gallery and stared at his friend. Tom just smiled.

"Something you need to understand about Johnny. It was always about him. His pleasure. His fun. What he wanted, he got. It was his motto – "my pleasure, my fun." What he wanted to do, we did. Illegal? He didn't care. None of them did," Rick said flatly.

"What was the second thing?" Lance asked, getting Rick back on track.

"Oddly enough, my own conscience. Something about Tom's beating changed me, I guess. I began having nightmares towards the end of Grade 10 and all through the summer. They started right after Tom's beating, now that I think about it. They were…warnings, almost, about what ended up happening this year," Rick said and briefly described some of his nightmares.

"Then there was the constant battles with Jordan's dad about seeing her. I was willing to give up the only family I really had just to be with her, and yet, no matter what I did, O'Reilly fought me," Rick continued. "Man, I thought he'd be glad, but he never was and it took me a long time to figure out why."

Rick took a couple of deep breaths before continuing. "Besides, I didn't like what I was becoming. A machine. One that reacted without thinking. I think if I'd stayed much longer, Johnny would've made me a killer. I know *he's* almost there – the attacks on me and Megs prove that. I couldn't stand looking at myself any more. Every time I looked in the mirror, I didn't see Rick or Moneyman. All I saw was a spoiled rich kid, breaking the law for fun and that wasn't the way Nana had raised me. I decided I had to get out," Rick said softly and looked at Delaney who had come for support. The principal smiled as Rick said, "Before Nana ended up scraping me up off the ground with Johnny's steel in me."

It wasn't easy, but Rick managed to describe the battle to break free of the Knights and how Blade had responded. He spared nothing. He laid his soul bare for everyone to see, things he hadn't told Jordan and even one or two that hadn't come out in his sessions with Tony. Details, little things that made the initial attacks on the girls make more sense, all tumbled out without hesitation.

"Doing okay, Rick?" Lance asked when Rick finally paused for breath and to take a quick drink. The lawyer was concerned Rick was showing as little emotion now as much as he had shown when he first started testifying. Tony just nodded as he glanced over his shoulder. His little brother was doing okay. Not great, but okay.

Rick nodded, too. He knew what was coming next and Lance gave him a small smile, trying to encourage the teen. "Okay, Rick, we've covered everything up to Megan's disappearance. You take your time, but start with the fight in the cafeteria. Okay?" Lance asked quietly. He didn't need to tell Rick where to stop.

"Yes, sir," Rick said hesitantly. He took a couple more deep breaths, fixed his gaze firmly on Tony's face, then launched into a graphic description of the entire time Megan had been gone, working his way up to the attempted murder. He spoke in a flat and unemotional tone, until he began to describe the attack. He had just started talking about it when he made the mistake of looking up at Lance. The prosecutor had shifted a bit and, instead of looking at Lance, Rick looked right at the defendants' table. Brain and Crank were laughing so hard they were crying, while Mark looked sick.

Rick couldn't handle anymore. He broke down and cried, "Your honour, please," he begged, holding his head in his hands while the two Knights roared with laughter.

"Enough. Lunchtime, folks. Court's in recess until 1:30 p.m.," Prokovic said, banging down his gavel without hesitation, impressed with how well Rick had done. He knew he wouldn't've lasted nearly as long as Rick had.

The court cleared quickly, except for Jordan, who came to the stand. She stood by Tony for a couple of minutes before she went to Rick. "Rick?" she said, touching his shoulder.

Rick drew a shuddering breath and dried his eyes. "Hey, babe," he croaked hoarsely, reaching up to hold her hand.

"Great job, son," Tony said proudly, handing Rick another glass of water and some tissue to wipe his eyes.

Rick gulped the water down, then snorted. "Yeah right, Fish," Rick said as he stretched carefully. His shoulders hurt from the tension and he still had a long way to go.

"I'm serious, bro. You did great. You probably would've made it further if you hadn't looked at them. C'mon, you two. I'm starved. Let's get some lunch and then I need to find a place to work on those shoulders, Rick. At least try to get you more relaxed before you're on cross this afternoon," Tony said as he put his chair back.

After lunch, Rick climbed back into the witness stand, much more relaxed and Tony returned to the gallery, confident Rick would get through the rest of the day on his own. "I'm sorry, your honour," Rick apologized immediately. The judge just waved the apology away.

"Understandable, Richard. I'm actually surprised you made it as far as you did. Before we continue, Mr. Tarbot, this court has a warning for your clients. One more outburst like this court saw before lunch and they will be removed. Understand? Good. Now, Mr. Blackstone, are you finished?" Prokovic asked, turning back to the prosecutor.

"Just a couple more questions, Rick. As horrible and as hard as it is, I really need you to go back and describe the attack at Blade's, okay? Be as detailed as you can, and by that I mean, who did what to you, okay? Take your time, and look right here at me," Lance said, standing right in front of Rick so he couldn't see past him, locking himself in place so he didn't move, either.

Rick nodded and described the entire attack from start to finish, as much as he could remember, at least. "I don't remember much past Johnny backhanding me off the chair, so I don't know how many more times they hit me. The next thing I do remember was gravel hitting me in the face. I opened my eyes as far as I could and realized I'd been dumped somewhere. I wasn't sure where, but I knew I had to get to the main road.

"It took me a long time to crawl probably ten feet to the main road. I collapsed again, and then nothing until the hospital two or three days later when I heard this weird drumming and someone literally calling me back from as close to death as I wanna get for a very long time. I managed to gasp out my story, and then nothing again until Tony brought Jor to see me after they found Megs. Sorry I wasn't faster, cuz," Rick apologized to Megan.

"Thank you, Rick. You did a fantastic job. You okay, son? Need another break?" Lance asked as he went back to his table.

"Okay, I guess, and, no sir, I don't wanna another break," Rick said. He stretched his arms up as far as he could and felt his back crack. He sighed and Prokovic smiled.

"Anything further, Mr. Blackstone?" the judge asked as Rick sipped at some water.

"Nothing further, your honour. I'm finished," Lance said and sat down.

"Mr. Grimes, your witness," the judge ordered, turning the floor over to the defence.

Josh asked a few questions about the final beating, and about the attacks that had happened over the rest of the year, focusing on Mark's involvement. Rick looked at the youngest Knight and said, "Most of the time, Mark held back. Johnny used him more for lookout than attack. I mean, honestly, he's the smallest of us all and he just can't fight as well as the rest of us. He's gotta piercing whistle, though, that can be heard over just about anything, except maybe an AC/DC concert, one no other Knight can match. That night, I know he beat me, but I can clearly remember when Johnny told him it was his turn, he hesitated for a moment. I don't think he wanted to do what Johnny asked him to do. Then he began to wail on me. I could feel the skin on my face tearing and I knew the little bugger had his ring on. But I'll always wonder if he beat me 'cause he wanted to or he didn't wanna disappoint the cousin he adored. Doc couldn't fix my face to keep me from getting any scars. I'll bear these for the rest of my life," Rick said bitterly, indicating the scars on his cheek.

"Nothing further, your honour," Grimes said as Mark flushed with shame.

"Need another break, Richard?" the judge asked again while sending a warning glance to Owen. Everyone knew Tarbot was going to be absolutely vicious on this cross.

"No, sir. Besides, I'd rather get it over with," Rick said shortly. He was proud of how he'd managed to hold things together since lunch, but when Julien Tarbot stood at the podium, forcing Rick to look right at the defendants' table, Rick tensed visibly and the teen sternly reminded himself to remain calm. He could do this.

Tarbot started off with some easy questions about the gang life and the things the gang did, things which Rick had willing participated in. Questions designed to make Rick relax. Rick knew it was too good to last and he was right.

"Richard, why'd you really try to return to the gang? It was, after all, in direct violation of your court order," Tarbot pointed out.

Shaking his head, Rick sighed. *Here we go again*, the teen thought miserably. "To save Megs, Tarbot, and 'fore you ask how I knew Johnny had taken her without helping him do it, let's just say I know how the bastard thinks."

Rick drew a breath to continue, but Prokovic spoke first. "Richard, I need to interrupt you here and remind you of something. Although you may not like him, this court needs you to be respectful. In the future, you will refer to the defense lawyer as either 'Sir' or 'Mr. Tarbot.'" The judge smiled at Rick to soften the reprimand.

Rick flushed and glanced at the judge. "Sorry, your honour. Anyway, 'sir,'" – Tony smirked and chuckled softly at Rick's attitude – "the thing's this: it may've been Johnny's idea, but the plan, from start to finish, was pure Brian. Why they came up with this specific idea, I don't know, but once Johnny did, it was all Brian.

"It's the reason we call him Brain. He's smarter than Johnny. Hell, he's smarter than all of us put together and I'm sure he figured he'd get away with it. This whole year? Planned, start to finish, by Brian. The letters. The physical attacks against the girls. The decision to focus on Megs simply because I was so close to her. All planned and executed by Brian," Rick said shortly.

"But *why*, Richard? Why would the Knights try and get you back? After all, you wanted out," Tarbot asked.

Rick shrugged. "Johnny wanted me back, period. Once you're in, you're a Knight for life, according to Johnny. And he used those three right there to try and beat that into me. I guess Johnny saw something in me, something he wanted for the gang, and what Johnny wants, Johnny gets. He saw something in all of us or he wouldn't've offered us the life. I mean, not everyone has what it takes to be a Knight. But what it was, I don't know. You'll have to ask him," Rick said shortly. He could feel the tension beginning again as he fought to control his bouncing legs. *Hold on, Rick*, Tony begged silently as he, too, noticed the signs. *You can do it.*

"So you violated your probation," Tarbot said with a smile.

"Objection, your honour: the witness has already answered this question several times," Lance said, standing before Owen could say anything.

"Sustained. Mr. Tarbot, move on, or dismiss the witness," Prokovic said firmly.

Tarbot questioned Rick on the attacks on him over the summer and the school year, wanting Rick to detail who had done what to him. Rick's responses were short, clear and under control, but Tony was beginning to worry. Rick had been under too much strain for way too long and there was no way he'd be able to hold up much longer.

"Can he hold up?" Owen asked quietly, as he noticed the tension on his client's face was matched the by the concern on Tony's.

"Barely, and only if Tarbot doesn't ask him *the question*," Tony said with a nervous chuckle.

Rick sat waiting for Tarbot's next question. "You've answered most of my questions, son. Now…"

"*Don't you ever call me that*! I am not your son! The only one who has any right to call me that is sitting right there!" Rick interrupted harshly, biting off each word, pointing to Tony.

Tarbot blinked, surprised at Rick's angry response. "My apologies, Richard. What I wanted to know was how does your father feel about your gang life?" Tarbot asked, trying to appear curious and failing miserably.

"I don't know, and to be perfectly honest, '*sir*,' I don't care. Ask *him*, if you can find him. My old man's curiously disappeared. Oddly enough, right after Nana paid a six million dollar ransom to your clients there. And the old man hasn't given a damn about me since I was six," Rick snapped harshly. He ran a hand through his hair, visibly steeling himself before continuing.

"And as for Mom, don't even *think* about asking about *her*. I won't play that game, not this time. I haven't seen her in over ten years and it hurts worse than any beating Johnny or his boys ever gave me. I won't talk about her," Rick growled, unable to control his anger any longer. He began to shift and he wasn't sure how much longer he could hold on without going after Tarbot or the two Knights sitting at the table, smirking.

Tony knew it, too. *Hold on, son*, the cop pleaded silently, trying to catch Rick's eye. *You lose it now, they walk.*

Blackstone rose. "Your honour, please. This witness isn't on trial. Most of Mr. Tarbot's questions've already been asked and answered, several times, I might add. Unless Mr. Tarbot has any further questions that pertain to the charges against *his* clients, I respectfully ask the court to move him along," Mr. Blackstone said mildly.

Tony stood from his seat in the gallery and spoke quickly. "If it pleases the court, may I comment?" Prokovic nodded in approval. "Your honour, I'd really rather not have to sedate Richard to calm him down, and at the rate the defence's going, I may not have a choice."

"I agree, Constable. Mr. Tarbot, do you have any further questions that pertain to the case and not to the witness's personal life?" the judge asked pointedly.

"Nothing further, your honour," Tarbot said, disgusted as to how his cross had transpired.

"Very well, then," Prokovic said firmly. "The witness may stand down."

Rick stood, his legs shaking, and managed, somehow, to stumble to his chair. He fell heavily into his seat and finally let his whole body shake from the day's intense emotions. He only vaguely heard Tom called to the stand.

"Great job, son, really great job. Hold on for a bit more. It's not gonna be much longer today," Tony whispered as he used one hand to massage Rick's neck.

Rick leaned forward, put his head in his hands, leaning carefully on his elbows – trying to put as little pressure on his shoulder as possible – and massaged his pounding temples in time to Tony's circles on his tense neck. He heard neither Tom's testimony, nor the cross, until Tom raised his voice.

"Don't you ever tell me I don't remember who hit me! That son of a bitch hit me so hard my jaw cracked, and he *stood over me, laughing about it!* If Rick hadn't gotten me into the boxing club, the next time someone hit me, it might've killed me!" Tom shouted. The

Kid had stood up in the witness box, his face flushed and had pointed at Brain.

Rick looked at his friend, *and second in command of a gang I don't want*, he thought, and spoke without regard for the court, "Enough, Angel. Stand down," Rick said firmly, catching Tom's eye.

Tom sat down, heavily, lowered his eyes and took several deep breaths. "Sorry, your honour. It won't happen again," Tom apologized. Prokovic nodded and motioned to the lawyer to continue. Tarbot took up his line of questioning and finished without any further interruptions.

Lance stood quickly before Prokovic could dismiss Tom. "Redirect, your honour?" At Prokovic's curious nod, Blackstone asked, "Tom, who formed the Grey Angels?"

"I did. Me, Carl, and two other boys from the boxing club," the Kid replied evenly.

"Why?"

"To take back our school from the Knights. We were tired of the destruction and the blitz attacks. To protect people like Jordan and Megan and others the Knights had gone after, especially those they targeted more than once. To let Johnny and his bullies know they couldn't just do what they wanted. It was our school, not their playground," Tom explained.

"Was Rick ever a member?" Blackstone asked.

"Initially, no. We formed up while he was in juvy in December. When he came back to school in January, he had to point something out to me. I'd begun to act just like Johnny – standing with my back to the wall, eyes that never stopped moving, always having at least one other Angel watching my back. I was walking – no, strutting around arrogantly, and looking for fights. Like Rick, I had begun to develop what he calls the gang reflexes – the ability to sense when someone's behind me, and react. I hadn't even realized it was happening and now I can't get rid of them," Tom said quietly.

"And his advice was?" Lance asked.

"Two things. Did I form the Angels to *fight* the Knights or to *become* the Knights? And...think of him and what he'd been going through. To avoid the gang mentality. It's been a struggle, but I've managed to bring the Angels back to what they started as. I owe him my life, literally," Tom said. "Now, although he really doesn't wanna, the Angels've chosen him to lead us. Their choice, not his. I'm his second, and I usually make all the decisions, but we are his. And proud of it, too," Tom said, standing tall in the stand.

There was nothing further from either side and the teen was dismissed. Judge Prokovic looked at his watch. "Okay, folks. Today's been long enough. Court's in recess until 9 a.m. tomorrow," he said and banged down the gavel.

"Rick, I'm so sorry, but I never expected Prokovic's ground rules," Lance apologized quickly, knowing he had to make up for the morning's near disaster. "Seriously, you okay?"

Rick waved away the apology. "Don't worry about it, Lance. I made it through it, somehow. Thanks, Fish," Rick said with a small smile. The cop nodded.

Standing to stretch, Rick looked back at Tom and pointed a finger at the Kid. "You've gotta learn control, Kid. He damn near had you. Don't ever give in to that kind of baiting," Rick said sagely, trying to break the tension.

It worked. Everyone chuckled as they filed out of the courtroom. "I know, Champ, but that slimy bugger tried to tell me you had hit me, not Brian. That's what got my goat," Tom explained.

Rick begged off dinner with the O'Reillys and Tony, telling Jordan he'd call later and then drove home alone. He needed some time to himself. He did his physio while his supper was cooking, all the while itching to hit the bag for a bit. He flopped in his favourite chair with his supper and turned on a football game, not really watching at first, but eventually, it got exciting enough for him to get into it. He was starting to relax. He knew his part was over, but starting tomorrow, Tarbot would have his chance at everyone else. *How much does he really know?* the teen wondered as he fell asleep. He could hardly wait for the morning to find out.

Chapter 60

The first witness called the next morning was Marshall. The cop settled into his seat in the witness stand, confident and relaxed, even though this was the first time he'd ever testified in a trial of this magnitude.

Blackstone led Marshall through the investigations he was primarily involved in, letting Marshall describe the first time he met Rick. "Call it a cop's instinct, but from the moment I met him, something told me Rick didn't do anything. I watched him very carefully and nothing. For the longest time, though, we couldn't find any evidence that didn't point to Rick. I don't mind saying it quickly became annoyingly frustrating, to say the least," Marshall said.

"Constable Andrews, you're Constable Whitefish's partner, correct?" Lance asked.

"Yes, sir," Marshall replied.

"Someone who should've been investigating the crimes with him, correct?" Lance continued.

"Yes, sir," Marshall replied again, wondering where this was going.

"Yet you were assigned to "guard" Rick after he was released, cleared of all charges in the assault of Jordan O'Reilly, isn't that correct? Why?" Lance asked quietly.

So that's what he's leading up to, Marshall thought. He hesitated, not really wanting to put more heat on Seamus. Tony caught his partner's eye and mouthed, "Truth."

"Yes, sir. I was ordered to Glencrest by the inspector. Inspector O'Reilly didn't trust Rick, plain and simple. He wanted him watched – well, spied on, really – even though the court ordered all charges dropped. He never explained why and I never asked. I'm still new enough at this precinct to just do as I'm ordered," Marshall explained with a shrug. No matter how he looked at it, it was a poor excuse.

"What did Inspector O'Reilly actually order you to do?" Lance asked. The prosecutor wanted Seamus' manipulation of the investigations to come out during his questioning, not Tarbot's cross.

"Inspector O'Reilly was very specific. Rick was never to be outta sight. The kid could go to the bathroom without me watching, but that was about it. He wanted me to gain Rick's confidence and trust, so he'd talk. Confess. Whatever. Find the evidence to put Rick away, that's all the inspector wanted. The longer I was with Rick, though, without getting the evidence the inspector wanted, the angrier he got. At me," Marshall said shortly. *Sorry, boss*, the cop thought grimly as Seamus hung his head in shame.

"Did the inspector ever ask you to create evidence?" Blackstone asked.

"No, sir. Thankfully, no one was ever asked to do that. It was just focus on Rick, no matter what. Even if the evidence didn't actually point to Rick, the inspector tried to twist it around until it did. The longer I was at Glencrest with Rick, the angrier he got and the dirtier I felt. Spying on him made me sick. I began to question what I was doing on the force, not just what was I doing at Glencrest. Honestly, Mr. Blackstone? I firmly blame myself for Megan's November attack. Not the attack itself, but the fact that Rick was blamed," Marshall said, disgusted all over again. He'd thought he'd dealt with those feelings, but apparently not.

"What do you mean?" Lance asked, curiously.

"Remember Rick was never to be outta my sight. Well, he'd had enough of being spied on. So he decided he was gonna take a good, long hot bath that day, at least that's what he told me, and that was the one place we'd agreed he could have some privacy. He filled the tub, turned on his music, and slipped out the window. He went for a walk and was the one who actually found Megan. Unfortunately, he was found standing over her unconscious body with no one else in sight. 'Course he was blamed. Who wouldn't've blamed him? And, every single day, I hate myself for what happened to him, spending almost three months in juvy for no reason," Marshall snapped roughly.

"One last question, Constable, then I'm through. How would you characterize the investigations?" Lance asked.

Marshall didn't hesitate this time. "Obsessive, sir. Totally obsessive. The only rule was to focus on Rick, no matter what evidence we found. The biggest problem we faced, though, was the *initial* evidence pointed to Rick. Always. The Knights were very good at making sure Rick was blamed. I admire them for that, really. It made it so damn hard to look at other suspects. It was always Rick's word against the evidence, and Inspector O'Reilly never trusted or listened to Rick.

"After spending time with Rick after Jordan's attack, I noticed one thing immediately. Rick complied, 100%, with his court orders. Never deviated at all. Rick was willing to live with the rules, even if he didn't like them. Still wasn't good enough for Inspector O'Reilly. Especially in January, after all the charges were dropped," Marshall said, sourly.

"What do you mean, Constable?" Lance queried.

This time Marshall did hesitate, long enough for Prokovic to look at the cop and order, "Answer the question, Constable."

"Yes, sir," Marshall said with a sigh, and bracing himself for the reaction in the courtroom. What he was about to say could fry Seamus and possibly cost him his job. "In January, when Rick was cleared of Megan's November attack and the charges dropped, Inspector O'Reilly didn't come to the hearing; he was that confident Rick would be found guilty. Constable Whitefish and I had to tell him Rick was released, all charges dropped. Not five minutes after being told and less than an hour after Judge Neils ordered Rick to be left alone, the inspector dragged me back out to Glencrest and ordered me to continue spying on Rick," Marshall said, anger colouring his voice.

"He did *what*?" Lance blurted out. He turned to glare at O'Reilly before turning back to Marshall. "He deliberately violated Rick's rights and *no one said a word*?" Lance was livid.

"That's right, Mr. Blackstone, but it was because of what Rick did. Despite how angry Rick was over the whole thing, he agreed to it on one condition – Inspector O'Reilly left Jordan alone and let her live her life. Rick and Jordan would be allowed to see each other, and Mickey would leave them alone. If the inspector didn't agree, all Rick had to do was call Judge Neils' direct line. Rick had started dialling the number when the inspector finally agreed," Marshall explained quickly.

"And after Megan disappeared?" Blackstone asked, once again in control.

"Initially, the investigation focused on Rick, until we found a black and silver bag with a vial of sedatives in it; on the vial was a fingerprint that didn't match Rick's. But even with all of this evidence, and even once we were able to tie everything together, we still had to fight the inspector. No matter how it looked, he wanted to pin the whole damn thing on Rick," Marshall said bitterly.

"When did that finally change? I mean, if Inspector O'Reilly wanted Rick put away for life, he wouldn't've let you focus on any one else. What made him change his mind?" Blackstone asked.

"When he saw Rick after he was almost killed. If he hadn't seen that, I don't think he ever would've been able to focus on someone else. Sorry, boss," Marshall said sadly, as Seamus looked at him in despair.

"Nothing further, your honour," Lance said, sitting down, still a little shaken at Marshall's testimony.

"If no one has any objections, we'll recess for lunch and reconvene at 1 p.m.," the judge said banging his gavel.

After a leisurely lunch, Marshall returned to the witness stand. "Okay, Mr. Grimes, your witness," Prokovic said after everyone had returned to their seats.

Josh Grimes only had a couple of questions for Marshall, then sat down. The same with Tarbot, much to the annoyance of Judge Prokovic.

"If I'd known that the two of you were gonna ask Constable Andrews so few questions, we wouldn't've broken for lunch. Do not waste the court's time again, gentlemen," the judge said and motioned Lance to call his next witness.

That was the pattern for both Jordan and Mickey. Their testimony, including cross, was under an hour for each of them. Jim took the stand as the last witness of the day, describing the injuries he treated on each girl, in each assault, and Rick's attempted murder and the probable causes.

As the doctor returned to the gallery, Prokovic looked at the two defence lawyers. "We're gonna break early today, gentlemen. When we reconvene in the morning, I suggest you be prepared for your cross examinations of the witnesses, although that is entirely up to you. Otherwise, it would be greatly appreciated if you could let the court know if you plan on presenting any kind of defence, and have some meaningful cross. If you aren't, I won't ask you do to any cross. Agreed?" Prokovic said.

"We apologize, your honour, as it was not our intention to waste the court's time. It's just we didn't have any questions for these last few witnesses which would've advanced our defence. As we know Inspector O'Reilly, Constable Whitefish and Miss Attison are the final three witnesses for the prosecution and are scheduled to start testifying tomorrow, we assure the court the defence'll be more than ready for our cross," Tarbot said reassuringly.

Prokovic just nodded. "Very well. Court's in recess until 9 o'clock tomorrow morning," the judge said, and left the courtroom.

Rick watched everyone but the O'Reillys drive away then turned to Jordan. "Supper and movie, sweets?" he asked shyly.

"Don't be out too late, kids. Ye'll need to be awake in court," Seamus warned absently as he walked to his truck.

"He's scared, Rick," Jordan said as they drove to their favourite restaurant. "He knows tomorrow's not gonna be very pleasant and he's scared."

"I'm scared for him, Jor," Rick said as they sat down to order. Tomorrow, they would find out how much Mendez really knew and Rick was sure he didn't want to know the answer.

He was sure it was going to be way too much.

Chapter 61

When Seamus took the stand the next morning, Rick could tell the inspector hadn't slept most of the night. The dark circles and bags under his eyes were the first clues, and he shuffled a bit on his way to the stand. But, tired or not, he sat tall and proud in the witness chair and answered all of the prosecution's questions as honestly as he could.

Finally, Lance looked at the inspector and said, "Inspector, we've heard your own constable describe your handling of all of these investigations as obsessive. How would you describe them?" Blackstone asked. Seamus sighed and shook his head.

"There's no other way *to* describe them. No matter what me officers told me, I tried to twist it around to make Rick fit evidence that just wasn't there. Everything, when ye place it in context, was circumstantial," Seamus explained. He hesitated then spoke very quietly. "Me obsession nearly cost me me family and Nana Attison two of her grandchildren."

"Explain, please," Blackstone said curtly.

"Me hatred of Rick forced Jordan to sneak around behind me back to see him at juvy, thanks to the help of a certain Constable Whitefish to whom I shall remain forever grateful, and I ended up getting so mad at her I figuratively tied her to her brother, Mickey. He was her keeper, and if that wasn't bad enough, she was forced to hide her journals and any of Rick's gifts so I couldn't find them. I knew if I did, I'd get more than mad at her. I even threatened to hurt her, physically, if I found anything.

"Mickey was never to let her out of his sight, at home or at school and if she went into the bathroom at school, Megan had to go with her so she wouldn't sneak away. I turned me son into an angry, bitter young man who blindly trusted his father, who was just as angry and bitter. If I told him the moon was made of purple cheese, he would've fought anyone who tried to tell him differently," Seamus said regretfully.

"In me drive to keep Rick away from Jordan, no one but Rick saw the attack on Megan coming. He kept trying to tell everyone the Knights were up to something, but no one paid any attention, except maybe Tony. Excuse me, Constable Whitefish. I certainly didn't, and, what with the letters and phone call transcripts, we certainly had enough warning she was in danger," Seamus continued sadly.

"While I never threw a single punch or held a knife to them, what the Knights did to Rick, Megan, Jordan and all the others this past year can be squarely blamed on me and me obsession with Richard Attison. But, dear God, don't let them walk because I screwed up," Seamus said, looking at Judge Prokovic who didn't even acknowledge the plea.

After the prosecutor had sat down, Josh Grimes climbed to his feet and asked, "What, if anything, in all of your investigations, led you to finally focus on someone other than Richard Attison?"

"Honestly, Mr. Grimes? The lack of any real, tangible *physical* evidence against the boy. The *only* time we found his fingerprints on anything was during the very first investigation into the destruction of the playground equipment near his house. The fingerprints were on a can of spray paint Rick swore had been used by your client, Mark Chilton. Otherwise, everything was purely circumstantial. 100%. No trace was ever found on him or the victims. All of the gang wear we found was washed or wiped clean. There wasn't one wound ever found on Rick and given the damage on both girls from their attacks, there should've been *something*, especially considering we know both girls fought back.

"It's only when you put it all together with that notebook of Brian Townsand's does it all make sense. Sick sense, but sense nonetheless," Seamus explained. With that, Josh thanked Seamus and sat down.

Julien Tarbot stood with an oily smile, making everyone in the court uneasy. Rick tensed, wondering what the crummy lawyer would ask and dreading the answers Seamus would be forced to give.

"Inspector, you say you were obsessed with keeping Richard away from your daughter. When did this obsession start?" the lawyer asked finally, after letting Seamus stew for a few moments. It seemed to be his favourite method of unnerving a witness. It usually worked.

Rick groaned softly and nudged Tony. "Fish, he knows about the fight," the teen whispered, worried he hadn't mentioned it during his testimony and wondered how this would look.

"Yeah, Rick, but does he know everything?" the cop whispered back. Both Rick and Tony hoped not.

The pair turned their attention back to Seamus' testimony in time to hear the inspector describe the fight between himself and Rick, again, with one small deletion. In less than ten minutes, the ordeal was over, they thought.

"Inspector, what ever happened to the service pistol Richard held to your head after he knocked you down?" Tarbot asked innocently.

"Objection! Relevance? The inspector's not on trial here, and I fail to see what this fight has to do with the charges against the *defendants*. Mr. Tarbot's constantly trying to put the witnesses on trial," Blackstone objected immediately.

"He knows everything," Tony said sourly. Rick could only nod as Tarbot tried to explain.

"Agreed, Mr. Blackstone. Mr. Tarbot, the fight itself between the inspector and Richard *may* be relevant, but after the last punch was thrown, nothing else is. Neither Richard nor Inspector O'Reilly is on trial here. *Your clients'*re the defendants. Move on," Prokovic ordered.

Tarbot frowned. The objection had forced him to revamp his strategy with his cross-examination of Seamus. He quickly reviewed his notes, then raised his head and spoke. "Inspector, please remind the court what evidence was found at the scene of Megan Attison's kidnapping."

"One of Rick's "Moneyman" bandanas, some writing on the wall, in what appeared to be blood which actually turned out to be blood-red marker, and, tucked behind the lockers was a small black bag containing a vial of fast acting, powerful sedative, and what appeared to be small darts, but no type of gun," Seamus replied immediately. "That gun has never been found in any of our searches of the defendants' homes."

"And what did the writing on the wall say?" Tarbot asked.

"Rick'll take good care of her," Seamus replied.

"Rick'll take good care of her," Tarbot repeated quietly. He glared at Seamus. "With that writing and the bandana, why on earth did you look at someone else? That's good enough for me to want someone arrested," Tarbot pointed out.

Seamus nodded. "I agree, Mr. Tarbot, and at first, I didn't wanna look at anyone else but Rick. But the longer I stood in that crime scene, the more I realized the whole thing seemed...contrived, I guess is the best word for it. Too perfect. The writing was just at the right height so as not to be missed. The bandana was lying just so, with "Money" clearly showing so it would catch any light passing over it and I'm sure we never would've found the black bag if a flashlight hadn't caught the silver zipper. I don't think it was actually supposed to be found or even left behind. It was their second mistake. Their first was taking Megan Attison, and trying to blame Rick," Seamus snapped.

"What was so significant about the black bag?" Tarbot asked.

"At first glance, nothing. We just grabbed it because it was there and we just kind of glanced at it to see what was in it. Later, when Constable Whitefish examined it, he found several small darts, the kind used in a handheld tranquilizer gun, and a bottle of fast acting sedative that could be loaded into the darts," Seamus said. "And like I've already stated, the gun has never been found and I doubt we ever *will* find it."

"And this vial was significant, why?" Tarbot pressed quickly. Seamus' answer seemed to surprise the usually calm lawyer.

"Because, on that vial, we found a single fingerprint that couldn't be matched to Rick. We were able to compare it to a fingerprint taken from Brian Townsand after a follow-up interview done by Constable Whitefish, where he left behind an empty pop can, in full public view. No search warrant was required," Seamus said with a slight smile.

"Nothing further," Tarbot said quickly and sat down. Seamus watched him have a muttered, angry conversation with Brain.

"Ladies and gentlemen, it's now 11:30 a.m. I suggest we break for an early lunch, one hour please. Mr. Blackstone, do you still plan on calling Constable Whitefish this afternoon?" Prokovic asked.

"Yes, your honour. Constable Whitefish, after Rick, is our main witness," Lance said. *If you don't count a surprise witness sitting at the defence table,* the lawyer thought smugly.

"Very well. Court is in recess until 12:30 p.m.," Prokovic said, banging down the gavel.

Tony sat still as the courtroom emptied. In less than an hour, he would have to bear his soul and he knew the prosecution's whole case rested on his testimony and his alone.

"Creator, I beg you. Give me strength," he whispered as he stood to go for lunch.

Chapter 62

"Call your next witness, Mr. Blackstone," Judge Prokovic said.

"Constable Tony Whitefish," Lance said as he turned to face the gallery.

Tony squared his shoulders as he stood. He stopped and smiled down at Rick before heading to the stand. His boots rang in the sudden silence of the courtroom. Everything that had happened in the last ten months was about to come out. *Ready or not, here we go*, Rick thought as he watched his best friend stand and swear to tell the truth.

As he sat down, Tony took a couple of deep breaths to calm his sudden nerves and focus his thoughts. After all, this wasn't the first time he had testified at a trial, but it was the first trial in which he was so intimately involved. Then Lance Blackstone began his questioning and Tony focused all of his attention on his testimony.

Unfortunately, Blackstone had no rhyme or reason to his questions, as he jumped from the trials and frustrations of one investigation to another. Finally, annoyed, Tony interrupted Lance's questions. "Look, Mr. Blackstone. Do my memory a favour – pick an investigation and stick to it. You keep jumping around like this and I *am* gonna forget something critical and that's gonna lead to doubt," Tony pointed out. *And give Tarbot ammo on cross*, he didn't add.

Lance nodded and then focused on the very first investigation, and the first time Tony had ever met Rick. "Did you start looking into the Knights then?" Blackstone asked after Tony outlined what the investigation had turned up.

Tony shook his head. "Logically, why would I? It was literally Rick's word against the physical evidence. A clear case of "I swear I didn't do this, but these guys did," and nothing to back it up. It was only after I got to know Rick better I began to see a very disturbing pattern," Tony said with a shrug.

"Constable Whitefish, you're a cop, the arresting officer in Rick's initial case of Destruction of Public Property. How and why'd you become Rick's counsellor? Wouldn't that be a conflict of interest? And that first session you had with him, what was it like?" Blackstone asked.

"As a cop, you often see a lot of the same troublemakers arrested over and over, and I was tired of arresting the same kids constantly. Most of them weren't bad kids, they just didn't have anyone to talk to and figure out what was going wrong in their lives. So Inspector O'Reilly and I created the Youth Justice League with the help of some counsellors at the youth centre downtown. I figured it wasn't fair that I created the League and provided the counsellors with their clients, yet never helped with it. I've taken all of the requisite courses and I'm a certified youth counsellor," Tony said as he looked at Rick.

"As for a conflict of interest, I cleared it with Inspector O'Reilly. Since the case in question was closed with a conviction, he didn't feel there would be a conflict, although that was brought up with the later investigations. But let me tell you, none of that mattered the first time I sat in that office with Rick, though. It was brutal. I've never met or worked with anyone like Rick before. There was so much pent up anger and resentment, and Johnny knew how to use it for maximum results. When I asked him questions in that first session, trying to get an understanding of the gang member in front of me, well, getting an answer from him was like pulling teeth without anaesthetic," Tony said, with a smile at Rick. The teen flushed as he recalled that session. It was the turning point of his life, he knew and he was thankful for it.

"What happened, Constable?" Lance asked as he noticed Tony hesitate.

"I just wanted Rick to answer a question, any question. I made the mistake of asking him about his mother. Lord, I've never seen anyone get that angry that fast. It was twice as bad as during the transfer hearing three weeks ago. He just...exploded. That's the only way to describe the sudden violence. He tried to attack me, but I was able to avoid the wild swings easily. I doubt I could do that now, he's that good a boxer. Then, once he had physically exhausted himself, I got him under control, and we talked for probably a good three or four hours. By the end, I knew I had only scratched the surface.

"He was a strong, wilful, violent, bully boy when I first met him. Now, he's a strong, wilful, and kind kid that'll literally die to protect someone he cares about. I've learned as much from him as he did from me. I can only say that while Rick has made a lot of progress in the last ten months, he's still got a long way to go. And I'll be right beside him as he does," Tony said with another smile at Rick.

"What were some of your other sessions like?" Lance asked.

Tarbot spoke up quickly. "Your honour, all of this is very interesting, if a little boring. However, I fail to see the relevance of these little chats between Constable Whitefish and Richard and this case," Tarbot objected for the first time in the whole trial.

"Your honour, I'm merely trying to show how the gang life has affected Richard, and how in helping him deal with it, it has also shaped how Constable Whitefish conducted his investigations. These "chats" would provide the best background possible," Lance explained.

Judge Prokovic hesitated. While he thought the sessions would be very interesting to hear, he realized they probably didn't have much to do with the matter at hand. As much as he hated to give Tarbot even this small win, he really had no choice. Trying not to show any emotion, Prokovic made his ruling.

"Objection sustained. Constable, unless there was something in your sessions that actually has anything to do with the crimes the defendants are accused of, they aren't relevant to this trial. Mr. Blackstone, move on," Prokovic directed. Tarbot just grinned at his small victory.

Tony held his hand up to stop Lance from asking any questions while he thought about his sessions with Rick. "Sorry, Mr. Blackstone, but as near as I can remember, there was never anything in the sessions that would pertain *directly* to the charges against the defendants. It was more about how Rick was gonna get outta the Knights and stuff like that. Let's go," Tony said and waited for Lance's next question.

Although he didn't like it, Blackstone nodded and returned to the investigations, guiding Tony through each one, searching for the smallest detail. When Lance focused on the day of Megan's kidnapping, even he was surprised at some of Tony's answers.

"Once I got to the school and found out what had happened, the first thing Inspector O'Reilly did was to order me back to the precinct and off of the investigation. Said I was too close to Rick and I couldn't be impartial," Tony said. "I pointed out he hated Rick too much to be impartial, but he's my boss and he was adamant that I leave."

"What did you do?" Lance asked.

"Defied orders, sir. While the inspector was off with the principal and the crime scene technicians investigating the hall where Megan was kidnapped, I snuck into the gym where all the students were waiting and talked to the O'Reilly twins," Tony explained and then went on to detail their conversation and the scene in the cafeteria.

"And afterwards?" Lance asked.

"I left the school and went to Glencrest," Tony said.

"To arrest Rick," Blackstone stated.

"No, sir. To hide him. I knew if Inspector O'Reilly found Rick at home, he'd arrest the boy and forget to look at all of the evidence," Tony said quietly. In the stunned silence of the courtroom, Tony went on to describe the initial days of the investigation, including how he had worked himself to the point of exhaustion and had collapsed at least twice at his desk.

"Based on what we found in the black bag, specifically that vial, we began to look into the break-in at Dr. Jim's clinic as a *possible* tie-in to this investigation. After all, there aren't that many places in town you can get this type of sedative. In fact, we found there's only two – the clinic and the hospital. Dr. Jim provided us with access to patient records, with him present to preserve patient confidentiality, and we discovered Brian Townsand had visited the clinic about a week prior to the break-in. Dr. Jim remembered taking him over to the cabinet where the sedatives were kept as the teen had asked for something for his younger sister who was having trouble sleeping, due to being bullied at her own school.

"Brian was the only Knight at the clinic prior to the break-in. It wasn't much, but it gave us another possible suspect to look at. His fingerprint was found on the vial, although at the time we lifted it we didn't know it was his," Tony explained.

By now, Blackstone had regained his composure at Tony's admission he had hidden Rick away and returned to his questioning. "Where did you do the initial interview of Brian Townsand?" the prosecutor asked.

"It was done in the principal's office at Colonial High," Tony said.

"With a lawyer or parent present, I presume?" Lance asked.

"No, sir. Although I did advise him he could have one, he declined and at 17, he's old enough to make his own decision about that, in my books, anyway. I did, however, have the school principal sitting just outside the office door, and the door was open so he could hear everything I asked Mr. Townsand," Tony said, stunning Blackstone again. "In fact, sir, it wasn't actually an official interview. It was merely a follow-up on the investigations. We were, at Inspector O'Reilly's orders, re-interviewing everyone that might know anything about all of the incidents throughout the year, and that included the Knights. Brian Townsand was a suspect, *in my mind only*, because of the *possible* connection to the vial. He wasn't under arrest. It was merely a conversation with one of Rick's known associates," Tony explained.

"How did you get the fingerprint?" Blackstone asked, after a couple of false starts.

"I offered Brian a can of pop. He drank it and left it behind. Since it was in public view, I could collect it without a warrant. I compared the print lifted off of the vial to one lifted off of the pop can, determined it was a match and then compared it to what we call a ten-card. This is a card that has someone's fingerprints on it after they are arrested for a crime, which Brian Townsand had been in the past, and obtained an arrest warrant executed at lunch at Colonial High approximately five days later. We were unable to locate him until then," Tony explained.

Lance glanced at the clock. He knew it was getting late, but he didn't want to interrupt Tony's testimony and the judge didn't seem to care about the time. He pressed on.

"Were you able to talk to Brian Townsand right after you arrested him?" Lance asked.

"Unfortunately, no. He was actually arrested the same day Rick was found after his brutal attack. I wasn't personally able to talk to Brian until almost a week later. And while I didn't, I know others did in order to get a preliminary statement. I also know he wasn't able to talk to a judge until several days after his arrest due to a sudden massive backlog at court," Tony explained. "His parents were informed but no lawyer was sent right away, not even a public defender. Why, I have no idea, but it was noted in his arrest file."

He paused long enough to take several sips of water and slip a throat lozenge in his mouth. Then he continued. "It was after Rick's "funeral" before I was finally able to go back and actually interview Brian. I asked him several times if he wanted either a parent or a lawyer present and he constantly refused. Said his dad would kill him just for being arrested and he didn't need a lawyer since he wasn't talking. I asked him about the attacks on both Miss O'Reilly and Miss Attison and he denied ever laying a hand on either one of them.

"I finally got frustrated enough at his lack of answers I showed him the pictures we had taken at the hospital after Rick's beating. I've never seen anyone go so pale. He was not expecting them, nor the rest of the evidence we had. His handwriting on the wall, confirmed to be his by his English teacher, Mr. Robson, the fingerprint on the vial. Not even the news Rick was "dead" and "buried" could get him to break," Tony said. A couple of more sips of water and Tony launched into a brief description of Rick coming to in the hospital, then what they found at Blade's.

"After all of this, Rick coming to, telling his story and all of the evidence we've just covered you found at Johnny Chilton's, did you then find Megan?" Lance asked.

"No, sir. We had plenty of evidence Johnny and the others had assaulted Rick in that house – blood evidence on a chair in the kitchen, Mark's signet ring with some blood and tissue on it, bloody clothes in Johnny's room, the photos. Just...box after box of evidence that *something* happened in that house. We did find a spot in the basement with had an army cot, thin blankets, some bloody rope and bloody pillows. We were eventually able to prove forensically Miss Attison had been kept there, but she wasn't there at that time. We had no idea where Johnny had taken her," Tony said. He rubbed his face. He was beginning to get very tired and he was worried about messing up.

"I know you're tired, Constable, but just a couple more questions and then I'll be finished for the night, 'kay? Now, after you finished gathering this evidence at Chilton's, what did you do?" Blackstone asked.

"Took it all back to the station, laid it out for Mr. Townsand to see and brought him up from Holding to have a good long look at it. After a couple of false starts, he finally got the message he was being hung out to dry by the gang. But he refused to actually say Miss Attison might be at Eric Jones'. He actually said, "Well, obviously Megs wasn't at Blade's or we wouldn't be having this conversation." Constable Andrews confirmed Johnny had been gone since the day after Rick's attack," Tony said, and took a couple more sips of water before continuing.

"Mr. Townsand looked at me like I was an idiot and said, "Since he's not at my place, and Pup lives with him, he's gotta be at Crank's." When I asked him where Crank – that's Eric Jones – lived, he wouldn't give me Eric's address. Just told me to look under Eric's real name, because he didn't want the Knights to think he'd given them up.

"The last thing I asked him, as we left the interrogation room, was if he was scared of Blade – also known as Johnny Chilton – and I don't think I'll ever forget his final words to me. He looked at me with a "duh" look on his face and said, "Man, get real. 'Course I am. Only a madman, or Moneyman, ain't scared of Blade." I thought about it and realized he was right. Rick had never really been scared of Johnny, just very respectful of his power. I honestly think, had Rick remained with the gang, he would've eventually challenged to be lead. He's a much more complete leader than Johnny ever will be," Tony finished quietly.

Rick looked at Tom, who flushed. The Kid understood now why Rick didn't want to lead the Angels, but they both knew it was way too late.

"Based on that evidence and Brian's admission, we were able to get a search warrant for Eric's place, including arrest warrants for the other three Knights. Upon executing said warrants, we found Johnny, Eric, and Mark in the living room with about $1,000,000 of the ransom money. The other five remains missing to this day. The three were arrested and separated immediately. It took us a while to search the house but we finally found Meg, excuse me, Miss Attison, beaten, starved and stabbed, in a small room above the garage," Tony finished.

"Thank you, Constable. Nothing further," Lance said and sat down.

"Mr. Grimes, Mr. Tarbot, you may begin your cross in the morning," Prokovic said before either lawyer could move. "Court's in recess until 9:00 a.m.," he continued and banged his gavel.

"Wow! What an afternoon," Tony groaned as he stood by the prosecutor's table. His back cracked as he stretched.

"You surprised me a couple of times there, Tony," Blackstone admonished. "You missed a point or two in our reviews."

"I know, Lance, but as long as I caught them by surprise too, I think you'll agree it was worth it. And I'll guarantee you Brian didn't tell Tarbot he was the one who gave up Meg's location," Tony snickered.

"Yeah, but is hiding me gonna come back to bite you?" Rick wondered.

Tony wondered the same thing. How much did Tarbot really know?

Chapter 63

The next morning, Tony returned to the witness stand, more nervous than he had been the day before. If he thought yesterday was hard, today was going to be pure hell.

Josh Grimes stood after Prokovic had opened court and looked at Tony. "Good morning, Constable, ready to begin? Good. Now, tell me, please, what evidence did you find against my client, Mark Chilton?" Josh asked.

"There was no forensic evidence found against any of the accused in Jordan O'Reilly's attack, except that which pointed to Rick. It appeared to us as if gloves had been used and discarded. There were some skin cells found on the rope used to tie Megan Attison to the tree, but we were unable to match them to anyone at the time," Tony said. "We have since linked the skin cells though D.N.A. to Johnny Chilton."

"What about the letters from throughout the year?" Josh asked.

"Again, nothing definite against your client, Mr. Grimes. The letters were all typed except the signature, a pair of stylized M's that're known to be Rick's gang sign," Tony explained.

"And the later attacks on Richard and Megan?" Josh pressed.

"In searching the Chilton home after Rick came to, we found a signet ring with blood and skin caught in it, although an attempt had been made to clean it. We were able to match it, again through D.N.A., to Rick. It was also consistent with the facial damage to Rick's face and Rick did remember Mark had been wearing it during the assault. The ring was found in Mark's room and it has been confirmed that it belongs to him," Tony said.

"Was there anything in Megan's assault connected directly to Mark?" Josh asked.

"No, sir. There was nothing forensically to link Mark to anything but the last attack on Rick," Tony said firmly.

"Thank you, Constable. Nothing further," Josh said as he sat down.

"Mr. Tarbot, do you think it would be possible to finish your cross no later than 1:00 p.m.?" Prokovic asked, glancing at his watch.

"Shouldn't be a problem, your honour," Tarbot agreed with that oily smile of his and then turned to Tony with a sneer. This time there was no waiting. He launched immediately into his cross.

"Constable, if there was no physical evidence against my clients, why've they been arrested and charged with the same crimes that Richard Attison was accused of?" Tarbot demanded.

"In case I wasn't clear before, Mr. Tarbot, let me be perfectly clear now. At the *time* of the original assaults against Miss Attison and Miss O'Reilly, there was no physical evidence to implicate anyone, really," Tony said firmly.

"Except Richard Attison," Tarbot interjected quickly.

"If you look at it properly, even that evidence was inconclusive. Yes, we found Rick's bandana at Miss O'Reilly's attack, but nothing else. No hair, no blood, no fibres, no fingerprints that didn't belong there. Same goes for Miss Attison's original assault in November," Tony stressed.

"You call finding his Knight's jacket at the scene nothing?" Tarbot asked, incredulous.

"Now get your facts straight, Mr. Tarbot. Rick's leather jacket was not found at the scene of Miss Attison's attack, which was in the woods about a 15-minute walk from her house. It was found in the spare bedroom closet in his house at Glencrest – a perfectly natural and logical place for it to be," Tony chided softly.

Tarbot frowned, as if Tony's explanation didn't match what he had been told, looked at his notes and then continued to hammer at Tony for the rest of the morning. Tony stuck firmly to his story, even though Tarbot doubled back on questions, asking the same question two or three different ways, all in a vain attempt to catch Tony in a lie.

Tony just took it all in stride. "Like or not, Counsellor, the evidence we now have points clearly at your clients and Johnny Chilton. Why fight it?" Tony asked mildly and was immediately censored by the judge.

Finally, after three hours of gruelling questions, Tarbot let Tony stand down, without scoring a single point against the cop. With a small smile, Tony stood up to step down, but the prosecutor spoke up. "Redirect, your honour," Lance said quickly.

Tony tilted his head, but didn't sit down. "Go ahead, Mr. Blackstone," Prokovic said with a frown. *What else could he possibly want to know?* the judge wondered.

"Constable, I need to know one thing – why, with all of the evidence against him, circumstantial or not, why did you believe in Rick's innocence?" Blackstone asked quietly.

Tony hesitated for a moment, looking at Rick. He was about to tell everyone the real reason why he believed in Rick, something only Runningbear knew. Rick looked back, wondering what was going on in his friend's mind. When Tony finally began to speak, his voice was quiet enough everyone had to strain to hear him.

"Wow, Mr. Blackstone, I...I wasn't expecting that question and I want everyone to understand something right now. What I'm about to tell you's only known by one other person – my shaman. Not even Rick knows," Tony said. He took a deep breath and continued softly, "It wasn't the evidence or lack of it. It wasn't Rick's continual protests of innocence. It wasn't anything in any one investigation that made up my mind. It was Rick himself.

"That first time he sat in my office at the youth centre and told me about his mother and the problems at home, I realized how much he was like the teens on my reserve. Like...I was at that age. Tough. Arrogant. Boss cock of the walk. He reminded me so much of me before my shaman dragged me into the tepee for my first vision quest I honestly thought I was talking to myself," Tony said quietly. The court was deathly silent as the cop continued.

"I saw a lot of me in that boy and in that instant, I just knew while, yes, Rick was very capable of violence, he was innocent of the violence he was accused of. It just wasn't in him to strike out against the weaker ones. It just kept getting stronger – this conviction. The longer I counselled him and the more I got to know him, the stronger my belief in my little brother grew," Tony continued softly.

"And the Knights? Other than the evidence, why did you believe they were guilty?" Lance asked.

Tony hesitated again. What he said here could be used as grounds for an appeal if he wasn't careful. "You mean, other than gut instinct, Mr. Blackstone? Again, my past. There was a group of boys like the Knights on the reserve, known as The Pack. Attacking without warning or reason, and vicious to boot. A gang...I was part of," Tony finally admitted, shocking Rick, and the Angels. The gasps echoed in the courtroom, making Tony flush with shame.

"Like Rick, I was sucked into the life and, like Rick, I managed to get out. I owe my life to my shaman, Runningbear. He made me get out because he saw more potential in me than just a gang banger. About a month later, The Pack's leader, Grey Wolf, got himself killed by the reserve police trying to steal a car. The rest of the gang woke up pretty quick after that, especially those who actually saw Grey Wolf gunned down like the rabid dog he'd become. The whole reserve was devastated. So was my shaman. Grey Wolf was his only son," Tony said sadly.

"When I first met the Knights during a quiet investigation into Tom Shelley's attack at the end of last school year, I was struck as to how much Johnny reminded me of Grey Wolf. They're both intense, single minded and fanatically loyal...to themselves, not the gang. As I began to dig more and more into the events over the year, I started to see a disturbing pattern – the Knights were always just in the background whenever Miss O'Reilly's and Miss Attison's accidents at the school would happen, but no one would ever remember seeing them until well after the fact and Rick had already been firmly blamed," Tony said and then paused.

"You take all of that, plus the physical evidence, and it pointed to the Knights. That's part of police work, sir. Trusting your gut won't let you down," Tony said with a shrug.

"Thank you, Constable. You may step down," Lance said.

"Before you call your final witness, Mr. Blackstone, we'll break for lunch. Court's in a one hour recess." The gavel banged as the judge stood and left.

Rick ate quietly, thinking about Tony's revelations that he had been in a gang, and Megan's upcoming testimony. It all made sense now – no wonder the cop had been able to understand Rick and the gang. He'd lived through it himself. He glanced at Megan. She was going to get pounded on this afternoon, he knew, but he couldn't help her get through it. She looked over at him and smiled. "I'll be okay, Rick. Trust me," she said softly.

As she settled into the seat, Megan was almost overcome by nerves. Her shoulder immediately began to ache and her mouth was suddenly very dry. She motioned to the bailiff for a glass of water, which she sipped at gratefully.

"Ready, Megan?" Lance asked when she finally put her glass down. She nodded.

Blackstone started with the very first day of school and her initial meeting with the Knights. "Awkward, to say the least. I was an object to be tossed aside, so they could disappear until lunch. Instead of leaving me alone, though, Rick introduced me to the O'Reilly twins. Sometimes, I think they saved my life. It gave me something to focus on during that month," Megan said softly.

And so it went. Lance asked about each attack and what she remembered and how the reactions of everyone, especially Mickey, affected her relationship with Rick. "I still can't figure out what kept me blaming my cousin. Mickey instinctively pushed me to blame the one person that had come between him and his twin, someone Mickey's always had trouble with. So I never knew if I was blaming Rick because he was actually guilty, which I know now he never was, or because Mickey wanted me to. I still don't," Megan said sadly.

"Was that what led to the confrontation in the cafeteria the day you were kidnapped?" Blackstone asked and then just let Megan talk about her captivity.

When she finished with her rescue by Tony, Lance thanked her and sat down. "Mr. Grimes?" the judge asked.

"Thank you, your honour. Miss Attison, I really only have one critical question for you. At any time, to the best of your recollection, did my client, Mark Chilton, ever attack you?" Josh Grimes asked, knowing this was the only point he had to score with this witness.

Megan paused for a long time and recalled every thing she could, then shook her head. "No sir. I don't ever recall Mark actually hitting me during my captivity with the Knights. As for November, I couldn't tell you for sure who hit me. Everyone had their faces covered. Mark would actually bring me water or soup, when he could sneak it past Johnny. I remember once, he brought me an extra blanket while Johnny was out of the house. Johnny took it away a couple of days later when he found it," Megan said. "Mark...cared, I guess you could say."

"Thank you, Miss Attison. Nothing further," the young lawyer said and sat down, satisfied he'd done his job.

"Mr. Tarbot, this is your only warning, don't harass or badger this witness. I read the transcript from the transfer hearing and I wasn't impressed. There'll be none of that in my courtroom. Understand?" Prokovic warned.

Nodding, Tarbot stood, adjusted his coat and began his questioning. For more than an hour and a half, he hammered on Megan, but the young girl never wavered in her testimony.

"I'm not sorry to blame your clients, Mr. Tarbot," Megan said firmly after the lawyer paused in his questioning. He cocked his head as she continued.

"No, sir, I'm not sorry at all. They've terrorized me, my family, my school and my town and they didn't seem to care who they hurt or how badly they hurt them. And that included my cousin and myself. They only cared about themselves. Anyone who tried to stand up to them was promptly beaten down," she snapped.

"Since you're old enough to do the crimes, I say you're old enough to do hard time," Megan finished with a sharp nod.

There wasn't much more Julien Tarbot could say after that and he let Megan step down. He advised the defence was declining to call any witnesses. Lance was a bit surprised, but not overly so.

- 573 -

He had kind of expected it. After all, it's up to the prosecution to prove the defendants had committed the crimes, not the defence to prove they didn't.

"Very well, gentlemen, we'll break early today then. Tomorrow you'll present your closing arguments. I expect them to be short and to the point. No long winded sermons. Understood? Good. This court stands in recess until 9:00 a.m." With the sound of the gavel echoing in the room, Prokovic left.

Lance turned to Rick and said, "You gonna be here tomorrow, son? You don't have to, y'know."

"Until the judge finds them guilty, I'll be here. They need to see me to remember what they've done," Rick said grimly.

It wasn't easy to drag himself from the warm bed the next morning. Standing at the speed bag, Rick once again did a slow run through of his workout. He nodded when he felt the muscles protest.

Dressing quickly, he wolfed down some breakfast and drove to town. Tony was standing in the foyer of the courthouse, talking to his partner while waiting for court to begin.

"Morning, little brother. Sleep good?" Tony said with a smile.

"Not bad, Fish, not bad. Actually, pretty good. No dreams of any kind lately. You, on the other hand, look strong enough to take on a grizzly. This time off's really done you some good, bro," Rick said, smiling back. Tony had more colour and the bags were gone from around his eyes. There was a spring in his step that hadn't been there since Christmas.

"It has, and we both return to active duty next week, but that's not why I'm in such a good mood," Tony said, his grin getting wider.

"Spill it, Fish. What's up?" Rick asked.

"Sheona's agreed to marry me, and I want you to be my best man," Tony said. He laughed at the stunned look on Rick's face, while Marshall congratulated his partner.

"Hey, Champ, don't worry about our counselling or calling me in the middle of the night," Tony said suddenly, knowing what was bothering Rick.

"Sheona doesn't like me, Fish. I've pulled you away from enough of your dates to know that," Rick protested weakly, although he was very happy for his friend.

"She understands, little brother. Now. But, yeah, it was hard at first. Having explained some of the things you've gone through has helped. You probably didn't notice, but she's been sitting at the back of the courtroom, taking notes. This is her first major trial coverage for the newspaper, so she knows the whole story by now. She knows you'll be in counselling for a long time yet. We still have lots to talk about," Tony said with a chuckle.

"Now you're here awfully early," the cop pointed out.

"Need some help, bro. For my shoulder and my boxing," Rick amended quickly when he saw how concerned Tony became almost immediately. He showed the partners his routine and the point where his shoulder began to ache. Both made suggestions and then the trio just talked about the mundane world of boxing until court was called into session.

Lance watched silently while the defendants were brought in. He had sent them an updated witness list a week ago, but since Tarbot hadn't raised an objection or threw a fit, Blackstone figured the lawyer hadn't even looked at it. *His loss*, the prosecutor thought.

"Mr. Blackstone, you advised the court this morning you wanted to call a last minute rebuttal witness and I will agree. Has the defence been advised of this witness?" Judge Prokovic asked as he sat down.

"Yes, your honour. I gave them the updated list last week. I wasn't 100% sure I was gonna call him or not, but I decided, while I was reviewing my notes for my summation, I needed to," Lance explained.

"Very well. Mr. Tarbot, Mr. Grimes, any objections? No? Go ahead, Mr. Blackstone. Call your witness," the judge ordered.

"The Prosecution calls Mark Chilton to the stand."

Chapter 64

Rick had to bite his tongue to keep from laughing at the look on Brain's face. If he was as smart as he thought he was, he would've realized something was up early in the trial. Mark was just as guilty as the others, yet his lawyer hadn't tried to present any defence.

Mark stood up in the silence and began to walk to the stand. The sudden movement startled Brain awake. "Pup! How could ya? How the hell could ya turn on yer own cuz? On the Knights? We're family, man!" Brain shouted, incensed.

Mark just glared at his former mates as he stomped up to the stand. It didn't take long for Blackstone to establish why he had called Mark as a rebuttal witness. He backed up Rick's testimony and then some. Details about the whole school year were bad enough, but when Mark started talking about the attack on Tom and the Slayers, even Rick blanched at the amount of detail the boy knew.

"'Fore a rumble, Johnny always bitched about Rick talking to the other street kids, like Jimmy and his crew, but he'd do the same thing. Only Johnny's info came from Mendez and his boys or the older gangs, the ones the Knights hadn't already creamed. Guys Johnny admired and wanted to be like," Mark said roughly.

"How's it you know so much?" Lance was curious.

"Simple. I never let Johnny think I was important enough to kick out of the room. I stayed in the background and never said a word. As long as I did, Johnny and the others would talk and ignore me," Mark said with a shrug.

Blackstone nodded and thanked the teen. Josh Grimes stood and approached his client. He was going to be the one who brought out why Mark had turned and what he was getting in return, as Lance had agreed to.

"Mark, you're taking a hell of a chance, y'know. Especially when your cousin finds out about this. So why'd you decide to do this? Why *did* you turn?" Josh asked quietly.

"What Johnny did wasn't right, not to Megs. Made me sick. She didn't deserve anything that happened to her after she was grabbed. The beatings. No food. No water. And slicin' her? No way, man. I didn't sign up for that crap. She didn't deserve none of that. That's not what Brian had planned, no way. She was supposed to go back, unharmed," Mark said harshly.

"What happened?" his lawyer asked.

"The plan was to keep our faces covered with plain, black bandanas, not wear the gear and not use any names. Johnny didn't care and he didn't listen to Brian. Johnny decided she needed to know right from the very beginning. Don't think he actually planned to give 'er back at all, let alone alive. He didn't care about nuthin', man," Mark said. "He wanted to brag."

He continued before his lawyer could ask another question. "Rick made his choice when he signed up. He got what he deserved, I guess, but Megs didn't ask for any of this. Johnny was just playin' with 'er. He wouldn't've cared one damn bit if she'd died. Not a bit. He didn't care

about Rick and he sure as hell didn't care about his best mate sittin' in jail. You wanna know why I turned, Brian? That's why. He wasn't my cuz anymore. He'd become vicious and cruel and what he did was *wrong*. Don't you get it, man? He's evil. He's not the guy I wanted to be when I grew up. Not anymore," Mark snapped. Brain just glared at the youngest Knight.

"Mark, did you make a deal for this testimony?" Josh asked quietly.

"Sure did, Grimes. A year total to be served here, and away from the rest of the Knights, with a chance for parole after six months. Two years probation and a chance. To do what, I don't know, but they promised me a chance," Mark said with a shrug, pointing to Lance and Rick.

"Thank you, Mark. Nothing further," Josh Grimes said as he sat down.

The judge glanced at his watch. "Your cross'll wait until after lunch, Mr. Tarbot. And just remember – no badgering," Prokovic warned once again before clearing the courtroom.

After lunch, Mark returned to the stand to let Tarbot hammer on him. The lawyer asked question after brutal question and Mark never lost his temper, not once. He'd often respond, "Don't care, Tarbot, if you believe me or not, but it's the truth."

Rick was impressed by Mark's testimony, especially on cross. The kid had guts to sit there and not lose it. Rick knew he would've blown up at Tarbot at least once, but Mark never did. *Then again, he hasn't been nearly beaten to death, either,* Rick admitted to himself.

Finally, Tarbot could ask nothing more and Mark was led away to begin serving his sentence away from Brain and the others.

"Now, gentlemen, no more surprise witnesses, I hope? Good. Summations in the morning. I wanna be reviewing all of the evidence by noon. Court's in recess until ten tomorrow morning," Prokovic said and banged his gavel.

The sound jarred everyone out of the spell Mark's testimony had woven. Rick stood and stretched, knowing this part was almost over. Out of the corner of his eye, he saw Brain turn and glare at him.

"You did this, Moneyman!" Brain shouted suddenly and launched himself over the rail separating the gallery from the rest of the courtroom.

Rick had expected something when he first noticed the glare Brain giving him. So when the Knight launched himself over the rail, Rick instinctively moved to one side and swung. His punch landed squarely on Brain's chin, knocking the teen to the floor, dazed.

"Leave us alone, Brian. Me, Mick, Mark, the girls, all of us. The Knights're finished," Rick snarled back, standing over the dazed Knight.

"Bailiff, restrain that defendant and get them both outta my courtroom," Prokovic ordered from where he stood, watching, on the bench.

Rick never relaxed his pose until the door slammed behind Tarbot. He could still hear Brain shouting about how Blade would get them all, no matter what. He turned with a grin to Tony and the others, feeling good for the first time in months.

"Knew he was gonna do something, Fish, but didn't think I could take him. Not with one punch," Rick laughed. His shoulder didn't even hurt!

"I don't think he even noticed the judge was still in the room. He did more damage with that attack than Mark or you did with your testimony, son," Tony replied, leading the way out of the room.

The next morning, Rick was a nervous wreck. He couldn't eat any breakfast and his hands twitched, wanting – no, needing – to do a workout. By the time he sat down next to Tony, he was a bundle of nerves and Tony could tell.

"Relax, little brother. This is only the summations. What're you gonna do when it comes time for sentencing?" Tony said in a low voice.

"You're sure Prokovic'll convict?" Rick asked, running a nervous hand through his hair.

"Look, Rick, I can't see any other verdict. They didn't put up any real defence, they just seemed to try and make Prokovic think they had nothing to do with any of it. Now, granted it's up to the prosecution to prove a case and the defence doesn't have to say a word, not even cross if they don't want to, but still most try and do something," Tony pointed out.

Rick didn't reply as Brain and Crank were led in, Brain in shackles, and a set of burly bailiffs standing behind each of them. Tarbot looked mad enough to spit nails and Rick was willing to bet it wasn't over the shackles.

Judge Prokovic walked in and settled behind the bench. He made no mention of the extra bodies at the defendant's table, but merely nodded to Blackstone.

Lance stood, straightened his tie and jacket and began his summation. He didn't go over every piece of evidence, but focused more on Rick's story, with Mark and Tony's testimony as backup. With all he wanted to review, he still managed to keep his summation to about a half an hour.

"A little longer than I really wanted, Mr. Blackstone, but you've made your point as eloquently as ever. Mr. Tarbot, you may begin," Prokovic said and motioned to the defence lawyer.

Tarbot spent his summation focused on the lack of record his clients had and Rick's arrest and convictions for at least one of the crimes his clients were now accused of. He spent most of his time on the lack of forensic evidence against his clients and the overwhelming evidence against Rick.

It took all of Rick's and Tony's self-control not to jump up and protest the blatant lies Tarbot was spouting. Even Lance looked annoyed, but it was Owen St. James who stole Tarbot's thunder.

"And so your honour, I ask you to return a verdict of Not Guilty for my clients. After all, we all know who has the sealed criminal record and who doesn't," Tarbot concluded and sat down with a smirk, one that quickly disappeared when Owen stood to speak.

"Your honour, a moment, if it would please the court," Owen said quietly as he stood.

"You have something you wish to say, Mr. St. James?" Prokovic asked. *Like a protest against the criminal record crap*, the judge thought.

"Yes, your honour, I do. I feel it's vital to remind the court my client, Richard Attison, does not, in fact, have a criminal record, sealed or otherwise. All charges've been dropped and Richard's record's completely expunged. Should Mr. Tarbot insist on continuing to slander my client's good name, I will have no choice but to file a Defamation of Character suit against him," Owen said, with a pointed look at Tarbot.

Tarbot blanched as the gallery snickered. Prokovic, however, maintained a straight face. "I hadn't forgotten, Mr. St. James, but thank you for that reminder. Mr. Tarbot, you can rest assured I've forgotten those unnecessary comments regarding Richard's criminal record. Now, having heard all of the evidence, all of the witnesses and your summations, I'm gonna retire and consider my verdict. There will be no decision until at least noon tomorrow," the judge said, then paused to wait while the muttering stopped in the gallery.

"I understand what these boys've been accused of, and the crimes are indeed heinous. I've seen many grievous crimes tried in these hallowed halls, trust me. However, I will *not* decide their fate in less than five minutes. They deserve better than that, no matter what my decision turns out to be. Please understand I have more than just their lives to consider. Court's in recess until 1:00 p.m. tomorrow, at which time, I will render my verdict."

Chapter 65

Rick rose late the next morning. He had talked late into the night with Jordan about their future. And for a change, his dreams had been pleasant. No nightmarish assaults and no dreams of dying and leaving her all alone. They had been all about living a very long and happy life with her.

Rick threw on his sweats and a muscle shirt and stood, once again, before his speed bag. He did his stretches and physio, his hands twitching violently with the desire to pound on the bag.

"Just five minutes," Rick decided quickly and swung into his routine. He didn't even last that long before his still-healing left shoulder gave out. He groaned as he rubbed it.

"Dumb move, Champ," Tony chuckled from the door. Rick jumped and fled to the other side of the room.

Tony didn't move. "Whoa, easy, son. It's just me. You were hitting the bag so hard, you didn't hear me come in," Tony said in the tense silence.

Rick took several deep breaths and tried to calm his pounding heart. He moved away from the wall to settle on the end of the bed. He couldn't help the shakes he got, and wondered when this jumping at sudden noises would end.

"Little brother, I'm sorry. I didn't mean to scare you," Tony said, moving quickly to squat in front of Rick, concerned.

"I'm okay, Fish," Rick said, finally getting the shaking under control. "I just can't believe I didn't hear ya come in." Rick sat there, rubbing his aching shoulder.

Tony found the muscle cream on Rick's dresser and motioned to his young friend. Rick stripped down and sighed in relief as Tony's strong hands gently eased away the aches. Tony spoke quietly as he massaged.

"You were going hard and your rhythm was off. Look, I know how bad you wanna get back to boxing, Champ, but this is exactly why you have to take it slow and steady. You've just set yourself back about a week. Come and see Aaron again today after court," Tony advised. "Let's see if we can't get you back boxing sooner rather than later. I don't want you doing this again."

Rick just nodded, mad at himself for re-injuring his shoulder. Once Tony finished, Rick changed quickly and then eased his left arm into his sling. Normally, he'd been doing without it, but after his stupid move this morning, he figured he should take it easy for the rest of the day.

Since Rick couldn't drive safely, Tony slid behind the wheel of the Firebird and started it up. They pulled out, with Marshall close behind.

"Is this really necessary, Fish?" Rick said sourly as he shifted around, trying to get comfortable.

Tony laughed. "Well, I honestly didn't *intend* to drive you today, little brother. Marsh and I've been reinstated and needed to bring some info on another case out to Seamus and thought we'd stop and chat before heading in," the cop explained as he navigated a corner. "Of course, I didn't count on you trying to dislocate your shoulder."

Rick laughed, and the rest of the trip was spent talking about anything and everything. For Rick, it was a chance to reconnect with the only father figure he had now and for Tony, it was a chance to be the father Rick needed.

Tony parked the car and turned to face Rick. "Rick?"

"Yeah?" Rick replied, hesitantly.

"No matter what happens today, you've won. Understand?" Tony asked. Rick nodded. "And, I want you to remember this – I'm proud of you...son." For once, Tony said that word as if he really meant it – Rick was his own son.

Rick climbed out as he thought about what Tony had just said. *Fish is right*, Rick realized. He'd broken free of the Knights. He'd won his girl and the respect of her father, even if Seamus didn't always truly trust him. Her brother and Rick had an uneasy truce, but they were working on it. And he had a big brother, alright a surrogate dad, and a ton of good caring friends. Tony was right. He'd won.

Rick and the partners met up with Megan and the O'Reillys at the courtroom door. "Afternoon, folks. Shall we?" Owen said and led the way into court.

Inside, it was packed. Tom had called out the troops and the Grey Angels were there en masse. It made Rick proud to see them there, everyone in their grey shirts, sending a strong message to the Knights. No more.

"Morning, Kid," Rick greeted Tom. He nodded to Carl, David and Jesse as they gathered around.

"Champ. What's with the wing?" Carl asked, returning Rick's nod.

"Pulled a stupid and tried the speed bag," Rick shrugged and sat down, not wanting to talk about it.

Carl shook his head and smiled. "Hmph. Brilliant, Champ." Tom just chuckled softly.

At exactly one, the defendants were led in and Judge Prokovic followed shortly afterwards. "Be seated, please," he said and waited for everyone to settle down.

"Good afternoon, everyone. Let me begin by stressing there'll be *no* interruptions while I'm reading my verdicts. Richard, control these Angels of yours," Prokovic said sternly.

Rick and Tom both nodded and both gave stern warning glances to the Angels, who all nodded. Silence reigned as Prokovic shuffled the papers and handed a copy to the court reporter. Rick suddenly couldn't breathe, couldn't think, couldn't focus. All he could do was pray.

"First of all, I'd like to say at times, the evidence presented made the verdicts seem clear cut – other times, not so easy. I've reviewed all documents introduced and logged into evidence, including the notebook discovered at Mr. Townsand's home, and I've read it, cover to cover. I've reviewed the testimony of all of the witnesses that was presented. I've made a very hard decision, but one I believe is fair.

"Now, will the defendants please stand while I read the verdicts?" Prokovic requested.

This is it, Rick thought. He groped blindly for Megan's hand and lowered his head. He couldn't bear to look at the Knights if the verdict wasn't guilty. All around him he could feel the support of his friends and family, but it was Tony's arm around his shoulder Rick felt the most comfort from.

"We'll begin with Brian Townsand. On the first count of the indictment, Kidnapping, I find the defendant...guilty," Prokovic said firmly.

As the judge continued to read the verdicts, Rick just sat there, head down and tears falling. He could feel Megan sobbing beside him as guilty verdict after guilty verdict was announced. The relief was almost too much to bear.

Only once the last verdict was read did the cheers finally erupt, almost deafening in their volume. It took the judge several minutes to calm everyone enough so that he could finish.

"The defendants're hereby ordered remanded into custody. Sentencing'll be in two days, gentlemen. Court's in recess," the judge said and banged down his gavel.

For once, Brain and Crank didn't have anything witty to say. They were led away in shocked silence, the door to the courtroom closing behind them with soft finality.

Everyone began talking at once, yet Rick heard none of it. He just kept hearing "Guilty" over and over and now realized the twins and his cousin were safe at last. He was so absorbed in his own thoughts he heard nothing around him and jumped a foot when someone touched his shoulder.

"Sorry, Richard. This was the easy trial, son," Judge Prokovic said kindly as Rick raised his tear-stained face. "Chilton'll fight a lot harder, especially when he hears about Mark turning," he said as he sat down with the family.

"Yeah, I know, but at least they're safe now," Rick said fervently as he looked around.

"So're you, Rick," Lance pointed out.

"Maybe so, Lance, but I made my choices a long time ago, when I joined up. Megs and the twins? They never asked for any of this. No one did," Rick said with a shrug.

"Neither did you, Rick," Tony said sharply. Rick waved the comment away.

"Whatever, Fish. It doesn't matter anymore. I've always known what would happen if I left, Johnny made that plain from day one. I've understood and accepted that. I just never thought it would be this bad," Rick said flatly. He shifted his shoulder as it began to throb.

"Rick, you don't have to be here for sentencing, if you don't want. I'll give them as much as I can, but it probably won't be more than three years, no matter how violent the crimes. I'll tack on as much probation as I can. Sorry, kids, but I can't give them adult sentences in this case. There's not enough physical evidence to give it to them," Prokovic said as he saw their faces fall.

"Three years? Why can't it be more?" Megan said bitterly. The judge didn't say anything else as he left.

Rick couldn't say anything. This part was over and the next couple of weeks would be tense, waiting for Blade's trial to start. Silently, he left the courthouse and drove to the youth centre, his mind focused on anything but a very bitter Blade and another trial from hell.

Chapter 66

Rick decided not to go to the sentencing for Brain and Crank, and it wasn't a hard decision, either. He'd had enough of them for a very long time. He knew they'd been given the maximum sentence Prokovic could give them, but it galled Rick all they could get was three years with a year and half probation afterwards. Because the crimes were so bad, Prokovic decided there would be no chance for parole. The two Knights would have to serve their full sentence.

Rick was glad. Both boys had been sent to a juvenile facility in a city more than five hours away so Mark would be safe. With the first trial now over, Rick could focus whole-heartedly on the physio Aaron had set up. Rick had a goal to be back boxing full-time by August. With physio in the morning and tutoring in the afternoon, Rick lived at the youth centre, something he really didn't mind.

The nights were the best, though. Rick spent every single night with Jordan at dinner, the movies, long horseback rides and solitary conversations at the house. The only rule Seamus imposed was Jordan back at her house by dark, unless they chose to go to a late movie. Thank God for cell phones. None of that mattered to Rick. It was time he was given with Jordan he didn't have to fight for.

But no matter what else the pair did, they spent most of the time talking. That is, Rick talked and Jordan listened. It was one way Jordan was dealing with what had happened to her boyfriend. For Rick, it was a different form of counselling, a way to deal with some of the nightmares and memories.

Although Rick didn't return to formal counselling with Tony right away, Rick made sure he stopped into the office between physio and tutoring to chat whenever Tony was at the centre. Rick wasn't avoiding his counselling, but he wanted to really think about what Tony wanted. It wasn't going to be easy to talk about the life. He really wanted to forget all about the Knights.

The day Blade's trial was due to start dawned clear and warm. Rick rose early and stood in front of his speed bag, hesitating for a long time. The past two weeks' intense physio had done Rick a lot of good. His shoulders no longer hurt when Aaron put him through his physio, but the physiotherapist stubbornly refused to give into Rick's pleas to try the bag. He wanted Jim to clear Rick first.

Rick thought about the nightmares still wracking him at night. Talking with Jordan had eased some of them, but Rick figured the rest would only ease once he could finally box again. Standing there in front of his bag, Rick made up his mind. He took several slow swings at the bag and smiled when he felt only some slight stiffness in the left shoulder. But no pain. Grinning even more, Rick swung into the first boxing routine in almost three months.

It was an hour later when Tony and Marshall showed up, knocking on the front door. The partners entered and heard the rhythmic thump-thump-thumping of the bag. Tony glanced at Marshall, who raised an eyebrow and followed his partner back to Rick's bedroom. They stood in the doorway, watching silently.

"I know you're there, Fish. Hey, Marsh," Rick said. As usual, his eyes were closed and his hands moved automatically. Tony couldn't see a single hesitation in the swings and the rhythm was perfect. His toes began tapping automatically.

"How long, Champ?" Tony asked, not moving.

"'Bout an hour," Rick said, glancing at the clock as he finished with a flourish. His left shoulder throbbed and he grimaced.

Tony didn't say anything as he grabbed the muscle cream and motioned for Rick to lie down. Hurt at the sudden and angry silence from his friend, Rick slowly stripped off his shirt and laid down. Tony smoothed some cream into the teen's sore shoulders, and began to rub, gently but firmly. The longer the silence stretched on, the more Rick wondered if Tony was mad or not.

"Fish?" Rick asked attentively.

"Jim clear you?" Tony wanted to know as he continued.

"I see him tomorrow morning before court. Honest, Fish, it's only throbbing a little, but it felt good. Please don't be mad at me," Rick begged. "I had to try."

"Come on, Fish, go easy on the kid," Marshall spoke up suddenly in Rick's defence. "We've both seem him do much harder workouts. Relax, man," Marshall said as Tony continued to massage Rick's shoulders. Finally, Tony sighed as he finished up and dried his hands.

"I guess there's no damage done, Rick. I was just surprised you'd try without getting cleared. Relax, little brother. I'm not mad at you," Tony said, suddenly smiling at Rick. He was actually surprised Rick had waited as long as he did.

"Now, go clean up so we can head into town," Tony said, giving Rick a gentle push towards the bathroom.

Twenty minutes later, the trio headed into town, Tony riding shotgun with Rick, and Marshall following behind. As he drove, Rick kept looking at Tony, wondering why he had come to see him.

"Alright, Fish. What's up? Why're you and Marsh really here?" Rick finally asked.

"Well, Nana asked us to make sure you got to the courthouse today. She figured you might be a little afraid of going by yourself," Tony began hesitantly.

Rick snorted as Tony continued. "I also wanted to talk to you, see how you're doing. Still coming back to counselling, son?" Tony asked.

"Eventually, but just not right now, Fish. Remember how I said I needed a friend, not a counsellor, for a while?" Rick asked, reminding Tony of that conversation at the centre over a month ago.

"Yeah, and I thought that we were gonna do that," Tony said as Rick entered city limits.

"We were, but *Jordan* needed me to talk to her. She needed to understand, in my own words, what happened to me, not just that one day but right from the very beginning and she didn't wanna just hear the testimony. She wanted to hear about it from me. Fish, it's been incredible! She doesn't flinch or push me away. She still loves me," Rick said, still amazed at the love in his girl.

"Did it help you, Rick?" Tony asked as they pulled up to the courthouse.

"With the nightmares? Somewhat. Some've gotten worse, some better and some've gone completely," Rick said. He parked the car and stared at the courthouse. The sunshine lit the building, making it seem so happy and cheerful, yet once inside the doors, Rick just felt overwhelming oppression.

"You okay, son?" Tony asked as Rick stopped just inside the doors.

"I really hate this place, Fish," Rick muttered sourly. He rubbed his shoulder absently.

Tony came over and put his hands on Rick's shoulders. His dark eyes were full of understanding and compassion. "Me too, son. Me, too. C'mon. Let's go put him away," Tony encouraged. Taking his strength from his best friend, Rick squared his shoulders and moved towards adult court.

A lady's shy voice stopped them just as they found the courtroom for Blade's trial. "Constable Whitefish?" she asked.

Rick turned around and came face to face with a vaguely familiar looking lady. Tony smiled at her. "Marian, how are you?" the cop said, shaking her hand.

"Better, now that he's not at home. Saw Mark yesterday at the young offender's centre and he seems better, too. And I have a new job. I'm working at the medical clinic now for Dr. Jim. He's paying me well enough I only have to work one job. I've moved to a new house and things're looking up," Marian Chilton said. Tony just smiled, not wanting to let Blade's mother know he'd had a hand in getting her the job and the new house. "But I've interrupted you and your young charge here. I'm sorry."

"That's quite alright, Marian. I've someone I'd like you to meet. Rick Attison, Marian Chilton," Tony said, introducing Rick to Blade's mother.

Rick froze. "Johnny's mom?" he gasped.

"You're the one my Johnny nearly killed!" Marian whispered, horrified, at the same time.

Rick studied Blade's mother for a moment, then said," Yes, ma'am. In your kitchen, while he had my cousin tied up in the basement. He's mean, cruel and vicious. And I'm gonna put him away for good. I'm sorry, ma'am," Rick said, trying not to be angry at her for letting it happen.

Marian smiled as she heard the anger in Rick's voice. She totally understood. "Don't be, lad. There's nothing to apologize for," she said, unconsciously mimicking Nana. "My...son, as much as I loved him when he was younger, *has* become evil. I've no problem with what you plan. How about we put him away – together?" Marian offered, stunning Rick briefly.

"Yes, ma'am," Rick agreed, smiling back, knowing he could grow to like Marian Chilton. He led the way into the crowded court with Tony and Marian following. Nana and the rest of his family sat behind Lance, leaving space for Rick and the two cops.

Tony looked at Rick after making sure Marian had found a seat. "She's just as terrified of Johnny as you were at one time, so she really understands why you wanna put him away," Tony said.

"Where's all the people? Did the jury get picked already, Fish?" Rick asked as he sat. Owen had reminded his client the night before this was adult court and anything Prokovic or Neils may have tolerated wouldn't be allowed by these judges, so Rick knew he'd have to be strong.

Owen answered Rick's question. "Johnny chose Trial by Judge alone. There's no jury. Here we go, folks," Owen said as the far door opened.

"This'll all be over by the end of the summer, Rick. Remember that," Megan said as she sat down with the twins right behind Rick. He cringed as Megan had unknowingly used Blade's favourite threat.

"Easy, little brother, she doesn't know," Tony said, as he noticed Rick's reaction.

Rick didn't respond. He had been watching Blade and Tarbot as they had entered. Blade was scowling and Tarbot looked ready to murder his client. The two continued to argue in low tones as they settled at the defendant's table.

Rick couldn't hear the words but he knew the tone. "Johnny's up to something, Fish. You better let Lance know," Rick warned. Tony looked at the defendant and then leaned forward to tap Lance on the shoulder where he sat with the lead adult prosecutor who'd asked Lance to help out with the trial, since Lance knew so much about the case and the defendant.

Just as Tony sat back, court was called to order and Assistant Chief Justice Andrew "Stonewall" Cottrell entered. He sat down behind the bench, an imposing figure that dominated, not just the judge's bench, but the whole courtroom. He let his eyes roam over the court and they settled on Rick.

The judge's black eyes bore into Rick's; unflinching, Rick understood. Cottrell would not tolerate any emotional breakdowns. Rick nodded – once – and Cottrell swung his gaze over to the defendant's table to stare at Blade. Blade just stared back with the sneer Rick knew so well plastered to his face.

"Be seated," Stonewall Cottrell ordered finally and banged his gavel sharply. "This court is ready to begin Crown vs. Johnny Chilton. Mr. Blackstone, thank you for joining us in Adult court. I know how crowded your Youth court is. We appreciate it. Now, is the prosecution ready?" the judge asked.

"Yes, your honour. The Prosecution is ready," Lance said as he half stood.

"Mr. Tarbot, we meet again. Is the Defence ready?" Cottrell asked.

Tarbot leaned over and muttered a question to his client. Blade shoved him away angrily. "Just do as yer told, Tarbot or piss off and I'll do it," Blade snapped.

"Mr. Tarbot, we have a very long way to go. Do not try my patience," Cottrell snapped.

"Your honour, over my objections, Johnny Chilton's electing to change his plea at this time," Tarbot said, disgusted. He was sure he could've beaten the charges, but Blade stubbornly refused to take on both Rick and Mark.

"Your Honour, is the defense trying to be funny? If so, he's failing – miserably," Lance said heatedly, quickly standing. The courtroom was filled with stunned murmurings at this sudden turn of events.

Rick couldn't believe his ears. After everything this year and all of the bragging Blade had done and now he was giving up? Rick wasn't sure if he should laugh, cry or jump up and tell Blade to quit screwing with his mind.

"Sit down, Mr. Blackstone. Mr. Tarbot, why've you waited until today to tell the court this? Surely you could've told everyone sooner and spared the witnesses some stress," Cottrell demanded.

"Because I just found out about it this morning, your honour. My client had been advised last week that his cousin, Mark Chilton, was planning to testify against him. This morning, when we met for our final pre-trial meeting, Mr. Chilton informed me he was changing his plea. I've been trying to talk him out of it ever since," Tarbot explained sourly.

"Are you changing your plea to Guilty, then?" Cottrell asked Blade.

"Yep," Blade drawled lazily.

"Have you arranged a plea bargain, Mr. Chilton?" the judge asked.

"Not with my office, your honour," Blackstone snapped quickly.

"Nope," Blade said at the same time.

"Are you hoping for a lighter sentence by changing your plea, young man?" the judge asked.

"Don't care, man. My boys'll fix'em. Maybe Mendez'll help, too. The punk won't know where. Won't know when. Moneyman, get used to lookin' over yer shoulder, man," Blade growled as he glared at Rick.

Rick surged to his feet. "Anytime you wanna face me like a man, I'll take you on, you bloody coward," Rick snapped back, as Tony and Marshall grabbed his arms to hold him back.

"Order!" Judge Cottrell snapped, banging his gavel. "Mr. St. James, control your client or I will!" The judge waited patiently until Rick had sat back down.

"Sorry, your honour. It won't happen again," Rick said, ashamed of losing control.

"Thank you, Richard. Very well, let the record show Johnny Chilton has changed his plea from Not Guilty to Guilty. As there is no plea bargain in place, there is no requirement for Mr. Chilton to admit or fully disclose what he has done; however, the charge must be read into the court records. At this time, the Court requests Mr. Blackstone to provide a summation of the facts of this case. Mr. Blackstone, please proceed."

Nodding, Lance stood, took a moment to compose his thoughts and his notes, and for the next several minutes, gave a summation of the charges against Blade. While Lance read, Blade stared over his shoulder at Rick, who resisted returning the stare.

"Thank you, Mr. Blackstone. Do you or Mr. Tarbot have any issues with sentencing being done at this time? No? Do any of Mr. Chilton's victims wish to make a statement at this time?" the judge asked, looking at the gallery.

No one moved for a long time. Rick finally took a deep breath and stood. The judge smiled slightly at the courage he knew it was going to take Rick to do this. "Somehow, I thought you might, Richard. Go ahead, please," the judge said gently.

"Johnny, when you made me a Knight, I'd never been happier. You gave me something I hadn't had for a long time – a brother and a family. I would've died for you, brother, until you decided Jor was a problem. And because of you, I damn near did die. If you'd just left her and Megs alone, we wouldn't've had a problem and none of this would've happened," Rick began quietly, not moving from the gallery. Blade didn't turn and look at Rick, so Rick moved to stand in front of the witness stand where Johnny, and everyone else, could see him.

"But I chose to leave, and you should've respected that. Or at the very least, been man enough to come after *me*. But no. You decided to go after a kid who still suffered from panic attacks and blinding headaches because of what you did to him the first time. You went after two beautiful ladies, tormenting and torturing one of them instead of facing me.

"Now, thankfully, you've finally decided to do the right thing and not make all of us go through this again. Although you damned near killed me and Megs, I'm gonna do something I don't think anyone here thought I'd ever do – I'm gonna forgive you for what you did," Rick said. The court was deathly silent as Rick took another deep breath, although Rick heard someone whisper, "He's forgiving him?" and who was quickly shushed.

"But, you can't be allowed to keep doing this. You have to go away for a very long time. I won't live my life in fear of you or the Knights. You deserve to rot in jail for the rest of your life. You remember *this*, Blade. I didn't beg. *And I never broke!*" Rick finished with a snarl. Tony was so proud of his little brother at that moment he thought he'd burst.

Rick stomped back to his chair while Judge Cottrell made a couple of notes. "Anyone else? No? Thank you, Richard. Mr. Chilton, I'm ready to pronounce sentence. Please stand," Cottrell ordered.

Blade surged to his feet and stood, waiting for his punishment. "Yong man, you've been charged with some very serious crimes, and although one of your victims has forgiven you, I'm afraid I must agree with another of Richard's statements. You *are* going away for a very long time," Cottrell began and then read the list of charges against Blade.

When he finished, he looked at Blade and asked, "Mr. Chilton, do you have anything to say at this time, before I pronounce sentence?" At Blade's indifferent shrug, Cottrell sighed and said, "Okay, son. Just remember you had your chance. Now, as you have pleaded Guilty, I will take that into consideration, but the attempted murder charges alone're enough to warrant a life sentence. And, although there was no evidence presented to the court formally in this case, I was aware of the severity of all of the evidence, and I hereby sentence you as follows." Cottrell began with the lesser charges of Harassment and moved on to the more serious charges. In all, it took ten minutes for Blade to be sentenced.

"So, young man, to summarize. You've been sentenced to life in prison with no chance at parole for at least 30 years, including good behaviour. I would like to recommend you get some help and improve yourself. You need some serious help. Court is adjourned," Cottrell ordered, smacking down his gavel sharply.

Blade didn't move for a moment, then he suddenly whirled and started towards Rick who hadn't bothered to sit back down. Blade was grabbed by a couple of bailiffs and dragged from the courtroom. "Remember, Moneyman!" Blade shouted once before the door slammed behind him.

The courtroom erupted into cheers and laughter as Blade disappeared. Everyone, that is, except Rick. He stood by Jordan in stunned silence.

"Rick, what's wrong? You should be the happiest of all of us," Nana said, puzzled.

Rick just shook his head. "I am happy, Nana. I just can't believe it's all over. I never thought he'd give up. It's not like Johnny to just give up," Rick said quietly.

"Rick, love, who cares? It's over!" Jordan cried happily. "It's over!"

Tony nodded and put his arm around Rick's shoulder, giving him a hug. "It's over, son," he said, smiling at Rick. Rick leaned into Tony's hug, knowing he wouldn't've made it to this day without Tony, his big brother and surrogate dad.

"It's over," was echoed as the twins, Megan, Nana, Ian, Marshall, Seamus and Tom all joined together arm in arm.

Rick looked at his family and friends. "Round one – Blade. Round two – Rick. Round three – Justice," Rick said softly.

"What, Rick?" Jordan asked, puzzled at Rick's comment.

Rick just laughed. "Nothing, sweets. You're right. It's over," Rick said happily and pulled her into a hug.

Chapter 67

"What're you two doing? Leave that! Frank can finish up," Nana scolded with a smile as she came out on the back porch, squinting in the bright sun.

Rick grinned down at her from the top of the ladder where he was hanging patio lanterns for the party that night. It was the last day of summer and Nana was having a bar-b-que for all of Rick's and Megan's friends. Nana hid a smile as she thought about the phone call she'd just received. It wasn't just friends here that night.

"Just gotta couple more to hang, Nana, then we're gone," Megan said as she handed Rick another hook. Her cousin screwed it into the porch façade and hung the final couple of lanterns.

"How's that, Megs?" he asked as he jumped down and gathered up his tools.

"Looks cool, Rick. Shall we?" she replied as she indicated Nana's folded arms and gentle smile.

Rick gave Nana a quick kiss on the cheek as they left. "Later, Nana," they called as they took off.

Rick glanced at his watch, then at Megan. "Mind if I work out, cuz? It's barely ten and I told Mick we'd be over around lunch," Rick said as he led the way into his house.

"Mind if I watch?" Megan asked.

"Never. Just don't talk to me. Throws off my rhythm," Rick said with an indulgent smile. *How things have changed,* Rick thought.

Nodding, Megan flung herself on Rick's bed with a book while Rick slipped off his shirt and stood in front of his speed bag, concentrating. Megan tried not to flinch as she saw the vivid scars that stood out on his torso from the past year. Each one reminded her of what he had gone through, and not just for her.

As she continued to study him, Rick took several deep breaths to relax and tried to put his cousin out of his mind. As usual, he stood with his eyes closed, listening to the sounds of the farm come through the window – the horses whinnying to each other in the distant pastures. There were birds chirping in the nearby trees while Rick could hear Frank talking and directing the other hands to get the farm ready for the party.

Suddenly, Rick swung into his workout, the rhythmic thumps of his hands hitting the leather bag filling the room. Megan lifted her head slightly and made sure Rick was truly involved in his workout before shifting to a more comfortable position on the bed. She knew he'd be at this for a while.

Rick didn't slow down. He focused on his workout and let his mind wander back over the most incredible month he had ever experienced in his 17 years.

The day after Blade had stunned everyone by changing his plea, Rick had met with Jim. It was going to be the final check-up before Rick could be cleared to go back to boxing, at least that was Rick's hope. His cast had been off for a couple of months, but he still had some pain. Rick was getting the strength back, thanks to Aaron's physio. The sling had gone into the garbage the night before and Rick had used the speed bag just the one time, without Aaron's or Jim's clearance.

Rick sat in the examination room, waiting for the doctor. *Man, Doc's taking his time*, Rick mused as he glanced at his watch. He got up and began to pace. Still no Jim. Rick looked at the shadow he was casting on the wall and shrugged. *Might as well get a bit of a workout,* he thought as he began to shadow box. *My timing sucks right now.*

Perhaps five minutes later, Jim walked in, catching Rick in the act. "So, Tony wasn't lying. You've gone back to boxing. Without clearing it with me first," the doctor stated, standing in the door, his arms folded and a frown on his face.

Rick flushed. "I've only done one workout on my speed bag and now this. Aaron won't let me do anything, I swear," Rick protested weakly.

"Sit!" Jim ordered roughly. Rick climbed back on the table after stripping off his shirt. He waited patiently while Jim examined the wrist and both shoulders. The doctor wasn't mad at Rick – he, like Tony, was actually quite surprised Rick had waited as long as he had.

"Any soreness? Tenderness? Stiff?" Jim asked as he gently manipulated Rick's left shoulder.

"Mainly just the first stab wound," Rick said. Jim's fingers probed gently until Rick gasped at the sudden pain. "Right there!"

"Sorry, Rick. That tenderness is to be expected. It was the deepest, all the way to the hilt, if I remember correctly," Jim said as he washed his hands and began to make some notes in Rick's file.

Rick slipped his shirt back on, trying to be patient, but failing miserably. "Come on, Doc. Tell me," he protested finally.

"Tell you what, Rick? That you can box again?" Jim asked, distracted. He hid a smile at the impatience in the question.

"Well, yeah," Rick said, puzzled. He couldn't understand why the doc was being so stubborn.

Jim put his pen down and looked at Rick. The teen was anxious enough and Jim didn't think it was worth the extra stress to hold out. "Of course you can, Rick. Just promise me you'll wear a brace on the wrist for the first little while until you get the strength back completely," Jim grinned.

Rick whooped, pumping his fist happily. Jim laughed at the teen's enthusiastic response. "Thanks, Doc. I can really box again?" Rick asked.

Jim laughed again. "Absolutely. Just be careful of those ribs when you spar for the first little while, okay? They'll break a bit easier right now," Jim said as he went back to making notes in the file.

Rick shrugged on his leather coat and hesitated by the door. "Doc, have I thanked you?" Rick asked quietly.

"Look at me, Rick," Jim said, just as quietly. The teen looked at the doctor. "You've been in trouble for as long as I've been at this clinic, and I've watched you struggle to grow up, suddenly and without parents to guide you. When Jordan was attacked and

Seamus accused you, I knew he was wrong. I knew deep down you'd never hurt those girls.

"I saw in you the trust, loyalty and love Seamus just couldn't for a while and that was why I helped you. I gave you the time you needed to clear your name," Jim explained.

"Now, get out of here. Go and just be a good guy."

Rick flexed his left hand as he drove to the centre. He was itching to get back in the ring, but he knew Aaron would make sure he took it slowly and so would Bob and Derrick. In fact, Rick was pretty sure the whole club would be careful. For the first little while, anyway.

Tony met Rick at the front door as usual and led his friend to the office. "Jim called. Said he cleared you," the cop said as he perched on the desk.

Rick laughed as he sat down. "Yep. Thanks for ratting me out, bro. He just about skinned me before he cleared me, Fish," Rick said, grinning at his friend.

Tony laughed, too. "My pleasure, Champ."

"I'm still supposed to take it easy, though. Fish, I can't thank you enough for helping me. I know you could've lost your job because of me, and no matter what you say, I was never worth that," Rick said seriously.

Tony just stared back at the young man. Rick had been greatly changed by the past year and so had Tony. Rick had learned, the hard way, other people mattered and it wasn't always about him. He had taken Tony's lessons to heart and Tony was really proud of how things had turned out. They both knew Rick still had a long way to go, but Tony could now take on another kid, if necessary. He'd work Rick into his schedule, no matter what it took.

"You bet, Champ. I could've lost my job. So could've Marsh, to be honest. After Judge Neils cleared you, Seamus should've lost his too, but because you spoke up at his disciplinary hearing in his defence, he suffered only a reprimand in his file and he's still in charge. We all accepted the risk. Without it, we wouldn't've found Meg. Y'know?" Tony said.

Rick didn't say anything for a while. Tony could see Rick was slightly upset and Tony wondered what he had said to upset the teen. Tony decided they were too good of friends to dance around the issue. "What's wrong, Rick? What did I say?" Tony asked bluntly.

Rick flushed. "Fish, you asked me once to talk about the life," Rick began hesitantly.

Tony nodded. "Still do. Especially to some of your Angels. You've got some big issues there," Tony said, worried.

Rick snorted. "No kidding, Fish, and this is exactly why I didn't wanna lead. But it's only really five guys I'm worried about. I've gotten through to the rest. I'll give you their names and see if they're the same ones you're worried about. I just can't get through to them, no matter what I say. They've gone after the Slayers and the Hit Squad, and more than once, even though those gangs haven't gone after each other. But, I'll only talk on one condition," Rick said, looking right at Tony.

The cop leaned back and slipped an envelope out of Rick's file. "Find your mom?" Tony asked, sitting back up, knowing what Rick needed with everything else was settled.

"Find Mom," Rick agreed.

"Here," Tony said, handing over the envelope.

"What's this?" Rick asked, puzzled.

"When we began talking, I did some digging, especially after that first session. You were so hurt by your mom leaving, I thought we might get to this point one day. I actually found her quite easily. She's remarried and you've got two half-sisters. I contacted her when you were in the hospital, but you were under enough stress I forced myself to wait until you asked," Tony said quietly.

Rick turned over the envelope and realized his mom lived only two towns away. "So near and yet so far away," Rick whispered, hurt even more. With a sudden movement, Rick ripped open the envelope and began to read greedily.

"Hello, Rick. My darling son, you're lying in a hospital bed, beaten, dying and all alone. And while I'd love to be there, I don't dare. Not yet anyways. I don't wanna run into your father, but I need to say good-bye. And explain. There's just too many unanswered questions.

"Constable Whitefish's done the one thing your father never could – find me. I thought I'd buried my past deep enough no one could ever find me, but I never counted on the determination of a cop, especially one hell bent on helping a good friend. And he really cares about you, Rick," the neat handwriting flowed across the page.

Rick wiped at his eyes before he could continue to read. "I'm sorry I left you and Nelson with that idiot, but I had no choice, honestly. Your father made me sign a pre-nup agreement, one cutting me off financially if I left, and he made sure to include any children we had were to stay with him. In other words, love him, tolerate what he did or get left out in the cold.

"By the time you were six, I couldn't stand the alcohol, the constant stream of women he'd brought to the house – right under my nose – and the horrible gambling addiction. Your father never laid a hand on me, but I was a beaten woman when I left," the letter continued.

Rick was getting angrier and angrier as he read. Michael had done his very best to destroy their family, deliberately, and Rick had paid the price. *If I could get my hands on you, you bastard,* Rick snarled silently as he struggled to read the rest of his mom's letter.

"Nelson managed to get away, I know, but left you to become your father's whipping post. I also know you ended up in a gang, and, according to Constable Whitefish, you've just about died more than once because of it.

"You have a step-father and two half-sisters that desperately want to meet you. Jeff Dunn loves me for me and, while he doesn't have Michael's money, we want for nothing. Jeff, Melissa and Julia can't wait to meet you. They already know and love Nelson, but I made your brother swear not to tell you until you were ready to find me yourself."

Rick could barely read the words as his eyes filled with tears. "Rick, son, I'm sorry. It isn't enough and it doesn't make up for eleven years of pain and heartache, I know, but it's all I have. I wish I could go back and take you with me, consequences be damned, but I can't. I know you must hate me, but I'd like to meet the man my boy's grown into.

"If you want to get together, Constable Whitefish knows how to get a hold of me. Know this, though, my son. I love you and I always have."

It was signed "Mom."

Rick let his tears fall. He hadn't driven his mom away. It wasn't his fault. His mom still loved him. "I love you too, Mom," he whispered as he dried his eyes.

"Now you know the truth, son, and from someone other than me. Your father drove Kara away, not you. *Now* are you ready to forgive yourself?" Tony asked quietly, knowing exactly how Rick was going to react.

"*Father?* I've got no damn father!" Rick snapped, coming out of his stunned silence.

Tony didn't say anything for a moment. "No father, except maybe you, Fish," Rick finished quietly, finally acknowledging what Tony really meant to him.

Tony nodded. "Gladly, son, gladly. Now, how're you doing?" Tony asked with a small smile. He was proud to be Rick's surrogate father. He was a good kid. Now.

"Honestly, Fish? Not well. I'm gonna take my frustrations out on the bag, 'kay? Unless you've got Michael hiding somewhere nearby?" Rick sighed and stood up.

Tony laughed. "Sorry, Champ, not today. Off you go, then, but no more than an hour and stay outta the ring until you're a bit stronger, 'kay? You're just not physically ready for that today. Meet me back here and we'll talk some more," Tony said as he stood up.

Rick turned to leave, but Tony's rough voice stopped him. "Rick?"

"Yeah?" Rick said without turning around. He wasn't sure if he wanted to see Tony's face. He might just break down and bawl again.

"I'm glad you're back. I've missed our sessions, little brother. I've learned as much as I've taught. Thank you...son," Tony said, his voice gravelly with emotion, really meaning it.

Rick turned slowly around. "You're thanking me, Fish? After everything I did to you? How could you thank me?" Rick asked harshly.

"Because of what you gave me – my own family away from the reserve. Someone to care about, besides Sheona. Someone to be a brother to, after living in a family of all girls. Someone to be a father to, and I'll even make it official, if you want. No? It doesn't matter. Family's important to me, and mine's so far away. Now, go on. Do your workout and we'll talk some more in an hour," Tony said firmly. *If I don't get him outta here quickly, I'm gonna start babbling and bawling like an idiot*, Tony thought, struggling to hold onto his composure. Rick really meant a lot to the cop and they both knew it.

Rick watched his friend struggle with his own emotions, then nodded. He left the office, closing the door softly behind him. Tony took a deep breath and composed himself. He had to wait a couple of more minutes before he could pick up the phone and place a very important call.

Chapter 68

Rick found his way to the boxing gym, calling out greetings to his friends and stopping to talk to a couple of his Angels, all the while thinking about the letter and what Tony had said back in the office.

The boxing club were all waiting for Rick inside the door. Carl and Tom were both grinning. Even Bob was smiling. "Hey, Champ. Glad you're back," Carl said, bouncing with excitement.

"Sorry, Carl, not yet. Gimme a week or so to get back into shape and get my timing back," Rick laughed as Carl's face fell.

"Here we go, Champ. Physio first, then come and see me," Bob said, handing Rick over to Aaron, who put Rick through his paces.

When Rick finally came over to Bob, the coach looked at him and frowned, trying to decide how to proceed. "Okay, Rick. I wanna see how much you've lost. Speed bag. 15 minutes. Go," Coach ordered.

Closing his eyes, Rick took a couple of breaths to calm his pounding heart. Once Rick felt he was ready, he swung. Bob watched, smiling slightly. Despite how long Rick had been away and how badly he'd been injured, his hands and muscles still remembered that pattern taught so long ago.

Fifteen minutes wasn't very long, but Rick was more than ready to quit. Between the physio and the workout, his shoulder was throbbing. So when Bob called, "Time, Champ," Rick finished with a flurry, took a deep breath and opened his eyes.

Bob nodded happily at Rick. "Good job, Champ. Just wanna show you a couple of corrections. You've been gone so long you've accidentally gotten sloppy on a couple of things," Bob said and went through the motions. Rick followed his coach's movements a couple of times, tried a single run through of the whole workout, then nodded.

"Good. Now, how's the shoulder?" Bob asked just as Rick heard the whisper of movement behind him.

A hand landed on Rick's shoulder and Rick reacted on pure instinct. He turned and struck out blindly.

"Rick, NO!" Bob shouted. It was too late. Rick had already thrown his punch and nothing could stop it. Tom shoved Aaron down and Rick's fist connected solidly, dropping the Kid, dazed, to the floor.

"Kid!" Rick cried, horrified.

Tom sat up groggily with Bob's help. "What broken wrist? Nothing wrong with your shoulder, man. Gang reflexes, check," Tom chuckled good-naturedly as he rubbed his sore jaw.

"God, Tom, I'm so sorry," Rick apologized as he knelt by his friend. Bob hid a smile. *Rick Attison, apologizing for hitting someone. Can't wait to tell Tony,* Bob thought, amazed at the change in Rick.

"Relax, Champ. I'm cool," Tom said as they both stood.

"Dumb move, Aaron," Rick glared at his physiotherapist.

"I know, Rick, and I'm sorry. I totally forgot to let you know I was there. Now, can I please check your shoulder?" Aaron asked, moving behind Rick when the teen nodded. Rick relaxed, stood there, letting Aaron probe and poke and didn't feel a bit of panic.

"Rick, it's a bit swollen and I won't let you do any more today, at least not here. You may start to use your bag at home, but no more than 15 minutes at a time. Understood? We need to get the endurance back," Aaron said, coming around to face Rick.

Rick nodded. "That's cool, Aaron. Coach, call Fish and tell 'im I'm about 15 minutes out, 'kay?" Rick said as he headed to the showers. Exactly 15 minutes later, Rick knocked perfunctorily on Tony's door and strode confidently into the room. He was so focused on the cop he missed the smiling family of four completely.

"Hey, Fish, I'm back. Man, it was good to be back in that gym, I'm telling you, but Aaron just about got flattened. Idiot forgot to warn me and grabbed me from behind. Missed him and got the

Kid instead. Now I feel…" Rick's voice trailed off as he recognized the woman standing next to Tony.

She was older, of course, but yet unchanged. Her hair was still the same golden brown Rick remembered and her eyes were the same blue as his. She was slender, and, in fact, Rick thought he was looking at a female version of himself. As he studied her, Rick was startled to realize he now looked down at his mom. When he was small, she'd seemed so *tall* to him.

"Mom?" the teen whispered, frozen.

"Hello, son," Kara Dunn said. She held open her arms, and after a long moment of hesitation, Rick slowly walked toward her. The moment his mom's arms tightened around him, Rick felt eleven years of anger, hatred and misery melt away. He was six again, and Mom had just met him at the door after school.

Rick couldn't stop himself. He held on tighter and began to sob. He was finally home.

When Rick finally raised his head to look down at his mom, he could see she had been crying, too. He realized they were alone in the office; he had been so wrapped up in his mom he hadn't heard Tony and the rest of the Dunns leave.

Rick guided Kara over to the chairs in front of Tony's desk. While Rick loved his mom and knew she loved him, he was still angry and hurt. At least now, he'd finally get some answers.

"Why, Mom? Why no calls? No contact at all? Michael's always blamed me, y'know. You get told something long enough, you believe it. No matter what anyone's told me, I've spent the last eleven years thinking I drove you away. Why'd you leave me?" Rick asked angrily.

"That idiot!" Kara snapped just as angrily. "No wonder you've struggled so much!"

Kara sighed as she calmed down. "Believe me, Rick, *Michael* was the one who drove me away. You had nothing to do with it. He was so kind and gentle when we dated and Nana was ecstatic when we became engaged. She spared no expense on the wedding and she was just as shocked as I was when Michael's lawyer showed up, right before the ceremony was to begin with the pre-nup," Kara explained.

"What a nightmare! It was either sign or go out into a church full of people and call off the wedding. I swore to my mother and Nana I loved your father," Kara continued, but Rick interrupted harshly.

"Don't call Michael my father! Tony's been more a father in the past year than Michael ever was," Rick snarled, making Kara flinch.

"I'm sorry, Rick, you're right. Well, after the wedding and our honeymoon, I finally read the agreement and was horrified to learn I wouldn't be able to leave him. If I did, I'd lose any children we had and all support. Because I signed it willingly, there was no way out of it, and Michael took advantage to really begin drinking, gambling, and sleeping around. He'd even bring his floosies to the house and sleep with them there," Kara said bitterly.

"It didn't get any better, Mom. But even if you couldn't talk directly to me, why didn't you contact Nana? She'd've made sure that I knew," Rick said bitterly.

"The one time I tried, Michael was at Glencrest and intercepted the call. He told me if I tried again, he'd have me arrested and charged with harassment. So...I never tried," Kara explained.

She looked at Rick and held out her hand. "I'm sorry, Rick. It's not enough, I know and I really wish I could change what happened, but I can't. Can we start again, son, please?" Kara asked wistfully.

"You've gotta understand something about your son, Kara," Tony said, coming back into the room.

Rick jumped to his feet, knocking over his chair, and ran behind Tony's desk. His heart pounding, he looked down and saw his fists were clenched, and knew he could've gone for Tony or one of the Dunns without realizing it. He also knew his face was flushed in anger.

"Sorry, son, I thought you heard me knock," Tony said quietly as he remained in the door, keeping himself between Rick and his sisters.

"Rick?" Kara asked, a little frightened at the reaction she had just seen.

Rick took a couple of deep breaths to calm his pounding heart. "Fish, dammit, next time make sure!" Rick snapped. Tony nodded without moving.

Rick turned to his mom. "Look, Mom, I'm not gonna lie to you. It's gonna be rough for a while. The gang damn near killed me and I could do the same to you or the girls without meaning to. When someone comes up behind me, I tend to swing first, and ask questions later, especially since the attack," Rick began. He didn't trust himself yet, so he didn't move.

"And...I'm gonna have to deal with you back in my life. Eleven years is a long time to get over. I have anger management issues still, thanks to Michael, and, well, I tend to get angry quickly and sometimes for no apparent reason. As long as you all understand, I'm willing to try," Rick said, finally coming to stand by his mom.

Tony looked at Rick and saw he had calmed down enough that it was safe to let the girls in. The cop turned to Jeff Dunn and said quietly, "Remember, let him make the first moves. No sudden movements and don't talk too low. Your voice sounds a lot like Michael's when you do. Ready?" Tony asked and stepped aside.

"Rick, I'm Jeff Dunn, your step-father and these're your half-sisters, Melissa and Julia," Jeff introduced himself briskly. He stood with his arms around his daughters' shoulders until Rick moved to greet them, with a hesitant smile on his face.

Rick bent down to look at Melissa and Julia. "Hey, girls. How're ya doing?" he asked softly.

"G...G...Good," Melissa said nervously. Julia just clung to her father.

Rick looked at them for moment, then reached back and pulled his chair closer to sit down. Tony watched silently as he remained by the door, leaning against the jamb with his arms crossed, knowing he could have the girls out of the room before Rick could blink if he had to. Rick extended his hands to his sisters. Jeff had to encourage the girls a bit, but they took Rick's offered hands. He smiled at them as he pulled them in closer, trying to put them at ease.

"Look, Jules, Mel. I know what you just saw was pretty scary, and I'm sorry. I've been told it's pretty bad to watch," Rick said softly as he pulled them into a three-way hug. He could feel them both relax the longer he held them. "So, I'm gonna make you a deal, 'kay? I promise I'll try not to scare you if you don't come up behind me and try and scare me. Deal?"

As he waited for them to agree, he glanced at Jeff. The girls' dad motioned to his ribs and Rick grinned. He slid his hands down to their ribs and tickled them both. As they dissolved into giggles, they both nodded and flung their arms around their brother. Rick and the other adults laughed as Rick returned their hugs and stood up.

"Nice to meet 'cha, Jeff," Rick said, extending his hand. As Jeff shook it, Rick could easily understand why Kara had been attracted to him. He was the same height and weight as Michael. He had the same colour hair, although his eyes were a deep ocean blue, while Michael's were icy blue. And that's where the similarities ended. Michael's eyes were cold and filled with hate whenever he looked at his son. Jeff's sparkled with laughter and love when he looked at his wife and daughters, and now his step-son.

"Welcome, Rick. It's nice to finally meet you, son." Jeff's voice did indeed sound like Michael's and yet it didn't.

Son. Rick hesitated when Jeff called him that. He looked at Tony, then back to Jeff. Tony didn't move, but spoke softly. "I'm proud to be a surrogate father, Rick, but you need a real dad. I'm happy to be big brother. Let Jeff be dad," Tony encouraged.

Rick didn't say anything until he felt a little tug on his hand. He looked down at Julia. "Please, Rick? Nelson's so far away," she said in a clear, piping voice.

"On one condition," Rick said. "Well, two I guess."

"What's that, son?" Kara said.

"I wanna stay at Glencrest and I wanna keep my name. As much of a pain as Michael was, I'm kinda proud to be an Attison, y'know?" Rick said sheepishly.

Jeff came over and stood in front of Rick. "Rick, I wanna adopt you to give you the added protection of a legal set of parents. Nana's good, but, given what Kara and Tony have both told me about Michael, I don't trust him and I don't want him coming after you. Or your mom," Jeff said firmly. "I wanna adopt you, but I don't wanna change you. If you wanna remain an Attison, that's cool with me."

Rick felt his sisters snuggle up and his mom looked so uncertain about the man standing before her as her son. Jeff stood and waited patiently, in front of all of them.

"You gotta deal, Jeff," Rick said. Tony smiled and slipped out of the room. He closed the door behind him and left Rick alone – with his family.

"He's gonna be just fine," Tony said softly as he went back to the gym to watch the boxing club and resisted the urge to leap up in the air and shout. "Yep, he's gonna be just fine. Thank the Creator."

Chapter 69

Finding his mom again seemed to set the tone for the remainder of Rick's summer. He'd spend the mornings with his tutor now and the afternoons boxing. His return to the ring, at his insistence, the day after he'd met the Dunns, ended with him on the mat for the first time ever, with Carl laughing at having beaten the Champ.

That didn't last too long before Rick's timing suddenly came back with a vengeance. Their third session, three days after Kara came back into Rick's life, Rick and Carl were sparring and Carl gave the Champ the opening he needed.

Carl looked up from the mat. "Did it again, didn't I, Champ?" he laughed and hauled himself up. Derrick would work with Carl and the next session would find Carl on the mat again. And again. And again.

After boxing, Rick and Tony would talk. And talk. And TALK. Nana had expedited Rick's adoption, but Rick still felt a little odd having Kara back in his life. The instant family made him very nervous since he had no idea how to be a big brother and he still hesitated when he talked to Jeff. He looked way too much like Michael for Rick to be comfortable right now. What made Rick the most nervous was being alone with the girls. He wasn't sure if he'd ever be comfortable with sisters.

And the more he talked to Tony, the more Rick realized he needed to talk about his life in the gang. If nothing else, it might help him deal with the nagging memories that refused to go away.

"Fish, I'm ready," Rick announced one day, striding into the office. He flopped into his chair, flushed and angry.

"What happened?" Tony asked, surprised at Rick's entrance.

"Jesse and David just won't listen. Caught them going after Julio and Santana of the Slayers," Rick said, disgusted. He finally understood what Tony had gone through in their first few sessions and he had a whole new appreciation for his big brother. "Again. Third time this month alone."

"Tom can't get through to them, either?" Tony asked with a sigh. He was just as frustrated as his young friend at these two very stubborn Angels.

Rick shook his head and found himself sitting, a week later, in the front row of the small auditorium at the centre, waiting for Tony to get the rest of the kids to their seats. He nodded to Tom, Jesse and David.

"Champ," the trio said as they sat, Tom right next to Rick and the other two on Tom's other side. Rick didn't say anything, but he could hear his two Angels muttering Fish had it all wrong. They weren't gang members. *And that, my friends, is why you need to hear this, this way,* Rick thought grimly.

Tony stood up in front and whistled for attention. Once everyone settled down and the muttering had subsided, Tony began. "Afternoon, guys. I called y'all here today to listen to a guest speaker. And I really want you to *listen*. This speaker has done something very few people have ever done, myself included – and I'm gonna let him tell his story, his way. Folks, meet Moneyman," Tony said and tossed Rick something as the teen stood up.

Without even thinking about it, Rick shrugged into his jacket and tied on the bandana, not needing a mirror to make sure "Money" faced the front. It was incredible to watch the transformation two pieces of clothing made in him. He could hear the muttering begin as many in the audience actually recognized who was standing in front of them, arrogance and attitude oozing out of every pore.

"Name's Rick "Moneyman" Attison, a Black Knight. And I knows some of ya. You," Rick drawled, pointed to one kid in the second row who was now cowering in his seat. "You, I gave a black eye and a couple of broken ribs because ya wouldn't get outta my way. You, whipped ya in the alley behind Mahoney's, twice. You, I watched you just about get killed. Twice," Rick said, looking right at Tom, dropping the gang speak when he looked at his second-in-command.

"I was a bully and proud of it. I was an angry, violent young man and it almost cost me my life and the life of my cousin, Megs. There was only one thing I wouldn't, couldn't do – and that was going after the little kids – those smaller than me. Johnny loved it and it made me sick," Rick said with considerable heat.

He motioned for Tom to join him on stage. Then he looked right at Jesse and David. "You two know the Kid's story. Johnny and Eric just about killed him. He suffered blinding headaches and panic attacks for months afterwards. He formed a new group called the Grey Angels. You two belong," Rick said, pointing at them.

"You were two of the Angels who *begged* me to lead the Angels, yet, dammit, you won't listen to me. So if you won't listen one-on-one, listen to my story from start to finish right now. And it starts right here," Rick said harshly as he threw his jacket and bandana in the garbage. He turned and looked at the two Angels squirming in their seats, embarrassed at being singled out. There may have been twenty people in that audience that day, but Rick was talking to only two of them. And they knew it.

"The Kid could've been killed that day, or in September when Johnny went after him again. I thought getting him into the boxing club would help him, but it gave him the skills that damn near turned him into Johnny. I've managed to convince him, and most of the rest of the Angels, that's where a gang belongs – in the trash," Rick said, pointing to the garbage again.

"Jesse, David, listen to me. *You don't need a gang to give you anything!* We'll always be there to give you friendship, but we'll never replace the love of your family." Rick looked over and pointed at Tony. "My best friend, big brother and surrogate father, Fish, taught me that," Rick said with a smile at the cop.

"Now, sit up and listen. Listen good, you two. I'll guarantee, once you hear the whole story, you'll run away from being a gang banger," Rick said.

He talked for more than an hour, leaving nothing about the gang life unexposed. Tony was totally impressed with his friend. Rick spoke with passion and never took his eyes off the two Angels, who were finally sitting up and paying attention to their leader.

Rick finished up by saying, "Look, guys, you're both great guys and fantastic fighters, don't get me wrong. But when you go *looking* for trouble, it usually finds you. In spades. The hardest lesson you'll ever learn is when to walk away from a fight. If you get into a fight, ask yourself this – why? Why did you get into the fight? And remember – did you join the Angels to fight Johnny or become him?" Rick finished.

There was some scattered applause, then Tony opened the floor for questions. Most of the kids took advantage and asked some pretty pointed questions. Rick took his time and answered them honestly. Once or twice he turned the questions over to Tony or Tom, surprising them both.

But it was David's last question that really caught Rick off guard. "Champ, you were a banger for a long time, right?" he asked.

"It was only three years, but, at times, it felt like forever. I was angry for a lot longer than that. Why?" Rick asked.

"Do you hate Johnny?" David asked after a moment's hesitation.

Rick thought about it for a moment. "No, I don't hate Johnny. I hate what he turned me into. Or almost did. Angry. Resentful. Willing to hurt almost anyone just for Johnny's approval, just like I did for my old man, until I figured out Michael didn't give a damn about me. I was a machine. One that reacted without thinking. I was very close to being capable of killing. That's what Johnny was trying to get me to be capable of and I'm glad I got out when I did," Rick answered patiently.

He hesitated for a second then peeled off his white t-shirt and stood up straight. There were several gasps as the kids looked at all the scars that criss-crossed his torso. Only Tony and Megan had seen him like this. He never showed Jordan because he knew how much they bothered her. Even Tom was shocked. These scars were bad enough. The ones no one could see, the mental ones, were twice as bad.

Rick thoughtfully traced the one in his left shoulder. "This is the one that almost killed me," Rick said to the stunned crowed. David and Jesse both turned away. "Don't look away, you two. Every time you think the gang's the way to go, remember this scar. Think about being on the receiving end of a wound like this or being the one that delivers it.

"It's taken me almost three months to heal physically, never mind mentally. I doubt the nightmares'll ever go away," Rick said softly.

"Champ, can I ask you one more thing?" Jesse asked hesitantly. Rick nodded, but he wasn't prepared for the question. Not one bit.

"If Johnny was here, right now, what would you say to him?" Jesse asked.

Rick hesitated for a long time. It was something Tony had asked him several times, but Rick never could give the cop a satisfactory answer. He wondered if he'd be able to give one now.

Tony winced as he heard the anger in Rick's voice as he began to talk. "Why? That's all I'd wanna know. Why he made me like this and why'd he tried to kill me. All I wanted was friendship, loyalty and protection, especially from my old man. Johnny wants something he can only find in the gang. He'll look for it in jail, too. Meanwhile, he's left a lot of us, this town included, broken and damaged. But all I'd wanna know is why he did this to me," Rick growled, his breathing ragged as he struggled to control a sudden surge of rage.

Tony immediately ended the session, and with Tom's help, cleared the auditorium. Rick had thrown his shirt back on and was pacing on the stage, muttering under his breath. Tony gathered up Rick's coat and bandana and tidied up a bit. Still Rick hadn't calmed down.

"Champ, you okay?" Tom asked, prudently standing out of Rick's reach, just in case.

Rick shook his head, realized he had worried them both, and smiled. "Not really, Kid, but it doesn't matter. I just wasn't expecting that question. From you, bro, okay, but not from anyone else," Rick said. He looked at Tony out of the corner of his eye. "Did it work, though? That's what I wanna know," he said.

Before Tony could answer, Jesse and David came back into the room. Both looked very uncomfortable. "Champ. Kid. We're sorry. We didn't know," David said, hanging his head in shame. Jesse couldn't look at either one of them, he was so embarrassed at what he had been doing. *No more,* he swore to himself. Rick just nodded and the pair left. Tony didn't say a word until the door closed behind them.

"Yeah, it worked," Tony said with a grin as they walked out into the early summer night.

Chapter 70

Rick just let his hands continue to swing at the bag as he realized the talk he had given to his Angels had done him a lot of good, too. He began to really see a lot of improvement in his own behaviour, even though he still had days when he'd be a brat or a jerk, especially to Tony. Tony put up with it because they were family and the days were so few and far between. But only for so long, before he'd give Rick a thorough dressing down.

Found a mom, gained a new dad, two sisters and have a great home, Rick thought as he finished with a flourish. "Ouch," he groaned as his shoulder began to throb. He'd really overdone it today.

"No kidding, ouch. You've been at it for almost two hours and really hard for the last half hour. Thinking about that talk you gave again?" Megan asked as she grabbed his muscle cream. Wordlessly, Rick towelled off and sat on the floor in front of his cousin. This was something only Tony or Megan could do for Rick. Not even Jordan, someone Rick trusted immensely, could be behind Rick, at least not yet. *Must have something to do with what we've both been through,* Rick thought as Megan gently worked on his shoulders, easing the aches. It wasn't the first time and it wouldn't be the last, Rick knew and he was grateful.

Swinging up into the saddles on Mystique and Cherokee twenty minutes later, Rick marvelled at how good Megan was getting at those massages. She would tell him, when he asked, she liked to help since she felt safe with him. He was just glad he had regained Megan's faith and trust and he vowed he wouldn't ever give her a reason to doubt him again.

Mickey and Jordan were waiting, on matching black thoroughbreds, at the gate as Rick and Megan rode up. After exchanging greetings, Rick silently led the way down a slightly challenging trail leading to a large clearing he had found on a solitary ride a week earlier.

The four friends just let the horses wander free, knowing they could be re-captured with only a whistle. While the others wandered around, laughing and talking, Rick leaned against a tree at the edge of the clearing, thinking about how far he had come, especially this summer, and how far he knew he still had to go.

The longer Rick stood, leaning against that tree, the more he felt someone staring at him from the woods. The Watcher, as Rick had named him, was making Rick uneasy, and it wasn't a feeling Rick liked. It wasn't the first time since Blade's trial Rick had felt like this, and yet it was very different from the way he had felt before Megan's disappearance.

The feeling was just as nebulous as before, yet it had no rhyme or reason and Rick couldn't stand it. He couldn't figure out what was causing it. It wasn't focused on any one person and every time he tried to analyze the feeling, it would slip away, leaving Rick feeling like he was trying to hold sand in a sieve. Time was slipping away from him again, he knew, only this time, Rick wasn't sure what to do.

Rick felt the Watcher's eyes still on the back of his neck and he turned slightly to look over his shoulder. He stared into the dark underbrush, but couldn't see anyone in the deep gloom. He didn't need this. Not today. He was stressed enough with the party, for some reason.

"Crap," Rick said quietly, but loud enough for Mickey to hear it and come over.

"What's up, Rick?" the teen said, as he kept an eye on the girls on the far side of the clearing.

"C'mon, man, what's up? What do you see?" Mickey asked again, coming to stand next to Rick. He noticed right away Rick was staring blankly off into the trees.

"Rick?" Mickey tried one last time, marvelling at how far he'd come since Megan's kidnapping.

"There's something out there, Mick. Something's coming again. Something's after...me, this time. I think," Rick said softly.

"The feelings're back? Is it aimed at anyone in particular?" Mickey deliberately avoided mentioning either girl, but both boys turned automatically to watch their girlfriends as they laughed at something Megan had just said.

"Yeah, it's back, Mick, with bells on, but no, I can't focus it on anything or anyone really and that's what's driving me batty. There's no actual threats, this time. No hint of danger. I'm just uneasy all of the time. It's like someone's watching me, but I can't see them. Oh hell, I'm so used to being in danger, I'm probably just making it all up," Rick shrugged, trying to ease Mickey's fears.

Mickey looked at the kid who had been such a pain in the butt to him since Rick had first laid eyes on Mickey's baby sister. "Rick, you and I've been at each other almost from the moment you first laid eyes on Jordan. You've taken away my sister, but you also gave me the greatest gift in the world when you introduced me to my lass," Mickey said softly.

"Yeah, so?" Rick agreed, wondering what Mickey was getting at.

"Let it go, Rick. They're gone. Maybe it's only for three years, but they're gone. Trust me, you don't have to look over your shoulder and watch out for them any more. Please, I'm begging you, don't leave Jordan alone," Mickey begged.

Let it go, Rick mused. *Mickey's right. I have to let it go.* He smiled suddenly at Mickey. "I won't. Promise," Rick vowed.

He waved to the two girls as they walked across the clearing. Neither girl invoked that uneasy feeling, and Rick realized Mickey was right. By focusing on those stupid feelings, he was leaving Jordan alone and unprotected. And that just wouldn't do.

Rick strode across the clearing to meet the two girls. He grabbed Jordan around the waist and swung her around and around. Laughing, Rick lowered her down and kissed Jordan until she was breathless and clinging to him.

"Love ya, sweets," he whispered as he held her close, and slipped something out of his pocket.

He dropped to one knee, and took Jordan's left hand. She gasped as she looked down at the ice blue diamond and emerald ring now on her third finger.

"Your dad'll kill me, but I don't care. I know we're only 17, but I wanna be with you for the rest of my life and I've known for a long time now. Marry me, sweets. Please?"

As Jordan let out a squeaking "Yes," and kissed Rick, Megan smiled at Mickey. She rubbed the ring Mickey had given her. It was a promise, she knew and he'd ask her soon enough. Once he got over the shock of his sister being engaged.

At least we'll never be alone, Megan thought as she embraced her boyfriend.

Holding onto Megan, Mickey looked at the radiant face of his sister. "Dad's gonna freak – right after he kills me," the Irish teen muttered in Megan's ear.

She laughed as she pulled free and swatted Mickey's arm playfully. "Will you please chill? It's not like they're gonna get married today, silly. Rick's thinking a couple of years. At least," Megan grinned at her boyfriend.

Mickey glowered at her. "You knew," he accused her.

Rick turned when he heard Mickey's tone. "'Course she knew, Mick. Who'd ya think helped me design the ring, man? Sure wasn't gonna ask you," Rick snorted.

Mickey didn't say anything. He glanced at his sister and saw how hurt Jordan was by his hesitant response. He sighed and pulled her close. "I'm sorry, sis, but you're being taken away from me again. By him. And I can't follow," he whispered, his voice breaking.

His twin hugged him. She understood how Mickey felt. It was like she was being torn in two. "I know, bro, but you'll follow soon enough. It's not for a couple of years at least. We've gotta finish high school first. Mick, please, don't spoil this," Jordan begged.

Rick stood back and held his breath. Mickey would fight tooth and nail to hold onto his twin, and without his support, Rick knew he stood a snowball's chance in hell of getting Seamus' permission to marry his girl. *O'Reilly still may not let me*, Rick thought as he waited.

Mickey stood back from Jordan and sighed again. He didn't know what to do. He just didn't know. On the one hand he was happy for his sister – she was finally going to be with her man. On the other hand, he was losing her. Forever. And it *hurt!*

"Mick, please?" Jordan whispered. She groped blindly for Rick's hand. Why couldn't her brother be happy for her?

"I may not like it, sis, but you've got my blessing, if that's what you want," Mickey said finally. Jordan laughed and hugged her brother.

Holding her in one arm, Mickey stuck out his hand. Rick grasped it gratefully. "Thanks, man," Rick said.

"You just take care of her, or I'll hunt you down, boy," Mickey growled. Then he laughed.

Rick laughed and swung Jordan around and kissed her again. Everything was going to work out just fine, he knew. No matter what happened, he had his girl.

"Hey, lover boy, time to ride. We're late!" Megan exclaimed as she glanced at her watch. She whistled for the horses and the four friends rode quickly for home.

Frank met them at the gate to the paddock. "Leave them, kids. Your friends're beginning to arrive. Scoot," he scolded them good naturedly.

Laughing, the four headed up to the house, arm in arm. Long before they saw any of their friends, they could hear the chatter and laugher. Over it all, Nana's welcoming voice.

She grinned when she saw the four teens walking up. "You're late. Where on earth have you been?" she called cheerfully.

Jordan giggled and held out her left hand. "We rode out to the clearing and Rick proposed!" the teen gushed, while Rick smiled indulgently.

Nana smiled. "Finally. He's had the ring for a couple of months now and was just waiting for the right time to ask. Now, get going. You're late," she said again, shooing them all away.

"Sorry, Nana," Megan said as she and Mickey headed in one direction while Rick and Jordan headed for the boxing club.

"Hey, Champ, Jordan. How's things?" Tom said, and tossed them each a cold pop from the cooler at his feet.

"Doing good, Kid," Rick said, nodding to the Angels that were around. "Stand down, boys. Today, we don't worry about a thing," Rick ordered, finally comfortable with his role with the Angels. The Angels nodded and some took off to be with other friends.

Those remaining were also part of the boxing club. Tom turned to Rick and said plaintively, "Champ, Carl beat me. Again. What am I doing wrong?"

"Simple. You're rushing. Trying for the fast take down. Just because I can doesn't mean you can. Patience, Kid. You keep giving Carl the left side ribs, just like he does with me, and he knows it. Follow this," Rick said and swung suddenly. Tom blocked quickly and the two were immediately involved in an impromptu sparring match. It didn't take long for Rick to prove his point.

"Got it, Champ," Tom groaned from the grass, where he lay, gasping, on his back. Off to the side, Jordan and Tom's girlfriend, Yvonne, were laughing as Jordan showed off her engagement ring. Again.

Rick hauled Tom up and joined their girlfriends. Laughter and a cacophony of conversations rolled over Glencrest as the rest of the guests arrived. Rick excused himself from the boxing club and stood in the shadows of the porch, watching his family and friends. He suddenly needed some quiet time, away from the excitement.

He leaned on the rail and watched as Jordan showed her father, Tony, and Marshall her engagement ring. Seamus frowned, said something to which Jordan replied firmly and then he smiled and hugged his daughter. Seamus caught Rick's eye and nodded, once. Rick sighed and nodded back, grateful for the acknowledgement.

Rick continued to look around and saw most of the Angels cheering on Carl and Tom as they sparred, Tom looking like he was going to finally beat the bigger boy. Mickey was over by the bar-b-que talking horses with Frank, Megan, and Ian. Rick watched as Nana joined them a few minutes later.

Satisfied all was well, Rick decided to head over to Jordan, who was still with the trio of cops. The sound of one final car pulling into the driveway caught his attention, and he smiled as he recognized the car pulling to a stop.

Rick slipped down the stairs to greet his family. "Hi, Mom," he said softly, giving her a big hug.

"Hello, son. Are you sure about this?" she asked shyly.

Rick laughed as he shook Jeff's hand and hugged his sisters. Leaving his arms around their shoulders, Rick nodded. "Don't worry about Michael, Mom. He's long gone. And, of course I'm sure. Nana's been dying to meet the girls since I told her about them. I'm not ashamed of having an adopted family. I wanna show you all off. C'mon, let's go," Rick said and led the way to where the cops stood talking with Ian.

"Marsh, Inspector O'Reilly, Uncle Ian, I'd like you to meet my mom, Kara, her husband Jeff, and my sisters, Melissa and Julia. Y'all already know Fish," Rick said as the group came up to the adults during a lull in their conversation.

As Kara thanked Tony and Marshall again for helping Rick, Nana joined the group. "Hello, lad. Who are these lovely young ladies?" Nana asked, smiling at Melissa and Julia as they hid shyly behind their brother.

Rick eased his sisters forward. "Nana, this is Melissa and Julia, my sisters. Mel, Jules. This is my Nana, Megan Attison. Just call her Nana, everyone does," he said, making the introductions.

Nana smiled again and began to talk to the girls. They were excited to learn Nana had a couple of colts for them to come and help raise, that would be theirs and they would be able to learn to ride. Rick smiled as everyone settled into easy conversations, as if they had known each other for eleven years, instead of having just met.

"Hey, love," Jordan said, coming up beside Rick and slipping an arm around his waist.

"Hi, sweets. Mom, Jeff, Mel, Jules. I want you to meet my fiancé, Jordan O'Reilly, her twin brother Mickey and Mickey's girl, and my cousin, Megan. Jor, Mick, Megs, I'd like you to meet my mom, Kara Dunn, her husband Jeff and their daughters, Melissa and Julia," Rick said.

"Didn't you forget someone, mate?" a deep voice, tinged with a faint Australian accent, said from behind Rick.

To his credit, Rick managed not to jump out of his skin, or flee. Instead, he said, "No, Nelson. I haven't forgotten anyone..." His voice trailed off as he turned his head slowly. There stood Nelson, a big grin on his face, his arms around his kids, Cherie and Matthew and his wife, Donna, by his side.

"Nelson!" Melissa squealed and launched herself at her older brother.

"Come here, Mel, Jules," Nelson laughed and swung them both up into a bear hug, the girls laughing and screaming in delight.

Rick hadn't moved as his brother greeted his mom and Nana, who introduced her eldest grandson to everyone else. Nelson stopped and stood in front of his little brother. His wide grin slowly faded as he realized his brother wasn't happy to see him.

"Rick? What's wrong?" Nelson asked softly, finally noticing Rick was silently crying. He couldn't stand seeing his brother hurting and pulled Rick into a rough embrace.

Rick clung to his brother as if, by letting go, Nelson would disappear. "I can't believe you're here," Rick sobbed. It was almost too much. He had all of his family back.

"To stay, little brother, to stay. We've moved back to that plot of land Nana was gonna give me anyway. We started planning this about six months ago, and got the house built. I've gotta job with the company setting up an office here in Collingwood. Nana's gonna help us. We're here to stay," Nelson explained as he released Rick.

Rick sniffled and dried his eyes. Then he smiled at his niece and nephew. He gave them hugs and greeted his sister-in-law. Then he turned back to his brother.

"Mom tell you what's been going on?" he asked hesitantly.

Nelson shook his head. "A bit, but not the full story. Looks like supper's ready. Why don't you fill me in, little brother?" Nelson said and led the way to the tables groaning with food.

Nelson and Rick sat apart from everyone else and Rick caught his brother up on the last year of hell. When he finished, Nelson looked pretty gray, but he managed to keep from bolting from his brother. Rick didn't blame him. It was still hard to talk about sometimes.

Rick slumped in his chair as Nelson joined the rest of the family on the porch. Rick heard them talking and laughing as Jeff told a story. The Angels and the boxing club had grouped up and again Rick heard lots of chatting and laughing. Sitting in the late summer evening sun, Rick was surrounded by peace and contentment. Just not him.

He turned his head as he heard someone approaching. "You're awfully quiet all of a sudden, son," Tony said, dropping into Nelson's empty chair.

"Yeah, I know. I'm surprised Nelson didn't bolt from me. Fish, if everything's over and they're gone, why the hell'm I so jumpy and nervous? Am I just in the habit of looking for trouble?" Rick asked after a couple of minutes.

"Those feelings back?" Tony asked shrewdly.

"With bells on. I'm surprised I didn't flatten Nelson when he came up behind me. Fish, I feel like I'm being watched all the time," Rick said sourly.

"Now?" Tony wondered.

Rick nodded. The Watcher was back. Standing somewhere behind him. Rick ignored him for now, but motioned vaguely to the trees behind him.

"This isn't finished, little brother, not by a long shot. Johnny had a lot of connections and who knows how long his arm is. It'll be someone we'll never even think of, I'm pretty sure. Michael's still part of this. You and I both know in our hearts he orchestrated this kidnapping and then disappeared with the money. We just need to prove it. And what was Mendez really after with the Knights?" Tony said as he stood up.

Tony looked at his friend sitting morosely in his chair. "You've won the battle, little brother, but you haven't won the war

- 627 -

yet," Tony said. With that comforting shot, Tony walked away, whistling a jaunty tune.

Needing a bit more breathing space, Rick walked to stand at the far end of the house. The conversations faded as he walked around the corner and climbed on an old stump to think.

Deep down, Rick knew Tony was right. The war was far from over. Blade would make every effort to get both Rick and Mark. Rick was ready for anything his former leader could throw at him and he could only hope Mark was, too.

Rick was sure Blade was going to change his tactics this time. He wasn't going to go after anyone else trying to get to Rick. Blade would have to come after Rick and Rick alone. *What a comforting thought*, Rick thought sourly.

He could still feel the Watcher's eyes on him. He turned to face the woods across from the house. Whatever, whoever, was going to be coming after him was waiting, right now, in those woods, Rick knew, and he was sorely tempted to go and confront him.

Rick snorted as common sense reasserted itself. Trouble would find him soon enough, he was sure. Sighing, he climbed to his feet and looked between the woods and his friends. Jordan and Megan, especially, were surrounded by the Grey Angels, guarded without realizing they were being guarded.

Suddenly, Rick was angry. They shouldn't have to live their lives looking back over their shoulders. He turned to glare at the woods. "No way, Johnny. Not this time. You want me? Come after me. Leave them alone. Remember *that*," Rick said softly. He continued to glare until he felt the Watcher leave.

He turned back and sauntered to his friends. As he wrapped his arms around Jordan, he looked back at the woods and said even softer than before, "Remember."

Rick's saga continues in Grey Shadows. Grade 12 was supposed to be a year to get ready for university, so Rick knows it's going to be hard. Instead, Rick faces new challenges, new foes, a mother who tries to control his life and gains a new family and friends. How far is Rick willing to go this time to protect not only Jordan, but Collingwood?

Made in the USA
Charleston, SC
29 April 2016